In the blockbuster story~~~~~~
bara Taylor Bradford's hallmark, here is the extraor-
dinary novel of a remarkable man—and the women
who love him.

THE WOMEN IN HIS LIFE

He is Maximilian West—billionaire tycoon and corporate
raider extraordinaire. He is a figure of almost mythical
power—an enigma to all who know him, a stranger even
to himself. But when his world is suddenly and irrevocably
shattered, Maxim must make peace with his turbulent past
and begin to understand the remarkable women who have
loved him, protected him, and lost him: Ursula, his mother;
Theodora, his devoted nanny; Anastasia, an artistic French
beauty and his first love; Camilla, the renowned English actress; and Adriana, an American business tycoon.

From the streets of London to the suites of New York, from
the rise of Nazi Germany to the fall of the Berlin Wall,
THE WOMEN IN HIS LIFE takes us on an unforgettable
journey of survival, secrets, love, and redemption that mes-
merizes from the first page to the last.

BARBARA TAYLOR BRADFORD

Also by Barbara Taylor Bradford:

A WOMAN OF SUBSTANCE
VOICE OF THE HEART
HOLD THE DREAM
ACT OF WILL
TO BE THE BEST

THE
WOMEN
IN
HIS LIFE

Barbara Taylor Bradford

BALLANTINE BOOKS • NEW YORK

Grateful acknowledgment is made to the following for permission to reprint previously published material:

Campbell Connelly & Co., Limited: Excerpt from "There'll Always Be an England," by Parker and Charles. Copyright © 1939 by Dash Music Co., Ltd., 8-9 Frith Street, London WIV 5TZ. Used by permission. All rights reserved.

EMI Music Publishing, UK and Williamson Music: Excerpt from "I'll Be Seeing You," by Irving Kahal and Sammy Fein. Copyright © 1938 by Williamson Music Company Rights throughout the British Commonwealth are controlled by EMI Music Publishing, United Kingdom. Reprinted by permission of Williamson Music and EMI Music Publishing, United Kingdom.

EMI Music Publishing, United Kingdom: Excerpt from "Pack Up Your Troubles (In Your Old Kit Bag)," by Powell and Asap. Copyright 1915. Reproduced by permission of Francis Day and Hunter Ltd. London WC2H OEA.

Shapiro Bernstein and Co., Inc., and Walter Kent Music Company, Los Angeles: Excerpts from "The White Cliffs of Dover," by Walter Kent and Nat Burton. Copyright © 1941 by Shapiro, Bernstein, and Co., Inc., New York. Copyright renewed. Reprinted by permission of Shapiro Bernstein and Co., Inc., and Walter Kent Music, Los Angeles.

Library of Congress Catalog Card Number: 89-43432

ISBN 0-345-34573-8

This edition published by arrangement with Random House, Inc.

Manufactured in the United States of America

First International Ballantine Books Edition: January 1991
First U.S. Ballantine Books Edition: September 1991

Author photo copyright © 1991 by Lord Lichfield

This book is for Bob, who means
all the world to me, and without
whom it could not have been written.

Contents

Acknowledgments

I would like to thank a few people who in different ways were involved in the making of this book: firstly, Joan Blutter of Chicago, a friend of many years, who was always there for me and who grew to love my characters as much as I love them; Jane Ogden of Naples, Florida, another friend of long standing, who grew up as I did in wartime Britain, and confirmed that my memories had not been eroded by the passing of time.

Enthusiasm is not for sale; it can only be freely given. Susan Schuhart Zito, my assistant, has always had unflagging enthusiasm for my novels. I am grateful to her for helping to prepare the manuscript meticulously and for assisting with some aspects of the research.

Two other friends took the time and trouble to assist me with certain details and I am indebted to them: Bernard H. Leser, President of Condé Nast Publications Inc.; Shirley Burnstein of London.

I would like to express my thanks and appreciation to Trudi Gold of the Spiro Institute in London, who helped me to understand the situation regarding European Jewish immigrants to England in the 1930s and Britain's attitude toward these immigrants.

PART ONE

Maximilian

═══════════════════════════════

LONDON–NEW YORK

1989

A man who stormed and captured
so many citadels which in his
boyhood and youth must have
seemed as fantastical and
unobtainable as Ali Baba's cave.
A man of many lives.

Melvyn Bragg, *Richard Burton: A Life*

1

≡

𝒽ᴇ ᴄᴀᴍᴇ ᴏᴜᴛ ᴏꜰ ᴛʜᴇ ɪᴍᴘᴏsɪɴɢ ʜᴏᴜsᴇ ᴏɴ ᴛʜᴇ ᴄᴏʀɴᴇʀ of Chesterfield Hill and Charles Street and stood for a moment poised on the front step. It had rained earlier, and the dampness lingered and the air was raw on this chilly Thursday evening in January.

Normally oblivious to the weather, he found himself shivering and turned up the collar of his black trench coat. The weather underscored his morose mood, his sense of desolation. For a long time there had been a deep sadness inside him; tonight, for some reason, it seemed more acute than usual.

Pushing his hands into his pockets, he forced himself to stride out, heading in the direction of Berkeley Square. He walked at a rapid pace along Charles Street, his step determined, his back straight, his head held erect. He was dark-haired with dark-brown eyes, tall, lean, trimly built. There was an athletic hardness about his body, and this was echoed in his lean and angular face, its rawboned sharpness softened by a deep tan. He was an exceptionally handsome man, in his mid-fifties, and his name was Maximilian West.

He cursed mildly under his breath, wondering at the heaviness he felt, and regretting that he had agreed to this meeting set for such a late hour. He had done so impulsively—he who was rarely impulsive—out of deference to his old school friend Alan Trenton. Alan had made Maxim's presence tonight sound so vitally important. But eight-forty-five was late even for Maxim West, renowned though he was for being ready to do business at any time of the day or night, any day of the week; and he had another appointment, for dinner that evening. What saved the situation was that Alan's office was only a stone's throw away from the late-night dining club where he had a table booked for nine-thirty.

He circled Berkeley Square, dodging the traffic as he made for the far side, wondering why Alan needed to see him, what this was all about. When Alan had telephoned the house earlier, his voice had vibrated with urgency, yet he had been curiously reticent. Intrigued, Maxim had agreed to stop by, but now he was acutely aware of the time, reminding himself that Alan was talkative, could be a bit long-winded on occasion. He would have to keep his eye on the clock, move the meeting along with a degree of rapidity.

Oh what the hell, he thought, as he reached the corner of Bruton Street. Alan's been special to me for most of my life. I owe him . . . we go back so far, he knows so much—and he's my best friend.

Crossing the street, his eyes focused on the Jack Barclay showroom on the opposite corner, and when he reached the plate-glass windows he paused to admire the sleek Rolls-Royces and Bentleys gleaming under the brilliant spotlights. He was always promising himself one of these superdeluxe models, but he never seemed to get around to buying it. On the other hand, he did not have much need for a car for his personal use anymore. Corporate jets that sped around the world were more his style these days, and when he was on the ground there were company limousines at his disposal.

He walked on past the Henley car showroom and Lloyds bank, and pushed through the doors of Berkeley Square House. He nodded to the security guard, who touched his cap in recognition. This was the best commercial address in town and a powerhouse of a building. Here, floor upon floor, were housed the great international corporations and the multinationals, companies that had more financial clout than the governments of the world. Maxim thought of the buff-colored edifice as a mighty treasury of trade, for it did hundreds of billions of dollars' worth of business a year. And yet it had no conspicuous face; had long since blended into the landscape of this lovely, leafy square in the very heart of Mayfair, and most Londoners who walked past it daily were hardly aware of its existence. But it was the British base for an amazing number of megacorporations and the spot where the big bucks stopped.

Maxim crossed the richly carpeted white-marble hall,

stepped into the elevator and rode up to Alan Trenton's offices on the sixth floor. Responding to his knock, Trenton's secretary of many years opened the door and smiled warmly when she saw Maxim standing there. "Good evening, Mr. West. Oh dear, I'm so sorry. I mean—Sir Maximilian!"

He brushed aside her apologies and flashed a dazzling smile. "Hello, Evelyn," he said, shrugging out of his trench coat. She ushered him toward Trenton's inner sanctum. "He's waiting for you."

Alan Trenton was standing next to a carved mahogany console of Chippendale design, pouring Roederer Cristal Brut into a silver tankard. He was Maxim's age, yet appeared older. He was stout, of medium height, fair of coloring and slightly balding above a ruddy face.

"Maxim!" he exclaimed, his pale-blue eyes lighting up with the most obvious pleasure. He put the bottle of Cristal down with a clatter, and hurried across the room. Grasping Maxim's hand, he half embraced his oldest and dearest friend. "It's good to see you," he said.

"And you, Alan. It's been too long, and my fault."

"No problem, I understand," Alan beamed. "I know I've said it on the phone, but I feel I must say it to you in person. Congratulations, Maxim, on your very great honor."

"Thanks, Stubby," Maxim said, reverting to his old nickname for Trenton from their schooldays. "Who'd have thought it, eh?"

"*I* would've, Duke, that's who," Alan shot back, using the name he had bestowed on Maxim some thirty years before. "And thanks for coming at such short notice, I know how pressed you are."

"And why *am* I here?" Maxim's gaze turned quizzical, a dark brow lifted.

Trenton did not at first respond. He stepped over to the console, lifted the bottle. "A drop of bubbly, old chap?"

"Thanks, but not really," Maxim said, then realizing the champagne was in his honor, he added quickly, "Oh, why not? But do make it a drop."

Maxim watched as Trenton dispensed the champagne, waiting for him to come to the point of the meeting. But when he didn't, Maxim strolled into the middle of the room and glanced around.

Alan had recently finished redecorating his office, and Maxim liked the new ambience. A sense of elegance and warmth had been created, with pine-paneled walls, fine English antiques and bucolic landscapes of the English countryside hanging in elaborate carved and gilded frames. All bespoke Trenton's lifelong predilection for ancient objects and artifacts, which had developed into a very serious and consuming hobby. He had become a well-known collector, an avid bidder at auctions. All that oil money to spend, Maxim commented to himself. North Sea oil money. Big Texas oil money. He had encouraged Alan to pursue his own ideas, to expand the family business after he had taken over from his father, had backed him to the hilt in every way, giving him moral and financial support. The combination had worked, and Alan's great prosperity over the past fifteen years pleased Maxim tremendously.

A moment later Trenton handed Maxim the champagne. They clinked tankards. Alan said, "Here's to your title. Wear it in good health, old chap."

Maxim couldn't help laughing. "Thanks, Stubby, and here's to you." Maxim tasted the icy Cristal, liking its dryness. He took another sip, then said, "So, Alan, what *is* this all about?"

Trenton eyed him speculatively. "How would you like to be a white knight?"

Maxim stared at him. It was the last thing he had expected.

"To come to the rescue of Lister Newspapers, I presume," Maxim said at last, and it was Trenton's turn to be taken aback. "Someone else has already approached you!" he exclaimed, managing to make his words sound like both a statement and a question.

Maxim shook his head. "Not at all. But that's the only company in London facing a hostile takeover bid, at least that I'm aware of. And anyway, how come you're involved?"

"In actuality, I'm not," Trenton was quick to say. "I'm sort of"—he paused, groped for a word—"a go-between. It's John Vale, my merchant banker, who is the one involved. The merchant bank acts for Lister Newspapers and John is very close to the chairman, Harry Lister, and is seeking to help him. He's aware we're old friends and asked me to arrange this meeting."

"But it's hardly my bailiwick, I'm not interested in—" Maxim abruptly broke off as he saw the door open.

"Ah, there you are, John," Trenton said, hurrying to greet the newcomer, his hand outstretched. "Come in! Come in!"

"Hello, Alan," John Vale said, shaking Trenton's hand. He was in his late thirties, of average height, wiry, very English in appearance, with a fair skin, streaky blond hair and light-gray eyes behind thick tortoiseshell glasses. He allowed Trenton to propel him across the room to where Maxim stood.

"Maxim, I'd like to introduce John Vale of Morgan Lane," Trenton said. "And, of course, this is Sir Maximilian West, John."

"Glad to meet you," Maxim said.

"It's my very great pleasure, Sir Maximilian," John Vale responded, endeavoring to conceal his avid curiosity. Maximilian West was one of the world's most brilliant tycoons, and a buccaneer, like Sir James Goldsmith and Lord Hanson, both shrewd operators in the takeover game. West more than outmatched them, at least in John Vale's opinion.

Leaving the two men, Alan went over to the console, exclaiming, "Champagne coming up, John."

"Thanks," Vale replied, turned to Maxim and began to make small talk, all the while studying him. West was power personified; it seemed to emanate from him. Vale had not expected such a good-looking man, though. There was something spectacular about that wide engaging smile, the very white teeth, the dark eyes filled with vivid intelligence. And that tan! It was the golden tan of a playboy acquired in some exotic winter playground, not that of a workaholic conglomerateur who spent the majority of his time cooped up in boardrooms and circling the globe in his private jet. The clothes were equally unexpected, hardly the usual drab garb of a typical businessman. More like movie-star clothes, Vale thought, eyeing the gray pure-silk shirt, the pearl-gray silk tie, the superbly cut black gabardine suit that hung on West with such precision it had undoubtedly been engineered by the world's greatest tailor for a large quantity of money. But John Vale recognized at once that there was an intense glamour about Maxim West that had more to do with his own personal magnetism than with his sartorial elegance.

Trenton's voice interrupted Vale's thoughts and the discussion he was having with Maxim West about the filthy English weather and other trivialities.

"Here you go, John, some champagne, and now we can get down to business. Or rather, the two of you can. Although I've brought you and Sir Maximilian together, I intend to sit back and be the silent observer."

Maxim chuckled. "The day you do that I guarantee it'll snow gold bricks. You haven't paused to draw breath since you uttered your first word," he said, but there was no hint of criticism in his voice, only warmth and great affection.

Alan threw back his head and laughed. "I suppose there's some truth in what you say. And *you* should know—after the forty-five years or more we've been together."

The three men drank, and Trenton gestured to a group of chairs around a Georgian occasional table. "Shall we sit?"

Once they were settled, Trenton glanced at John Vale and said, "I told Maxim why I asked him to come over this evening. I think you should elucidate further."

Vale nodded, gave his attention to Maxim. "Firstly, I'd like to know whether you would be interested in being the white knight for Lister Newspapers."

Maxim frowned. "I honestly don't know. Just before you arrived, I had started to say to Alan that I didn't think a newspaper empire was my bailiwick exactly."

"But why not?" Trenton demanded peremptorily, forgetting his vow of silence of a moment ago. "Surely it's a perfect acquisition for you at this stage of your career. Think of the added power and influence you would have if you controlled Lister. A national daily, a national Sunday newspaper and a galaxy of prestigious magazines."

Maxim threw Alan a swift look but did not respond. Instead he addressed John Vale. "What makes you think I'd be acceptable to the stockholders?"

"Harry Lister is certain of it, so are the other members of the Lister board. I agree with them, as do the directors of Morgan Lane." Vale perched precariously on the edge of his seat, leaned forward and fixed his bespectacled, earnest gaze on Maxim. "You have the name, a formidable reputation and an extraordinary track record. You're not an asset stripper, far from it. The companies you have taken over have flourished under your good management. These things are tremendous points in your favor. Quite frankly, you're impressive, very impressive indeed, and that's why we're absolutely positive you'd be acceptable to the stockholders. Incidentally, so are Birch, Rider, stockbrokers for Lister Newspapers. They're as enthusiastic about you as we are, in point of fact."

"Those are very kind words. Thank you," Maxim murmured, and paused. He looked thoughtful, then said, "Arthur Bradley's International Publishing Group has tendered an offer of five hundred million pounds for Lister Newspapers. As a white knight I would have to top that offer by at least two hundred million pounds."

"Not necessarily," Vale shot back. "It could be less."

"Two hundred million, one hundred million, what's the difference—it's still a big ticket," Maxim remarked coolly.

"True," John Vale agreed. "But look at it this way, you stand to make a lot of money."

"I don't always consider how much I might make," Maxim replied in a quiet voice. "Rather, I ask myself, How much can I *lose*?"

"Oh, I'm certain you wouldn't lose," John asserted confidently. "I would like to give you some relevant information regarding Lister Newspapers, a few facts and figures."

"Go ahead." Maxim settled back in the chair, ready to listen, and at this juncture Alan Trenton rose. "If you'll excuse me, I'll attend to a bit of my own business," he murmured and went to the far side of the office where he sat down behind his desk. He studied the faxes and telexes from New York, which had come in earlier, wrote replies to be dispatched in the morning, perused other urgent papers, making notations on them.

At one point he looked over at Maxim and John Vale, who were still deep in conversation, and decided to leave them to their own devices for a short while longer. There was nothing pertinent he could say, little he could contribute to their discussion. It was best he remain out of it altogether.

Swiveling the desk chair, Alan sat gazing out the window that overlooked Berkeley Square. His thoughts drifted aimlessly for a few seconds and then settled on Maximilian West, as they generally did when Maxim was in close proximity. It was difficult not to focus on him, so powerful were his charisma and his presence.

"Best friends till the day we die," they had sworn at boarding school, and curiously enough this boyhood vow was holding true. And that's all that matters in the long run, isn't it, Alan thought. To know in our hearts that we're always there for each other, that we can rely on each other no matter what.

It delighted him to see Maxim in such great form. If one judged by his appearance, he led a life of ease and pleasure, in one of his many beautiful houses or on his floating palace of a yacht. But Alan knew that nothing was further from the truth. Maxim worked around the clock, was never off a plane, kept up the most killing pace—and yet somehow he managed to appear remarkably unruffled. In fact, Alan often thought that Maxim thrived on it all. In the past nine years Maxim had been under excessive pressure and not so readily available, traveling the world at large as he did. Also, London was more of a stopping-off point for him these days, even though he had his head office here and the house in Mayfair. Greener fields, in the shape of Manhattan, beckoned.

Alan wished he saw more of him. They spoke frequently on the telephone and grabbed a quick bite or a drink together occasionally, but this was not quite the same as lunching and dining in a leisurely fashion, the way they had in the past. They had been inseparable as boys, equally close in their teens, and their friendship had continued into full manhood.

Spinning the chair again, Alan fixed his eyes on Maxim and observed him carefully for a few seconds. His old friend appeared to be quizzing John Vale, asking some hard questions, no doubt. Vale was responding alertly, looking suitably impressed by his inquisitor. But then there was nothing unique about that. Everyone was impressed by Maximilian West. Startled, too, more often than not, when first meeting him. He was never what anyone expected him to be. Nor did he ever do what people anticipated he would do. He had always been a maverick.

In his mind's eye Alan suddenly saw Maxim as he had been at fifteen, remembered that ghastly day when two boys from another school, bullies both, had picked on Maxim, sneered at him, called him filthy names, been immeasurably cruel as only the young can be cruel. Maxim, ashen-faced, his dark eyes blazing with rage, had instantly turned combative, and had raised his fists like a boxer about to go on the attack. Ready to do battle for his best friend, Alan had brought his hands up too, wanting to fight at Maxim's side. And then the unexpected, the unanticipated, had happened, startling the crowd of boys, and him most of all. Maxim had dropped his arms to his sides and walked away without uttering a word, his head held high, his immense pride and dignity forming a shield around him. The group of boys who had been watching and jeering had fallen silent, had parted ranks to let him pass, intimidated by the cold, implacable expression on Maxim's face, by his lofty demeanor.

Alan recalled how he had run after Maxim, wanting to give him comfort. But Maxim had not needed sympathy; he had even refused to discuss the matter, had turned morose and moody for the rest of the day. It was only later that night, after lights-out in the dormitory, that Maxim had finally mentioned the incident. As if in answer to Alan's unspoken question, he had hissed in the dark, "I walked away because those cowards weren't worth fighting! I didn't even want to soil my hands by touching them!" Then he had gone on to say, "One day I'll be cock of the heap, just you wait and see, Stubby." And then in a fierce whisper he had added, "I'm nobody now! I have nothing now! But no matter how long it takes, I promise you I'm going to be *somebody*. And I'm going to have *everything*."

He was. And he did. He had made it all come true, perhaps beyond even his own wildest dreams.

Maximilian West was a man with the world at his feet.

Consequently he was envied by most men. Alan did not envy him; he was filled only with admiration for his friend. He knew what a difficult road Maxim had traveled, the enormous leaps he had made, the chances he had taken. His was an extraordinary success story, an epic story, really. He had become a great magnate; his name was one to be truly reckoned with on the international business scene, and in the last fifteen years he had gone from millionaire to multimillionaire to billionaire.

And only a couple of weeks ago, on the last day of December, the Queen's New Year Honours List had been announced. Among those titles and honors put forward by the prime minister for the Queen's approval was a knighthood for Maxim, in recognition of his enormous contributions to British industry at home and abroad. He was now Sir Maximilian West and could be thus addressed, even though his investiture at Buckingham Palace was not for three more months, in March.

Cock of the bloody heap indeed, Alan thought, and smiled. It was a deep smile, one of genuine pride and satisfaction. He reveled in Maxim's successes and triumphs, was always there on the sidelines, applauding. Maxim had been his hero at school. In a way, he still was. Alan supposed he always would be.

He glanced at Maxim again, admiringly. How wonderful his dear old friend looked.

But wait—no, he doesn't, Trenton suddenly thought, startling himself, and sitting up with a little jolt. He looked harder at Maxim.

The dazzling façade was intact, but now, instinctively, Alan knew there was something terribly wrong. It was not possible to be close to a man for almost forty-seven years and not know him inside out. There was a shadow at the back of Maxim's eyes that Alan had not seen there for years; he wondered why he hadn't noticed it when Maxim first arrived. Perhaps because he'd been too busy congratulating him on his knighthood. Maxim's got trouble, serious trouble, Stubby decided. Is it the women? I hope to God not, he's had enough trouble with women to last him a lifetime. Well, whatever's wrong, and there *is* something, I'll offer to help. That's what a best friend is for.

Now Alan looked quickly at the watch on his wrist, the gold Patek Philippe that Maxim had given him last year for his fifty-fourth birthday. He saw that it was exactly nine-fifteen. Earlier, on the phone, Maxim had said he would have to leave by nine-twenty. Alan knew that in one second, certainly not much longer, Maxim would stand up, make his good-byes and be gone. He was precise in a multitude of ways, and punctuality was one of them.

Anticipating Maxim's imminent departure, Alan went over and joined the two men as Maxim was saying, "The figures you've given me are interesting, but I'm still not sure I want to jump into the fray and make a counteroffer for Lister. I really will have to give the matter some thought."

Vale swallowed hard, striving to hide his disappointment that the meeting had not been more conclusive. "Yes, of course, I understand perfectly. And I'm sure you understand that speed is of the essence. Lister Newspapers are wide open right at this point, exposed in so many ways. They're a sitting target for other corporate raiders. That's what worries us the most, that someone else, another company, might enter the bidding and go after Lister." Vale exhaled heavily. "You know what that could mean."

"Only too well. *A bidding war.*" Maxim stood. "If you drop the documents off at my house tonight, as you suggested, I'll study them later."

Vale also rose, nodded. "Yes, I will. And thank you very much for your courtesy, and for listening." He extended his hand, added, "I'm most appreciative, Sir Maximilian."

Maxim took Vale's hand. "Now, if you'll excuse me, I really must go." He glanced conspiratorially at Alan, winked and said, "I have a dinner engagement and I would hate to keep the lady waiting."

"I'll walk you to the lift, Duke," Alan said, taking hold of Maxim's arm and ushering him out. He wanted to get Maxim alone, to ask him what was the matter, what he could do to help.

When Trenton returned to his office a few seconds later, John Vale peered at him and, with anxiety in his voice, asked, "Well? What did he say?"

"Nothing. At least, not about Lister Newspapers and his intentions. He wouldn't, you know, not even to me. He's very secretive about his business, always has been. I can tell you for a fact that he shreds every document that passes through his hands. Afraid of leaks, I suppose."

"Nobody knows him better than you, Alan. What is your assessment? What do you think our chances are?"

Trenton pursued his lips, pondered briefly. "I honestly don't know." He sat down heavily and looked off into the distance, a reflective expression on his face. At length he said, "If it *feels* right to him, he'll go with it."

"What do you mean exactly?"

"That's what Maxim has always said to me—that a deal's got to feel right. He goes on instinct. Gut instinct. He ignores analysts, reports, valuations, advisers. Gut instinct, that's what guides him."

"Do you really believe that?" Vale sounded doubtful.

"Oh yes, I do! More important, Maxim believes it. But what he really means, of course, is that he relies on his experience, his expertise, his great knowledge. Plus his instinctive feel for the particular deal, the particular situation."

Trenton picked up his champagne and sipped as he mulled something over.

"You asked me what my assessment is, John," he went on at last, "and it's this. If Maximilian West feels right about making an offer for Lister Newspapers he will do so. And if he feels wrong, or if he has no feeling about it whatsoever, then he'll pass. That's the way he is. Very cut and dried. *Precise.* It's his nature, always has been. Certainly he won't keep you dangling. You'll get a decision, and an answer, very quickly."

"That's good to know at least. And by the way, Alan, whatever the outcome is, I'm indebted to you. I don't know how to thank you for arranging this meeting."

"Very easily, old boy. Take me to dinner as you promised. *Now.* I'm starving."

John laughed. "That makes two of us. I booked a table at Mark's Club. Let's walk over there, and after we've dined I'll leave the papers at Maxim's house in Chesterfield Hill. He said you'd give me the exact address."

"Of course." Alan pushed himself up. "I'll clear my desk, then we'll be off."

As Trenton shuffled his papers Vale said, "I hadn't expected him to be such a handsome man. I've seen photographs of him in newspapers and magazines and none of them do him justice."

"No, they don't. But then a lot of Duke's appeal lies in his personal charisma. I don't suppose you can take a photograph of that."

"Why do you call him Duke?" Vale asked.

"After Archduke Maximilian of Austria who became emperor of Mexico in 1864," Alan explained. "Maxim was being a bit imperious with me one day at prep school, and I dubbed him that. He thought it was hilarious. . . . Anyway, the name stuck."

"I see. Is it true what they say about him?"

"They say a lot of things. What in particular are you referring to?"

"That Maximilian West cares about only four things. The prime minister. The United States. Making money. And screwing."

Alan started to laugh. Recovering himself after a brief moment, he said, "I know he holds Mrs. Thatcher in the highest regard, is a great admirer of her policies, especially when it comes to business. And let's face it, old chap, he's flourishing under her regime. She's just had him knighted. Most certainly he loves the United States, he's been straddling the Atlantic for a decade or so. He spends as much time there as he does here, you know."

A mischievous gleam entered Alan's eyes, "And for as long as I can remember, Maxim's been very intense about making money, *and* making love to the ladies. Oh yes, he's a bit of a lady-killer, our Maxim is. As for the ladies, they, of course, find him quite devastating."

"All those wives, all those mistresses," Vale murmured, a hint of awe echoing. "How on earth has he managed to juggle them, and apparently with such adroitness, too?"

"I wouldn't know."

"Haven't you ever asked him?"

"Good Lord, of course not. I've never had the nerve."

In fact Alan was lying. He had no wish to discuss his best friend's unorthodox personal life any further with John Vale. He had said enough as it was. There had been a great deal of gossip about Maxim over the years and he was hardly going to add to it. That would be the worst kind of betrayal.

I know far too much, Alan thought as he locked the top drawer of his desk. All those confidences Maxim has shared over the years. And continues to share. But his secrets are safe with me. And he knows that, knows I will take them with me to the grave.

2

☞OR THE SECOND TIME THAT EVENING MAXIMILIAN WEST found himself shaking off a feeling of heaviness as he traversed Berkeley Square.

Heading back in the direction he had walked earlier, his destination now was No. 44, directly opposite Alan Trenton's office building, on the other side of the plane trees in the park in the middle of the square. There, in the basement of a beautiful old house, was one of the most exclusive nightclubs in Europe—the famous Annabel's.

Founded in the summer of 1963 by Mark Birley, and named after his wife, Lady Annabel, from whom he was now divorced, it was the chicest of watering holes for the rich and famous, where the international jet set rubbed shoulders with movie stars and magnates and members of the British royal family. For the past twenty-six years it had remained very much the in spot, yet it had now gone beyond being merely fashionable; it had become legendary. It was Maxim's favorite place to dine in London.

Within minutes of leaving Alan's office, Maxim was nodding to the uniformed doorman who hovered outside, ducking under the green awning and hurrying down the flight of steps into the club.

A bevy of smiling familiar faces greeted him as he entered, and after shedding his trench coat he went over to the reception desk, where Ted was waiting to welcome guests, as he usually was most nights of the week.

Maxim accepted Ted's congratulations, signed the book and walked through into the bar–sitting room. Seeing that it was still relatively empty, he sat down at a small table in the corner, to one side of the brightly burning log fire. A waiter was instantly by his side; he ordered vodka straight with ice and lime, then settled into the squashy sofa, welcoming the comfort and warmth and the sense of ease that had always come to him here.

He had been a member since the club first opened, and he liked the atmosphere, the intimacy created by the blazing fire, the soft lights and deep sofas, the aroma of masses of fresh flowers in antique containers, the beauty of dark-red Oriental rugs and pumpkin-colored walls covered with a diversity of paintings. There were wonderful dog portraits, cartoons by Landseer, Munnings and Bateman, oils of elegant women, some nude, some clothed. At first glance the paintings seemed to have been put together with careless abandon, yet one could see there was nothing haphazard about their placement if one looked more carefully. They never ceased to delight his eye, and to amuse him.

To Maxim, Annabel's was more like an extension of Mark Birley's own house than a restaurant and nightclub, and perhaps this was the key to its enormous success. The bar area had the feeling of a country drawing room in a manor house; it could never be mistaken for anything but an English drawing room, what with its mixture of chintzes and paintings and flowers, its mellowness and charm. And then there was the gracious staff to be thankful for, the excellent service and finally the type of unpretentious food—for the most part, English cooking at its best—that Maxim preferred.

In his opinion there was nowhere in the world quite like Annabel's, and it was one of the things he sorely missed about London when he was away. He had not been in town for some weeks—maybe that was part of his problem; and in any case he was especially glad to be back in his special haunt tonight. Invariably the tensions of the day left him the instant he stepped through Annabel's portals. Here, he felt insulated against the world, cocooned within the familiar, pleasant surroundings. A home away from home, he thought, then added sardonically to himself, Except that I prefer this place to home. And, in fact, I don't have a home anymore, do I?

Reaching for the drink, he took a quick swallow, leaned against the cushions and forced himself to focus on the meeting he had just had in Stubby's office.

He realized he was curiously ambivalent about going after the Lister newspaper empire, and he wondered why. Before he had a chance to ponder the reasons, he saw Louis, the manager, heading in his direction, his face wreathed in smiles. They were old friends, had known each other for well over thirty years, ever since Louis had been the maître d' at the Mirabella Restaurant in Curzon Street, just around the corner from Annabel's. There was a unique camaraderie between them that sprang from many shared experiences in the past as well as the genuine affection they had for each other.

Maxim jumped up, beaming, and as they shook hands Louis congratulated him on his knighthood. They stood talking, catching up on each other's news; then after a few minutes Louis was summoned to take a phone call, and Maxim sat down again and picked up his drink. But immediately he found himself rising once more as Graeme Longdon came floating into the bar–sitting room on a cloud of perfume.

Graeme Longdon, his personal assistant, thirty-seven years old, was a tall, beanpole-thin American, with curly brown hair shot through with a hint of auburn and the brightest of green eyes. Not classically beautiful in the strict sense of the word, she was nonetheless a lovely young woman, very arresting, with a broad brow, high cheekbones above rounded cheeks, and a full, wide mouth. She was from Richmond, Virginia, and was independent, feisty, outspoken and something of a maverick. Maxim considered her to be one of the smartest people he had ever known, and she was his good right hand.

Tonight she was dressed in a superlative black velvet suit, which to his discerning eye was most obviously an haute couture number from Paris. The jacket above the pencil-slim skirt was trimmed across the shoulders and yoke with jet-bead embroidery and silk tassels. Her long, shapely legs were encased in sheer black hose, and she wore a pair of elegant black satin pumps. The only pieces of jewelry she wore were large diamond earrings shaped like flowers, and, on her wrist, a narrow diamond watch designed by Cartier in the thirties.

Maxim went to meet her, took hold of her elbow and guided her to the corner table.

"You look lovely," he said, in a voice that conveyed real appreciation of a pretty woman.

"Thank you, Maxim," she said, turning to him with a wide smile. "I always feel I must get myself done up in my best clothes to come to this place, so I dashed back to the Ritz to change. Sorry I'm late, Boss," she said with her usual breeziness.

"You're really not late," he said, returning her smile, and as usual faintly amused by her irreverent manner and her persistence in calling him Boss. When she had first come to work for him and had started to address him in this way, he had been irritated and tried to make her stop. But she had ignored his protests, and Boss it had remained ever since. He had grown used to it by now, and he no longer minded. He admired her, not the least for being herself, for not compromising her personality to suit somebody else's idea of the proper corporate image. She was honest and forthright and rather blunt, unnervingly so at times. Graeme had nicknames for others in the company, at least those she dealt with on a day-to-day basis. Most of the names were highly appropriate, and some disconcertingly so.

"You're worth the wait, Graeme—you look positively gorgeous tonight. While we have a drink before dinner, tell me what happened after I left the office. And would you like a glass of champagne, as usual? Or something else?"

"Champagne, Maxim, please." Graeme put her black velvet evening purse on the table and made herself comfortable on the chair opposite him, crossing her legs and adjusting her skirt. There was an air of urgency about her; it was as though she could hardly contain herself.

Now she bent forward, her manner suddenly grown confidential, her vivid eyes more alive and eager than ever, her intelligent face flushed pink with excitement. "I've come to a conclusion about the Winonda Group. After being on and off the phone with Peter Heilbron in New York for the last couple of hours, I think we should go for it, make a bid! It's a *cinch* for us. The perfect company for a takeover despite what appear to be certain problems. I've studied the last two telexes from Peter and—"

"If they're sensitive, I presume you've shredded them," Maxim cut in.

"Of course!" She looked at him askance. "Am I not your clone, Boss?"

Maxim bit back a smile, made no response.

Graeme rushed on, "Winonda has a number of unprofitable divisions, but these would be easy to liquidate. We would keep the profitable divisions, of course, and simply reorganize them, give them a bit of the West International streamlining."

She paused when the waiter brought the flute of champagne to her and waited until they were alone before continuing, "What makes the deal so attractive to me is the real estate Winonda owns just outside Seattle. It looks worthless at first glance, and especially so on paper. Undervalued, actually. It's run-down, and it's in a very bad area. However, I know it has *great* value, that it's a *big asset.*"

Maxim stared at her, lifted a brow.

Graeme went on. "It's a big asset because a Japanese company wants to buy it. They're in the process of buying up the entire area, actually, and they want the Winonda real estate so that they can tear down the existing buildings, redevelop the land by constructing a hotel, a shopping mall and offices on it."

"Then why hasn't Charles Bishop sold to them?" Maxim frowned. "That strikes me as particularly odd. He's extremely shrewd, very fast."

"He turned them down flat. Didn't want to know what they were offering, apparently. And not because they weren't offering plenty. I believe they went as high as two hundred and seventy million."

"What's the catch?"

"There isn't one, at least not for us. If we owned Winonda, we could sell the real estate holdings tomorrow, and to the same Japanese company. They're waiting in the wings. They'll wait in vain, of course, as long as Bishop's the president of Winonda. His father died in a Japanese prisoner-of-war camp, that's why he won't strike a deal with them."

When Maxim said nothing, Graeme remarked in a low voice, "Put very simply, he's letting his personal feelings get in the way."

Maxim looked thoughtful. After a moment he glanced at her. "You have good vibes about this deal, don't you?"

"Absolutely!"

"So do I, and I have from the beginning, ever since you put forward Winonda as a possibility for us. Call Peter tomorrow, tell him to get the acquisition team moving at once. And good for you, Grae. I'm impressed. You must have done a great deal of research."

Graeme shook her head. "A little, but not as much as you probably think. By one of those odd coincidences, my cousin Sara lives in Seattle now. She's with a bank. I asked her about Winonda, after you'd told me to go ahead and analyze the situation. She mentioned that some Japanese company had been sniffing around. She'd heard about their interest in the Winonda real estate through her boyfriend, who's a partner in an accounting firm. There was a nasty leak from somewhere, I suspect."

She grinned at Maxim. "I guess you're right about shredding machines, Boss. You can't be too careful. In any event, I ran with the information Sara had passed on to me and had it checked out. It proved to be correct." Graeme stopped, cleared her throat. "The stockholders of the Winonda Group might not be too happy to learn that their president passed up millions of dollars for a parcel of real estate that nobody else seems to want. Poor judgment on Bishop's part, wouldn't you say?"

"Yes, but I can understand his reasoning in some ways. In the final analysis, though, you're right."

"As the president and CEO of a public company he ought to have put personal sentiments aside," she said, in a voice that was surprisingly cold and deliberate.

Maxim gave her a swift look. He knew how tough, even ruthless, she could be at times, but her assessment of Bishop seemed to him harsh. Fleetingly a faint shadow crossed his face. He frowned. Suddenly he didn't wish to continue this conversation, and so he reached for his glass.

Graeme was about to ask him if something was wrong and then changed her mind. A muscle twitched on his cheek; he appeared strained all of a sudden, and she wondered why. He was such a private man, never revealing much about himself or his feelings, and she knew he hated anyone to pry, to try to get behind that impenetrable façade of his.

She lifted her flute of champagne. "Cheers," she said. "Here's to the Winonda Group. And to us."

Maxim said, "To Winonda. And to you."

They fell silent for a moment, both caught up in their own thoughts, and it was Graeme who spoke first. "How did your meeting with Alan Trenton go?"

"It wasn't with Alan, as it turns out. Oh, he was there, of course, but he wanted me to meet his merchant banker, John Vale of Morgan Lane. He had a proposition for me."

"What kind of proposition?" she asked, her eyes lighting up. Like Maxim, she was excited by business, and the prospect of a new deal gave her a high in much the same way it did him.

"To come to the rescue of Lister Newspapers," he said.

Graeme let out a long, low whistle. "My, my, that *is* something," she said in a soft voice. "*And?*"

Maxim told her what had happened earlier that evening, leaving nothing out, and Graeme listened avidly, giving him her full attention, wondering what he would do, asking herself whether he *would* go after the Lister empire. He was tough-minded, fearless when it came to business, but not really a gambler; Lister might well prove to be a gamble. Rectitude and prudence Maxim had in abundance, and she admired those traits in him. Yet, over the seven years she had worked for him, there had been times when he *had* taken real chances, and now, on reflection, it occurred to her that they had been rather big chances at that. Would he consider Lister Newspapers worth the risk? One never knew with him, he was so hard to read accurately. He called her his good right hand, but most of the time she didn't know what his left hand was doing.

Perhaps it was the contradictions, the unexpected in him that people found so fascinating—and irresistible. She stifled a sigh, realizing she had always been a little bit in love with him, even though he had never displayed one iota of interest in her. Not as a woman, at any rate. Oh, he paid her lovely compliments, said flattering things about her work, but that was as far as it went. She was his executive assistant, and therefore off limits. He was far too involved with his business ever to mix it with anything that remotely smacked of pleasure, sex or love.

And besides, he was married. And there were hints of another woman besides. Still, there were times, like now, when they were not in a work environment, when she sat looking at him, listening to his voice, savoring his company, when she fell completely under his spell as a woman. He was the most lethally attractive man she had ever met.

It was not only his face, his powerful dark gaze, his elegance and distinction; it was also the enigma of him. For there was something deeply mysterious about Maximilian West. And there was also, of course, his charm. Maxim had fatal charm, the kind that makes women commit terrible indiscretions. He was a natural-born lady-killer who, without doing one single thing, had women flinging themselves at him. On yet another level there was the intellect, the brains, the drive, the energy, the ambition and the success. It was a combination that spelled one thing—power. And power was exciting to her, an extraordinary aphrodisiac like no other she had ever known.

"You look as if you're drifting off," Maxim said, somewhat sharply for him.

Graeme said, "Sorry, Boss, I *am* concentrating." She offered him a bright, reassuring smile. "Let's see if I can sum up for you—John Vale of Morgan Lane wants you to be white knight for Lister. Everyone involved wants it. But you're not interested, are you?"

"No," he admitted, "I don't think I am."

"Are the figures that poor?"

"On the contrary, they're quite impressive. In fact, the company's in great shape." He frowned. "It's *me*, Grae. I'm just not excited about it—not excited *enough*, anyway. No fire in my gut. I don't know why, exactly, but I don't want to pick up my sword and go into combat for a newspaper empire. That's more up Rupert Murdoch's alley. Come to think of it, John Vale ought to have asked Rupert to be the white knight, not me. He's dropping the Lister accounts off at the house later, and I suddenly wish he weren't. I don't think I even want to look at the wretched papers, never mind study them."

"Do you want me to do it for you?"

He motioned to one of the waiters and ordered two more drinks. "We'll see," he said. Then he turned to her and put his hand on her arm. "Grae, I don't think I'll stay in London for the weekend after all."

"That's no problem, I'm ready whenever you say. When are we leaving? Tomorrow or Saturday?"

"I'm going alone. Tomorrow. On the morning Concorde."

Unable to disguise her surprise, she stared at him. "Oh" was about the only word she could muster.

"Normally I would say, Come back on the Concorde with me, but I'd like you to stay in London, follow through on a few things for me. You should be able to finish up by the end of the day tomorrow. You can fly back to New York on the company jet whenever you like. Tomorrow night, Saturday, Sunday or even Monday. The plane's at your disposal."

"London on the weekend doesn't appeal to me especially," she murmured, "but maybe I will stay in Europe. I could go to Paris for a couple of days—that might be fun."

She hesitated a moment before she leaned across the table to give him a penetrating look, and say in a low conspiratorial voice, "No problems at the New York office, I hope?"

"No, no, if there were, you'd be the first to know. I'm going back a little earlier than I'd planned, to see to a personal matter. I want to get it out of the way this weekend."

Instantly she thought, It's a woman and he's got trouble with her. But she merely said, "What is it you want me to do for you here in London?"

"There are a couple of banking matters to attend to. Also, rather than canceling it, I'd like you to take my place at the meeting with Montague Reston and Gerald Sloane. There'll be no problem, you can handle it."

"Okay, whatever you say. But I'll need a briefing on the Reston deal."

"Of course. First let's order dinner, I see Louis heading our way."

3

*I*T WAS ONE-FIFTEEN IN THE MORNING BY THE TIME Maxim got back to his house on the corner of Chesterfield Hill and Charles Street. He had escorted Graeme to the Ritz Hotel after their dinner at Annabel's, and had then walked home, crossing Piccadilly and heading through Half Moon Street into Mayfair. There was no longer any hint of rain, the air was crisp and dry, and usually he would have enjoyed the short walk. Yet all evening he had been fighting a feeling of weightedness, almost of oppression.

He let himself in, locked the front door behind him and hung his coat in the hall closet. He paused for a moment, listening. The house was quiet, perfectly still; nothing stirred. The staff had gone to bed, were no doubt already fast asleep, and the only sound was the hollow ticking of the antique grandfather's clock in the imposing marble foyer, where he stood.

Turning off the light, Maxim went up the curving staircase, more slowly than usual, to the second floor. In the master bedroom he shed his clothes, hoping that once he had on his pajamas and dressing gown, he would feel more himself.

Marco, the butler, familiar with Maxim's habits of working

late, studying documents and balance sheets well into the early hours, had turned on the lamps and banked up the fire before retiring to his own quarters. The silk-shaded lamps cast a rose-ate glow throughout and the logs burned brightly in the grate behind the mesh fire screen, throwing off welcome heat. Maxim seated himself at the escritoire, glanced at the telephone messages Marco had placed under a glass paperweight and put them to one side. None were of any great importance, they could be dealt with before he left for the airport in a few hours. Picking up a pearl-handled paper knife, he slit open the manila envelope that John Vale had dropped off earlier and took out the sheaf of papers.

It was with only the smallest degree of interest that he looked over the accounts of Lister Newspapers that he had fanned out on the desk in front of him. One of Maxim's greatest assets had always been his ability to read a financial statement well, and to size up a company quickly and with his own special brand of business acumen. This he did now, determining at once that Lister Newspapers was indeed a good buy, and by anybody's standards. Excellent, in fact. Then why did he feel no quickening of his pulse, no excitement in his veins, no thrill at the thought of going after it? Indisputably, his attitude had not changed since the meeting in Alan Trenton's office. He simply was not interested in making a play for this company.

Or was that true for *any* company?

It struck Maxim, and with some force, that he wasn't particularly interested in the Winonda Group either; and combined with everything else, this made him sit up with a start. What had caused his sudden change of heart?

Earlier, when he had told Graeme to go ahead, it had been for a variety of reasons. It was one of her bigger deals, and he knew how much it meant to her; he had no wish to disappoint or discourage her. Also, right at the outset he had recognized that Winonda would be an important acquisition for them, an enormously valuable asset to West International when it came to the overall picture of the conglomerate. But he had to admit, with surprise, that he much preferred that she handle the deal herself, with the help of Peter Heilbron and the financial team in the New York office. He didn't want to be the chief combatant in the actual battle; he had no interest whatsoever in being out there on the front line, a position he normally enjoyed. He would give advice from the trenches, but this time his staff would have to do the hard hand-to-hand fighting.

Maxim frowned. Why this sudden reluctance to put himself in the middle of the action? He had never felt this way before.

He had always thrived on being at the center of the action, at being the pivotal point. Was business beginning to bore him? Was that what was wrong with him? But how could that be? Business was his life, wasn't it? Anastasia had always said so.

At the thought of his first wife he winced, ran his hands through his hair distractedly, suddenly conscious that this was not the first night he had felt this way. He had not been himself of late.

He kept up the façade, of course, that dazzling façade of charm and magnetism that the world had come to expect. But inside, at the very core of his being, he was conscious that he felt empty. A bleakness had crept into his soul, he knew not from where. For some reason he felt joyless most of the time now, and increasingly he fought a terrible melancholy he could not fully comprehend.

Now he felt a deeper despair begin to settle over him, a feeling of panic, of claustrophobia. He felt as if he were suffocating, and he had the most pressing urge to open the windows, to get out of the room—a compulsion to run and not stop running until he had put great distance between himself and this place. He wanted to be far, far away. But where?

Whatever in the world was happening to him?

A chill coursed through him; he shivered; he realized it was a feeling others had described, a feeling that someone had walked over his grave. With this strange thought, gooseflesh prickled his arms and face. He would have to take hold of himself!

He glanced around his study. Whyever would he want to escape this room? He did not understand. It had been his favorite place in the entire house, filled as it was with treasures from which he had always drawn comfort and pleasure. Each item had been lovingly placed here by Anastasia and himself—and he recalled the satisfaction they had derived from searching out the antiques, the objets d'art and the paintings in England and on the Continent.

They had found the ancient oak boiserie that paneled the walls in an old manor house in Normandy. The French writing desk where he now sat had been discovered in an antiques shop in the Rue du Bac on a weekend trip to Paris. The wall sconces were picked up when they were traveling through Tuscany, while the remarkable horse paintings by Stubbs had been bought from a peer of the realm whose country seat was in Yorkshire. Altogether it was an eclectic mixture that somehow worked, mostly because the pieces were compatible with one another and shared one important quality, that of excellence.

Although the possessions in his study were beautiful, not all of the items were of great value. Yet they had always meant a lot to him. Now, seemingly, they no longer mattered.

Not only irritated with himself but also a little alarmed, Maxim walked over to the handsome William and Mary inlaid chest under the window, opened a bottle of carbonated water and poured himself a glass. He took a long swallow, breathing deeply, then he carried the glass back to a chair in front of the fire and sat staring into the flames. A look of abstraction settled over his face.

After a while, he felt calmer, and as he began to piece together patterns in his behavior in the last few months he began to see things as they actually were. With a rush of clarity he understood his dilemma. Quite simply, *he was a man in crisis.*

This sudden self-knowledge came to him from the deepest, innermost part of his psyche, and while it gave him a bitter jolt, on another level he realized he wasn't totally surprised. There had been other clues, from time to time, over the years. He sat up straighter; his eyes were blazing and he closed them convulsively, momentarily stunned.

But it was true; there was no point in denying it any longer— he had been doing that for long enough. He was at a critical point in his life; he could not go on any longer, could not live the way he had been living, with his personal life in such a shambles. And yet he did not know what to do about himself . . . or about his life.

For the first time he could ever remember, he felt immobilized by uncertainty, rendered helpless by indecision, and by situations he himself had created. He felt he needed to escape from people, from his life.

Setting down the crystal tumbler of water, Maxim propped his elbows on his knees and dropped his head into his hands. He was completely at a loss. For once he had no solutions to his problems. After a few minutes he lifted his head and forced himself to relax. And he began to ruminate on his life.

He knew that his dear old friend Stubby believed he had everything—that the world believed he had everything. Yet it struck him that, except for business success, in reality he had nothing. Because of his business acumen, he had power, fame of a kind, money to burn, houses, a yacht, a slick private jet, the other grand accoutrements of privilege and wealth. He hobnobbed with people who were as rich and famous as he was. Too, there was his knighthood, a great honor. While he was proud of all this, in fact none of it now filled the terrible void in his life.

He was alone. And lonely.

He was estranged from the people he needed to be closest to. The women he was involved with no longer brought him joy. His children seemed lost to him. Perhaps that was only temporary, perhaps there was a chance with Alix; nevertheless, he could not turn to them at this moment. And now he had to face the possibility that his work, that most enduring of all his passions, his greatest pleasure and triumph, was beginning to pall on him.

The idea was insupportable. In truth, it frightened the hell out of him.

Well, Maxim, he said to himself. Your bottom line at the moment is appalling. *Dismal*, in fact. You are in the red on every personal level . . . an emotional bankrupt.

His feeble attempt at humor did not lessen the misery. He had become a deeply unhappy man, that was the crux of it.

But then, had not happiness been an elusive stranger—transient at best—for the better part of his life?

He tried to think when it might have been that he had felt happy, and a cynical laugh rose in his throat. Happy—what an overworked word that was. Who the hell is happy?—at least for very long, anyway. The fortunate people he knew seemed content, or to have gained a certain kind of peace, but could they be called *happy*?

Rising, he began to pace the floor restlessly, his mind suddenly whirling in dizzying circles.

Eventually he was able to calm himself sufficiently to look at things more clearly, to regroup his thoughts, redirect his focus and to concentrate on the women in his life.

Two women, to be exact.

Adriana. His wife. And *Blair*. His mistress.

Blair was pushing for marriage. Adriana would not acknowledge that such a word as divorce even existed. And he was caught between the two of them, each more intransigent than the other.

He was not so sure he wanted to continue living with Adriana. On the other hand, did he really want to divorce her? What were his true feelings about Blair? Would marrying her solve his problems? He remembered something, and it made him laugh out loud. A famous wit had once said that when a man married his mistress he created a job vacancy. If he married Blair would he then be tempted to fill the vacancy? Find himself a new mistress to replace the one who had become his wife?

What a cynical thought *that* was. He laughed again, without a trace of mirth. Had he become the kind of man who would always need a mistress whatever the circumstances in the marriage? Perish the thought, he added under his breath.

In his mind's eye, Maxim pictured the people who were important in his life. How did *they* view *him*? He did not have to ponder that for more than a second.

To Adriana I am the faithless husband wanting to escape the marital bonds.

To Blair I am the lover grown ambivalent, distracted, less caring, in my preoccupation with my work.

To Anastasia I am her best friend, but only a friend, nothing else.

To my children I am the busy tycoon, the father who has no time for them. I have been cast in the role of the heavy. I am important because I pay their bills, but in their eyes I am no longer the loving father they once adored.

To my mother I am the son she is the proudest of, her favorite perhaps, and yet half the time she is disapproving of me because she cannot condone my private life, my personal behavior.

But I am *not* the person they think I am, he said to himself. None of their perceptions of me is accurate; they don't really know me. On the other hand, I don't really know myself, not anymore. Why am I here, what is my purpose on this planet? Is it merely to make money, run the business? In the last analysis, what is it all about?

To Maxim, these admissions were so staggering, so unacceptable that he caught his breath in surprise, and he paused in his pacing. He had to stop this! He must not validate these thoughts by giving them any kind of credence whatsoever.

Ultimately, though, he was unable to banish these disturbing self-revelations. All were inescapable truths. And so no matter which way he twisted and turned everything around in his head, he finally had to admit to himself that he would have to face up to what was disastrously wrong with his life, his deep unhappiness with it. And the sooner the better.

It was three o'clock when Maxim went to bed.

He did not really sleep, merely dozed fitfully on and off for several hours. Finally, around six, he got up, and showered and shaved. Marco brought him a pot of coffee and toast, and while he had his breakfast he wrote a detailed memo to Graeme, explained what he wanted done in London, and outlined the strategy for the meeting she was to have with Montague Reston.

At exactly eight-thirty he left the house carrying his trench coat and a briefcase, his only piece of luggage, and was driven off to Heathrow in one of West International's limousines. At the airport he was swiftly checked in, and went immediately to the Concorde departure lounge, where he sat reading the morning newspapers until boarding time, at ten o'clock.

Fastening his seat belt and settling down, Maxim glanced around and was relieved to see the plane was not as jam-packed as it had been on the last few occasions he had flown it. He had chosen to go on to New York by Concorde rather than travel on his personal Grumman Gulfstream jet because it was much faster, only three hours and forty-five minutes—even less time if there were no strong head winds.

Maxim opened his briefcase, took out some papers and buried his head in them for the first hour of the flight. He accepted a cup of tea, refused all other drinks and snacks, and gave his entire attention to his business papers. When he had done as much work as he could, he locked the folders in his briefcase, settled back and closed his eyes. He found it impossible to sleep, but he did manage to relax enough to get some rest. Half an hour later he roused himself and looked out the window.

They were floating through a vast stretch of cumulus clouds, soaring higher and higher above the Atlantic. As he stared into the infinite space, he contemplated Alix, his daughter. She was the reason he had decided to return to New York a few days earlier than he had originally planned. He wanted to see her, to talk to her, to spend some time over the weekend with her. Now that he was resolved to put his life in order, he was even more desperate to put things right with his firstborn child. They were both at fault, she more than he in so many ways. Nevertheless, he was quite prepared to take full blame for the rift that had developed between them. He would apologize, ask her forgiveness if necessary. In fact, he would do just about anything to win her trust again, to have this young woman back in his life.

4

▬▬▬▬▬

𝒜 FEMALE VOICE HE DID NOT RECOGNIZE ANSWERED THE telephone. "Alix West's office. May I help you?"

"I'd like to speak to Miss West, please," Maxim said.

"I'm sorry, but Ms. West isn't in today," the young voice informed him. "May I ask who's calling?"

"This is her father. To whom am I speaking?"

"Oh, good morning, Sir Maximilian!" the voice said in a tone that now sounded awed. "This is Geraldine Bonnay, her new assistant. Alix flew to California this morning. On business."

"I see. When will she be returning to New York?"

"Hopefully on Monday, Sir Maximilian. It's a quick trip. She has a meeting with a client in Beverly Hills tomorrow and is flying right out again on Sunday. Unless there are unexpected problems, of course. She'll be calling me sometime tomorrow. Can I give her a message?"

"No, not really," Maxim began, and paused, thought quickly. "As a matter of fact, Miss Bonnay, I'd really rather you didn't say I telephoned today. I have something special for her—a surprise," he improvised. "So please, not a word. It would only spoil everything."

"Of course, Sir Maximilian! Not a word!" Geraldine Bonnay assured him, sincerity echoing down the wire. "And just in case you do change your mind and want to talk to her tonight, or on Saturday, Alix is staying at the Bel-Air Hotel."

"I think not . . . the surprise, you know. But thank you for the information anyway."

"Oh it's my pleasure, and it's been lovely talking to you!"

"Likewise, Miss Bonnay. My thanks again. Good-bye."

Maxim let his hand rest on the phone for a moment, fighting back his disappointment that Alix had left New York the very same day he had arrived. He had so wanted to see her, to spend time with her. He ought to have called her in advance, made sure she was going to be in the city for the weekend, but if he *had* phoned from London to alert her to his arrival, she, more than likely, would have fled. Or found plausible reasons why she couldn't see him. Surprise was always the most successful technique to use with Alix, he had discovered long ago.

He sighed, facing the fact that there was no doubt in his mind that Alix still harbored a grudge, even though she persisted in denying this. He was equally convinced that her smoldering dissatisfaction with him was more than likely being fanned into a roaring bushfire by her brother, Michael, who had always had an enormous influence over Alix, ever since their childhood, much more than anyone else did and in an infinite number of ways. Furthermore, Michael had his own ax to grind these days—he, too, was full of grievances and resentment, and not a little anger. Maxim was fully aware of that anger and the frustration in Michael, even though he denied there was anything wrong, just as his sister did. Children, Maxim muttered to himself. People. Why does everything seem so difficult? As if life isn't hard enough without having children inventing problems and blowing things out of all proportion!

Shifting slightly in the chair behind his desk, he turned his head and let his gaze rest on the photograph of Alix that stood framed in silver, with other family portraits, on the ebony table near the window. It had been taken six years ago to commemorate her twenty-first birthday, and he was struck again with what a lovely young woman that tomboy of a child had grown up to be. So fair, with creamy skin and delicate bone structure

in a face whose expression was invariably so serene, so calm
it made him catch his breath. But most beautiful and striking
were her eyes. Widely spaced and enormous, they were an unusual pale gray-green and filled with pellucid light. Alix was
tall and lissome, with a fine athletic body, and she moved with
elegance and grace. Aside from her great looks, his daughter
had a quick, intelligent mind, and was extremely clever, most
especially when it came to business and finance. In fact, she
was as smart as her brother, perhaps even a fraction more as-
tute than he, which was saying a great deal because Michael
was brilliant.

Alix had wanted to come and work with him since her teens,
and he had been thrilled at the idea of having his daughter in
the business. Everything had been planned most carefully. And
then four years ago, just before she was supposed to start at
the New York office, they had quarreled badly. It had been
about her entanglement with a man he considered to be highly
disreputable; and there had been several other problems that
now seemed too petty to recall. She had gone off in a huff and
started a business of her own.

She had opened an office in the middle of Manhattan, setting
herself up as an art and antiques broker working primarily with
English and European dealers and leading art galleries.

She bought and sold only the most sought-after items, the
kind of rare, precious and costly objects and paintings that generally made it to the auction floor of Christie's and Sotheby's.
Some few years earlier she had taken courses at Sotheby's in
London, and her knowledge of paintings and objets d'art was
considerable. Also, she had been gifted with the critical eye of
a true expert, who recognizes excellence instantly and can just
as quickly and easily spot a fake. These attributes, plus her extraordinary taste and natural head for business, had proven to
be an invaluable combination. She had been successful right
from the start and he was inordinately proud of her. Nonetheless, he still longed for her presence at his own office; it would
be good to have her working alongside him.

Perhaps it was not too late. Maybe he could still lure her
into West International—once they had made their peace. And
he was determined that they should do that. He heard his
mother's voice reverberating in his head: "It's never too late
to repair damages of the heart, Maxim. It's never too late to

start over again, to come back to a loved one by mending a quarrel." His mother had said that to him countless times over the years and he had always believed her. He still did. He had to, because that belief reinforced his hope that he would win Alix back, that they would be as close as they had once been.

He had never missed anyone as much as he missed his daughter. And now, especially. He felt quite lost, really.

The fact that he would have to put off seeing her, now, for several days, was like a physical pain in the region of his chest, an ache. He hurt in a way he never had before.

But no, actually that wasn't strictly true. He *had* experienced this same kind of longing, once before—this yearning for someone. It had been a long, long time ago.

And it had been for Ursula.

Once again Maxim's eyes strayed to the photograph of Alix. She had the same fine blond hair and flawless complexion as Ursula, the same lovely, luminous eyes full of dreaminess and tranquillity.

Ursula. He realized he had thought of her more often recently; he began to wonder why she had been so much on his mind of late. Was it because his painful feelings about Alix echoed his feelings about *her*, the other woman he had loved with such intensity and so completely? These feelings had been buried a long time, and buried so deeply that he had been momentarily startled, a few weeks ago, when her face had sprung wholly formed into his mind for the first time in years. His memories of Ursula now were very clear.

He unlocked the top drawer of his desk and reached into the back to take out the black leather wallet that he kept there for safety. He opened it and looked at a picture in it of Ursula. It was a black-and-white shot, faded now, but time had not dimmed the lustrous eyes, the bright curving smile so full of trust and hope.

The wallet was worn, the leather cracked in places. He smoothed his hand over it, remembering. It had belonged to Sigmund. . . .

When he slipped the memento back into the drawer, he was surprised at the tightness in his throat, the way his eyes smarted. Resolutely pushing back this rush of emotion, Maxim stood up and walked across the cream-colored stretch of carpet. He stood staring out through the metal-mesh curtain that covered the plate-glass window of his office high up in the Seagram Building, and focused his attention on Park Avenue far below, but in his present mood he hardly saw anything. The melancholy that had beset him in London in the early hours of the morning had persisted, and now, to make matters worse, he found himself dwelling on the past. He brought his concentration to bear on the present; he had to make some plans. He had come to New York for the weekend, hoping to see his daughter; well, Alix was not available until Monday, perhaps even Tuesday. Today was Friday. The whole weekend stretched ahead.

What to do? Where to go?

He had a variety of choices, yet none appealed. There was his apartment on Fifth Avenue, but if he went there he would undoubtedly have a confrontation with Adriana, whose sole purpose in life these days seemed to be to fight with him. He could go to the house he owned in Sutton Place, where he had installed Blair, but if he did he would be exposing himself to a weekend of Blair's nagging and veiled threats, which in fact were not particularly veiled anymore. There was his farm in Connecticut, but Adriana might conceivably hear of his arrival in New Preston, and come rushing out—to fight with him in the country instead of the city. She was certainly combative enough, at the moment.

What he really wanted was to be alone. Entirely alone.

There was only one place for that, and it was the perfect place—his beach house in East Hampton. Closed for the winter though it was, the house was more or less kept ready for his arrival at any moment. It was a year-round house, insulated for the cold weather, and in the winter months the heat was kept on a low temperature at all times. Elias Mulvaney, his gardener and handyman, watched over the house, checked on it every day or so. And Mrs. Mulvaney went in to dust once a week. All he had to do was telephone Elias and instruct him to go over to the house later that afternoon to turn up the heat, and arrange for Mrs. Mulvaney to come in on Saturday and do a few chores. It couldn't be simpler.

Maxim turned away from the window and strode back to his desk, pleased with the idea of driving out to East Hampton for a couple of days alone. He would be able to indulge himself in that rare commodity—solitude—and try to sort out his thoughts. He could listen to music, take long walks on the beach. But mostly, he would endeavor to bring a semblance of order to the chaos in his head, and heart.

His private life had long needed to be put in order, yet he had not been able to commit himself to any action. Perhaps the time had come to make some decisions about Adriana and Blair. Only then would he be able to take himself in hand, get to the root of the personal crisis that threatened to engulf him, and in so doing resolve his inner conflicts.

He opened his address book, picked up his private phone and dialed Elias Mulvaney's number on Long Island. It rang and rang, but no one answered. He glanced at the clock on the desk; it was just eleven. No doubt Elias was making his daily rounds, checking on other homes, doing odd jobs for the permanent residents in the village who also employed him on a part-time basis. And Mrs. Mulvaney was more than likely out marketing for the weekend groceries.

No problem, Maxim murmured to himself, I'll reach one of them sooner or later. He pressed the intercom. "Douglas, would you come in, please."

"Of course, right away."

Within seconds, Douglas Andrews, Maxim's private secretary at the New York office, hurried in carrying a sheaf of papers. A New Yorker born and bred, Douglas was thirty-three, short, fresh-faced and dark-haired, with a pleasant, outgoing disposition and a willingness to work around the clock. He had been Maxim's private secretary for five years and was devoted, loyal and fiercely protective.

"Here are the legal documents on the Mystell deal that you asked me for. Peter Heilbron's secretary just dropped this memo off for you, regarding the Blane-Gregson takeover," Douglas said. He placed the papers in an empty chromium tray on the right-hand corner, then sat down in the chair facing Maxim.

"Thank you," Maxim said, glancing at the pile in the tray. "I'll attend to those shortly. There's a couple of things I'd like you to do, Douglas. First, rent a car for me, please, and have it outside at four o'clock. Send one of the secretaries over to Bloomingdale's food department to buy some provisions for me—a cold chicken, potato salad, a piece of Brie, some French bread and a carton of milk. That should do it."

"I'll get on it right away." Douglas could not quite keep the surprise out of his voice, and he gave Maxim a curious stare. "Are you going somewhere?" he asked.

An imperceptible smile flicked across Maxim's face. "Looks that way, doesn't it. I think I'll go to the beach cottage in East Hampton, for the weekend. Alone. I want a little peace, some quiet time to think. And I don't want *anyone* to know where I am."

Douglas nodded. "Of course. Absolutely. I'll deal with the car and send Alice over to the store. But are you sure that's enough food for you? Maybe she should buy more."

"No, no, the chicken and the salad will do me fine for tonight, and I can pick up some groceries in East Hampton on Saturday morning."

"You're pretty brave, leaving at four o'clock," Douglas volunteered, frowning. "You'll have all that commuter traffic on the Long Island Expressway to contend with. It might be a better idea to drive out to the Hamptons later—say, around six or so."

"Oh, it's not all that bad in winter."

"Well . . ." Douglas's voice trailed off as he could see that Maxim was already thinking about something else. He got up, headed for the door.

Maxim reached for the documents in the chromium tray, and called, "Oh yes, please ask Peter if he can have a quick lunch with me. And if he's available, let the Four Seasons know I'd like my regular table today, if possible. Around one."

"Yes, Sir Maxim," Douglas murmured, opening the door, and closing it quietly behind him. He wondered if Maxim really was going to spend the weekend alone—or did he have an assignation with some new lady love? Lucky devil, Douglas thought, he's got it all, and then some. What I wouldn't give to be in his shoes.

But would I really? Douglas asked himself as he sat down at his desk a moment later. Would I want Adriana for a wife? And as for that girlfriend over on Sutton Place, she's not much better. Graeme Longdon called her Miss Greedy Guts, and Graeme was right.

How did such a *prince* of a guy get himself in such a situation? Douglas had come to the conclusion that men who were brilliant in business were not necessarily always smart when it came to the women in their lives.

He dialed Peter Heilbron, head of West International's acquisition team. "It's Doug, Peter. The boss wants to know if you can have a quick lunch with him today. Downstairs. At one. I hope you can, because he seems a bit down in the mouth to me."

"Of course—I'll make myself free," Peter said quickly. "And what exactly do you mean by 'down in the mouth'?"

"Well, when the boss walked in this morning I thought he looked preoccupied. Or 'troubled' may be a better word. And a bit sad, or so it seemed to me. None of that's like him. You know what an expert he is at veiling his feelings."

"Yes, I do. Is it business, do you suppose, or personal?"

"I'm not sure. . . . personal, probably."

"It has to be, because as far as I can see there are no problems here, or at the London office that I know of . . . and I'd know—" He cleared his throat. "Whatever it is, it can't be too serious, or he would have mentioned it. Maybe he's just tired."

"Sure," Douglas said, deciding that discretion was the wisest policy when it came to the subject of the boss. He had no intention of speculating, or gossiping with Peter. "He *has* been traveling a lot these past few weeks. By the way, nobody knows he's in town except you and me and your secretary. He wants to keep it that way."

5

It took Maxim two and a half hours to drive from Manhattan to East Hampton, and by the time he reached the charming old village on Long Island the bleak January sky, so cold and remote and colorless, had long since turned gray and then the color of pitch. Only a few stars dotted the horizon, far out over the black and endless sea, and the moon, clear, high-flung and silvered, was obscured by scudding dark clouds.

Maxim glanced at the clock on the dashboard as he turned off Ocean Avenue into Lily Pond Lane; he noted that it was almost six-forty-five. Not bad, he thought, as he drove on, heading toward the Georgica Beach end of the lane where his cottage was located.

Within a few minutes he was pulling up outside.

The cottage had gray shingles, white shutters, a black door and neat squared-off chimneys. Set a little back from the road, it was fronted by sloping lawns, now covered with a sprinkling of hoarfrost, along with a number of giant oaks, which offered privacy the year round and plenty of cool leafy shade in the heat of the summer.

Although it was not a large house by Maxim's standards, it more than adequately filled his needs. It was spacious without being sprawling, and the layout was well planned: the hall, big family kitchen, dining room and study were at the front of the house; the living room, which flowed into a library, was at the back. These two adjoining rooms overlooked the swimming pool, a small pool house and flower gardens; nestling at the far end of the rear lawn, beyond the flower beds, was a copse that gave the property additional privacy.

The upstairs consisted of two floors. On one were the master bedroom, bath and dressing rooms; on the other, two guest rooms with their own bathrooms, plus a third, larger bedroom that had been converted into an office, equipped with two desks, a typewriter and a computer, plus fax, telex, Xerox and shredding machines, as well as a battery of telephones. Because of this superefficient office, which Maxim thought of as a command post, he could come to the cottage whenever he wished but still be in touch with his business empire around the world. Often he brought along Douglas Andrews and Graeme Longdon, sometimes Peter Heilbron, to work on pending deals, especially in the summer months, when they were glad to escape from the sweltering heat of the city for a few days.

After parking against the curb, Maxim took the Bloomingdale's shopping bag from the backseat and got out of the rented Jaguar.

It was a bitter night, with an icy wind blowing in from the

Atlantic. He glanced around. The lane was in total darkness; there was not the slightest glimmer of light from any of the other houses. But as he strode rapidly up the path between the lawns the moon came out from behind the banked-up clouds and bathed the cottage and the path with silvery radiance. For a few moments it was like daylight.

Out of the corner of his eye Maxim noticed a station wagon parked a bit farther along and wondered absently whom it belonged to as he hurried around to the side entrance of the cottage. He let himself in through the kitchen door and switched on the lights. Pushing the door closed with his foot, he carried the bag of food over to the circular table that stood in the center of the room.

The blue-and-white tiled kitchen was spotless. Everything gleamed brightly, and the room looked as if Mrs. Mulvaney had only just cleaned it. Perhaps she did do it today, Maxim thought. He had not succeeded in reaching either of the Mulvaneys before leaving the office, and aware of their diligence and reliability, it now struck him that they might easily have been here when he was ringing them at home.

Maxim shivered, conscious of the chill in the air. The heat was on as usual, but he realized that it needed to be turned up on a cold night like this. Still shivering, he headed in the direction of the front hall, where the controls for the heating system were located in a cupboard under the stairs.

Pulling open the door leading into the hall, Maxim suddenly stopped dead, one foot poised on the step. He had heard a faint noise, a pinging sound, like metal hitting metal. It was barely discernible, but puzzled, Maxim stepped out into the hall.

Light from the kitchen streamed around him, and he could not fail to see the television set standing on the floor, along with various pieces of equipment from the office upstairs.

Once more there was that odd pinging sound, then a small crash, a muffled curse. The noises were coming from the living room.

Immediately all of Maxim's senses were alerted to trouble. Apparently there was someone in the house besides himself—an intruder, no doubt about that, a burglar, judging by the things stacked up in the hall.

Moving stealthily and noiselessly, Maxim crossed the hall and opened the door a crack. The living room was dark, as was the adjoining library, but in the library he could see the small circle of light from a flashlight, which was being trained around the room.

Deciding that surprise was his best tactic, Maxim struck the master switch on the wall, and instantly, six table lamps in the two rooms blazed to life, flooding the area with brilliance.

Startled, the intruder swung around and saw Maxim. He was not very tall and was slightly built, dressed entirely in black. He was holding a large black nylon laundry bag that bulged and was obviously filled with loot.

The burglar stood gaping at Maxim.

"Drop that bag!" Maxim yelled, his expression one of utter fury. The man continued to gape; there was a dumbfounded look on his face, and he appeared to be momentarily paralyzed.

With a rush, Maxim sprinted across the floor, toward the intruder, confident he could tackle and overpower him before calling in the police. But just before Maxim reached him, the burglar pulled out a gun and fired.

Maxim felt the bullet slam against his chest and went down at once with a thud, sprawling between the living room and the library. The look of astonishment on his face changed to one of stunned shock.

Maxim thought: *This can't be happening to me . . . it can't be ending like this . . . not after all I've been through. . . . I can't be dying at the hands of a petty thief. . . .*

The burglar stood stock-still, listening. He wondered if anyone had heard the shot, then dismissed the idea at once. There was nobody around. These houses were summer places. That was why he had headed for the area earlier. He'd already pulled two other jobs down the block. Easy pickings they'd been. He hadn't had to waste anybody in the other houses, though; no one had walked in and surprised him. Shame about the guy who just had. But he'd had to protect himself. The guy was big, powerful, could've taken him easy.

He walked over to the body and looked down at it dispassionately. The man he had shot was lying on his side. He did not stir. Blood stained the front of his pale-blue shirt, was already seeping into the gray carpet, turning a patch of it a funny rust color.

Shoving the gun back into the waistband of his pants, the

burglar quickly returned to the library, grabbed a few more silver trinkets and threw them into the laundry bag. Glancing about, satisfied that he had ripped off the best of the small stuff here, he left the living room and switched off the lights as he headed out. He went through to check the kitchen, turned off the lights there and returned to the hall.

He stood listening again.

The darkened house was totally silent. So was the street. Nothing moved. No cars drove past. Methodically he began to carry the pieces of equipment and the television set to the front steps. Once everything was outside, he dropped the latch on the door and pulled it tightly shut behind him. Still moving with speed and expertise, he went up and down the path until all of his booty had been stowed in the station wagon. Sliding in behind the wheel, he drove off without a backward glance.

He did not see anyone or any traffic as he sped down Lily Pond Lane. He knew he was safe. Nobody ever came out here in this kind of freezing weather in the dead of winter. The body would not be found for weeks. And anyway, he couldn't be linked to the man's death. He had been smart, cool. He hadn't left a single fingerprint, not even half of one. He knew better than that. He always wore gloves when he pulled jobs.

Elias Mulvaney sat at the kitchen table in his small, comfortable house behind the railway station in East Hampton. He was enjoying the warmth of the blazing fire, his second cup of coffee and a jelly doughnut on this icy night, and thinking about the afternoon he and Clara had just spent at their daughter's house in Quogue.

It had been a red-letter day for them, visiting with their first grandchild, reveling in her good health and prettiness, and in Lola's happiness. She and Mickey, her husband of ten years, had been waiting a long time for this baby. Yep, it's been the grandest day, Elias thought, and it has given Clara a real boost, made her forget her rheumatism. Clara had stayed on in Quogue for the weekend. Elias was certain she would be fussing and bustling, playing mother hen to the child and Lola, but he didn't think there was any harm in that. None at all. Do her good, he decided, and, picking up his mug, drank the rest of his coffee.

The shrilling of the telephone broke the silence in the

kitchen, made Elias sit up with a start. He rose and ambled across the room to answer it.

"Mulvaney here."

"Good evening, Elias, this is Douglas Andrews."

"Hello, Mr. Andrews!" Elias exclaimed warmly, his grizzled, weatherbeaten face lighting up. Douglas Andrews had been a favorite of his for several years. "How've you been?" he asked.

"Very well, thanks, Elias. And you?"

"Can't complain," Elias replied.

"I'm calling you because I've been trying to reach Sir Maximilian at the cottage, but there's no reply. I was wondering if you'd heard from him this evening."

"Well, no, I haven't," Elias said, sounding surprised. "Been in Quogue all day, didn't get back until seven. I didn't even know Sir Maxim was out here."

"He did try to get hold of you several times today. Obviously, since you were in Quogue, there was no answer. He left the city around four-fifteen. I rented a Jaguar for him and he was driving himself. I figured it would probably take him about three hours, or thereabouts, and I started to call him around seven-thirty. I have a number of messages for him. I don't understand why he's not there, since it's now eight already."

"Yes, Sir Maxim should have reached East Hampton by now," Elias agreed. Because Douglas Andrews sounded so worried he tried to reassure him. "Mebbe the line is wonky in some way or other, it's been mighty cold and windy out here these last few days, and we've had a lot of rain."

"Yes," Douglas said and paused. He took a deep breath, then continued, "I must admit, I'm growing concerned. I hope he hasn't had an accident on the road."

"Oh, I'm sure he hasn't," Elias said. "Sir Maxim's a careful driver, you know that. There's more'n likely a good explanation."

"It's very important that I speak with him tonight, Elias, and I wonder if you'd mind going over to the cottage, checking things out for me."

"Sure, I'll go immediately, that's no problem. Just give me your number so I can call you the minute I get there." As he was speaking Elias picked up the pencil near the message pad, licked the point and quickly scribbled down Douglas's number as it was given to him.

They rang off, and Elias hurried out into the passageway. He opened the top drawer of the chest, took out his bunch of house keys and slipped them into his trouser pocket. Hanging on a coat stand near the door were his down-filled parka, a woolen scarf and a cap with earflaps, and these garments he took down and put on. He picked up his gloves and left at once.

The pickup truck Elias used for running around the village was parked in front of his house, and he clambered in and drove off down the street.

Once he had crossed the railway tracks he sped through the village, heading for Lily Pond Lane, driving through streets unimpeded by traffic this evening. East Hampton was deserted, and it looked as if every one of the locals had left along with the summer residents. Within minutes Elias arrived at the gray-shingled cottage.

He walked briskly to the Jaguar parked immediately in front of him, shone his flashlight on the windows and peered inside.

Then he began to walk up the path between the frost-covered lawns. As he approached the house he suddenly experienced such a strange sense of apprehension that he was startled enough to stop dead. He had been born and brought up in East Hampton, and in all of his sixty-five years of living here he had never felt uneasy or afraid. But at this moment he was filled with trepidation, and he did not understand why. It was eerie.

Elias looked up at the house. The moon was high, a great chunk of silver shining vibrantly, casting its bright glow across the lines of the roof, the chimneys, the towering trees. The cottage was thrown into relief against the dark backdrop of the sky and the copse, and it looked unnaturally gloomy and somber, almost sinister. No welcoming lights winked in the windows as they did when Maximilian West was in residence.

If Sir Maxim is inside, then why are all the lights turned off? Elias asked himself, and he continued to stare at the house worriedly. He knew Sir Maxim had arrived because of the Jaguar. He wondered if Sir Maxim had had a heart attack or a stroke, and was lying somewhere in the house, stricken and unable to phone for help. Sir Maxim was a young man, and he looked healthy enough, but you never knew about anybody these days. On the other hand, he could have gone for a walk. Elias dismissed this idea the moment it entered his mind. Who would go wandering around the neighborhood on a bitter-cold night like this? It then occurred to him that someone driving his own car could have picked up Sir Maxim and taken him out to dinner.

This last theory was the most reasonable explanation so far, and a feeling of vast relief washed over Elias. He hurried up the path, strode purposefully around to the side of the house and stopped at the kitchen door.

Even though he was now convinced that Sir Maximilian West had gone to dinner with a friend, Elias nevertheless rang the doorbell several times. When there was no answer, he took out a bunch of keys, found the right one and let himself into the house. He switched on the lights, closed the door behind him, and walking into the middle of the room, he called out, "Hello, hello, anybody home?"

His question was greeted by total silence, but this did not particularly surprise him. He looked around the kitchen, spotted the Bloomingdale's shopping bag and, checking its contents, saw that it was filled with provisions for the weekend. He then went to the door leading into the main entrance hall, determined to investigate further on the off chance that Sir Maxim had been taken ill.

When Elias opened the door, such a strong sense of foreboding assaulted him again, the hackles rose on the back of his neck and he shivered. Telling himself he was being a stupid old fool, and clamping down on this unexpected and ridiculous feeling of dread, he put the light on, glanced about and saw that there was nothing untoward here in the hall.

Reassured, Elias walked across to the double doors of the living room, flung them open and flicked the master switch. Instantly he saw the body on the floor.

He gasped, then exclaimed out loud, "Oh my God!" His chest tightened, and for a split second he was rooted to the spot, his eyes staring.

After a moment or two Elias managed to take hold of himself and he walked over to the body. The shock he experienced was like a violent punch in the belly, and he gazed down at Maximilian West disbelievingly, feeling as though his legs were turning to jelly. He thought he was going to keel over as he gripped the back of a chair to steady himself.

After calming himself he stepped closer, saw the blood, the gunshot wound, and his heart sank with dismay. The injury was obviously serious. He knelt down, peering into Maxim's face. It was ghastly, the color of bleached bone. Elias searched for signs of life, brought his head nearer to Maxim's chest. He was breathing. Just barely. Elias took hold of his wrist, felt for a pulse. It was faint but it was there.

Elias straightened, his face stark, his eyes glassy with shock. Who had done this? And why? Rage flooded him, and he thought of searching the house looking for clues, but he quickly changed his mind. Whoever had shot Sir Maxim had doubtless fled without leaving any evidence. Besides, it was vital that he get help immediately if he was to save Sir Maxim. He went to the desk, picked up the phone and dialed.

"East Hampton Village Police. Officer Spank speaking."

"Norman, it's Elias here. I'm at the West house out on Lily Pond Lane. Sir Maximilian West has been shot," he said shakily. "I just found him. Call Southampton Hospital for an ambulance. He's alive, but he looks as if he's lost a lot of blood. Tell them to hurry. And you'd better get here as fast as you can."

"As soon as I've contacted the hospital I'll be over," Norman Spank said. As an afterthought, he added brusquely, "Don't touch anything, Elias," and he promptly hung up.

Elias sat down heavily in the chair near the desk, fumbled in his pocket and pulled out the piece of paper on which he had written Douglas Andrews's phone number in Manhattan. He dialed it, and as the number began to ring he braced himself to give the young man the terrible news.

Maxim floated in space . . . in a great white void . . . in a vast nothingness.

He wanted to open his eyes but could not. He felt as if they were permanently sealed.

Where was he?

He did not know. He hardly cared. His body, which a moment ago had seemed weightless, now felt as heavy as lead and immovable.

Gradually he became aware of voices. A man's voice, clear, resonant, a voice he had never heard before. The man was saying something about blood transfusions, a bullet that had lodged near the heart.

And then Maxim heard a woman speaking. Her voice filled the air . . . it was light . . . musical . . . and it seemed familiar, yet he could not quite identify it.

"He's not going to die, is he, Dr. Morrison?" the woman asked.

"We're doing everything to save his life," the man replied. His tone was somber. "He lost a lot of blood at the time of the shooting, and as I have explained, the operation to remove the bullet has been delicate, complicated. He *is* in a very serious condition—I'm not going to mislead you about that."

"But he does have a chance, doesn't he?" the woman persisted.

The doctor did not answer immediately. Then he said, "Fortunately, Maximilian is a healthy man, he's very strong. That's an important factor. And he is in the best of hands here at Mount Sinai. He's getting superior care and treatment, and he is being monitored night and day."

Maxim made a supreme effort and finally he managed to lift his eyelids. He blinked, adjusted to the light, swung his eyes from side to side, taking everything in.

He saw a man in a white coat. That must be the doctor.

Then he became aware of others standing at the bottom of the bed.

The women.

They were grouped in a semicircle. He was conscious of five pairs of female eyes focused on him intently, watching him, waiting. *His mother. His first wife. His third wife. His mistress. His daughter, Alix.*

All of the women in his life, assembled here, at his bedside.

He snapped his eyes shut. He did not want to see them, to deal with them.

Everything suddenly came back to him. He remembered driving to Long Island in the rented Jaguar, going into the cottage in East Hampton, surprising the intruder. Then the man had pulled a gun and shot him. He could not remember anything after that.

The doctor in the room had just mentioned Mount Sinai. So he had been brought to New York. How long had he been here? He had no idea.

He wondered if he was going to die. He didn't want to die. He wanted to live.

Teddy. Where was Teddy?

Maxim tried to open his eyes, but the effort to do so was far too great.

He wanted Teddy. She could save him. She had always saved him in the past. Once, long ago, she had said he was like a cat with nine lives. How many of his nine lives had he used up?

He could not die now. He must live. He had so much to do. So much to put right.

Maxim tried to speak, but the words would not come out of his mouth.

Teddy. Oh, Teddy, where are you? Help . . . help . . . me. . . .

He felt himself drifting back into the vast white nothingness, that great vaporous void that had engulfed him before, and he fought it, but it was too strong for him in his weakened state and it overwhelmed him.

PART TWO

Ursula

BERLIN

1938

Thou shalt not be afraid for the terror by night;
nor for the arrow that flieth by day;
Nor for the pestilence that walketh in darkness;
nor for the destruction that wasteth at noonday.
A thousand shall fall at thy side,
and ten thousand at thy right hand;
but it shall not come nigh thee.

—Psalm 91

6

≡

THE WOMAN STOOD BEFORE THE EMPIRE-STYLE CHEVAL mirror in the bedroom, staring hard at her reflection. Slowly she turned, studying the gown. She had bought it on a trip to Paris three years ago and it was by Jean Patou, her favorite couturier. She had worn it only once since then, and now she saw that it had retained its incomparable style and elegance, as had the other Patou creations she owned.

Tonight she had wanted to wear a simple dress, which was why she had chosen this particular one, a floor-length column that fell in fluid lines from shoulder to hem. The sleeves were long, the bodice plain, the neckline high, skimming across the throat, while the back was worked into a draped-cowl effect. Made of matte crepe and cut with superb skill, it was the color, nevertheless, that caught the eye. Called Patou blue, it was almost, but not quite, violet.

This vibrant shade was the ideal foil for the woman's Nordic coloring. Her hair was a shining gilt, her skin creamy, her eyes a misty gray-blue, luminous, fringed with thick blond lashes. She was of medium height, but her slender figure and long coltish legs made her look taller. Her feet and ankles were delicate, well shaped, and she had aristocratic hands, slim, with tapering fingers. It was the combination of her physical attributes, her ability to wear clothes well and her inherent good taste that gave her an elegance of appearance that was quite singular. The overall impression she projected was a mixture of femininity, breeding and intelligence. Her name was Ursula Westheim. She was thirty-four years old.

Satisfied that the gown was appropriate not only for the reception and dinner at the British embassy, which she was to attend that evening, but also for her mood of reserve, her sense of restraint, she slowly walked toward the dressing table. But when she came to the white marble fireplace she paused, and stood warming her hands at the huge log fire that took the chill out of the air on this cold winter night.

After a moment she found herself turning inward, sinking into her myriad thoughts, as she was wont to do of late. Introspective of nature though she was, this characteristic had grown and magnified, become more pronounced in the past year. She had to watch herself, particularly at social functions, since she had developed a habit of drifting off, carried along by her thoughts into a place known only to her and where no one else could follow. Her husband, Sigmund, endeavored to understand, and he was infinitely patient with her, and gentle, but she was aware that his family, most especially his mother and his sister Hedy, found her remote, impenetrable. She could not help this. Her inchoate thoughts were like monsters in her mind, forever present yet not wholly formed and therefore all the more troubling.

She lived with a nagging anxiety that never seemed to leave her these days. Moreover, she no longer felt safe anywhere, except perhaps when she was in this house. It was her haven, her bastion against the ugliness in the world outside its doors, her strong citadel. There were moments when she truly wished she did not have to leave it, for, in a certain sense, there was very little for her beyond these walls.

The Berlin she had been born in, and where she had grown up, no longer existed. Today it was a city of fear, of brutality and thuggery, of grimness and virulent rumor, of treachery and betrayal. The Gestapo, the secret police, stalked the streets, the beer halls and the cafés; frozen-faced SS men were everywhere one looked, as were Hitler's unholy gang of thugs, posturing and looking ridiculous in their operetta uniforms, for all the world like toy soldiers playing war games—except that their games were dangerous, deadly, and played with evil intent.

Last year she had been at a reception at the French embassy on the Pariserplatz when Hitler had walked in suddenly, flanked by Goebbels and Göring and several of his other cronies. She had been startled to see how small they were, how unimpressive and ordinary, looking quite different in reality than they did in their photographs in newspapers, which made them seem invincible. She had thought they appeared foolish in their fancy-dress uniforms, and for a brief moment it was difficult to take them seriously as they strutted past, arrogant, vulgar, and bloated with self-importance. But that moment had been fleeting, for indeed she took them seriously. *Very* seriously. The power they embodied was only too real. And it was a terrifying power.

She was forever asking herself how such a large number of people had allowed themselves to be led by the nose by a man like Hitler, a former vagabond and derelict who wasn't even a German but an uneducated Austrian corporal who could not speak the German language properly. Yet, amazingly, many believed he had only the welfare of the German nation at heart and had fallen under his spell; his great magnetism had made his demagoguery mesmerizing. Weren't the people aware of the horror implicit in his terrible creed? He was leading them down a road to hell. How could they possibly think he was their saviour?

She had voiced these thoughts to her dearest friend, Renata von Tiegal, recently, and Renata had said, "The Germans have a tendency to love false gods, to worship false idols. And don't let any of us forget that."

And then Renata's husband, Reinhard, had remarked in a regretful voice, "Hitler should have been stopped years ago. The Western Alliance could have done it. But they didn't, and now I'm afraid it's too late. For us. For them."

Kurt von Wittingen, who was also present that evening, had finished softly, "The British, the French and the Americans failed to understand one basic fact. That the Nazis didn't want power because of the economic situation. They just wanted power."

Well, now they had power, didn't they? The ultimate power. Ursula shivered involuntarily, gripped the mantelpiece, and rested her forehead on her hands. She closed her eyes. *What to do? What to do?* This question was her constant companion, endlessly reverberating in her head. Panic flooded through her, but after a moment she got a grip on herself. What she would do, what they would all do, was simply keep going. That was the only answer. There was no alternative. One day at a time, she told herself, I'll get through one day at a time.

She lifted her face, and her eyes swept the room. How normal it looked and therefore reassuring. Her bedroom was truly beautiful, such a tranquil setting, with its mixture of pale greens in the watered silks that splashed over the walls, hung at the windows, covered chairs and a chaise lounge. The furniture was French, finely scaled antiques from her favorite Louis XVI period, and here and there were scattered exquisite trinkets and small objects that she had collected over the years or had inherited from her family. Rose-quartz boxes, miniature watercolors, antique porcelain snuff boxes and vinaigrettes, Meissen figurines and silver-framed photographs of family and friends, those whom she loved the most.

And everywhere there were bowls of fresh hothouse flowers spilling their bright colors and fragrant scents into the room, which glowed at this hour with the muted light from crystal lamps shaded in pink silk.

The superb bedroom was made all the more superb by the art. Her eyes came finally to rest on the paintings by Renoir, and she admired them yet again, as she did almost every day, and as usual she was awed. How magnificent they looked against the pale-green walls. Two were paintings of nudes, another was a portrait of a mother with her two daughters, and the fourth depicted a garden in summer. To Ursula their tints were breathtaking: shell-pink and pearl, deep rose and lustrous gold, soft pastel blues and greens and the most glorious of yellows. All were light-filled, warm and sensuous, and wondrous to behold. They were part of the Westheim Collection, which had been started by Sigmund's grandfather Friedrich in the late nineteenth century, immediately following the historic first Impressionist showing in Paris in 1874, and she considered it a privilege to have them hanging here in her home.

Sighing under her breath, Ursula roused herself, aware that Sigmund had returned from the bank some time ago, and that he was already dressed in his evening clothes and waiting for her downstairs. Now she must hurry. Punctual himself, he disliked tardiness in others. She went to the Venetian mirrored dressing table positioned between two windows that soared to the high ceiling and opened the black leather jewel case resting on top of it.

Automatically, almost perfunctorily, she put on a pair of simple diamond earrings, slipped on her diamond engagement ring next to her gold wedding band, and locked the case. She would wear nothing else, none of her important pieces. She loathed ostentation at the best of times and these were the worst. And why encourage the envy of others, she found herself thinking.

Stepping away from the dressing table, Ursula gave herself a final cursory glance and smoothed with one hand her short, wavy blond hair before walking over to the wardrobe where her coats and capes were kept.

There was a knock on the door, and before she could respond, it flew open and her personal maid, Gisela, hurried into the room. "You are ready to leave, Frau Westheim? Which fur will you wear?"

Ursula smiled her lovely smile, and in her low voice she said, "I'm not taking a coat, the velvet wrap will do nicely, Gisela. If you would be good enough to get it out for me, please. Oh, and I will need a pair of white kid gloves. If you'll wait for me for a moment, I'll be right back."

"Yes, Frau Westheim."

Ursula stepped out into the bedroom corridor, pushed open the door exactly opposite hers and went inside. A night-light on the bedside table glowed faintly in the dim and shadowy room. She tiptoed over to the bed and looked down at the small boy sleeping there so peacefully with one of his small chubby hands resting under a pink cheek. Bending over him, she stroked his blond hair and gave him a light kiss.

The boy stirred. A pair of eyes opened and a sleep-filled voice murmured, "Mutti? I've been waiting for you, Mutti."

Ursula felt a rush of surging warmth, and she smiled. She experienced such infinite joy when she was with this child. There was a chair near the bed and she pulled it closer, sat down, took his other hand in hers. "I was dressing, *mein Schatz.* Papa and I have to go out this evening."

"Papa came to kiss me. He's buying me a pony next summer," her small son confided, now wide awake. His brown eyes gleamed with excitement as they fastened intently on hers.

Ursula leaned forward to kiss him again. He nuzzled his warm little face against her cheek and, putting his tender young arms around her neck, clung to her. She held him close, stroking his head with one hand. She loved this four-year-old boy so very much. Her only child. Her heart. *She was so afraid for him. Nothing must happen to him. She must protect him with her life.*

Pushing away the troubled thoughts with which she now lived daily, she took a deep breath and said, "Your pony will be waiting for you when we go to the villa in the Wannsee next summer. Papa will have it taken there for you."

"Mutti?"

"Yes, Maxim?"

"Will Papa show me how to ride it?"

"Of course he will," she said, smiling.

"What's the pony's name?"

"I don't know. We haven't found the right one for you yet. But we will. Come now, it's time to go to sleep."

Still holding her child in her arms, she leaned forward and laid him against the snowy linen pillows, but he did not want to let go of her and clung to her more tightly than ever, almost fiercely. Gently she unclasped his arms and sat up. Touching his face lightly with her fingertips, she spoke to him with great tenderness. "You're such a good little boy, Maxim, a sweet boy, and I love you very, very much."

"I love you, Mutti."

"Good night, *Mäuschen*, sweet dreams," she murmured against his cheek.

"Night." He yawned and his eyelids began to droop, and Ursula knew he would be fast asleep before she even reached the door. She crept out silently and returned to her bedroom, where she collected her wrap, gloves and evening bag.

"Good night, Gisela," she said, pausing in the doorway and turning around. "And please don't wait up for me."

"But, Frau Westheim, I always help you to—"

"No, no, it's not really necessary," Ursula interrupted softly. "I can manage by myself, but thank you anyway." She walked along the corridor to the staircase, which swept grandly down to the vast baronial entrance foyer. The Westheim house was a mansion on the Tiergartenstrasse, near the Tiergarten, in a charming residential area of Berlin.

Halfway down the stairs, Ursula stopped, stood stock-still listening, her head on one side.

Sigmund was playing the piano in the music room, and the melodic strains of Beethoven's "Moonlight Sonata" came wafting to her on the warm air. It was beautiful . . . delicate . . . but so ineffably sad. Her throat ached with unexpected emotion, and inexplicably tears sprang into her eyes. And she realized that tonight for some reason this particular piece of music seemed to move her especially, perhaps more than it ever had before.

She stood for a moment longer, composing herself. She marveled at Sigmund's touch—it was magical. If he had not been an investment banker, she believed he could easily have become a classical concert pianist, such was his talent. But banking was in his blood. Centuries of it. Passed down from father to son, ever since Jacob Westheim, the founding father of the dynasty, had opened the original merchant bank in Frankfurt in 1690. The entire family had moved to Berlin over a hundred years ago, and the Westheim private investment bank in the Gendarmenmarkt, Berlin's financial district, dated back to 1820.

The clock in the foyer began to chime and the pendulum struck six times, announcing the hour and cutting into her thoughts. She hurried down the stairs, deposited her things on an antique loveseat below a Gobelin tapestry, then crossed the black-and-white marble floor, heading in the direction of the music room. Here she paused in the doorway, watching her husband, thinking how handsome he looked in his dinner jacket and black tie.

The moment he saw her Sigmund stopped playing, sprang up and came swiftly to meet her. Brown-haired with bright-blue eyes and a warm, sincere smile, he was about five foot eleven, slender, compactly built, a good-looking man with a strong, well-defined face. He was thirty-six years old, and had been married to Ursula for fifteen years.

He put his arm around her, bringing his lips to her cheek. They had known each other all their lives, and their parents had always hoped they would marry, and when they did, two elite German families had been united. But it had not been an arranged union. Theirs was a true love story. They had fallen in love as children and had never wanted anyone but each other. It was a perfect match.

Sigmund broke their embrace, held her away from him and looked down into her face. "You are very beautiful tonight, Ursula."

A faint smile touched her lips and her eyes signaled her deep love for him, but she made no verbal response.

He put his arm around her and walked her back toward the foyer. "I was going to have a glass of champagne with you before we left, but I'm afraid that's no longer possible. I think we must leave. I promised Irina we would meet her at the reception, and I don't want to keep her waiting, since she's going there alone."

Ursula nodded. "Of course, darling."

Her voice was so low it was barely audible. Sigmund came to a dead stop, glanced at her and tilted her face up to his. He frowned when he saw the worry in her eyes and the gravity that had suddenly settled on her face. "What's wrong? What is it?"

"I wish we didn't have to go, Sigmund."

"But you were enthusiastic when the invitation came. Why this change of heart at the last minute?" He sounded puzzled.

"I was never *that* enthusiastic," she replied. "Not really."

"It's important that we make an appearance, you know. The ambassador *is* expecting us."

For a moment she did not speak, and then she said slowly, "There will be Nazis there."

"That's true, yes. But then there are Nazis everywhere these days. You mustn't let it concern you."

Again she was briefly silent before saying, more vehemently than was usual for her, "But it does concern me, Sigi, we're Jews."

"And Germans, Ursula. *Real* Germans, just as our forefathers were for centuries before we were born. Remember, we are both from great and ancient families, and furthermore, as an investment banker, I am extremely important and useful to the government and the state, as I have so often pointed out to you. You *know* they need me to help them build the economy, and for my foreign connections, the bankers and industrialists I'm acquainted with, and also for the foreign currency and gold the bank deals in." He put his arm around her again and held her close to him, finishing confidently in a reassuring voice, "We are not at risk, Ursula, please believe that."

She leaned away from him and looked up into his face, giving him a penetrating stare. "The Nazis fill me with dread. I detest being anywhere near them. I hate having to even breathe the same air."

"I know, I know. But, Ursula, many of our good friends will be present this evening, and you'll be with them. Renata and Reinhard, Kurt and Arabella von Wittingen, and Irina . . ."

His voice trailed off—he was not sure how to make her feel better at this moment.

"Yes, many of our friends *will* be there, Sigi," she concurred softly, "including those who are now members of the Nazi party. I'm uncomfortable with them, too, these days."

A nod indicated that he acknowledged the truth of her comments, and he grimaced, then cleared his throat. "But I'm afraid we can't possibly cancel at this hour, and we really must leave. *Now*, darling. Quite aside from not wishing to keep Irina waiting, I don't want to offend Sir Nevile Henderson by being late."

"Yes, of course," she said at once, forcing a smile, putting on a bright face, instantly trying to change her demeanor. There was nothing to be gained by upsetting him further. "I'll be fine, Sigi, please don't worry about me."

Looking relieved, he smiled into her eyes, took her arm and squeezed it, and together they hurried out of the music room into the foyer, where Sigmund picked up her wrap. He was placing it around her shoulders when Walter, the butler, came through from the servants' quarters at the back of the house. Walter inclined his head respectfully, went immediately to the clothes closet and brought out Sigmund's overcoat.

"Thank you, Walter, but I think I'll carry it," Sigmund said.

The butler folded the coat neatly and handed it to him, and ushered them out, wishing them a good evening.

7

≡≡≡

THE CAR WAS WAITING IN FRONT OF THE HOUSE. KARL, the chauffeur, greeted them respectfully and held the door open for them. Sigmund told him they were going to the British embassy, and a second later Karl pulled away from the curb and headed along the Tiergartenstrasse in the direction of the Hof-jägerallee.

Ursula glanced out of the window as the car sped past the Tiergarten, the lovely public park that had been the private hunting forest of the Brandenburg princes several hundred years ago. How forbidding it looks tonight, she thought, bringing her face closer to the glass. The trees, bereft of leaves, were stark, skeletal black images silhouetted against the cold and fading sky of early evening. She felt suddenly chilled and nestled deeper into her velvet wrap.

And then in her mind's eye she pictured the park as it was in the summer months, when it was breathtaking in its beauty—the rolling expanse of grass, the abundant weeping willows, the lime and the horse chestnut trees lushly green, the flower beds bordering the paths bursting with blossoms of every hue. Of the flowering bushes in full bloom, the lilacs were her favorites, dripping their plump May blossoms of pink and white and mauve, filling the air with a delicate, haunting fragrance.

Laid out in the manner of a natural English park, landscaped in parts, and scattered with artificial ponds and flowing streams, the Tiergarten had majesty and serenity, and it was a place of happy memories for her. She had gone riding in it as a child and a young girl, and still rode there when the weather was good. She had also been partial to walking along its winding paths beneath the canopy of cool and shady trees. In the past it had been with Sigmund; now she went there with Maxim and his nurse. Occasionally she would stroll through this gentle green enclave by herself, when she wanted to be alone or to think. It was, for her, still a place of peace and safety, a refuge amid the turbulence of life in Berlin today. And the beauty and simplicity of nature soothed her, were a balm to her troubled spirit.

When Sigmund made a remark to her about his mother, she searched his face in the dimness of the car and put a hand on his arm lovingly, knowing how concerned he was about her. They talked about the senior Frau Westheim, who had been in precarious health since her husband's death two years before, and then about his sisters, Hedy and Sigrid, and their relationship with their mother. They briefly discussed the happenings of the day before lapsing into silence, and for a short while they were caught up in the intricate web of their own private thoughts.

Ursula, who not only adored Sigmund but respected his judgment, wanted desperately to believe that he was correct in his assertions about their situation in relation to the Nazi regime. But her intelligence and her woman's intuition were at odds with his assurances. They were saying entirely different things to her, were alerting her to trouble. Her deepest instincts told her that something horrendous was coming, although what this was, what form it would take, she could not say. Stiffening, she sat up straighter in the corner of the car. Was it this awful foreboding that was at the root of her anxiety and apprehension? She was convinced it was. She felt an overwhelming sense of despair and her blood ran cold.

Sigmund's thoughts were also troubled. It was perfectly true that he felt reasonably secure in Berlin, despite the climate of the times, for although measures had been taken against Jews, the entire Westheim family had been left alone, along with other prominent and wealthy Jewish families who were important and useful to the state. Not one piece of Westheim property had been touched and the bank had not been closed down. Nor had he been forced to take on Aryan partners, as some Jewish businessmen had. And yet, lately, he had started to harbor a disturbing suspicion that the situation was going to change for every Jew living under the rule of the Third Reich.

Only a few minutes ago he had been reassuring his wife, speaking brave words to her, having no wish to increase her smoldering anxiety. But *he* must confront the possibility that they might soon be in danger. Not to do so would be sheer folly. Perhaps it would be wise to leave Berlin, to leave Germany, as so many already had. He was a wealthy man. Conceivably he might be able to buy their way out, purchase exit visas and new passports. But he would need assistance to do that, the right introductions to those who could produce the necessary documents. He was fully aware that bribery, graft and corruption were commonplace in the Third Reich; it was only a question of knowing exactly *whom* to go to in order to get what he needed. He had friends who could probably guide him in this, ease the way for him. But would they? And whom could he trust? He ran a few names through his head, pondered them carefully.

Karl swept off the Hofjägerallee, took the car around the circle that was the Grosser Stern, passed the Siegessäule, the winged-victory column that dominated its center, and headed down toward the Brandenburg Gate.

Ursula stared in front of her as they drove under the triumphal arch of the gate and focused her eyes on the Unter den Linden ahead. The Nazis had defaced this wide and stately avenue, the most glorious of all the boulevards in Berlin, by erecting rows of soaring columns down its center and along its sides. Each one of these columns was surmounted by a giant Nazi eagle, and because the columns were floodlit they were thrown into dramatic relief against the darkening night sky. Typical Nazi theatrics, Ursula thought, loathing what she saw. To her the columns were towering reminders of the tyranny and menace the Third Reich represented. She averted her eyes.

They were passing the Pariserplatz. Her parents had owned a house on that elegant square, and she had grown up there, had been married to Sigmund from that house, and it was there that her mother had died in 1935, and then her father, only last year. The square that had played such an important part in her life evoked a time past and the Berlin she loved that tragically was now gone forever.

She sighed under her breath and endeavored to shake off her despondency. Karl had turned right and was driving up the Wilhelmstrasse, where the British embassy was located at No. 70. They were about to arrive at their destination. She adjusted her expression and fixed a smile on her face as she had learned to do.

There was a lineup of cars in front of theirs. Some were official and from various ministries; others were diplomatic and bore stiff little flags on their hoods, and she recognized the colors of Italy and America and Spain.

A moment later Ursula was alighting from the car, and while she waited for Sigmund to come around from the other side, she glanced up the Wilhelmstrasse. Only a few doors away from her stood the Reich Chancellery, where Hitler was ensconced with his sinister henchmen, and she could not help wondering what diabolical schemes they were hatching at that very moment. Her spirits shriveled at the thought, and a shudder ran through her.

And then Sigmund was by her side, smiling down at her, and

she smiled back feebly. If he noticed her wan response, he showed no sign of it, but simply took her elbow and led her forward through the huge doors above which the Union Jack fluttered in the cold wind.

The sight of the red, white and blue flag lifted her spirits. It was not merely a banner of colored cloth that was the national emblem of Great Britain, but a symbol of justice, democracy and freedom.

Sir Nevile Henderson, His Britannic Majesty's ambassador in Berlin, stood in the hall situated between the two reception rooms at the top of the broad staircase, greeting his guests as they arrived. He was his usual smiling self, debonair and full of charm.

Sigmund and Ursula edged along slowly behind the other guests, until at last Sir Nevile was shaking her hand and warmly welcoming her, before turning his attention to Sigmund. The two men exchanged pleasantries for a few moments, and then together she and Sigmund stepped away and headed for one of the two rooms where drinks were being served before dinner.

The reception was already in full swing and the room was thronged. There was not only an aura of glamour about the gathering but also a feeling of tension and excitement in the air, as there generally was at such affairs in Berlin these days. This was especially so at the foreign embassy parties, which tended to be international in scope.

Shimmering crystal chandeliers blazed from the high ceiling; masses of flowers were banked around the room, adding to the festive mood, and a small string quartet played quietly in a corner. White-gloved waiters in tailcoats were fleet of foot among the crowd, expertly balancing immense silver trays that held either glasses of champagne or assorted canapés. And gazing down on the scene was the life-size portrait in oil of King George VI, newly crowned last year, who had stepped into the breach after his weak and shallow brother, Edward, had abdicated in order to marry Mrs. Simpson, the American adventuress.

"It's quite a turnout this evening," Sigmund murmured in Ursula's ear, escorting her into the room and glancing about. Instantly, a waiter stopped in front of them to offer them champagne. Sigmund thanked him, took two flutes, handed one to Ursula and clinked his glass against hers. He looked about. "I don't see Irina, do you?"

Ursula followed his gaze, swiftly surveyed the gathering. "No, I'm afraid not, Sigi, perhaps she's in the other reception room. It certainly is a motley crowd tonight."

She saw that the diplomatic corps was present in full force and spotted several ambassadors she knew by sight, as well as the familiar faces of two British foreign correspondents who were talking to their American colleague William Shirer. Mingling among them were government ministers, military officers, high-ranking Nazis, members of the German aristocracy and prominent Berliners.

Some of the young internationals who lived in Berlin were also present. She knew from Irina that they were popular with the staffs of the British and French embassies because they were charming, entertaining and good-looking, and enlivened these formal diplomatic functions. The majority had titles and were Hungarians, Slavs, Lithuanians, Austrians, Poles, Rumanians or, like Irina, White Russians. With their families, they had been displaced from their homelands by the erratic swings of political power in a shifting Europe inexorably changed some twenty years ago, first by the Russian Revolution and then by the collapse of the Austro-Hungarian empire.

Ursula's eyes roved the room. Elegance was the order of the evening, it seemed; everyone was very well dressed. The men wore dinner jackets or military uniforms; the women were decked out in their finery, most of them boasting a certain chic, a stylishness that was eye-catching. A few women clinging to the arms of some of the Nazis looked out of place, flashy in their gaudy dresses splattered with diamanté, their hands, arms and throats plastered with vulgar jewelry.

In the crowd she saw a familiar burnished head, a piquant smiling face in which vivid blue eyes danced, and a small hand waving in greeting to her.

Ursula's face instantly lit up. "Sigi! It's Irina, over there!"

"Yes, I just saw her myself. Come on, darling."

He took Ursula's arm and they hurried over toward their friend, who came to meet them halfway, her black lace dress of ballerina length swirling around her slim ankles. A moment later they were hugging and kissing each other, and laughing.

Irina had a gay and effervescent personality and was full of joie de vivre. It struck Ursula, as it often did, that her friend's extraordinary life, a life marked by tragedy, upheaval and turbulence, seemed to have done little, perhaps even nothing, to scar her.

Princess Irina Troubetzkoy and her mother, Princess Natalie, had fled Russia in 1917, when the Romanov autocracy fell, and after the Bolsheviks had murdered Prince Igor Troubetzkoy. Irina had been six years old, her mother twenty-five, at the time, and they had lived as refugees in Lithuania, Poland and Silesia before journeying to Berlin. They had settled in the city ten years ago, which was when Ursula and Sigmund had first met them. Recently Irina's mother had married a widowed Prussian baron, and for the first time in their twenty-one years of exile the two women had a real home at last.

Irina, Sigmund and Ursula were talking about her mother and the change for the better in Princess Natalie's fortunes when Irina began to chuckle.

Sigmund stared at her, raising a brow, and asked, perplexed, "What is it? Has either of us said something that amuses you?"

Irina shook her head. "No. I was just thinking that my mother has now acquired a degree of respectability since her marriage to the Herr Baron." She looked around, then dropped her voice, "As far as the Nazis are concerned, that is. How ridiculous when one considers that she has always been a woman of rectitude and impeccable moral character, with a spotless reputation, quite aside from the fact that she's of royal blood and is a cousin of the late Czar." Irina leaned closer to them and confided softly, "Incidentally, Goebbels just attached a label to us foreign exiles. *International garbage* he calls us, and very disdainfully, too."

"Ah yes, Dr. Goebbels—" Sigmund began, but bit off the rest of his sentence.

A pair of SS officers, typical of their breed—cold-faced and blue-eyed with short-cropped blond hair and ramrod-straight postures—were drawing to a halt in front of them. They clicked their heels together, bowed stiffly and focused their penetrating eyes on Irina. Both flashed a smile, and one of them said, "*Guten Abend, Prinzessin.*"

"Good evening," Irina responded, repeating his greeting politely, even proffering a smile. But her eyes, which were the color of violets, were glacial.

The officers bowed courteously and moved on, perfectly in step like carefully programmed robots.

"And that's *Nazi garbage*," Irina whispered. "A couple of Heydrich's hatchet men. I felt like spitting in their faces."

Ursula put a gentle hand on her arm and murmured, "Please, do be careful what you say, Irina, you never know who's listening."

"Yes, informers are all over the place," she muttered in agreement. "One doesn't know whom to trust these days." Irina now spoke in a voice so inaudible the Westheims had to draw closer to her in order to hear what she said as she added, "But a foul regime such as theirs needs informers in order to function, to flourish."

Renata von Tiegal, who had been scanning the reception room from the entrance, saw them and hurried over. She was always dramatic-looking, and tonight more than ever, gowned in scarlet silk, the vivid color setting off her inky-black hair and ivory skin.

"Hello!" she cried. "I was looking for you across the way. How is everyone?" Her dark eyes and wide smile radiated affection.

"We're all fine," Sigmund said, answering for the three of them. "And you look superb this evening, my dear."

"Why, thank you, Sigi," she said.

Ursula slipped her arm through Renata's and asked, "And where's Reinhard?"

"In the other reception room." Renata glanced about her. "What a happy crowd it appears to be tonight."

"But everyone is happy in Berlin," Irina said, softly, her voice dripping sarcasm. "They're full of relief that Hitler averted war when he signed the Munich Pact with the British prime minister and the French premier in September."

"Berliners have their heads stuck in the sand," Renata responded, and made a sour face. "How can anyone think that that odious little man has stopped a war?" When Irina was silent, she turned to Sigi. "Do *you* believe he has?"

"I'm hoping against hope," Sigi answered.

Irina looked over her shoulder to make sure no one was eavesdropping on their conversation, saw that they were quite isolated where they stood, then remarked quietly, "Hitler might have duped Chamberlain and Daladier, bluffed them into thinking that he wants peace as they do, but he hasn't convinced me and my mother, or the baron for that matter. Helmut thinks he aims to go against the Western democracies next year."

Renata said, "I suspect your stepfather's not far from the truth."

"I pray that Helmut is wrong." Sigmund's voice was as somber as the expression on his face.

Renata began to shake her head. "I tremble at the thought of the poor Czechoslovakians. When Hitler marched into the Sudetenland last month *they* were finished."

"Please, don't let's talk politics tonight," Ursula whispered. "Not even here in the relative safety of the British embassy. It makes me nervous."

"You're absolutely right," Sigmund agreed. "It's a dangerous game anywhere these days." Out of the corner of his eye he noticed that the von Wittingens had just arrived, and wanting to bring this conversation to a close and needing an excuse to speak privately to Irina, he said, "Come along, Irina, my dear, let's go over and have a word with Kurt and Arabella, and find ourselves a little champagne on the way."

Irina agreed and the two went off.

Left alone together, Renata turned to face Ursula. "Are you feeling all right, Ursi?" she asked, frowning and peering at her friend. "You look so very pale tonight."

Ursula was silent for a moment, and then giving Renata a very direct look, she confessed, "I live with the most corrosive anxiety, Ren. It's perfectly awful, and very debilitating. And although I try desperately to control myself, I'm filled with terrible apprehension most of the time."

Renata's face reflected her sympathy and her understanding. "We all feel the same way, and with good reason. We're in the hands of criminals. Let's face it, the German government is being led by a bunch of gangsters."

"Keep your voice down," Ursula cautioned in a whisper, "the Gestapo's everywhere. Even at this party, I'm sure."

"Yes, you're probably right," Renata replied dully, adopting the same whispering tone.

Automatically they both edged farther into the corner. Re-

nata stared at Ursula in despair and let out a weary sigh. "Why
did we bother to come here tonight, knowing the place would
be teeming with *them* and the SS and God knows who else?"

"To be together in a friendly atmosphere at a friendly embassy where there are still a few civilized people left to talk to,
and to have a pleasant evening with each other, that's why,"
Ursula murmured, and squeezed her arm comfortingly.

"Hello, you two," a husky, very English voice said behind
them. They swung around to greet Arabella von Wittingen.

Tall, slender and elegant this evening in a bottle-green brocade dinner suit composed of a long skirt and a tailored jacket,
Arabella had fair hair, light-blue eyes and skin like a peach.
She was the former Lady Arabella Cunningham and the sister
of the Earl of Langley.

Her pretty mouth twitching with amusement, Arabella said,
"I can hardly believe my eyes! A member of the ambassador's
staff must have gone slightly *mad*. What an invitation list! Some
of the raciest ladies in Berlin are present this evening, not to
mention those *cuties* over there, the ones draped all over the
Nazi officers." She laughed. "The three of them look as if
they've just stepped out of Madam Kitty's front door," she continued, referring to the most famous brothel in Berlin. "Out
of several *beds* in Madam Kitty's, I should have said," she
added as an afterthought, and laughed again.

Ursula chuckled and exclaimed softly, "You're as irreverent
as ever and brutally honest, but then that's why we love you,
Belle darling."

These three women did love each other, and they had been
devoted friends for the past eighteen years. They had met in
1920, when, at the age of sixteen, they were pupils at Roedean,
the famous English girls' school near Brighton. In the two years
they had attended the school they had been considered a daunt-
ing trio—intelligent, confident, self-assured, independent and,
at times, rebellious. The friendship had continued after their
schooldays, and Renata and Ursula had frequently gone to stay
with Arabella at Langley Castle in Yorkshire, which was the
family seat, and Arabella had journeyed to Berlin to visit both
girls at different times. In 1923 she and Renata were brides-
maids at Ursula's marriage to Sigmund. After the wedding, Arabella had gone with Renata to stay at the home of her fiancé,
Graf Reinhard von Tiegal, at his schloss on the edge of the for-

ests of the Spree in the Mark Brandenburg, a country area outside Berlin. It was there that she had met Prince Rudolf Kurt
von Wittingen, with whom she had fallen in love, and he with
her. They had been married a year later, after which Arabella
had come to live in Berlin permanently. The three women had
drawn closer than ever, and became as inseparable as they had
been at school in England in their teens.

Their irrepressible laughter broke the tension Ursula and Renata had been experiencing before Arabella's arrival. Now Renata motioned to a waiter. "Let's have another glass of
champagne," she suggested to her closest friends, her expression brightening considerably.

"That's a good idea," Ursula said, and helped herself to a
flute of the wine. "It's ages since we've had a quiet moment
together without our children. Why don't we go and sit over
there and talk for a few minutes."

"Splendid," Arabella said, and Renata agreed. They strolled
over to a group of chairs arranged in front of a window, where
they made themselves comfortable and began to talk about inconsequential things, each of them wanting desperately to
create a sense of normalcy about their lives in these most abnor-
mal times.

They did not move until their husbands came back with
Irina, to escort them in to dinner. And later they agreed that
for them this short interlude had been the best part of the evening at the British embassy.

8

$\mathcal{I}$'M GLAD YOU TOLD HENRIETTA WE HAD TO LEAVE,"
Theodora Stein said, looking across at her boyfriend, Willy
Herzog, who stood on the other side of the small foyer, putting

on his overcoat. "I have to get up early tomorrow." She made a face at the thought.

Willy nodded as he reached for his hat. "We'll only get a few hours' sleep, that's true, it's an early start for me, too. It was a grand party and I enjoyed myself, but it's going on a bit too long."

Theodora glanced at the door to the living room through which could be heard voices raised in revelry, laughter and gramophone music. She shrugged her shoulders. "But then, how often are you twenty-one, Willy?" Since this was a rhetorical question, she did not expect an answer, and she rushed on, "I suppose Henrietta wanted to make the most of this very special birthday. And I don't blame her. I know I will when *I'm* twenty-one. I plan to have a fancy party too."

Willy flashed her a wide grin. "Will I be invited?"

"*If* you're still around, Willy Herzog. *If* you haven't sailed off to America as you keep threatening to do," she shot back, giving him a flirtatious look. "Are you still planning to go over there to join your uncle Nathan in Brooklyn and study to be a dentist?"

"*Doctor*," he corrected. He frowned. "It's the getting of the American visas, Theodora. *Very* difficult it is. They're extremely hard to come by, I think I told you that before. Anyway, my father has a friend in Frankfurt who has a friend who knows a consular official who *might* be able to help us. For the right price. That's why my father went to Frankfurt yesterday, hoping to bribe this man and get the three visas we need—for himself, and for my sister Clara and me."

Willy cleared his throat. "I'd like to go to America . . . want to go . . . but . . ." He hesitated and cleared his throat again, looked down, studied his shoes. Then he fixed his gentle hazel eyes on Theodora. "I don't want to leave *you*," he announced, surprising himself and startling her. There, it's out at last, he thought. He had finally said it, had had the courage to tell her what had been on his mind for weeks. Relief surged through him as he stood gazing adoringly at Theodora.

Stupefied, totally at a loss for words, she gaped back at him in amazement.

Willy flung down his hat and, pulling her into his arms, held her close. "I love you, Teddy," he said against the top of her head, kissing her silky fair hair. "I do, I love you."

"Oh . . . Willy . . . Is this a proposal, then?"

There was a small silence.

He said at last, "Do I want to marry you? Yes . . . *yes* . . . and *yes*, it's a proposal."

"*Oh, Willy!* I don't know what to say! I'm only nineteen and you're only nineteen. We're so young. And—"

"Don't you love me?"

Now it was Theodora's turn to be silent.

She wondered if she did love him. She wasn't sure. Perhaps she did. He was very nice-looking and quiet and studious, and serious about studying medicine, and he had lovely manners. Mrs. Mandelbaum, Henrietta's mother, was always saying Willy was a real *mensch*. And it was true, he was a *haimisher mensch*, so easy to be around, very comfortable. Yes, Willy was a good man. He went to *shul* regularly, and in the year she had known him he had never done a thing to upset her, had never put a foot wrong. But *marriage*? She hadn't thought about *that* before. But she could do worse. Much worse. Besides, she didn't mind it when he kissed her. In fact, she liked it. He had soft warm lips and sweet breath and he always smelled fresh and clean, of soap and Kölnisch Wasser. And he was gentle with her, never tried to force her, or make her do anything wrong. When he kissed her she always got a funny feeling inside, and her heart pounded and she grew warm and flushed. Yes, Willy *was* special, now that she really thought about it. She didn't want to lose him. Quite suddenly she knew she would never find anybody who was better than Willy.

She said slowly, "I *think* I love you, Willy." There was a little pause, and she said more firmly, "Yes, I *do* love you."

"Oh, Teddy! I'm so happy. And *will* you marry me?"

There was another pause before she said, "Yes, Willy Herzog, I will."

He put his hand under her chin and lifted her small heart-shaped face to his, kissed her pretty upturned nose, her eyelids and finally her sweet lips. They held the kiss, making it last, and they clung to each other tightly until they had to break away to catch their breath.

Willy pressed her head against his shoulder and stroked her hair, and in silent communion they lingered in their embrace. They knew that a commitment had been made, by each to the other, and it was a serious moment, meaningful and precious to them both, and they did not want to let it go.

Finally Theodora gently pushed Willy away, extricating herself from his arms. "Look at the clock, Willy, it's almost midnight. We *have* to leave, I'll hardly get any sleep before I have to be up to take care of Maxim. The little one's always awake early."

"Yes, we had better go. Come on."

"Let me put my hat on first. It's a cold night, and even colder on the back of your motorbike."

Theodora took down her green-and-blue tartan tam-o'-shanter from the coat stand, and looked at herself in the Biedermeier mirror as she put it on, then tightened her matching scarf around her neck. She fished a woolen glove out of each pocket of her navy-blue winter coat, and said, "I'm ready."

They let themselves out of the Mandelbaums' apartment and Willy closed the door behind them; pausing on the landing, he took hold of Theodora's shoulders and gently turned her face to him. "So, we have an understanding, Theodora? You *will* meet me under the *chuppa* and become my wife?"

She nodded solemnly and her expression was serious, but her light-green eyes were shining and danced with happiness. "Yes, Willy. *Yes* to both your questions. And I shall write to Aunt Ketti in London to tell her. As my only living relative she'd want to know that I'm . . . engaged . . . to be married."

"And I shall inform my father, when he gets back from Frankfurt, and I shall also tell him that I can't go to America. Not without you. We'll have to get a visa for you too, Teddy. I'll stay in Berlin until we can *both* go to Brooklyn to my uncle Nathan's."

She smiled and nodded and took his hand in hers, and together they went down the steep flight of stairs and crossed the vestibule of the apartment building.

As Willy opened the door leading into the street, Theodora stiffened and grabbed his arm. "Listen! Isn't that the sound of breaking glass?"

"You're right, it is. I hope it's not a burglar trying to get into Mr. Mandelbaum's jewelry shop. I'd better go and see. Wait here."

"No! Don't go out, Willy! It's dangerous!" she cried.

He paid no attention to her warning, and hurried into the

narrow street, where he immediately collided with a storm trooper who stood staring up at the building. The man grabbed Willy by the shoulder and swung him to one side. "Hey, you! Watch it! Watch where you're going, you clumsy dolt!"

"I'm very sorry, sir," Willy said politely, struggling to break free from the man's grip, but it was tenacious. "Please, let go of me."

At this the storm trooper tightened his hold, peered at Willy in the pale light coming through the door's transom from the vestibule. "Why should I let go of you? You might be a Jew for all I know. Is this a Jewish house? Are you a Jew?"

Theodora, who had been listening with growing alarm, could no longer contain herself. She rushed outside before Willy had a chance to answer and perhaps unwittingly say the wrong thing.

"Let him go!" she yelled, running right up to the storm trooper. "Let him go at once!" she repeated, her voice rising shrilly. "We haven't done anything."

"You have if you're Jews. Are you stinking shitty Jews?" He grinned and sadistically twisted Willy's shoulder back so far that Theodora winced and sucked in her breath.

Willy gritted his teeth and did not cry out once, despite the sharp pain.

"Come on, confess it," the storm trooper snarled, "this *is* a Jewish house, and you're *both* Jews."

"We are not Jews! What kind of a thing is that to say!" Theodora exclaimed. And with immense hauteur she drew herself up to her full height of five foot five, and faced him down unflinchingly.

"My name is Theodora Marie-Theresa Schmidt and this is Wilhelm Braun, and we're both good Catholics and good Germans." She gulped and took a deep breath. "And yes, we are good Nazis." She thrust her arm straight out in front of her in the Nazi salute. "*Heil Hitler!* Long live our magnificent Führer! Long live the Third Reich!"

The storm trooper gaped at her in astonishment.

And so did Willy. When she had rushed out into the street, his heart had almost stopped and he had been terrified, more for her than for himself. But now he knew she was going to get away with this act she was pulling because the storm trooper would think that no Jew would dare to confront him

like this. Her anger and her arrogance were so perfectly simu-
lated and she spoke with such conviction, who could doubt that
she was telling the truth? It was quite a performance, and Willy
marveled at it.

Theodora continued to rail at the man. "You've got a flashlight in your hand," she bellowed. "Shine it on us. Shine it on
Willy. Go on, do it! You'll see he's not a Jew!" Before the storm
trooper could stop her she leaned forward and snatched the
flashlight out of his hand, turned it on and leveled it at Willy.

Willy held his breath, once again petrified for her, for them
both.

"Take your hat off, Willy!" She spoke so imperiously, he did
as she said, pulling off his hat with his free hand, while praying
under his breath.

"Look at him!" she ordered the storm trooper. "*Look at him!*
He has sandy-red hair and more freckles than you've ever seen
on anybody, and hazel eyes. Is that a Jewish face? No, it's an
Aryan face."

Dramatically she turned the flashlight on herself.

"And just look at me. I'm the Nordic type personified." She
pulled her long hair over her shoulder. "See, I have fair hair
and green eyes and skin the color of a rose. Do I look Semitic?
Of course I don't, because I'm not."

At last the storm trooper found his voice. "Looks can be very
deceptive," he snapped. Nonetheless, some of the bluster had
gone out of him, and he seemed uncertain in the face of her
anger and the torrent of words uttered in such superior and
confident tones. But he continued to hold on to Willy, even
tightening his grasp.

Theodora drew closer and said icily, "What you say is true.
Looks *can* deceive. And perhaps *you* are not all *you* appear to
be. I said *Heil Hitler* before. Why didn't you respond in the
same way, as you're supposed to? I hope you're a loyal party
member." She threw back her shoulders proudly and, tossing
her head, spoke more arrogantly than ever. "My father is SS
Gruppenführer Schmidt. He is a good friend of Reichsführer
Himmler. He knows him very well." Summoning every ounce
of her nerve, Theodora now waved the flashlight in front of the
startled storm trooper's face. She stared at him, as if commit-
ting his face to memory. "What's your name, Corporal?" she
asked, her eyes narrowing.

The storm trooper reacted as she had expected he would, furiously pushing her arm away. "Get that light out of my eyes!" he yelled, and leaning toward her he grabbed the flashlight.

Unperturbed, Theodora said, "Did you hear me, Corporal? My father is a friend of Himmler's, and he's a powerful man in the SS. He's not going to be happy when he knows we've been detained by you in this way. I asked you your name, Corporal. *So, what is it?*"

It was apparent the storm trooper had believed everything Theodora had said thus far, and this second reference to Himmler, head of the SS, seemed to galvanize him. Abruptly he let go of Willy.

Instantly Theodora took hold of Willy's arm and pulled him close to her side. "Come on, let's go," she said.

"Yes, you'd better get off," the storm trooper exclaimed sharply, stepping back. "Go on, go home! A lot's about to happen. Soon it won't be safe on the streets. We're after Jews tonight." He laughed raucously and slapped his thigh, as if it were a huge joke, and then, abruptly turning from them, he walked on down the narrow street, shining his flashlight on the shop windows.

Willy gasped, "Look what he did to Mr. Mandelbaum's storefront—"

"Hurry, Willy! *Hurry!*" Theodora hissed, catching Willy's hand in hers, and they ran in the other direction, away from the apartment building and Mandelbaum's jewelry shop, and out onto the Kurfürstendamm. They immediately saw there was havoc on the street, so they went on as fast as they could, their feet pounding the pavement until they reached the lamppost where Willy had parked his motorbike. They were relieved to see that it had not been touched, but they knew they had reached it just in time. They clambered on, breathing hard as they settled themselves on the saddle.

"Hold tight!" Willy ordered, and Teddy wrapped her arms around his waist as the bike leaped forward and headed down the Kurfürstendamm at breakneck speed.

Vans and trucks were now pulling up all along this wide avenue lined with shops and cafés and apartment buildings. Storm troopers and thugs were spilling out, brandishing hatchets, guns, clubs and truncheons. Like fevered maniacs, they were rushing in every direction, smashing the windows of Jewish-owned stores, throwing goods out into the street, destroying the fronts of cafés and hacking at the doors of apartment buildings. Combined with the earsplitting noise of shattering glass were the sounds of splintering wood and the bloodcurdling cries of triumph from the frenzied mob led by storm troopers.

Theodora was shaking. Holding on to Willy tighter than ever, she shouted in his ear, "*Faster! Faster!* Get us away from here!"

He gunned the bike forward with a screeching of tires, and within minutes they were leaving the Kurfürstendamm behind them. Willy was making for the Stülerstrasse, which flowed into the Tiergartenstrasse, where the Westheim family lived and where Theodora worked as the nanny to young Maxim.

They were on the Fasanenstrasse now. Just ahead of them was the lovely old Central Synagogue, and as they approached it they were horror-struck. Thugs and storm troopers were breaking all the windows and setting the building on fire with flaming torches.

Willy accelerated his speed to the maximum, dangerous though this was, and shot ahead to escape this scene of violent destruction. But not before they had seen the scrolls of the Torah and the ark of the covenant lying among the debris in the street. Alongside were torn prayer books and shawls, and all were being trampled underfoot by the wild mob shrieking with hysterical laughter and shouting obscenities about Jews.

"I can't believe they're burning down the synagogue," Theodora wailed in Willy's ear, and she began to sob and pressed her face into his back.

Willy desperately wanted to stop to comfort her, but he did not dare, not until they were out of this area and in a safer part of Berlin. He pushed the motorcycle harder, as hard as he could, and eventually he was cutting across the Kantstrasse and speeding down the Budapesterstrasse. This was a long and curving avenue that led directly into the Stülerstrasse. With enormous relief he saw that the street was quiet, entirely deserted, as he entered it; in fact, it might as well have been on another planet, it was so peaceful. He parked by the side of the road in the shadow of some trees and jumped off the bike.

Theodora was still weeping, now shaking her head from side to side, her hands pressed to her streaming eyes. "God forgive me! God forgive me for denying my heritage, for denying my religion, for denying myself and all that I am!"

Willy took her in his arms, and she sobbed uncontrollably, clinging to him. He stroked her back, trying to calm her.

With great gentleness he said, "God does forgive you. I know He does. You saved us, didn't you? With your quick thinking and your cheek. You've got a good Jewish *kop* on your shoulders, Teddy. And *chutzpa*. A lot of *chutzpa*. That's what saved us."

"I shouldn't have denied we are Jews," she whimpered. "It was wrong, Willy."

"It saved us. And that's all that counts."

She looked up into his grave face and asked tearfully, "Why, Willy? *Why?* Why are they doing this? And why are they burning down the synagogue?"

He was silent for a moment, and then said in a voice that was anguished, "The Nazis have turned prejudice into hatred, and tonight we are witnessing a Nazi rampage against us and our homes, our businesses and our places of worship. They are torching, vandalizing and desecrating everything that belongs to Jews because they hate us with a terrible, *terrible* vengeance."

"*Oh, Willy.*"

He held her close to him again so that she would not see the sudden tears misting his eyes.

Theodora was endeavoring to stem her sobs, heaving and catching her breath in little spasms, and after a short while she was quieter, in control. "Willy?"

"Yes, Teddy?"

"They want to murder us all," she whispered against his shoulder.

He did not respond. He knew she was right. And he was afraid.

9

THEODORA FELT CONSIDERABLY SAFER ONCE SHE WAS IN-
side the Westheim mansion on the Tiergartenstrasse.

She locked and bolted the door behind her, and then leaned
against it, trying to compose herself. She was no longer racked
by sobs and the tears had dried on her face, but she was still
profoundly disturbed. The violence she had just seen on the
streets, the ferocity of the attack on the synagogue, were indeli-
bly imprinted on her mind.

After taking several deep breaths and steadying herself, she
walked quickly across the black-and-white marble foyer, the
metallic click of her heels against the floor the only sound in
the huge and silent house. Obviously everyone was sleeping
soundly, unaware of the riots outside. The mobs had stayed
away from this exclusive residential district, occupied mostly
by wealthy Gentile families, and had apparently concentrated
their attacks around the area of the Kurfürstendamm.

An antique porcelain lamp on a chest to one side of the Gobelin tapestry had been left burning for her—no doubt by Frau
Westheim, upon her return from the dinner at the British embassy. It illuminated her way up the grand staircase.

When she reached the landing at the top of the stairs, she
turned on the lights and made her way along the main corridor.
She stopped at Maxim's door, stood listening, then opened it
gently and peeped inside.

The tiny night-light on the bedside table made a faint glow,
and it comforted her to see that the child was sleeping so peacefully. Closing the door carefully so as not to awaken him, she
turned around, and rather than going to her own room, which
was next to Maxim's, she went toward his parents' bedroom
instead. Lightly she rapped on the door.

She waited several moments, and was about to knock again, when the door was opened by Sigmund dressed in pajamas and a dark silk robe.

Taken by surprise that it was she, and not one of the servants, he stared at her, frowning. "Theodora! What is it? What's wrong? You're as white as chalk." He squinted at her in the dimly lit corridor.

He was about to say something else when Theodora put her finger to her lips, shook her head and glanced over at the child's room. "Shhhh," she whispered, "we don't want to awaken Maxim."

Sigmund nodded, and opened the door wider to let her in.

Ursula was out of bed and slipping on her peignoir, worry clouding her smoky-blue eyes.

When she saw Theodora's white face and the shock in her eyes, the girl's distress instantly communicated itself to her. "Teddy, whatever is it? Why, you've been crying. What has upset you so?"

Theodora stood in the center of the beautiful bedroom with its green watered-silk walls and many exquisite objects and great works of art, and wondered where to begin, how to tell this refined and aristocratic couple about the hideous violence and destruction she had just witnessed out there in the center of the city. And for a second she could not find the words.

Her mouth trembling, she stared at Ursula.

Ursula looked at the girl with an expression of deep concern. Theodora was her charge, whom she had taken into her home three years ago, after the death of Frau Rosa Stein, Teddy's mother and widow of Dr. Johann Stein. Until his death in 1933, the doctor had been the Westheim family's devoted physician for many years. When Teddy had come to live with the Westheims at the age of sixteen, Ursula had been fulfilling a deathbed promise to Teddy's mother to look after her until she came of age or got married. Ursula took the promise seriously, and although Teddy was Maxim's nanny, the girl was treated with the greatest kindness and affection, and almost as though she were a member of the family.

Now Ursula said gently, "Teddy, dear, please tell us what has happened to you."

Theodora nodded, and words began to tumble out of her in a great rush. "Out there. In the streets. The Nazis have gone crazy. They're doing terrible things. Demolishing Jewish property. Smashing store windows, café fronts. Battering their way into apartment buildings. And they've burned the Central Synagogue. *Burned it to the ground.* I saw them doing it with my own eyes!"

"Oh, dear God! Dear God!" Ursula cried. Her face turned ashen, and an internal shaking seized her. Reaching out, she got hold of the back of a chair to steady herself, and that sense of dread, which she had pressed back for weeks, rose up in her and lodged like a stone weight in her chest.

Anxiously she swung her eyes to Sigmund, and they stared at each other disbelievingly. They were appalled at what they had just heard.

Turning back to Teddy, Ursula said, "Thank God you weren't hurt. You're not, are you?"

"No, I'm not, Frau Westheim."

"You weren't out alone tonight, were you, Teddy?" Sigmund interjected.

"I was with Willy, Herr Westheim."

"Willy?" he repeated, with a questioning look.

"Professor Herzog's son," Ursula cut in swiftly. "He's studying at the university, and he's been taking Teddy out on her days off for about a year."

"Yes, of course, now I remember." Sigmund focused his bright-blue eyes on Teddy again. "How did you get home? How did you manage to get through the demonstrations?"

"On Willy's motorcycle. He drove like a maniac. But he had to. It was awful, frightening, especially on the Ku'damm and the Fasanenstrasse."

"Oh, Teddy, Teddy," Ursula said, her voice low and strained, "I've warned you not to stay out late at night. These are terribly dangerous times we're living in."

"I know. And I'm sorry, Frau Westheim. I know you worry about me. But Henrietta's birthday party went on much longer than we expected. We kept trying to leave. Finally we got away around midnight. The violence was just beginning."

Ursula frowned, thinking that their unimpeded journey across the rioting city was nothing short of miraculous, and she probed, "No one bothered you? Stopped you? Shot at you?"

"No, not when we were riding the motorbike. But . . . well . . . there was a little incident as we left the apartment. Willy acci-

dentally barreled into a storm trooper outside the Mandelbaums' building, and he grabbed hold of Willy, started to
question—"

"*Storm trooper!*" Ursula's eyes opened wider, and she
brought a hand up to her mouth. Civilian mobs were one thing;
the involvement of storm troopers meant something entirely
different—and much more threatening.

"Yes, a storm trooper," Theodora said, and graphically recounted what had happened between herself and the Nazi when
she had rushed out to confront him on the street. She did not
leave out one single detail.

Ursula was aghast throughout this recital, and when Teddy
finished, she exclaimed, "What you did was terribly, *terribly*
dangerous! The consequences for you and Willy could have
been disastrous. *Horrendous.* The storm trooper could have
beaten you up or killed you. What's perhaps even worse to contemplate, he could have dragged you both to Gestapo headquarters for questioning. People who have been made to take
forced trips to the Prinz-Albrecht-Strasse haven't always come
out of there alive. And *if* they have, they've often been mindless
wrecks because of the torture inflicted on them."

Teddy went cold, realizing that everything Ursula Westheim
said was true. She bit her lip and said in a chagrined voice, "I
just reacted . . . without thinking. I was certain my insolence
and superior manner would convince him I was not Jewish. I
was right about that, Frau Westheim—he really did believe my
father was in the SS, and that he was a friend of Himmler's."

"Teddy did what she thought was the best thing, I'm absolutely sure of that, and certainly she used her wits," Sigmund
said to Ursula. Then he glanced at Theodora and shook his
head. His kindly eyes were grave when he murmured after a
slight pause, "I don't think you should tempt Providence again.
It might not work a second time."

"Yes, now I realize that," Teddy admitted. "Willy was
scared when I was shouting at the storm trooper. Scared for
both of us, he told me later."

"And where is Willy?" Sigmund asked. "Is he downstairs?"

"No, he went home. His father's away and he was worried
about his sister, Clara, being alone in their flat."

"But it's dangerous out on the streets," Sigmund responded.
"You should have insisted that he stay here tonight."

Ursula said, "I'm certain Willy is all right, Sigi. He lives not far from here, just behind us, near the Landwehrkanal."

"Willy *must* be safely home by now," Teddy asserted. "It would only take him a few minutes on the motorbike, and everything was quiet in the neighborhood when he dropped me off."

Sigmund went across to one of the windows, parted the silk draperies and anxiously looked down into the Tiergartenstrasse. He saw that the street below was indeed empty, and this reassured him that the boy had undoubtedly made it home without running into more trouble. Nevertheless, he pointed to the phone on Ursula's writing desk, and said, "I think we will all feel much better, Teddy, if you ring Willy."

"Yes, Herr Westheim," Teddy replied and did as he asked. The phone in the Herzogs' apartment was picked up after only two rings, and Willy was on the line. "Yes?" he said warily.

"It's Teddy," she answered. "Herr Westheim asked me to ring you up, Willy, to check that you'd arrived home all right." He told her that he had done so without any sort of incident and without seeing one single person.

After hanging up, Teddy turned to Sigmund. "He's fine, he said he got home in a few minutes. The streets around here *are* quiet, Herr Westheim."

Sigmund nodded, immense relief showing on his face.

"*Storm troopers*," Ursula said and gave Sigmund a meaningful look. "So apparently the government is no longer simply turning a blind eye to these anti-Semitic demonstrations. *Now*, seemingly, it is actively involved in them."

"That's the way it looks," Teddy said. "I saw a lot of storm troopers on our way home. They were leading the mobs—" Theodora broke off as a wave of nausea unexpectedly swept over her. She swayed on her feet, and wondered if she was going to faint.

Ursula ran to her immediately and put an arm around her to support her. She helped Teddy remove her coat and tam-o'-shanter, mothering her as she would Maxim. Taking her hand, Ursula led her over to the fireplace, where a few embers still glowed in the grate. Glancing over her shoulder at Sigmund, she said, "I think a glass of cognac would help. Teddy's hands are icy."

"Of course. I'll get it right away."

Sigmund strode into the adjoining room, his upstairs study, where he sometimes worked and where there was a small but well-stocked liquor cabinet.

Meanwhile, Ursula and Teddy seated themselves on the chaise and Ursula tried to warm the girl's hands by rubbing them with her own.

Theodora looked at her suddenly, and exclaimed, "They were so *vicious* when they attacked the synagogue. They set fire to it! I couldn't believe such a dreadful thing was happening." This scene stood out with such agonizing clarity in her mind she began to weep, and the tears rolled down her cheeks unchecked. Ursula gently wiped the tears away with her fingertips in trying to comfort her.

Sigmund was back within seconds, carrying a silver tray with three liqueur glasses of brandy. "I think we *all* need a drop of this," he said.

Theodora took a big swallow of the brandy and felt the warmth of it in her throat at once. She took another swallow and, putting the glass on a nearby table, looked from Ursula to Sigmund. "Thank you," she said softly, her expression one of deep gratitude. "Thank you for being so kind to me always."

Sigmund had tossed back his small glass of cognac in one quick gulp, and now he said, "I must go and make several phone calls . . . to Hedy, to make certain she and my mother are all right. I'm absolutely positive they are, out there in the Grunewald. Sigrid, of course, is in Hamburg with Thomas on business, so we don't have to be concerned about them. And then I must reach the night guard at the bank, check out the situation in the Gendarmenmarkt."

"Yes, you had better do that," Ursula concurred.

Sigmund nodded and disappeared in the direction of his study.

Theodora, who had been fumbling around in the pocket of her blue wool dress, pulled out her handkerchief and blew her nose. "I'm sorry I broke down before, Frau Westheim. But I couldn't help it. This has been the most terrifying experience. I know one thing . . . I'll never forget the ninth of November. . . . Henrietta Mandelbaum's twenty-first birthday and the night the Nazis torched the Central Synagogue. No, I'll never forget it," she finished vehemently. "Not as long as I live."

"I don't think anyone will," Ursula replied.

She walked over to a window, drew open the draperies and stood looking out at the sky. It was jet-black and littered with bright stars, and on the horizon she could see a jagged patch of red flaring upward. *Fire*, she thought. *They're burning something else in another part of the city. Another synagogue perhaps. Or someone's home. Or both. Where will this end? Dear God, where will this end?* She felt chilled to the bone, icy all over.

Sigmund did not remain on the telephone for very long, and he soon returned to the bedroom, saying with obvious relief, "I spoke to Hedy. The Grunewald is as peaceful and sleepy as it always is, and the night guard at the bank tells me nothing untoward is happening down there in the financial district. So perhaps the demonstrations on the Ku'damm and the Fasanenstrasse are simply isolated incidents, started by the rowdies and thugs who are so frequently out of control—"

"I doubt that," Ursula remarked in the softest of voices. "Not when there are storm troopers involved. This is much more serious than anything we've ever seen before."

"Perhaps," Sigmund muttered noncommittally. Privately he agreed with her, but he did not want to increase her alarm, nor did he wish to frighten Theodora further—she had been through enough as it was this night.

Abruptly Ursula said, "It's the beginning."

"The beginning, Frau Westheim? Of what?" Theodora asked.

There was a silence before Ursula replied. "The beginning of the end of the Jews in Germany."

After Theodora had gone to bed, Ursula and Sigmund sat together on the chaise, endeavoring to analyze the dramatic events of the night, trying to understand what they predicted for the future.

At one moment, Ursula turned to him, and said slowly, "Stop trying to protect me by not telling me what you *truly* think, Sigi. I'm far too intelligent to be duped, especially by my own husband, a man I've known since childhood."

"Yes, you are," he said with a faint sigh. "And I only meant the best for you."

She tried to smile, unsuccessfully. "As always, my dearest Sigi, as always."

She held his hand very tightly and after a while said in a voice choked with emotion, "We have to leave, Sigi . . . leave this house . . . leave the villa in Wannsee . . . leave the bank . . . leave the art collection . . . leave all of our possessions . . . and go. We have to leave Berlin, Sigi. We have to get out of Germany."

"Yes, I know," he said somberly. "I've known it for a long time, really, but I suppose I haven't wanted to face it." He sighed again. "The entire family must get out. And Theodora. We cannot leave her behind, that would be unthinkable. She will come with us. I must get exit visas for everyone, and entry visas for another country."

"How?"

Indeed *how*, he thought, but he said, "To be honest, Ursula, I don't know . . . *yet*. But I will. And very soon. Certainly I've got one thing in my favor."

"What is that, Sigi?"

"Money."

10

ENTSCHULDIGEN SIE, GNÄDIGE FRAU," THE BUTLER SAID, apologizing for disturbing her.

Ursula looked across at him from the Louis XVI writing desk at the far end of the bedroom, where she sat working on some papers. "That's perfectly all right, Walter. What is it?"

"Die Gräfin von Tiegal ist da, gnädige Frau."

Ursula was momentarily startled. "The Countess von Tiegal is *here*?" she repeated.

Walter nodded. *"Ja, gnädige Frau."*

"Please show her into the library, and I'll be down in a moment. Offer her coffee, and I'll have a cup, too. Thank you, Walter."

"*Gnädige Frau*," he murmured, backing out and quietly closing the door behind him.

Ursula slid her papers into the top drawer of the desk, locked it and pocketed the key. She smoothed down the skirt of her dark-gray woolen dress with both hands as she walked over to the dressing table, where she glanced at herself in the mirror. Her face was drawn, her mouth pale and tense, and there were dark circles under her eyes. This hardly surprised her, in view of the events of the previous night. She had not slept, had lain awake until first light, worrying and pondering their predicament and their future. Sigmund had not slept either, and he had risen at six and gone off to the bank very early. He had already spoken to her on the telephone several times since leaving the house, keeping his promise to stay in touch, to inform her of any new developments after the night of havoc in the city.

She ran a comb through her short blond hair, smoothed it abstractedly, then walked to the door while looking at her wristwatch. It was still early, not quite nine o'clock. She knew why Renata was downstairs, asking to see her. She had come out of genuine concern for them, and Ursula was immeasurably touched by the gesture.

A moment later she was hurrying down the stairs, crossing the vast hall and pushing open the double doors of the library.

Renata was standing looking out the window. She swung around when Ursula entered and ran to meet her. She caught hold of her almost roughly, hugged her close, saying, "Oh, Ursi, Ursi," several times before releasing her. "Forgive me for bursting in on you like this without warning," Renata went on, "but I wanted to speak to you urgently, and our phone isn't working. For some reason, it seems to be out of order this morning."

"It was good of you to come, Ren, and I'm glad you're here. You always make me feel better. Walter is bringing us coffee. Come."

Arms linked, the two women walked over to the Biedermeier sofa and sat down. Drawing back and looking at her closely, Renata said, "Of course you know that last night's riots were not only in Berlin, they took place all over Germany and Austria as well. Yes, I can see from your face that you do."

"The whole thing is incredible. Almost impossible to believe."

"And even harder to bear! You've seen the newspapers? Heard the radio?"

"The papers yes, but I haven't listened to the radio." Speaking quickly, Ursula explained how they had learned about the demonstrations from Theodora in the middle of the night, and recounted the girl's experiences.

Renata paled as she listened, and exclaimed, "Teddy and her friend were extremely lucky—they could easily have been killed. Quite a few people were."

Ursula stared at her. "*Jews* were killed."

"Yes." Renata leaned closer. "Listen to me, Ursula, you must—" She broke off as Walter knocked, then came gliding in with the coffee tray.

"*Danke schön*, Walter," Ursula said.

The butler deposited the silver tray on the occasional table in front of the sofa and discreetly withdrew.

In hushed tones, Renata continued urgently, "You must make plans to leave Germany. It's not safe for you here anymore."

"I don't think it has been for a long time. We should have gone last year—even the year before, perhaps. But we believed in German law and order, and we thought we were safe. We also drew comfort from the belief that Hitler couldn't last, couldn't possibly stay in power. Many Germans did, and not all of them Jews, you and Reinhard included. But we were all wrong. Now I don't think there is any turning back. This is the end. For Jews anyway."

"For us all." Renata looked at her intently, her dark eyes very bright and blazing with anger. "That damned megalomaniac Hitler is leading us into a dark abyss of brutality and murder. Germany is being destroyed from within by him and his depraved cohorts. They're nothing but terrorists, for God's sake!"

"I read in the papers that the Nazis are saying last night's demonstrations were spontaneous. *That they were provoked*," Ursula said. "And all because of that seventeen-year-old German Jewish refugee living in Paris, Herschel Grynszpan, who shot and killed Ernst vom Rath, the third secretary at the German embassy in Paris. You see, Renata, they're blaming the Jews yet again."

"We read that story, but Reinhard is convinced the riots were not spontaneous, that they were cleverly and expertly orchestrated by Heydrich and the SS. And he's right, I'm certain. What's more, we both believe there are bound to be additional demonstrations, and many other acts of brutality directed against Jews." Renata shook her head and finished in a worried voice, "We think Hitler wants to kill every Jew in the land, Ursi."

"But that's inconceivable," Ursula stammered. "How can Hitler kill an entire people? Millions of people. No one could do that. . . ." Her voice trailed off helplessly.

"He aims to try." Renata's tone was grim. "Read *Mein Kampf* again. And believe it this time."

"We are *Germans*," Ursula began, and stopped abruptly. She clenched her hands and took a deep breath. "Our families, Sigi's and mine, have been here for hundreds and hundreds of years. . . ." Once more she came to a halt as her voice cracked, and she looked away, steadying herself. "But we must leave our country . . . yes . . . we must leave this country we love . . . if we are to survive. . . ."

Feelings of compassion and loving friendship washed over Renata, and she reached out to put her hand on Ursula's arm consolingly. Ursula turned, and they shared a look that was direct and intimate and full of truth.

Tears welled up in Renata when she saw her friend's deep anguish and the profound sorrow darkening her soft gray-blue eyes. "I don't want anything to happen to you!" she cried fiercely, her voice choked. "I love and care for you, and for Sigi and little Maxim. So does Reinhard. We will help you in any way we can, do anything to help you leave Germany safely. And you must leave, darling, you know you must . . . to save yourselves."

"Yes." Ursula sat staring into the distance, her eyes focused on the pale-blue sky outside the tall window, and with an unexpected rush of clarity she finally understood what it was that had haunted her for so long a time. For a while she was so shaken and alarmed that she was unable to say anything, but at last she turned her head and looked deeply into Renata's eyes once more.

Renata felt as if Ursula were staring into her soul, and, shivering slightly, she said, "Why are you looking at me like that? Whatever is it?"

"A moment ago I said that it was inconceivable . . . that Hitler cannot kill an entire people. *But he can.* Oh yes, he can. *I know that now.* The knowledge is deep within me, in my bones, in the very pores of my skin. For months I've had desperate feelings gnawing at me . . . the ones I've spoken to you about. I thought they were feelings of apprehension and dread, but they weren't. What I've harbored within me all this time is an overwhelming sense of doom. *We are doomed, my family and I.*"

"My dearest, my most beloved friend—" Renata found she was unable to continue, so overcome was she by the pain she felt for Ursula. What her friend was facing was monstrous: uprootedness, flight, exile. But if she and Sigi and little Maxim stayed they would be hounded and brutally persecuted. The evil of it filled Renata with rage, and she cried passionately, "Those Nazi bastards! This shouldn't be happening! It shouldn't! It's wrong!"

"Don't, darling. Please don't. We'll be all right. Somehow."

Renata reached for Ursula's hand and clasped it in hers, and they sat motionless, unable to continue the conversation.

After a while Ursula cleared her throat and said in a voice that was oddly calm, "Sigi does have a plan of action, you know. He's working on it right now. He has a good contact, apparently. He's hoping to buy exit visas for us. And new passports." She paused, then went on, "You see, last month we had to take our passports to be stamped—with a *J*—for Jew."

Shocked, Renata looked at her in consternation. "How ridiculous! What evil nonsense!"

"Yes, but the Nazis have made this a law, and we had to comply."

Renata made an effort to suppress her immense anger and control her flaring emotions, thinking that if Ursula could be so brave, so contained, then so must she. She even managed to force a smile onto her face when she said, "Reinhard and I want you to come out to the Mark Brandenburg and stay at the schloss. Until you leave Germany it will be much safer for you at our country estate than in Berlin."

When Ursula did not immediately respond, Renata brought

her face closer to her friend's and said, "Look, it could take Sigi several weeks to get the necessary documents together, to arrange everything to facilitate your departure."

"It might, that's true. And thank you for inviting us to the schloss. It's so kind and thoughtful of you. But I can't leave Sigi alone here in Berlin. You know how much he needs me. We've never really been apart since we were children, except when I was at school in England with you and Arabella."

"He can see you on weekends. He can drive down to the Mark Brandenburg with us every Friday afternoon. Please say yes."

Ursula remained uncertain. "Let me think about it and discuss it with Sigi."

The telephone began to ring and Ursula immediately went to answer it, wanting to pick it up before the butler did.

"Hello?" she said, fully expecting to hear her husband's voice, but it was Arabella von Wittingen at the other end. She listened for several moments, then murmured, "Thank you, Belle, and I'm all right, really." She listened again, then quickly explained, "Their phone is out of order, Ren is here. Do you wish to speak with her?" Ursula stood with the receiver pressed to her ear, nodding her head several times before she said, "Yes, Arabella, that's fine. Yes, good-bye."

"She's coming over here, isn't she?" Renata said as Ursula put down the phone.

"Of course. I suppose we both knew she would. And I'm sure you've gathered that she's been trying to telephone you."

Renata nodded.

"Arabella is in her most Bolshie and defiant mood this morning," Ursula confided. "She insists that the three of us go out to lunch. To the Adlon Hotel."

Straightening up on the sofa, Renata threw her a questioning look. "Are you up to it? And do you think we *should*?"

Ursula was thoughtful, wondering whether or not it would be a wise thing to do. And then she, who of late had sometimes been so fearful about going out, suddenly had no qualms at all. Her own sense of defiance and her pride made her say, "Of course I'm up to it. And why shouldn't we go to lunch at the Adlon? We're as entitled as anyone else, aren't we?"

"Indeed we are!" Renata agreed. "Let's do it!"

Ursula walked back to the sofa and looked down at the silver tray, shaking her head. "We've been so busy talking we never drank the coffee, and now it's probably quite cold. Shall I ask Walter to brew some more?"

"Not right now, thanks. Let's wait until Arabella gets here. You know what she's like about her morning tea. She's bound to ask you for a pot, so we might as well share it with her." Renata walked over to the window overlooking the Tiergarten-strasse, then swung around to face Ursula. "I heard on the radio earlier that the Nazis have already given last night a name. They're calling it *Kristallnacht*—crystal night. Because of all the broken glass, I suppose." Renata shuddered, and grimaced in utter disgust. "How despicable the Nazis are! Imagine using a pretty and poetic name like that to describe a night of such unspeakable savagery!" She shuddered again. "It's beyond comprehension."

"Everything that's happening is beyond comprehension," Ursula said.

11

*T*HE TIERGARTEN WAS DESERTED.

As Sigmund walked down the path he realized it would not be anything *but* deserted in bitterly cold weather such as they were having in Berlin this December. And that was precisely the reason it had been chosen for the rendezvous. A park without people was a safe park.

He had no idea whom he was to meet.

Irina had slipped a note to him two nights ago, during drinks at the von Tiegals' house, where he and Ursula were attending a small dinner party. Within seconds of pocketing it he had excused himself and hurried to the bathroom in order to read it, impatient to know what it said.

The note had been brief and to the point.

Tiergarten. Saturday. 11 A.M. Hofjägerallee side. For identification your contact will say: The blue gentians are not in bloom today. Destroy this note.

After reading the note a second time, he had set fire to the bit of paper with his cigarette lighter, held it until it was almost burnt through, then dropped it into the toilet bowl and flushed it away. Returning to the living room, he had found Irina in conversation with Reinhard, and he had simply touched her elbow, as if by accident, to let her know he had read the note and destroyed it. He knew better than to discuss anything in front of others, even their closest and most trustworthy friends. A slip of the tongue might put others in grave danger.

Sigmund had asked Irina for help the evening he and Ursula had attended the reception and dinner at the British embassy, which had been the ill-fated night of the Nazi riots—*Kristallnacht.*

Without ever having been told, he knew intuitively that Irina would be closely tied to one of the secret movements that aided Jews, Catholics, Protestants, dissidents and so-called political offenders of all kinds who sought to flee Germany and the persecution of the Third Reich. From a few bits of information he had picked up here and there and at different times, he was aware that there were several such movements operating in Berlin; all were run by German aristocrats, for the most part, although some of the young international émigrés were also apparently involved. All were opposed to Hitler and his regime, and violently anti-Nazi.

When he had approached Irina four weeks ago, he had not made any reference to the various resistance movements, deeming it wiser not to do so, and had merely asked her if she could put him in touch with someone who might help him get exit visas. She had replied that she would see what she could do, and a week later she had invited Ursula and him to dinner with her mother Natalie and the baron, at the baron's house on the Lützowufer. She had found an opportunity to get him alone for a moment, had murmured that the matter was in hand, and that there was no need for him to approach anyone else. "Patience, Sigi. Trust me," she had said softly, before gliding away to speak to another guest. Three more weeks had gone by until she had finally passed the note to him on Thursday. He had been vastly relieved, and had hardly been able to contain himself until today.

As he continued along the same path that ran parallel with the Hofjägeralle, walking in the direction of the Siegessäule, Sigmund saw a man coming toward him. He was tall and thin, dressed in a dark-green loden coat and a Tyrolean hat, and was striding purposefully, swinging a walking stick. He seemed oddly familiar to Sigi, who within seconds was filled with dismay. He had recognized the man; it was Kurt von Wittingen. The last person he wanted to run into when he was on this delicate mission was a friend who would engage him in conversation, and in the process most probably scare off his contact. But Sigmund knew there was nothing he could do. He was trapped. He could not turn around and walk in another direction because Kurt had already seen him, was raising his stick, waving it in greeting. There was nothing for it but to act in the most normal way, chat for a few minutes and then walk on. Fortunately the weather played in his favor. It was so icy he was sure Kurt would not wish to linger.

A moment later the two men were shaking hands, greeting each other warmly. After the initial greetings were over, Kurt said, "It's far too bitter to stand here chatting like this."

Relieved to hear him make this comment, Sigmund instantly agreed. "Yes, it is. Very nice running into you, Kurt, give my love to Arabella, and we'll see you next week. I must be on my way."

Kurt said, "I'll walk with you."

Sigmund's dismay spiraled into alarm. When his contact saw him with a companion, he or she would not dare to approach him and would simply disappear, he was quite convinced of that. For a split second panic rendered him speechless. He stood staring at Kurt, desperately wondering how to get rid of him courteously, and without giving offense.

"It's all right, Sigi," Kurt said. "Relax. *The blue gentians are not in bloom in the Tiergarten today.*"

Sigmund was not sure that he had heard correctly, and he continued to stare at Kurt, looking dumbfounded.

"Let's start walking," Kurt said swiftly, and set off at a brisk pace.

Recovering himself, Sigi fell into step. "Why didn't Irina tell me *you* were my contact?"

"She wasn't sure it *would* be me. So why risk exposing me unnecessarily, albeit to a very old and reliable friend?"

"I understand."

"The eight exit visas you require are for Ursula, Maxim and yourself, and your immediate family. And Theodora. I am correct, am I not?"

"Yes. I would like to get new passports for all of us. Passports not stamped with a *J.*"

Kurt threw him a quick glance and frowned. "I am *positive* I cannot get new passports, Sigi. Does it really matter that those you have are stamped with a *J?*"

"No, I don't suppose so." Sigmund cleared his throat. "But I was hoping that if you *could* get them, they could be issued under a different name. At least, for the Westheims."

"Why a false name?"

"Look, I've not been touched so far, nor has the bank been taken over by them, because I've been extremely useful to the government in various financial transactions, notably those to do with foreign currencies and such. And I'm still very useful to them. Very frankly, I just don't think they'd like it if I tried to leave Germany at this time. They might even try to prevent me from going, if they got wind of it. And so obviously if I were traveling out under a different name I would not be so easily spotted."

"Yes, of course, I see what you mean. But I know I cannot get you new passports. I'm so sorry, but that's not something *my* contact could pull off."

"All right, never mind."

"Arabella tells me that you and Ursula are coming to supper on Monday night. You must bring the eight passports with you then. I will need them for the exit visas. Put them in the inside breast pocket of your overcoat. I will take them out of your coat at some point during the evening."

"No problem. I'll collect the passports from my family tomorrow."

The two men walked on in silence for several seconds, and then Sigmund said worriedly, "Are you sure you can procure the exit visas?"

"I won't lie to you, Sigi, I don't know that I can," Kurt said. "It won't be easy. But I have a good source and I am extremely hopeful. Let's just say that I'm ninety percent certain."

"I have money on me, in my overcoat pocket. A great deal of cash. Do you want it now?"

"No, I don't, but thank you for offering."

"What about entry visas to another country?"

"They're not going to be easy to get, either."

"Have you any idea which country we might be able to go to?"

Kurt shook his head. "Not at this moment. I doubt that it will be America, though. The U.S. Congress doesn't seem willing to modify the immigration laws, to allow any more Jewish refugees from Germany to enter the country. Nor does Roosevelt seem prepared to act."

"What about England?"

"I believe that's your best chance, since the British have been very generous about taking in Jewish refugees from Europe for some time. And anyway, my influence and contacts are much stronger with the British diplomatic service. Never fear, I will pull every string available to me."

"I know you'll do your damnedest. Where will we actually go when we leave Berlin?"

"To one of two cities, Lisbon or Paris. But more than likely it will be Paris, where you could pick up your entry visas from the British embassy, if you don't have them in your hands when you leave Germany."

"Have you any idea when that will be?" Sigi asked.

"I daren't promise anything, or give you a specific date. But I don't think it will take much longer than a month to get the documents. Let's say early January."

Sigmund nodded. "I *can* tell Ursula, can't I? Just to alleviate her awful worry about Maxim's safety."

"Yes, but do warn her not to discuss your plans with anyone outside the family. And don't tell her who is helping you. The less you say, and actually the less you know, the safer it is for me, Irina and our friends. And for you too, in the long run," Kurt said.

"You have no cause to worry, Kurt. I will be discreet, and so will Ursula. And not one member of my family will know any of the details, only that we are going to leave. I realize that there will be hefty payoffs involved, and I would simply like to add that money is no object."

"I know that, Sigi. I also know that it is now impossible for

Jews to transfer any assets abroad. I hope you took care of that some time ago." Kurt gave him a questioning look.

Sigmund nodded. "I managed to get some money out."

"But not enough, perhaps. You must have Ursula sew her most valuable jewelry into the linings of the clothes she will be traveling in, such as a suit jacket and its skirt, her top coat, even under the lining of her hat. That is the best way to get valuables out undetected. And have your mother and sisters do the same thing."

"I will."

"Oh, and one other thing, they must do this themselves. I'm not suggesting for one moment that your servants are disloyal, but it's wise to be cautious. One never knows about anyone these days. Brother is informing on brother, so just be careful in front of the servants. The last thing you want is the Nazi guards at the border alerted that you are carrying valuables. They would confiscate everything."

"I am quite positive our servants are trustworthy—they have been with the family for years. However, I will naturally heed your advice," Sigi promised.

"And also be careful what you say on the telephone—at home and at the bank. Phone tapping has become a favorite Nazi pastime," Kurt remarked in a disdainful tone.

"Do you think my phones are tapped?" Sigmund asked swiftly.

"I'm not sure. Possibly they are at the bank. Just be *aware*, that's all."

"I have been for a long time."

"Good. That's it for now. We will go our separate ways. And when we meet again socially we will obviously not discuss this meeting, or anything else pertaining to the matter."

"Absolutely not," Sigi concurred.

"Once I have the documents in my hands, I will arrange a rendezvous for us. We will meet somewhere exceptionally safe," Kurt said. "And you must be prepared to travel immediately, of course. So be ready. And you must travel light. Take only one suitcase each, if possible. If it's not, then do not take more than two each, at the most."

"I understand." Sigi came to a halt and turned to face the other man. "I don't know how to thank you, Kurt, I really don't. I am overcome with gratitude for what you're doing for me and my family. The words *thank you* somehow don't seem to be quite enough."

"Thanks are not necessary, my dear old friend. I am glad to help you. And for your own sakes, I'm glad you're going. It's obvious, after *Kristallnacht*, that this country is in the hands of mass murderers." A terrible sadness came over Kurt's sensitive, gentle face and he sighed heavily. There was a slight pause before he went on quietly, "Stay calm. Try not to worry. Everything is well in hand. With a bit of luck you'll soon be out of Germany. In the meantime, just continue to go about your business in the most natural way." He thrust out his hand.

Sigi took it, clasped it strongly. "Thank you again, Kurt, and from the very bottom of my heart. I will never forget this, never as long as I live. You are a true friend."

Sigmund stood for a moment watching Kurt's retreating figure. Then he turned up the collar of his overcoat, thrust his hands in his pockets and walked in the direction they had just come from. He could not wait to get back to his house on the Tiergartenstrasse to tell Ursula the good news.

His thoughts zeroed in on Prince Rudolf Kurt von Wittingen as he hurried along the path. He trusted Kurt implicitly. And if anyone could pull this off, he could.

For several years Kurt had been a senior consultant to Krupp, the German armaments king. As such he roamed all over Europe, frequently traveled to England and the United States, handling top-level negotiations, entertaining foreign dignitaries and acting as a sort of roving ambassador for the Krupp organization. Sigi now realized that this job was the ideal cover for Kurt. He was able to come and go in almost perfect freedom. He had access to all kinds of important people, who in turn were extraordinary sources of information, and probably privileged information at that.

This aside, Sigmund knew for a fact that Kurt was a fervent anti-fascist, an idealist who happened to be a realist, in that he viewed the totalitarian dictatorship that was Germany through clear, unblinkered eyes. Naturally he would be involved in some sort of resistance movement because of his convictions.

Sigmund wondered why he had never thought of all this before. Perhaps because of the Krupp connection, which was undoubtedly the *real* reason why it existed in the first place. It was a red herring to throw people off the scent. A protection for Kurt. He was above suspicion as Krupp's envoy.

And then there was Graf Reinhard von Tiegal. Sigmund considered his other close friend. The count belonged to an ancient Prussian family of Junkers, the conservative landholders who were descended from the Teutonic Knights. And so by reason of birth and upbringing Reinhard also detested everything the Nazis stood for, and believed them to be criminals of the most despicable kind.

Was Reinhard involved in the resistance to Hitler? Sigi asked himself. More than likely, he decided after only a moment's thought. And because he knew how dangerous it was for both men, the knowledge that they were fighting the Nazis with whatever means they had moved him immensely.

As long as there were men of honor and humanity in Germany, then Hitler and his evil regime would eventually be overcome and ultimately destroyed.

Ursula looked up quickly as Sigmund walked into the library, and she angrily threw down the newspaper she had been reading.

"I don't know why I bother with the papers anymore!" she exclaimed, gesturing to the pile of discarded periodicals at her feet. "They're only full of Hitler's vile lies and propaganda, courtesy of Goebbels!"

Sigmund sat down on the sofa next to her. "I suppose we all keep reading the newspapers hoping against hope that we'll glean a little bit of real news."

"Yes, you're right, darling," she agreed.

Sigmund took her hand in his and smiled into her drawn face. "*I* have some *news*, Ursula," he said softly. Moving closer to her, he kissed her cheek, then whispered against her hair, "I saw my contact a short while ago. The plans are progressing. We're getting out. Hopefully within the next four to five weeks, if all goes well."

"Thank God! Oh, thank God!" she gasped, holding on to him tightly. "Maxim's going to be safe, Sigi. Our little boy is going to be safe. And that's all that matters."

12

$\mathcal{M}$AXIM STOOD OUTSIDE THE LIBRARY, LISTENING.

The door was open a crack and he peeped through it. Just as he thought, his grandmother was sitting near the fireplace in her favorite chair, the one in which she always sat when she came to visit them. She preferred its straight back—he had heard her say that to Mutti and Papa many times. She sat staring into the fire, her hands resting on top of her black cane with its polished silver handle, which gleamed brightly in the firelight.

He liked her cane, which had belonged to his grandfather. Grandfather Westheim had died two years ago. He remembered many things about him, and he missed him very much. When Grandfather Westheim used to come to visit them he would lift Maxim up on his knee and tell him stories, and sometimes he would take him for a drive in his big black motorcar with Manfred, the chauffeur, at the wheel. They would sit on the backseat together and talk of many Important Things, like The Bank, where he would work with his papa when he grew up, and which would be his one day. After their drive they always stopped at Grandfather's favorite *Konditorei* and had an ice cream and sometimes cake as well, and Grandfather would smoke a cigar and sip a small cup of strong coffee, very black and very sweet, something that he was not allowed to have.

He wished his grandfather would come back. But dead people never came back. Not ever. Being dead meant that you had gone to Heaven to live with God, his papa had told him that. Grandfather Neuman was dead, too. He had died last year, and Mutti had been very sad and had cried a lot, and he had cried too, partly because his mother was crying and that made him sad. But he had loved Grandfather Neuman as much as he had loved Grandfather Westheim.

Suddenly he wondered if the grandfathers ever met each other in Heaven and sat and smoked their cigars and drank cognac and talked about Important World Matters, as they had when they had not been dead. He hoped they did. He wouldn't like them to be lonely in Heaven. Grandmama Neuman was another dead person, but he had never known her. At least, he had only been one year old when she had died, just a little baby, not grown-up as he was now that he was four, and so he couldn't remember much about her, not really. There was only Grandmama Westheim left. "We must treasure her," his mother kept saying.

Maxim bent over and pulled up his sock, which had slithered down around his ankle.

As he straightened he heard the rustle of silk and a small sigh, and he smiled inside, waiting. Then he heard it . . . the low whistle like a bird chirping in the Tiergarten. He pursed his lips and gave a little whistle himself, and waited again. The trilling response came almost immediately, and he pushed open the big double doors with both hands and bounded into the room, laughing as he rushed to her, exclaiming, "I am here, Grandmama! I am here!"

She laughed, too, as he stopped in front of her, and she leaned forward, proffering her cheek to him.

He gave her a big kiss, then stood back regarding her, rocking on his heels. His grandmother was dressed in a black lace and silk dress, as she usually was, with the long string of shiny white pearls like fat peas hanging around her neck and the sparkly clips on her ears. She had lots of silky white hair piled on top of her head, with tortoiseshell combs pressed in at each side to hold it there. Her skin was funny, all wrinkly like scrunched-up paper, but she had smooth, pink apple cheeks and bright shining eyes that reminded him of round blue pebbles.

He loved her a lot.

"Don't do that, Maximilian. Don't rock back and forth in that fashion," his grandmother scolded, but her voice was gentle.

"Sorry, Grandmama."

She took the box that lay on her lap and handed it to him.

"This is from Auntie Hedy. She wasn't able to come tonight, but she sent this to you and many kisses as well."

"Oh, thank you, Grandmama!" he cried, taking the box from her. Excitedly he tore off the fancy colored paper, lifted the lid and looked inside.

"Oooh!" he cried when he saw the six candy pigs lying side by side in the box. They were plump and rosy, with beady eyes and yellow bows, and they looked delicious. His mouth watered.

"They're made of your favorite marzipan," his grandmother said, smiling at him. "But you're not to eat even *one* before dinner. Your mother will be cross with both of us, if you do."

"I won't, I *promise*, Grandmama," he said, careful to be the polite and obedient boy his grandmother expected him to be. After putting the lid back on the box, he placed it on a nearby table, picked up the torn paper from the floor, crumpled it in a ball and threw it into the fire.

Then he stepped closer to his grandmother, put one of his small, chubby hands on top of hers and began to pat it. "Gangan," he said, reverting to his babyhood name for her. "Can I ask you something?"

"Anything in the whole world, Maxim."

He held his head on one side and wrinkled his nose. "How do you know when to whistle?"

"What do you mean?"

"How do you know I'm there, outside the door?"

Her mouth twitched in amusement but she kept a serious face and said, "Well, I don't *really* know that you're there. I *hope* you are—I suppose I sort of *feel* that you are—because I love you."

He nodded solemnly. "I *like* our game, Grandmama."

"So do I." Margarete Westheim leaned back in the chair and studied her only grandchild for a moment. She loved him so much she sometimes thought her heart would break from it. The knowledge that she would have to leave him was an agony. Her only regret about dying, and die she must one day in the not too distant future, was that she would miss all those years of his growing up, the wonderful years. He was such a beautiful boy, full of life and laughter and mischief, and so bright, and intelligent beyond his years. She prayed to God every night that Sigmund would succeed in getting the child out of Germany.

Like her son and daughter-in-law, she was terribly afraid for him. A pestilence stalked this land. A shiver ran through Margarete, and she wondered where God was in this godless nation. But then what could *He* do? Evil was man's invention, not God's.

"Is something hurting, Gangan?"

Startled out of her brief reverie by his piping child's voice, Margarete looked at him quickly. "No. Why do you ask that, darling?"

"You have a funny look on your face, a puckery look, like you're going to cry."

"I'm fine," she reassured him with a quick smile, suddenly aware of the worry in his child's eyes. She opened her black beaded evening bag and took out a small item wrapped in silver paper and handed it to him. "Here you are, Maxim, here is your Friday pocket money."

"Oh, Grandmama, thank you, *thank you.*"

He unwrapped the silver paper, his eyes shining as he stared down at the coins in his hand. *Four marks.* His Gangan always gave him four now. Last year he had received three. Next year she would give him five. She had told him that. One mark for every year he had been born. He leaned closer to her, kissed her cheek and beamed into her face as he slipped the coins in his pocket, playing with them for a moment, liking the way they jingled.

The door opened and Maxim turned to see his father standing in the doorway. He flew to him at once, crying, "Papa! Papa!"

His father caught him, swung him up and kissed him and carried him in his arms as he strode across the floor.

"Good evening, Mother," Sigmund said.

"Good evening, Sigi," she responded, her clear blue eyes so like his lighting up at the sight of him. He was her youngest son, the third one she had borne. His two elder brothers were both dead over twenty years now, killed as boys in the trenches of the Somme in the Great War. Two sons she had sacrificed for the Fatherland.

Sigmund put Maxim on the sofa and went to kiss his mother before sitting down next to his son. He said to her, "I understand from Ursula that Hedy is not coming this evening, that she's not feeling well. Nothing too serious, I hope?" A dark brow lifted.

"A cold, Sigi, that's all." Frau Westheim sighed. "There's always *something* with Hedy these days. That girl would be better off living in a warmer climate, I do believe."

"Wouldn't we all," Sigmund murmured and continued, "She has not seemed well since she broke off her engagement to Paul."

"No, she hasn't," Frau Westheim agreed, and looked into the fire, a faraway expression on her face.

Watching her, Maxim thought, Gangan looks unhappy. I wonder why? He glanced up at his father, his wonderful papa, and smiled at him adoringly.

Sigmund stared down into the small, bright face, smiled back and said, "Do you remember what I told you last Friday evening? When I was speaking to you about the standards I want you to have when you are a big boy, and when you are a man?"

"Yes, Papa. You said a gentleman never tells a lie."

"That's correct, Maxim, but now I'm afraid I must amend that statement."

"Oh." Maxim looked surprised. He was not sure what the word "amend" meant, but he was reluctant to admit this, so he kept silent.

"I don't suppose you know what 'amend' means, do you?" Sigmund said, as if reading his mind.

"No."

Sigmund took his child's hand in his lovingly. "I thought as much. It means *to change* or *revise.* And I wish to revise what I said to you last week, change my opinion. . . . I believe it is perfectly all right for a gentleman to tell a lie, if it is a matter of life and death . . . if it is to save his life. Or the lives of others, of course."

Maxim nodded.

"Do you understand me?"

"I think so, Papa."

"Very good, Maxim. You're a clever boy, I know that, and you are learning quickly. Now—there is something else I want to tell you, and it is this: a man must have valor, honor and nobility if he is to be of great character. I want you to remember that when you grow up."

"Yes, Papa, I will."

His grandmother said, "Your father's brothers, Heinrich and Peter, had valor . . . they were very courageous . . . they went to fight for their country in the Great War and they were not afraid. That is what valor means."

"My dead uncles—they were *brave,*" Maxim said with a little frown.

"Yes, your dead uncles were," his grandmother answered. "And your grandfathers were both men of honor because they never did anything that was cruel or wicked, unjust or dishonest—"

"Dinner is ready, everyone," Ursula announced from the doorway. "Marta is waiting to serve."

"We shall come at once, my darling," Sigmund said, rising immediately. "Now, Maxim, run along with your mother. We will follow." He lifted the boy down from the sofa, then reached into his pocket and took out a slip of paper. "Here you are. I have written out the new words for you, as well as their meaning."

Maxim took it and put it in his pocket. He kept all these pieces of paper that his father had been giving him for the last few weeks. "Thank you, Papa, and I *will* remember."

Sigmund gazed down at him, marveling at the beauty and brightness of the boy. He really was exceptional, highly intelligent and articulate for his age, an extraordinary child. He stroked Maxim's blond head, and then, after helping his mother out of the chair, he escorted her slowly across the room.

Maxim ran ahead to Ursula, who stood waiting in the doorway. She took his hand in hers and together they crossed the baronial marble entrance hall toward the dining room.

"And what was Papa telling you tonight, my darling?"

"He said that when I grow up I must be a man of valor, honor and nobility."

Ursula said, very softly, "If you are, then you will be exactly like your father."

Maxim shut his eyes tightly and listened as his mother performed the ritual of blessing the *Shabbat* candles.

"*Baruch ata Adonai, Elohaynu melech ha-olam, asher kid'shanu b'mitsvotav v'tsivanu l'hadlik nayr shel shabbat,*" she said slowly in her light clear voice, which he always loved to listen to, and most especially when she spoke Hebrew. She made the words sound like music.

"Amen," he sang as she finished, joining in with everyone else. And then he opened his eyes.

They all sat down around the large table with its snow-white cloth and silver candelabra and crystal goblets that sparkled in the candlelight. Papa was at the head, Mutti at the other end facing his father, and he and Theodora sat together opposite Grandmama.

Now it was his father's turn to perform the ritual.

He blessed the red wine in a little silver cup and said the *Kiddush* in Hebrew, and then he murmured another blessing, this time over the *chollah*, the two twisted loaves of bread in the silver basket under the embroidered linen napkin.

Once the blessings were finished, his father lifted the napkin, made a little ceremony of breaking the bread, and passed it around to everyone at the table. And at last Marta was allowed to serve the food, which Frau Müller had been cooking all afternoon in the big kitchen. Marta always served the dinner on Friday because it was Walter's night off, when he went to see his daughter and her children. Maxim knew a lot about the butler's grandchildren. Walter told him many things when he sneaked into the kitchen on baking days. Walter would sit him at Frau Müller's baking table and give him a *Berliner Pfannkuchen* oozing jelly, and a glass of milk, and talk to him, and slip him another jelly doughnut when no one was looking. Except that Frau Müller always noticed. "You spoil that child," she would tell Walter, who fortunately never paid any attention to her. Walter and he were *very* good friends.

Maxim settled back in the chair, waiting.

Everything always happened the way he knew it would, and as it had for as long as he could remember. "The rituals of the Sabbath are important to us all, and should be properly observed," his mother had often told him. He liked rituals and looked forward to them. They were special, somehow.

Friday was his favorite night of the week, and for lots of reasons. For one thing, he and Teddy were permitted to have dinner with his mother and father in the grand dining room, instead of eating alone together in the nursery as they generally did, except on Teddy's day off. For another, he was with Mutti, Papa, Teddy and Grandmama, the four people he loved the most in the whole wide world. Also, he got to stay up late, and the things he enjoyed the most were served. Piping-hot chicken soup, then a roasted chicken, all golden and crisp on the outside and juicy on the inside, or beef flanken or perhaps steamed carp, and there would be little potato pancakes and apple sauce, or sweet shredded carrots and potato dumplings. And at the end of the meal there was always something wonderful, such as apple strudel, which melted in the mouth.

Yes, Friday was the *best* night of the week. It was like the beginning of a holiday. His father did not go to The Bank on Saturday and Sunday, and so they did many things and had such a lot of fun together. Friday night was . . . was . . . *festive.* Yes, that was it exactly. Except that tonight no one seemed very festive. His mother was quiet, so very still. She had been like this for ages, and he kept wondering why. He had asked Teddy, just the other day, and she had not really given him an answer. All she had said was that his mother had *things* on her mind, and even though he had pestered her a lot she had not told him anything else.

Mutti did not seem to laugh very much anymore, and her beautiful face was sad, like the time when Grandfather Neuman died. He thought she was cross with him, but Teddy said this wasn't so, and he believed Teddy. She always told him the truth. Besides, he hadn't been a bad boy. In fact, he had been an angel lately, or so Teddy said.

The tantalizing aroma of chicken soup floated delicately in the air. Maxim's nose twitched and he salivated when Marta placed one of the steaming porcelain bowls in front of him.

"*Danke schön, Marta,*" he said, and picked up his silver spoon. He dipped it in the clear golden liquid, scooped up a sliver of carrot and a curly bit of noodle, and took his first mouthful. It tasted delicious. This was definitely the soup he liked the best. He wished they had it every day.

His father and his grandmother talked nonstop about this and that, and occasionally his mother joined in, but he and Teddy were as quiet as mice, as they always were, not speaking unless they were spoken to, when they had to reply.

After they had all finished the soup, Gerda, the other downstairs maid, took the bowls away and Marta came gliding in from the kitchen carrying a silver platter on which there lay a huge steamed carp.

Maxim could see the fish if he sat up really straight in the chair and craned his neck. Marta showed the fish to his mother, who nodded and said, "It looks wonderful, Marta. My compliments to Frau Müller. Please be kind enough to serve it."

"It seems to me that it would be a nice change for you if you went to stay with Renata at the schloss for a few days," Sigmund said, looking down the long stretch of table at Ursula as the dessert was being served. "And I'm sure Maxim and Teddy would enjoy it too."

At the mention of his name, Maxim sat up in the chair and looked from his father to his mother alertly. His dark eyes gleamed, and before he could stop himself, he exclaimed, "Oh yes, Mutti, please let's go!"

Ursula glanced at him. A faint smile touched her mouth. "Would you really like to do that, *mein Schatz*?"

"I would, Mutti, and so would Teddy. Wouldn't you, Teddy?" He turned to Theodora, gave her a pleading look.

Teddy said, "I think Maxim would benefit from a change of air, a few days in the country."

Sigmund smiled. He was delighted to have his son and Teddy as his allies. He had been quite certain that Ursula would object, that she would not wish to go away, although in his opinion she truly needed a break from Berlin and its tensions. Maxim's enthusiasm would undoubtedly sway her, he now believed.

Just as Sigmund had thought, Ursula nodded her assent. "All right, Maxim, we'll go in the middle of next week, let's say on Wednesday." She focused her gaze on Sigmund, and added, "But only if you promise to join us on Friday, Sigi."

"I do promise," Sigmund said at once. "I understand from Reinhard that Renata is going to invite Arabella and the children if you accept, so it will be nice for Maxim to be with them."

"Yes, it will," Ursula agreed. The thought of the trip to the Mark Brandenburg and being with her two best women friends cheered her, and she suddenly felt lighter in spirit. Turning to Maxim, she said with a loving smile, "It's been snowing in the Mark so we'll be able to play outside with the other children. We'll go tobogganing and perhaps we can even skate on the lake."

Maxim nodded excitedly. The prospect of this trip thrilled him and it showed on his animated little face. Laughing gaily, he cried, "And I will build you a beautiful snowman, Mutti, and one for you too, Teddy." He looked from one to the other, and his mother smiled at him and Teddy murmured her thanks, and this made him glow inside.

As he picked up his fork and cut into his apple strudel, he thought he was going to burst with happiness. Friday night had been extra-special this week. They were going to stay at the big old castle, where he always had fun with Gretchen, Diana and Christian, and his mother was smiling again, which was the most important thing of all.

13

THE FORESTS OF THE MARK BRANDENBURG, ONCE THE DO-main of the conquering Teutonic Knights, stretched for miles in the marshy region of Prussia. Drained by three rivers, the Havel, the Spree and the Oder, it was an area of many lakes, crisscrossed by countless canals and little waterways that connected its quaint villages.

At the edge of one such old and charming village stood the great schloss of Graf Reinhard von Tiegal. The back façade of this ancient and picturesque castle faced sloping lawns and formal gardens, and beyond these were the pine forests that were part of the immense von Tiegal estates, owned by the family since the sixteenth century.

On this Sunday morning, early in January of 1939, the forests looked quite magical, completely garbed in white. Snow and dripping icicles covered the trees, weighted their branches down in places, and underfoot the narrow, winding paths were obscured by new layers of snow that had fallen during the night and then frozen. In the brilliant golden sunlight streaming in through the trees everything glistened as if it had been dusted with silver.

The only sound in this vast and silent white wonderland was the crunch of heavy boots sinking into the crisp snow as Sigmund and Kurt plowed forward through the forest on their morning walk. Both men had come to the schloss to join their wives for the weekend, Sigmund driving down to the Mark from Berlin on Friday evening, Kurt on Saturday afternoon.

Heavily bundled up though they were, in thick green loden coats, Tyrolean hats, woolen scarves and gloves, and with their trousers tucked inside their ski boots, they nevertheless moved at a relatively brisk pace, since there was an icy, cutting wind.

Neither of them spoke for a while, wrapped in their own thoughts yet perfectly comfortable in their companionable silence, as old friends frequently are.

It was Kurt who broke the silence by saying, "I have news for you, Sigi."

Sigmund looked at him alertly. "You do? Please, tell me quickly."

"I will have the exit visas for you tomorrow or on Tuesday. However, there has been a slight snag. I can only get three."

Sigmund's heart sank. He stopped abruptly and stared at Kurt, unable to keep the dismay from showing on his face. "What happened? What went wrong?"

"Nothing went *wrong*. Very simply, my contact feels he must move carefully. For the moment, at least. To avoid arousing suspicion." Kurt took hold of Sigmund's arm. "Come, let's keep walking. We don't want to freeze to death out here." The two men set off again, and the prince continued. "Eight visas are a lot to get all at once, and especially since only a week or two ago my contact managed to help a large family leave, after numerous delays. *Nine* people, actually. But quite aside from his own sense of caution, *his* contact at the Foreign Ministry is somewhat nervous just now. Nonetheless, my friend promises to have three more exit visas for you in a couple of weeks, and the last two by the end of the month. No later. Please don't worry, it's going to be all right. Now, we need to know who will be using the first three visas. I presume you want to get Ursula and Maxim out immediately. Will you go with them?"

"Ursula and Maxim *must* go at once. But I cannot," Sigmund said without hesitation. "I must stay behind until everyone else has left."

"I rather thought you'd say that," Kurt murmured. "So who will accompany Ursula and Maxim? Your mother?"

Sigmund shook his head. "My mother wouldn't go, not without my sisters. She would never leave her daughters behind, I can assure you of that. She will tell me that she is an old woman, that her life is virtually over anyway, and she'll refuse. And so I think it will be best if Theodora travels with Ursula and Maxim. In two weeks, when you have the second set of visas, Sigrid, her husband and Hedy can leave. I will take my mother out with me at the end of the month."

"I guessed you wouldn't even contemplate leaving Germany until the entire family was safely in another country," Kurt said. "I should have the three relevant passports back in my hands by Tuesday—Wednesday at the latest. I will bring them to you at the house."

"Thank you very much, Kurt. Ursula is prepared, and she can leave immediately. Your contact—" Sigmund broke off, hesitating, then said, "Your contact *is* fairly certain he can get the other visas, isn't he?"

"Yes." Now it was Kurt who stopped abruptly, and he swung around to face Sigmund. The look he gave him was very direct. "*He is absolutely sure.* I promise you, Sigi."

Sigmund returned his friend's gaze, and their eyes locked and held.

For a fleeting moment Kurt thought he saw a flicker of doubt or worry, or perhaps a mingling of both, in Sigmund's eyes, and he said, "You must believe me—my source is extremely reliable. He wouldn't say he could get the visas if he thought he couldn't, if he had any reservations whatsoever."

There was a small silence; finally Sigmund nodded. "As long as you have confidence in him, Kurt, that is good enough for me."

Even though they were now in the depths of the forest, Kurt dropped his voice to a lower pitch, more from habit than from anything else, and said, "Look, to make you feel more secure about everything, I will tell you who is helping me. And you. It's Admiral Canaris."

Sigmund's jaw dropped. He was thunderstruck and he gaped at Kurt. "*Wilhelm Canaris!* But he's head of the Abwehr."

"Yes. And as head of German military intelligence he is invaluable to me. And in many more ways than I can ever tell you."

"*Canaris*," Sigmund repeated wonderingly.

It was obvious to Kurt that Sigmund was stunned by what he had just told him, and he said, "By birth, upbringing, tradition, instinct and conviction, Admiral Canaris detests Hitler and all that he stands for, as do many of the men who work under him. And, incidentally, there isn't one ministry in the entire government that doesn't have two or three men, sometimes even more, who feel the same way."

"Like the admiral's contact in the Foreign Ministry?"

"Exactly."

"I must admit, you startled me, took my breath away, when you mentioned the admiral," Sigi said. "Who would guess he is an anti-Nazi!"

"His hatred of them is quite known—in a select circle. You could say it's a sort of . . . well, it's an open secret really. And there happens to be a number of generals who think exactly as he does. But it would be useless for them to work *openly* against Hitler, not to mention extremely foolhardy. Each of them would find himself swinging at the end of a rope if he did."

"So Canaris and the others are fighting Hitler from within—on the inside," Sigi asserted.

"That's correct. Canaris believes that Hitler will eventually bring about the total collapse of Germany. I happen to agree," Kurt said with a heavy sigh. "And he and I are both convinced that Hitler will definitely go to war with England sometime this year. . . . A lot of people believe that, actually. He wants to engulf the West."

"You sound pessimistic, Kurt."

"I feel *very* pessimistic." The prince shook his head. "The future looks bleak, very bad; war *is* inevitable. And Germany must lose that war if it is to survive as a nation, and regain its humanity."

"Yes," Sigi said in the quietest of tones.

They walked on together, each of them preoccupied with dire thoughts, but after a few seconds Sigi muttered thoughtfully, "If Hitler forces Chamberlain's hand and Britain *does* go to war, France will join in the fight as England's long-standing ally, and co-signer of the Munich Pact."

"Undoubtedly." Kurt shook his head and cursed mildly under his breath before exclaiming, "That fool Chamberlain! He always buys Hitler's talk of appeasement—empty words—of no value. There's only one politician in England who genuinely understands Hitler's warlike intentions, his eventual aims and the overall situation, and that's Winston Churchill."

"But he's a lone voice, Kurt. No one is listening to Churchill," Sigmund pointed out.

"Unfortunately. It's a great pity Churchill isn't prime minister." Once more Kurt sighed in frustration, and then went on rapidly, "But to get back to Ursula's travel plans. I do think it would be a good idea to have her leave by the end of this coming week. I want you to buy train tickets for Paris, Sigi. Plus *return tickets*."

"Yes, I will. But what about the entry visas for England?"

"We decided that it would look better if Ursula appears to be taking Maxim on a vacation to France, hence the return tickets. Therefore she *cannot* have the entry visa for England in her passport when she leaves Germany, and obviously neither can Maxim or Theodora. Ursula will be able to pick up the documents they require at the British embassy in Paris. I have arranged everything, and she will get the entry visas immediately, without any problem. Rest assured."

Sigmund nodded. "I have every confidence in you, Kurt, and again I thank you for all that you are doing for me, and for trusting me enough to tell me about Canaris. And of course I realize the necessity for total secrecy about the admiral and his activities."

"I know you will be discreet, and after all the years of close friendship we have enjoyed, our trust in each other goes without saying. Now perhaps we ought to return to the schloss and join Reinhard. I believe he's expecting Adam von Trott for lunch. He's staying with friends nearby. You know Adam von Trott zu Solz, don't you?"

"Not very well. I've met him with Reinhard a few times. Weren't they at Oxford together?"

"Yes. Adam is a Rhodes Scholar."

"He's half German, half American, isn't he?"

"That's correct. He had a rather famous American ancestor,

as a matter of fact. John Jay, who became the first chief justice of the U.S. Supreme Court, was his great-great-grandfather. Jay was also a statesman and diplomat of great repute."

"I didn't know that. It will be nice to see Adam again," Sigmund said. "If I remember correctly, he's with the German Foreign Office."

14

$\mathscr{A}$ RAMBLING CENTURIES-OLD CASTLE STANDING ON A small rise, its turrets and towers and onion-shaped cupolas glittering in the radiant sunshine. Dark-green pine forests frosted with ice, encircling the white-stone schloss, rising up behind it like a giant ruff. Children brightly dressed, playing in the snow under a sky so crystal clear it looked like polished blue glass.

Such was the scene that confronted Sigmund and Kurt as they tramped out of the lower forest, where they had been walking and talking for the past half hour. And it was a scene of such simplicity, gentleness and innocence that both men stopped to stare, entranced, carried back to their own childhoods. They glanced at each other and knew they shared identical thoughts.

Sigi said softly, as though to himself, "Nothing must happen to those children, Kurt. They must not come to any harm."

"They won't. Not if I have anything to do with it," Kurt vowed vehemently. His own children, thirteen-year-old Christian and nine-year-old Diana, were helping Maxim to build a huge snowman, which dwarfed the smaller boy somewhat, although this did not seem to bother him. Eight-year-old Gretchen von Tiegal was pushing a wheelbarrow full of snow over to her nanny, Irmgard, who, along with Teddy, was fashioning an ice castle for Gretchen. Both young women were working intently at their task, completely absorbed in what they were doing.

"Cooee, all of you!" Kurt called. He and Sigmund waved to the group as all eyes turned toward them.

"Cooee!" the children and the nannies cried in unison, waving and laughing before turning back to their sculptures of snow.

"They want to finish before lunch," Sigmund laughed. "So that we can come and admire their handiwork."

Kurt also chuckled, and the two men veered to the left, taking a path that led up to a side wing of the castle; the path had recently been cleared of snow by one of the gardeners, so they were able to cover the distance at a rapid pace.

Once inside the little entrance hall, with its wood-paneled walls and blue-and-white tiled floor, they shed their outer garments, replaced their ski boots with shoes, and climbed the narrow, twisting stone staircase that spiraled up to the floor above, and Reinhard's study.

The door was ajar. Sigmund pushed it open and walked in, closely followed by Kurt.

Adam von Trott zu Solz had already arrived, and he and Reinhard were standing in front of the blazing fire, drinking champagne. Greetings were exchanged, and Reinhard said to the newcomers, "A glass of this? Or would you prefer to fortify yourselves with something stronger?"

"Champagne for me, please," Sigmund said. "How about you, Kurt?"

The prince nodded. "I'll have the same, thanks." He took a gold cigarette case out of his tweed shooting jacket, and offered its contents to Sigi and Adam. Sigi took one; Adam declined.

As he lit his cigarette Sigi looked across at Adam von Trott. He had forgotten how good-looking Adam was. Tall, rather rangy in build, he was very personable, with a great deal of natural charm.

In contrast to him, Reinhard was shorter, with dark-brown hair and eyes, and a somewhat burnished, weatherbeaten complexion, that of a man who spends a lot of time outdoors. He was exuberant and outgoing by nature, and full of easy laughter, although that laughter had been mostly absent in the past year.

His face was very serious now as he carried the crystal goblets of sparkling wine over to Sigmund and Kurt. Retrieving his own glass from the mantel of the huge stone fireplace, he lifted it in the air. *"Prost!"*

"Prost!" the others said.

After a few sips of champagne, Reinhard said, "I think Hitler is losing his self-control. I understand from certain sources of mine that there have been a lot of mad outbursts lately, in the inner sanctum of the Reich Chancellery. And then there's *Kristallnacht* to consider. I lay the blame for that unconscionable brutality entirely on him. Nobody will ever convince *me* that he didn't sanction it, indeed encourage the riots. And it seems to me that his megalomania is getting out of hand. Very frankly, I believe it's started to take him over, and who knows what he'll do next, what atrocities he'll commit if he isn't stopped."

Kurt frowned. "What are you leading up to, Reinhard?"

"Tyrannicide. He won't go willingly, so he has to be assassinated."

"Do be careful!" Kurt hissed, striding over to the door, which was still ajar, and looking out into the corridor. To his relief it was deserted, and he closed it firmly before he rejoined the others at the fireplace. "Careless talk can do a lot of harm to a lot of people," he said, giving Reinhard a cautionary look. "I know you are going to say that you trust the servants and everyone else living under this roof, but we must all be circumspect in what we say, and *wherever* we are."

"I'm not planning to assassinate Hitler. I'm only theorizing about it," Reinhard pointed out. "But you're absolutely right, Kurt, of course." There was a slight pause before he said in a much lower voice, "Don't you all agree with me that tyrannicide *is* the only answer?"

The other men were silent.

Sigi spoke at last. "It's not enough to assassinate Hitler. His evil partners in crime would have to be killed as well."

"That is correct," Kurt agreed swiftly. "Killing a tyrant is one thing, but here there's a whole government to be taken into consideration. Any plot to kill Hitler would have to be very comprehensive in scope. There would have to be plans to seize power instantly, the minute he was dead. A list of men to run the government would have to be drawn up beforehand, and they would have to take control immediately."

"Yes," Reinhard said thoughtfully. He walked over to the window, stood looking out, then swung around to face his guests. "I want democracy for Germany, not dictatorship."

"Of course you do. That's what we all want," Adam said.

"I know that." Reinhard shook his head. "And we'll never have it as long as the Nazis are in power. To get rid of the Nazis effectively, we have first to cut off the head of the beast, the master of the vermin. Which brings me back to my first point. . . . There are a lot of committed anti-Nazis around . . . someone's got to formulate a plan for killing Hitler."

"Yes, but—" Kurt began, but he stopped abruptly at the sound of knocking.

The men exchanged worried glances only a split second before the door flew open.

Renata stood on the threshold.

"You startled us!" Reinhard exclaimed.

"Oh, I'm sorry, I didn't mean to," Renata said. "Are the ladies allowed up here for a glass of champagne before lunch, or shall you come down to join us?"

"We'll be down in a moment," Reinhard told her.

"Very well." She smiled and disappeared, quietly closing the door behind her.

"You see what I mean. That could have been anyone," Kurt was quick to point out. "I think we would be wise to drop this conversation, for the time being at any rate."

Reinhard nodded in agreement. He looked out the window again and exclaimed, "Now, who can this be arriving just before lunch? A fellow on a motorcycle, no less, and he doesn't look remotely familiar to me."

"Motorcycle," Sigi repeated, instantly thinking of Willy Herzog. "It might possibly be Theodora's boyfriend. Sunday is her day off when we're in Berlin," he murmured, hurrying over to the window. He glanced down, saw that the young man was already parking the motorbike. "Yes, that's Willy," Sigi said. "I suppose he's come to make his usual Sunday call."

"Teddy! Teddy! Look, there's Willy!" Maxim shouted, and he began to wave at the young man standing on the wide flagstone terrace that ran along the back façade of the schloss.

Theodora glanced across at Maxim, then looked up toward the terrace and exclaimed, "Good Lord, it *is* Willy! I thought you were teasing me, Maxim." Thrusting the garden trowel into a snowdrift, she climbed the slope, carefully straightening her tartan tam-o'-shanter as she did.

Willy grabbed hold of her when she reached him, hugged her tightly and kissed her cheek, not giving her a chance to say a word. When they finally drew apart, she cried, "Goodness, Willy, whatever are you doing here?"

"I came to see you, of course."

"I realize that . . . but such a long way, Willy."

"Not so long. It only took me a few hours on the bike. When you told me on the phone yesterday that Frau Westheim planned to stay on at Schloss Tiegal for several more weeks, I thought I should come. I've something to discuss with you, and it's always better to talk in person, isn't it?"

"Is something wrong?" Anxiously she searched his face.

He shook his head. "Do you think I could go to the cloak-room, and also get a cup of hot coffee or tea? It was *cold* riding that bike."

"Of course, Willy. How rude I'm being. First I'll show you to the cloakroom, and then I'll ask Cook for something hot. And of course you must stay to lunch. I know Frau Westheim and Countess von Tiegal will insist that you do. . . . I hope you won't mind eating with the children and Irmgard and me?"

"No, of course not. And thanks, I'd like to stay. Who's Irmgard?"

"She's the nanny here," Teddy explained, and moving to the edge of the terrace, she called out, "Maxim!"

"Yes, Teddy?" he answered, raising his little face, looking up the slope, shielding his eyes against the sun with one hand.

"I'm taking Willy to the kitchen—to get a hot drink."

"Can I come?"

"No, Maxim! You stay here and play."

"But I want to say hello to Willy!"

"You'll see him later. He's going to have lunch with us."

"Hooray! Hooray!" Maxim cried, waving his spade in the air.

"Don't worry," Irmgard called. "I'll keep an eye on Maxim for you."

"And so will I, Teddy," nine-year-old Diana von Wittingen volunteered.

"I'm not a baby!" Maxim shouted.

"Thanks, to both of you," Teddy cried, and swinging around she took hold of Willy's arm. "Come along, let's get that coffee for you. You can drink it in Irmgard's sitting room, which I'm sharing with her. There's a big fire in there, and you can get warm in front of it. You must be frozen."

"I am," Willy admitted.

Theodora now gave him a penetrating look. "And then you can tell me what's troubling you *so much* it brought you all this way on a motorcycle to talk to me."

"It's like this," Willy said, looking across at Theodora. "My father hasn't been able to get entry visas for America, as you know. But he has been promised *one* for Palestine by a Jewish organization in Berlin, which will also obtain an exit visa. He should be getting both in a week or two."

"And he wants you to use them, Willy, isn't that so?"

"Yes," Willy muttered, sounding as miserable as he suddenly looked.

"Then you must."

"I *can't*," Willy exclaimed. "Don't you see, I can't go without you, Teddy."

"You *must*, Willy, you have no alternative," Teddy said very gently, leaning forward, putting her hand on his arm.

"I won't leave you behind in Berlin," he protested, his voice shaking.

He seemed close to tears, but Teddy was fully prepared for such a moment as this, fully prepared with all the right words—and lies, if necessary. In November, when Herr Westheim had asked her for her passport, and had explained that he was hoping to get her out of Germany with his family, he had sworn her to secrecy. "No one must know," he had said. The Nazis might stop the Westheims from leaving if they discovered their plans, because of his importance to the Ministry of Finance and the state. She had understood everything, and had given her word to him.

It was on this same Saturday afternoon that she had told the Westheims about her unofficial engagement to Willy, had confided that Willy hoped the two of them would be able to go to America eventually, along with his father and sister. The Westheims had immediately exchanged worried looks, and Frau Westheim had said, "Of course we can't force you to leave with us, Teddy, nor would we want to. However, don't forget that you are my charge. I promised your mother I would look after you, and it would distress me to leave you behind. Very honestly, I think you should get out when you can. Just as Willy should, if he has the opportunity, even if it means going without you. In any case, there's no guarantee that Professor Herzog is going to succeed."

Herr Westheim had then interjected: "It's highly unlikely that he will, Theodora. The United States is not going to admit any more European Jews. The quota is used up." On hearing this dismal news, she had looked from Herr Westheim to Frau Westheim, and had exclaimed, "But I can't just *disappear*! Willy would be frantic." Ursula Westheim had taken her hand, had said, "Yes, you can, Teddy. And when we arrive at our destination, you can phone Willy to explain everything. He will be *relieved* to know you are safe. Trust me, he will."

Quite suddenly she had realized that what Frau Westheim said was true. Anyway, Willy had a far better chance of making it safely out of Germany alone, without her hampering him. Something else had struck her that afternoon, and she had wondered out loud what she would say to Willy if he asked for her passport. "He won't," Herr Westheim had assured her, "the Americans are not issuing any more entry visas. But should he do so, then you must simply say you have sent your passport in for renewal. Don't say I have it, and remember, don't mention our plans, whatever you do." For a second time she had promised not to reveal a single thing.

In the end, of course, the Westheims had managed to persuade her to abide by their wishes. After all, her mother had had great faith in them, and had entrusted her well-being to them until she was twenty-one, and she must respect that. They were older and cleverer than she, and they knew best.

And as the weeks had slowly passed she had begun to acknowledge to herself that they had indeed been correct in what they had said to her. Chanukah had come and gone, and then Christmas, and finally New Year's Eve. It was suddenly 1939, and Professor Herzog had still not heard a word from his friend in Frankfurt who had a friend who knew an American consular official. Willy had confessed to her one night that he had given up all hope of the American visas ever being issued. Several times she had been on the verge of confiding that her aunt Ketti in London was endeavoring to get a British entry visa for her, but she had always remained silent, always curiously, inexplicably tongue-tied on this subject.

Now here was Willy at the schloss with his latest news.

As she looked into his pale, stricken face her heart went out to him. He was concerned about leaving her behind, and yet there was no way she could alleviate his worry by revealing the truth. Certainly she could not tell Willy about Sigmund Westheim's plans for them. Nothing on this earth would make her put the family in jeopardy. She trusted Willy Herzog, trusted him with her life. On the other hand, it was not up to her to put little Maxim and his parents at risk in any way whatsoever.

And so she must convince Willy that he should take advantage of the visa his father had been offered and leave Germany, whatever lies she had to tell him to accomplish this end.

Rising, she went and sat next to him on the sofa in front of the fire. She took his hand and squeezed it, then brought it up to her face and rubbed it against her cheek in a gesture of tenderness and love.

After a moment she said, "I want you to go to Palestine, Willy. In fact, I insist that you go. Listen to me. Frau Westheim is planning to stay at the schloss *indefinitely.* When you phoned yesterday, I said we'd be staying a few weeks because I didn't want to upset you. But actually we won't be coming back to Berlin for a very, very long time. The Westheims believe it's safer here in the country. And it is. We'll be fine, living with the von Tiegals. And once you get to Palestine you can try to get entry visas for your family. And for me. And as soon as you do, I'll come and join you."

"It worries me to leave you behind, and—"

"You'll have a much better chance of getting those visas in Palestine than you would here," she cut in swiftly.

"I don't know about that," Willy said, his expression doubtful.

"Oh yes, you *will.* Honestly, Willy. Herr Westheim told me it's easier to get a visa for a country when you're actually in that country. You know, a visa for someone else. He understands these things. He's a banker, don't forget." Teddy paused, took a deep breath. "My aunt Ketti in London is trying to get me an entry visa for England," she blurted out, telling him at last, knowing that she must now use this as a weapon of persuasion.

Genuinely startled by this last announcement, Willy stared at Theodora. "Why didn't you tell me?"

Teddy bit her lip. "I'm sorry, Willy, I should have." She sighed. "I suppose I was reluctant to tell you that I might leave Berlin before you, and also I don't like discussing such things, in case they don't happen. I'm a bit superstitious in that way. Aunt Ketti is hopeful, though. Very hopeful indeed." This last statement was not strictly true, but Theodora smiled, and warming to her subject, she went on, "I will give you Aunt Ketti's address before you leave this afternoon, just in case. Listen, by the time you get to Tel Aviv or Jerusalem, or wherever you're going, I could be sitting in Belsize Park Gardens with my aunt. Think about that, Willy. It should cheer you up." She sat back, beaming at him confidently, her face a picture of truth and sincerity.

Willy studied her carefully, his eyes narrowed. "Are you *sure* your aunt Ketti can get a British visa for you?"

"Well, she certainly has all the right connections," Teddy said. "So you see, you must go to Palestine. We'll meet up when this mess is over. . . . Herr Westheim says there's going to be a war." When he did not respond, she exclaimed in a cheery voice, "Look, Willy, either you'll come to London, or I'll come to Palestine, and together we'll go to America!"

For the first time since he had arrived at the schloss Willy smiled. "*America!* Oh, Teddy, that's where our future is. And it's a wonderful dream to hold on to . . . something to look forward to, and keep us both going while we're apart." He put his arm around her and drew her close to him. "You will write to me, won't you?" he asked anxiously, holding her tighter.

"Every week," Theodora promised, flooded with relief that she had managed to persuade him to go to Palestine without her. And she was happy in the knowledge that once he was there, Willy Herzog would be safe.

15

$\mathscr{M}$AXIM SAT ON THE CARRIAGE SEAT GAZING UP AT HIS father.

"Why aren't you coming with us, Papa?" he asked tremulously. Until this moment of departure he had not known that Sigmund was staying behind in Berlin; his young face registered acute disappointment, and worry flickered in his brown eyes.

"Because, Maxim, they need me at the bank next week. But as soon as I finish my work I shall come and meet you in Paris," Sigmund explained, hoping to reassure the child.

"*When*, Papa?"

"In about two weeks. And when I arrive we shall go away immediately for our seaside holiday."

"*Where*, Papa?"

"To the south of France—to Monte Carlo or Cannes. Or perhaps we'll go to San Remo in Italy, possibly even Corsica. But I'm certainly going to choose a warm climate so that Mutti can rest, and you and I will have a fine time together."

A smile touched the boy's mouth, but it was fleeting, and he said in a plaintive voice, "Please come soon, Papa. *Please.*"

"I will, I promise," Sigmund said, "Now, let me take off your overcoat, it's rather warm in the compartment." He lifted Maxim down, removed his coat and handed it to Teddy, who stowed it away on top of their three suitcases in the luggage rack above.

Sigmund bent forward and picked Maxim up in his arms. He held him tightly, pressing the boy's head into his shoulder, loving him so much. He drew back after a moment and smiled into his face as he put him down on the seat. He reached out and straightened his little blue tie, and then smoothed his fair head with the same loving hand.

Still smiling at him, Sigi said, "I want you to be a good boy, Maxim, and take care of Mutti for me. And Teddy too, until I can get there."

Maxim nodded, looking very solemn. "Yes, I will, Papa, but don't be long, will you?"

"No, I won't." Sigmund leaned closer and kissed Maxim, who put his arms around his father's neck and clung to him. They had never been separated for longer than a day or two, and knowing his father was staying in Berlin now alarmed and frightened him, even though Teddy and his mother were with him on the train.

Sigmund hugged his son once more, then released him and turned away, clearing his throat and blinking rapidly. His eyes were suddenly wet and it took him a moment to compose himself. Once he had done so, he turned to Teddy and offered her his hand. She clasped it tightly, and then impulsively Sigmund pulled her to her feet and enveloped her in a warm hug.

"Look after them for me, Teddy, and take care of yourself," he said quietly, when they drew apart.

"I will, Herr Westheim, and please try not to worry."

Sigmund nodded, and glanced down at his little son, whose eyes were fastened on him so intently. "You'll enjoy the train journey, Maxim. It'll be like an adventure for you, and before you know it, you'll be in Paris . . . on holiday. Mutti and Teddy will take you to see the Eiffel Tower and all the other sights."

"Yes . . . Papa, will Gangan come with you?"

"She will indeed."

A joyful smile suddenly lit up Maxim's face. It made him happy to know that his grandmother was coming on holiday with them. Soon everyone he loved in the whole wide world would be with him. He settled against the seat and picked up the small wooden horse his papa had given him yesterday. It was exactly like the pony he was going to buy for him. He had told him so. "And you'll have it very soon, I promise," his papa had added. He could hardly wait. It would be lovely to have the pony. He had wanted it for so long. In the summer he would ride it in the garden in Wannsee.

Seeing that Maxim was occupied with the little carved horse, Sigmund left the carriage quickly, wishing to curtail these prolonged good-byes that were painful to him and everyone else. His heart was very full, and he was aware that Ursula was on the verge of tears. She followed him out of the carriage and onto the platform, where they stood together talking.

Maxim pressed his nose to the window, watching his parents. But he could not hear what they were saying, and so he went back to examining the wooden horse, banging his heels against the bottom of the carriage seat until Teddy told him, rather sternly, to stop at once, which he did.

Despite the bustle and din on the crowded platform, Ursula spoke very quietly, not wanting to be overheard. She took Sigmund's hand in hers. "I wish I hadn't agreed to this. I hate to leave you behind. I think we should all go together. Please, Sigi, let me take Maxim and Teddy off the train now, while there's still time."

"No, absolutely not," he replied in a low but emphatic voice. "I told you, I don't want you to wait until the end of the month. I think it's better this way, that we go out in twos and threes— less noticeable, for one thing. In ten days or so Hedy, Sigrid and Thomas will be joining you in Paris, and then I will follow with Mother."

"Yes, Sigi, I know. But I loathe leaving like this, I really do. I'm worried about you. Anything could happen," she whispered.

"Nothing is going to happen. I want you and Maxim out of Berlin. I'll breathe a little easier knowing that you and he are safe."

The train started to hoot loudly, emitting clouds of steam and smoke, which enveloped them, and a guard came hurrying along the platform holding his red flag and blowing his whistle. The departure of the Berlin–Paris train was imminent and last-minute passengers pushed past them, intent on boarding at once.

Sigmund and Ursula were jostled closer together and he took her in his arms and kissed her. "I love you, Ursula."

"I love you, Sigi, and with all my heart."

He heard the tremor of strong emotion in her voice and he put his hand under her chin and lifted her face to his, gazing into her smoky-blue eyes. "Come now, no tears, my love. I'll soon be with you and Maxim. You and he are my life, and nothing is going to separate us. Not for very long, at least."

"Yes," she said, striving for control, clutching him fiercely.

All their lives they had loved each other, all their lives they had been together, had hardly ever been apart, except for their school years. Leaving him like this made her feel as if part of her body were being wrenched away from her.

"You'd better board," Sigi said, and added sotto voce, "And be careful on the train. *Be wary*, darling. Keep your eyes and ears open, and say very little to anyone. Just be polite, that's all that's necessary. No complicated conversations."

"Yes," she murmured.

"It looks as if the train's thick with SS officers, army personnel and Gestapo, but there's nothing very unusual about that, so don't worry. Some of them are probably going on leave, others following military orders."

She nodded.

Sigi went on quickly, in the same undertone, "And remember, there will be police at the border, as well as immigration and customs officials. And Gestapo agents. But that is quite normal these days, routine. As long as you remain your usual calm self everything will be all right."

"Yes, Sigi, I understand." Ursula's throat was tight and she was incapable of saying anything more. She pivoted swiftly and walked to the train.

Sigmund followed her and helped her up the steps. "Go on," he said, "go to the carriage." He banged the door shut, but immediately she pushed down the window and reached her hand out to him. He grasped it in his.

Slowly the wheels began to turn, grinding and screeching against the iron tracks, moving at a snail's pace at first. He walked along the platform, still gripping her hand, staring up into that face he had known and loved since he was a boy. The lovely face was pale now, but the valedictory smile she gave him was brave and he smiled back, but then her smile slipped and her face crumpled and the tears she had been holding back trickled down her cheeks.

"Don't, darling, don't," he said, squeezing her hand encouragingly, reassuringly, but when the train picked up speed he had to let go of her fingers.

He raised his arm in a farewell salute as the train slid out of the station, and he stood quite motionless on the platform, staring after it until it had completely disappeared from sight.

Only then did he finally turn away and leave the Schlesischer Bahnhof, making for the Westheim bank in the Gendarmenmarkt.

16

ᑌRSULA HUNG OUT OF THE WINDOW FOR AS LONG AS SHE could see Sigmund. But when the train rounded a bend and he was lost from view, she closed it and turned away.

She hurried along the corridor until she found a toilet. She went in, locked the door and leaned against it, pressing her handkerchief to her streaming eyes. But within seconds she had managed to calm herself, knowing that Maxim and Teddy would be wondering where she was, and that Teddy in particular would also be worrying about her.

When she looked in the mirror above the washbasin, she saw that her face was streaked with tears, her nose shiny. Rummaging around in her handbag, she found her compact, powdered her face, added a touch of rouge and outlined her mouth with pink lipstick. She placed her fedora-style hat in the washbasin along with her bag and ran a comb through her short blond hair. She put the hat back on and stepped back to review her image.

She nodded to herself, satisfied that she looked quietly elegant, dignified and dull, which was exactly what she and Sigi had intended.

The most important thing on the journey to France was not to draw attention to herself. This was the reason she had chosen the tailored, heather-colored tweed suit with a plain white silk blouse, the dark-gray fedora and a heather-tweed topcoat. The only ornaments she wore were her gold wedding band, a utilitarian watch and simple pearl studs on her ears.

Ursula had helped Theodora to select her own clothes just

as carefully, and together they had picked out a navy wool suit, a matching sweater and a navy topcoat. As always, Teddy wore her dark green-and-blue tartan tam-o'-shanter, from which she refused to be parted.

"Don't you remember, Frau Westheim, my aunt Ketti gave it to me three years ago when I went on holiday to London. She bought it for me at the Scotch House, and it's my lucky hat," Teddy had explained when they were packing. And she had answered, "Of course, Teddy dear, wear it by all means." And Teddy had.

Ursula picked up her handbag, slung it over her arm and left the toilet. She walked down the corridor somewhat unevenly, swaying from side to side, occasionally stretching an arm out to steady herself against the wall as the train hurtled along the tracks at gathering speed.

She, Maxim and Teddy had been the only occupants of the carriage when she had left it to follow Sigmund onto the platform. Now, when she opened the door and stepped inside, she saw that it was full. But of course it would be; Sigi had told her the train was completely booked. He had been unable to get them either a compartment to themselves or sleepers. In fact, he had considered himself lucky to find three tickets available when he had tried to get them, and for the day he wanted them.

Apologizing to the other passengers as she moved past them, Ursula took her seat between Maxim and Teddy.

Maxim was engrossed in one of his picture books, but he looked up as she sat down. "Where were you, Mutti?" he asked.

She leaned closer to him and whispered, "I had to powder my nose, darling."

Teddy had a book on her lap, but she was not reading it. She looked extremely relieved to see Ursula, and gave her a faint smile.

Ursula smiled back.

Teddy nodded imperceptibly, picked up the novel and buried her face in it.

Ursula allowed her gaze to discreetly wander around the carriage.

Sitting in the window seat, immediately facing Maxim, was a middle-aged officer dressed in the field-gray uniform of the German army. From the insignia on his high-necked tunic she saw that he was a colonel. He had a briefcase open on his knee and was studiously perusing a sheaf of papers, appearing to be totally absorbed in them.

Seated next to him was a thin young woman who looked to be in her early thirties. She had a narrow face and was nondescript in appearance, except for her eyes, which were a startling blue and extremely piercing. She sat rigidly in her seat, her face stony, staring across at Ursula with unblinking intensity.

Ursula shivered involuntarily, finding those eyes unnervingly cold and calculating, and she glanced away at once, wondering if the woman was with the colonel. If she was, he was paying scant attention to her.

Now Ursula focused on the SS officer in the corner, who sat opposite Teddy. His face looked as if it had been cut from cold steel, his mouth had a cruel set to it, and his expression was disdainful. Oh, what a typical Nazi *he* is, she thought. Perhaps the young woman was with him. Two of a kind, she added under her breath. The SS officer also had a briefcase open and he was reading documents, and then, as if he were aware of Ursula's gaze resting on him, he suddenly raised his eyes and looked at her, frowning slightly.

Quickly she averted her face and looked out the window. The train was now slowing, pulling into the Friedrichstrasse Bahnhof, its second stop in Berlin, to take on additional passengers. Within a few minutes it was steaming out again, but it would stop one more time, at the Zoologischer Garten station, before heading in the direction of Hannover, Cologne and beyond.

Leaning her head against the seat, she closed her eyes, trying to relax her muscles, which were stiff with tension. It was difficult for her to believe that they were actually sitting on this train, which today and tonight would push its way through the very heart of Germany on its journey west to France. Everything had happened so fast she still felt slightly disoriented, and a bit breathless. Less than a week ago, at the schloss in the Mark Brandenburg on Sunday night, Sigmund had told her they must return to Berlin the following morning, explaining that they would soon be leaving the country. And then on Wednesday evening, not long after arriving home from the bank, he had asked her to join him in the library for cocktails. She had thought nothing of it, and had gone downstairs a few minutes later, to be confronted by Kurt von Wittingen, who was looking extremely serious, and an equally concerned Sigi.

Without much preamble, Kurt had taken her fully into his confidence and had told her everything. He had then handed the three passports to her, and when she saw that Sigmund's was not among them she had protested violently, and had refused to leave without him. Despite her fierce opposition to the idea, Kurt had managed to convince her after several hours that she must go.

Last night she had endeavored to talk Sigi into allowing her to remain until the entire family could leave together, but he had been adamant, would brook no argument from her. And so in the end she had had no alternative but to do as her husband said.

"Please present tickets, passports and any other travel documents." A man's loud, gruff voice shattered the quiet of the carriage.

Ursula's eyes flew open and she sat up straighter on her seat, her attention directed on the doorway. The conductor was framed in it, and standing immediately behind him were two official-looking men dressed in dark coats and snap-brimmed hats.

She pulled her passport and Maxim's out of her handbag, along with the train tickets, and offered them to the conductor. Teddy did the same.

The conductor glanced at the tickets first, then opened Ursula's passport. His eyes rested on it for a moment, and he stared at her closely before handing it to the man nearest to him without making any comment. Next, he examined Maxim's, passed it on while carefully scrutinizing the child, and then opened Teddy's, giving it the same attention as the others. This, too, was handed over at once.

While the men studied their papers, the conductor collected the travel documents belonging to the other passengers; he flipped through them and held them out to his companions. These papers were given only a cursory glance before being returned to the conductor, who immediately distributed them to their owners.

Ursula looked across at the conductor, now fully expecting their documents to be passed back to her. He stared at her icily and with the two men stepped out into the corridor, where they stood conferring with one another. Several times they turned their heads to look at her, peered at the passports they were holding, and went on talking between themselves.

Gestapo, Ursula thought, feeling unnerved.

She gripped the frame of her handbag tightly to stop her hands from shaking. A feeling of enormous fear swept over her—but she could not afford to panic, not under any circumstances. So she immediately made a desperate effort to push it aside, to still her nerves. Keep a cool head, Ursula, stay calm, she cautioned herself, remembering Sigi's instructions to her. She tried to take comfort from the fact that their passports and exit visas were in order, and that their tickets, from Berlin to Paris and back, were valid. The only thing was, their passports were stamped with *J* for Jew. So what, she thought. All the Nazis can do is harass me, humiliate me on this train. I can live with that quite easily. I am taking my child to safety and freedom and that overshadows everything else.

They can do much more than harass me, she thought, stiffening on the carriage seat. Alarm seized her, and in an instant that alarm turned to stark fear. They could take her and her child and Teddy off this train at any point during the journey and arrest them, if the whim struck. *Kristallnacht* had unleashed more ugliness and brutality, cruelty and pain for so many. Jews all over Germany had been sent to concentration camps. They were still being sent, and property, businesses and possessions were being confiscated daily by the Third Reich.

She thought of her jewelry stitched into her clothes and tightened her hands on her bag, conscious that they were beginning to shake again. God knows what the Nazis would do to her if they did arrest her and found the diamonds in the hem of her skirt and inside the lining of her jacket. The consequences were unthinkable. But she did think of them: *imprisonment, most certainly—torture and death, perhaps*.

Those men were taking far too long examining their papers. Her heart shifted within her. Oh dear God, dear God, don't let them interfere with us, don't let them take me away. I must get Maxim and Teddy to France, where they will be safe. That's all that matters.

She swallowed, fixed her eyes on the wall opposite, forcing herself to think of Arabella and Renata and their schooldays at Roedean together. "Focus on good things, positive things that will make you feel truly strong," Sigi had said last night. "And most especially when you feel nervous," he had thought to add.

And so that is what she did, remembering those youthful days and her dearest friends with the greatest of love and affection. She had spoken to Ren and Belle yesterday, talking only about inconsequential things. Her trip had not been discussed; the three of them knew better than that these days. So many phones were being tapped by the Gestapo. In any case, Ren and Belle would have learned from their husbands that she was leaving. Nothing else needed to be said between them.

Ursula continued to stare at the wall. Her face was without expression. She was determined not to display any signs of weakness or look in the direction of the Gestapo agents, who continued to talk outside the compartment. And Gestapo they most certainly were. She had no doubt of it.

Paris. That was another positive thought, and she hooked in to it. The first thing she would do when she arrived at the Plaza-Athénée Hotel tomorrow was telephone Sigi in Berlin. If he had reminded her of this once, he had done so half a dozen times in the past twenty-four hours. But she had not needed to be reminded, as she had pointed out to him. How relieved he would be when they were in *la belle France* at last. Her dearest Sigi. She loved him so.

The conductor was standing in front of her, and his sudden presence made her jump. Her heart began to thump in her chest, and she gaped at him speechlessly, wondering what was coming, steeling herself for the worst.

He handed her the tickets and passports without uttering a single word.

"*Danke schön,*" she heard herself saying, and she was surprised at how steady her voice sounded.

The conductor nodded curtly, and moved on to Teddy, who also thanked him politely when her documents were returned to her.

And then he was gone, striding down the corridor with the Gestapo agents hurrying after him.

Teddy and Ursula exchanged looks of relief, and then Ursula put her arm around her child and sat staring at the drawings in his picture book without seeing anything at all.

Her mind was still fogged by fear, and she knew that it was

going to take her a while to recover her equilibrium. She had a strong desire to let out a sigh of the most profound relief, but she did not dare, because even this might betray her in some way. A wave of nausea swept over her, and suddenly feeling weak in the legs, she realized that the last few minutes had been a major ordeal. But her shakiness would disappear in a short while; all she had to do was sit here quietly until it did.

Everything was going to be all right. Unexpectedly she felt quite certain of that. *They were going to make it.* She must hold these thoughts to her, they gave her additional strength.

About an hour after the departure of the conductor the door slid open again. This time a steward in a white jacket was standing there, and he quietly announced to the occupants of the compartment that those who wished to partake of lunch could now be seated.

Immediately Ursula stood up, took Maxim's picture book away from him and lifted him down off the seat. "Come along," she said softly, taking him by the hand. Teddy rose and the three of them filed out of the carriage.

They swayed their way down the corridor in the direction of the dining car, and paused when they came to the first vacant toilet. Teddy opened the door, ushered Maxim inside and instructed him to wash his hands.

"Yes, Teddy," he said and closed the door behind him.

The moment they were alone Teddy spun toward Ursula and took hold of her arm anxiously. Breathing heavily, she peered into Ursula's face. "I was so worried, Frau Westheim," she whispered. "I really thought we were going to have trouble with those men. Do you think they were Gestapo?"

With a swift nod Ursula affirmed this, and she brought her finger to her lips, warning the girl to be absolutely silent.

Lunch passed uneventfully, and after Ursula and Teddy finished their coffee they all returned to the compartment. Maxim soon began to doze, feeling sleepy after his lunch and lulled by the movement of the train. Teddy read her book, and Ursula let herself drift with her thoughts. None of the other occupants of the carriage addressed a single word to her, and she did not speak either. She was relieved not to have to be sociable, and to be left alone.

Although the behavior of the conductor and the two Gestapo

agents had unnerved her earlier that morning, she had managed to take hold of herself, and had remained calm, a model of self-possession. Assiduously she had schooled herself not to contemplate what might happen when they reached the border town of Aachen very early the next morning, and thus far she had been successful. She simply continued to focus on plans for the future, heeding Sigi's advice to hold only positive thoughts in her head.

17

*L*ATER THAT EVENING, AT SEVEN O'CLOCK, THE SAME steward appeared in the doorway of the carriage and announced that dinner was about to be served.

Ursula, Maxim and Teddy wended their way down the corridor, all three of them glad to stretch their legs, and to escape the confines of the compartment and the cold and watchful faces of the other passengers with whom they shared it.

By the time they entered the dining car it was filling up, but a large table for four was still available. The pleasant waiter with the friendly smile, who had served them at lunch, showed them to it, then went on to explain that they would most probably have to share it with someone else.

Ursula, Maxim and Teddy had only just settled into their places when another passenger was ushered to the table to be seated. It was a gray-haired, middle-aged woman dressed in black.

"*Guten Abend,*" the woman said as she sat down.

Both Ursula and Teddy said good evening in response, and they turned their attention to the menus. Before Ursula had a chance to suggest something to Maxim, he tugged at her sleeve. "Yes, darling, what is it?" she asked.

"I'd like chicken soup, please, Mutti."

"Oh dear, I don't think there is any." She scanned the menu again. "There's lentil, though."

"Chicken soup's my favorite."

"I know. But if it's not on the menu, I can't order it for you. Have the lentil soup. I'm going to, I think."

Maxim nodded. "All right."

Teddy said, "That's what I'll have, please."

"I'm sure it's excellent," Ursula murmured. "Now, Maxim, what will you have after the soup? There's—"

"Chicken or carp, *Mutti*."

She shook her head. "I'm afraid not, darling, neither is on the menu. But here's *Wiener Schnitzel*, *Bratwurst* or—"

"But we always have carp or roast chicken on Friday. And where are the *Shabbat* candles, *Mutti*? You have to bless them," he cried in his ringing child's voice.

Ursula blanched and threw a quick, worried look at the woman who sat next to Teddy. She had been watching them surreptitiously, and listening.

Helplessly, Ursula gazed across the table at Teddy, who was as startled as she, and had turned deathly pale. They both began to talk at once to try to drown out Maxim's voice as he began to prattle on again about the *Shabbat* candles.

Eventually he stopped talking, since neither his mother nor Teddy was paying any attention to him.

Ursula said, "I'm sorry, Teddy, I didn't hear you."

"I said I thought I would have the *Bratwurst*, please. And that perhaps Maxim should have the veal sausage too, since it's the lightest thing on the menu."

"That's a good idea." Ursula cast another glance in the woman's direction. She was now diligently studying her menu.

Maxim said, "But I don't want—"

"Listen, darling, there's one thing on the menu that you really love. Apple strudel. You can have it for dessert," his mother said.

A happy expression spread across his face and he nodded enthusiastically. "But where are the candles—"

"Now, Maxim!" Ursula exclaimed, instantly cutting him off. She turned into him, so that her body hid him from view, and bent down, said in a low voice, "Shhh, *mein Schatz*, I don't want you to discuss the things we do at home. Those are private matters, and are not talked about in public. Do you understand me?"

"Yes, Mutti." He looked up at her and smiled that funny little smile of his that always tugged at her heart.

Ursula smiled at him and said, "That's a good boy." She straightened, and shared a knowing look with Teddy. And then craning her neck, she looked down the restaurant car, finally caught the eye of their waiter and motioned to him. Within seconds he was standing to attention at their table, his pencil poised above his order pad.

Ursula told him they would all like to have the lentil soup, the *Bratwurst* with mashed potatoes and red cabbage, and that two would have the strudel to follow. "No dessert for me, thank you," she said. "Just a cup of black coffee."

The waiter nodded, said they had made good choices, and then gave his attention to the fourth person at the table. The woman asked him a question about the *Kasseler Rippchen,* a pork dish, and he started to explain that it was served with sauerkraut.

"Speak up, speak up, please," the woman shouted, leaning closer to him, cupping a hand around her ear.

The waiter immediately bent down and began to explain about the dish carefully, and in a much louder voice.

It was obvious to Ursula and Teddy that the woman was stone-deaf. Teddy rolled her eyes heavenward, and then looked across at Ursula pointedly.

Ursula was relieved that the woman hadn't heard Maxim's reference to the *Shabbat* candles. Many Germans were anti-Semitic and had been brainwashed by the Nazis into believing the Jews were responsible for all of their troubles. The woman was obviously just another passenger, with no special powers, as far as they were aware. On the other hand, if she knew they were Jews she might conceivably make a fuss, insist on changing tables, and so draw unwanted attention to them. If she was prejudiced, that is—not every German was. Still, thank God she was deaf. Now they had a chance to relax if only for a short time over dinner. Ursula was not particularly hungry, but Maxim and Teddy needed their nourishment, and she wanted them to eat in peace.

Another thought struck Ursula all of a sudden and she frowned to herself. What if the woman wasn't deaf at all, but merely pretending to be? But why would she do that? There was no reason. She was a stranger on the train who did not know them. And so Ursula dismissed the idea at once, refusing to become paranoid.

She began to talk to Teddy and Maxim about Paris, an innocuous subject, one that was perfectly safe.

Ursula led Maxim down the platform, holding him tightly with one hand. In the other she carried her suitcase.

Teddy walked along next to her, carrying her own case and Maxim's. Since it was cold on this early morning, they stepped forward quickly, following the other passengers who were making for the German customs and immigration shed at the far end of the platform. They had reached the railway station at the border town of Aachen about ten minutes ago, and the conductor had gone down the corridor of the train, opening carriage doors, telling the remaining passengers to take all of their belongings when they alighted. And to have their papers ready. The crowd ahead of them was not very large, and it was apparent to Ursula that many people had left the train during the night, when it had stopped at different towns.

She paused abruptly and Teddy immediately followed suit and threw her a questioning look.

"Give me your ticket and passport, Teddy dear," Ursula said, putting her case down, holding out her hand. "I think it will be easier if I deal with our papers. You can look after Maxim."

"Yes, Frau Westheim," Teddy said, placing the two cases on the platform, opening her bag and taking out her passport and ticket. She gave them to Ursula, who thanked her and put them inside her own purse. Ursula held Teddy's eyes and mouthed above Maxim's head, "*Stay calm.*"

Teddy nodded.

As the two women and the child started walking again, the SS officer who had occupied their carriage dashed past them at breakneck speed, veered to the left, and went barreling out through the exit door. Ursula was glad to see the back of him. Although he had paid no attention to them, he had somehow been a sinister presence on the entire journey.

Upon entering the customs and immigration shed, Ursula saw that there were three tables. Behind each one sat a member of the border police, all of them identifiable because of their uniforms. But hovering in the background, under the windows set high on the wall, were several men in civilian clothes. She was quite certain they were Gestapo.

Sigi had told her the secret police were everywhere, and that she should not worry, so she took a deep breath and marched forward determinedly. Her face was calm, her expression neutral, but her smoky-blue eyes were wary, missing nothing as she came up behind a young couple. She glanced over her shoulder and gave Teddy a warm smile, one that she hoped was reassuring.

When it was finally her turn, Ursula stepped up to the table, looked steadily at the uniformed policeman, opened her bag and gave him their three sets of papers.

The policeman spread them out before him on the table and examined them for a moment or two, then he lifted his head and eyed her coldly. "What is the purpose of your journey to France, Frau Westheim?"

"I am taking my child, and his nurse, Fräulein Stein, on a holiday."

"You have return tickets for Berlin. When do you plan to return to Germany?"

"In several weeks. About four weeks, to be precise."

He said nothing as he cast his eyes over the three of them, scrutinizing them fixedly for the longest minute. Eventually he asked, "Are you taking any valuables out of Germany?"

"No. No, I'm not," Ursula said in a clear, strong voice. "We are not. No."

"Put the suitcases up here on the table. I want to see inside them," the policeman ordered.

Ursula did as he said, lifting her own onto the table first. He made a thorough search, rummaging through her clothes, feeling the sides and bottom. He then went through the other two cases before asking for their handbags. The contents were tipped out of her bag and it was carefully checked, as was Teddy's, before everything was put back.

Once again, the border policeman studied their passports, finally stamped each one with a sharp thud and handed them back to her with a curt nod of dismissal.

"*Danke schön*," Ursula murmured, picking up her own suitcase and the one belonging to Teddy. Turning to her, she said, "Let's go. Attend to Maxim, and I'll handle these."

"Yes, Frau Westheim." Teddy took Maxim's hand in hers, lifted his suitcase, and together they followed his mother, although it was a trifle difficult to keep up with her. Ursula was hurrying so fast she was almost running out of the customs-immigration shed.

Thank God, thank God, it was easier than I imagined it was going to be, Ursula thought. Her heart soared. They were home free. Well, *almost.* Nevertheless, she could not keep the happy smile from invading her face.

As she came out of the shed and turned right, about to walk along the platform and back to their carriage, Ursula found herself face-to-face with the army colonel who had been seated opposite Maxim all the way from Berlin.

He was blocking her path.

She moved slightly to one side, attempting to walk around him, but he moved also, and so blocked her path once more. The smile on her face congealed. Swiftly, she glanced back, checking on Teddy and Maxim.

They were only a few steps behind her, but Teddy was now standing perfectly still, watching her uncertainly, and grasping Maxim's hand more tightly than ever. She was frightened, her eyes stark in her white face.

Swinging back to the officer, Ursula gasped, "Please. We must get on the train. We have been through customs. And immigration. Please. Let me pass." She was terrified that this man was going to prevent them from leaving Germany.

"Frau Westheim," the colonel said.

Aghast, Ursula could only stare at him. My God, he knew her name! Who was he? What did he want? She opened her mouth. No words came out.

Pitching his voice to a lower key, he said, "Don't be alarmed. My name is Oster. Colonel Oster of the Abwehr. I am a friend of Kurt's."

For a split second Ursula did not comprehend what the colonel was saying, and she continued to gape at him blankly.

"You'll be crossing the border into Belgium in a short while, and within the hour you'll be in France," he went on softly. "You are safe, Frau Westheim. Good luck." He half smiled, and then clicking his heels together and lifting his arm, he said in his normal voice, "*Heil Hitler!*"

"*Heil Hitler!*" Ursula responded automatically, suddenly understanding everything. She motioned to Teddy to join her and then turned back to look at the colonel. To her astonishment he was not there. Her eyes searched for him on the platform, but he had disappeared. Literally, into thin air.

"Is everything all right, Frau Westheim?" Teddy asked, hurrying up to her with Maxim in tow.

"Yes," Ursula said, "*Very.* Now, let's go and get on that train that's taking us to Liège, and from there to Paris."

"What did that man want, Mutti?" Maxim asked.

"I'll tell you later," she said.

It was not until they were settled in the carriage and rolling slowly out of the railway station that Ursula realized something. The army colonel called Oster, who had wished her luck, had done so in English.

18

THE BERLIN–PARIS TRAIN THUNDERED INTO THE GARE DU Nord, and came to a shuddering stop with a screeching of wheels.

Ursula glanced at her watch; it was 6:30 A.M. With typical German efficiency the train had arrived exactly on time. She stood up, and as she did so she realized that the tension that had built up inside her on the journey was now beginning to evaporate.

Maxim was safe. Teddy was safe. She was safe. Soon the entire family would be safe. The rest of them would come to Paris by the end of the month and they would all go south for a holiday. And then they would embark for England afterward and the start of a new life there. The future looked very bright to her, and she felt happier and more optimistic than she had for several years.

Moving swiftly, Ursula pulled their suitcases off the rack and then bundled Teddy and Maxim down onto the platform, handed out the suitcases one by one to Teddy, and alighted herself.

A porter was quickly found, and trundling their luggage ahead of them on a rickety barrow, he led them out of the immense and cavernous old railway station to a taxi stand.

Within minutes the three of them were squashed together in the backseat of an ancient taxicab and rumbling their way across Paris to the Plaza-Athénée Hotel on the Avenue Montaigne.

Paris, Ursula thought. *Paris*. I can hardly believe I'm actually here. She glanced out of the window, just to reassure herself that she was. Even in the cold, wintry light of early morning the city had a unique kind of beauty—muted, gentle, misty, a mingling of pale grays and smudged blacks. Like a painting in grisaille, she thought.

Maxim rested his head against her arm and snuggled into her body. She glanced down at him. My poor little boy, she thought, he must be exhausted after the long overnight journey. She was worn out herself, and grubby, and she suspected that Teddy felt exactly the same way.

Ursula turned her head and caught Teddy stifling a yawn. "I know how you feel," she said, "but we'll soon be arriving at the hotel. I think we should have a light breakfast and then go to bed for a few hours. We need to rest after sitting up all night on the train."

"Yes," Teddy agreed, and peered at Maxim. She saw that his eyes were closed, and added softly, confidingly, "It was the strain that was the worst, Frau Westheim. We were both so worried something would go wrong, weren't we?"

"Yes."

Teddy continued, in the same soft voice, "The army colonel who spoke to you at the border station gave me a fright. For a minute I thought something awful was going to happen, that in some way he would prevent us from leaving Germany."

"So did I."

"I was afraid to speak about it on the train," Teddy now admitted, "even after we crossed the border into Belgium. But

I couldn't help wondering about him, Frau Westheim. I mean, it was so peculiar, wasn't it? He never spoke to you once during the entire journey, and then suddenly he approaches you at the station in Aachen."

"But only after we had passed customs and immigration, Teddy, don't forget that. Perhaps he didn't dare reveal himself to me before then, certainly not on the train in front of the SS officer and that strange young woman. He is a friend of a friend, and I'm positive he was on the train to keep an eye on us."

"Oh!" Teddy exclaimed, looking surprised. "Do you mean he was there to intervene if we ran into . . . trouble?"

"I'm not sure. Perhaps he couldn't have done that exactly. But who knows, maybe he could have. He told me his name was Oster, and that he was with the Abwehr."

Teddy looked at her quickly. "He was our guardian angel."

"Perhaps he was."

The two women fell silent, and not long after this conversation the taxi pulled up outside the Plaza-Athénée. It took Ursula only a few seconds to pay the driver and organize their luggage, and then she ushered Maxim and Teddy into the lobby. Here Ursula was immediately greeted by the head concierge, who knew her from her previous visits over the years, and by the manager, who hurried forward to meet her. He chatted amiably as he escorted her over to the reception desk, and once she had registered he showed them to their rooms on the sixth floor.

As they entered the elevator he told her she would be occupying her usual suite, but that an adjoining second bedroom had been opened up to accommodate the three of them. Having their old suite pleased Ursula, brought a smile to her face.

"Yes, yes, Sigi, everything is fine!" Ursula cried, her voice rising to compensate for the static on the line, the poor connection to Berlin. "The journey was quite uneventful."

"Are you comfortably settled in?" Sigi shouted back.

"Yes, we are," Ursula responded, watching her words, knowing she must be absolutely circumspect in what she said, in case the line at the house in the Tiergartenstrasse was tapped. "I'm in our old suite," she added, thinking that at least there was no harm in saying this to him.

She heard the pleasure enter his voice as he said, "I'm glad you are. Familiar surroundings are important. Now you must relax, and have a pleasant holiday."

"Yes, yes. Is everything all right with you?"

"Things are just the same as they were yesterday, when you left. Give Maxim my love, kiss him for me, and say hello to Teddy."

"I will."

"Good-bye for now. We'll speak in a few days."

"Good-bye, Sigi. Take care."

Ursula replaced the receiver slowly, and stood for a moment by the bed, her hand resting on the phone. Before she left they had agreed that their calls must, of necessity, be brief and to the point, but how unsatisfactory this was, she had now just discovered. She had wanted to tell him about Colonel Oster being on the train, their guardian angel, as Teddy had called him, and talk about a few other things as well. Never mind, she thought, I will be able to tell him everything when I see him.

Ursula hurried through the sitting room and entered the second bedroom of the large suite. Teddy had Maxim's suitcase open on one of the twin beds that stood side by side, with a small night table between them, and she was unpacking his clothes; Maxim hovered near the washbasin in the adjoining bathroom, drying his hands on a towel.

"I just spoke to Herr Westheim, Teddy. He says hello to you."

Teddy smiled and nodded and went on taking out the child's underclothes and jumpers, placing them on the bed in a neat pile.

Maxim ran to his mother, and she bent down and kissed his cheek, and gave him a big hug. "That's from Papa. And he sends his love to you," she said.

"Is he coming soon?" Maxim asked, looking up at her.

"Yes, *mein Schatz.*"

"I'm hungry, Mutti."

"We shall have breakfast immediately. Soft-boiled eggs and bread and butter and jam and hot chocolate. Would you like that?"

"Yes, please, Mutti."

"And you, Teddy dear? What will you have?"

"The same, thank you, Frau Westheim."

"Once I've ordered breakfast, perhaps you should put a call through to Willy Herzog in Berlin," Ursula went on, looking at her. "To let him know that you are here in Paris."

"He had to go to Frankfurt on Thursday with his father and sister," Teddy explained. "They'll be away for a week. I thought I'd write to him today, or tomorrow, and post it immediately, so that it'll be there waiting for him when he gets back."

"All right. But remember, the rest of our family are still in Berlin, so do be most careful what you say."

"Oh, I will!" Teddy cried. "I was just going to tell him that I was on my way to see my aunt. He'll understand exactly what I mean at once. He knows I have only *one* aunt, and that she lives in London. Yes, he'll understand that I've left Germany for good, and that I'm safe, Frau Westheim."

"I'm sure he will. He's very intelligent." Ursula picked up the phone and called room service; once she had ordered breakfast, she took Maxim by the hand and led him into the sitting room.

"Papa and I always stayed in this suite when we were in Paris, and there's something I want to show you," she said, going over to the tall window. Opening it, she stepped out onto a small terrace, which overlooked the trees on the Avenue Montaigne, where she and Sigi had so frequently breakfasted in summers past. "Come along," she said, beckoning to Maxim.

The child clambered out onto the terrace and she picked him up in her arms and then turned around, so that the two of them were facing the river Seine. "Look, Maxim, over there! Do you see it? The Eiffel Tower."

That extraordinary edifice made of interlocking steel girders soared into the sky, dominating it, glittering brightly in the clear morning sunlight that now streamed out from behind the banked-up gray clouds.

Maxim caught his breath in surprise. "It's so tall, Mutti, the tallest building I've ever seen!"

"We can go to the very top of it, if you wish."

"*To the very top!*" he cried, turning to look at her, his dark, soulful eyes huge in his little face.

"Yes, and you can see the whole of Paris from there. I once went up to the top with your papa, and it was a most wonderful sight."

"When can we go?" he asked, his excitement growing.

"Tomorrow, Maxim, I promise."

She put him down on the terrace and gave him a gentle push forward. "Go along inside, darling. It's chilly out here, and I don't want you to catch cold."

Ursula sat at the escritoire in the sitting room, staring down at the list in front of her. It did not seem possible, and yet she had done it. Everything she had set out to do had been accomplished.

They had been in Paris for six days, and for most of that time she had behaved like a whirling dervish, rushing from place to place attending to business. Of course on Sunday, the day after they arrived, she had devoted herself to Maxim. She had taken him and Teddy to the top of the Eiffel Tower, as always keeping any promise she made to him, and afterward to see some of the other famous sights in Paris. In the afternoon they had gone for a drive through the Bois de Boulogne, before eating an early dinner at a charming bistro on the Left Bank. On Monday morning, bright and early, she had gone to the British embassy in the Rue du Faubourg Saint-Honoré, where she had met with Mr. Stiles, a consular official who had been expecting her. He had had the three entry visas for Great Britain waiting for her when she arrived at the appointed hour, and had presented them to her at once. He had been a pleasant man who had told her to get in touch with him if she needed anything else during her stay in Paris.

After lunch, on that same day, she had visited a luggage store where she had purchased extra suitcases, explaining to Teddy that since they had brought so little with them they were going to go shopping for clothes later in the week.

On Tuesday morning she had kept the appointment she had previously made with Monsieur André Mallet, head of the Banque Mallet, which was situated on a side street just off the Place Madeleine. After discussing a variety of financial matters with him at great length, she had withdrawn a substantial amount of money from the Westheim account to cover her current expenses. And then, once the business appointments were out of the way, she had occupied herself with shopping for two days. Maxim and Teddy had been taken to numerous shops and department stores, where Ursula had purchased warm and attractive winter clothes for them and good strong shoes guaranteed to keep them dry in the rainy English weather.

Now, this afternoon, she planned to select a few outfits for herself. But she had no intention of visiting Jean Patou or, for that matter, any other famous dress designers. Haute couture clothes were an extravagance she could no longer afford, but this did not trouble her in the least. She had much more pressing and important priorities these days: her family's survival, to mention only one.

The telephone next to her on the desk began to shrill loudly, and she picked it up at once. The hotel operator told her she had a call from Berlin coming through, and would she please kindly hold on. A few seconds later Sigi was on the line, asking her how she was.

"What a wonderful surprise!" she exclaimed, her heart lifting on hearing his dear, familiar voice. "I thought you wouldn't call until tomorrow or Sunday. I am well, we are all well. How are you?"

"I am fine. And things at the bank are fine, just the same as usual."

She knew instantly, and instinctively, that things weren't fine at all, that there was something dreadfully wrong. His voice was flat, very tense, and the strain in it was pronounced.

"Sigi, what is it?" she cried, sitting up in the chair, holding herself stiffly.

"It's Mother. I'm afraid she's quite poorly. She had . . ."

His voice faded away and there was a great deal of static on the line and a peculiar echoing sound as if they were talking down a long tunnel. It was another bad connection.

"Sigi! Sigi! I can't hear you! What did you say?"

"I . . . Mother . . . had a stroke . . . in the early . . . Thursday . . ." His voice disappeared, then came back. "I spent most of yesterday with her . . . Sigrid . . . Hedy . . ."

"Oh, my God! Your poor mother! Oh no! Not Margarete! Oh, Sigi, I'm so sorry." She clutched the phone, her heart in her throat—she was so stunned and filled with dread that she could hardly speak. Swallowing hard, she asked, "What do the doctors say? What's the prognosis?" She held her breath, silently praying as she waited for his answer.

". . . not sure . . . cannot be moved . . . she cannot join the boy. . . ."

"Sigi, you keep fading away. *Can you hear me?*"

"Yes . . . I can."

"Will she get better?" Ursula screamed.

"We think so. We hope so." His voice was now quite distinct and very close, as though he were in the next room. The line was finally clear. "But she cannot take her holiday just yet. *Do you understand me?*"

"I do. Can the others?"

". . . don't want to . . ."

"*You?* Can *you*, Sigi?"

"I . . . hopefully . . . as planned. I have to go now, my darling. I . . ." The static obliterated his voice completely.

"Give my love to your mother!" Ursula shouted. "To everyone. I'll wait for your next call. And, Sigi—"

The line was abruptly cut at the Berlin end of the wire. Ursula was left holding a dead phone in her hand. She replaced it and sat staring at the wall, reeling from Sigi's bad news, so unexpected, so shocking. Poor Margarete. How tragic and distressing that she had had a stroke at this time in her life. Sigi's mother had never completely recovered from her husband's death and her health had been failing of late. And surely this stroke was too much for a frail old lady to bear. Ursula was extremely fond of Margarete, and her compassionate, loving heart now went out to her, and to Sigi. Her husband had always been close to his mother. . . .

Ursula froze in the chair.

A terrible truth came to her. As long as his mother was ill and incapacitated and could not be moved, Sigi would not leave Berlin. Not the Sigmund Westheim she knew. He had too much integrity and responsibility and devotion to abandon the mother he loved, to flee to freedom and safety without her.

19

$\mathcal{U}$RSULA CROSSED THE ROND POINT AT THE LOWER END of the Champs-Élysées and walked down the Avenue Montaigne, shivering slightly, even though she was wearing a thick cream wool suit, a heavier cream-and-coffee wool plaid cloak to match, and a tight-fitting cream felt cloche that entirely covered her silver-gilt hair.

It was an exceptionally cold afternoon early in February. A biting north wind was blowing down from the plains of eastern Europe, and she quickened her step, craving the warmth of the hotel after her long walk back from the Banque Mallet near the Madeleine.

When she had set out earlier, Maxim had wanted to accompany her, but she had insisted he stay inside today. She was relieved now that she had been adamant with him, had remained unmoved by his cajoling and pleading to come with her. He had developed a slight head cold, and despite the radiant sunshine and the vivid blue sky, the weather was pernicious; the last thing she needed was for her child to become sick.

It was exceedingly worrying to her, and dismaying, that illness was dogging the Westheims at this time. Margarete was still paralyzed from the stroke that had felled her in the middle of January, and only a week ago Hedy, Sigmund's youngest sister, had fallen on the front steps of the house in the Grunewald and broken her shoulder. As a consequence of these health problems, none of the family members remaining in Germany had yet come to Paris, and the longer she sat waiting for them the more anxious and nervous she became. She continually willed herself to be patient, but this was a hard task for her under the present circumstances. She had always been a person of decision and action, and she had lately discovered that playing a waiting game was debilitating, since it was alien to her nature.

As she drew closer to the hotel she sighed to herself, then tried to push to one side the dismal thoughts that had preoccupied her for most of the day, and that now jostled for prominence in her mind. Ursula felt it was her duty to have a positive demeanor, to be cheerful around her child and Teddy. Not that Teddy needed any cheering up at the moment. Her worry about Willy Herzog had been completely alleviated with the arrival of Willy's long letter from Palestine, which had been forwarded to her from London by her aunt Ketti Berners.

"He's out! He's safe! He's in Tel Aviv!" Teddy had shrieked with her usual exuberance, waving the letter in the air, before hurrying to her room to reply to it at once. Ursula had been as joyful as the girl on hearing this good news. It was always heartening for her to learn that another person had managed to escape the Nazi tyranny, had made it out of Germany to freedom in another country.

The uniformed doorman touched his cap and acknowledged her with a friendly nod when she approached the hotel. He opened the door for her, and she swept into the lobby.

Ursula stopped at the desk, where Charles, the head concierge, greeted her with a bright smile. "A gentleman was here a short while ago, looking for you, Madame Westheim," Charles said. "He went into the Relais Plaza for tea. He asked me to tell you that he would wait there for you."

Ursula was startled, and she frowned. "Did he give you his name?"

"No, madame."

"Thank you, Charles," she murmured, pulling off her gloves and going directly to the Relais Plaza to look for her mysterious visitor, wondering who it could possibly be. Pushing open the door, she entered the small restaurant linked to the hotel by a short corridor, and paused in the doorway, scanning the room.

He saw her before she spotted him.

He rose and came quickly to meet her.

Ursula caught her breath in happy surprise and her face lit up at the sight of the tall, thin, fair-haired man in the dark business suit who was smiling broadly at her. There he was, larger than life, their dear, dear friend Prince Kurt von Wittingen.

"Kurt!" She moved forward, both hands outstretched to him.

He took them in his. "Hello, Ursula," he said, leaning into her, kissing her cheek. "Come, my dear, let us sit down." As he spoke he led her to his table in the corner, and after motioning to a waiter and ordering a pot of the China tea that he knew she preferred, he went on: "I'm sorry I wasn't able to let you know in advance that I was coming to Paris. I arrived early this morning from Berlin, and I was picked up at the Gare du Nord by an associate, who took me directly to a business meeting. After that there was a luncheon, and another meeting, and I was never alone for a single moment. It was quite impossible for me to telephone you."

"Oh, Kurt, that's all right. It doesn't matter, really. It's just so wonderful to see you. I'm glad I returned to the hotel when I did—it would have been an enormous disappointment to me if I had missed you, just awful, in fact."

"I would have waited for you, my dear. I wouldn't have left without seeing you."

She nodded, gave him a small smile. "How is Sigi?" she asked, anxiously searching his face. "Have you seen him?"

"Yes, a few days ago. And he is well. I told him I would most likely be in Paris this week, and he sends his dearest love to you and Maxim. Ursula, he especially asked me to tell you that you must not worry. He is doing the best he can, and he hopes his mother will be well enough to travel soon. She is now improving, and very rapidly, it seems. He wanted you to know this."

"Thank God! I've been so concerned about them, and sitting here waiting is dreadfully nerve-racking, as I'm sure you can imagine. And, of course, the phone calls are extremely frustrating. We're both afraid to say too much, for fear the phones at the Berlin end are tapped, as you suggested they might be. But quite apart from this, the connections are terrible. Half the time we can hardly hear each other. Still, I do live for those calls."

"So does Sigi. They have kept him going."

"As they have me, Kurt. Do forgive me, I'm being so rude, not asking about Arabella and the children. How are they?"

"In fine form, and Arabella sends her love, as do Renata and Reinhard. We miss you very much, you know."

Her lovely luminous eyes filled with tears. "Oh, Kurt, I miss all of you," she murmured, her voice husky with emotion.

He took her hand in his and held it tightly, his gentle face full of sympathy. "I know, I know. It is terribly hard for you and in so many different ways, but you are in the best place at the moment. Believe me, you are."

"Yes." She picked up the pot of tea that the waiter had brought while they had been talking, and poured herself a cup. There was a tiny silence, and then she glanced at Kurt and confided in a low voice, "I had hoped that at least Sigrid and Thomas would join me here, but I suppose Sigrid doesn't want to leave her mother, and certainly Thomas won't leave without his wife."

"You are quite correct, and of course Sigrid feels she's needed in Berlin more than ever at the moment, because of Hedy's broken shoulder."

"Poor Hedy, she's always been accident-prone, and her injury must be excruciatingly painful. But I gathered from Sigi that she *is* mending."

"So I understand."

Ursula now said in an even quieter voice, "Where does the family stand, as far as exit visas are concerned?" Her gray-blue eyes held his.

He returned her gaze steadfastly. "The three I was expecting in the middle of January were given to me then, and they have been passed on. And I received the last two at the end of last month. Sigi already has them in his possession."

"So everyone could travel now."

"Yes, if Frau Westheim were well enough."

She smiled with relief. "Well, that is certainly good to know." She reached out, touched his arm affectionately. "Thank you, Kurt, for everything you've done for us. You have been so very caring, and a true friend."

"You know I will always do anything to help you and Sigi."

Leaning closer, Ursula said, "There was a man on the train . . . a Colonel Oster. He said he was a friend of yours . . ." Her voice trailed off, and she gazed at him questioningly.

"Indeed he is."

"*You* arranged for him to be on that train. It wasn't a coincidence, was it?"

"No, but I didn't actually arrange it. I simply asked my contact if someone could be in your carriage, certainly near you, in order to keep an eye on you until after you passed border controls."

"And Admiral Canaris agreed?"

Kurt nodded.

"The admiral has also been wonderful to us," Ursula said. "He's another person we will never be able to thank enough. Not ever, as long as we live."

"You have thanked him actually, and in a very special way."

"How?"

"Sigi gave me quite a lot of money for a fund the admiral controls . . . a fund that he uses to help people without money get out of Germany . . . Jews, Catholics, political refugees. So you have done your bit, so to speak. The admiral was very grateful."

"I am glad we were able to help with such a positive gesture. It's important to come to the aid of other people who are in trouble, especially those who are less fortunate than oneself."

Kurt smiled at her, then glanced at his watch. He grimaced and shook his head sadly. "I'm afraid I haven't got much longer, Ursula. I must keep my last business appointment at the other side of Paris before I take the night train to Zurich."

"Oh, Kurt, it's been so quick, such a short visit. . . ." She broke off, glanced away so that he would not see the tears starting to gather in her eyes. She longed desperately to detain him, needing his understanding, his warmth and his friendship so much at this moment. He had played an important role in her life because of her relationship with Arabella, and his presence this afternoon had brought her such a great measure of comfort.

Kurt asked for the bill and then put enough money on the table to cover it before helping her up from the banquette. He took his briefcase and overcoat from the chair nearby, and led her out into the lobby.

Kurt said, "I have a few minutes to spare, Ursi. May I come up to the suite to see Maxim?"

"That would be lovely, Kurt." She broke into smiles. "Maxim will be so thrilled to see you."

"Uncle Kurt! Uncle Kurt!"

Maxim slid off the sofa where he was sitting with Teddy reading one of his books, and hurtled across the sitting room.

Kurt quickly placed his briefcase and overcoat on a chair in the small foyer and swept the boy up into his arms to hug him close. A second later he put him down on the floor, lowered his lanky frame into a hunkering position in front of him and looked into Maxim's flushed face. "Hello, Maxim, I came all the way from Berlin to see you."

"Is Papa here?" Maxim asked excitedly, looking past him to the door. "Did you bring my papa?"

Kurt shook his head. "No, old fellow, I didn't," he said in a gentle voice. "But I did bring much love and many kisses from him, and he told me to tell you that he will be here in no time at all."

Maxim beamed with happiness on hearing this news. "Soon? Will Papa come soon?"

"Indeed he will." Kurt straightened and stood up, took Maxim's hand and together they walked into the sitting room. After greeting Teddy, Kurt seated himself on a chair, picked up the little boy and settled him comfortably on his knee.

Maxim peered into his face. "Did Christian come? And Diana? Are they here?"

"No, they're not, Maxim. They're with their mother in Berlin."

"I wish they were here, then I could play with them, couldn't I?"

"Yes, you could. Now, tell me what you've been doing in Paris, old fellow."

Maxim, who was an articulate child, started his recital by explaining that he had been to the top of the Eiffel Tower with his mother and Teddy, went on to enumerate the other sights they had seen, and listed everything they had done since they had arrived in Paris. The prince listened attentively, nodding, and smiling lovingly at the boy.

From the doorway, Ursula stood watching them, her eyes bright with pleasure. Kurt von Wittingen's unexpected visit had been an enormous boost to her flagging morale. But, perhaps even more important, his news from Berlin about her mother-in-law's improved condition had given her renewed hope that she and Sigi would soon be able to travel. Ursula was now convinced that they would be with her in the next couple of weeks, and her spirits soared.

20

*H*OW IS YOUR AUNT?" URSULA ASKED TEDDY WHEN THE young woman returned to the sitting room of the suite in the Plaza-Athénée after making her weekly telephone call to Ketti Berners in London.

Teddy gave her a happy smile and sat down opposite her. "Aunt Ketti is very well, and she can't wait for us to go to London, Frau Westheim. She's looking forward to meeting you and Maxim, and she told me, once again, how grateful she is to you for everything you've done for me, and most especially for getting me out of Germany."

"I never had the slightest intention of leaving you behind," Ursula replied. There was a small pause before she went on, "You haven't told me very much about your aunt, except that she's your father's sister and that she's a widow."

"Yes, my uncle Harry died two years ago. Aunt Ketti is about sixty-one, and she has one daughter, my cousin Rachel, who lives in Brighton. Rachel's married and has a baby girl called Harriet."

"Your aunt has lived in London for a long time, hasn't she?"

"About thirty years or more. She married my uncle in 1904, when she was twenty-six, and that was when she moved to England. She's English now, an English subject, I mean."

"And was your uncle an Englishman?"

"Yes, but of German extraction. My uncle Harry once told me that his parents left Berlin in about 1860, when there was apparently a big influx of the Ashkenazim into England, and he and his two brothers were born in London. You'll like Aunt Ketti when you meet her, Frau Westheim, she's a fine woman."

"If she's anything like your father, she must be very special indeed." Ursula walked over to her bedroom, opened the door

quietly and slipped inside. She tiptoed over to the single bed
next to hers, where Maxim lay curled up under the covers, satisfied herself that he was sleeping soundly, and immediately returned to the sitting room.

Teddy had picked up her embroidery while Ursula was out
of the room, and without lifting her head, she said, "He *is* fast
asleep, isn't he?"

"Yes," Ursula murmured, and leaned back against the chair
and closed her eyes.

Teddy glanced up from her needlework, on the point of making a comment about Maxim, but when she saw that Ursula
was resting she refrained. In repose Ursula's face looked weary
and vulnerable, and a little sad. She's tired, Teddy thought,
tired of waiting all these weeks for the family to come, tired
of marking time since January. It's just not in her nature to
be so inactive. Still, there's very little she *can* do except sit and
wait. At least I have Maxim to keep me busy with his lessons
and his walks and his care in general. Poor Frau Westheim is
lost. If only we were in London, she could be looking for a
home for us, a flat or a house, and getting it furnished and ready
for Herr Westheim and the rest of the family, keeping herself
busy. This awful waiting and the inactivity are destructive to
her.

Teddy sighed under her breath, and, resuming her needlework, thought of the way Ursula had led her life in Berlin.
There she had had two houses to run, the mansion in the Tiergartenstrasse and the rambling old villa out in the Wannsee,
and the servants to deal with, plus her various charity commit-
tees to attend and friends to see and a social schedule to organize. It struck Teddy that there had never been a single moment
when Ursula Westheim had not been run off her feet. How different was her life in Paris. . . .

Quite suddenly Ursula opened her eyes and sat up. "Teddy?"

"Yes, Frau Westheim?" Teddy said and looked across at her.

"What is your aunt's house in London like? Is it large?"

"Fairly large. She rents out the flat in the basement, as well
as the one at the top of the house in the attic, which she had
converted recently. But she still has two floors to herself, and
a lovely garden at the back with a lawn and a rockery and an
apple tree. She lives in Belsize Park Gardens, in a pleasant area
near Hampstead."

"It sounds very nice indeed. Teddy—" Ursula paused and hesitated briefly, then plunged on, "Do you think your aunt would let you and Maxim stay with her for a few weeks?"

Teddy glanced up from her embroidery, and although she was startled by this question, she nodded. "I'm sure she would. But why do you want us to stay with her?"

"Because I'd like to send you and Maxim to London ahead of me. I would then follow later this month."

"Oh" was about all Teddy could think of to say, and she stared hard at Ursula, her eyes full of questions. After a moment she asked, "Why aren't you coming at the same time as we are, Frau Westheim?"

"I came to a decision the other day," Ursula began and stopped. After a second she went on slowly, softly, "I'm going back."

Teddy frowned. "*Back*," she repeated, looking puzzled. "I'm sorry, I'm not following you."

"I'm going back to Berlin."

Teddy was so flabbergasted she was speechless. However, she found her voice very quickly, and cried in a fierce whisper, "You can't, Frau Westheim! You can't!"

"Yes, Teddy, I can."

"But it's not safe in Berlin," the girl exclaimed.

"Perhaps it isn't. Nevertheless, I have to return. I have to help Herr Westheim. He needs me. Instinctively, I *know* he does. Together, we must bring his mother out. And his sisters. It's the only way. We must do it *somehow*."

Teddy was not only shocked by Ursula's sudden and dramatic announcement, but exceedingly frightened by it. Memories of *Kristallnacht* still lingered. They were extremely potent, vividly etched on her brain, and they continued to fill her with dread whenever she reluctantly cast her mind back to that horrifying night. And certainly things had not improved in the Third Reich since then. If anything, they must have worsened. She wondered how to convey her own terror to Ursula, how to persuade her not to return there, but she was at a loss. Teddy knew Ursula Westheim well, knew how stubborn she could be, and how difficult to dissuade once her mind was made up.

Ursula leaned forward and fastened her gaze on Teddy.

"I realize you're wondering how to talk me out of my plan, but you can't. Look, it's already March and soon it will be spring, and I can't just sit here waiting, leaving things to chance. I'm frantic about the family, I've no idea what's happening anymore. You've heard me on the phone to Herr Westheim. The calls are hopeless, frustrating, since neither of us dare speak openly to each other. However, one thing I'm certain of—he needs assistance with his mother. His sisters are lovely women, but, unfortunately, they have never been very decisive, and under the present circumstances I don't believe they are of much use to him. *But I can be.* And I know Prince and Princess von Wittingen will be as helpful as they possibly can . . . they'll do whatever is necessary to get us out, with the cooperation of Admiral Canaris and Colonel Oster of German military intelligence."

Teddy remained silent, and Ursula hurried on, "And there's another thing. We both know from what we've read in the French newspapers that war is inevitable between Germany and England, and France is bound to join in. We don't know when it will come—the situation gets more explosive by the day, and obviously I don't want the family to get stuck in Berlin. I *must* act now while there's still time."

Leaning back in the chair, Ursula waited for Teddy to respond. But again no words were forthcoming, and so she added quickly, in a more insistent tone, "I'm *needed* in Berlin! Don't you see that?"

"Yes, I suppose so," Teddy mumbled, desperately endeavoring to quiet her fears.

"I knew you would understand. I really would appreciate it if you would telephone your aunt tomorrow morning and ask her if you can stay with her for two weeks. And I will have a word with her myself, of course."

"She'll try to talk you out of it!"

"No, she won't, because I'm not going to tell her about my trip to Germany. I shall merely say that I have business in Switzerland, and that I think it would be more suitable for you and my son to go to England. That *is* the wisest thing to say, don't you agree, Teddy?"

"Yes, Frau Westheim," Teddy said miserably, her voice a whisper.

Ursula jumped up, suddenly full of energy and vigor after days of lethargy and despair, and hurried over to the desk, opened the top drawer and took out two envelopes. These she brought to Teddy, and after showing them to her, she continued in the same brisk and businesslike tone, "I shall give these letters to you on the day you leave for London, and in the meantime they'll be locked in the desk here. The first is addressed to Mr. Henry Rossiter, of the Rossiter Merchant Bank in London. I have already spoken to him on the telephone, and he is expecting to hear from you, once you have settled in at your aunt's house. You must go to see him and give him my letter. It confirms in writing my verbal instructions to him, which, in essence, are to give you money as and when you need it. Our funds here in France are in the process of being transferred from the Banque Mallet to the Rossiter Merchant Bank. I arranged this transaction several days ago. I want you to remember that you have access to those funds for yourself and Maxim until we arrive."

"I don't need any money, Frau Westheim," Teddy protested. "My aunt will provide for us while we're staying with her."

"I realize that, Teddy. However, it makes me feel better, easier within myself, knowing that you can draw on the money in case of an emergency."

Teddy nodded, realizing that there was no point in arguing with her.

Ursula rushed on: "The second letter is addressed to you. However, you must not open it unless something happens to me and my husband. If I should die, and he survives me, then you will give him the letter. I have asked Mr. Rossiter to provide us with a safety deposit box at the bank, and you will place the letter in it for safekeeping."

"Yes, of course. But nothing is going to happen to you or Herr Westheim!" Teddy announced emphatically, forcing a smile and inwardly praying that she spoke the truth.

"There's something else I must mention," Ursula went on. "When we left Germany, some of my jewelry was stitched into my traveling clothes. Mostly my diamonds and sapphires. After we arrived in Paris I took the jewelry to Monsieur André Mallet of the Banque Mallet, who has been keeping it in a safe for me. Tomorrow it will be on its way to the Rossiter Merchant Bank in London. Monsieur Mallet is sending it by bonded courier. The jewelry must also be put in the safety deposit box with the letter, and before you leave I'll make a list of everything for you."

Teddy nodded, she understood.

"There's one last thing. I know you are very capable, Teddy, and that you speak good English, but Mr. Stiles at the British embassy here in Paris is going to have someone from the British Foreign Office waiting for you when you pass through immigration in England. Just in case you need help with any of the formalities."

"Thank you," Teddy said and looked closely at Ursula. "You didn't tell Mr. Stiles you were going back to Germany, did you?"

"Of course not!"

"If you had, he would have objected too, and *he* would perhaps have tried to stop you!" she exclaimed with her own brand of feistiness.

Ursula was silent, realizing this was true.

After a moment she rose and joined Teddy on the sofa.

Taking her hand, she squeezed it, then said quietly, but with an air of immense confidence, "Try not to worry, everything's going to be all right. I just know it is, Teddy dear."

Four days after this conversation took place, all of the necessary arrangements had been made for Teddy and Maxim to travel to England.

Aunt Ketti Berners had immediately agreed that they stay with her until such time as Ursula and Sigmund arrived in London.

"I will be at Victoria Station to meet the boat train from Paris," she told Teddy, and had repeated this to Ursula, before going on to say how excited and delighted she was that they were coming, and that she was truly looking forward to receiving them in her home.

For several weeks Ursula had wrestled with the problem of what to do that would be best for them all, and she had been caught on the horns of the most agonizing dilemma. She loved her child and her husband equally, and it had never been a question of choosing between them, but rather of deciding on the best measures to take. Measures that would guarantee that they would ultimately be reunited.

Sigi, seemingly, was immobilized in Berlin, but for what reason other than his mother's health she did not know. Nor did she have any means of finding out, unless Kurt von Wittingen passed through Paris on business again and brought her news. Yet this was most unlikely; he had told her as much when he had dropped in unexpectedly for tea, over a month ago now.

At one point last week she had considered telephoning either Arabella or Renata, but had dismissed the idea. Their phones had more than likely been tapped for the longest time, and she had no wish to create difficulties for her two dearest friends. And anyway, she was not sure what they could have told her, even if she had telephoned. Certainly no more than Sigi was saying when he called, for, like him, they would have been afraid to speak out.

And so finally she had made the decision to go back to Berlin. Her aim was to aid Sigi in moving the family as soon and as rapidly as possible. There was no question in her mind that together she and he could do it. They had always been a good team, even as children.

Sigi already had the five exit visas from Admiral Canaris, and once she was in Berlin she would literally force Sigrid and her husband, Thomas Mayer, to leave at once. She had worked it all out in her head in advance and it was a good plan: the Mayers would tell their servants they were going to Hamburg on business, as they frequently did, and they would take Hedy with them—as a companion for Sigrid, the story would be. As soon as the three of them reached Hamburg they would book passage on any boat leaving for England, even a cargo steamer if there was nothing else available. Hamburg was a busy North Sea port, and there would be no problem for them to find some kind of vessel.

Meanwhile, she and Sigi would take his mother to Switzerland, ostensibly for medical reasons. Her idea was that they would travel by car, taking the route from Berlin to Frankfurt and on to Stuttgart. From there they would go to Mannheim and Konstanz, sleeping overnight at most of these places, and resting whenever necessary, to give Margarete a respite from all the traveling. They would cross the German border into Switzerland near Konstanz, which would bring them relatively close to Zurich, where they had Swiss banking friends who would assist them, if this was required.

Ursula was absolutely convinced that Admiral Canaris would be willing to help them one last time, and that he might also be able to facilitate an easy crossing at the border—hopefully without too much close scrutiny from the German border police.

There was no doubt in her mind that Maxim would be safe while she and Sigi were engaged in these activities, and she drew comfort from this knowledge. She had implicit faith in Theodora Stein. The young woman was responsible and trustworthy, and loving Maxim the way she did, as if he were her own child, she would never let anything happen to him. Teddy would protect him with her life, in the same way she herself would. And so she had no qualms about sending him to England in Teddy's care, and England *was* the best place for him, a democratic and civilized land where justice and fair play were common everyday standards, a country whose treatment of Jews had always been less harsh and far more generous than most other places in the world.

Furthermore, she was satisfied that Ketti Berners was a solid, upstanding woman. Certainly the several conversations she had had with her on the phone over the past few days had only served to reinforce the feeling that she was as admirable as her late brother, Dr. Johann Stein. There was not the slightest question in Ursula's mind that Maxim and Teddy would be well looked after by this woman, who sounded unusually loving and seemed the personification of kindness.

And yet on the morning they were to leave, Ursula felt a heaviness descend on her. There was a terrible ache in the region of her heart, a constriction in her throat as she buttoned Maxim's jacket after breakfast, getting him ready for the journey. He was such a little boy, only four and a half years old, and still a baby in so many ways.

For a moment she wavered, almost changed her mind, realizing that she could hardly bear to let him out of her sight for a single second, much less several weeks. But then she remembered what was at stake in Berlin, and she took firm control of her emotions.

"Come and sit on the sofa with me for a moment, *mein Schatz*, I want to talk to you," she said gently, lovingly, smiling at him.

"What about, Mutti?" he asked, staring up at her with those large, liquid brown eyes that always touched her heart, but never more than they did today.

"About the trip to England," she answered as they settled

on the sofa next to each other. From the corner of her eye she could see Teddy on the phone in the adjoining bedroom, undoubtedly calling the concierge for porters to help with the many suitcases.

Clearing her throat, Ursula continued, "Teddy is going to take you to London by yourself, Maxim. You're going to stay with her aunt Ketti. I can't come today, but I shall be there very soon."

Alarm instantly struck his small face. His eyes opened wide and he cried fretfully, "But why aren't you coming with us, Mutti? I want you to come too!"

"Sssh, sweetheart, there's no reason to get upset." She took his hand in hers and held it tightly. "I have to go to Berlin tomorrow, to help Papa. We must bring your grandmother to England. Remember, I told you she was ill, and Papa cannot manage to do everything for her himself. He needs me to take care of Grandmama on the journey, she's an old lady, and she needs proper looking-after, you know."

"I don't want to go without you!" Maxim wailed. His upper lip began to tremble, and he flung himself against her and burst into tears.

Ursula wrapped her arms around him and held him close to her, stroking his hair, hushing him gently. It was hard for her to part with him, even for so short a time. They had waited so long for him, for so many years of their marriage, and she loved him so very much. He was part of her . . . her heart.

Tears welled and she was choked, unable to speak, and she simply sat there holding her little son in her arms, rocking him to and fro, her love enveloping him.

Finally, when she was composed enough, she said, "I'll be with you in ten days, not much longer, *Maüschen*, and then we'll be together again . . . you and me and Papa . . . just as we always were in Berlin."

The child drew away from her and peered into her face, and then he put a chubby hand against her cheek and stroked it. "Promise, Mutti," he whispered, his voice still tearful.

"I do. *I promise.*" Ursula took a handkerchief out of her suit pocket and wiped his damp cheeks. "There, that's better, my little love," she said, smiling at him. "No more tears. We won't be separated for long, and you have sweet Teddy to look after you until I get there."

Maxim nodded and gave her a faint smile in return. "And when you come, will you bring Papa and Gangan with you, Mutti?"

"Of course! That's why I'm going back . . . to get them."

He gazed at her thoughtfully and then he tilted his head on one side, and said, "You won't lose me, will you, Mutti?"

Taken aback by this question, and instantly noticing the worry settling on his face, she exclaimed, "How could I lose you! Whatever makes you say a thing like that, darling?"

"Teddy read me a story once . . . about a boy called Hans . . . his mother lost him . . . and she couldn't find him . . . not ever. I don't want to be a lost boy. Don't lose me, Mutti. *Please*."

"Never, darling! *Never, never, never!* You're far too precious. And I love you far too much." She reached out for him again and brought him close into her arms and hugged him, and he clung to her tenaciously, with all his might.

The sudden sound of knocking on the door made Ursula release him and she stood up quickly. At this moment Teddy came hurrying into the living room exclaiming, "That must be the porters!" She went through into the foyer and opened the door to let in the two bellboys standing there.

"Maxim, would you like to take them into the bedroom, show them the suitcases that are to be taken down to the lobby?" Ursula suggested, wanting to distract him and also to speak to Teddy alone for a moment.

"Oh yes, I would!" Maxim cried, jumping down off the sofa and running over to the bellboys.

The two women watched him usher them into the bedroom, and then turned to look at each other.

Ursula said in a very low voice, "I won't leave for Berlin until I know you've arrived. I'll wait here at the hotel until I hear from you."

"I'll telephone you as soon as we get to Aunt Ketti's."

"You do remember everything I've told you, don't you, Teddy?"

"Every single thing—all of your instructions. I have the two letters in my handbag, along with the cash you gave me, and the list of your jewelry."

"I have great faith in you, Teddy, and in your abilities. If anything should go wrong—" Ursula's throat closed and she glanced away, suddenly unable to continue. But shortly she was able to proceed, and she did so in the same quiet tone. "If we don't make it to England, you will look after Maxim for me, won't you? For as long as it's necessary."

"You know I will!" Teddy caught hold of Ursula's arm reassuringly. "But you'll be looking after him yourself. You'll be with us soon. Everything will go according to your plan."

"I hope so." Ursula stepped closer and embraced Teddy warmly. "Take care of yourself, and of Maxim," she said.

"I will, Frau Westheim, and remember, you have nothing to fret yourself about."

"I know. Now, I think that perhaps we should get off to the Gare du Nord. Although I'm going to miss you both most dreadfully, I'm glad I'm putting you on that boat train to London." There was a pause, and she stared into Teddy's face, and the smile she gave her was brave. She finished softly, "You'll be safe there, the two of you."

PART THREE

Theodora

LONDON

1944

There shall no evil befall thee,
neither shall any plague come nigh thy dwelling.
For he shall give his angels charge over thee,
to keep thee in all thy ways.
They shall bear thee up in their hands,
lest thou dash thy foot against a stone.

—Psalm 91

21

$\mathcal{I}$T WAS A PERFECT SUMMER EVENING ON THE LAST DAY of August.

The brilliant sun had disappeared, its last flickering rays painting the rim of the sky with liquid crimson bleeding into saffron and amethyst and the palest of lilacs before dropping down behind the dim horizon. The sunset had been one of such incredible beauty that Theodora had caught her breath in surprise and delight. Now the sky was turning a deep pavonine blue and filling with dusky clouds; twilight was rapidly descending, casting pearly and opalescent tints over the verdant lawn, the old apple tree, the fragrant rose bushes and the rockery scattered with pretty alpine flowers.

In the garden spread out in front of the stone-paved terrace where she sat, all things appeared transfixed. Nothing moved. Not a blade of grass, nor a leaf, nor any living creature stirred, and there was a hush over everything, as if the little garden lay under a vast body of pale, transparent water that was entirely motionless.

Teddy rested her head against the back of the canvas deck chair, listening to the silence, enjoying the quiescence that enveloped her. There was a heaviness in the air, but she did not find this unpleasant; it was a balminess really, and it added to the tranquillity she was feeling.

Theodora had had such a hectic day she was glad of this brief respite before she started to prepare supper. Maxim and his school friend Alan Trenton, who was staying with them for a few days, had kept her busy since early morning. Walking on Hampstead Heath—"exploring," they called it; racing down to the Two Blues Tea Room in Hampstead village for a mid-morning snack of tea and biscuits; afterward, up to the heath again, to sail their boats on Whitestone Pond, and finally back down to the house for lunch.

She had made them sausages and chips and baked beans, their particular favorites at the moment, and there had been the rare luxury of two fresh eggs, which the grocer, Sam Giles, had let her have the day before. She had queued up for half an hour outside the shop along with the other women waiting patiently to buy their groceries for the weekend. When it was her turn, Mr. Giles had glanced at her three ration books, leaned over the counter and whispered conspiratorially, "You've got enough coupons left for two eggs, Miss Stein," and then he had brought out a brown paper bag surreptitiously, and, with sleight of hand, had quickly passed it to her. "Put this in your basket, ducks, and don't say a word to anyone. I don't want a riot on my hands, I've only got nine eggs in the entire shop, and two dozen women wanting them."

Teddy had thanked him profusely, and had carefully carried the precious eggs back to the house, gratified that Sam Giles liked her, and that she had been a favored customer over the years. Everything was scarcer than ever these days, especially fresh eggs, sugar, meat and imported fruits. They had not seen an orange, a banana or a grapefruit in the shops for years, and food rationing meant dreary meals most of the time. Something rare was therefore the greatest of treats, and it had given her immense pleasure to observe the way the boys' eyes had gleamed at the sight of the eggs when she had put their plates in front of them.

In the afternoon, Aunt Ketti had provided yet another treat. She had taken them to a matinee at the local picture house, to see Claude Rains in *The Phantom of the Opera*, which had come around for the third time since it opened the previous year. The four of them had enjoyed it enormously. The Technicolor film had been just ghoulish enough, and sufficiently scary, for the ten-year-olds to take great delight in it, and on the way home they had pranced ahead of Teddy and Ketti, pulling grotesque faces and aping Claude Rains emoting in the bowels of the Paris opera house.

Ten years old, she mused. How the time had flown since she and Maxim had come to England five years ago. Her only regret was that the Westheims had not been able to join them yet. Their whereabouts, their well-being and their safety were forever on her mind. Not a day went by without her thinking of them, and every night before she went to sleep she prayed for them, for their deliverance. Sometimes she found it hard to believe that Maxim was already ten, but indeed he was, and he was grown up in so many different ways. She supposed this came from being away at boarding school with boys of his own age, out on his own, in a certain sense. He had become much more independent this past year. But that was all to the good. While he was the center of her life, she did not want Maxim to become a namby-pamby boy, permanently attached to her apron strings and forever reliant on her. Steadfastly she had encouraged him to stand on his own two feet, and, much to her satisfaction, he had done so.

Academically, Maxim was brilliant. When he was eight he had passed the entrance exam for Colet Court with the greatest of ease, and had won such high marks that even Aunt Ketti had been impressed. Teddy was particularly proud of the way he had breezed through the exams because the scholastic standards of the famous old school were extremely high, and also because she herself had tutored him.

After they arrived in England in March of 1939, she had sent him on her aunt's recommendation to the little elementary school in Belsize Park near Aunt Ketti's house. He had started in September, a few months after his fifth birthday on June 12, and he had settled in at once, had swiftly adapted himself, chameleonlike, to the English and their curious ways. There had never been any problems with him at the local kindergarten, nor at Colet Court thus far.

She had taught him English in the first five months they had lived with Aunt Ketti, before he had started in kindergarten, and he had proven to have an aptitude for languages. Now he spoke flawless English with a perfect English accent, and he was becoming fluent in French as well, which he was learning at the preparatory school.

Even though he had been only five when he started at the kindergarten, Teddy had realized almost at once that the curriculum was not challenging enough for him, for he was an exceptionally clever boy. And so she had begun to teach him herself on weekends, giving him lessons in more advanced English history, geography and mathematics. The last, even at that age, had been his favorite subject; he had a unique affinity for numbers. Since attending Colet Court, math had become his forte; his teacher claimed he was a mathematical genius, only echoing what Teddy herself had believed for a long time.

The sudden shrill, insistent wailing of the air-raid siren disturbed the peace and tranquillity of the garden. It cut off her ruminations about Maxim, brought her out of the deck chair with a leap, the war impinging on her consciousness once again, as it did at some point every day.

There was a clattering sound behind her, and when she swung her head she saw that her aunt, Maxim and Alan were rushing through the French doors that led from the back parlor out into the garden.

"Doodlebugs again, Teddy!" Maxim cried, using the nickname for the V1 flying bombs, which the Germans were systematically launching against England from sites across the English Channel. As he spoke he was helping Aunt Ketti down the stone steps.

"That's one thing I'm *absolutely* certain of!" Teddy called back, beckoning to them urgently. "Let's take to the safety of the shelter at once. Get a move on, the three of you! *Please.*"

"We're right behind you, lovey," Aunt Ketti assured her.

Teddy raced ahead to the air-raid shelter at the bottom of the garden, which had such a large quantity of sandbags protecting its roof of corrugated iron and earth that it looked like a dugout in the trenches on the front lines.

Running down the three steps and wrenching open the door, she picked up the flashlight that was kept on the floor immediately inside, turned it on and made for the table straight ahead of her. Three large white candles in jam jars and two kerosene lamps stood on the table, and she had just finished lighting them when Aunt Ketti came in with the boys.

Ketti closed the door firmly behind her and went to her usual chair, sighing under her breath as she did. Five years of war, bombings, peril and fear, of deprivations and anxieties of all kinds, plus living in the shelter on a daily basis, had wearied her in a variety of different ways.

The Anderson air-raid shelter was of reasonable size, and there was ample room for the four of them. The local air-raid warden, Jock Philips, and two of his helpers had built the shelter for Aunt Ketti. This had been in September of 1939, not many days after the British government, provoked to the limit of its patience by Hitler's ruthless invasion of Poland, had finally declared war on Germany, as had France.

The three men had done an excellent job of erecting the shelter, which was actually prefabricated and came in sections. To be effective, the tunnel-shaped shelter had to be partially sunk into a hole in the ground. Its walls, floor and curved ceiling were made of corrugated-iron panels, and these were joined together to form the whole. Earth was then piled on the roof outside and covered with sandbags for extra protection.

Bunk beds, stacked one on top of the other, stood against a wall, and there was a cot alongside another; such items as two chairs and a worn Oriental rug added small but welcome touches of comfort. A paraffin stove occupied a corner, and this provided necessary heat in the cold weather.

Placed against a third wall was their all-important storage cupboard. Aunt Ketti and Teddy had stocked this to the hilt with tinned food, such as Fray Bentos corned beef, Spam, Heinz tomato soup, baked beans, fruits, cocoa, Ovaltine, powdered milk and powdered eggs, and many Tizer bottles, emptied of their soda pop and filled with water in case the mains were hit and there was a water shortage. A Primus stove for cooking, several pans, a whistling kettle, plates, mugs, cutlery and a thermos flask were ranged along the top of the cupboard, while a tea chest next to it contained a first-aid box and extra gas masks for them, just in case the Germans did use poison gas after all; a second tea chest held soap, toothpaste and other toiletries, plus towels, hot water bottles, thick wool blankets, sweaters, scarves, woolen caps and gloves.

The two women had endeavored to stock the air-raid shelter with all the basic necessities of daily life. These were the essentials they knew they would require, should the house suffer a direct hit in one of the many bombing raids, when they would then be forced to live in the shelter permanently. Or until they could make other arrangements.

Maxim, who had led Alan over to the cot, now said, "Sit here, Stubby, I've got a new jigsaw puzzle, and we can have a go at it, if you like."

"Bang-on, Duke!" Alan exclaimed, flopping down on the cot unceremoniously. He lolled back on one elbow, stared up at Maxim and asked, "What's the subject this time?"

"A good one," Maxim answered, taking the puzzle out of the tea chest. "Saint George and the dragon, and it looks jolly difficult."

"It won't be for you," Stubby shot back, grinning. "Come on, open it, and let's start putting it together."

"You open it, Stubby." Maxim dropped the box on the blanket, and added, "I'll get the tin tray from under the cot, so that we can set the puzzle up properly on a solid base." Once Maxim had produced the tray, the boys bent their heads over it, and soon they were so engrossed, sorting through the hundreds of pieces of the jigsaw puzzle, they were entirely oblivious to Teddy and Aunt Ketti and even the air raid outside.

Teddy had seated herself in the chair opposite Aunt Ketti, and said to her softly, "I hope we're not in for a long night of it again."

"You never know with the V1s. It depends on how many they're going to fire at us in the next few hours," Ketti answered dourly. "Hitler's secret weapon has turned out to be a rather diabolical one, hasn't it, Theodora?"

"Yes, it certainly has. . . . So many people killed these past few months, hundreds in the London area alone. It makes my heart ache just to think about it." She shook her head. "I remember what Mr. Churchill said on the wireless in July—that civilian deaths from the flying bombs have been on such a scale there's been nothing like this since the Blitz. The way those bombs suddenly zoom over unexpectedly is horrible. They petrify me, Aunt Ketti."

Ketti shuddered, made no verbal response, merely nodded. But she grimaced angrily to herself as she reached for the knitting bag she kept in the shelter, cursing under her breath the Mad Austrian, as she called Hitler, and the Nazis. Heaving a sigh, she took out the Fair Isle sweater she was making for Maxim, and within seconds her knitting needles were rapidly clicking away.

At sixty-six, Ketti Stein Berners was a most handsome woman, who did not look her age. Perhaps this was because she had led a good life in England, a sheltered life, wrapped by her late husband in a cocoon of love and tender care and comfort. Snow-white though her hair was, her face was plump, pink-complexioned and almost without a wrinkle. Certainly it belied her age, as did her trim figure, her considerable vigor and vitality. She had sympathetic brown eyes, a warm, outgoing nature and a cheerful disposition. Her only regret in life was that her beloved Harry had died of a heart attack long before his time. Harry Berners, the only man she had ever loved, had left her comfortably off; his two brothers, his partners in the clothing-manufacturing business he had founded, continued to pay her his full salary and his share of the profits, and they would do so until the day she died. After that, her daughter, Rachel, would receive a share of the profits for as long as the Berners brothers remained in business.

Abruptly Ketti stopped knitting, lifted her head and listened alertly.

So did Teddy and the boys.

A loud roaring noise drew closer, then became deafening, alarming them because it was immediately above their heads. They knew it was a flying bomb, and their fear showed on their faces. The roar of the engine reached a crescendo, then cut out, and there was a sudden deathly silence for a second or two, followed by a crash and the most shattering explosion.

"Oh my God! The house!" Ketti shrieked in panic, her eyes widening. "We've been hit! The house has suffered a direct hit!"

"No, it hasn't, Aunt Ketti," Maxim said. "The explosion would have been ten times louder if the doodlebug had dropped on our house. I think it fell a few streets away."

"Maxim's right, Mrs. Berners," Stubby asserted, as always agreeing with Maxim. "I bet there's a big crater, too, wherever it fell. There always is."

"Poor souls. Poor, poor souls," Ketti murmured, shaking her head with sadness. "Every night . . . nothing but death and destruction. And grief for so many . . ." Her voice trailed off in anguish.

She thought of her daughter, Rachel, and her little granddaughter, Harriet, in Brighton, and she prayed to God that they were safe in their own air-raid shelter. She also prayed for her son-in-law, Gerald, who was somewhere in Italy with General Alexander and the British army. Keep them safe, dear God, she said in the silence of her heart. Keep my family safe . . . and keep all of our brave fighting men safe, wherever they may be.

"A flying bomb is the size of a Spitfire," Maxim suddenly remarked, startling Ketti, making her sit up with a jerk.

She looked across at him, frowning slightly, as he continued, "It's a pilotless aircraft, Aunt Ketti, and very large. That's why it makes such a gigantic crater when it crashes."

Stubby nodded, his pale-blue eyes and his little freckled face growing very serious. "My father says we'll beat 'em yet, though, beat the Jerries and the Eyeties. Our fighter planes and antiaircraft guns are shooting down a lot of flying bombs, and we're building new antiaircraft sites all along the coast of the English Channel."

This was said with such authority, Ketti glanced at Stubby in surprise. "Such knowledge for children to have!" she cried, genuine horror reverberating in her voice. "Such a *terrible* knowledge . . . of guns and fighter planes and death . . . Ach! . . . I can't stand it! I cannot wait for this horrendous war to be over, so that our children can forget about airplanes and bombs and tanks and guns and bullets, and go back to being children, playing children's games."

Teddy nodded. "I know exactly what you mean, Aunt."

"My father says the war *will* be over soon," Stubby now announced. "He says we'll be having victory celebrations next summer."

"And let's hope your father is right, Alan," Teddy murmured. She rose and went to the storage cupboard. "How about a nice cup of tea to calm your nerves, Aunt Ketti?"

"My nerves don't need calming, Theodora. On the other hand, I wouldn't mind a rosy lea. You know I rarely say no to that."

"I could do with one myself." Teddy picked up the Tizer bottle, poured water from it into the kettle, lit the Primus stove and placed the kettle on it to boil.

" 'A rosy lea, *a cup of tea*. A twist and a twirl, *a girl*. Apples and pears, *stairs*. Whistle and flute, *suit*,' " Stubby recited in a gleeful voice, grinning at Maxim.

Maxim burst out laughing. "I love the cockney rhyming slang. You promised to teach me more of it, so go on, let's hear it."

" 'Trouble and strife, *wife*,' " Stubby began, and stopped, his repertoire having petered out.

"*And?*" Maxim pressed, staring hard at his friend.

Stubby made a face, shrugged and admitted, "That's all I know, Duke." His smile was a bit rueful, as he added, "I'll try and rustle up some more next week, before we go back to school. I'll ask Mrs. Threscoe, you know, our charlady. She's a real cockney, born in the sound of Bow bells . . . that's where you have to be born to be a cockney, in case you didn't know."

"I *did* know, because you keep telling me. Listen, Mrs. Threscoe promised to take us to see the costermongers, to meet the Pearly King and Queen. But she never did, did she?"

"That's because the Pearly King of the costermongers is in the Royal Navy, off fighting the war. She'll take us, though, when the Jerries have surrendered and he comes home to the East End. That's where the costermongers live, down the Mile End Road, Duke. But come on, let's keep going with the jig-saw."

"All right," Maxim agreed, searching through the pieces on the cot, looking for one that might complete the dragon's head.

"Would you boys like something to drink?" Teddy asked as she poured hot water over the tea leaves she had just measured into the large brown teapot, the one Aunt Ketti insisted produced the best cup of tea in the world.

"Yes, please," Maxim said and glanced at his friend. "How about you, Stubby? Would you like a dandelion and burdock?"

"Whiz-o! Smashing!" Stubby burst out, and then instantly remembering his manners, added swiftly in his most polite voice, "If I may, Teddy, please."

She nodded. "Very well, but only one glass each, I don't like you drinking too much of this bottled pop."

22

TEDDY SAT SIPPING HER TEA, ENDEAVORING TO IGNORE the air raid that was still raging outside. This was difficult to do, however, for the continuing bombardment and explosions, the antiaircraft guns, the high-pitched whine of the ambulances

and the clanging bells of the fire engines created a cacophony
of sound that easily penetrated the corrugated-iron walls of the
shelter, and it was nerve-racking.

She dreaded to think of the havoc in the streets, of those who
were injured or dead or dying or who had lost loved ones or
their homes. Every night it was the same, lives torn asunder
by this foul and senseless war.

At one moment she glanced around, thinking how well their
shelter had served them so far. All through the Battle of Britain, during those long and dreadful months of 1940 when England had stood alone after the fall of France. London and most
of the big provincial cities had been turned into piles of rubble
by the thousands of bombs that had been dropped on them,
and thousands of people had been maimed or killed. Everyone
had suffered terribly through those days and nights of relentless
pounding by the Dornier and Heinkel bombers of the Luftwaffe, never knowing whether or not they would live to see another day.

But eventually those brave boys of the Royal Air Force, he-
roes all, had beaten back the Luftwaffe, described by journalists
as "the greatest air fleet ever assembled by any nation." Summer had turned to autumn, winter had come and gone, and at
the start of the new year, 1941, the British were still surviving,
and they had continued to survive for three more years.

How lucky they themselves had been, not to suffer so much
as a single scratch. Now their Anderson shelter was protecting
them once again, this time against the lethal flying bombs that
had started to rain down in a never-ending torrent in June, taking the whole country by surprise and terrorizing them all.

Teddy prayed constantly that Maxim, Aunt Ketti and she
would live to see the end of this war. The danger was not yet
over, for them and the rest of England; on the other hand, she
was inclined to agree with Stubby's father's prediction that the
Allies would be victorious by next summer. The defeat of the
Third Reich, which she had once believed to be an impossibility, miraculously now seemed imminent. Much had happened
lately to send their hopes soaring.

Two months ago, on the sixth of June, a great armada of
ships had sailed from England to France, and British and
American troops had stormed the beaches of Normandy.
D-Day had been an outstanding success for the Allies. And just

a week ago, at noon last Friday, the twenty-fifth of August, the Free French army, led by General Jacques Leclerc and backed up by American infantry, had poured across the bridges of the Seine in an endless stream. French tanks had rumbled into the city, the foot soldiers taking possession of the streets, and within hours General Leclerc had liberated Paris from German occupation and domination. Later that same evening, the commanding German general, Dietrich von Choltitz, was captured, and the last of the German troops finally surrendered. General von Choltitz had then handed the French capital back to the French.

The following morning, General Charles de Gaulle had marched down the Champs-Élysées from the Arc de Triomphe to the Place de la Concorde, leading a triumphal parade amid the tumultuous cheers and rejoicing of exultant, flag-waving French citizens.

She, Maxim, Aunt Ketti and Stubby had seen these memorable events on the Movietone News at the local cinema on Tuesday night, and the liberation of Paris had also been much reported in the British newspapers.

Teddy kept herself well informed about the progress of the war by reading the *Daily Express* and several other papers every day, and she and Aunt Ketti listened to the daily news bulletins on the wireless, and most particularly when Winston Churchill broadcast to the nation. Teddy revered Winnie, as he was affectionately called by the British people, and she had ever since he had become prime minister on May 10, 1940. She remembered that date very well indeed, for it happened to have been the day following her twenty-first birthday.

To Teddy, Churchill was the quintessential man of honor and bravery, the embodiment of all that was best in this island race of Britons—stoical, determined and just. He was an inspiration not only to her and every other ordinary person in England but also to those in the fighting forces, and he gave each and every one of them a bit of his tremendous courage, imbued in them his own strength of will to keep on going against all odds.

In part, he did this through his extraordinary mastery of rhetoric and magnificent oratory, which never failed to move her deeply. His words captivated her, they reverberated in her head. Much of what he had said at different times she knew by heart, and she frequently found herself drawing strength from his words when the situation looked bleak or when she was filled with despair.

Her mind slid back to the time she had first heard him speak, in the summer of 1940, just after Dunkirk, when he had said, "We shall fight on the beaches, we shall fight on the landing grounds, we shall fight in the fields and in the streets, we shall fight in the hills; we shall never surrender." And as she had sat glued to the radio that day, her own courage had been fortified and renewed.

In that same month of June, not long before France fell, when the world had wondered out loud what England would do, Winston Churchill had vowed that the English would battle on alone. And he had told his countrymen and -women, in that majestic and sonorous voice of his, "Let us therefore brace ourselves to our duties and so bear ourselves that, if the British Empire and its Commonwealth last for a thousand years, men will still say, 'This was their finest hour.' "

And she, German Jewish refugee that she was, had wept as she had listened to him. For her deepest emotions had been stirred, and she was filled with pride and love for this man who was setting such a valiant example for them, and for the rest of the world. She had taken heart after hearing this speech, for she had come to understand fully that with a leader like Churchill, the British could not fail to win the war. However long it took, they would inevitably succeed, because *he* was determined to lead them to victory.

And in this summer of 1944 they *were* winning.

It will soon be over, Teddy thought. The hostilities will end, and we will be able to start leading normal lives again . . . and we will be able to pick up the threads of the past. . . .

The sound of the All Clear signal going off roused her at once and brought her to her feet, as it did Aunt Ketti, who pushed her knitting into its bag and threw it onto the chair she had just vacated.

But the boys remained glued to their jigsaw puzzle, and did not bother to lift their heads as Teddy flew to the door. She jerked it open, peered out and turned back to her aunt. "There it goes again, Aunt Ketti! The All Clear at last, thank God! We can go back to the house. Come along, Maxim, Stubby."

"May we bring the jigsaw puzzle with us, Teddy?" Maxim asked, looking up at last.

She nodded, and stepped outside into the garden.

Teddy stared up into the heavens from which the murderous bombs had so recently fallen. The ink-black velvety sky was incredibly beautiful, glittering with brilliant stars and swept by searchlights that continued to crisscross the dark clouds with giant beams of blazing white light. Here and there the sky glowed scarlet from the many fires burning where bombs had fallen in different areas. Tonight, as on so many other nights, London was aflame.

Casualties and pain, grief, despair and devastation, Teddy said to herself, that's all we live with on a daily basis. She felt a sudden heaviness settle on her when she realized that they would have much, much more to live through before peace came to this turbulent world so riven apart by the fighting.

She began to walk up the garden path at a rapid pace. The muggy August air was acrid now with the smell of smoke, high explosives, burning wood and metal. Despite the warmth of the evening, she could not help shivering when she envisioned the damage that must have been done only a few streets away from where they lived. The sound of ambulances and fire engines only reinforced this assumption, and led her to believe that there were many losses on every level. And she knew that the Red Cross, the St. John's Ambulance Brigade and other emergency units would be at work throughout the night.

Climbing the front steps, she pushed open the door to the back parlor and paused on the threshold of the darkened room. Earlier, when the air-raid siren had sounded, Aunt Ketti had run out and left the wireless on in the kitchen. Now, along the corridor floated the familiar voice of the Forces Sweetheart, as Vera Lynn had come to be known through her radio show, *Sincerely Yours*.

Teddy leaned her head against the doorframe, listening to Vera's rendition of one of the most popular songs of the war years. " 'There'll always be an England, while there's a country lane, wherever there's a cottage small beside a field of grain. There'll always be an England, while there's a busy street, wherever there's a turning wheel, a million marching feet.' "

Teddy's throat tightened as she continued to stand there for a moment longer, listening to Vera finishing the song. And she found herself unexpectedly confronting an inescapable fact: *she did not want to live anywhere else but England.*

She thought of Willy Herzog, and her heart sank. He wanted to go to America more desperately than ever, at least so it seemed to her from his letters these days. Perhaps there was a way to persuade him to change his mind, to persuade him to settle here in London. Certainly she must try. It struck her that this was imperative, and then with a rush of genuine insight into herself, she realized how much this country had come to mean to her. She felt safe here, secure, and she had become very anglicized in the last five years, as had Maxim. She knew this was partially because of Ursula Westheim, who had wanted them to love this country, and who had never stopped talking about England when they were in Paris in 1939. Ursula had extolled its virtues, telling them it was the best, the fairest, the most democratic and civilized place in the world, and Teddy had discovered this to be true. And then there was her aunt Ketti, who in the forty years she had lived here had become a true Londoner.

Teddy had to admit that becoming so English herself was her way of denying Nazi Germany, of negating the country of her birth in her mind because its anti-Semitism was so painful to her. And as far as Maxim was concerned, he wanted to be like the other boys at school. She was well aware how much children hated to be singled out as being "different" from their peers.

She heard her aunt behind her on the stone steps, and, crossing the parlor, hurried down the corridor to the kitchen. After checking that the blackout curtain was properly drawn, she turned on the kitchen lights, pushed aside her worrisome thoughts about Willy and the future, and set about the task of preparing supper.

It had become the custom for Ketti and Teddy to sit down together in the back parlor at the end of the day to share a pot of tea and chat for a while before retiring. Tonight was no exception to this rule.

After Maxim and Stubby had gone upstairs to bed, Teddy and Ketti washed the dishes and put everything away, and then Ketti retreated to the other room to wait for her niece, who always made the tea.

"It's such a warm night," Teddy said a few minutes later, coming into the parlor carrying the silver tray of tea things. She placed this on the antique butler's tray table near the fireplace, and went on, "Shall I turn off the lamps and open the French doors?"

"Why not, Theodora, it's very humid, isn't it?"

After she had given Ketti her cup of tea, Teddy turned off the lights, drew back the heavy blackout curtains and flung open the glass doors leading into the garden.

There was a high, full moon riding the dark crest of the clouds, and it silvered the apple tree, the rose bushes and the rockery filled with alpine flowers that was Ketti's pride and joy. A slight breeze had blown up and it rustled the leaves of the old tree, and swept the heady fragrance of the last of the summer roses toward them on the pleasant night air.

The two women sat in silence, looking out at the garden, beautiful now in the moonlight and uncommonly peaceful. Once more the war seemed remote to them both, far, far away after the air raid of an earlier hour, which at this moment in time might not have even occurred. They sipped their tea, not talking at all, lost in their own reveries.

It was Ketti who finally spoke first. Quietly she said, "Children know too much about too many things these days, and well before they *should*, in my opinion."

"I suppose they do," Teddy acknowledged. "It's the times we're living in, I'm afraid."

"That's true, and between the wireless and the newsreels at the picture house and the newspapers, it's not possible to hide anything from them these days, I'm sad to say," Ketti added.

Teddy was silent, caught up in her thoughts, until she suddenly blurted out, "Where will I find the wisdom to raise him, to bring him up properly, Aunt Ketti?"

Ketti put her cup back in the saucer with a clatter, startled by these words, which she found quite extraordinary. They literally took her breath away. "What*ever* makes you ask me a thing like that, Theodora?" she demanded, her voice rising to a higher pitch.

"I can't *help* asking it, when I think of Maxim and the way he is these days," Teddy replied. "He's so clever, so smart. I don't have to tell you that he's a quite remarkable little boy, since you know that already. But I wonder if you've ever realized how much he is aware of?" She did not wait for a response, and rushed on, "His teachers at Colet Court keep telling me that he's a brilliant student . . . and imagine, I used to think I was prejudiced because I love him so much, but I've discovered I'm not prejudiced at all. Maxim *is* unique, Aunt Ketti, and sometimes I think he knows more than I do. About almost everything, too. So who am I to bring him up . . ." Her sentence trailed off and she sat back, staring at her aunt, looking glum in the dim light.

Ketti rose and went over to the glass doors, which she closed. After attending to the blackout curtains and switching on a lamp, she sat down again and examined Teddy closely through narrowed eyes. "This is the first time you've ever spoken so negatively, Teddy dear. You sound as if you think the Westheims won't be bringing him up themselves." There was a moment's hesitation before she leaned forward. "Have you had bad news from Germany? Is there something you're not telling me?"

Teddy shook her head, but she sounded worried as she said, "No, I haven't had *any* news, good or bad. You'd be the first to know if I had. However, I'm not stupid, and even if they weren't arrested and taken away to one of those hideous camps, even if they *are* still in Berlin, how could they possibly be *alive*? Berlin has been razed to the ground by British and American bombers. You know the raids have been far heavier than usual of late, and on a nonstop basis."

"The raids in London have been just as grim and *we're* alive, aren't we? So you see, we mustn't give up on the Westheims. And even if they *were* taken to a camp, they may well be surviving." Ketti paused, took a deep breath, and finished emphatically, "Certainly *I* will not give up hope for them."

"I try to believe they're alive, Aunt Ketti! *I do!* I have to, for the child's sake. But it's been so long since we've heard anything . . . *years.* And Arabella von Wittingen, Ursula's friend, hasn't been in touch for ages either. I can't help wondering if that's because she knows something *new* . . . something she's afraid to tell me."

"Nonsense, Theodora! The princess is a true aristocrat, and as such she would never shirk her duty, even if that duty meant she had to be the bearer of bad news!" Ketti exclaimed. "I believe in my heart of hearts that Ursula and Sigmund Westheim are alive. You must believe that too, Teddy dear. You must have *faith,* as I do."

Her aunt's positive attitude seemed to have the right effect on Teddy, and she brightened. "Yes, perhaps you're right, Aunt Ketti, it's ridiculous of me to be so pessimistic, I realize that," she said, "and especially since I've nothing to go on. Besides, Ursula Westheim is a clever and resourceful woman. If anyone can survive under difficult and extreme circumstances, she can. I agree with you, I'm sure she and Herr Westheim are all right. And the rest of the family. She would see to that."

"Maxim's grandmother probably has passed on, God rest her soul," Ketti murmured softly.

"She was frail, yes, and the stroke she had five years ago paralyzed her. . . ." Teddy did not have the heart to continue.

Ketti inclined her head slightly, sat back in the chair and sipped her tea.

A silence fell between them again.

Teddy, in particular, was lost in her thoughts about the Westheims and Maxim, and an abstracted expression glazed her eyes.

Ketti cast a glance at her, and then poured herself another cup, nibbled on a ginger biscuit and carefully observed her niece. She's such a good girl, Ketti thought, the best, so straightforward and honest. There's not a devious bone in her body. And she's strong of heart. And loyal and kind and loving. She loves that child too much, though. Yes, she's building a tragedy for herself, going on as if Maxim's hers. He's not, and his parents will come and take him away one day, and then where will she be? Heartbroken, I've no doubt. *Oy vey is mir,* such *tsuris* will we have when that happens, oh yes, trouble and then some. What she needs is to be married. That will help to soften the blow when the Westheims take Maxim away from her, as they will once the war ends. After all, he is *their* child, not hers, whatever the situation of the last years has been. Yes, marriage is definitely the solution. Marriage, and babies of her own to love.

Ketti cleared her throat and ventured carefully, "Talking of absent friends, what about Willy Herzog? I haven't heard you mention him lately."

Teddy looked at her aunt, then lifted her shoulders in a light shrug. "I had a letter from him the other day, opened by the

British censor, of course, because of the foreign postmark. But they needn't have bothered. There was very little in the letter, and Willy didn't have much to say about anything." She let out a small sigh. "I'll never understand why Willy left Palestine and went to Shanghai. I realize it's an international city, but what can that possibly *mean* to Willy?" She shook her head in bafflement and instantly answered her own question. "It means nothing to him, that's what! His moving there has never made the remotest bit of sense to me."

"Nor to me, Teddy. It always seemed to be a *meshuggeneh* thing to do, a crazy idea, if you want the truth," Ketti said quietly, and added, "China is so very, *very* far away."

"So is America," Teddy muttered.

"What do you mean, dear?"

"You know very well Willy wants to live in America when the war is over."

"So you've told me. But I thought you were keen to go there too." Ketti gave her a questioning look.

"I was, when Willy and I were in Berlin," Teddy answered quickly. "But it struck me tonight, and very forcibly, that I don't want to leave London. I'd like to spend the rest of my life here, Aunt Ketti. I feel comfortable with the English, and you're here, and you're the only family I have. Besides, Maxim likes living in England. He loves Colet Court, and he can't wait to go to St. Paul's School when he's thirteen, and later to Oxford University when he's old enough. So I couldn't go to America with Willy anyway, because of Maxim." She paused and glanced at her aunt. "Well, I couldn't, could I?"

Ketti stared at her, dumbfounded by her statements, and perturbed about her attitude toward Maxim. She said slowly, pointedly, "When the Westheims get here you can do anything you want, Teddy, since they will be raising their own child."

"Oh yes, I know they will. And look, don't misunderstand me, Aunt Ketti, when I say this—but if something *has* happened to them, God forbid, then I am responsible for Maxim until he's grown up. I *promised* Frau Westheim I would bring him up until he could take care of himself. And even looking on the positive side, and believing they *will* come to London eventually, I would still prefer to live in England. Aside from anything else, I want to be near Maxim, to visit him at school, and see him from time to time. That's only natural, under the circumstances, don't you think?"

"Perhaps," Ketti said in a low voice.

She was thoughtful for a few seconds, and then she murmured in her most gentle and loving tone, "I hope you don't mind my saying this, but from the way you're speaking, *bubeleh*, it sounds to me as though Maxim means more to you than Willy Herzog."

Teddy opened her mouth to say something and then, obviously changing her mind, she closed it.

Ketti probed: "Don't you love Willy?"

"I don't know," Teddy said after a moment, speaking the truth. "And I'm not even sure that I want to marry him anymore."

"You told me he is a real *mensch*, and a good Jew who goes to *shul* regularly, that he is reliable and studious, and all these things seemed to please you. But if I recollect correctly, and I *do*, you have never actually used that most important word in relation to Willy. The word *love*, Teddy. You've never said to me that you *love* Willy."

"I was never entirely certain that I did, I suppose," Teddy said, sounding regretful. "I was young then, back in Berlin, only nineteen, and I thought I wouldn't find anyone who was nicer than Willy, *better* than he is, because he *is* a good person, and that's why I said I'd marry him . . . I think."

Ketti was quiet, but her mind was turning with great agility and rapidity. What I need is a *shadchen.* Ach! What good will a matchmaker do me, when all the nice Jewish boys are off fighting this terrible war. Never mind. I must go and talk to Rebecca Cohen. And Sarah Levine. Tomorrow. I'll go tomorrow. Fine sons they both have. Fine sons their sisters have. All single. A fine Jewish boy *I* will find for my Theodora, my only niece, my brother's only child. An English Jew to be her husband. That's what I need for her.

"Is something wrong, Aunt Ketti?"

"No, no, why do you ask?" Ketti cried, sitting up with a jerk, looking across at her niece, giving her the sweetest of smiles.

"You look troubled, that's all."

"I'm all right, Theodora. Perfectly all right. I was just thinking about . . . er . . . thinking . . . *thinking* that five years is a long time for you to have been separated from your Willy

Herzog. And these past five years have changed you, Teddy.
Living here has changed you, the war has changed you, being
entirely responsible for Maxim and making all the decisions
about his education has changed you. And you've grown up
a *little*. No, I correct myself, you've grown up a whole lot.
You're twenty-five now, not nineteen, and Willy is also twenty-
five, and I'm quite positive that he, too, has been changed by
his experiences and the life he's lived in Palestine and Shanghai."

Ketti paused and gave Teddy a meaningful look as she finished slowly, "Why, you could say that you and he will be like
total *strangers* when you meet again."

"Yes," Teddy said, her voice almost a whisper. "I've already
thought of that."

23

"CAN WE GO TO LYON'S CORNER HOUSE FOR LUNCH?"
Maxim asked, looking at Teddy.

She returned his glance and nodded as she reached into her
bag for money and their clothing coupon books. "Yes, we can,
and I think we'll have it next, before we look for that raincoat
for you. As Aunt Ketti always says, I'm feeling a bit peckish.
Are you?"

"Yes, I am."

Teddy and Maxim stood together at the counter in the boys'
clothing department in Selfridge's store, waiting patiently for
the young woman who was serving them to check if she had
a third shirt in Maxim's size. The girl soon returned, shaking
her head and grimacing. "Sorry, madam, but those *are* the last
two in your boy's size. Would you like to look at some jerseys
perhaps?"

"No, thank you very much. We'll take the two shirts and

leave it at that for today," Teddy said, and handed her the clothing coupon books and a pound note.

The girl made out the bill, clipped the coupons out of the ration books, counted Teddy's change and gave it to her, along with the books and the bill.

The girl grinned at Maxim and remarked, "Summer hols never seem to last very long, do they? Now it's back to school, eh? Grim thought."

"I like school," Maxim told her.

The girl gave him a glance that was entirely skeptical, and raised an eyebrow rather expressively. With a small smile she moved along behind the counter and began to attend to another customer waiting with her young son.

Teddy winked at Maxim conspiratorially, put an arm around his shoulders and hurried him through the boys' clothing department, across the main hall of the large store, and out into Oxford Street.

The two of them walked toward Marble Arch, where Lyon's Corner House was located, not talking as they hurried along, dodging in and out between the other pedestrians. It was a Saturday morning at the beginning of September. The sky was a radiant blue, without a cloud and shimmering with pale sunlight. It was a soft day, balmy, and unusually warm for September, a day for the garden rather than the hard city streets.

Teddy wished they were sitting in the shade of the apple tree, sipping a cool drink and reading. But there had been no avoiding this shopping expedition, since Maxim had to return to school in a few days, and he certainly needed the extra shirts and a new raincoat. He was growing so rapidly, getting taller every day. All arms and legs, or so it seemed to her, and he was tall for ten.

Maxim suddenly said, in a slightly indignant voice, "That girl who served us in Selfridge's didn't believe me, when I said I liked school."

Teddy looked at him out of the corner of her eye. "Not everyone does, you know. Unlike you," she said, and started to laugh. The laughter instantly froze on her lips and abruptly she stopped walking and looked up at the sky. Maxim did the same thing, as did the other people hurrying along both sides of Oxford Street.

The high-pitched roar was only too familiar and frightening

to Londoners. It was a flying bomb, one of the pilotless aircraft, and it was zooming across the blue sky toward them at a relatively low level. The air-raid siren was already wailing in unison, and the combined noises were obliterating the sound of the traffic.

For a moment Teddy and Maxim were mesmerized as they stared up into the clear, wide arc of the sky. The bomb was flying at a level so low they could easily see the insignia of the swastika painted on its fat underbelly.

People began to scream, and to scatter in all directions, running in search of shelter or some form of protection.

Teddy grabbed hold of Maxim's hand and, shouting "Come on!" dragged him out into the middle of the road, as far away from the storefronts as possible. The bomb was now casting a giant shadow over Oxford Street, and over the crowds, and then its engine cut out, which always happened before the craft started to fall. Reacting instinctively Teddy pushed Maxim down onto the ground and flung herself on top of him, shielding his body with her own.

Other people were also dropping to the ground in a similar fashion, hoping to protect themselves as best they could from the flying bomb. A bus screeched to a standstill; passengers jumped off, along with the driver and the conductor, all of them seeking to take cover, or to at least minimize the risk of injury by lying prone.

A taxi swerved, and came to a halt close to Teddy and Maxim. The cabbie leaped out, flattened himself on the road next to Teddy, and shouted to her, "Crikey! It's a bleedin' Jerry buzz bomb, an' right over our bleedin' heads!"

The cabbie wrapped his arms around his head and hissed at her, "Do the same as me with your arms, ducks. Protect yourself, as well as your lad. Against the glass. It's the shattering glass from the store windows as does the most bleedin' harm. Folks get slashed to ribbons by the flyin' glass."

"I know," Teddy yelled back, and took the cabbie's advice, covering her head with her arms.

"Look after yourself as well as me," a muffled voice from underneath her body instructed, and she replied, "I'm fine, Maxim, don't worry." But her words were drowned out by the sound of the crash and, a split second later, a terrific explosion.

The cabdriver was the first to raise his head and look around.

He stood up, briskly brushing down his trousers as he did. "We was lucky, ducks," he said to Teddy. "It could have come down right on top of us. But the bleeder fell somewhere behind the Cumberland Hotel. Down Edgware Road. Poor buggers, whoever it was that got it."

Teddy looked at him speechlessly, willing the shaking in her limbs to stop, and for a moment she was unable to get up off the ground.

In the distance there was the sudden roaring sound of another flying bomb, and like the first it was heading in their direction. Everyone looked at the sky, and the screaming started all over again.

The cabbie gave Teddy his hand and pulled her up, and Maxim scrambled to his feet. The cabdriver said, "The bleedin' Germans don't know when to stop! Take your lad and run to the tube, ducks. This bloomin' raid ain't going to be over for a bit, mark my words."

"Yes, that's where we'll go," Teddy exclaimed. "And thanks."

Without giving his abandoned taxi a last glance, the cabbie began to sprint toward Marble Arch. Teddy retrieved the paper bag of shirts, took Maxim's hand, and together they ran as fast as they could, hard on the heels of the friendly cockney cabdriver, following him to the tube station at Marble Arch.

The cheery little cabbie had disappeared in the crowds thronging the underground station by the time Teddy and Maxim raced down the steps.

The platform was jammed with people, mostly women and children who had been visiting the shops, out on a Saturday morning jaunt. There were a few men, but not many. Most of the menfolk of England were with the fighting forces—in the army, the navy or the air force.

Panting and heaving, Teddy and Maxim stopped at the bottom of the stairs. They were lucky enough to find a corner spot near the flight of steps and sat down, wedging themselves close together to make room for someone else.

Unnerved by the ordeal they had just gone through, they sat for a long time in silence, calming themselves, collecting their scattered senses.

"Don't be afraid, Maxim, we're safe here," Teddy said to him at last.

"I'm never afraid when I'm with you, Teddy," Maxim replied, and took a handkerchief out of his pocket. He spat on it and began to pat his knee with the damp cloth.

Leaning forward, Teddy exclaimed, "Did I hurt you when I pushed you to the ground?"

Maxim shook his head and grinned at her. "It's just a graze, and it doesn't smart, honestly. Well, not really."

She frowned and bent over him, examining his knee. "It doesn't look bad—still, it ought to have some iodine on it. . . ." She raised her head and scanned the crowd. "Usually there are Red Cross nurses covering all the underground stations during a raid. But I don't see one, do you?"

He shook his head. "Anyway, I'm not hurt. Please don't fuss, Teddy, I'll wash my knee in the men's toilet at Lyon's Corner House. We're still going there for lunch, aren't we?"

"At this rate, if the raid keeps up, it'll be more like tea that we'll be having," she muttered.

Maxim did not respond. He leaned back against the base of the steps, stretched out his legs and sat staring at his shoes for a long time, looking preoccupied and thoughtful. At last he turned to her and said in a low voice, "Thanks for shielding me the way you did."

"I will always protect you, Maxim. For as long as I live. You're my boy, and I love you very much."

"I love you too, Teddy."

Maxim did not say anything after this, and neither did she. But in a short while his hand crept into hers and he drew even closer to her, resting his head against her bare arm. And they sat quietly, feeling safe together, as they had for so long, and knowing that whatever else happened, they had each other.

Suddenly, unexpectedly, the voice of a stranger rang out in the underground, a woman's beautiful soprano reaching high to the ceiling as she began to sing, " 'There'll be bluebirds over the white cliffs of Dover, tomorrow, just you wait and see. There'll be love and laughter, and peace ever after, tomorrow, when the world is free.' "

As the woman went on singing, people began to join in, lending their own voices to hers as she picked up the verse, and soon the whole underground station reverberated with the wonderful sound of the crowd, Teddy and Maxim included, singing their hearts out. " 'The shepherd will tend his sheep, the valley will bloom again and Jimmy will go to sleep in his own little room again. There'll be bluebirds over the white cliffs of Dover, tomorrow, just you wait and see.'"

Once the song was finished, the woman stood up and shouted, "We're not going to let the Jerries get *us* down, are we?"

"*No!*" the crowd bellowed back.

"Then let's keep on singing!" the woman shouted.

"How about *Pack Up Your Troubles in Your Old Kit Bag*?" an elderly lady cried.

"You've got the wrong war, ducks!" their little cockney cabbie retorted, unexpectedly popping up next to Teddy and Maxim, and grinning at them in his cheery fashion.

"Let's have *I'm Gonna Get Lit Up When the Lights Go Up in London*," another person called out.

The crowd roared its approval of this suggestion, and the soprano started it off and everyone followed her lead. When this number was finished she began another, and then another, and another after that, and the crowd sang along for the next hour.

Teddy and Maxim joined in, enjoying themselves, the raid certainly not forgotten but pushed to one side for a while. And they found themselves enveloped in the extraordinary warmth and friendliness of these Londoners with whom they now shared a common fate as well as the common bonds of courage, perseverance, cheerfulness and defiance.

It was an air-raid warden who broke up the sing-along when he pushed his way down the crowded steps, blowing his whistle enthusiastically. Voices fell silent at once and dozens of pairs of eyes were focused on him intently.

"The All Clear has just gone off," he called to them. "You can leave, it's safe now. But file out in an orderly fashion, please. We don't want any accidents down here. There's enough trouble up there."

Maxim sprang to his feet and helped Teddy to get up.

"I'm going to have beans on toast," he said to her as they slowly mounted the steps, following the horde of people out of the underground. "What are you going to have for lunch?"

"The same, I suppose. There's never much choice these days,

lovely, is there?" she answered, and realized that she was quite hungry. Survival, she thought. That's what it's all about. I must make sure we survive until Hitler is defeated and the world is a free place again.

24

$\mathcal{M}$AXIM PLACED THE TWO NEW SHIRTS ON TOP OF THE other clothes in the suitcase on his bed, closed the lid and locked it, and carried the case to the door.

Then he turned around and walked back to the chest of drawers near the window, where he stood for a moment looking at the photographs. He always did this before returning to boarding school, and over the past two years it had become something of a little ritual.

There were three pictures, and they were large, framed in silver, and carefully arranged in a semicircle on the chest. One of them in particular held Maxim's attention and he stared at it intently. It was his favorite because whenever he remembered the day the picture had been taken he experienced a surge of happiness and the sadness inside him went away for a while.

The photograph was of the four people he loved the most in the whole world. He was in it, too, and it had been taken on his fourth birthday in 1938, in the garden of their country villa in the Wannsee, near the two lakes of the same name, on the outskirts of Berlin.

Aunt Hedy had been the photographer, and she had arranged the little family group exactly the way she had wanted, had seated them on the lawn underneath the linden trees down by the edge of the little lake, the Kleiner Wannsee.

He sat between Mutti and Papa. His grandmother was next to his father, and Teddy was on the other side of his mother, and they were all smiling and their faces looked radiant in the bright sunlight filtering through the leafy branches of the trees. It was a happy picture, just as the day had been a happy one, and it had remained etched in his memory.

When he closed his eyes, as he did now, he could picture everything exactly the way it was that afternoon, could conjure it up, so that every nuance was vivid, every detail crystal clear, and he could relive it again. . . .

He was four years old today.

He stood in the vast garden shielding his eyes against the bright-yellow sun. The day was beautiful. The sky was blue, filled with puffball white clouds, and down at the bottom of the sloping green lawns the lake glittered like glass and the big white sails of their boat billowed about in the wind.

His nose twitched. He caught a whiff of lilacs mingled with the scent of roses, and a tangy smell wafted up from the lake. He ran across the lawn to the table under the weeping willow tree. It was spread with a white damask cloth and set for eight with his mother's fine bone china. Nearby, on another table, were piled many beribboned boxes, full of fanciful toys and games and picture books, he was quite sure of that.

He heard his mother's voice calling him, and suddenly she and Papa were standing there next to him, smiling, and hugging him, and out of the corner of his eye he saw Aunt Sigrid and Uncle Thomas walking across the lawn to join them. Behind Uncle Thomas walked his chauffeur, Heinz, who was carrying a very large object wrapped in brown paper. Heinz put the package down in front of him, and Aunt Sigrid cried, "It's for you, darling!" and she helped him to rip the paper off. And then before his eyes stood the most beautiful rocking horse he had ever seen, with a golden mane and flaring nostrils and a polished saddle trimmed with silver bells.

Papa placed him on the rocking horse and pushed him, and he rode it excitedly for a while, and Aunt Hedy took many photographs of him until finally his father said, "Enough," and lifted him down. Next, everyone gave him the other presents in the pretty boxes, and Aunt Hedy said, "Now I want a family group," and she led them to the linden trees and they sat down, while she snapped and snapped her camera.

Walter suddenly appeared on the terrace, and led the way down the steps and across the lawn, carrying the big silver tea

*tray, and behind him came a small procession composed of
Marta, Gerda and Anna, the three maids from the mansion in
the Tiergartenstrasse, and even Frau Müller, the cook, was in
the little procession. The trays the four women held out in front
of them were laden with tea sandwiches and fancy cakes and
marzipan pigs and a* Schwarzwälder Kirschtorte *oozing rich
brown chocolate and cherries and whipped cream, which Frau
Müller had made specially for his birthday as an extra treat.*

*His grandmother took his hand and led him to the table. "You
have the place of honor, sweetheart," she said, and then they ate
the special birthday tea and everyone chattered and laughed and
was happy.*

*Not long after tea was finished, Walter came walking down
the terrace steps again, this time bringing a birthday cake with
four red candles on it, and everyone sang the special birthday
song, and he sang it too, which made them all laugh. And when
the song was finished he huffed and puffed and blew out the candles and made a wish, just as Mutti had told him to do, and
everyone kissed him and hugged him again, and it was the best
day, the happiest day he had ever spent. . . .*

After a few seconds, Maxim opened his eyes and stared again
at the photograph taken on his fourth birthday. It had been
the last birthday he had spent with his parents. They had
planned to be in London with him and Teddy to celebrate his
fifth, but they had not come because Gangan was so sick and
they had been unable to travel. And then the war had started
and they were trapped in Berlin. He had celebrated six birthdays without them and this thought made him very sad.

He thought about his parents every day, wondering where
they were and what they were doing, and he worried a lot about
them. He knew bad things were done to Jews in Germany;
Teddy had told him that when he was seven. "You're old
enough now to know," she had said, and had gone on to explain
that this was the reason his father had wanted them to leave
Germany in the first place. But he was sure his parents were
safe. He had always been close to them, and he believed he
would have known if something terrible had happened to them,
would have felt it in his heart if they were dead. And so, like
Teddy and Aunt Ketti, he truly believed they were still alive.

He loved Teddy very much, and he knew she loved him.

When he was small, and Mutti had not come, he had cried a lot, and Teddy had rocked him in her arms and comforted him, and made him feel safe. He did not know what he would do without Teddy—she was the most important person in his life after Papa and Mutti. When his father and mother finally arrived, they would all live together in a big house here in London, perhaps in Regent's Park or Hampstead. He supposed Aunt Hedy would live with them too, but he did not know whether his grandmother would, since he was not sure whether or not she had died. Gangan had been a very, *very* old lady even six years ago, and then she had fallen ill, and perhaps by now she had gone to Heaven to be with Grandfather Westheim. He would miss her if she had.

Maxim's glance shifted to the other photographs.

One was of his parents in 1935. Teddy called it "the portrait" because they were posed together in evening clothes, his mother in a white satin gown with a little cape and glittering diamond necklace, his father in white tie and tails.

The third photograph was of Mutti and Teddy and him standing outside the Plaza-Athénée Hotel in Paris, and it had been taken by the head concierge, who was always so nice to them.

Stepping closer to the chest, Maxim now pulled open the top drawer, took out Papa's black leather wallet, which had been given to him the day before he and Mutti and Teddy had gone to Paris. He opened it and took out the enlarged snapshot of Mutti, which was his father's favorite.

His mother was standing on the jetty at the villa in Wannsee, with the lake shimmering in the sunlight behind her. How beautiful she was with her halo of blond hair, her bright, curving smile, her lovely, lustrous eyes. He kissed her face and then quickly slipped the picture back into one side of the wallet. In the other section were the pieces of paper his father had given him when he was little, but he did not take them out because he knew the words very well by now. "These are the standards by which to live your life," Papa had told him. He had not understood some of the things his father had written down, at least not then, for he had been only a little boy, only four. Now that he was ten and grown up, he knew what the words meant, and he intended to live by those standards, which were his father's.

Returning the wallet to its customary place in the drawer, Maxim picked up the carved wooden horse that his father had also given him just before he had left Germany. He touched the little horse gently, thinking first of Papa and then of Mutti, loving them so much.

He shut his eyes tightly, squeezing back the tears that suddenly pricked behind his lids. "Be safe," he whispered out loud. "Be safe. Come back to me, Mutti and Papa. Please, please come back to me."

He stood there for a long time, clutching the little horse and swallowing his tears as the sadness returned and once again filled him up inside.

"Maxim! Maxim!" he heard Teddy calling from downstairs. "It's time to go!"

He put the horse next to the wallet in the drawer and closed it, and gave the photographs a last lingering glance before running to the door. Picking up his suitcase, he took a deep breath, threw back his shoulders and went out.

"I hate railway stations!" Maxim announced as he and Teddy walked down the platform at Victoria.

Teddy glanced at him swiftly, and although she made no comment her heart shifted inside her.

"You always have to say good-bye at railway stations," he muttered, and abruptly stopped walking.

She also stopped and turned to look at him. His fresh young face, so healthy and rosy and lightly tanned by the summer sun, had suddenly set in rigid lines and she saw his mother's stubbornness in his tightened mouth and in the proud tilt of his little chin.

"I know, darling," she said softly, putting the suitcase down, reaching out and squeezing his shoulder.

"I had to say good-bye to Papa at the railway station in Berlin and to Mutti in Paris, and whenever I go back to school it's *you* I leave behind, and I don't like the feeling it gives me inside."

She pulled him to her and hugged him close to her body. "I'm not going anywhere, I shall always be here for you, and anyway you're clever enough to know there *is* a difference when *we* say good-bye. The circumstances *are* different from those other times."

"I suppose . . . but I still hate railway stations!"

"It'll be different soon, Maxim. Once the war is over, Colet Court and St. Paul's School won't need to be evacuated any longer and will return to London, and you'll be able to become a day boy and live at home."

He nodded and his face began to brighten. "Stubby's father says that our two schools have played a big part in the war effort. After all, Colet Court houses recruits, and St. Paul's is General Montgomery's headquarters. He's an old boy of St. Paul's, don't forget."

She laughed. "How could I! Neither you nor Stubby is likely to let me. In any case, once things return to normal the two schools will be housed in their old buildings in Hammersmith again. And speaking of Stubby's father, isn't that Stubby himself standing over there looking rather forlorn?"

"Gosh, it is! I wonder where Mrs. Trenton is? She usually brings Stubby to the station herself. Come on, Teddy, let's go and see what's up." So saying he hitched his satchel of books over his shoulder and hurried off, looking behind him once and beckoning to her.

"Don't trail your new raincoat on the ground!" she shouted after him, following more slowly, hampered as she was by the large suitcase, her purse and a carrier bag full of sandwiches and buns for their lunch.

"Hello, Teddy," Stubby said politely as she drew closer.

"Hello, Alan. Where's your mother?"

"She had to dash off, she's got an appointment in Whitehall this morning. At the Ministry of Works. Something to do with Dad's business. She's been sort of trying to run it since my uncle had a heart attack, while Dad's in the RAF. She knew you were bound to arrive any minute with Duke, and that you'd see me safely on the train."

"And here comes the train for Crowthorne now!" Teddy exclaimed. "As well as a few of your schoolfellows, it seems. Isn't that nice, you'll be able to sit together."

Maxim and Stubby followed her gaze and groaned loudly and in unison when they saw the stragglers coming down the platform.

"We don't want to sit with *them*," Maxim muttered, rolling his eyes heavenward. "They're too *young*, Teddy. Can't you see that?"

"Last term's new boys," Stubby explained.

"We'd like a carriage to ourselves," Maxim said. "We can, can't we, Teddy?"

"I suppose so. There aren't many people waiting for the train, and certainly not as many boys as I'd expected."

"A lot went back yesterday," Stubby told her and grinned hugely. "I expect their mothers wanted to get rid of the ugly blighters!"

"And you two are beautiful, is that it?" she asked, raising a brow.

Typical ten-year-olds that they were, they made ugly faces for her and she began to laugh, enjoying them, and her spirits lifted at the sight of their youthful antics. And she was pleased that Maxim's mood had changed. He'll be all right, she thought, more than all right.

But sitting on the bus going home to Belsize Park Gardens, Teddy wondered if she had made a mistake sending him away to school. In view of the Westheims' absence, perhaps it would have been wiser if she had kept him by her side.

On the other hand, he was such a brilliant boy he deserved to be in the best school. Aunt Ketti had recommended St. Paul's and its preparatory school, Colet Court. The prep school and the college, being connected as they were, welded the juniors and the older boys together as a unit. Also, the ancient public school had a great liberal tradition, seemed to be totally without prejudice, and there were a number of German Jewish refugee boys at the school.

Henry Rossiter, of the Rossiter Merchant Bank, had wholeheartedly endorsed Ketti's suggestion, and had said that the Westheims would certainly approve of her choice of schools for their son. He had also pointed out that Teddy had plenty of money for the school fees, books and the uniform, although the latter was not mandatory at the moment because of clothes rationing.

And so she had sent him there, and it had hardly been her fault that the two schools had been evacuated to Wellington College in Surrey in 1942, just when Maxim was starting at Colet.

I did the right thing, she reassured herself, and she sat back in her seat and opened the *Evening Standard* she had just bought at the railway station. The headlines brought a happy smile to her face. The Allies were in the process of liberating the whole of France.

25

I'M SO GLAD YOU CAME, THEODORA!" LYDIA PELL EXclaimed, her face lighting up at the sight of Teddy on the doorstep of her mother's house in Hampstead. "Come in, come in, don't stand outside in the cold."

"Hello, Lydia," Teddy said, smiling affectionately and stepping inside. "I said I'd try my best to come, and here I am," she went on, taking off her scarf, shrugging out of her coat, putting them into Lydia's outstretched hands.

"It was Aunt Ketti who was being a bit difficult, but only because she'd arranged for me to go with her to Mrs. Levine's house for supper tonight. But without telling *me*," Teddy explained. "She finally came around to seeing my point of view and she understands now that it's not fair to accept invitations for me without first finding out if I'm free!"

Lydia gave Teddy a swift look and asked, "Does Mrs. Levine have a son?"

"Yes. Two, in fact. They're both in the services. Why?"

"I bet one of them is home on leave," Lydia said and chuckled. "Knowing your aunt Ketti, she's more than likely trying to fix you up with a nice young man."

"Oh, she wouldn't do that!" Teddy exclaimed, looking at Lydia askance.

"I wouldn't be so sure if I were you," Lydia retorted, still chuckling. She hung Teddy's coat and scarf in the coat closet, linked her arm through her friend's and said, "Let's go in and join the others."

Together the two young women strolled across the entrance hall in the direction of the drawing room.

From behind its closed door came the sound of a piano being played with superb skill, and Teddy instantly thought of Sigmund Westheim, who had been such a virtuoso himself, and her throat tightened with unexpected emotion. She could not help wondering where he and Ursula were at that moment, and if they were all right. Lydia pushed open the door and led her inside, and she quickly clamped down on her troubled thoughts to arrange a bright smile on her face.

Teddy knew this room very well. She had spent many enjoyable evenings here with Lydia since they first met four years ago, and she always felt comfortable and at home in it.

Mellow, and filled with a certain kind of old-world charm, it had strong echoes of a country house in the way it was decorated: warm and welcoming with soft creamy walls, heavy red-brocade draperies, a matching red carpet stretching wall to wall, with an Oriental rug in front of the fireplace. The sofa and chairs were covered in a floral chintz that had once been vivid and colorful but had long ago faded into softer tones, and scattered about were antique pieces of furniture made of ripe old woods. There were good oil paintings and watercolors on the walls, and a beautiful Queen Anne mirror hung above the fireplace.

In the grate a huge log fire burned brightly; crystal vases brimmed with gold and bronze chrysanthemums, and a brass jug on the baby grand was resplendent with burnished copper beech leaves. All contributed to the feeling of autumn, which abounded throughout, and on this chilly October night the room appeared more inviting than ever.

A small group was gathered around the piano. Archie, Lydia's brother who was in the Royal Air Force, stood with his arm around his girlfriend, Penelope Jardene. Two of his former school friends from Eton, Tom Andrews and Victor Spencer, both fighter pilots like Archie, were leaning over the piano, and so was Victor's current girl, Daphne Hodges.

Lydia announced, "Here's Theodora at last!" and whoever it was playing the piano stopped, and the others turned around to greet her warmly, and she smiled back at them and said, "Hello, everyone."

Propelling Teddy across the room, Lydia murmured to her,

"The only person you don't know is the chap who was just playing the piano so exceptionally well. He's with the Number Thirty-two Squadron at Biggin Hill in Kent—Archie's squadron. His name is Mark Lewis."

On hearing his name mentioned, Mark pushed back the piano stool and strode around the group of friends to meet Theodora.

Lydia said, "Teddy, this is Mark, and Mark, meet my very dear friend Theodora Stein."

"Hello, Theodora," Mark said, stepping toward her, his hand outstretched.

Teddy put her hand in his, said, "Good evening, Mark," and stood staring into his face, one of such boyishness he did not look old enough to be a fighter pilot. And then she became aware of his eyes. They were of a brown so dark they were almost black, and there was an expression in them that was quite unfathomable. Old eyes in a young face, she thought, old eyes that have already seen too much killing and death and destruction. And it was then that she recognized the enigmatic expression for what it was—a mingling of pain and too much sadness.

"I've been playing favorite songs for the chaps," Mark told her, breaking the silence between them. "What's your favorite song, Theodora?"

"I'm not sure," she replied, suddenly feeling shy and tongue-tied. She slid her hand out of his, and took a step backward, realizing that he was having a peculiar effect on her.

"No requests, then?" he asked.

She shook her head, still incapable of speech.

He half smiled, turned away, walked over to the piano and took up his seat once more.

Daphne said, "If no one has a request, please play my second favorite, Mark. It's 'I'll Be Seeing You.'"

"All right," Mark said, and grinned. "Providing you sing it, Daphers."

"Agreed!" Daphne cried. "We'll all sing it, won't we?"

"Of course we will," Victor said, and as Mark struck up the refrain that is exactly what they did.

While the singing was under way, Teddy sat in a chair near the fire, and a few seconds later Lydia came over, bringing her a glass of white wine.

"Don't you want to sing along with them?" Lydia asked,

handing Teddy the crystal goblet, and sitting down on the arm of the chair.

"Thank you," Teddy said, accepting the wine. "Sing-songs are very nice, and jolly, and usually I enjoy them, but I just don't feel like joining in tonight. Don't ask me why."

"Neither do I, to tell you the truth," Lydia confessed. "The sing-song seems to be the most popular pastime there is these days, and it certainly puts a stop to any decent conversation, doesn't it?"

"It does," Teddy agreed. "Still, *we* must seem rather aloof, even a bit churlish, sitting over here by ourselves. Perhaps we ought to join them, we don't *have* to sing, I suppose."

"Come on, then," Lydia said, standing up. "I'd hate anyone's feelings to be hurt."

Teddy stood with Lydia near the piano, listening to Mark's playing. His talent as a pianist was undeniable, and for the second time that evening she was reminded of Sigmund Westheim. Poignant memories assailed her, and she was carried back to the music room in the mansion on the Tiergartenstrasse, and for a moment she was wrapped in sadness and her sense of loss was so acute it resembled physical pain. She took a deep breath, willing the pain to go away, reminding herself that the war would soon be over now, that in due course the Westheims would come to England, and that they would be together. Things would again be the way they had been in Berlin. The past would become the present—and the future.

This thought, hardly a new one, immediately cheered her, as it usually did, and she took a sip of the wine and looked over the rim of the glass at Mark Lewis.

As the young airman continued to play she studied him, filled with curiosity about him. He was good-looking, with smooth, round cheeks, a wide brow, and a full and generous mouth. His hair was dark brown and wavy, brushed straight back from his forehead, and he had thick, curving brows above those soulful, expressive eyes. Broad-shouldered and muscular, he had towered over her when they had been introduced, and she decided he must be all of six feet, perhaps more than that. Even sitting down at the piano he looked tall.

Unexpectedly, he lifted his head and stared at her, and their eyes locked. Try though she did, Teddy discovered she was unable to look away. The intensity of his gaze held her. And it unnerved her, made her heart begin to pound in a most unreasonable and unfamiliar way, and she felt the color rushing up to flood her face.

She was finally able to avert her gaze, but within a split second her eyes were inevitably drawn back to his. The look he gave her was more direct than ever and seemed full of meaning.

Teddy dropped her eyes, endeavoring to compose herself. When she looked up again, she saw that he was still watching her closely. Then he smiled at her, and it was the loveliest of smiles, and it seemed to reach deep inside her to touch her heart, and she understood that something important was happening between them at this moment, and she was afraid.

Lydia whispered in her ear, "I'm going to the kitchen to give my mother a hand with supper. Excuse me a moment," and she moved away from the piano as she spoke.

Teddy immediately swung around and hurried after her friend.

Drawing alongside her, she murmured, "I haven't said hello to your mother yet. I'll come with you, and perhaps I can also be of some help."

"I'm quite sure Mother has done everything, Teddy dear, but by all means come along, and at least we can carry the food into the dining room for her."

Teddy followed Lydia out into the hall. They were making their way down the corridor to the kitchen at the back of the house, when Teddy said quietly, "Mark is tremendously talented, isn't he?"

"Yes, he is," Lydia agreed. There was a short pause and then she glanced at Teddy over her shoulder. "I think he is very taken with you, my dear."

"What do you mean?" Teddy asked, her eyes widening.

"He was looking at you, Teddy, you know, in *that* way."

"What way?"

"The way a man looks at a woman when he's attracted to her, and interested in pursuing her."

"Oh," Teddy said, at a loss for words.

"Do you like him?"

"I hardly know him, Lydia!"

"What I meant was, do you like the look of him."

"Yes," Teddy admitted, and then shyness seized her and she

stammered, "I—I—I think he's very good-looking, actually, and he seems very nice, very pleasant."

"Mark's quite something, in my opinion. I wish he were interested in me, but he isn't. I suppose I'm not his type." Lydia eyed her, and a smile slowly spread across her face. "But I believe *you* are, and that's why I wanted you to come this evening."

"Do you mean you're *matchmaking*?" Teddy said, frowning, and then giving her friend a hard stare.

Lydia grinned, "Yes, I'm afraid so. But look, why not? What's wrong with getting two people together?"

Teddy was silent, and then she suddenly said, "I hope Mark doesn't think you're doing that. I'd feel awful if he did, and I'd also be very embarrassed."

"He has no inkling. *Truly.* By the way, quite aside from being such a nice person, Mark's a war hero. He has the DSO, and the DFC, and oodles of other decorations."

"But he's so young!" Teddy exclaimed in surprise. "Still, I can well imagine that he is brave."

"He has a certain look about him," Lydia murmured thoughtfully. "A special look, one I can't quite define. And I understand from Archie that he's very dependable and patriotic. Incidentally, he's not as young as he *looks* and you think."

"How old is he?"

"Twenty-five, a year older than Archie. Your age, actually."

"I see."

"He's one of The Few, you know."

"A Battle of Britain pilot!" Teddy exclaimed, impressed. "Then that explains all the medals," she added and thought of Winston Churchill's words about those young men, none of them much older than twenty, who in 1940 had defended England in the skies. "Never in the field of human conflict was so much owed by so many to so few," Churchill had said, and ever after that speech to the House of Commons, those valiant Battle of Britain fighter pilots had been known as The Few, and referred to as such by everyone. Being a Battle of Britain flyer had become a special kind of honor in itself, even for those who had not won medals.

26

<hr>

$\mathcal{J}$ULIA PELL WAS PEERING INSIDE THE AGA OVEN WHEN
Lydia and Teddy walked into the spacious family-style kitchen,
and she turned around at the sound of footsteps on the tiled
floor.

Her face lit up at the sight of the two young women. She
was extremely fond of Teddy, and she cried, "There you are,
Theodora! I'm delighted you are here tonight after all."

"So am I, Mrs. Pell," Teddy responded, walking over to her
friend's mother and embracing her. Mrs. Pell returned the loving gesture with genuine warmth, and when they drew apart,
Teddy asked, "What can I do to help?"

"Nothing right now, my dear, but thank you so much for
offering. Do go and sit at the kitchen table and finish your wine,
and you, too, Lydia. Everything's under control. In a few minutes I'll start taking the food out of the oven, and then you can
both pitch in, good sports that you are."

So saying, Mrs. Pell hurried over to the pantry and immediately came out carrying a large glass bowl, which she placed
on one of the countertops, and then returned to the pantry
again.

Watching her move around the kitchen with speed and efficiency, yet also with lithesome grace, Teddy could not help
thinking how much Lydia resembled her, and in so many ways.

Julia Pell was tall, willowy, a striking woman with dark-red
hair, cornflower-blue eyes and hundreds of freckles on her
creamy-toned skin. Lydia had inherited her mother's height
and figure, her sparkling blue eyes and fiery hair, as well as her
elegance of movement, her happy-go-lucky disposition. It
struck Teddy that tonight more than ever they seemed like sisters rather than mother and daughter. She was extremely fond

of both women, who had proven to be good friends to her over the past few years. When she and Lydia had first met, they had taken to each other at once, and Mrs. Pell's response to her had been as spontaneous and warm as her daughter's.

Julia and her husband, Michael, were both descended from Anglo-Irish Catholic families and had been born and brought up in Ireland. Although they had lived in London for their entire married life, and their children had been born here, they still maintained a home in Donegal, the house that Michael had inherited from his father, and where, until 1939, they had spent their summers. "When the war is over and we can all travel again, you must come and stay with us at Dromlochan, and for the whole summer," Mrs. Pell had said on frequent occasions to Teddy, and she had graciously included Maxim, Aunt Ketti and even the Westheims. Teddy had been touched by this generous invitation, and she hoped they would all be able to go to Dromlochan one day. For a long time she had itched to visit Ireland, and it had become one of her ambitions for the future. The Pells had two other children: Siobhan, who was in the Women's Land Army in Scotland, and Niall, an officer with the merchant marine on the Russian convoy run. Both were as unorthodox, friendly and easygoing as the rest of the family.

Mrs. Pell made a final trip to the pantry and came out carrying another cut-glass bowl.

"Well, my darling," she said to Lydia, "I've blown every one of our ration coupons on this supper for Archie and his friends! However, I do think it's been worth it, and certainly your brother is about to savor some of his favorite dishes."

Lydia laughed and said, "They're undoubtedly Daddy's favorites, too. I wish he weren't up north tonight. He'd enjoy them as much as Archie."

"Yes, that's true, he would, but what can one do, my darling?" Julia did not wait for an answer and rushed on, "He had to be at the munitions factory in Leeds today, come hell or high water, and the trains are so *frightfully* slow at the moment he would never have got back in time for supper anyway. So it's much better that he spend the night at the Queens Hotel in Leeds, and travel home comfortably tomorrow."

Teddy said, "Whatever's in the oven smells delicious, Mrs. Pell."

Julia beamed at her. "Doesn't it just," she agreed, and continued in a confiding manner, "The butcher let me have some ground beef—in exchange for all of our ration coupons for the next few weeks, of course! And with it I've made a huge cottage pie, Archie does love that so. And I've got an apple tart baking as well. I had some bottled apples put away, you see, for a special occasion, and tonight seemed as good a time as any to use them."

Lydia said, "I thought you were making a trifle, Mummy."

"Oh, but I did, my darling!" Mrs. Pell glanced at the glass bowls. "Two, actually, though I am rather *afraid* they're very much wartime trifles, since there are no bananas available. Or any of the other fruit I need, for that matter. Oh, well, never mind." Julia Pell shrugged and let out a chuckle. "Thank goodness for sponge cake, jelly, Bird's Eye custard powder, and sherry. Lots of the latter, I might add. It does give a trifle a special flavor."

"Good Lord, Mummy, you haven't gone and done it again, have you!" Lydia exclaimed, looking across the kitchen table at Teddy, rolling her eyes and grimacing theatrically. "My mother has recently acquired this knack for making sherry-drenched trifle that gets us all positively squiffy, truly and absolutely pie-eyed!"

Julia Pell protested this statement, but before Teddy could think of an appropriate comment, Archie's ginger head appeared around the kitchen door.

"How much longer until supper, Mother?" he asked. "The troops are getting more ravenous by the minute. I won't be able to restrain them soon . . . they'll be descending on you like the Mongol hordes."

"Actually, Archie, supper is ready now," Mrs. Pell answered her son with a bright smile. "Do show your friends into the dining room, please. Lydia and Teddy are about to bring everything in, and they will help me to serve."

Supper at the Pells was always a boisterous affair when Archie was home on leave, and most especially when he invited his chums along for the evening.

And as usual the boys of the Royal Air Force took over. They recounted hair-raising stories about flying, gave vivid accounts of the narrow escapes they had had, told all kinds of jokes, laughed a lot, ribbed each other and everyone else unmercifully, and in general kept the womenfolk well and truly entertained throughout the meal.

Teddy, who could hold her own with anyone, and was spirited and vivacious of personality, found herself silent for once, almost withdrawn. And she was aware that this was because of Mark Lewis. He sat next to her at the dining table, and she was acutely conscious of his presence. Several times he had addressed remarks to her, and she had responded politely, but she had not initiated any conversation with him, even though she longed to do so. Her own reticence surprised her; she was rendered completely tongue-tied by this man.

Her problem was herself, she knew that, and she tried to come to grips with her inner feelings. From the moment she had met him she had responded to Mark Lewis, on every level, as a woman. She found him overwhelmingly attractive and physically appealing, and on the surface he was genial and charming. Yet intuitively she knew he was also a young man of character, one who was strong and brave, and she felt there were hidden depths to him, sensed that he was a person of feeling, sensitivity and gentleness.

In the five years she had been living in London, Teddy had met several young men who had shown an interest in her, and who had wanted to take her out. Each time she had declined, and she had never dated anyone since leaving Berlin. This was not only because of her commitment to Willy Herzog, but because she had not been attracted to those other men. In consequence, her fierce response to Mark had shaken her considerably; she was taken aback at herself. There was no possible way she could deny that she was as interested in him as he seemed to be in her, because she was, and she wanted to see him again, to be alone with him and get to know him better.

Earlier, when he had pulled the chair out for her at the dining table, he had accidentally brushed his hand against hers, and she had almost jumped out of her skin. His fingers on hers had been like an electric shock, and she had pulled her hand away quickly, even though she had not wanted to do this at all, had wanted to entwine her fingers with his. She was flooded with emotions that were unusually strong—and wholly unfamiliar. She had never experienced anything like this before in her entire life. Not even with Willy, her fiancé. Poor Willy. Just a short while ago her thoughts had swung to him, so far away in Shanghai, and she had admitted that there was no future for them together, whether Mark Lewis was around or not. Mark had nothing whatsoever to do with her sudden self-revelation. Her aunt had said that she and Willy would be like total strangers when they met again after their long five-year separation, and she acknowledged to herself that Aunt Ketti was right.

All her instincts told Teddy that Mark Lewis would ask to see her again, and she had every intention of agreeing to do so. He might turn out to be a flash in the pan for her, and she for him, and in all truth she had no idea what would happen between them, if, indeed, anything at all. But she was certain of one thing. She did not love Willy enough to marry him. She harbored only sisterly affection for him, and she now understood that this was all she had ever felt. She had not been in love with him in Berlin in 1938, but in love with love, in love with the idea of marriage, and that was why she had said yes to Willy. But those were the wrong reasons to marry anyone.

"How long have you known the Pells?" Mark asked, startling her. He pushed his chair away from the table slightly, turning to face her, and crossed his long legs.

"About four and a half years," Teddy replied.

"I suppose you met them through Lydia?"

"Yes, we do war work together."

"War work," he repeated and stared at her, frowning. "You can't mean you both work in a factory. Or do you mean that?"

"No. I was referring to the work we do at the first-aid station on Haverstock Hill, and as volunteers for the Red Cross," Teddy explained.

"Oh, I see. So you don't have a job, then?"

"No . . . well, not really," Teddy hesitated, wondering whether to tell him about Maxim. She decided against it. "Both Lydia and I are involved in our volunteer war work on a full-time basis," she murmured.

Mark nodded. "And do you live near here, Theodora?"

"Yes, in Belsize Park Gardens."

"With your parents?"

"Do you always ask so many questions when you first meet someone?" Teddy asked quietly.

He had the good grace to laugh. "No," he admitted, and flashed his most charming smile, showing his even white teeth. He sat back in the chair, draped one arm over it in a nonchalant manner and gave her a long, meaningful look. "Only when I'm intrigued by someone," he said in a low, husky voice.

Teddy could not fail to miss the innuendo, and she was at a loss for words. She tried to look away from those dark, piercing eyes focused so unblinkingly on her, and she discovered she could not. And then she began to blush under his close and fixed scrutiny, and she was mortified with herself. Teddy was wondering how best to steer the conversation in another direction when Mrs. Pell saved her the trouble.

"Let's have coffee in the drawing room," Julia Pell announced, rising from the table and sweeping through the door into the hall.

Everyone else trooped out of the dining room after her.

At the end of the evening Mark asked Teddy if he could drive her home and she accepted his offer.

Now the two of them sat in his red MG sports car cruising down the hill from Hampstead village in the direction of Belsize Park Gardens. For one who had asked so many questions earlier, Mark was curiously uncommunicative on the short drive to her home. And Teddy herself was as quiet as she had been at the Pells, hardly opening her mouth except to give him directions.

Finally when the car came to a standstill outside her aunt's house, he turned around in the seat to face her and said, "I'd like to see you again, Theodora. Will you come out with me?"

"Yes."

"Such a weak little yes," he said gently. "You are the shy one, aren't you?"

"I'm not really. It's just that—" She broke off, looked at him in the murky light of the car, took a deep breath and said, "I'd like to go out with you. I *want* to . . . very much."

"Good, I'm glad," he said, his deep-timbred voice full of warmth. "What about tomorrow evening?"

"I can't, I promised to visit a friend who is sick, and it wouldn't be very nice to disappoint her."

"I understand. Unfortunately, I'm busy on Friday."

"So am I."

"I hope you're free on Saturday, Theodora, because my leave is up on Sunday."

THE WOMEN IN HIS LIFE

"Oh yes, Saturday would be fine."

"Then we'll go dancing," he said, smiling at her in the darkness of the car.

27

HE TOOK HER TO THE SAVOY HOTEL IN THE STRAND. They had dinner in the beautiful room overlooking the river Thames, and danced to Carroll Gibbons and his orchestra.

Teddy thought she had never seen anyone as handsome as Mark Lewis. Tonight he wore his blue Royal Air Force uniform with his decorations on the left side of his jacket, and it was a shock to see that boyish face above those war hero's emblems that proclaimed his bravery as a fighter pilot.

Several times during the evening she had noticed that men as well as women cast admiring glances in his direction, and at one moment an older gentleman in a dinner jacket, dancing with his wife, had spoken to them on the dance floor.

"It's young men like you for whom we have to be thankful," the stranger had said. "Well done, well done, your country's very proud of you."

Mark had murmured something and smiled at the man and his wife, but he had made no comment to her as they had continued to move around the floor to the strains of "Besame Mucho." And then, quite unexpectedly, he had tightened his grip on her, pulled her closer to him, much closer than before, and she had trembled in his arms and worried that he would hear the sound of her rapidly beating heart. But of course he had not. How could he.

Now they were sitting at the table, sipping the champagne he had ordered to go with dessert, and talking. So far this evening they had spoken only in generalities. They had shared their mutual worry about the V2s, the horrendous new German flying bombs that did far more damage than the V1s, and that were currently being hurled on London. They had discussed the progress of the war, the Allied victories in Italy and other parts of Europe, and Mark had echoed what everyone was saying—that the war would be over by next summer. But they had not touched on anything else. It was almost as if they were both reluctant to take the initial step of asking the first truly personal question of each other.

Teddy continued to be thrown off balance by Mark Lewis, and her emotions were churning inside her, just as they had at the Pells' several nights ago. Yet she was determined not to allow her nervousness to show, and she had been skillful in masking this, outwardly appearing to be cool, contained, and very much in control.

"I'm sorry the pudding is taking so long," Mark said, making an apologetic face. "Would you like to dance while we're waiting, Theodora?"

She shook her head. "Not at the moment, if you don't mind. And you can call me Teddy if you want, Theodora's such a mouthful."

He smiled at her. "No, it isn't, I think it's a beautiful name. Thee-o-dor-a . . . it's very melodic to me. Of course, Teddy is more . . . *cozy*. In any case, I shall call you by both names, sometimes Theodora, sometimes Teddy."

She nodded, leaned back in her chair, took another sip of the champagne and gave him a lovely smile. Then she turned her head toward the orchestra and sat listening to the music, tapping her foot under the table, glad that she had spent the five pounds on the smart new evening dress, which was long and svelte-looking and in the latest color called dusty pink. She knew it was flattering. She had seen it in the model room at Harrods, and had known at once that it would suit her. With the gown she wore a strand of pearls, pearl studs in her ears, and an amethyst bracelet, all of which had been her mother's, and her mother's engagement ring was on her right hand.

Earlier that evening, when she had finished dressing and had come downstairs, Aunt Ketti had caught her breath and told her she looked beautiful, but she hadn't really believed her. And then Mark had said exactly the same thing when he had arrived to collect her, and she had believed *him*, because she wanted to, she supposed.

She had taken him into the drawing room to meet Aunt Ketti, who had asked him to take off his overcoat, sit down and have a drink, but thankfully he had declined, explaining that he had a cab waiting. He said that the cabdriver was a bit Bolshie and wanting to be on his way back to the West End, and so they ought to hurry.

When they stepped into the cab a few minutes later, Teddy had given a little sigh of relief that they were out of the house and on their way to dinner. Aunt Ketti had previously asked her a multitude of questions about Mark, which she had been unable to answer, and she had not wanted her aunt to start probing again, asking him awkward questions about his family and, even worse, his religion. She did not care what he was. He was the most fascinating man she had ever met, and, as far as she was concerned, that was all that mattered.

Although Teddy had no way of knowing it, Mark Lewis was as overwhelmed by her as she was by him, and now, as she sat lost in her thoughts, with a dreamy expression on her face, he was doing his level best to keep cool. His main concern was to conduct himself like a mature man and not like a schoolboy having his first crush who was out on his first date with the object of his infatuation, even though he did seem to fit this role.

He lit a cigarette and looked across the table at Teddy in the candlelight. She had a face that was positively angelic, and he had never seen a woman as beautiful as she, except perhaps for Ingrid Bergman in one of her recent movies, *Casablanca*; Teddy strongly resembled her, with her rounded face, high cheekbones, small, straight nose and wide mouth with a full, voluptuous lower lip. Although her hair was fair, her brows were dark and thick, and natural in shape, thankfully not fashionably plucked into sharp thin lines.

Her eyes were large and of the clearest green and heavily lashed. They were not only lovely but bright with intelligence, which convinced him there was a keen brain behind that madonnalike face.

Mark picked up his glass and took a gulp of champagne, suddenly wishing it were something much stronger. Teddy unnerved him. He longed to know more about her, yet he did not dare ask her anything. She had already implied he was being

nosy, and he had considered himself rebuked by her at the
Pells' on Wednesday.

Was it only Wednesday that they had met?

Mark felt as though he had always known her. He had
thought about her incessantly over the past few days, and
dreamed about her every night, and he was aware that she was
the most dangerous woman he had ever met. Dangerous because he could so easily fall in love with her, become serious
about her. He had known quite a few women in the past five
or six years, but he had never felt like this before . . . so . . .
so . . . *undone.*

Theodora Stein was different from those other women in his
past, infinitely different. There was something about her that
tugged at his heartstrings, made him want to protect and cher-
ish her as well as possess her physically. *Theodora Stein*, he repeated to himself. He wondered if she was Jewish; his mother
had wondered the same thing out loud at lunch today.

"With a name like Stein she has to be," his mother had said.
He had explained that he didn't know, and why did it matter
what she was? Jew or Gentile, it made no difference to him.
It was a remark he instantly regretted; he should have known
not to say it. "You had better find out. You know what your
father's like," his mother had warned, and he had groaned to
himself, wishing he had never mentioned Teddy to her. But he
had, and she would tell his father, had probably already told
him over dinner, and tomorrow at Sunday lunch there would
most probably be an inquisition. There always was when he
showed an interest in a woman. This was because he was the
eldest son now. His brother David, his most beloved darling
David, whom he had adored and hero-worshiped all his life,
had been killed in the North African campaign. He was supposed to take his place. As if anyone could take the place of
another human being who was unique unto himself. But he was
expected to do just that, and go into the family business, as
David had been going to do. And he was also expected to do
the right thing by the family by marrying the right kind of
woman one day.

Oh, bugger it, Mark thought, I'm going to go out with
whomever I wish, and marry the woman I *love*, when I find
her and when the time comes, whether she's Jewish, Catholic,
Protestant or Hindustani. I must please myself as well as the

old man. After all, it's my life, not his, and I can't *be* him, just as I can't *become* what David was. I shall do as I want. *To thine own self be true.*

The thought of his father galvanized Mark into verbal action, and leaning forward he took a deep breath and plunged in. "I want to get to know you better, Teddy," he said, "and I want you to know me, too. But that will never happen if we just sit here listening to the music and smiling at each other. However, I must admit, I do hesitate to ask you about yourself, because you sort of rebuked me the other evening, and I—"

"Rebuked you! But I didn't mean it to sound that way!" Teddy exclaimed. "I hope I didn't offend you?"

He smiled at her and shook his head. "No, you didn't. Anyway, now it's your turn . . . you must ask me anything you wish and I'll answer you truthfully, I promise."

"No, Mark, it's *you* who must ask *me*. . . . I owe you that for making you feel so uncomfortable on Wednesday."

"All right, if you say so." There was a little pause and he leveled his eyes on her as he asked slowly, "Is there anyone that you're going out with, Teddy, a sweetheart who's perhaps away in the forces?"

"No," she answered at once, giving him a direct, straightforward look. "There *was* a boy . . . once. But I haven't seen him for almost six years. He lives abroad. He's become . . . just a friend."

"And you haven't dated anyone in all this time?"

"No."

"But a beautiful girl like you! Why, Teddy, you must have had a few admirers, surely?"

"Yes, I have," she replied somewhat shyly. "But I didn't go out with any of them. . . . I wasn't interested in them."

He stared hard at her, reached out and put his hand on hers. He felt it trembling under his, and this pleased him. He leaned closer and whispered, "Are you interested in *me*, Theodora?"

She was so overcome by her feelings for him she could not speak, and she swallowed several times, merely gazed back at him, her lips slightly parted. Then finally she nodded her head.

A glow spread through him and he tightened his grip on her hand and said in the same low voice, "You simply can't imagine how very happy that makes me. And, Teddy, I'm terribly interested in you, but then you know that."

She continued to gaze at him, and her eyes were shining with joy, and there was a faint blush on her cheeks.

Eventually Mark said, "It's your turn to ask me a question."

"What about you?" she said in a faintly quavering voice after a short pause. "I mean, is there someone you've been seeing?"

"Absolutely not! There have been women, I'm not going to deny that, of course, but there's no one special, and there hasn't been for the longest time." Not ever, if the truth be known, he thought. Not in comparison to you, my darling.

At this moment the waiter arrived with the dessert. Their conversation was momentarily curtailed as they watched him spoon out the piping-hot bread-and-butter pudding, which they had both ordered and were now no longer interested in eating.

Once the waiter had departed, Mark said, "I thought I might meet your parents when I came to collect you tonight. Were they out?"

"My parents are dead, Mark," Teddy replied very quietly.

"God, how stupid I am! And so very clumsy. Do forgive me. I'm so sorry—"

"Please, it's all right, you couldn't have known. In any case, they've both been dead for a very long time."

"And that's why you live with your aunt?"

"Yes. What about your parents? Are they alive?"

"They are. Do you have any brothers and sisters?"

She shook her head. "I was an only child. Do you?"

"A younger brother, Lionel. He's away at school. At Harrow."

"Harrow! That's a marvelous school! Winston Churchill went to Harrow."

"So did I," Mark said.

"Did you really! Have you ever met Winston Churchill?" she now asked in an eager voice.

"Once."

"How lucky you are. I wish I had. He's the greatest man in England. In the world, actually, at least in my opinion. He's my hero."

Mark smiled at her, and he wanted to say he wished *he* were her hero, but restrained himself. Instead he asked, "And where did you go to school, Theodora?"

"I went to a school you couldn't possibly know . . . in Berlin."

Mark was taken aback by her answer, and he stared at her, frowning slightly. "What on earth were you doing in Berlin? Were your parents living there for some reason at the time?"

"They were Berliners. I am a Berliner. I was born there."

"You are a *German*?" Mark's voice reverberated with incredulity.

"I am."

"But you don't sound it. What I mean is that you don't have a German accent. You speak perfect English, and beautifully, I might add."

Teddy explained, "My mother taught me English when I was small. She spoke it well herself, and we came frequently to England to see Aunt Ketti before the war, when I was growing up. You see, she's lived here for over thirty years; her late husband, Uncle Harry, was an Englishman. Anyway, I've spoken English since I was five years old. Perhaps that's the reason I have no accent. When children learn a second language at a very young age they generally speak it without any kind of accent."

Mark continued to stare at Teddy and suddenly something clicked in his mind. "How long have you lived here?"

"Five years. I came here in the spring of 1939, via Paris."

He nodded, wondering if what he now suspected could possibly be true.

Teddy saw a look cross Mark's face, and it was an expression she could not quite fathom. She was not certain if it was one of perplexity or confusion or worry, or a combination of all three.

"I'm Jewish," she blurted out, and then she sat back in the chair and returned his stare, wondering if this was going to make any difference to him. She fervently hoped it wouldn't, that he was not one of those hateful people who were prejudiced.

Mark did not respond at first. He just sat looking at her in amazement. And then he smiled an odd little smile before he stretched his hand across the table and took hold of hers. "So am I, Teddy," he said. "As my father would say, our family is also of the Mosaic persuasion."

28

THEY SAT STARING AT EACH OTHER ACROSS THE DINNER table, both equally engrossed in what the other had to say.

Mark spoke about his family, and then talked at length about the family businesses. He told her that he was expected to go to work in the organization with his father when the war ended, and that he would take over when his father retired. He went on to explain that music had always been only his hobby, that he had never intended to make a career on the concert platform, so that he was not one bit disappointed about his future because the world of business excited him, which was the absolute truth.

In turn, Teddy filled him in with details of her early life in Berlin and her sojourn with the Westheims at the mansion on the Tiergartenstrasse. Then she carefully recounted the experiences she had had just before she left Berlin, along with a blow-by-blow description of *Kristallnacht* on November the ninth, a date she would never ever forget. She even told him about her relationship with Willy Herzog, leaving nothing out. After touching on her stay in Paris with Ursula Westheim, she ended up speaking about her subsequent journey to England with Maxim, the life she had made for them in London, and finally she confided her concerns about Maxim and the future.

Mark listened attentively to everything she had to say, and when at last she finished, he took her hand in his, and his face was sober when he asked, "And Frau Westheim and her husband are still in Germany?"

"Oh, yes, I'm sure they are," Teddy responded. "I would have definitely heard from them if they had managed to leave. And there would have been some sort of message from Princess von Wittingen, if anything . . . if anything *awful* had happened to them. But there's been nothing but silence." Teddy's smile was confident as she concluded, "They're in hiding somewhere and they're quite *safe*, of that I'm convinced. And Aunt Ketti agrees with me."

Mark nodded. It was on the tip of his tongue to bring up the heavy Allied bombing raids on Germany and the concentration camps, both dire threats to the safety of the Westheims, but he bit back his words. He had no desire to alarm her, or to spoil their wonderful evening together, by raising unpleasant facts that neither of them could do anything to alter. Instead, he raised his glass of champagne to her, and said, "A toast to you, Teddy! I'm full of admiration for you. It strikes me you're a wonderfully loyal girl, and a very courageous one, quite aside from being the most beautiful I've ever known."

"Thank you," she said, smiling with happiness. "I don't know about courage, though, I just do what I have to do. As for my looks, well, I'm not all *that* beautiful, Mark."

"To me you are. . . ." He paused, and added in a lower tone, "You're also very dangerous."

"*Dangerous!*" She gave him an odd look through narrowed green eyes and frowned at him. "I can't *imagine* what you mean!"

"I say *dangerous* because I could so easily become serious about you, Teddy."

She gaped at him, at a loss to know how to respond to this declaration. And then quite suddenly she admitted to herself that she felt exactly the same way about him. When she first met him she had been afraid of him—because she had sensed *his* danger to *her*, had understood her own vulnerability to him.

Mark had been studying her, and now he leaned across the table, put his hand over hers again. "I've never said that to anyone else, Theodora, you do believe me, don't you."

"Yes."

"Do you think . . . could *you* become serious about *me*, Teddy?"

"I could, Mark," she answered in a voice that was clear and firm and strong.

He squeezed her hand, thrilled at her response. "Come on, darling," he said, using this term of endearment for the first time. "I want to hold you in my arms and dance with you," and so saying he led her away from the table, her hand gripped in his.

The lights were very dim in the room as a whole, and on the dance floor they were virtually nonexistent, and so the atmosphere was highly conducive to romance, and perfect for young lovers caught up in the fears and dangers and tensions of war.

Mark took Teddy in his arms when the Carroll Gibbons orchestra began to play one of the most sentimental love songs of the time. As they moved slowly around the room to the music, holding each other tightly, Teddy sang the chorus softly, in a low voice that only Mark could hear: " 'I'll be seeing you in all the old familiar places that my mind and heart embraces all day through. In that small café, the park across the way, the children's carousel, the chestnut trees, the wishing well. I'll be seeing you in every lovely summer's day, in everything that's light and gay, I'll always think of you that way, I'll find you in the morning sun, and when the night is new, I'll be looking at the moon, but I'll be seeing you.' "

She did not know the verse, and so she hummed the rest of the number, now pressed so close to him she could feel the brass buttons of his uniform hard and sharp against her body. And she thought: I'm falling in love with him, I knew I was going to at the Pells'. And she had no regrets; she was filled with the most total kind of happiness she had ever known.

Mark glanced down at Teddy. Her face was upturned to his and he saw the radiant joy reflected on it, and he drew even closer, brought her head against his shoulder and kissed her hair tenderly. He would never forget this moment or this song for as long as he lived . . . he had just realized he had found the woman of his life.

He brushed his lips against her cheek without breaking the rhythm of their steps, and they danced around the floor once again.

And they went on dancing for the rest of the evening as if in a dream.

They walked along the Embankment in silence, holding hands.

It was a cold, clear night without a cloud and there was a full moon, and even though the wind blowing up from the Thames was sharp with frost, neither of them noticed.

Teddy was bundled up in her aunt's sheared-beaver coat, borrowed for the occasion, with a pink, lacy, mohair scarf covering her hair, and Mark wore his heavy RAF overcoat, peaked officer's cap and white silk flyer's scarf wrapped around his neck.

But they were both too preoccupied with themselves to be aware of such a mundane thing as the weather; they were oblivious to all else except each other and their emotions.

The stretch of the Embankment behind the Savoy Hotel, which they had just left, was as dark as pitch because of the blackout regulations; not a crack of light was visible from the hotel windows, and all the street lamps were doused for the same reason. But the bright moon lighted their way, and at one moment Mark lifted his eyes to the sky and said, "It's perfect weather for flying, Teddy. I'd love to be up there with you in my plane, taking you for a spin right now. It's so breathtaking on a night like this, awe-inspiring, really." As he spoke he looked down at her and caught his breath. Teddy was gazing up at him as raptly as she had been on the dance floor. In the moonlight her face was clearly illuminated, and once again he saw her adoring expression, recognized her enchantment with him shining forth from her eyes, and his heart missed a beat. He pulled her to him almost roughly, wrapped his arms around her and kissed her fully on the mouth.

She returned his kiss ardently, wanting this as much as he did, and she clung to him, and when they managed to let go of each other at last and drew apart, they were breathless, thrown off balance by the impact of their first real physical contact. They stared at each other wonderingly.

"Oh, Teddy, my darling . . ." he began, and then fell silent. It was his turn to be inexplicably tongue-tied, and he simply stood staring at her in the moonlight, marveling at her beauty and the feelings she aroused in him. But within seconds Mark drew her to him again and whispered against her hair, "You know, I've been wanting to kiss you all evening. In fact, ever since the first night I met you at the Pells', if you want the truth."

"And I've wanted you to kiss me," she answered without the slightest bit of guile, in her honest fashion.

This admission thrilled him, and unable to restrain himself, Mark began to kiss her even more passionately than before, his mouth warm, loving, seeking. And she responded with equal passion, wrapping her arms around his neck and parting her lips at last to let his insistent tongue slide in next to hers. He allowed it to rest there for a moment of quiet and profound intimacy, and then he began to caress her tongue with his own, slowly, languorously. With a sudden, swift movement he brought his hands up to her face and, cupping it, began to devour her mouth with a hunger that was surprising to him as well as to her.

She grew more inflamed, and an extraordinary heat suffused her entire body, settled in the pit of her stomach; she swayed slightly in his arms, overcome by strange new feelings and urgent desires and longings hitherto unknown to her.

For his part, Mark was slightly dizzy himself, and their passionate kissing was arousing him to such a degree his legs were shaking; he thought for a moment that they were going to buckle under him. He could hardly contain himself, and so he withdrew his mouth from hers reluctantly, and took a deep breath of the frosty air, endeavoring to calm his racing heart, his flaring sexual desire for her. In a short while he slackened his grip on her, released her from his embrace and said gently, "It's cold out here, and late, Theodora darling. I'd better get you home. Your aunt will be wondering where you are. And worrying."

"It's all right," she responded, touching his arm. "I am twenty-five, you know. I don't have to answer to my aunt."

"I know that," he said with a quirky smile, looking amused. He continued, "But I wouldn't want to find myself in her bad books. That wouldn't bode well for the future, now, would it?"

"No," she agreed, pleased by his words.

Mark now took charge, and purposefully so, tucked her arm through his, and falling into step they set off at a brisk pace, soon left the Embankment behind them and made their way up the Strand, all the while looking for a cab. They had reached the Nelson monument in Trafalgar Square before they found one, the only one in the vicinity, in fact.

"Belsize Park Gardens, number forty-three," Mark told the driver. They sat close to each other on the seat, holding hands tightly as the taxi rumbled on its way, making for north London.

Mark wanted to take her in his arms, to start kissing her

again, but he resisted the temptation, knowing that under the circumstances this would not lead anywhere, and that he would only end up feeling more frustrated than he already did. There was even a brief moment when he thought of telling the cabbie to turn around and drive to Farm Street in Mayfair, where his mews house was located, but he did not. With any other woman he would hardly have hesitated, and once there he would have had little or no compunction about seducing her. But he would not do that to Teddy. She was different. She was special. She was going to be his wife.

The streets were relatively empty of traffic, not only because of the hour—it was now one o'clock in the morning—but also because of petrol rationing, which kept motorists at home. In consequence, there were few vehicles on the road, and in a very short time they were pulling up outside her aunt's house and alighting together.

Mark took Teddy's arm and led her up the flight of steps. After she had inserted the key in the front door, he turned her to face him.

"Thanks, Teddy, for coming out with me. I had a grand time, and it's really meant a lot. More than I can ever say, darling."

"It's *I* who should be thanking *you*, Mark, and I do." She stood on tiptoe and kissed his cheek. "And this evening's meant a great deal to me, too."

"I'm so glad." He looked serious when he added, "There's something I've been wanting to ask you for the last couple of hours."

"What is it?"

"I want you to be my girl, Teddy. You will, won't you? I haven't misread your reaction to me, have I?"

"No, you haven't, and of course I'll be your girl." For always, she thought. For the rest of my life. But she did not voice these thoughts, just stood and smiled at him instead.

"Thank God I've found you!" he cried and swept her into his arms, kissed her on the lips and hugged her hard. When he let her go, he said, "I told you I have to have lunch with my parents tomorrow. But I'll ring you up before I go back to Biggin Hill."

"I'll be in all day, Mark, I'll wait for your call. Good night now."

"Good night, darling."

He ran lightly down the steps. Before he stepped into the waiting cab he turned to wave, and she waved back, and then she went into the house and closed the door behind her.

Teddy stood for a moment in the darkness of the hall, trying to catch her breath, to quiet her rapidly beating heart. She was reeling from the impact of him, still felt startled by the power of their physical attraction for each other. She had not realized she was capable of such intense passion, or that such strong and overwhelming feelings could even exist between a man and a woman.

29

AFTER HANGING UP THE SHEARED-BEAVER COAT IN THE hall closet, Teddy crept gingerly up the stairs, having no wish to disturb her aunt. But when she reached the landing at the top she smiled to herself. She might have known that Aunt Ketti would not go to sleep before she arrived home. Her aunt's bedroom door stood ajar and lamplight was streaming out onto the darkened landing. Teddy crossed the floor in several swift strides, popped her head around the door and exclaimed, "I'm home, Aunt Ketti! And you certainly didn't have to wait up for me!"

Ketti was propped against the snowy antique linen pillows in her large comfortable bed, holding a library book in her hands. She put this down and smiled at her niece. "Hello, Teddy dear, and I know I didn't, but I wasn't at all tired. In any case, I wanted to hear all about your evening. I also thought it would be nice if we had our usual cup of tea before going to sleep. We've never missed our little ritual yet, except when I've been in Brighton visiting Rachel."

"I'll run downstairs and make a pot immediately."

"Everything's ready for you in the kitchen, dear. All you have to do is boil the water."

"I'll be right back," Teddy said, and hurried off.

True to her word, she returned after only a few minutes, carrying the silver tea tray, which she placed carefully on the window seat. She poured two cups, passed one to her aunt and then sat down with her own cup in an easy chair nearby.

Ketti took a sip of the tea, put the cup and saucer on the bedside table, and gave Teddy a long and careful look. "Did you have a lovely time?" she asked at last. "Where did Mark take you?"

"To the Savoy Hotel, for dinner and dancing, and yes, I had a marvelous time."

Ketti studied her thoughtfully for a moment. "Mmmmm. Stars in your eyes, I see."

Teddy nodded, and all at once her face became serious, grave almost. "Yes, that's true, very much so, Aunt Ketti. Mark is absolutely wonderful—" She broke off, looking as thoughtful as her aunt, then confided, "I think I'm falling in love with him."

Ketti threw Teddy a penetrating glance, and clucked sharply under her breath. Her expression altered slightly; worry settled in her eyes. She said in a voice that had become rather fretful, "Teddy, Teddy, all this is going too *fast*, most assuredly it is. Yes, *far* too fast, in my opinion."

"No, it isn't! I know how I feel, and so does Mark!"

"I don't want you to get hurt."

"What do you mean?"

"You hardly know him! Why, Teddy dear, you only met him three days ago—"

"Mark will *never* hurt me, I'm sure of that!" Teddy exclaimed, cutting her aunt off. She rose, crossed to the bed and sat down on the edge of it. Clearing her throat, she went on more softly, in a gentler tone, "Well, there's one thing that should please you, at least."

"And what's that?"

"He's Jewish."

It was immediately obvious from Ketti's face that she was indeed delighted to hear this news, and her expression instantly changed for the better, and her eyes brightened. "Well, that's a blessing! When people are of the same religion it saves a lot of heartache in the end. Is he Orthodox or Reform?"

"Reform. However, I got the impression Mark isn't especially religious himself, although he did say his father was constantly worried that he might marry out of the faith."

"Don't tell me he's proposed to you already!" Ketti cried, sitting up straighter in the bed, her eyes flying open in surprise and alarm.

"No, of course not! Don't be so silly!" Teddy retorted, and shook her head, amazed that her aunt would even think such a thing. "We were simply telling each other about our lives," she continued, and then suddenly she began to laugh. "But just now, on the doorstep, he *did* ask me to be his girl. And I accepted."

"*Naturally.*" Ketti sipped her tea, replaced the cup in its saucer with a clatter and probed, "What else did Mark tell you about himself and his family?"

"He has a brother, Lionel, who's at Harrow, and he went there himself. He was just starting at Oxford when he joined the RAF at the beginning of the war. Oh, by the way, Mark is fourth-generation English, his great-great-grandfather came here from Odessa in the early 1800's."

"Russian, eh? And Ashkenazi! Good, very good." Ketti nodded to herself, looking pleased as she mulled this information over. "More than likely their original name was Lewenstein, before it got shortened and anglicized to Lewis. I have a friend, Riba Lewis, whose family also came from Odessa years ago. Goodness me, could it be that she's a relative of theirs? What does his father do? Did Mark mention that?"

"Yes, he did. They have a company called Lewis and Sons, which his father runs. They're diamond merchants in Hatton Gardens. And they have several other related businesses, including a jewelry shop in Regent Street—"

"Not Tannen and Graf!" Ketti interjected, giving her niece a swift glance. "Now, don't tell me that Mark comes from *that* family."

"Why yes, he does, Aunt Ketti. You've got a peculiar look on your face. Is something the matter?"

"Is something the matter, she asks me," Ketti muttered and sighed to herself. "Oh dear no, nothing's the matter. At least,

I don't believe it is. Tannen and Graf, eh? So, Mark is a grandson of old Isadore Tannen."

"Do you know his grandfather, Aunt Ketti? Tell me about
him, tell me more about the family," Teddy said.

"Ach, such a long *megillah* that is! But, since you ask, I'll
try, and I'll make it as brief as possible. Isadore Tannen used
to own Tannen and Graf, and *he* inherited it from *his* father,
who in turn got it from *his* father. Mark's mother, Isabelle, is
Isadore's only child, and the store is hers now, given to her by
her father, of course, some years ago. Isadore is a very old man.
Very old, yes, in his nineties, and the store has been run for
a long time by Isabelle's husband, Charles Lewis, who is
Mark's father. The Tannens were German Jews originally,
Tannenbaum was their actual name, shortened years ago to
Tannen—easier for the English to pronounce, and much more
English-sounding. But Isadore Tannen is what I term a *fancy*
Jew, extraordinarily rich, living in grand houses, full of preten-
sions, and one who likes to call the English aristocracy his *land-
sleit*," she finished, a hint of sarcasm echoing in her voice.

"And the Lewises? Do you know anything about them?"

"Now, there's a different kettle of fish. Intellectuals, think-
ers, musicians, painters, although I must add that they've always been rich, too, and a trifle fancy, like the Tannens. But
they've also been great philanthropists. As Mark told you, they
came from Russia a century ago, and some of them set themselves up as diamond merchants, which they had been in Russia. And other members became moneylenders and bankers;
still others went into the arts. They're a big family, with many
branches, if I remember correctly."

"I see . . . have you ever met Mark's parents?"

"Very briefly, at a charity event once. I will say this for Isabelle Lewis, she is a doer of good works, and has given millions
to deserving causes, mostly to do with children and the sick.
Her husband is equally philanthropic, like his father before
him."

"And how do you know so much about the Tannens and
the Lewises, Aunt Ketti?"

"We Jews in London *do* know a lot about each other," she
answered. "In a certain sense, it's a small community, and anyway, I suspect we all make it our business to know about each
other. But actually, if you want the real truth, my friend Riba

is related to Mark's family, and most of my knowledge about them comes from her, she's a second cousin of Mark's father. Riba is married to one of the Levines, and, in fact, I think you might have met her with me."

"I believe I have, Aunt Ketti. And isn't it a small world?" Ketti nodded.

There was a little pause, and then Teddy asked, "Why were you looking so strange a moment ago? Don't you like Mark's family?"

"What's to like or dislike, since I don't *know* them personally. I only know *of* them. Good heavens, my dear, they don't socialize with the likes of me."

"I'm not following you."

"They're very snobbish, they have their own little clique. And they're very anglicized," Ketti added.

"But so are you, Aunt Ketti! You've been here for thirty-odd years or more, and I can't think of anyone who's more English than you. You're a *real* Londoner."

"That's true, yes, but *I* wasn't born here, nor do I have English-born ancestors. Also, I come from a different echelon than they do. I'm sort of . . . well, middle-class, wouldn't you say? They're the upper crust. Why, one might say they're more English than the English."

"I've heard that before!"

Ketti lifted a brow. "Now it's my turn to say, What do you mean?"

"The German Jews were more German than the Germans."

"Sadly, yes."

A sudden thought occurred to Teddy and she exclaimed, "Do you think Mark's family might not consider me good enough for him? Is that what you're implying?"

"Certainly not! You come from a fine, highly educated family, with doctors and professors as your antecedents. You're good enough for anybody, as far as I'm concerned. Seemingly, Mark thinks the same thing."

Teddy smiled, "Yes, Aunt Ketti, I believe he does."

Ketti returned Teddy's smile. "And what have you told Mark about *your* life?"

"*Everything.*"

"Have you, now! And does he know about Maxim?"

"Of course he does!" Teddy looked at Ketti aghast. "Why wouldn't I tell him about Maxim?"

Ketti merely shrugged and did not answer.

Teddy continued, "Mark thinks I'm sending Maxim to *exactly* the right school, and he wants to meet him at Christmas, or before, if that's possible. And I know they're going to like each other very much. In fact, they're going to get on like a house on fire."

"I'm sure they will," Ketti soothed, fully aware that Teddy's voice had risen an octave. She now stifled a yawn, glanced at the carriage clock on the mantelpiece. "Good heavens, we *have* been talking, haven't we? It's turned two o'clock, already. Come, Teddy dear, give me a good-night kiss and let's go to sleep."

Teddy bent forward and embraced her aunt affectionately, and then she got up off the bed and gathered the teacups together. "I'll take these downstairs and rinse them before I go to bed."

Ketti nodded and leaned back against the pillows, and once Teddy had left and closed the door, she turned off the lamp and settled down for the night.

However, Ketti soon discovered she could not fall asleep. Her mind was suddenly alive with thoughts of the Tannens and the Lewises. She could not help wondering what their attitude would be if Mark became seriously involved with Teddy and wanted to marry her. She knew enough about them to understand that the two clans were ambitious and class-conscious, and had always set their sights high when it came to marrying off their young. They were the elite of English Jewry and prominent in society, and they were not likely to let anyone forget that.

A nice English Jewish boy she had wanted for her Theodora. One so high-born she had not quite bargained for.

As he had promised, Mark telephoned Teddy on Sunday, before he returned to the No. 32 Squadron at Biggin Hill. And he did so every day thereafter.

On the days he did not ring her she knew he was on a flying mission somewhere over Germany, and her heart was in her mouth until she heard his voice again. A responsible and devoted person by nature, Teddy was always concerned about the welfare of those she loved, and now she had another and special person's well-being to occupy her thoughts. Quite aside from their telephone calls, Teddy and Mark wrote to each other regularly, quickly got to know each other better, and drew closer and closer as the weeks sped by.

Unexpectedly, in late October, Mark managed to get a twenty-four-hour weekend pass, and rushed up to London. Since he wanted to see his parents and Teddy, and did not really have the time to do both, he decided on the most practical solution. He took the three of them to dinner at Claridge's on Saturday night.

As it turned out, Isabelle and Charles Lewis were just as enchanted by Teddy as was their smitten son. His mother appreciated her natural beauty and air of refinement, her obvious innocence and lack of sophistication. Isabelle Lewis decided that this young woman looked as if she would bear children well, and made up her mind about Theodora on the spot. It seemed to her that she would make her son an excellent wife—if it went that far.

As for Mark's father, he too was full of enthusiasm for Teddy. Like his wife, he thought she was lovely. This was a major consideration in his son's case, since he knew how necessary physical beauty was to Mark, who had always fallen for a pretty face. Charles was well aware, just from looking at her across the dinner table, that Teddy would satisfy Mark on every physical level. But what delighted him most was Teddy's wholesomeness. The other young women Mark had brought home in the past had always struck him as being racy, and had dripped with "war paint," as he termed cosmetics. Good in bed, no doubt, but unqualified disasters in the drawing room, he had always thought privately to himself. And, of course, Theodora Stein was Jewish, a fact that was of vital consideration to Charles Lewis. If his son was as serious about this girl as he appeared to be, then marriage would be the inevitable outcome of the relationship. And he could not have borne it if Mark had married out of the faith. So he gave Teddy his stamp of approval, albeit silently at this moment.

The minute she met Isabelle and Charles Lewis, Teddy knew that Mark's parents were not *quite* the way Aunt Ketti had painted them to be, when she had heard about the dinner earlier in the day. They did not seem to have any pretensions of grandeur, nor did they strike her as being snobs. Teddy thought they were a pleasant, charming couple who appeared to be fair-minded and not a bit judgmental, and they showed a warm interest in her. Furthermore, they put her at ease immediately.

And so the evening at Claridge's was a success, and the future looked bright for the young lovers.

Teddy could not wait for Maxim and Mark to be introduced, and luckily it happened that Mark's next weekend leave fell at the same time as half term at Colet Court, when Maxim was home from prep school.

The two were friends from the moment Mark walked into the back parlor at No. 43, looking so dashing in his RAF uniform, and shook Maxim's hand. Mark asked the boy if he would like to go for a spin in the MG, and perhaps to sail his boat on Whitestone Pond in Hampstead, and Maxim was thrilled.

All through that weekend, as Teddy watched them enjoying so many different things together, talking about football, cricket, flying, airplanes and sports cars, she came to understand how much Maxim must have missed a masculine influence in his life at home, with only her and Aunt Ketti for company. And momentarily she was sad, thinking once again about Sigmund Westheim. He and Ursula were rarely far from her thoughts, and she prayed every day for their safety and longed for the war to be over so that they could come at last to England.

On Sunday night, after Mark had gone back to his squadron, Teddy and Maxim had their supper together in the dining room. They were alone, since Aunt Ketti had gone to play cards with Sarah Levine, and at one moment he suddenly looked across at her and said, "Is Mark your sweetheart, Teddy?"

Coming out of the blue as it did, the question startled her, and for a second she was silent. And then she said, with a small smile, "I suppose you could call him that."

"Does that mean you're going to marry him?"

Giving Maxim a very direct look, she said carefully, "I don't know, darling, he hasn't asked me."

"But if he did ask?" Maxim insisted.

"I might."

There was a short pause, and then the boy asked so quietly she could hardly hear him, "What would happen to me?"

"Nothing would happen to you!" Teddy exclaimed, sitting up in her chair, frowning. "You'd be with me. And in any case, if I ever did decide to marry Mark, or anyone else for that matter, I certainly wouldn't do so until your parents were here. Surely you know that."

Maxim nodded. "You've always said we'd live together. You and me and Mutti and Papa. If you married Mark, I suppose you'd have to live with him, wouldn't you?"

"Yes. But we'd find a house or a flat very close to your parents', and I'd see you every day, and nothing would be very much different," she reassured him quickly, sensing his insecurity. She looked across at him, smiling, her love and devotion reflected in her eyes.

"I know," Maxim said, but nevertheless a glum expression settled on his face and he glanced down at his plate.

Teddy was now watching him closely, suddenly worried about him, wondering how to make him feel better, when he lifted his head and stared back at her. There was such bereftness in his eyes, such a stricken expression on his face, she sucked in her breath in concern and her chest tightened.

"Maxim, whatever is it? Don't you like Mark Lewis?"

"Yes," he muttered. "He's nice . . ."

"Well then, what is it, darling?"

His voice was very small and it quavered slightly when he said slowly, "What if Mutti and Papa don't come? What if . . . what if something's—" The boy broke off, unable to voice his fears about his parents, and he sat back in his chair, biting his lower lip, fighting the sudden rush of emotion filling his throat.

Teddy was alarmed by his words, and she immediately jumped up and went to sit in the chair next to his. She put an arm around him and held him close.

After a moment she said gently, "They're safe, Maxim. Try not to worry. And they *will* come to London, once the war ends and things get back to normal. But whatever happens, I want you to remember that I will always be here for you, and I'll look after you, until you're grown up if necessary. I've told you that many times before, now, haven't I?"

"Yes," he whispered against her shoulder, fighting back his incipient tears.

"You're *my boy*, don't forget, and I love you very much."

30

Maxim's half term was over a few days later, and he returned to Colet Court, and Teddy went back to her voluntary work at the local Red Cross office.

It seemed to her that after this the weeks rushed by, and almost before she could catch her breath Maxim was home again in December for the holidays. Christmas and the New Year were the best they had spent in years—they both agreed wholeheartedly on that. This was not only because Mark was present—he was with them for part of the festivities, and made a great fuss over Maxim and Teddy—but also because the news about the war grew better and better every day, and filled them with hope.

As January of 1945 turned into February, Allied troops were spreading out across the whole of Europe, and the entire country was betting that peace would come in the spring.

One day toward the end of April, as Teddy stood in the kitchen preparing breakfast for Aunt Ketti and herself, she could not help thinking about Stubby's father's prediction. It suddenly struck her that Mr. Trenton had been right in the end. All the British newspapers were saying that the collapse of Nazi Germany was only a matter of weeks away, and Arthur Trenton had constantly told her and the boys that they would be celebrating victory well before Maxim's eleventh birthday in June.

Teddy sighed to herself as she put the cups and saucers on the big wooden tray. There were times, like this morning, when she could hardly bear the waiting . . . her mind was forever focused on the Westheims. It had been a long time . . . six years since Paris, when Ursula had put them on the boat train to Victoria Station. How proud she and Sigmund would be of Maxim today. What a truly remarkable boy he had turned out to be. So brilliant at school, yet not at all vain or boastful about his scholastic achievements, and he was such a nice boy as well, and so normal. At Christmas, when Mark's mother had met him for the first time, she had said he was a little gentleman, and this had caused Teddy to fill with pleasure, and her pride in him knew no bounds. His parents would be surprised, of course, when they saw him. He had sprung up even more than ever in the last couple of years, and he was tall for his age: he looked older than he was.

Teddy heard the rattle of the letter box in the front hall, and she wondered if it was the post or the newspapers that had been pushed through. After carrying the tray of breakfast china into the dining room, she walked down the hall to the front door; the morning papers were on the floor, and she picked them up along with the post, which lay underneath.

The postman came early today, she thought, tucking the newspapers under her arm, and, shuffling through the envelopes, hoping to find a letter from Mark. Her face lit up at the sight of his handwriting, and, wasting no time, she hurried back to the kitchen, flung the newspapers and the mail down on the kitchen table and ripped open his letter. As always, it was loving and romantic, and full of plans for his next weekend leave, and for the future. She read it through twice, and still smiling, she slipped it into her pocket.

As she swung around, intending to fill the kettle for the tea, her eye caught the *Daily Express*, which lay front page up on the table, and the smile on her face congealed. She grabbed the paper, stood staring at the headlines and the photographs, her eyes widening with shock, her face freezing into rigid lines of horror.

Names of places leaped off the page at her. *Ohrdruf* . . . *Belsen* . . . *Buchenwald*. The most fearful words stabbed at her eyes. *Death camps* . . . *atrocities* . . . *inhumanity* . . . *extermination* . . . *Jews* . . . *millions murdered* . . . *genocide*.

She lowered her eyes to the pictures, which stunned and horrified her further, so graphic were they in the foul, inhuman story they told of the most unspeakable brutality and cruelty, a terrible testimony to the pitiless torture and mass murder of innocent people.

Teddy's hands began to shake, and she had to put the newspaper down on the table. She closed her eyes, not wanting to see or read anything else, but then she forced herself to open them at once. *She had to know more.*

She stood with her head bent over the table, her eyes scanning the photographs. Half-naked people, emaciated beyond recognition as human beings, were living skeletons, hollow-eyed and hairless, staring vacantly out from behind the barbed-wire fences of the camps. And yet more photographs . . . of gas ovens and torture chambers, of heaps and heaps of bodies dumped haphazardly like so much rubbish in mass graves, of experimental medical laboratories, and lampshades made of human skin, and mountainous piles of discarded false teeth and eyeglasses and shoes, and more bodies, and still more, of men and women and little children and even babies, all victims of the Nazi death machine.

Teddy brought her hands up to her mouth as the first sob broke from her throat. Scalding-hot tears fell down her face and splashed onto the newspaper, and she wrapped her arms around her body, rocking back and forth, crying out, "Oh God, no! Oh my God, no! It's not possible! It just can't be . . . it *can't* have happened!" But she knew it had.

She fell into a chair, her legs collapsing under her, and she doubled over in anguish, clapped one hand over her mouth once more, to again stifle the scream of pain and outrage rising in her throat.

After a while Teddy was able to calm herself sufficiently to reach for the other newspapers. She was fully aware that to read on would be harrowing, but it was imperative that she know everything there was to know.

The *Daily Mail* carried as many photographs as the *Express*, as did the *Daily Telegraph*, and the accounts she read in all three papers were virtually the same, reporting the ghastly and horrendous facts. British and American troops had entered camps in western and eastern Germany in the last few days, and what they had found there had been overwhelming in its indescribable horror. The first camp to be liberated was Ohr-druf, near Gotha, and there the Americans had discovered ditches filled to overflowing with four thousand bodies, including Jews, Russian prisoners of war and Polish slave laborers who had been systematically starved to death, or so neglected and denied medical treatment they had died of disease, or had been murdered. When the British entered Belsen they had been shocked and appalled by what they had found, and the Americans, who had liberated Buchenwald, had reacted in the same way, stunned by the scenes that had confronted them. General Bedell Smith, General Eisenhower's chief of staff, was quoted as saying that among the newly liberated camps Buchenwald was "the acme of atrocity."

Waves of nausea washed over Teddy; she swayed in the chair and thought for a moment that she was going to vomit, to be violently sick, but the feeling passed. She put the *Telegraph* on the table with the other papers, reeling from what she had read, her mind unable to absorb any more.

Teddy sat for a while at the kitchen table, staring blankly into space, but finally she roused herself, rose and put the kettle on, stood near the stove waiting for it to boil. She made the morning tea in the brown pot that Aunt Ketti preferred, put a cup and saucer and a small pitcher of milk on a tray, doing everything by rote. All she could think of were the horrifying reports in the papers.

Carrying the tray upstairs, she pushed open the door to her aunt's room and went inside. Light was filtering in through the blackout curtains. She glanced at the bed, wondering whether her aunt was awake, when Ketti said in her usual bright voice, "Good morning, Theodora. This *is* a treat, getting a cup of tea in bed."

"Good morning," Teddy replied quietly, hardly trusting her own voice, placing the tray on the window seat. She then drew back the curtains swiftly, and brilliant sunlight streamed into the bedroom, making her blink.

Teddy carried the cup of tea over to her aunt, who now sat propped up against the pillows.

"Thank you," Ketti said, and instantly noticed that Teddy's hand was shaking as she passed her the cup, and, glancing at her face, saw that it was white and drawn. "Teddy, you look awful, whatever is it? Is something wrong?"

Teddy could only nod.

"It's not Mark, is it? Nothing's happened to him, has it?" Ketti cried, sitting bolt upright with alarm.

"No, it's not Mark," Teddy said, and sat down heavily on the edge of the bed. Not knowing quite how to begin, she started in a roundabout way, saying slowly, "Aunt Ketti . . . that committee you're on, the refugee committee affiliated with the synagogue . . ."

"Yes, what about it?" Ketti asked with a puzzled frown.

"You've told me stories, horrendous stories, which came from some of the European refugees your committee has been trying to help."

Ketti nodded. "You're referring to the dreadful things they said happened in the concentration camps, aren't you?"

"Well, they're true. *Absolutely true*," Teddy whispered hoarsely. "And they're *not* concentration camps, they're *death* camps. The proof is in this morning's papers, proof for the whole world."

Ketti pulled back slightly, staring at her niece, finding it difficult to comprehend what she was saying. "I don't understand," she muttered, shaking her head from side to side.

Teddy explained. "In the past few days, British and American troops have started to enter those camps, to liberate them, and what they've found is so ghastly, so horrifying, it's beyond understanding. Unbelievable cruelty, and human degradation of such enormity it staggers the mind. Millions have been slaughtered. Jews, Russians, Poles, Slavs, and Gypsies, but mostly . . . Jews."

The cup and saucer Ketti was holding began to rattle in her hands, and Teddy leaned forward, took them from her, placed them on the bedside table before she spilled the tea all over herself.

"It doesn't seem possible," Ketti whispered, her skin turning the color of putty, her eyes wide and staring in her stark face. "They couldn't . . . they wouldn't *dare*—"

"They did!" Teddy said in a low, fierce voice. "The British newspapers are calling it genocide."

Later that day Ketti went looking all over the house for Teddy, concerned about her. She found her in Maxim's room, sitting in a chair, staring at the photographs of the Westheims on the chest of drawers. Teddy looked around as the door was pushed open, and Ketti knew that she had been weeping.

"Are you all right, my dear?" Ketti asked.

"Yes."

"Am I intruding?"

"No, come in."

Ketti did so, and sat down on the edge of the other chair. She was aware that Theodora was terrified for the Westheims, but she had been afraid to mention them thus far today. She still hesitated to do so even now, for fear of upsetting Teddy further.

Almost as if she knew what her aunt was thinking, Teddy said, "Ursula and Sigmund have been the focus of my thoughts ever since I read the newspapers, Aunt Ketti, as I'm sure you probably realize."

"I do, Teddy. You care for them deeply, so it's obvious you would be more worried than ever about them after . . . after what we've read."

"I haven't been able to get the newspaper photographs out of my head . . . those horrible images. Oh Aunt Ketti!" she cried, her voice anguished. "What if Sigmund and Ursula *did* end up in one of those monstrous places?" Her voice faltered and her eyes filled. "I'm in agony about them, and I don't seem able to think straight."

Ketti said, "I know it's hard, but you must be hopeful, positive. And you must remember that the last message you received from Arabella von Wittingen was very reassuring."

"But that was such a long time ago, several *years* now."

"Never mind." Ketti bent forward, and continued in her most reassuring voice, "The princess hasn't been in touch since then, I know that. On the other hand, maybe this only means that things are status quo. She told you then, when she telephoned from Switzerland, that the Westheims were staying with the von Tiegals at the Schloss Tiegal in the Mark Brandenburg, where they were safe. And you've said over and over again to me that they *would* definitely be safe there."

"Yes, and the von Tiegals could easily be hiding them. There are dozens of passages and dungeons underneath the castle, which is centuries old. I think there are even some secret rooms and corridors." Teddy looked across at her aunt and went on, "I don't doubt they're all right if they're at the schloss. But I can't help wondering if they remained there. This has always been my worry . . . that they left for some reason, and went back to Berlin. Once in the city, they could have been arrested and sent . . . to a camp, or they could have been killed in an Allied bombing raid."

"We've gone over this so many times before, Teddy dear, and I'm not trying to dismiss your concern or diminish your reasons for it. God only knows, you have good cause to worry about Ursula and Sigmund. But you must hold the thought that they are surviving, wherever they are, whatever their circumstances. If you don't, you'll drive yourself mad."

Teddy was silent.

Ketti said slowly, softly, "And Teddy dear, there's Maxim to think of, the boy needs you so very much."

"I'll never give up hope for them," Teddy said. "I will go on believing they are alive until I have proof . . . proof that they're not."

31

THE RED-WHITE-AND-BLUE UNION JACK HUNG OUT OF every window, fluttering in the breeze.

People danced in the streets, cheering and singing, laughing and crying; they hugged and kissed one another, friends and strangers alike, and were filled with jubilation, happiness and pride.

Brilliant light streamed out of windows no longer blacked out against enemy bombers, and bonfires blazed the length and breadth of the land and effigies of Hitler were devoured in their flames. And the pubs were filled to overflowing with the revelers, who toasted the boys in blue and khaki, and one another, and cried, "Long live Winston, he's brought us through!"

It was the night of Tuesday, May 8, and the whole of England was rejoicing. The day before, in the early hours of Monday, May 7, at 2:41 A.M. precisely, General Alfred Jodl, the representative of the German High Command, and Admiral

Hans von Friedeburg, empowered by Grand Admiral Karl Doenitz, the designated head of the German state, signed the act of unconditional surrender of all German land, sea and air forces in Europe to the Allied Expeditionary Force and simultaneously to the Soviet Union. The war with Germany was suddenly, and finally, at an end.

Great Britain was victorious, and the British were celebrating Victory Day in Europe. They had taken to the streets to do it, and what better place to share their joy with their ecstatic fellow citizens on this national holiday, which would forever after commemorate the destruction of the most evil regime in the history of the world.

Teddy and Aunt Ketti were among the thousands of people who stood near the House of Commons, waiting for the prime minister to make a speech. He had spoken to the nation on the wireless at three o'clock that afternoon, but the crowds still wanted to hear more from this British bulldog, their beloved Winnie, their great leader—possibly the greatest leader their country had ever known—who had brought them to a victory hard won and honorable.

The roar of the crowd and the cheering were overpowering, deafening, when he appeared on the balcony of one of the government buildings at ten-thirty that night, wearing his "siren" suit and giving his famous V-for-Victory sign with his right hand.

A sea of faces stretching for miles stared up at him. And as he began to speak Teddy and Ketti and the thousands swarming around them fell silent, and the most extraordinary hush of reverence and respect descended on the streets of Whitehall.

"*My dear friends,*" Winston Churchill began, "*this is your hour. This is not victory of a party or of any class. It's a victory of the great British nation as a whole. We were the first, in this ancient island, to draw the sword against tyranny. After a while we were left all alone against the most tremendous military power that has been seen. We were all alone for a whole year. There we stood, alone. Did anyone want to give in?*" Churchill paused and in answer to this question the crowd roared, "No!" "*Were we downhearted?*" the prime minister demanded. "No!" responded thousands in one voice.

The prime minister said, "*The lights went out and the bombs came down. But every man, woman and child in the country had no thought of quitting the struggle. London can take it. So we came back after long months from the jaws of death, out of the mouth of hell, while all the world wondered. When shall the reputation and faith of this generation of English men and women fail? I say that in the long years to come not only will the people of this island but of the world, wherever the bird of freedom chirps in human hearts, look back to what we've done and they will say, 'do not despair, do not yield to violence and tyranny, march straight forward and die if needs be—unconquered.' Now we have emerged from one deadly struggle—a terrible foe has been cast on the ground and awaits our judgment and our mercy."*

Teddy discovered that tears were streaming down her cheeks, and she fumbled with her handbag, to search for her handkerchief, then mopped her wet cheeks.

"Are you all right, my dear?" Ketti asked, taking Teddy's arm, peering into her face.

"I'm fine, Aunt Ketti." Teddy blew her nose and blinked back her tears. "Mr. Churchill always manages to move me with his words. He speaks such truths in his own very special way, and he's so reassuring and inspiring. There's no one like him."

Apparently the thousands in the streets listening now to the end of his speech agreed with her. As Winston Churchill finished speaking they began to shout and cheer, and they cheered him until they were hoarse, and then they started singing "For He's a Jolly Good Fellow" and "Land of Hope and Glory." Ketti and Teddy joined in, warbling like full-blown cockney sparrows. And it struck Teddy suddenly, as she sang, that this war had been punctuated by rousing Churchillian speeches and by singing, and that somehow his words and the popular songs had kept them going, had been their mainstay when the future looked bleak.

The prime minister waved and left the balcony, and slowly the crowds began to disperse and stream away, and the two women moved with them. It was growing late, and Teddy and Ketti had had a long and busy day, one that had been thrilling but also wearing. Near Victoria Station they managed to find a taxi and clambered in thankfully. They were glad to be by themselves at last, and away from the milling crowds.

Teddy glanced at her aunt, and despite the dim light in the

cab she noticed how worn-out she looked, and exclaimed, "Why, Aunt Ketti, you're absolutely exhausted!"

"I'm afraid I am a bit, aren't you?"

"Yes," Teddy admitted. "But it's been worth it, celebrating the downfall and defeat of the Nazis and the Third Reich."

It was Theodora's twenty-sixth birthday the following day, May 9, and that afternoon Aunt Ketti gave a small tea party for her, to which Ketti invited Teddy's dear friends Julia and Lydia Pell.

They came promptly at four, each carrying a prettily wrapped present, which Teddy opened, and, as always, she was touched by their thoughtfulness. From Mrs. Pell she received a hand-painted silk scarf in pretty tones of lilac, magenta and pink, and from Lydia a string of amethyst beads, which were quite beautiful. "You spoil me, and you're far too extravagant," Teddy said, kissing first Mrs. Pell and then Lydia. "Thank you both very much."

A short while later Aunt Ketti brought in the silver tea tray and the four women sat down around the Queen Anne tea table that was laden with a mixture of thin finger sandwiches, scones and an iced birthday cake boasting a single candle. They were halfway through the tea when the doorbell rang.

"Who on earth can that be?" Ketti asked, frowning. "We're not expecting anyone else, are we, Teddy?"

"No, I'll go and see who it is," she volunteered, springing up and hurrying down the corridor to the front door. She jerked it open to find Mark standing on the doorstep, much to her surprise.

"Happy birthday, darling!" he exclaimed, stepping inside the hall, hugging her, picking her up and swinging her around so that her feet left the ground.

"But you've already wished me that on the telephone," Teddy said, as he put her down on the floor at last and planted a kiss on her cheek.

"But I wanted to say it in person, and with this," he explained, presenting her with the package he was holding. He added, "It's a bottle of Dad's best pink champagne."

"Oh, how lovely of you, Mark, thank you. Come on, Aunt Ketti is with Lydia and Mrs. Pell in the drawing room, we're having tea. Perhaps you'd like a cup, and a piece of birthday cake?"

"No, thanks," he said, smiling, "I much prefer the champagne."

The others were equally surprised to see Mark when Teddy ushered him into the room, and after he had greeted them in his genial way, he set about opening the bottle. "It's cold enough to drink now," he assured Teddy as she took the champagne flutes out of the china cabinet. "My father always keeps a few bottles on ice for emergencies, and I bagged one from his cellar for this very special occasion." The cork in the Dom Pérignon popped like a gun going off, and some of the frothy wine rushed up and spilled out of the neck of the bottle. "Whoops!" he exclaimed, quickly pouring the champagne into the flutes, "I mustn't waste any of this precious stuff."

Mark lifted his glass and toasted Teddy, and so did everyone else, and they clinked glasses and sipped the wine, and then Mark put his flute down and turned to her. "May I speak to you alone for a moment?" he asked.

"Of course." Teddy threw him a swift glance, wondering if something was wrong. He sounded unusually serious, even grave.

They excused themselves, and Mark escorted her down the corridor, through the back parlor and out into the garden. Mark was aware that Teddy liked to sit under the old apple tree reading or sewing in the warm weather, and it was to this favorite spot that he now brought her, holding her hand in his.

He gazed down into her baffled face and said, "You know I love you, Teddy, that I want to marry you, and I know you love me. But you've never agreed to become engaged. You've said over and over again that you wanted to wait until the war was over. Well, it *is* over now. Please say *yes*, please become my fiancée today."

"Yes, I will, Mark," she said after the merest hesitation. Her sudden joy was muted by her nagging worry about the Westheims, but she did not allow this to show. She looked up into his adoring face and the smile she gave him was radiant.

He reached into the pocket of his flying jacket, took out a black leather box and handed it to her without a word. But his eyes were fastened on hers and he watched her closely.

Teddy slowly opened the box. A breathtaking square-cut

emerald ring with diamonds on either side was nestled in the folds of the white satin. "Oh Mark! It's *beautiful!*"

"As you are, my Teddy," he said, and then asked, "Do you really like it?"

"How could I not! It's magnificent!"

"Emerald is your birthstone, as well as the color of your eyes, and that's why I chose it. And happy birthday again, darling."

"Oh, Mark."

He took the ring out of the box and slipped it on the third finger of her left hand. "Now it's truly official," and so saying he swept her into his arms and kissed her on the mouth.

After a short while the two of them walked slowly up the garden path holding hands, and went back into the house to announce their engagement to Aunt Ketti and the Pells. Neither her aunt nor her friends seemed in the least surprised to hear this news. They congratulated them warmly, and Ketti said, "We've been expecting it, you know, for ages. And the three of us were only just saying that we've never seen anyone more in love than you two."

Everyone laughed at this comment, and the newly engaged couple thanked Ketti and the Pells for their good wishes, and another toast was made.

Mark immediately put his glass down after only a sip and said, "I have to go, Teddy. I've got to get back to Biggin Hill. My pass is for a few hours, that's all. Courtesy of a very romantic squadron leader, who agreed you should have your ring on your birthday. And who, by the way, insists on being present at the wedding."

Teddy said, "Then we must invite him."

Mark took his leave of Aunt Ketti and the Pells, and Teddy accompanied him to the front door, where she stood on tiptoe to kiss him good-bye.

When they drew apart, Mark murmured softly, "Let's set a date for the wedding."

Teddy's face instantly changed. "You know I can't, Mark! Not until I hear from the Westheims, find out when they're coming. I've always told you I couldn't get married without Maxim's parents being present."

"But it might be months before you hear anything from them! Things are a mess in Germany, there's nothing but chaos over there right now!"

"I understand that, Mark, but knowing Ursula Westheim, I'm quite certain she'll find a way to be in touch with me soon. Or someone else will be, on her behalf."

"All right," Mark said in a resigned voice. "We'll wait for a while before we get married." He smiled at her and Teddy smiled back and she did not notice the uncertainty in his eyes. Nor did she realize at this moment that she would wait in vain to hear from the Westheims. In the weeks that followed there was no news of them. And they did not come.

32

FINALLY TEDDY WENT BACK TO GERMANY TO FIND THE Westheims. She felt as though she were in an alien land.

She did not recognize the city where she had been born and had lived until she was almost twenty. There was nothing left standing to recognize. Berlin looked like a moonscape covered with deep craters and weirdly shaped mountains made of debris.

The city had been turned into a wasteland by Allied bombers, which had flattened five hundred thousand buildings, a third of those in the city, and in so doing had destroyed most of central Berlin. What had not been laid waste by Allied bombs had been demolished on May 2, when the city had fallen to Marshal Zhukov and the advancing Red Army. Ruthlessly the Russians had turned twenty-two thousand guns on what remained, a barrage of unprecedented intensity, and had thus reduced everything that had been left standing to rubble and dust.

Teddy was stupefied by what she saw. A voracious reader of international news, and especially news about Germany, she had followed the events of the past few months scrupulously. Nonetheless, she had not envisioned that the city would be as

ravaged as it was, or that it would have such an air of desolation
about it.

She returned at the beginning of October, traveling from
London to Berlin by train. The many arrangements for her
journey had been made with the help of Mark's father and Julia
Pell. Charles Lewis had made certain that all her papers were
in good order, and had insisted on paying for the trip, even
though she had not wanted him to do so. He had won the argument, and she had given in gracefully.

It was Lydia's mother who had found her accommodation
in Berlin. Julia Pell had arranged for her to stay with a woman
called Anne Reynolds, who held an important administrative
position with the International Red Cross, and had been a
friend of Julia's for over twenty years. Now a widow, Anne
Reynolds had lived in Germany with her husband before the
war, spoke fluent German and knew the country well. These
were just two of the many reasons she had been selected for
her high-powered job.

According to Julia Pell, Mrs. Reynolds had been sent to Berlin in July, when the British, American and French troops had
entered the city to join with the Russian army in the four-power
control of Berlin. She had been allocated a small apartment in
Charlottenburg, which was one of the areas in the British Zone,
and she had written back to Julia Pell to say that although her
quarters were not very large, Theodora was most certainly welcome to stay as long as she wished. In her letter she had added
that she constantly traveled around the British Zone of West
Germany on Red Cross business, and that it was more than
likely Teddy would have the place to herself most of the time.
And as it happened, this was the way it turned out.

After greeting her cordially when she arrived at the flat on
Sunday afternoon, Anne Reynolds apologetically explained
that she had to depart almost immediately for Frankfurt on an
assignment.

"I'm afraid I only have time for a cup of tea with you before
I leave," she said as they sat down together in the sitting room.

"That's all right, Mrs. Reynolds, I do understand," Teddy
said, taking to her at once. A tall, striking woman in her late
forties, with blond hair and a typical pink English complexion,
she had a friendly smile and an assertive yet sympathetic way
about her.

"Please make yourself comfortable, while I brew a pot," Anne Reynolds said, "and I'll be back in a moment." Then she changed her mind and said, "Now that I think of it, why don't you come to the kitchen with me, I'll show you where everything's kept, and we can chat at the same time."

"I'd like that, Mrs. Reynolds, and thank you so much for letting me stay here. It's very generous of you to take in a stranger like this," Teddy said, her gratitude very much apparent on her face.

Anne smiled at her, and as she led the way to the tiny kitchen, which was more like a large walk-in closet than a room, she remarked, "Julia Pell cares about you a great deal, thinks of you as another daughter. And since she's one of my oldest and dearest friends, I was delighted to be of help to someone who obviously means so much to her. Besides, there are no hotels left standing, so I don't know where else you would have found accommodation. The Kaiserhof, the Eden and the Adlon have been destroyed beyond recognition, and so have most of the smaller hotels. Rooms are at a premium." She sighed heavily, and added, "Most Berliners are living in cellars or are camping out in the ruins. The city's in a mess, and refugees are still pouring in daily."

"Where from?" Teddy asked.

"Everywhere really. Mostly they're returning Berliners who left during the war, but there are refugees coming in from other parts of Germany, who think they will be better off here." She shook her head and grimaced. "They're not, of course. Conditions are terrible, and I've never seen such overcrowding in my life."

Anne lit the gas under the kettle and told Teddy, "We have our work cut out for us, I don't mind telling you. Almost all of the hospitals are gone, blown apart in the bombing raids, and those that are left are very badly damaged. There's also a shortage of medicines, food and fuel. The hospitals are full—jammed, actually—and tuberculosis, typhoid and diphtheria are the cause of most deaths." Anne paused and asked matter-of-factly, "By the way, you *were* immunized for the last two, weren't you? I told Julia you *must* be."

"Yes, I was," Teddy replied.

She thought of Ursula and Sigmund, and wondered where they were, if they were among the refugees streaming back into

Berlin. She was about to mention them to Anne Reynolds, then
changed her mind, deciding to do this later when they sat down
for their cup of tea.

"Disease is rampant in the city, Theodora," Anne informed
her. "You could say it's in the very air we breathe, since there
are still thousands of dead bodies that have not yet been buried."

"My God, that's appalling!" Teddy cried, both flabbergasted
and horrified. "Where are they?"

"In the rivers, under the piles of rubble, and lying in very
shallow graves in gardens. Not conducive to a healthy atmosphere at all. And, of course, there are rats everywhere."

Teddy shuddered and her skin crawled at the thought of the
vermin. "It must be horrible out there in the streets."

"I'm afraid it's really quite ghastly," Anne answered. She
shook her head sadly. "We have an immense task, but we do
try to do our best. For everyone."

"I know from working with the Red Cross in London how
extraordinary the international division is," Teddy said. "I
don't know what the world would do if our organization didn't
exist. I'm so proud to be associated with it."

"So am I," Anne murmured, and began putting cups, saucers and a small bowl of powdered milk on a tray. Once she
had done this, she opened two cupboards, turned to Teddy and
explained, "Here are utensils, china, that sort of thing. In here
are basic staples, and food. There's plenty of that, mostly tinned
stuff, though, such as corned beef, Spam and soup."

She opened another cupboard and went on, "There are a few
luxuries here . . . tinned fruit, sugar and chocolate biscuits,
courtesy of the PX and a friend of mine who's a major in the
American army. He very kindly keeps me supplied, and on a
regular basis, so do feel free to use whatever you wish."

"Thank you, Mrs. Reynolds," Teddy murmured. "You're
being extremely kind and I'm very appreciative." It struck her
now that she would have been floundering in Berlin without
the help of Anne Reynolds, and she could not help thinking
how lucky she was to have friends like the Pells, and a future
father-in-law as caring as Charles Lewis. Between them they
had made her personal search for the Westheims possible, and
certainly easier than it would have been otherwise.

*   *   *

Later, as they were drinking their tea in the little sitting room, Teddy was about to bring up the subject of the Westheims when her friendly hostess began to enlighten her about everyday living in Berlin. Teddy had no alternative but to bide her time.

"After Germany capitulated to the Allies, the Russians soon got certain services working again," Anne explained. "Such as gas and electricity. Plus the underground, trams and trains, so we're able to get around the city. There are also a few ramshackle old taxis, but not many, because of the petrol shortage. But stay in the British Zone," she cautioned, "don't wander into the Russian Zone by mistake, it's dangerous, there's still a lot of rape going on."

"I understand."

"The telephone service isn't what it should be yet," Anne added with a wry smile. "Sometimes it works, sometimes it doesn't. If you want to call your aunt later, to let her know you've arrived safely, you could give it a try. I can't guarantee that you'd get through, though."

"That's very kind of you, and I will attempt to call Aunt Ketti tonight, if you don't mind," Teddy said, "and I insist on paying for any calls I make."

"Don't be silly," Anne murmured dismissively.

Teddy now said, "You haven't mentioned the Westheims, so I assume the International Red Cross hasn't turned up anything regarding their whereabouts yet. Or come across any other information about them."

Anne shook her head. "No, I'm afraid not, I would have told you the moment you walked in if I'd had any news."

Teddy bit her lip tensely, looking troubled.

"Try not to be downhearted," Anne said gently, softening her rather efficient manner. "Even though there is no information so far, in actuality this doesn't mean very much. Things are terribly chaotic, as I've already explained. Millions of displaced people are on the move in Europe—ten million, to be precise. Records have been destroyed, either in the bombing raids or by the Nazis when they realized defeat was upon them. Then again, many of the agencies that might be able to help you locate them are understaffed. It truly is a herculean task, trying to trace missing people, so it may take a while. But you will find them, I feel sure of that."

Teddy nodded, praying that Mrs. Reynolds was correct in

her assumption that she would succeed in what she had come here to do.

Anne gave her another reassuring glance, then motioned to the desk near the window. "I've written down the names and addresses of the agencies you must visit tomorrow, as well as my office number. Elizabeth Jefford, my secretary, is efficient, knows her way around the British and American zones very well, so don't hesitate to call her if you need any kind of help. And there's a set of keys to the flat on the desk alongside the pad."

"Thank you, Mrs. Reynolds, thank you for everything."

"Thanks are not necessary," Anne said, "I'm happy to be of some help. As a matter of fact, I wanted to tell—"

"There's one other thing," Teddy said, swiftly cutting in. She leaned forward urgently and rushed on, "If I don't have any success with the agencies here in Berlin, I would like to go to the Schloss Tiegal in the Mark Brandenburg. I realize it's in the Russian Zone, but perhaps I—"

Now it was Anne's turn to interrupt. "You don't have to go there, Theodora," she said. "I was about to tell you that Julia wrote to me some weeks ago, explained that the Westheims were staying at the schloss when you last had news of them. And so I asked my American friend Major Evans to have the schloss checked out. Fortunately he was able to do so, managed to cut through the usual Russian red tape. He discovered that the schloss hadn't been damaged in the war, even though Potsdam and Brandenburg had been badly bombed."

"That's wonderful news!" Teddy cried, her eyes instantly brightening.

"Yes, it is. Since the schloss wasn't bombed, we know the Westheims couldn't possibly have been killed in a raid there. However, the schloss is uninhabited, deserted except for a caretaker who was put in by the Russians. They have requisitioned it, and I understand from Major Evans that they are going to turn it into a barracks."

"And this caretaker had no information?" Teddy asked quickly, fixing her intent gaze on Anne.

"None. Apparently all he said was that everyone had gone away."

"It seems as if the Westheims have disappeared without a

trace, doesn't it?" Teddy muttered glumly, her excitement of a moment ago completely evaporating.

"Yes, that's true," Anne agreed. "On the other hand, there is no reason yet to believe they're dead."

Anne now rose and went out into the foyer, where she took her overcoat from the closet. Slipping into it, she said, "I'm afraid I really must leave for Frankfurt. Keep your spirits up, and try not to fret, Theodora. And don't forget, my secretary is there if you need anything, she'll do her best to help you. I'll see you at the end of the week."

"Good-bye, Mrs. Reynolds, have a safe trip," Teddy said.

The following morning Teddy left the flat in Charlottenburg early, and took the underground to the Bahnhof Zoo, which was the station closest to the Tiergartenstrasse.

It did not take her long to arrive at her destination, and after alighting from the train she walked up the Budapesterstrasse and into the Stülerstrasse, heading in the direction of the Tiergarten, the lovely old park that she had so often frequented with Maxim and Ursula.

Teddy hurried along at a brisk pace on this misty and drizzly October day, glancing from side to side, struck with dismay when she saw the devastation all around her. She wondered whether there was any point in going to see if there was anything left of the Westheim mansion. No buildings were standing on these two streets, so why should the Tiergartenstrasse be any different? she asked herself. Berlin was a ruined city. She had seen that with her own eyes yesterday, and Mrs. Reynolds's descriptions had only confirmed that *everything* had been blown to smithereens.

Drawing closer to the Tiergarten, she came to a sudden stop, and could not help gasping in astonishment. She was astounded by what she saw. Not a single tree was left standing, and the denuded park looked barren and desolate under the curdled gray sky.

After a moment, Teddy became aware of a curious chip-chip-chipping noise that sounded like metal hitting stone, and she turned around, wondering what it was.

A few yards away a woman was working among the piles of rubble littering a stretch of ground where there had once been a house. The woman was hacking at a brick with a broken chisel, removing ancient plaster from around its edges. And then she placed the brick into an improvised wheelbarrow made from a pair of small wheels and an old wooden box strung together with string and bits of wire.

Teddy walked over to the woman and addressed her politely. "*Bitte* . . . what happened to the trees in the park? *Please*, can you tell me why the park is so ruined?"

The woman glanced at Teddy, looked her up and down with wary eyes, not responding at first. Then she said in a clipped, harsh tone, "You must be a stranger to Berlin to ask a question like that."

"Yes, I am. The trees in the Tiergarten," Teddy repeated. "What happened to them?"

"They were cut down," the woman said flatly. "For firewood. The Berliners needed to keep warm during the war. There was no other fuel."

"Yes, I see, I understand," Teddy said. "*Danke* . . . thank you very much." She inclined her head and walked away rapidly, conscious of the woman's hostility.

Within a few seconds Teddy was at the center of the Tiergartenstrasse, where the Westheims' beautiful mansion had been. Her steps slowed and she stood gazing across the dirt and the mud and the puddles to the pile of rubble it had become.

Memories rushed at her, bright and sharp and in focus, and for a fleeting moment she was carried back in time to the old days, and she thought of the happy hours she had spent in that house with Maxim and his parents.

And she saw them then in her mind's eye.

Ursula, so lovely in her blond freshness, and refined and elegant, moving about the house and the garden with such grace; and Sigmund, so handsome, kind and gentlemanly, sitting at the piano in the music room, playing his beautiful music. And Maxim running to them, calling their names, his young face shining with adoration for them. The memories were bittersweet, for she was caught between the past as it had once been and the present as it was in all its pain and ugliness. She felt a strangling sensation in her throat, and tears pricked behind her lids, but she blinked them away at once.

It was ridiculous to think about that house. It had only been bricks and mortar, and therefore of small consequence. What truly mattered were the couple who had owned it and had made it into such a wonderfully loving and happy home for their child. And also for her.

Teddy turned away, filled with sadness. She slowly retraced her steps down the Tiergartenstrasse and swung off it at the intersection between the Hofjägerallee and the Stülerstrasse, making for the Lützowufer, where the von Tiegals had lived, in an apartment overlooking the Landwehrkanal—and Willy Herzog's home had been close by as well.

But before she even reached the Lützowufer she saw that this area was another blighted wasteland, and so she turned and walked back to the Bahnhof Zoo station. There was nothing for her here.

I cannot linger in the past, she thought, or dwell on the memories. The present is the only thing that counts now. My objective in Berlin is to find the Westheims, and that is what I must do.

Teddy held this thought for the rest of the day as she visited the various agencies on Anne Reynolds's list. These included several Jewish refugee groups and Zionist organizations dealing with missing persons, and also the Society of Friends, run by the American Quakers, who were doing relief and reconstruction work in the war-torn city. Everyone she met was as helpful as they could possibly be. Each agency gave her long lists of names of those who had been sent to camps or deported by the Nazis or who had been reported as dead. The Westheims were not on any of them.

"Don't give up hope," the American woman at the office of the Society of Friends said. "And check all the agencies daily, since new names are constantly being added."

Teddy thanked the helpful Quaker and returned to the flat in Charlottenburg. She made a light supper and then went to bed, determined to start her search again tomorrow.

33

≡

*I*T DREW HER BACK LIKE A MAGNET, THAT AREA OF THE
Tiergarten and its environs, where so much of her life had been
spent in the past.

After her first visit, on that drizzly Monday morning, she
had returned several times, enticed by a place she found irresistible because it was both familiar and loaded with poignant
memories. But on each occasion she had found nothing worthwhile, and certainly nothing that would help her in her search
for the Westheims. And she had always come away from there
brimming with frustration and heightened anxiety, vowing
never to return.

But one Saturday afternoon, two weeks after she arrived in
Berlin, Teddy took herself off to the Tiergartenstrasse yet
again. The difference was that today she had a purpose, a real
reason for being there. Elizabeth Jefford, Mrs. Reynolds's secretary, had suggested to Teddy that she talk to the *Trümmerfrauen*, the rubble women, who worked the city in groups,
cleaning up the debris and collecting the bricks that could be
used again, once the rebuilding of Berlin commenced.

Elizabeth had explained to her on the telephone the previous
night that the *Trümmerfrauen* had developed their own intricate networks, had their own grapevines, and thus were extraordinary sources of information about everything—from the
black market to missing people. The women apparently worked
in and around the streets where they had previously had homes,
and where most of them still lived in makeshift quarters. Elizabeth had pointed out to Teddy that perhaps one of them might
have seen something or met someone or heard gossip that could
be useful to her in her search for Ursula and Sigmund.

And so she had come here again. *Just one more time*, she

had said to herself a short while ago, as she had taken the underground train that had brought her to the Bahnhof Zoo station. Now she walked along the Tiergartenstrasse at a slow pace, all the while glancing around alertly.

It did not take her very long to realize that there were no women working the rubble today. Her disappointment was so acute she suddenly understood how high her anticipation had been since her conversation with Elizabeth last night.

Just as Teddy was giving up hope of finding any of the *Trümmerfrauen*, she spotted three of them standing near a pit on a piece of land that had been partially cleared of rubble. They were talking among themselves and sharing a cigarette.

Teddy came to a stop a short distance away and stood watching them with interest for a few seconds. Each woman took several deep drags of the cigarette, then handed it to the next one, and Teddy saw at once how much they were enjoying this little luxury, making the most of it.

Elizabeth had warned her not to go empty-handed. And so in her bag were a pack of Lucky Strikes and three chocolate bars from the special cupboard in the flat, gifts Mrs. Reynolds had undoubtedly received from her boyfriend, the American major. Mrs. Reynolds was in Bonn with him this weekend, and Elizabeth had told her to take the items with her today, assuring her that Mrs. Reynolds would not mind. Teddy was now very glad she had listened to her, that she had this extremely precious supply on hand. A bribe of cigarettes or chocolate would surely help to loosen tongues, which otherwise might remain still.

The women stopped talking when Teddy approached, and turned to look at her. Their faces were closed and inscrutable, their eyes cold, and she remembered the blatant hostility of the only other rubble woman she had spoken to when she had asked about the lack of trees in the Tiergarten. She hoped these three would be a little more friendly.

"Please . . . can you help me," Teddy said.

The women simply stared at her, made no response.

She began again. "*Bitte* . . . I'm looking for some friends, or information about them . . . a couple I used to know before the war. They lived along there—" Teddy paused, and pointed down the Tiergartenstrasse. "In one of the big houses, one of the grand houses. Herr Sigmund Westheim, Frau Ursula Westheim. They had a small son, a lovely boy called Maximilian."

Three pairs of eyes bored into her. Not one pair blinked, nor did a single eyelash flicker.

Teddy focused on the woman nearest to her. "Perhaps you knew the Westheims?"

"*Nein.*"

"Did *you* know them?" Teddy said to the woman in the center of the trio who was at that moment drawing on the cigarette. The woman exhaled, shook her head. "*Nein.*"

Teddy decided there was not much point in asking the third woman. These *Trümmerfrauen* were obviously not going to be of any help to her. At least, not without a little encouragement. She opened her bag, took out the pack of Lucky Strikes.

"*Zigarette?*" Teddy asked, offering the pack around. Each of them took one, said "*Danke*"—but only thanks, nothing more—and carefully stowed the cigarette in a pocket.

"*I must find these people,*" Teddy began again, and more emphatically, hoping for success this time. "If you know anything at all, or have heard anything about them, please tell me. *Please.*" She let her intense gaze rest on each woman individually, and her eyes were full of entreaty.

There was a long moment of silence, and at last one of the women spoke. She said, "That mansion was bombed like all of them on this street, you can see that for yourself. No one survived."

"Some people who lived on the Tiergartenstrasse *did* survive," one of the women swiftly contradicted, and then she volunteered, "There's a rubble woman who works on the Lützowufer. She knew lots of people in this area before the war. Go and talk to her."

"I will!" Teddy exclaimed, her face lighting up. "Who is she? What's her name? How will I recognize her?"

"I don't know who she is, or her name. I've only heard about her," the friendliest of the three now said. "Ask around, one of the other *Trümmerfrauen* will point her out."

"Thank you! Thank you so much!" Teddy cried. "You've been most helpful."

Buoyed by renewed hope, Teddy set off at a rapid pace, and by the time she reached the bridge that led over the Landwehrkanal into the Lützowufer she was almost running. Finally, she came to a halt, and stood catching her breath, looking up and down the street. To her dismay, and further disappointment, it was even more deserted than the Tiergartenstrasse. And it was eerily silent.

Because there was little or no traffic in the Berlin streets these days, human voices were clearly audible, as were footsteps. But these sounds were strangely and most noticeably absent this afternoon. So was the constant chip-chip-chipping noise made by the countless *Trümmerfrauen* cleaning up the bricks and stones they were salvaging.

Teddy exhaled heavily, wondering where the rubble women were; Elizabeth had assured her they worked seven days a week. Since she was here, she decided she might as well investigate the area further, and she set off again, shivering slightly and huddling into her topcoat. A chill wind was blowing across from the Landwehrkanal, and within seconds she understood why the street was deserted. The wind was whipping the dust from the rubble up into the air. It swirled around her, settling in her hair, on her cheeks and her lips, and she blinked rapidly as it got into her eyes.

There's no point walking through *this*, she thought, it's like a sandstorm. I might as well return to the flat in Charlottenburg. And so she turned around and hurried down the Lützowufer the way she had just come, heading for the bridge. She suddenly wished she had not bothered to make this little excursion after all. It had only been a wild-goose chase like the others.

The silence was suddenly broken by a child's piping voice ringing out clearly across the rubble. "Here, Grandfather! Here's another one!"

Teddy stopped, looking around, listening acutely.

There was no one in sight.

Then there was a burst of harsh coughing, and after a moment an old man's raspy voice said, "We have a good pile of tiles, Wilhelm. We have done very well today."

"*Ja, ja!*" the child responded, and he sounded excited.

Teddy had no way of knowing where these disembodied voices were coming from, but they had sounded quite close. She hesitated, wondering exactly where to begin looking for the old man and the boy in this rubble, when she heard the old man's coughing again. It came from a small mountain of debris a little way ahead of her, and to the right. She guessed the old man and the boy were working behind it.

Leaving the path, Teddy ventured into the rubble-strewn wasteland, and picked her way across the messy ground until she arrived at the mound. She walked around it to the other side, and stepped forward. "Excuse me," she said.

The old man and the boy were startled by her sudden appearance as if from nowhere; it was obvious that they had not heard her approaching.

They gaped at her, and the old man said quickly, in an aggressive and hostile voice, "Who are you? What do you want?"

Teddy detected a certain amount of fear behind the hostility, and wanting to put him at ease, she said mildly, "I am a stranger from another city. I am looking for one of the rubble women who works here on the Lützowufer."

"*Why?*" the old man asked.

"The *Trümmerfrauen* on the Tiergartenstrasse said she might be able to help me."

The old man laughed with some coldness. "How could a poor rubble woman help *you?*" he asked scathingly, his eyes running over her, swiftly assessing her, taking in her well-fed appearance, her cleanliness and her good clothes.

"She might be able to give me information about certain people who once lived here," Teddy explained in the same soft tone. "I am looking for these people. The woman I seek . . . well, I understand that she knew everyone there was to know in this district before the war."

"Maybe she did," the old man snapped. "I don't know. Nor do I know which rubble woman you mean. *Many* work this street, you can see what a mess it is. And they are not here today. You can also *see* that for yourself, you're not blind. *Go away!*"

"Will the women be here tomorrow?" Teddy asked patiently, and with her usual persistence.

"How do I know! I am not their keeper!" the old man angrily muttered, and dropped his eyes, began to fiddle with the stack of chipped white tiles in front of him, which he and the boy had obviously been diligently collecting.

The boy had been listening attentively and closely watching Teddy during this conversation. He said plaintively, "*Bitte* . . . do you have something to eat? I'm hungry." He put his hand out to her in a begging gesture, his expression pleading, and said again, "*Please*, do you have anything?"

Teddy looked back at him. His dark eyes were sunken hollows in his little white face, and she could not help thinking of Maxim. But this boy was not as healthy; he was small and thin and undernourished. Starving most probably, she thought. She put his age at about seven or eight, but his eyes were much older and knowing and very weary.

She opened her bag, took out a bar of chocolate and handed it to the boy without saying a word.

"*Danke!*" he cried excitedly, ripping off the silver paper and pushing the chocolate into his mouth wolfishly with both hands. Only then did Teddy truly understand how ravenous he was.

But after only a mouthful the boy called Wilhelm suddenly stopped eating and looked at his grandfather. He took the chocolate bar out of his mouth, broke it in two and gave half to the old man. "Here, Grandfather, you are also hungry," the boy said.

"*Danke*, Wilhelm." The old man smiled at his grandson, took the chocolate and began to munch on it.

Teddy stood watching them devour the chocolate. She had mixed feelings about the Germans these days. Her eyes came to rest on the old man and she thought: Where were *you* on *Kristallnacht*? I wonder. Where were you when they were shoving my people into the gas ovens and the torture chambers and onto the deportation trains? And what would you say now if I asked you these questions? Would you deny having been a Nazi? Would you protest that you had not known about the terrible things they did to the Jews? *But you all knew.* You and every other German were aware the camps existed. Not a single German alive today can deny that. And what would you do if you knew *I* was a *Jew*? Would you continue to eat my chocolate? *Eat* the chocolate of a dirty *Jew*?

Teddy curbed these thoughts immediately, before they got out of hand and made her angry, as they generally did once they were ignited. After all, not every German had been a Nazi, and the average person had been powerless, unequipped to do anything against Hitler and his band of thugs. Nor had anyone understood or guessed how far these criminals would go in their persecution of the Jews. No one had anticipated the massacre of millions. To everyone, Jew and Gentile alike, the systematic killing of an entire people had been unthinkable, had seemed downright impossible.

Shifting her gaze to the little boy, Teddy also reminded herself that one should not punish the children for the sins of the fathers. Opening her handbag, she brought out the other two bars of chocolate and gave one to the boy, one to the grandfather. They both seemed startled and surprised by her generosity, although happily so, and they smiled at her and thanked her profusely.

And then the old man suddenly bowed to her in the most elaborate way, and said in a gruff voice, "The *Trümmerfrauen* take their bricks to the storage place every Saturday afternoon. That is why they are not here, they get paid today. But they should be back again tomorrow." There was a little pause and he finished with a thin smile, "You see, they have nowhere else to go."

"Come tomorrow," the boy Wilhelm said with a huge grin, showing her his chocolate-covered teeth.

Teddy smiled at him. "Yes, I will," she answered, and then turning to the old man, she added, "*Danke*."

"And we thank you, *gnädige Frau*," the old man said with great politeness and bowed again.

There was only one rubble woman working on the Lützowufer when Teddy returned the following morning. Deciding to get straight to the point, Teddy walked over to her purposefully and said, "*Guten Morgen*."

The woman was standing near an old pram, piling bricks into it. She glanced up and looked at her, and then smiled, much to Teddy's amazement and considerable relief.

"*Guten Morgen*," the rubble woman said, returning her greeting graciously.

Encouraged by the woman's pleasantness and approachability, Teddy went on, "I am hoping you might be able to help me."

"I will be happy to if I can," the woman replied with the same courtesy as before.

Teddy said, "Yesterday I was talking to the *Trümmerfrauen* on the Tiergartenstrasse, asking them for information about people who used to live on that street. They told me to look for a woman who worked the Lützowufer, who may well have been acquainted with them, and who might know where they are now."

"I certainly know all the women who clear the rubble in this vicinity. What is her name, the one for whom you are looking?"

Teddy shrugged and said, "That's just the problem, I don't know her name. . . ." Her voice trailed off lamely as she realized how ridiculous she sounded.

The woman was again bending over the decrepit pram, covering the bricks with a piece of torn linoleum. She straightened up, threw her shoulders back and tossed her head slightly, and gazed at Teddy, focusing vivid blue eyes on her. "Then I'm afraid I cannot be of help," the woman murmured.

To Teddy there was something strangely familiar about the voice, the sudden gesture of the head, and she gave the rubble woman a penetrating stare, swiftly noting everything about her as a distant memory stirred.

Like the other *Trümmerfrauen*, this woman had covered her hair with a scarf, had wrapped it turban style around her head, and she wore an assortment of odd clothes. And yet despite her worn, patched coat and the man's boots on her feet, she had a distinct air of breeding about her, a certain dignity that commanded attention, and also the good manners, the pleasant demeanor.

It came together in a flash all of a sudden, clicked into place in Teddy's mind, and she had to stifle a small cry of recognition. Her heart tightened and she held herself perfectly still, hardly daring to breathe, and she said slowly, "Actually, *gnädige Frau*, I think *you* are the person I am looking for."

The rubble woman frowned and arched a brow. "I?" she said. "Oh, no, I don't think so. I'm sure not, in fact."

Teddy was now absolutely certain who she was and said, "Yes, I *do* know you. And *you* know *me*. I am Theodora Stein, Maxim's nanny!"

The rubble woman was flabbergasted and for a moment she could not speak, and then she gasped, "Is it *you*, Teddy? Is it *really* you?"

"Yes, it's me!" Teddy cried, and, stepping forward, took hold of the chapped, work-worn hands of Ursula's friend Princess Irina Troubetzkoy.

34

TEDDY AND THE RUSSIAN PRINCESS STOOD CLASPING hands and staring at each other incredulously. They were hardly able to contain their excitement; their delight and amazement at finding each other in the devastated and war-torn city was reflected on their faces.

After a moment the princess took a sudden step forward, put her arms around Teddy and embraced her and the two women clung together in the midst of the debris on the ruined Lützo-wufer.

When at last they drew apart the princess exclaimed, "*Maxim*. How is he? Is he all right? He must be quite grown up by now."

"Yes, he is," Teddy answered. "He's the most wonderful boy, and a brilliant student, and he's at a good school in England." Teddy stared hard at the princess, and, clearing her throat, said in a voice that sounded suddenly strained, "I came to Berlin as soon as I could, to look for his parents. Do you know what happened to them?"

The smile on Princess Irina's face faded and she shook her head rapidly.

"When was the last time *you* saw them, Princess Irina?"

"In September of 1941, when they were staying with the Graf and Gräfin von Tiegal at the schloss near Brandenburg," Irina replied. "This was just prior to my falling ill with bronchitis. When I recovered, and was finally able to leave my bed, I discovered they had disappeared."

"Had they gone into hiding somewhere? Or had they simply left the schloss?"

"I honestly don't know. It was . . . well, it was a mystery."

"Didn't the von Tiegals know anything, Princess?"

Again Irina Troubetzkoy shook her head, and her face showed overwhelming sadness. "They had also vanished—as if into thin air."

Teddy met Irina's steady gaze with alert and questioning eyes. "Did they vanish at the same time as the Westheims? Or later?" she probed.

"Actually, I am not certain. All I know is that the four of them were not at the schloss in November of 1941, which was when I went there hoping to see them again."

"But surely the von Tiegals' servants knew *something*. There were quite a few servants, as I recall, and Gretchen had a nanny, Irmgard was her name."

"Yes, I know," Princess Irina replied, leaning closer, giving Teddy a very direct look. "But by 1941 all of the male servants who had been employed at the schloss had gone off to fight the war, and the maids were in the munitions factories, or doing other war work. There was only an old housekeeper left when I went to the schloss that day in November. She told me the Graf and Gräfin had returned to Berlin some days before, that I would find them at their flat—the flat *here* on the Lützowufer, where we are standing now. But I didn't find them, no one was there, not even servants."

"And the von Tiegals never showed up? You never heard from them?" Teddy asked quietly, her eyes not leaving the other woman's face.

"No. Nor did I hear from Sigmund and Ursula. Not ever again. The house on the Tiergartenstrasse had been badly bombed earlier that summer, and so obviously they had not returned there. I went next to the villa in the Wannsee to look for them, but it was deserted. Locked and shuttered."

Teddy said, "I visited the villa at the lake last week. My friend Mrs. Anne Reynolds, who is with the International Red Cross, drove me out. I didn't expect to find the Westheims, but I felt I had to check the villa, just for my own satisfaction. Mrs. Reynolds and I both spoke to the woman who is living at the villa now. We didn't get anything out of her, and she denies any knowledge of the Westheims."

The princess nodded, and gave Teddy a pointed look. "The villa was taken over later by a high-ranking Nazi," she told her. "Things like that happened all the time in those days. Bigwigs in the Third Reich stole so much from so many."

"And especially from Jews," Teddy said, and hesitated for a moment before murmuring more softly, "But, Princess, didn't you try to investigate the disappearance of the Westheims and the von Tiegals? Check things out through—through the underground, the resistance?"

"*I* was a member of one of the resistance movements, Teddy, and naturally I tried to find out if my friends had managed to leave Germany. Or if they had been arrested by the Gestapo. But I wasn't able to turn anything up, no one did. We all drew a blank. But it was not *unusual* for people to simply disappear without leaving a trace. Millions did, *millions*, Teddy. And millions are *still* missing, their fates unknown."

"What about the rest of the Westheim family? Do you have any idea what happened to them?"

"Mrs. Westheim, Sigmund's mother, died in the spring of 1940. Of natural causes—heart failure. She had been ill for a long time, as you know. That same year, Sigrid and her husband, Thomas Mayer, were killed in a bombing raid, when they were in Hamburg, and poor Hedy was in the house in the Tiergartenstrasse when it was hit in the summer of 1941. I'm afraid she died with the servants who were in the house at the time."

On hearing this news Teddy became very quiet, and she stood staring at the princess, incapable of making any sort of response. Sadness filled her and tears came into her eyes when she thought of Maxim's aunts and his uncle Thomas. They had been so young, all of them in their twenties.

Teddy sighed, and she said in a sorrowful voice, "How tragic they're *all* dead. I was fairly certain Grandmother Westheim would be gone by now, she was so old and frail. But the others . . . I had hoped that one of them at least would still be alive . . . Oh God, all this is so hard to accept!"

"I know it is," the princess said, and shook her head, her expression as mournful as Teddy's. "Nobody wanted this war," she exclaimed, anger surfacing. "It was started by a madman, and it was so futile, so *unnecessary*. It need never have happened. And look how it's taken its toll on the whole world. Millions are dead, or maimed for life, we are all suffering terribly because of it and in countless different ways. Great cities throughout Europe have been destroyed, so much has been lost . . . so much is gone . . . forever."

Teddy looked off into the distance, caught up in her worried thoughts. Then she turned to face the Russian aristocrat again, and confided, "I don't know what to do anymore, Princess—" She broke off, lifted her shoulders in a gesture of helplessness. "I've been to all the appropriate agencies, the International Red Cross, Jewish and Zionist organizations, and the Quakers, to no avail. I've studied their many lists, gone over list after list of names, in fact, and neither the Westheims nor the von Tiegals are on any of them. It's so strange, it doesn't make any sense, how can they have just . . . *vanished*?"

"So *many* did, Teddy." The princess touched her arm lightly, and continued, "Let us not stand here like this. It would be much better if we went to my little abode to talk." She swung around, put her red chafed hands on the old pram and began to push it ahead of her, saying, "We will go to my house. It is not a grand place, but it is reasonably comfortable and it will certainly be much warmer than standing out here."

"Yes, it's colder this morning than it has been since I arrived in Berlin," Teddy remarked, and she followed the princess through the rubble, glancing around, looking for any sort of dwelling, however humble. But there were no houses standing, nor any other kind of structures, for that matter.

As she drew alongside her, Teddy could not help saying, "And where do you live, Princess Irina? Where is your house?"

"Oh, you can't see it from here," Irina Troubetzkoy answered with a curious little laugh. "I call it my *house*, but my little abode is actually a hole in the ground."

Teddy was so startled to hear this she was completely at a loss for words.

They had not gone much farther when the princess suddenly drew to a halt and pointed to a crater a few steps in front of them.

"*That* is my hole! I live down there—like a troglodyte." Irina looked at Teddy out of the corner of her eye and went on, "Don't be alarmed, it's not quite as dreadful as it sounds. Now—I shall leave my bricks here for the moment, and deal with them later."

The princess pushed the pram over to a heap of debris near the crater, knelt down, and began to carefully wedge stones around the front wheels.

Teddy also knelt and helped to put the stones in place, stealing a glance at Irina as she did. "Princess?"

"Yes?"

"Why are you a rubble woman?"

Irina Troubetzkoy lifted her head, rather proudly, and rested her bright-blue eyes on Teddy. She said, very simply, "Because I have nothing else to do." She gave a little sigh, then explained, "Besides, I get paid for the bricks, and I also get extra food rations." With a small smile, she went on, "And there is another reason, another consideration. I feel as though I am doing something useful and worthwhile, something for the future, by reclaiming the bricks with which Berlin can eventually be rebuilt. It gives me, and the other rubble women, too, a sense of purpose. And a stake in the future."

"Yes," Teddy said, nodding her head. "Yes, yes, I see what you mean." But she could not help thinking how different Princess Irina Troubetzkoy's life would have been if the Russian Revolution had not happened. Because her mother, the princess Natalie, had been born a Romanov and was a cousin of Czar Nicholas, Irina would have led an existence of ease and comfort and privilege at the Russian court. She certainly would not have been scrabbling around in the ruins of Berlin, salvaging bricks and living in a hole in the ground.

The princess scrambled to her feet, stared down at Teddy, who had remained kneeling in the rubble, and beckoned. "Come!" she cried, and moving to the crater, she stepped over the edge and disappeared from view.

Teddy stifled a cry, jumped up and ran after her, looked into the crater with trepidation, and saw that there was a steep flight of stone steps leading to the bottom. The steps were partly shattered, and she realized that they had been badly damaged by bombs. The princess was carefully maneuvering her way down them. Taking a deep breath, Teddy followed her.

"These steps used to lead from the kitchen to the cellars in my stepfather's house, when it was standing," Irina informed her. "And, as you can see, they're all that's left of the Herr Baron's mansion now, except for my little abode, of course, which is through the door straight ahead."

35

$\equiv$

THE PRINCESS PULLED AN IRON KEY OUT OF HER COAT pocket and opened the heavy wooden door. "Wait here for a moment, please, Teddy, while I light the oil lamps," she said, and stepped inside.

A moment later the princess was calling, "Come in, come in," and Teddy entered.

She found herself standing in a little cellar. It was illuminated by the lamps that had just been lit by Irina, and they flickered brightly in the murkiness of the interior. Teddy blinked several times, adjusting her eyes, and then looked around with curiosity.

The ugly cellar was furnished sparsely. An ancient threadbare sofa with sagging springs was set against the back wall, flanked on either side by small dark-wood tables on which the oil lamps stood, and a couple of armchairs faced the sofa. In the center of this grouping was a large wooden packing crate with a lace doily on top of it, and apparently this served as a coffee table. Against another wall rested an old-fashioned sideboard that had seen better days, and on top of it were a pile of books, a fat white candle in a carved wooden candlestick, and some chipped white china cups and saucers.

It was obvious to Teddy that the princess had tried to give the cellar some warmth and coziness, plus a few homey touches. A worn Oriental rug covered the concrete floor; several stained and crumpled red-velvet cushions dressed up the dark-blue brocade sofa, and a faded plaid blanket was thrown over the back of one of the armchairs. On the packing crate stood a bedraggled little bunch of artificial flowers in a jam jar. There was something pathetically touching about these grubby imitations of the real thing, and a lump came into her throat as she looked at them.

The princess had been observing Teddy keenly, and moving forward into the center of the cellar, she said in a brisk voice, "It's not much, I know, but it's better than what most Berliners have these days. Many of them are walking around carrying their possessions in paper bags, and camping out in the ruins the best way they can. *I am lucky.* This place is dry, and, most important, it's safe. And I can soon get it warm with the paraffin stove. Are you cold, Teddy? I will light the stove, if you are."

"No, no!" Teddy exclaimed. "I don't want you to waste your precious fuel on me. I'll keep my overcoat on."

"So will I," the princess said, "such as it is." She chuckled, glanced down at the shabby man's coat that was far too big for her, pulled it around her tightly, possessively, and added, "This belonged to my stepfather, and I do look dreadful in it, but it *is* warm." Gesturing to a chair, she hurried on: "Now, Teddy, please do sit down. I would like to offer you some sort of refreshment, but I don't really have much. Still, let me see what I can find."

"Thank you, but I don't want anything, Princess Irina, really I don't, I'm fine," Teddy assured her, and sat down in one of the chairs. She took off her woolen gloves and stuffed them in her pocket, then unwrapped her long tartan scarf to let it dangle loosely around her neck.

The princess took a seat on the sofa, opposite Teddy, and airily waved one hand around the cellar. "This was a storage room, a vault really, and the baron used it for silver, porcelain and household valuables of that sort," she explained. "Through there"—she motioned to the door near the sideboard—"is the wine cellar, although there's no wine in it anymore. The bottles were smashed in the raids, and the wine cave is now—my bedroom!"

Teddy eyed everything with great interest, and then asked, "Did you manage to salvage this furniture from the wreckage of the mansion?"

"Oh no, there wasn't much left of the house, or its contents, not after the Allies had bombed us eighty-two times in as many days. These sorry pieces were already down here. My stepfather had turned the two storage cellars into air-raid shelters for us and the household staff, in 1940. So you see, my little abode was ready and waiting for me after the house was hit the last time. That was when it was completely demolished."

"The baron . . . Princess Natalie . . ." Teddy stopped, suddenly wondering if she ought to continue. Perhaps the princess's mother and stepfather had been killed; she had no wish to upset Irina.

Immediately recognizing Teddy's dilemma, Irina said quickly, "It's all right, they are perfectly well, thank goodness. My mother and stepfather are living in the gardener's cottage on one of the baron's estates near Baden-Baden in the Black Forest. Naturally, the castle itself is closed up for the time being—it's too difficult for Helmut to run it without staff, fuel and other supplies."

"I'm glad to hear they're both in good health, and were not hurt." Teddy glanced around the dank, gloomy cellar, and suggested quietly, "Wouldn't you be better off living in the country with them, Princess Irina?"

"Not at all!" Irina shook her head vehemently, and frowned at the mere idea of this. Unexpectedly, a peal of laughter broke free, and she said, "They are an odd couple, the Russian princess and the Prussian baron. They are like—a couple of lovebirds, yes, I do believe that is the best way to describe them. And they much prefer to be on their own, I am quite certain of this. Besides, the cottage is small, and, as they say, three's a crowd." Irina sat back and crossed her long legs. "I like being in Berlin, in the center of things, as difficult as living here is these days. And at least I'm not in the Russian Zone."

"Mrs. Reynolds told me there's still a lot of rape going on, that it's not safe for women in the Red sector."

"And especially a White Russian such as myself! Can you imagine how the Bolsheviks would treat me!" Irina cried. "When they first captured the city in May, I was terrified. I hid in here for weeks, until the British, French and Americans came in to occupy their zones. . . . Enough of this, I am safe now."

Teddy looked thoughtful for a moment, then said, "But things are not especially easy for you, Princess Irina, even though you do have a roof over your head. I know food is short and I would like to come tomorrow with some groceries, a few luxuries. I know Mrs. Reynolds will gladly give them to me, she will want to help you, too, when she knows of your plight."

"That's not necessary, but thank you anyway, Teddy, it was kind of you to offer. I do manage fairly well, and when I feel the need I occasionally make a purchase in the Tiergarten."

"The Tiergarten?" Teddy repeated, giving the princess a quizzical look.

"There is a very active black market in the park," Irina explained. "For a price, one can buy butter, coffee, tea, chocolate bars, cigarettes and toothpaste. Many things."

"Even so, I would like to bring you some of those items. It's no trouble, really it isn't. I want to do *something* to help you. Please let me," she begged.

"Very well, Teddy, and thank you." The princess inclined her head graciously and a pleased expression settled on her face. "That is very, very kind of you. But then one does have to rely on the kindness of friends in times of great difficulty such as these."

Teddy said, "I have wonderful friends in London who helped me to come here to look for Herr and Frau Westheim. Do you have good friends, Princess? I mean in Berlin?"

"One or two are still left. Unfortunately, and very sadly, most of my friends have not survived the war." Irina leaned her head against the back of the sofa and closed her eyes, and when she opened them they were dark with pain and tears glistened on her lashes.

There was no way Teddy could miss the look of suffering on Irina's face, now so pale and drawn in the lamplight, and her heart went out to her. "I'm so sorry," she said. "So very sorry, Princess Irina."

"My friends were murdered, tragically murdered—" Irina Troubetzkoy's voice started to tremble and she was unable to continue speaking. She began to weep silently. After a second or two, she reached into her pocket and pulled out a piece of grubby rag and wiped her eyes with it.

"Forgive me," she apologized, forcing a smile, but a weak one. "I didn't mean to break down this way, but your kindness touched me, and when I thought of my poor friends—" Irina cut herself off and closed her eyes once more, repeatedly sighing to herself, as if her sorrow was too much for her to bear.

Teddy sat watching the princess, waiting for her to recover

her equilibrium, knowing there was not much she could do or say to help her assuage her grief. And for the second time that morning she could not help thinking what a hard and painful life this aristocratic Russian woman had led. Scrutinizing her face in the lambent light, Teddy noted its fine structure, the good bones, the perfectly shaped mouth and chin, and the smooth, wide forehead, the symmetrical auburn brows above those startlingly blue eyes. There were webs of fine lines around her eyes and her mouth now, but she was still a beautiful woman. Teddy guessed she must be about thirty-three or there-abouts, yet she looked older. No wonder, Teddy thought, after what she's been through.

Suddenly the princess sat up straighter and threw Teddy a quick glance. "Kurt von Wittingen and I worked together in the resistance, and we had a good friend, Admiral Canaris ... Wilhelm Canaris. It was the admiral who helped to get Ursula, Maxim and you out of Germany. Did you know that?"

"Frau Westheim told me."

"Wilhelm Canaris is dead," Irina announced quietly. "He loathed Hitler, and everything that that criminal stood for, and inevitably he paid for his beliefs with his life." She focused her attention on a distant corner of the cellar, momentarily lost in her own ruminations, and a few minutes elapsed before she continued slowly, "The admiral certainly took breathtaking risks in order to help the resistance, to help us aid those victims of the Nazis whom we were so desperately trying to save—" Irina broke off, left her sentence unfinished.

Teddy was watching her closely, and she saw an agonized look cross her face; she suddenly knew that the princess harbored some awful knowledge that she did not dare guess at, and she felt a shiver run through her. She held herself very still, waiting.

Rising jerkily, all of a sudden, Irina crossed to the sideboard, opened a drawer and took out a pack of cigarettes. Turning to face Teddy, she asked, "Do you smoke? Would you like one of these?"

Teddy shook her head. "No, thank you, and please take this." Opening her bag, Teddy took out a pack of Lucky Strikes, and put them on the packing crate next to the jam jar of faded silk flowers. "I hadn't realized you smoked—I would have given them to you before."

"My thanks, Teddy," Irina said, gratefully accepting the precious little gift. She walked back to the sofa and sat down again. Lighting one of the Lucky Strikes, she started immediately to speak about Wilhelm Canaris. "The admiral was arrested last summer, the summer of 1944, and accused of treason against the Third Reich." There was a short pause as she puffed on her cigarette, and in a low voice, she said, "He was hanged at Flossenburg concentration camp in April of this year, ironically just a short time before the Allies liberated the camp."

"So I read in the papers. How tragic that the Americans arrived too late to save him! It's heartbreaking even to think about," Teddy said, and fell silent, once again pondering the terrible death of this courageous man.

The princess was also quiet for a few moments, drawing on her cigarette, lost in her thoughts, surrounded by a haze of smoke. She took a deep breath, and said in a precise and careful voice to give weight to her words, "I hope they are beginning to understand in England that there were some very brave men in Germany, men who fought Hitler and his henchmen with all their might and tried to stop them. Men of great honor and integrity who wanted to save others from being destroyed by that foul regime of evil and tyranny, and who tried very hard to overthrow Hitler and the Nazis, and who ultimately lost their lives in so doing."

"Yes, they do know now," Teddy assured her. "I've recently been reading things about the German resistance, and the British papers called Admiral Canaris a hero, Princess."

"He was indeed."

"Maxim and I owe him our lives," Teddy said softly.

"True, yes, you do. But other people were involved in helping you to escape. Do you remember the colonel who traveled in your compartment on the train from Berlin to Aachen?"

"Colonel Oster," Teddy said. "Frau Westheim told me who he was, after we crossed the border into Belgium."

"He was on the train to keep an eye on you, to make sure all of you were safe, and that you got away. He, too, was a brave man. He was the admiral's assistant in German military intelligence, close to him, and most especially so because of their hatred of the Nazis."

Irina stubbed out her cigarette and sat back, folding her hands in her lap. She stared down at them. The events of the past few years were forever fresh and vivid in her mind, could never be forgotten. Without looking up, she told Teddy an astonishing story. "There was a plot to assassinate Hitler in 1944—imagine, just last year, yet it seems so long ago now, perhaps because so much has happened lately. It was called the July Twentieth Plot and it did not succeed, went horribly awry, unfortunately. Hitler was only *wounded*, not killed, as had been planned, even though Count Klaus von Stauffenberg placed the briefcase holding the bomb only twelve feet away from him. Despite his injuries, Hitler survived, and some of the plotters were captured immediately. Colonel von Stauffenberg was shot that same evening . . . at midnight in the courtyard of the War Ministry."

The princess reached for another cigarette, and continued: "The Gestapo thought Colonel Oster was involved, and he was arrested that month, held at Gestapo headquarters in the Prinz-Albrecht-Strasse. We were sure he was being horribly tortured. In fact, we were quite positive they were all being tortured. . . ."

"Who were the others?" Teddy asked in a whisper, hardly able to breathe.

"Adam von Trott zu Solz, Gottfried Bismarck, Fritzi Schulenberg, many others. None of those men broke under torture, they did not give our names or implicate us. No, they did not give us away. . . ." Irina Troubetzkoy stared into Teddy's eyes, and said, "I was deeply, *deeply* involved with the plotters, who were all my friends, but I was never arrested. They died protecting me, and other men and women as well."

"Oh, Princess Irina, how courageous of you! But you could easily have been killed yourself!" Teddy cried, and then she remembered that Irina had always appeared intrepid to her, and had carried her fearlessness like a proud banner in the past. Ursula Westheim had called her a heroic woman.

Irina nodded. "Yes, I could have died," she agreed. "But I didn't. *I was left to mourn.*"

There was a little silence; the cellar was deathly quiet.

Teddy wanted to mention Prince Kurt von Wittingen, to ask about his fate, but before she could, Irina started to speak again, as if it were a great relief to unburden herself to someone.

She said in the softest of tones, "So many of my friends *were* executed in the end, and some died most horribly. Adam von Trott was hanged from a meat hook with piano wire, and died very slowly of strangulation, in Plötzensee Prison in August of last year. And, Teddy, can you believe that they actually took photographs and made films of the meat-hook deaths to show to Hitler. *Sadists!* And Hans Oster was hanged in Flossenburg this past April, at the same time as Admiral Canaris. My heart bleeds for them all. I will never forget any of them. I think of each one every day, and I will until the day *I* die."

Teddy was so shocked and so profoundly affected by the things she had just heard, she could not speak for a while. When she did manage to speak, her voice was choked. "What a tragic, tragic waste! The world must be told about these horrendous crimes as they have been told about the camps. And they must never be allowed to happen again!"

Turning to look at Teddy, Irina took a deep breath, and said, "At least Hitler is dead. Although I can't help wishing he hadn't committed suicide in his bunker in April, that he could have been arrested by the Allies and properly tried for his crimes against humanity, along with the other criminals. The four-power international tribunal begins in Nuremberg next month, and the whole world will be watching. *Justice must be done*. It *must* be done, in the name of those millions who died, to ensure that they did not die in vain."

"It will be, don't worry," Teddy said grimly. "Those monsters are not going to get off scot-free. They're all going to be punished, to swing at the end of ropes. But actually, hanging is too good for them, in my opinion."

"An eye for an eye, a tooth for a tooth," Irina muttered almost to herself.

Leaning forward urgently, Teddy focused her eyes on Irina and said tremulously, "You haven't mentioned Prince Kurt von Wittingen. . . . *He* wasn't captured and executed as well, was he?"

"Not by the Nazis." Irina's bright-blue eyes clouded over, and she took a long draw on the Lucky Strike she was holding before elucidating further. "Actually, Teddy, no one really knows what has happened to him. Kurt was in Berlin this summer, I didn't see him myself, but another member of our resistance group, Wolfgang Schroeder, did. Wolfgang exchanged greetings with Kurt, and a couple of days later he saw him again—this time talking to some Russian officers in that part of Berlin which is now the East Zone. But Kurt has never been seen by anyone since then. He just vanished."

"Like the Westheims and the von Tiegals."

Irina made no response to this comment at first, then she murmured quietly, "It wasn't quite the same."

"Do *you* think the prince is dead?" Teddy asked.

"He might be. When Kurt did not surface at the end of the war, we thought that perhaps he had been injured in the last-ditch fighting. Some of it was still going on, even after the Russians had overrun the city and taken it. And so we searched every hospital. Berlin was turned upside down, and many people were questioned. Another member of our resistance group, Dieter Müller, made a second and more thorough search, but Kurt was never found. Nor was his body."

"Could it . . . could the prince's body be buried under the rubble?" Teddy ventured, recalling what Anne Reynolds had told her about the bodies rotting in the ruins of the city and in the river.

"That's always possible, of course," Irina conceded. "But Dieter Müller has another theory. He believes that Kurt was arrested by those Russian officers whom Wolfgang Schroeder spotted him with. Perhaps on that very day."

Teddy sat poised on the edge of her seat. She had listened attentively and was full of questions. But she asked the princess the most obvious one. "Why would the Russians want to arrest Prince Kurt von Wittingen?"

"Perhaps because they thought he was a spy," Irina suggested, and raised an eyebrow. "More precisely, a spy for the Americans, and that would surely make him an enemy of the Soviet Union. They're very paranoid, you know, these Bolsheviks, and especially about the Americans. In that respect they take after their leader, Joseph Stalin, another tyrant with blood on his hands."

"And *you*? What is *your* opinion? Do you believe that the prince was arrested?"

"I simply don't know, Teddy. I wish I did."

"I went to the von Wittingen house the other day . . . and of course you know that it is no more. Like the rest of Berlin, it's a pile of rubble. Is Princess Arabella in Zurich?"

"Yes, she is. She came back to Berlin as soon as she could this summer, but with Kurt missing, her home destroyed and nowhere to live, there was nothing here for her. She returned to Switzerland with Diana and Christian."

"I thought perhaps she had done that."

"Arabella is . . . Well, to be truthful, she's not herself anymore. Since Kurt's disappearance, her mind has—She's a little confused at times."

Teddy looked stricken. "How *dreadful*. Poor woman . . . But at least she has the children."

"Diana and Christian are a great comfort to her, yes."

The two women did not speak for a while, drifting with their own thoughts. Finally, it was Irina who broke the silence. "Oh dear, all we have spoken about are sad things, Theodora. Painful things. And when we haven't seen each other for six very long and trying years. It's my fault, of course, I'm the one who's been doing most of the talking." Irina sat forward eagerly, and, with a lovely smile, exclaimed, "I want to hear all about you and Maxim and the life you've made in London! *Everything* now, you mustn't leave anything out."

"I won't," Teddy promised, also smiling. "And actually I do have a lot to tell you." She reached into her bag, searched for the packet of snaps, and when she found it she said, "I have some beautiful photos of Maxim, I brought them with me for his parents. They're going to be so proud of him when they see him again. He's very grown up, the most wonderful boy."

Irina Troubetzkoy could not speak.

She stood up unsteadily and walked to the sideboard, where, with shaking hands, she made a pretense of looking for something in a drawer. It was imperative that Teddy did not see the anguish on her face, the tears that blinded her.

36

It WAS LATE IN THE AFTERNOON WHEN TEDDY RETURNED to the cellar on the Lützowufer the following day.

The princess had obviously been waiting for her, and the door was opened instantly, after only one knock. Teddy found herself being greeted affectionately and ushered into the little abode, as the princess insisted on calling the cellar.

To Teddy it was a miserable hole in the ground, dark, damp, fusty and unsanitary, and she could not bear to think of anyone living there, especially Princess Irina Troubetzkoy. Yet Teddy knew she was powerless to help her change her lot in life, at least at this moment. Last night she had spoken at length about the princess to Anne Reynolds, who had promised to keep an eye on her, and if possible make her life a bit easier whenever she could, and this had pleased Teddy.

Irina had lit the paraffin stove earlier and the cellar did not seem as cold and damp as it had been yesterday, even though it was a rainy day; the candle and the two oil lamps burned brightly and added to the feeling of warmth, the illusion of coziness.

After helping Teddy off with her coat, Irina said, "I thought you might like a little schnapps—it will warm you, Teddy, it's awfully cold out there this afternoon." She waved her hand in the direction of the sideboard, and then carefully placed Teddy's coat over a chair back.

Teddy glanced at the sideboard and saw that the princess had put out two chipped crystal glasses and a much depleted bottle of *Kirschwasser* from the Black Forest. "Thank you, that would be nice," she answered, even though she did not feel like cherry brandy just then. On the other hand, she did not want to offend the princess, who had obviously gone to a lot of trouble to spruce up the cellar and make it more inviting. And the precious drop of *Kirschwasser*, which was all there was left in the bottle, was yet another kind gesture from a woman in the most pitiful of circumstances.

"However, before we have a drink I would first like to give you this," Teddy said, picking up the shopping bag she had put down on the floor when she had entered the cellar. "I *was* able to get a few things for you, Princess Irina."

"How kind of you, Teddy," the princess said, her eyes lighting up.

Carrying the bag over to the sideboard, Teddy began to take out some food. "Here's a packet of Typhoo tea, real coffee, chocolate biscuits—delicious American ones, too—a loaf of bread and a quarter pound of butter. Then there're some tinned items. Spam, corned beef, salmon and sardines, all from the American PX, and a tin of powdered egg, one of powdered milk. Plus a few other things in the bottom of the bag. Come and look."

"My goodness!" Irina exclaimed, flabbergasted. She had not expected such a large quantity of foodstuff, and her face was a picture of gratitude as she joined Teddy near the sideboard. Almost reverently she touched the items that Teddy had already unpacked before peeking into the bag. Then she turned to Teddy in astonishment. "*Toothpaste, toilet soap*, and . . . oh, Teddy, how *wonderful*! A tube of Max Factor lipstick *and* Apple Blossom toilet water! Thank you, thank you." She took a step closer and, embracing Teddy affectionately, gave her a warm smile.

Teddy said, "I'm glad to help you in any way I can, Princess Irina."

"And *where* in heaven's name did you get all these wonderful things?"

"From Mrs. Reynolds, of the International Red Cross, the lady I told you about, and her secretary, Elizabeth Jefford. They both gave me some of their own rations, and Mrs. Reynolds was also able to get a few extra things for you from her friend Major Evans, who's with the American occupation forces. It was the major who contributed the red lipstick, Princess. And Mrs. Reynolds gave me the toilet water for you."

"How very generous and kind of them. You must thank

them all for me. Imagine, lipstick! It's marvelous to own a tube of it again."

"I think you're more thrilled about the lipstick than the food," Teddy exclaimed and began to laugh.

Irina also laughed. "Not really," she said. "But it's a treat to have something truly feminine after all this time, and years of deprivations of all kinds. Now, shall we have the schnapps?"

"That would be nice." Teddy walked over to the sofa and sat watching the princess pour the cherry brandy into the liqueur glasses.

This afternoon Irina Troubetzkoy looked more like the woman she had been before the war, almost her old self, Teddy thought. She wore a black wool dress, old-fashioned, very dated and obviously from the 1930s, thick black stockings and sturdy black walking shoes. Nonetheless, despite the drabness of the clothes, there was a certain elegance about her, a special kind of dignity that had a lot to do with her aristocratic bearing. Her hair was as magnificent as it had always been—a wonderful burnished auburn—and, surprisingly, there were only a few sprinklings of silver among its luxuriant waves. She found a way to wash it today, Teddy thought. Irina's face was also scrubbed and shining, not dust-covered as it had been the day before when Teddy had found her working in the rubble. And the princess looked her real age, not a woman in her late forties as she had appeared to be yesterday, and in the flickering lamplight she was as beautiful as she had ever been.

Irina gave Teddy the glass of *Kirschwasser*, and said, "I would like to toast you, Teddy, to say many, many congratulations on your engagement to be married." She clinked her little glass against Teddy's, and added, "I was so pleased when you told me about it."

"Thank you very much." Teddy took a swallow of the liqueur, being careful not to drink from the chipped side of the glass.

The princess also sipped her drink, and sat down in one of the chairs facing the sofa.

Teddy put her glass on the packing crate, opened her handbag and took out a small photograph in a leather frame. "I had snaps only of Maxim with me yesterday," she explained. "This is Mark, my fiancé." As she spoke she handed the picture to the princess.

"And what a nice-looking young man he is too, Teddy," Irina said, looking at the photograph. "And obviously very brave, if these decorations on his uniform are anything to go by."

"He was in the Battle of Britain."

The princess nodded and handed the frame back to her. "After you left yesterday morning, I remembered that you had been going out with Professor Herzog's son before the war. I believe they lived further down on the Lützowufer. As I recall, the young man went to Palestine in 1939. . . . Whatever happened to him?"

"Willy is his name, and he didn't stay very long in Palestine. He moved on, went to Shanghai. He's still there, but hoping to go to America one day," Teddy told her. "We wrote to each other regularly, and I never thought of another man until I met Mark. He and I truly fell in love, and it was only then that I realized I had to write to Willy and end our unofficial engagement."

"And was Willy Herzog heartbroken?"

Teddy shook her head and gave a little laugh. "No, he wasn't. He was rather relieved. He wrote back to congratulate me and explained that he, too, had met someone else, and had been wondering how to break the news to *me*. So, no broken hearts, and we have remained good friends. Actually, I should think Willy is married by now."

"And when are you planning to marry, Teddy?" the princess asked, and took a sip of the cherry brandy she was holding.

"Oh not yet for a while. I couldn't possibly get married without Frau and Herr Westheim being present. Mark understands that we have to wait until I find them, or until they get in touch with me, as I know they will."

Irina Troubetzkoy sat straighter in the chair, gaping at Teddy. She did not say a word, but simply sat there staring blankly, and her face turned very pale.

Teddy noticed the sudden change in her and asked, concerned, "What's the matter? Are you ill? Don't you feel well?"

Still the princess did not speak, and then, at last, she said faintly, "No, I don't. But I'll be all right. Just give me a moment. . . ." She placed the chipped liqueur glass on the packing crate and saw that her hand was trembling as she did so.

Clasping her fingers together to stop their shaking, she bent forward and focused a look on Teddy.

Returning the princess's penetrating gaze, Teddy couldn't help thinking that her eyes looked more startlingly blue than ever and very beautiful. Then she noticed they were glittering with tears, and that her face had turned white as chalk.

"Princes Irina, what's wrong? Whatever is it?"

"I have not told you the truth," the princess said in a voice pitched low. "While I have not exactly lied to you, I have been less than honest." She shook her head and made a small, self-deprecating grimace. "Why do I make excuses for myself? Why do I say that I have not lied to you, when I have? I have lied by omission."

"What . . . do . . . you . . . mean?" Teddy asked slowly, dragging the words out. They seemed to be stuck in her throat. She leaned forward herself, and frowned, examining the princess's face. And at that moment she had a premonition and a terrible sense of dread swept over her and her heart began to pound erratically.

"I omitted—" The princess stopped, took a deep breath, then continued in a quick rush of words, "I omitted to tell you something, Teddy. Something I know about Sigmund and Ursula. Something I ought to have told you yesterday. I was going to several times, but my courage failed me."

"What?" Teddy cried, her voice rising shrilly. "Tell me! Oh, please tell me!"

"Teddy dear . . . Teddy . . . you're not going to find them. And they won't find you, as you keep insisting they will. Ursula and Sigmund are not refugees trying to get back to Berlin, and they're not about to be released from the camps." Irina said very shakily, "They're not coming back. Not ever coming back."

The princess now rose quickly and went to sit on the sofa, and took Teddy's hand in hers.

Teddy's mouth had begun to tremble and her eyes were wide and staring in her pale face. She grabbed Irina's hand, peered deeply into her eyes and said in a strangled voice, "They're dead, aren't they? Ursula and Sigmund Westheim are dead."

The princess nodded. "Yes," she acknowledged in a whisper, and drew Teddy into her arms, held her close, with one hand pressed to her head.

Teddy was weeping uncontrollably. "I knew, really . . . deep down inside. I think I always knew," she sobbed, choking on her words. "I was always so afraid for them. They had a million-to-one chance of making it. I knew they wouldn't . . . but I couldn't admit it."

Irina cradled Teddy like a child and tried to soothe her, to console and comfort her, and the two women clung to each other. But at one moment Teddy pulled away and cried out, "*Oh God, why them? Why did it have to be them?*"

Irina Troubetzkoy shook her head. She had no answer for her, just as she had no answer for herself.

The sobbing of the two women slowly began to subside. They drew apart and wiped their eyes.

Teddy asked quietly, "Where . . . where did they die?"

Brushing her damp cheeks with one hand, Irina said, "Sigmund died in Buchenwald. In 1942."

"Are you sure?"

The princess nodded. "Kurt von Wittengen found out. Somehow . . . through the Krupp works at Essen . . . a group of inmates from Buchenwald were sent to work at one of Krupp's slave camps. Mostly women. One of them, a Polish countess, had known Sigi in Berlin. She had seen him in Buchenwald, and passed on word of his execution. He was shot." Tears filled Irina's eyes again, and she pressed one hand to her mouth, choking back a sob. After a moment she managed to say, "Kurt was able to find things out all the time. But he couldn't always do anything about what he knew. Only occasionally could he do that."

Teddy pressed back her tears, and asked, "*Ursula?* Was she in Buchenwald?"

"No. Ravensbrück. She died there in 1943."

"You're sure?"

"Yes, I am. A member of our resistance group, Maria Langen, was imprisoned in Ravensbrück from 1943 until the summer of 1944, when she was unexpectedly released. She knew Ursula and Renata in the camp. They were there together. Renata died in Ravensbrück too."

"Were they shot? How did they die?"

Irina bit her lip and began to blink. She averted her head, swallowing repeatedly, sat gazing straight in front of her, and held herself very still.

"*Please*," Teddy said. "*I must know.*"

Irina turned to face her, gave her a very direct look, and the tears could no longer be held back—they fell out of Irina's eyes and splashed down her face onto her hands in her lap.

In a voice that was barely a whisper, Irina said, "She was beaten to death."

"Oh, my God, no! No! No! No! Not Ursula," Teddy shouted, half rising from the sofa. "Oh God, no, I can't bear it! I can't bear it!" She was seized by a terrible weeping as the horror of Ursula's agonizing death struck at her, and at the thought of her suffering Teddy doubled over, in agony herself, and wrapped her arms around her body. She went on weeping until there were no tears left to weep, rocking back and forth, filled with pain.

Irina sat with her arm around Teddy's shoulders, endeavoring to comfort her while knowing there was no comfort that could be given. And the two women mourned for Ursula and Sigmund, overwhelmed by grief.

It took Teddy a long time to calm down, but eventually she was able to take control of herself. She reached for the schnapps, and after swallowing some of it, she asked softly, in a subdued tone, "How did Renata von Tiegal die? Was it . . . the same way? Do you know?"

"Renata *was* badly beaten. But she died from a burst appendix. It was neglected, she had no treatment, peritonitis set in and she was suddenly gone. This was a few months after Ursula died."

Teddy bit her lip, and looked away, then at last managed to ask, "And what about Reinhard von Tiegal?"

"We never found out what happened to him."

"Then he could still be alive," Teddy suggested, hope rising.

"I doubt it. Renata told Maria Langen in Ravensbrück that the four of them had left Schloss Tiegal because they had been warned they were going to be arrested. Sigi and Ursula because they were Jews, Renata and Reinhard because they were sheltering Jews. And also because the Gestapo apparently believed Reinhard was a member of one of the resistance groups, which he was, of course."

"And they didn't make it to a safe place," Teddy stated quietly.

"No, they didn't. They only got as far as Potsdam, when they were arrested. Renata and Ursula were taken to Ravensbrück. They never found out where Reinhard and Sigi had been sent."

"But why weren't any of their names on the lists with the various agencies I visited?" Teddy wondered out loud, looking at Irina, frowning in bafflement.

"I don't know," Irina answered, and shook her head very slowly, helplessly shrugging her shoulders. "We all know how zealous the Nazis were about making lists of those they arrested, lists of the numbers they had tattooed on the forearms of their victims. But in the same way, they were equally zealous in destroying their lists, once defeat was upon them, and when the Allies started liberating the camps." She repeated, "I just don't know how to explain it, Teddy. Their names had to have been on the camp lists that were destroyed by the Nazis."

"Yes." Teddy now looked at Irina very sharply. "Your friend Maria Langen from the resistance group . . . is it possible . . . could I go and see her, talk to her? Perhaps she could tell me more. . . ."

"Unfortunately she died earlier this year. God knows how she survived as long as she did. Poor Maria had been so mistreated she never properly recovered."

Teddy leaned against the sofa and said nothing.

Suddenly there was nothing to say.

She closed her eyes and retreated into her memories, and she saw Ursula's lovely face, heard her sweet and gentle voice, and a scream rose in her throat. She pushed it back and squeezed her eyes shut more tightly, squeezing back the tears. She could not bear to think of the horrifying way Ursula had died, beaten and tortured beyond endurance. And she knew that she would never be able to expunge the brutality of Ursula's death from her mind. It would haunt her for as long as she lived.

37

"You'll be quite comfortable in here, Miss Stein,"
Mr. Johnson of the Rossiter Merchant Bank said, showing her
into the small private room. "And if you would kindly sign this
card, I will bring your safety deposit box to you immediately."

"Thank you, Mr. Johnson," Teddy said, and sitting down
at the table, she signed the authorization card he put in front
of her and gave it back to him.

The bank official smiled pleasantly and went out.

Teddy sat back in the chair, waiting for him to return, staring at the painting on the wall opposite but not really seeing
it. The conversation she had just had with Henry Rossiter occupied her thoughts.

Mr. Rossiter had been saddened to hear the dire news she
had brought back from Berlin, but she realized now that he
had not appeared to be unduly surprised to learn that the Westheims were dead. After offering her his condolences in a gentle
and concerned way, he had told her that she was now Maxim's
guardian until the boy was twenty-one years old.

"This was Mrs. Westheim's express wish," the head of the
bank had explained. "And the letter that you brought to me
from her, when you first arrived in England in 1939, confirmed
a telephone conversation that she and I had about this matter,
just a week prior to your arrival. I thought you would like to
see that letter now." Henry Rossiter had passed it across the
desk; she had perused it quickly and handed it back to him.
"Is everything clear?" he had asked, and she had nodded. After
this, she had told him she wanted him to continue advising her
about the investment of the Westheim funds, had thanked him
for the guidance he had given her thus far. He had smiled in

285

his kindly way, assured her that he would help her in whatever way he could and had agreed to handle Maxim's money.

Teddy's thoughts were interrupted as the door of the private room flew open and Mr. Johnson reappeared. He hurried in, carrying her safety deposit box, which he placed on the table. "There you are, Miss Stein, and take your time," he said, and disappeared before she had a chance to thank him properly.

This was the first time Teddy had gone into her safety deposit box since the day she had acquired it, over six years ago, when she had locked the contents inside. She sat staring at the box for a very long moment before taking the key out of her purse to open it.

Ursula Westheim's jewels filled the box. The pieces were wrapped in the soft velvet-lined jewelry rolls that Ursula herself had purchased in Paris in 1939, on one of the days they had gone shopping together. Teddy picked up one of the jewelry rolls, opened it and gazed at the wide diamond bracelet that lay there glittering brilliantly in the light.

She touched the bracelet, remembering the last time she had seen Ursula wearing it in Berlin, and her throat tightened with emotion. The occasion had been a small dinner party at the mansion on the Tiergartenstrasse in 1937, and Ursula had never looked more beautiful. That night she had worn a burgundy velvet evening gown that had set off her fair skin, her pale blond hair, her ethereal beauty. Teddy felt the tears rushing to the surface, but she blinked them away, clamped down her grief for the dead woman.

Ever since Princess Irina Troubetzkoy had told her about Ursula's death a week ago, she had lived with nightmares, had rarely been able to close her eyes without seeing images of Ursula, a bruised and battered Ursula, tortured and beaten into insensibility by her Nazi tormentors in Ravensbrück. Only in the last few days had she begun to realize that the only way she could cope was to remember Ursula the way she had been in all her loveliness, and hold this picture in her head. But frequently the other horrifying images insinuated themselves into her mind, and when she imagined the agony Ursula must have lived through, she was in torment herself. And she wondered if she would ever obliterate those images. I must, she thought, for Maxim's sake, for my own sanity, and for Mark and our future life together.

After fastening the roll and laying it on one side on the table, Teddy removed all the other jewelry until she came to the envelope that lay in the bottom of the safety deposit box.

Ursula Westheim had given this envelope to her in Paris on the day she had taken Maxim and herself to the boat train bound for England. Across the large brown envelope Ursula had printed in bold block letters:

PRIVATE AND CONFIDENTIAL: TO BE OPENED IN THE EVENT OF THE DEATHS OF SIGMUND AND URSULA WESTHEIM.

And then underneath, in her flowing script, Ursula had written: *Miss Theodora Stein.*

Miss, Teddy repeated to herself, and thought, She was already making me English, even then. Swiftly she opened the brown envelope. Inside were two smaller white envelopes: one had her name on the front; the other was addressed to Maxim.

Teddy opened her own letter, and saw that it was written on the stationery of the Plaza-Athénée Hotel.

> *Paris*   *March 10, 1939*
> *My dear Teddy:*
> *If you are reading this letter, then my husband and I are already dead. I return to Berlin knowing there is a great possibility that neither he nor I, nor any of the Westheim family, will survive the persecution of the Third Reich. And if we do not die at the hands of the Nazis, there is always the strong possibility that we will be killed in the war between Germany and the Western Alliance, which we all know is now an inevitability.*
>
> *I therefore feel that I must write to you about a matter of tremendous importance regarding my son, Maximilian. I know that what I am about to say is going to come as a great surprise, and it may even shock you, but I want someone to know the truth, in the event that I do not survive. And it can only be you. Before I go any further, I must tell you that the words which I am about to write are for your eyes only. No one else must ever know the contents of this letter, unless, of course, you wish to tell Maxim when he is old enough to understand everything. However, I leave that decision to you. You must use your discretion, and you may come to believe that it is better he never knows.*

Perhaps it is wrong of me to burden you with this responsibility, but there is no one else I can entrust with this secret. And I do trust you implicitly, Teddy. I cannot advise you, I am afraid, for I have never really been sure what I myself would do, when Maxim was old enough to be told the truth. You are strong and clear-thinking and sensible, and I am certain that the decision you make will be the right one for my son, whom I know you love very much, as I do.

To begin my story, I must go back in time, to 1931. It was then that . . .

Teddy's eyes raced down the page, absorbing line after line that Ursula had written so carefully in Paris, six years past. The letter continued for another page, and when she had finished reading it Teddy sat back in the chair. She was stunned, and her face was a picture of disbelief.

And she fervently wished that Ursula Westheim had never written this letter to her.

Teddy left the Rossiter Merchant Bank and walked across Berkeley Square. It was a crisp, sunny winter's day, and she hoped that the fresh air would help clear her head. The letter she had just read troubled her deeply, but she knew she must put it out of her mind for the time being. There was something much more pressing and important with which she had to deal. Maxim was coming home from school for the weekend, was probably already there now, and she *must* tell him about his parents. But she had no idea what she would say to him—she constantly balked at the thought of it.

Near Marble Arch she hailed a cab and got in, and all the way back to Belsize Park Gardens she wrestled with her terrible problem. By the time she was alighting at Aunt Ketti's house she was certain of only one thing—that no matter what else she said, she could never tell Maxim exactly how his mother had died. To burden a child with that awful knowledge would be unconscionable.

He must have been waiting for her, watching the street from his bedroom window, for as Teddy came into the house Maxim was already clattering down the stairs.

"I'm here, Teddy!" he cried, racing along the hall, flinging himself against her body and hugging her. She hugged him back, and then looked up and saw Aunt Ketti standing in the doorway of the back parlor, observing them worriedly, her eyes anxious.

"Let me take my coat off, darling," she said to Maxim, and went swiftly to the coat closet.

Ketti said, "The train was on time for once, Teddy. Mrs. Trenton was at the railway station to meet Stubby. She invited Maxim for lunch tomorrow. But Mark rang up just before I left to say he has a pass for the weekend. You'll have to let Mrs. Trenton know what you want to do about Saturday lunch."

"Yes, Aunt Ketti, I'll ring her up later, and thank you for collecting Maxim from the station for me."

Maxim said, "Gosh, if Mark is coming up for the weekend, I'd like to see him. I mean, I see Stubby all the time, don't I? And I have lunch with him every day at school."

"That's true," Teddy said. "Perhaps Stubby can join *us*. It would be nice to spend the day with Mark."

She put her arm around his shoulder, and they continued down the hall together. Teddy paused at the door leading into the small den, and said, "Come in here for a moment, there's something I want to talk to you about."

"Gosh, you do sound serious!" he cried, frowning. "I hope it's not anything to do with school. Old Mr. Helliwell—"

"It doesn't have anything to do with school. You haven't done anything wrong," she said, pushing open the door and going inside.

Teddy sat down on the sofa and patted the cushion next to her. "Sit here with me, Maxim."

He did so, continuing to look at her with curiosity.

Teddy said, "I've been away for a couple of weeks. I've been to Berlin."

His dark eyes widened. "And you didn't tell me!" he said swiftly, sounding hurt, even a little accusatory.

"I went there to look for your parents, and I didn't want to get your hopes up."

"Did you find them?" he asked, sudden excitement flaring.

"No, I'm afraid not."

"Didn't you find *anything* out?" he demanded, his eyes impaling hers.

She swallowed. "No, not really. At least, not very much."

"But *what* exactly?"

"That they were with the von Tiegals at the schloss in 1941, and then the four of them disappeared. Vanished."

"But we already knew that!"

"That's all I could find out."

"I don't believe you," Maxim said, his face settling in rigid, stubborn lines. "I know you, Teddy, I've known you all my life. And you're far too clever not to have found out something else. I just *know* you *did*," he insisted.

"I didn't," she protested, shaking her head.

He was silent, staring at her.

Teddy could almost hear his mind working, and she held her breath. He was only eleven years old, but he was a boy of great brilliance and precocity, and therefore far too bright to be deceived. He would probe and probe. Her mouth went dry, and she wondered where she would find the words to tell him. Her eyes filled, and she blinked.

He noticed this immediately, and said, "Are they . . . are they . . . dead?"

"I'm so sorry, darling, so very, very sorry," she murmured, her voice full of love, and she reached for his hand.

He took it, held on to it tightly, and said in a small voice, "How did Mutti and Papa die?"

Teddy could not speak.

"In a bombing raid or . . . or . . . in the camps?" he asked hesitantly, his voice growing even smaller.

Teddy was still incapable of saying anything, but the tears spilled over the rims of her eyes and trickled down her cheeks unchecked.

"It *was* in the camps," he whispered so softly now she could hardly hear him. "Mutti and Papa died in the camps, didn't they?"

"Yes."

"Which one?"

"Your father in Buchenwald . . . your mother in Ravensbrück."

"*How?*"

"That I don't know. I really don't know. I promise you, I don't know how they died, Maxim," she said, her tone quietly vehement.

He sat looking at her speechlessly. His face was gray and his eyes had turned black with shock and anguish.

"Oh Teddy . . . Teddy . . ." he cried at last, and his face crumpled.

She reached for him as he reached for her, and she held him in her arms as he sobbed out his raw pain and grief for his mother and father. She rocked him to and fro, and endeavored to comfort him. She whispered: "I will look after you always, and so will Mark. I know it's not the same, but you will have us. You will be our boy."

He did not respond, but she knew he had heard her, and that he had understood, even though he went on weeping as though his heart was breaking.

Later, when he was calmer, she made him sit up on the sofa. After she had wiped his wet face with her handkerchief, she reached into her jacket pocket.

"The day we left Paris in 1939 your mother gave me a brown envelope, Maxim. Do you remember?"

He nodded.

"This was in it," she explained, and handed him the smaller white envelope with his name written on the front in Ursula's hand.

He took the letter from her and gazed at it. After a moment, he whispered, "I'd like to go to my room, Teddy, do you mind?"

"No, I understand," she said. She leaned back against the sofa and watched him slowly cross the room, and her heart ached for him. He was still such a little boy in so many ways, and yet he was so brave.

Maxim sat in the chair facing the chest of drawers on which the photographs of his parents stood. He looked at them for a few minutes before he opened the letter from his mother and began to read it.

Paris   *March 10th, 1939*
My dearest Maxim:
   I go back to Berlin with the realization that I may never see you again. Yet I return with a lighter heart than I have had for a long time, because I know you will soon be safe in England with Teddy. And there no harm will come to you. Your well-being and happiness have always been of

*paramount importance to Papa and me, and you must al-
ways remember this.*

*The only reason I go back to Berlin is to help Papa with
your grandmother, and to bring her out of Germany to
safety.*

*Papa and I waited for such a long time for you, and the
day you were born was the happiest day of our lives. You
are growing up to be such a fine boy, Maxim, and Papa
and I are so very proud of you.*

*If we do not come to England, Teddy will look after you
until you are grown up. Trust her judgment and wisdom,
and love her always, as she loves you.*

*Whatever happens, know that Papa and I love you very
much. You are the best part of us.*

I hold you in my heart always, mein Schatz.

*Your loving and devoted
Mother*

He put the letter down and fumbled for his handkerchief.
He wiped his streaming eyes, then stuffed the handkerchief
back in his pocket, and he sat for a long time in the chair, hurting inside, feeling as if part of him had been cut away.

Finally, he slipped the letter from his mother back in its envelope, and walked over to the chest. Opening the drawer, he
took out his father's wallet, tucked the letter inside, then placed
the wallet next to his little carved wooden horse and closed the
drawer.

"Mutti, Mutti," he whispered, filled with yearning, aching
for her. He could not bear that he would never see her again,
never hear her voice, or nestle in her arms and smell her perfume, lilies of the valley, that she had always worn. He could
not believe that he would never go walking in the woods with
his father again, or sailing with him on the lake, and that they
would never work together in the Westheim Bank when he was
grown up, as they had always planned. "Papa, Papa," he cried
out silently, and he felt as if his heart were being squeezed and
squeezed. He closed his eyes. And in his head he heard his father's music, heard the tinkling of the piano in his father's
house on the Tiergartenstrasse. . . .

He picked up the photograph of Mutti and Papa in evening

dress and stood looking down at it, and fresh tears splashed onto the glass. And Maxim suddenly understood that the sadness inside him would never go away. It would always be there. For the rest of his life.

PART FOUR

Anastasia

═══════════════

PARIS
1959

My beloved spake, and said unto me,
Rise up, my love, my fair one, and come away.
For lo, the winter is past,
the rain is over and gone.
The flowers appear on the earth;
the time of the singing of birds is come,
and the voice of the turtle is heard in the land.

—The Song of Solomon

38

SHE HEARD THE GIRL'S VOICE AS SHE CLIMBED THE BROAD staircase. It floated down to her on the warm July air, light, lyrical, full of music, a lovely voice all the more captivating because it was so natural and unaffected.

Ideal for stage or screen, Margo Derevenko thought, but thankfully she has no ambitions in that direction. And even if she did, her father would never permit her to become an actress. He knows too much about that tough and uncertain world to let her venture into it.

As Margot drew closer to the second-floor landing she paused to listen, one hand resting on the polished oak banister, the other holding a small basket filled with fresh-cut white flowers from her garden. The girl's words were clearer, more distinct now, and Margot realized she was talking to the dressmaker.

"And so, Marie, I said to the *clochard*, "Come with me, I know you are hungry. I invite you to the café across the street for lunch.' "

Marie sucked in her breath incredulously. "And did the *clochard* come with you to the café, mademoiselle?" she gasped.

"Of course not, Marie! He looked at me as if I had invited him to a funeral. *His own.* And so I said, 'All right, if you don't want to take lunch with me in the café, let us go to my parents' house. Our cook, Maruba, will make a splendid lunch for you, anything you fancy.' And can you imagine what happened, Marie?"

"No, mademoiselle, I cannot."

"He *refused.*"

"It is good that he did," Marie said after a moment, in a dry

297

voice. "I don't think your parents would be too happy if you entertained a tramp in their beautiful home."

Indeed we would *not,* Margot muttered under her breath. Anastasia said nothing.

A moment of silence ensued, and then the dressmaker went on to remark in a genuinely puzzled voice, "I do not understand, mademoiselle, why you asked this tramp to lunch in the first place."

"Obviously because he was *hungry,* Marie."

"But that is *his* problem. Anyway, these tramps of the Seine are all scoundrels."

"How can you say a thing like that! It's not their fault they've fallen on hard times, have been reduced to living that kind of life. I talk to them all the time, and visit with them, and believe me, Marie, the *clochards* are not a bit happy about living under the bridges of the river, sleeping outside in all kinds of weather, existing on nothing, scavenging for food."

"They bring on their own misfortunes."

"*I* don't believe they do, and *I* try to help them."

When Marie did not respond, the girl rushed on, "And I have succeeded in helping *one* of them—a lady *clochard.* She is now on the way to making a good life for herself."

"*Really,*" Marie said, sounding skeptical.

"Yes, it's true, I *did* help her. I persuaded her to give up the wine bottle, which she did, and she now has a job and somewhere to live."

"I see. And tell me, mademoiselle, do your parents know about your concern for the *clochards* of the Seine, and your involvement with them?"

"Of course, and they approve."

We do? Margot thought. Since when, I wonder? She now hurried on up the wide polished-wood stairs and stepped into the spacious first-floor hall, where the Degas bronze of the little ballerina took pride of place to the left of the gouache of ballet dancers in green dresses, also by Degas. He and Monet were her husband's favorite artists, and both were well represented in this house.

The huge double doors of the *petit salon* stood ajar, and Margot peered inside as she paused for a moment before entering, and caught her breath in surprise and pleasure.

Her eighteen-year-old daughter stood in the center of the

room and was slowly turning around, her arms outstretched, so that Marie could make a final check of the evening dress she had finished the day before. The dress, a gossamer confection of chiffon in a mixture of delicate blues and pale grays, floated around her like wisps of sea mist. If the dress was superb, then the girl was perfection itself.

The room was flooded with morning sun, which poured in through the tall windows and bathed the girl in its soft light. Her pale-blond hair, falling to her tiny waist, seemed to be full of sunlight and shimmered around her exquisite heart-shaped face, which gleamed like polished ivory. Her eyes, set wide apart and heavily lashed, were a lovely, misty, blue-gray color. Of medium height, the girl had long and graceful limbs; the floating, capelike sleeves of the dress fell away from the prettiest of shoulders and arms, while the pointed handkerchief hemline showed off her shapely ankles and dainty feet.

So beautiful she doesn't seem real, Margot thought, but then she never did, not even as a child. She's too exquisite and far too sweet and gentle for her own good. Idealist, romantic dreamer. Whatever am I going to do with her? She's much too impractical and trusting for this hard world we live in today. Sighing to herself, Margot pushed open the door and glided into the room.

"There you are, Anastasia!" she exclaimed, smiling at her daughter.

"Look, Mummy, isn't it gorgeous?" As she spoke Anastasia held out the skirt of the dress, did a little pirouette and ended up facing her mother, looking at her questioningly.

Margot nodded in approval, and looked at the dressmaker. "Good morning, Marie, and I see you have created another triumph."

"*Bonjour, madame.* It is not I that did that, but you," Marie replied, looking pointedly at Anastasia. Nonetheless, the compliment about her work pleased her, and she smiled at Madame Derevenko.

"I'm afraid I can't take all the credit for Anastasia," Margot said with a chuckle. "I believe her father had something to do with producing her."

Anastasia laughed with her mother. It was a light, tinkling laugh, which like her voice was as clear as a bell. "The dress really is divine, isn't it? Marie truly has outdone herself. *Merci beaucoup*, Marie," she said and made a small curtsy.

The dressmaker's face filled with happiness. She liked nothing better than satisfied customers, and most especially the Derevenko women, who were her favorites. She had made a great many clothes for them over the years, although recently they had been mostly for Anastasia. Madame favored haute couture more than ever these days. But what a joy it was to sew for this girl who did the garments such justice with her incredible beauty, her willowy figure and perfect carriage.

Margot was studying her daughter thoughtfully, and now exclaimed, "Opals! That's it! You must wear my opals with the new gown. They will go beautifully with the blues and grays in it."

"Oh, Mummy, thank you! How lovely of you to lend them to me."

"You're going to look ravishing, and you'll be the proverbial belle of the ball."

"Hardly. Yvette will be the star turn, and so she should be. After all, it's her special day," Anastasia pointed out.

Margot merely smiled, and then glanced around the small sitting room. Solange, the maid, had placed bud vases filled with water on the various occasional tables; now Margot moved around the room with her flower basket, placing blooms in the little cylinders and pots, then stepping back to regard them critically, her fair head on one side.

Anastasia watched her mother, thinking how talented she was when it came to artistic matters, such as flower arranging, table setting, and decorating a room. She was full of admiration for her.

Margot suddenly swung around and directed her hazel-eyed gaze at her daughter. "Daydreaming again?"

"No, Mummy," Anastasia laughed. "And I'd better go and change out of this dress. Marie, will you come and help me, please?"

"Of course, mademoiselle."

"Lunch at one in the garden, Anastasia."

"Yes, you've already told me," the girl said, and floated out on a cloud of chiffon and Ma Griffe scent.

*   *   *

The *hôtel particulier* owned by Alexander and Margot Derevenko was on the elegant Faubourg Saint-Germain, and it was
only one of a number of beautiful private houses standing on
this street behind forbiddingly high stone walls. The Faubourg
Saint-Germain is in the Seventh Arrondissement, which is part
of one of the most celebrated districts on the Left Bank, a district at once an enclave for aristocrats and a haven for students,
artists and writers.

In the vicinity of the house were the Rodin Museum, the
French Academy, the École Militaire, and the Hôtel des Invalides, housing the tomb of Napoleon I. Along with these historic
buildings, there were charming little bistros, antique shops and
art galleries located in the area, as well as two of the most famous hangouts for writers and artists in Paris, the Café des
Deux Magots and the Café de Flore.

The Derevenko house was hidden from pedestrians by mas-
sive dark-green doors that fronted on the street. Behind them
was a small concierge's cottage in a typical Parisian courtyard,
cobblestoned, with a fountain in the center and a horse chestnut
tree near one of the ivy-clad walls.

The house itself was elongated and had a façade of classical
design, with many tall shuttered windows and wide stone steps
leading up to a double front door. Inside were spacious rooms
with high ceilings that were airy and full of light, and they owed
their elegance and graciousness to Margot Derevenko's impeccable taste in antiques and furnishings. Her flair and talent at
combining and arranging these elements were in evidence
throughout the house.

The entrance hall on the ground floor led directly to the garden through a series of glass doors, and the garden itself was
something of a masterpiece, painstakingly created over the
years under Margot's loving guidance. Although she had lived
in France since her youth and had been educated at the Sorbonne, Margot was English by birth and upbringing. And so
it was to one of the great English gardens that she had turned
when seeking ideas for her own retreat in the heart of Paris,
drawing inspiration from the famous White Garden at Sis-
singhurst Castle. Like the one in Kent, this much smaller garden sitting in the shadow of the Hôtel des Invalides was a mingling of green foliage and flowers and flowering bushes of only
one color—white. It was the simplicity and purity of this green-

and-white theme that gave this formal Parisian garden its sense of coolness, serenity and elegance.

A lily pond surrounded by flagstones was at the edge of the lawn, which was encircled by luxuriant borders and beds filled to overflowing with white flowers of all kinds—azaleas, roses, tulips, narcissi, chrysanthemums and snowdrops, depending on the season. Beyond the flower beds were lilac and horse chestnut trees, as well as flowering bushes such as rhododendrons and hydrangeas, and surrounding the entire garden were high ancient stone walls covered with glossy ivy.

A flagstone terrace stretched the length of the house and overlooked the garden, and it was here that Margot and Anastasia sat having lunch at a wrought-iron garden table, shaded by a large sun umbrella. Maruba, their North African cook, had prepared a simple meal of grilled fish, a green salad and fresh sliced peaches soaked in champagne.

Between mouthfuls of fish, Margot said, "I wasn't eavesdropping before, but I couldn't help hearing your conversation with Marie when I was coming up the stairs. You must stop spending time with the *clochards*, you know. It's simply not right."

"I'm only trying to help them, Mother!"

"You can't help them. It seems to me that they have chosen that kind of life."

"How can you say such a thing? You sound like Marie! Anyway, who would choose to live in such extreme conditions?"

Margot shook her head. "Oh, darling, don't be naive. . . ." Her voice trailed off, and she was thoughtful before saying, "Your father and I worry about you. I don't think you realize how lovely you are, and who knows about these tramps—"

"They're gentle people!" Anastasia interrupted. "And not dangerous at all, which is what you're implying. They're not going to attack me, or try to rape me. You mustn't worry, and please don't be angry with me—I can't bear it when you and Daddy are cross."

"Good heavens, we're not angry, only concerned about your welfare." Margot smiled at her daughter. "Actually, your father and I are very pleased with the way you've passed your *Baccalauréat* with honors, and been accepted at the Sorbonne. In fact, I would say we're *more* than pleased, darling. However, we—"

"I know what you're going to say, Mummy," Anastasia exclaimed, cutting in again. "You don't want me messing around with derelicts."

"*Exactly.*"

"Those poor souls. I can hardly bear to think of their suffering, the way they live."

"Yes, it is sad, Anastasia. But the world is full of the most awful inequities, and it always has been, and there is little you or anyone else can do to help those poor creatures, I'm afraid."

"I don't believe that, Mummy. In my opinion even one person can make a difference."

Margot looked at her daughter and realized it would be wiser to let the subject rest for the moment. As sweet as Anastasia was, she was nobody's fool—she was in fact clever and quick-witted. And also extremely stubborn by nature. If Margot continued to berate her for her concern about the tramps the girl would only dig in her heels defiantly. They were leaving in a few days to spend the rest of July and part of August at their villa in Cannes, and then Anastasia was going to London to stay with her grandmother. She would be far away from her *clochards*, and in the autumn she was starting at the university, and the work schedule there would preoccupy her and more than fill her time.

And so Margot changed the subject, and said, "I am going shopping with Lucrezia this afternoon. Would you like to join us, darling?"

"Thanks, but I can't. I want to go and look for several history books I need. Yvette told me I would most probably find them at the old bookshop near the Quai Saint-Michel."

Margot nodded. "Don't forget, you're joining us for dinner tonight. Your father has people here from Hollywood."

"He told me. Where are we going?"

"La Tour d'Argent."

"It's going to be full of rich foreign tourists. You know what it's like in July."

Margot smiled. "But it's still very beautiful. Think of the gorgeous views of Notre Dame and the Seine. And the gorgeous duck. Besides, that's where the Hollywood people want to go."

"They always do," Anastasia murmured, then asked, "Is Daddy doing another American movie?"

"It looks like it. Drinks here at the house at eight o'clock, and then we'll wander over to the restaurant about nine."

"Don't worry, Mummy, I won't be late. I know how important these business evenings are to Daddy. And I promise to be on my best behavior." She gave her mother a sly little look and her mouth twitched as she added, "And I won't mention the *clochards*."

Margot burst out laughing. "Well, I must say, I'm glad to see your newly developed social conscience hasn't affected your sense of humor."

39

MAXIM WALKED AT A LEISURELY PACE ALONG THE quays that ran parallel with the Seine, enjoying a stroll on this pleasant afternoon.

He had just finished lunch with an American business associate who was on a trip to France, had concluded an excellent deal and was delighted. His first day in Paris had turned out exceptionally well.

When he came to the Quai Voltaire he paused, glanced up a narrow side street on his right, hesitating, wondering whether to go into Saint-Germain-des-Prés for a cup of coffee at the Deux Magots, and then decided against it. He was making for a particular corner of the city, and he did not want to sidetrack himself.

And so he strode on purposefully, heading in the direction of the Cathedral of Notre Dame, whose imposing Gothic towers were like giant sentinels silhouetted against the azure summer sky, perfect today and full of that soft light beloved by painters which was so characteristic of Paris. The waters of the Seine trembled in the hazy sunshine filtering through the leafy branches of the trees that lined the river's edge.

Paris was Maxim's favorite city. He preferred it to London, where he lived and worked, to New York, where he frequently went on business, and to Berlin, where he was born. And whenever he came back it always looked more beautiful than he had remembered it to be; it forever took him by surprise.

He had first seen Paris in the early part of 1939, when he and Mutti and Teddy had been fleeing Nazi Germany, and he had never forgotten that time of his childhood, those gloriously happy weeks with his mother, the last he had ever spent with her. A multitude of images were engraved on his mind, and the memories had remained ever constant, would be forever part of him.

Thirteen years had passed before he had visited the city again. He had first returned in 1952 to celebrate his eighteenth birthday; it was Mark who had thought of the trip and had also invited Stubby to join them as his guest. They had all had a wonderful time together, and Teddy, in particular, had thoroughly enjoyed herself. She had given birth to her second child in February of that year, a boy they named David, after Mark's brother, who had been killed in the war, and the prospect of a long weekend in Paris had excited her.

"It's just what I need," Teddy had exclaimed when Mark had told her what he was planning for Maxim's birthday. "I looked like a whale in a tent for so many weeks of my pregnancy, I can't wait to buy some smart new French clothes, now that I've got my figure back. So Paris it is!" She had enthusiastically agreed. But deep down inside, the real reason Teddy was glad they were going was that she had always understood how much Paris meant to her beloved Maxim, knew that he held joyous memories of the months he had spent there with Ursula. So for once she had not fussed about leaving their two-year-old daughter, Kay, in the care of the nanny and Mark's mother. She had even handed over the new baby with a smile on her face. Maxim's eighteenth-birthday celebration and the trip to Paris took precedence over everything else. Maxim was like her own child, and she thought of him as such, considered him to be her son. He was, and always would be, her pride and joy, and he could do no wrong in her eyes, and he was her favorite.

As it turned out, the trip to Paris in 1952 had been truly memorable, for Maxim's birthday had not been the only thing they had celebrated that particular June. Maxim and Stubby had spent some of their time whooping it up and congratulating each other because they had concluded their first successful business deal. A month before Maxim's birthday they had sold the land they owned in the East End to one of the big London builders, and they had made a tidy profit for themselves in the process.

This business venture had originally come about quite by accident, and because of Mrs. Threscoe, the Trentons' cockney charlady.

Stubby and she had had a soft spot for each other since his childhood, and over the years Stubby had become her most trusted confidant. In 1950, when her husband had been knocked down by a truck and had subsequently died of head injuries, Mrs. Threscoe, who was childless, had come weeping to Stubby with her problems. Jack Threscoe had left very little money; all of his savings were tied up in a piece of land in the East End, a bomb site, which he had purchased in 1946. With Jack gone, she was now ready to sell the land, *needed* to sell it, Mrs. Threscoe had explained to Stubby. But to her immense dismay nobody seemed to want it.

When Stubby had told his best friend the story, Maxim had mulled it over for a couple of days, and had then suggested that they look at the land themselves. "If we're going to be business-men, now's the time to start," he had said, and had pointed out that rebuilding was going on in various parts of London. "That land might have possibilities. Perhaps *we* should buy it, Stubby. We'd be helping Mrs. Threscoe out, and, with a bit of luck, it could prove to be a good investment."

As it turned out, Maxim was right.

Before the sixteen-year-old boys had purchased the Threscoe bomb site, Maxim had asked the opinion of Henry Rossiter, who was still in charge of his money. The merchant banker had called in his real estate experts, who had gone to look at the land; after receiving their report, he had informed Maxim that it would be a safe investment.

"You probably won't make a great deal of money on it when you sell, which obviously you will do one day, but you certainly won't lose," he had assured Maxim, and he had then purchased the land on their behalf. Mrs. Threscoe had asked for five thousand pounds, which gave her a decent profit; the boys had agreed to her price without haggling and had split the cost down the middle, thus becoming partners. Maxim had used money from the Westheim funds, which were in Henry Rossiter's control; Stubby, with permission from his father, had plunked down the entire legacy his uncle had left him, plus three hundred pounds contributed by his doting mother.

Two years later they had sold the Threscoe bomb site for twenty-five thousand pounds, and had made a straight profit of twenty thousand, much to their surprise—and everyone else's, in fact.

They were supposed to have started university that year, having graduated from St. Paul's School in July, at the age of eighteen. But they had rejected Oxford. Instead they had started their own company with the profits from the Threscoe deal.

Teddy had objected initially, and so had Stubby's father, but they had both been won over in the end, thanks chiefly to the intervention of Henry Rossiter.

"Forcing them to go to Oxford now is rather like closing the gate after the horses have escaped," Mr. Rossiter had said to Teddy and Mr. Trenton with a chuckle. "It seems to me that these two young bucks have embarked on commercial careers already, and rather successfully, I might add. So why stop them now? I think they're going to do very nicely for themselves."

Mark had tended to agree with the merchant banker. His endorsement of the scheme had ultimately convinced Teddy that she was not making a mistake by permitting Maxim to go into business, rather than continuing his higher education. And she had given him her blessing.

Maxim had planned to be a financier, and had never intended to open a real estate business, and if it had not been for Stubby he would not have done so. But because the East End property had turned such a good profit, Stubby had persuaded Maxim to stay in this field, at least for a while. They took offices in Jermyn Street, formed a company called Westrent, which was a contraction of their last names, and started to buy bomb sites wherever they could find them.

For the most part they concentrated on major industrial cities in the provinces, which had been heavily bombed by the Luftwaffe during the war. They concentrated on Leeds, Bradford, Sheffield, Coventry and Birmingham, managed to find suitable tracts of land at decent prices, sites that they considered to have great potential for future building projects. Once they had had the land cleaned of rubble and fenced in, they had sensibly held on to the sites until really good bids had been made. In some instances they had had to wait several years to make the right sales; ultimately, Westrent was profitable largely because of the postwar building boom in England in the mid-fifties.

The year 1952 was also the year Maxim decided to legally change his name. When he had first mentioned to Teddy that he wished to anglicize Westheim by dropping the *heim* and calling himself West, she had agreed it was a good idea, and, as his guardian, had given her consent. "Your parents planned to do that anyway," she had informed him. "In fact, your mother brought the matter up to me several times when we were in Paris in 1939. You know how much she loved England, wished us all to become English. She would be so pleased if she knew you intended to do this, and so would your father. He had wanted to adopt West as the family surname even before we left Germany, but the prince didn't think Admiral Canaris could get new passports."

So he had changed his name—and his nationality as well. He had become Maximilian West, naturalized British subject, with a British passport and the right to vote in the elections.

And in the ensuing years since his eighteenth birthday Maxim had not looked back.

When wheeling and dealing in real estate had become less challenging, and had actually begun to bore him, he had purchased several small, unprofitable companies: a printing plant in Wakefield, a bus company in Bristol and a brickyard in Nottingham. In a relatively short time he had put them back on their feet through a bit of brilliant reorganization and with the help of the new management teams he had sent in. Subsequently he had sold them, making excellent profits on all three. And thus a second company, Westinvest, was born.

Aside from his business acumen and his brilliance with figures, Maxim had the ability to understand and assess a balance sheet and all its ramifications immediately and with the greatest of ease. He also had imagination and vision, his gut instinct, which he always relied on, sometimes sweeping away analysts' reports and recommendations in favor of his own instinctive reaction to a deal, the "feel" he had for it. All of these elements

were important factors in his success, and were to stand him
in good stead for the future.

Now, at the age of twenty-five, he was managing director
of Westrent and Westinvest. He owned an elegantly furnished
flat in Mayfair and a sleek new wine-colored Jaguar. He belonged to some of the best private clubs in town, and cut quite
a swath in smart London society, escorting beautiful young
women, such as a couple of well-known starlets, and was considered to be something of a playboy by the British press. The
gossip columnists loved him. They were forever exclaiming in
print about his dashing good looks, his elegance and style, his
gorgeous female companions, the parties he gave and his
wealth.

He considered the parties and the women and his social life
in general to be all so much folderol, the fluff of life, and therefore of little value or consequence. The only thing that truly
mattered to him and gave him genuine pleasure was his work.

He had told Stubby that he intended to make a million
pounds by the time he was thirty. Stubby never once doubted
that he would. Nor did Maxim doubt himself, and making that
million was the yardstick by which he judged himself and his
achievements. And so he drove himself.

Five years to go, he thought, as he came to the Place Saint-
Michel, and stood at the curb waiting for the lights to change.
He smiled; he was quite confident he would achieve his goal.

As far as Maxim himself was concerned, the real secrets of
his success were single-mindedness of purpose, dedication,
hard work and the ability to put in very long hours without
suffering from fatigue. He was fortunate in that he had immense stamina, and needed only about five hours' sleep; he usually rose at four in the morning, was at his desk in the flat by
four-thirty, where he did paperwork until seven, when he left
for his office in Jermyn Street to put in a full day. He thought
nothing of working seven days a week, and for weeks on end
without a break. Maxim had long acknowledged that he was
a dyed-in-the-wool workaholic, which was why he guffawed
when the papers called him a playboy.

He thought of this now, and chuckled. *Some playboy*, he
muttered under his breath. If only they knew.

The truth was, the beautiful women he took out were mere
decorative accessories to wear on his arm. Of course, he *had*

fallen in love several times. And out of it rather rapidly. In between he had had numerous affairs. But none of the women had lasted very long with him. Simply put, he had never managed to find the right woman. He wondered sometimes what he was looking for exactly. Perfection? But he was smart enough to understand that there was no such thing as a perfect woman. Or man, for that matter. In any case, he did not want a paragon.

Still, true love *did* seem to elude him.

The lights changed to green, and Maxim crossed the Place Saint-Michel and headed toward the Rue de la Huchette.

As he walked down that narrow old street, he experienced a sense of nostalgia as he glanced around. On his left was the Hôtel Mont Blanc, where he and Stubby had stayed on a couple of occasions, and immediately opposite was the El Djazier, the North African nightclub that they still frequented, going there to drink mint tea, ogle the exotic belly dancers and eat couscous with harissa, the hot piquant sauce that blew his head off but that he nevertheless enjoyed. And a few yards farther along were the famous jazz joints, where some of the American jazz greats came to play and musicians of all nationalities came to listen, as did he and Stubby from time to time.

He paused when he saw the Rue du Chat-qui-Pêche.

It was only a little alleyway, but he had never forgotten this street because the name had so delighted him when he was a child. "It means the 'Street of the Cat Who Fishes,' " Mutti had said, translating the French for him. Filled with glee, he had laughed out loud, tickled at the idea of a cat who fished.

They had been on one of their outings, he and Mutti and Teddy. "Investigating the quaint bits of Paris," Mutti had called their excursions, and ever since those days this most picturesque area had remained a favorite. He often returned to walk around these narrow cobblestoned streets to browse in the bookstores and galleries.

Maxim went on walking up the Rue de la Huchette, past the little Greek and North African restaurants, until he came to the top of the street and into a wide, open area like a square called the Rue de la Bûcherie. Here he headed for one of the cafés that fronted on a series of little gardens and faced the Cathedral of Notre Dame, which stood on the Île de la Cité, one of the small islands in the Seine.

He found a seat at a sidewalk table, and when the waiter came to take his order he asked for a *citron pressé*. The afternoon had suddenly become very warm; he leaned back in the wicker chair, loosened his tie and undid the top button of his shirt, trying to cool off. Within seconds the lemonade arrived. Sipping it, Maxim relaxed and let his thoughts drift for a while. It was odd how childhood places always tugged at him and pulled him back. Whenever he went to Berlin, whether on business or to see Aunt Irina, he made a point of passing by the Tiergartenstrasse and the Tiergarten.

The lure of childhood memories, he thought, how strong it is with me. . . . I wonder if it's so with everyone else? Or is it because I lost so much when I was a child . . . had such irretrievable losses? Do I come back to Paris and Berlin in the hope of finding something that escaped me long, long ago? Am I on an eternal quest? What is it I hope to find?

The answers to his questions were elusive, as they always were. . . .

A short while later Maxim walked to Shakespeare and Company, the secondhand bookshop nearby that was run by a friendly American called Bill, with whom Maxim had been acquainted for the past few years. When he asked for the owner, he was told by the American girl working there that Bill would not be in the shop before six.

"Any message?" the girl asked, smiling broadly, showing her perfect white teeth.

Maxim shook his head. "Just tell him Duke stopped in to say hello, and that I'll try and come by tomorrow."

"Okay, Duke," the girl said, and went on arranging books on a shelf.

Maxim watched her for a moment, fascinated by her choices. They were an eclectic selection: novels by Richard Wright, Henry Miller, Lawrence Durrell and Anaïs Nin. These writers, all of whom he had read, had absolutely nothing in common with each other, as far as their writing was concerned. He could not for the life of him understand why the girl was placing them together. And then he remembered that they had all lived in Paris at the same time, and were friends. Obviously she saw this as some sort of link between them. The Paris clique, he thought, and smiled.

Maxim browsed in Shakespeare and Company for a while,

and to his delight he spotted a copy of *The Young Lions*, by Irwin Shaw, his favorite writer. He looked inside the book and discovered it was a first edition, published by Random House in 1948. He bought it at once, and left the shop clutching it, well pleased with his find. He had a whole shelf of first editions at the flat in London, and this copy of early Shaw would make a wonderful addition.

Crossing the square, Maxim went past the Hôtel Notre Dame and headed down the Quai Saint-Michel, walking in the direction of another secondhand bookshop, one of a slightly different nature. Arcel et Fils sold antique books, some dating back to the eighteenth century, and many were rare, others first editions, yet others genuine collector's items.

At the sound of the door opening, the owner swung around from the shelves where he was standing and peered down the shop. His face lit up at the sight of Maxim.

"*Monsieur West! Quel plaisir de vous revoir.*"

"And it's a great pleasure for me to see you, Monsieur Arcel," Maxim replied, walking forward, thrusting out his hand.

The owner of the shop shook it vigorously. "The book I wrote to you about is in the back room. I will get it. Please excuse me for a moment."

Maxim was looking forward to seeing this rare volume on antique jewelry, and hoped that it really was as special as Monsieur Arcel had indicated in his letter. If it was, it would make a nice present for Mark.

Maxim slouched against the counter, leaning on one elbow, and glanced around the shop. It was then that he saw the girl.

He straightened, looking at her alertly. She stood at the far end, silhouetted against the window. The light of the late afternoon sun surrounded her like an aureole, turning her long blond hair into spun gold. Her face was in profile, and it was exquisite. He noted the smooth brow, the small straight nose, the chiseled chin, the long neck rising from the white silk shirt she wore with a navy-blue cotton dirndl skirt. She was slender—willowy. Her bare feet were in sandals, yet despite her casual dress there was an elegance about her, an aristocratic dignity.

Maxim was fascinated. Who was she?

As if she were aware that someone was scrutinizing her, she turned slowly, and their gaze met.

Her eyes were large and luminous, a light gray-blue in color. A dreamer's eyes, he thought, unable to tear his gaze away from hers, mesmerized by her beauty. And yet there was something else, something more than her beauty that captivated him. There was a mysteriousness about her, and it made him catch his breath.

The girl suddenly smiled at him. It was the loveliest of smiles, lifting the corners of her pretty mouth in a tantalizing tilt, dimpling her cheeks, bringing a sudden gaiety and laughter to her sparkling eyes.

Maxim smiled back.

Unexpectedly he felt very happy, almost light-headed with happiness. He knew it was her smile that made him feel this way. It seemed to fill the empty places of his heart.

They just stood there staring at each other and smiling.

"Here it is, monsieur," the owner of the shop said, hurrying back from his private quarters, the antique book in his hands. "It is unique. And the illustrations are . . . *wonderful.*"

With reluctance, Maxim looked away from the girl, and glanced down at the book that the Frenchman had placed on the counter in front of him.

"Look at the illustrations," Monsieur Arcel exclaimed, opening the leather-bound volume at random, pointing to a page.

"Yes, I see what you mean," Maxim murmured, and then unable to restrain himself, he turned and looked over his shoulder, his eyes seeking the girl again. To his surprise and dismay she was no longer standing near the window. She had vanished.

Maxim looked at Monsieur Arcel, and asked, "The young woman who was standing there near the window. Did she leave?"

"Why, yes, Monsieur West, she slipped out a moment ago. When you were perusing the book."

"Excuse me." Maxim rushed to the door, and ran out into the street, looking up and down anxiously.

He spotted her a little farther along the quay. He was just in time to see her stepping into a taxi.

"Wait!" he cried.

The sound of the traffic drowned out his voice; she did not hear him.

Helplessly Maxim stood and watched the cab slide into the swiftly moving line of cars on the Quai Saint-Michel and disappear from sight. He sighed and went back into the shop, a sense of dejection descending on him.

"Do you know the girl who just left, Monsieur Arcel?" Maxim asked, striding back to the counter.

The old Frenchman shook his head. "I am so sorry, I do not. It is the first time I have seen her. Ah, but she *is* lovely, eh, Monsieur West?"

"She's the most beautiful girl I've ever set eyes on," Maxim said.

"I've never seen you looking so morose, Duke. Not for years," Stubby murmured, peering at Maxim across the dinner table. "For God's sake, do cheer up."

Maxim chose not to comment. He picked up the glass of good burgundy, which Stubby had ordered earlier, and took a swallow.

Stubby also drank, observing his friend over the top of the glass, his eyes thoughtful.

The two men were sitting at a corner table in Chez André, an excellent bistro on the Rue Marbeuf, not far from the Plaza-Athénée Hotel, where they were staying.

Ever since he had returned to the hotel at six-thirty Stubby had been disturbed by Maxim's glum demeanor. He took another sip of the red wine, put the glass down and remarked, "You look as if it's the end of the world."

"That's how I feel." Maxim returned Alan Trenton's steady gaze, then muttered, "I'll never find that girl again."

"I can't believe it!" Stubby cried, his blue eyes widening. "*You*, of all people, going on this way about a bloody female! *You!* And imagine, all these years I've believed that the only thing that really excited you, gave you pleasure, was business. It just goes to show what an idiot I am, doesn't it?" Stubby shook his head. "You've certainly fooled *me*, Duke."

Seeing the humorous side, Maxim had the good grace to laugh. "I *am* behaving out of character, aren't I?"

"I'll say."

The noise of the bistro swirled around them, and they did not speak for a while.

Maxim leaned across the table and asked, "Can I let you in on a little secret?"

"Why not? You've been telling me your secrets since you were eight. Why stop now?"

"I think I'm in love."

"Oh come on!" Stubby exploded, aghast. Then laughter burst out of him while he stared at Maxim, but quite suddenly it died in his throat and he said in a sober voice, "Good God, I think you mean it! But how can you have fallen in love with a girl you haven't even *spoken* to? *You,* Maxim! Women are usually the last thing on your mind."

"I know. And you're right, of course, Alan," Maxim said quietly, now feeling more than a little foolish. "I am being stupid, aren't I? Crazy. Let's forget about the girl and all that silliness, which is what it is, actually. Pure silliness. How did your meeting go?" he asked, changing the subject.

"Okay. More than okay. The French group are keen to do a deal. It was well worth my while, driving out to Versailles to see Monsieur Verland. They do have North African oil interests. Libya, I think. The bottom line is this: Monsieur Verland is prepared to come to London for talks, when Dad gets back from Hong Kong, so I think the old man will be pleased with with the way I've handled things." Stubby sat back in the chair and gave Maxim a faint smile. "But I can't help wishing I was still in business with you, old chap."

"So do I, Stubby. Come back! Tell your father the oil business bores you, that you want to work with me in Westrent again."

"I wish I could, but you know very well I can't. Dad's just not up to it these days, and if I did a bunk—it'd kill him, actually. He really needs me in the business with him."

"I know. But remember, you're always welcome—I miss you."

"I feel the same way, Maxim. We've always been good sparring partners, haven't we?"

"The best."

Stubby looked thoughtful. "The girl . . . how old was she?"

"Seventeen or eighteen, thereabouts. Why?" Maxim lifted a brow.

"She's probably a student. I bet she bought books at Arcel's shop, and that she'll go back. Why don't we stop in there tomorrow? It's Saturday, we've nothing better to do."

"Why? To what purpose?"

"We could ask old Arcel a few questions. He might know more than he realizes. We could jog his memory. You never know, she might have given him a clue to her identity, and he just doesn't realize it."

"Oh, Stubby, that's so far-fetched—it's clutching at straws. . . ." Maxim's voice trailed off.

But he would give anything to know who she was, and to find her again.

40

ᴀɴᴀsᴛᴀsɪᴀ SAW HIM BEFORE HE SAW HER. HE STOOD with his back to her, but then he moved his head slightly and she caught a glimpse of his face and her heart missed a beat. She did not have to look twice to recognize the man who had stared at her so penetratingly in Arcel's bookshop yesterday.

That he was a guest at the party celebrating Yvette's engagement to Philippe Arnaud was surprising in itself, but that she had spotted him among the two hundred people present, and so early in the evening, was remarkable. Even more amazing was the fact that he was actually talking to her *mother*. At least, the blond young man with him was engaged in conversation with her; *he* just stood to one side, listening politely. His companion and her mother appeared to know each other quite well, if their animated expressions were anything to judge by.

Anastasia hovered a short distance away, at the other side of the dance floor. She was standing next to an enormous potted orchid plant, one of the many exotic floral decorations used to enhance the tented gardens of the de Millinets' house in Neuilly-sur-Seine, near the Bois de Boulogne.

She stepped behind the plant so that she was partially hidden from view but able to observe her mother and the two young men quite clearly.

Anastasia and her parents had arrived at the supper dance about half an hour ago, and after greeting their host and hostess and congratulating the newly engaged couple, they had stood chatting with one another for a few minutes, sipping champagne and admiring the lovely setting and the elegant guests. The men were in black tie; the women wore evening gowns and were much bejeweled. It was an extremely chic gathering, and the crème de la crème of Parisian society mingled with movie people and members of the jet set.

After a while the three Derevenkos had separated and wandered off in different directions. Alexander Derevenko had caught sight of some of his cronies from the picture business, and had gone over to hobnob with them near the bar. Margot had glided across the dance floor to join her friends Lucrezia and Sophia. Anastasia had drifted about aimlessly, seeking her own friends. Somewhat to her surprise not many of them were in evidence, certainly none of the girls to whom she was especially close. She felt rather lost, especially since Yvette clung to the arm of Philippe, her betrothed, and was oblivious of everyone else. There was such a scarcity of young people, she began to wonder if this was going to turn out to be a boring party—for adults only. Perhaps the de Millinets had invited more of their contemporaries than their daughter's special chums. That was not uncommon on occasions like this.

And then a split second later, she had seen him. Instantly, she had thought: *Fate. We were fated to meet again. I just knew last night that it would happen.*

She had not stopped thinking about him since yesterday afternoon. The minute she had arrived home she had regretted her hasty flight from Monsieur Arcel's little shop on the Quai Saint-Michel. But the dark and handsome young man had had such an aura of sophistication and self-confidence about him, and he had stared so intensely with those piercing dark eyes, that she had suddenly felt frightened. And inadequate. Shy, gauche, schoolgirlish, and most certainly out of her depth. She was very inexperienced when it came to men. And so she had fled, run out into the street and hailed the first taxi she had seen.

But last night, when she had been dressing to go out to dinner with her parents and her father's Hollywood associates, she had decided to make herself look more grown up, older. "Practicing," she had muttered to herself as she piled her hair on top of her head, put on pink lipstick, dressed in one of her new and more sophisticated outfits, a black silk two-piece, and high-heeled black patent shoes.

Her father had looked slightly startled when she had joined him and her mother and their guests for cocktails in the garden. He had murmured that she looked chic, a word he had never used in relation to her before, and her mother smiled and nodded in agreement. Later, at La Tour d'Argent, she had noticed that quite a lot of people glanced her way, and admiringly so, and she had been pleased.

Last night she had been testing the waters, preparing herself, wanting to be ready when she saw him again. She was positive that their paths would cross; she had simply not known how quickly.

It was meant to be, Anastasia thought, staring at his well-defined profile. She wondered what to do. She acknowledged to herself that she ought to go and speak to him immediately, while her mother was engaged in conversation with the blond young man, so that her mother could introduce her.

She hesitated, and in that moment she saw that her mother was nodding graciously and walking away to join another group of friends nearby.

Now, Anastasia instructed herself. *Go now. Go before it's too late, before he disappears in the crowd.*

Skirting the edge of the dance floor, where people were already beginning to dance, she walked over to the other side of the tented garden, and stopped immediately behind him.

He was tall, taller than she had realized. At least six feet, and well built.

"Good evening," she said.

He swung around, so did his companion, and they both stared at her. She heard his quick intake of breath, observed his shock and disbelief, then saw pure pleasure invading his face.

"It's *you*!" he exclaimed.

"Hello."

He thrust out his hand. "I'm Maximilian West. Tell me your name immediately, before you disappear again."

She took hold of his hand. "I'm Anastasia Alexandrovna Derevenko," she said.

"What a lovely name. Hello, Anastasia. Hello. *Hello*." He turned to his friend. "Alan, this is Anastasia. The young lady from Arcel's bookshop."

"So I gather," Stubby said. "I can't begin to tell you what a pleasure this is, Anastasia. Apparently I was talking to your mother a moment ago. You *are* Madame Derevenko's daughter, aren't you?"

Anastasia nodded. A small frown furrowed her brow. "Have we met before?"

Alan grinned. "My parents have a villa in Cannes, and they are friends of the de Millinets. And yes, I think we did meet once. Rather fleetingly, a long time ago. You were about twelve, I believe." And then Alan said, "Excuse me, you two. I see an acquaintance of mine over there. Camilla Galland, the actress. I think I'll go and talk to her. She seems to be all alone, and looks a bit forlorn. See you later."

"I thought I'd lost you," Maxim said, after Stubby left. He was staring at her, continuing to hold her hand. "Actually, I thought I'd never find you again."

"I knew we'd meet," she responded with the same kind of unselfconscious honesty.

"You did?" He sounded surprised.

"Oh yes, I was certain."

"Why? I mean, what made you so sure?"

"It's Destiny."

He paused, peered at her. "Are you saying that I am your destiny, Anastasia?"

"Yes. And I am yours."

"I hope to God you are."

She half smiled, stood looking up at him, her eyes growing dreamier than ever. He was even more handsome than she had realized yesterday: his face was strong and masculine, his dark eyes brilliant, his nose straight and well shaped above a mouth she could only think of as beautiful—it was wide, full and generous. There's nothing mean about him, she thought, and he looks like a man of great heart. She could tell this from his eyes and his mouth, the expression on his face. His dark-brown hair had a slight wave in it, was brushed straight back from a broad brow. Straightaway she noticed how impeccably dressed he was. His dinner jacket had obviously been cut by the best tailor in Savile Row, and the dress studs down the front of his pleated voile shirt were small cabochon sapphires set in gold. Expensive but discreet, as was the paper-thin gold watch on his wrist. His faultless clothes and grooming pleased her. She liked men to be well dressed, just as her father was.

For his part, Maxim was staring down into a face that had haunted him for the past twenty-four hours. It was a face of infinite beauty and sensitivity, with that hint of mystery he had noticed yesterday. The face of an angel, he thought. A Botticelli angel. It was the eyes, of course, that so captivated. They were so luminous and light-filled that they appeared to be transparent, and were a lovely hazy-blue in color. They reminded him of Mutti's eyes.

It struck him that the girl appeared more grown-up tonight. To a certain extent it was the hairdo, upswept into a coil of plaits on top of her head like a small coronet. Plus the touch of pink lipstick, the mascara on her thick blond lashes. Yesterday she had not worn any makeup at all. The chiffon gown she was dressed in tonight and the delicate opal-and-diamond jewelry also enhanced her natural loveliness.

Finally he spoke. "What do you do, Anastasia?"

"I go to school. Or rather, I did until I passed my *Bac* earlier this summer. I shall be starting at the Sorbonne in the autumn."

"How old are you?"

"Eighteen. And how old are you, Maximilian?"

"Twenty-five, and call me Maxim."

"All right, Maxim. And what do you do?"

"I'm a financier."

She laughed. "At twenty-five!"

"Of course." He grinned at her. "I'm very clever."

"I'm sure you are." She laughed again. "Could we dance? I like this song."

"What's it called?"

" 'Darling, Je Vous Aime Beaucoup.' "

"It seems appropriate, let's dance."

Still gripping her hand, he put his other arm around her

shoulders, and led her to the edge of the dance floor, where he took her in his arms. For a moment he did not move, just held her very close to him, and she could feel his heart beating very rapidly, as hers was. They stood holding each other for a little longer, and then he guided her onto the floor.

"It's a charming song," he said, smiling, as they began to dance.

"A friend of my father's wrote it," she told him. "Anna Sosenko. She's also in show business."

"Does that mean your father is?"

"Yes, he's a film producer."

Once they fell into the rhythm of the music and were moving perfectly in step, Maxim slid one hand down her back and pressed her body into his, and Anastasia welded herself to him. They danced in silence, cheek to cheek, and she wished the dance would never end. And so did he.

Maxim kept her on the dance floor for several numbers, wanting to hold her forever in this intimate way, reluctant to let go of her. But at last he said, "Let's sit down and talk, Anastasia." Because there were serious matters to discuss.

41

HEY SAT AT A TABLE FOR TWO, HIDDEN AWAY IN A CORner near a bank of massed hydrangea, tulip and azalea plants, sipping champagne.

Maxim said, "I enjoyed meeting your mother, she's very charming. Is your father here tonight?"

"Oh yes, he's standing over there near the bar with that group of men. He's the one with the blue cornflower in his buttonhole." Anastasia smiled as she spoke. "Daddy always wears a flower. It's sort of—his trademark."

Maxim followed the direction of her gaze, craning his neck.

"Ah yes, I see him. He's a very handsome man." Turning to her, he remarked, "Your name is Russian, but I presume your father has lived in France for a long time?"

"He was born here. In 1918. My grandparents are White Russians who came to Paris in 1917, at the time of the Revolution, and they've lived here ever since."

"From speaking to your mother, I gather she is English."

"Yes, but her father had a French mother, and she's got French blood, and therefore so do I. Well, a drop anyway, and Russian and English; actually, I'm a bit of a mongrel."

"A thoroughbred, I would say."

Anastasia flushed at this compliment and murmured, "And you're English, aren't you, Maxim?"

"By upbringing, education and citizenship, but I was born in Germany."

"Were you really! I would never have guessed that." She leaned across the table eagerly. "But you do live in Paris now, don't you?"

"No, London. Unfortunately."

"Why do you say 'unfortunately.' "

He gave her a long, speculative look. "Because you're not there."

She stared back at him and her eyes danced. "I love London, and I go often to visit my English grandmother."

"We'll see each other when you next come."

Anastasia nodded. "Granny's expecting me in August."

"I'll collect you at the airport."

"That'll be wonderful."

Maxim looked at her carefully. He said, "Will they let you get married?"

"When?"

"Now."

"No, not yet. When I'm twenty. Perhaps. In two years."

"Next year?"

"Maybe."

"I'm serious, Anastasia."

"Oh, I know you are. And so am I."

They sat staring at each other, their eyes locked, and they did not speak for a long time, reflecting on each other's words.

Suddenly Anastasia said, "Come and meet my father."

They rose together and walked across the tented garden to the bar on the other side.

Alexander Derevenko's eyes lit up when he saw his daughter approaching, and it was quite obvious from the expression on his face that he adored her. Derevenko was tall, well built, an imposing-looking man, with dark curly hair, light-gray eyes and a somewhat broad Slavic face. He was dressed in a beautifully tailored silk-mohair dinner jacket; a deep-blue silk handkerchief flared in his breast pocket, matching the small fresh flower in his buttonhole.

"Anastasia!" he exclaimed, smiling at his daughter. "Where have you been for the last half hour?"

"Dancing—talking—with Maxim, Daddy." She glanced at Maxim, then back at her father, and went on, "I'd like to introduce him to you. Maximilian West . . . Alexander Derevenko."

"I'm very pleased to meet you, sir," Maxim said, taking her father's outstretched hand.

"My pleasure, Mr. West. Let me present my friends and associates, Ilya Lopert, Gregory Ratoff, Anatole Litvak and Sam Spiegel."

Maxim shook hands with the four men, who greeted him cordially before turning their attention on Anastasia, who was obviously a favorite of theirs.

Alexander addressed Maxim. "Do you know the de Millinets from Paris or Cannes, Mr. West?"

"From Cannes. But actually I don't know them very well, sir. They're friends of the Trentons, who are the parents of my best friend, Alan. I came with him tonight."

"Oh, are the Trentons here?" Derevenko asked. "I'd like to say hello to them. I've met them from time to time, over the years, mostly with the de Millinets in Cannes. Charming couple."

"They're in Hong Kong, Mr. Derevenko. That's why Alan and I popped over from London for the weekend. To attend Yvette's engagement party in their place, and also to do a bit of business."

"What type of business are you in, Mr. West?"

"Finance. I'm a financier."

"How interesting," Alexander Derevenko said.

Anastasia slipped her arm through Maxim's and announced,

"We'd better go and find Alan. We did promise to sit with him for dinner."

"Oh. Oh yes, that's right," Maxim said, quickly catching on, understanding that she wanted to escape.

With a smile, Anastasia blew her father and his friends several kisses, and then glided off on Maxim's arm.

"I'm sorry I had to tell a lie," she whispered as they moved away. "But if we hadn't escaped *then*, my father would have engaged you in an everlasting conversation about film finance, and all that sort of boring business stuff. I saw the gleam in his eye when you told him you were a financier."

Maxim grinned. "But I don't finance films."

"*He* doesn't know that, and in any case, we didn't want to get stuck with Mummy and Daddy for supper, did we?"

He shook his head. "And that was a good idea of yours. I do think we ought to look for Alan, find out what he's up to with Camilla Galland."

"Do you know her?" Anastasia asked swiftly, looking at him out of the corner of her eye.

"No, I've never met her. But I did see her last play in the West End. She's really rather a good actress."

"I think she's supposed to be in a film for one of Daddy's associates, Pierre Petrovicci, so perhaps that's why she's here tonight. Pierre is a close friend of Jacques de Millinet, whose bank finances a lot of movies, and especially for Daddy's little clique."

"Who *are* those four men I just met? What do they do?"

"They're lobby sitters," Anastasia replied, her eyes suddenly full of merriment. "My mother says they're the *greatest* lobby sitters of all time."

"I'm not following you." Maxim frowned in puzzlement. "Why does she say that about them?"

"Because they're always sitting in the lobbies of the best hotels around the world. The George Cinq and the Prince de Galles here in Paris, Claridge's in London, the Excelsior in Rome, the St. Regis in New York, and the Beverly Hills in Beverly Hills," she explained, laughing. "Having their endless business confabs. Talking picture deals." She laughed again and said, "But joking aside, they are rather important men in the film industry."

"But what do they *do*, actually?"

"Sam Spiegel's a wonderful producer, he made *The Bridge on the River Kwai* and *The African Queen*, to name only a couple of his great films. And now he's thinking of making one about Lawrence of Arabia, so Daddy tells me," Anastasia said. "Grisha Ratoff and Tole Litvak are both directors, and Ilya Lopert is a producer, like Daddy and Mr. Spiegel. One of his last pictures was *Summertime*. Daddy took us to Venice when they were making it, that's my most favorite place. Anyway, the film was lovely, very romantic—and sad. Perhaps you saw it?"

"As a matter of fact, I did. Katharine Hepburn and Rossano Brazzi, right? And what about your father? What I mean is, would I have seen any of his films?"

"I'm sure you must have. His last one was called *Eyes of Love*." There was a little pause before Anastasia added, "Camilla Galland was in it, although she wasn't the star. Janice Mills was the leading lady."

Maxim said, "I did see it, and it was terrific, a wonderful story. So you must know Camilla."

"Not really, but I have met her."

"I haven't. Shall we go over and say hello to her? Look, she's standing over there and she's still with Alan. She seems to have attached herself to him. Or vice versa." Maxim looked at Anastasia and winked, his expression turning wickedly suggestive. "Good old Stubby, I'm delighted he's found himself a girl for the evening."

"Stubby!" Anastasia exclaimed. "What a peculiar name."

Maxim couldn't help laughing at the look of disbelief on her face. "I suppose it is," he chortled. "And it's my fault. I once called him that at boarding school when we were about eight or nine, and I'm afraid it stuck. In retaliation, he nicknamed me Duke, after Duke Maximilian of Austria, because he said I was imperious."

"Are you?"

"Sometimes. At least, Stubby says I am."

She was reflective for a moment, then declared. "Duke is certainly a better name than Stubby."

"That it is," Maxim agreed. "Come on, let's join them."

"Hello, Anastasia, it's so lovely to see you again," Camilla Galland said, smiling sweetly, leaning forward and pecking her on the cheek.

Anastasia said, "It's nice to see you too. I'd like to introduce Maximilian West, he's a friend of Alan's."

Camilla and Maxim shook hands.

Alan told them: "We were just about to come and look for *you*. I think we ought to find ourselves a table—people are already beginning to sit down."

"Yes, we should do that," Anastasia concurred. "Yvette told me there wouldn't be any place cards this evening, so we can sit wherever we wish."

"That's a cozy table for four over there—let's grab it," Maxim said, as usual taking charge in his masterful way. He immediately guided Anastasia toward it, saying quietly, "I picked a small table because it's more intimate. Having just found you again, I don't want to share you with a lot of other people."

She gazed at him solemnly and admitted in a low voice, "And I don't want to share you either."

They stood staring at each other, oblivious to everyone else, and Maxim had to fight the temptation to kiss her. She took his breath away, made him forget everything. Swallowing hard, he propelled her forward, wondering how and when he could get her alone.

Once they were seated at the table, Maxim reached for her hand, held it tightly and said, "I believe it was tremendously lucky that Stubby and I came to this party tonight."

She nodded, sat looking at him with eyes grown dreamy, thinking how wonderful he was. She wished they were alone so that he could kiss her. She knew he wanted to, just as she did.

Camilla and Alan joined them at the table, and Camilla immediately engaged Maxim in conversation.

Stubby turned to Anastasia and said with a friendly smile, "Your mother told me you have a new villa in Cannes."

"Yes, in the hills above the town. It's very beautiful, and my mother loves it because the grounds are much larger, and she can garden away to her heart's content. I suppose your parents still have a house down there?"

Stubby nodded. "They bought another place a couple of years ago, too. Listen, maybe we can all get together later this

month. Maxim and I are planning to be down there at the end
of July. Will you be in Cannes then?"

"Oh yes."

Maxim, who had been listening to their conversation with
one ear while talking to Camilla, squeezed Anastasia's hand
and glanced at her quickly. He said, "I'll need your phone numbers in Paris and Cannes, and I'll give you mine, Anastasia,
so that—"

"Now I realize why I think I know you, Maximilian!" Camilla cut in, and rushed on, "I've seen your picture in the newspapers—in fact, I see it all the time. You're very popular with
the press."

Maxim hoped the actress wouldn't say anything about his
reputation for being a playboy, which was untrue and unde-
served. Much to his relief, Camilla did not mention this. Instead she said, "And you're a friend of Faith Carr's, aren't
you?"

"Yes, I am. So is Stubby. Her boyfriend, John Fuller, used
to be at boarding school with us. Is she a friend of yours?"

"One of my closest," Camilla answered, smiling at Maxim.

"Good old Johnny-boy, he's quite the lad," Stubby said,
grinning, and the three of them launched into a long discourse
about the engaged couple and their stormy on-again, off-again
relationship.

Anastasia sat back in the chair and sipped the iced water a
waiter had just poured, listening to her companions with only
half an ear. Her thoughts were focused on Camilla Galland.
There was something about her she did not like. Yet she could
not put her finger on exactly what it was about the girl that
so disturbed her. All she knew was that she felt slightly uneasy
in Camilla's company tonight, as she had when she had met
her in the past. Consequently, she was wary, on her guard.

The other three were laughing about something and there
was quite a lot of conviviality at that moment, but Anastasia
found herself growing suddenly quiet and withdrawn. She felt
like being an observer rather than a participant, at least for
now.

Maxim was busy talking and he did not seem to notice her
constraint, and for this she was thankful. The last thing she
wanted was for him to think she was aloof or snobbish. She
was not; it was Camilla's presence that made her feel cautious

and watchful. Once again Anastasia wondered why this was so. She hardly knew the English actress, had met her only a couple of times before, when Camilla had been in the movie her father had made last year. And if she was honest with herself, she had to admit that the young woman had always been cordial and pleasant. As she has been so far this evening, Anastasia thought, and glanced across the table at her, thinking that Camilla was rather pretty in an understated way. She was very English-looking with her reddish-blond hair, translucent complexion and light-green eyes. Anastasia knew she was about twenty-six, but she looked younger, despite the sophisticated black-lace, halter-necked gown she was wearing and all the costly jewelry.

I wonder who gave her the diamonds? This thought made Anastasia sit up in the chair with a small jolt. And then something clicked in her mind. Only last summer she had heard her mother and Aunt Lucrezia talking about Camilla Galland in the garden of Lucrezia's villa in Cannes. They had been speculating about who Camilla's current "protector" was, and discussing her extraordinary collection of jewels, and Lucrezia had said, "And she looks as if butter wouldn't melt in her mouth, doesn't she?" Both women had laughed knowingly, and her mother had said, "She bears watching, that one." And they had laughed again, then gone on to talk about the painting her father was thinking of buying.

Is that it? Anastasia now asked herself. Am I leery of her because of the things my mother and Aunt Lucrezia implied, or is there something else about Camilla Galland that bothers me? She was not sure.

Maxim said, "You're awfully quiet, Anastasia, and I can't say I blame you. Here we are, talking about people you don't know, and excluding you. How very rude of us." He stared into her face. "And you look so very pensive. What's the matter?"

"Nothing, really," Anastasia reassured him, smiling into his dark eyes.

"Come and dance with me," he said, rising and helping her out of the small gold-painted chair.

Once again Maxim held her very close on the dance floor, and she responded by clinging to him tightly. It was obvious to them both that each was overwhelmingly attracted to the other.

They had been dancing for only a few seconds when he murmured in her ear, "Yvette is your friend, so you must know this place well. Can't we escape for a while, to be alone? Go for a stroll somewhere? When we arrived tonight I couldn't help noticing that the grounds of this house are very extensive."

"They are, and yes, let's go for a walk, get a little air. It's stuffy here."

Hand in hand, Maxim and Anastasia left the dance floor. She led him through the tented parts of the garden and out onto the grounds, which were not covered by one of the three giant marquees erected specially for the engagement party.

It was a beautiful night, warm, balmy, gentle. The ink-black sky was sprinkled with dozens of stars, and there was a hazy full moon. The air was heavy with the scent of honeysuckle and roses and the profusion of other summer flowers.

Maxim breathed deeply of the soft air, and murmured, "It's such a beautiful evening, and you're so beautiful, my wonderful, incredible Anastasia." Putting his arm around her shoulders, he kissed her cheek lightly, and they walked on in silence toward the old walled rose garden. Yesterday when she had smiled at him he had experienced a sudden surge of unprecedented happiness and he had understood immediately that, for him, she was something very special. He felt happier now than he ever had since he was a small child, and the sadness inside him, ever constant, seemed to diminish a little when he was near her.

They wandered through the rose garden and sat down on a rustic iron seat. With one hand Maxim turned her face to his and looked deeply into her eyes, then found her soft lips with his mouth and kissed her ardently. She responded with equal fervor, and their mutual excitement mounted as their kissing grew more passionate and they were lost to the world in each other's arms. Anastasia was trembling inside, and swamped by fierce and overpowering feelings. She wanted to be with Maxim always, never to leave him again, and inexperienced though she was, she knew in the innermost part of herself that he was the right man for her. The only man she wanted. The only man she would ever want. She had understood this last night.

Maxim broke away from her gently and brought her head onto his shoulder, and as if he had read her thoughts of a second ago, he asked softly, "What made you say earlier that we were each other's destiny?"

"It was a powerful feeling I had after I'd seen you in the bookshop. I was absolutely positive we would meet again. I often get strong feelings about certain things—they're almost premonitions. My mother says I'm psychic, my father says I'm a witch." She sighed lightly, and stroked his cheek, and then whispered, "*Qué sera sera.*"

"What will be will be," Maxim repeated and kissed her gently, holding her very tightly in his arms. He never wanted to let her go. They belonged together, the two of them. Two halves come together to make a whole.

And in the rose garden at that moment something was settled between them, and they both understood this, unspoken though it was.

42

"I'M GOING TO MARRY MY BEAUTIFUL DREAMER," MAXIM announced suddenly to Alan Trenton. The two men were on the early morning flight to London on Monday morning, following their long weekend in Paris.

Stubby looked at his friend and said, "Yes, I know. In fact, I knew on Saturday night."

"Good God!" Maxim exclaimed. "We were that obvious?"

"To me at least. I can recognize love at first sight when I witness it—a *coup de foudre*, as the French say."

"Struck by lightning is right, old son. I've fallen terribly in love with her. I want her to be my wife, and the mother of my children, and I fully intend to spend the rest of my life with her. And I'll let you in on a secret, Stubby, the thought of being apart from her makes me feel genuinely quite ill." Maxim shook his head. "I've never felt like this before, I'm afraid I've fallen very hard."

"I can understand why, Duke—she's a beautiful girl, and she has a lovely warm and outgoing personality." Stubby hesitated a moment, and then added quietly, "She *is* very *young*, of course."

"That's true—on the other hand, at eighteen she's malleable."

"I wouldn't be too sure. Anastasia might not be quite as moldable, as pliable, as you imagine her to be."

Maxim raised an eyebrow and gave Stubby one of his penetrating glances. "What makes you say that?"

"From what I observed on Saturday night. For one thing, I think she has a lot of character, and strength of will—I bet you anything she's as stubborn as hell. Also, the girl's clever. A lot of things came back to me this weekend, things I'd heard about the Derevenko girl, indirectly, from my parents. She's apparently an outstanding student, remarkably intelligent, and she's also artistically talented like her mother, who by the way is a very well-known and highly-thought-of interior designer in Paris, in case you didn't know."

"Anastasia didn't mention that. I suspect we were too busy talking about ourselves."

"In short, the girl is exceptional, Maxim. I'm certain she's not the submissive type."

"Oh, I agree with you, Stubby, and I'm glad she isn't. Submissiveness is not a trait I especially require in a woman—you of all people ought to realize that by now. When I used the word 'malleable,' what I meant was a woman who was not set in her ways or rigid, one who was flexible, ready to learn. I want a woman who can keep abreast of me, grow as I grow. I don't want a woman made of putty, one that I can mold into exactly what I want her to be."

Don't you? Stubby wondered, but said, "Then I believe that in Anastasia you have found your ideal woman." Stubby shifted slightly in his seat, leaned closer and asked, "You say you're going to marry her. But what about her parents? I mean, won't they feel she's a bit young to be getting married this year?"

"Absolutely. But Anastasia thinks we can plan it for next year, when she's nineteen."

"So you've already proposed?" It was Alan's turn to raise a brow.

Maxim chuckled. "More or less, in a slightly casual way on Saturday night. But she knew I meant it, and I knew *she* meant it, when she said she was as serious as I was. We have an understanding, Alan. We really do." Maxim paused to glance out of the plane window, then instantly swung his eyes back to his friend and said, "It's a quite extraordinary thing, but she and I are truly on the same wavelength."

"Lucky blighter! I hope I can have that sort of relationship with a woman one day, feel so close and involved."

"You will, I've no doubt. What about Camilla Galland? You seemed quite cozy with her on Saturday night, and then you had a date with her on Sunday. Aren't you interested in *her*?"

"I could be, given half the chance. But she's not champing at the bit as far as I'm concerned."

"Is there a man in her life?"

"I gather there isn't, and that there hasn't been for a long time. Seemingly she was involved with someone, and very much so, but he died. Suddenly, unexpectedly. She's an interesting woman, Duke, and not at all like one might expect, given her glamorous looks and all that jazz. She's rather deep and reflective, has quite an intellectual turn of mind, and I discovered this weekend that she's very sensitive in so many different ways, not a bit the dumb blond starlet."

"I didn't think she was. She's far too good a stage actress to be dumb. Anyway, since she's not involved with anyone, you could ask her out again, couldn't you?"

"I have issued another invitation," Stubby confessed, grinning sheepishly, "and she accepted. We're having dinner at Les A. on Friday."

Maxim punched his arm lightly and laughed. "Now, why did I ever think you'd let the grass grow under *your* feet."

"Hang on a minute, I'm not the playboy—*you* are!" Stubby said.

"You know that's pure invention on the part of the British press," Maxim protested, as always reacting defensively even when he knew the remark was made in jest; he had not yet developed a sense of humor about it.

"I know, I know," Stubby said apologetically, "don't get excited, I was only kidding. And when are you going back to Paris to see your lady love?"

"This weekend. But not to Paris. To Cannes. Anastasia and her mother are going down to their villa on Wednesday, so I thought I'd hop on a plane myself on Friday morning, go down to the Côte d'Azur for a long weekend."

"Are you staying with them?"

"Wasn't invited, Stubbs."

"You can stay at my parents' villa if you wish. After all, it's standing there fully staffed, and with no one in it."

"Thanks, I appreciate the offer, but no thanks. I'm going to book a suite at the Carlton Hotel. It's more convenient."

"If you change your mind, let me know." Stubby sat back in the plane seat and then abruptly sat up, looked at Maxim and said, "How can you leave on Friday morning? I thought you had an appointment in Sheffield that day, with the managing director of Hardcastle Silversmiths? About buying the company?"

"Yes, I do, but I intend to change it. I'll go up to Yorkshire on Thursday. There won't be a problem."

Stubby exclaimed, "That clinches it, then!"

"What does?" Maxim looked baffled.

"The fact that you're putting a woman before a business deal. You've never done that before in your entire life. So Anastasia *must* mean the world to you."

"She does, and anyway, if I don't see Anastasia this weekend, I won't be able to do so until early August."

"Why? Aren't you coming to stay with us in Cannes in July after all?"

"I'm afraid I can't make it until the first week of August now, Stubby. I'm sorry about that, but it just can't be helped. I have to go to Berlin to see Aunt Irina, and then from Berlin I'm flying to New York for three days, for a meeting with some Wall Street bankers."

"It sounds as if you have a tough schedule this month, Duke."

"Oh, it's not that bad, and to be honest, I sort of thrive on it." There was a small pause as Maxim eyed Stubby, and then he said with a huge grin, "You will be my best man, won't you?"

Stubby grinned back. "Did you have to ask?"

*   *   *

Maxim sat waiting for Teddy in the Grill Room of the Savoy. The hotel was one of her favorite places, since it had such romantic connotations for her, which was the main reason he had chosen it. He wanted her to be in the right frame of mind when he told her about Anastasia.

He arrived first, and when she appeared in the entrance to the Grill a short while afterward he could not help admiring her. At forty Teddy had become a truly lovely woman. The years had treated her kindly, and her good marriage to Mark showed in her face, which had the bloom of happiness on it. There was an air of confidence, fulfillment and glowing contentment about her, and her eyes sparkled. Teddy, he thought, my dearest, dearest Teddy. Whatever would I have done without you? When I was growing up you were the rock of my life, and you've always been there for me, no matter what. He loved her very much, and her approval was very necessary and important to him.

Maxim rose as she came toward him, escorted by the head waiter, and he noted how chic she looked in her beautiful navy-blue linen Givenchy suit with a floppy silk rose on one shoulder, a smart little white hat and white gloves.

"You look stunning, Teddy," he said as she came to the table, and he kissed her cheek.

"Thank you, Maxim dear," she said with a bright and loving smile, sitting down and pulling off her gloves. "And you don't look too bad yourself. You must have had a good weekend in Paris."

He smiled. "What would you like?"

She eyed his glass. "If that's tonic water, which I feel certain it is, I'd like the same, please."

After ordering the tonic water for her, he leaned closer and said, "I'm going to see Aunt Irina in about a week. Would you like to come to Berlin with me?"

"Oh, Maxim, I'd love to!" Teddy exclaimed and then made a small moue. "I really *do* wish I could, but I can't. Mark and I have had a little holiday planned for ages, just the two of us, without the children. We're going to Donegal, to stay at Dromlochan. You know, the Pells' house, where we spent our honeymoon. The dates will clash, I'm afraid. But I have a couple of things for Irina, if you wouldn't mind taking them with you."

"Of course not." He cleared his throat, looked at her closely and said, "Teddy, there's something I want to tell you."

He sounded so serious, she stared hard at him and a small frown puckered her brow. "What? What is it? Is something wrong?"

"Not at all . . . I've met someone. I'm going to marry her."

Teddy's face lit up. "Oh, darling, I'm so happy for you! Who is she? And why haven't *we* met her, if you're so serious about her? Why haven't you brought her home to Eaton Square for dinner?"

"We've only just met, Teddy."

"When?" She sat back, her head on one side, and looked at him quizzically.

At this moment the tonic water was placed in front of her by the waiter, and Maxim waited until they were alone before he responded to her question.

He said, "It all happened this past weekend. Friday. Well, I *saw* her on Friday, I didn't actually meet her until Saturday."

"But it's only Wednesday!"

"Nevertheless, I know what I feel. It's something I've never felt before. She's the one. The only one."

Teddy was so flabbergasted she simply sat staring at him.

Maxim said, "You're going to love her, I know you are, Teddy. She's just the sort of girl you've always wanted for me."

"Oh, Maxim darling, it's so . . . so . . . *fast.* How could you possibly know, or be sure . . ."

"How long did it take *you* to realize what you felt about Mark, when you met him?" Maxim asked softly, giving her a pointed stare.

She was silent, thoughtful for a long moment. "Well, you have me there, I suppose. Just a few hours—well, a few days at the most."

"Exactly! One always knows how one feels about another person within a short time. A very short time, in my experience."

"That's true."

"And in any case, I'm not planning to marry her tomorrow, so we'll have a chance to get to know each other better."

"When *are* you thinking of getting married?"

"Next summer. We have to wait until then. You see, she's only eighteen."

Teddy was even more startled, although she endeavored to conceal this. But she did not succeed very well, and after taking a sip of the tonic water, she put the glass down on the table and gave Maxim a very direct look. "Who is she?" she asked.

"Her name is Anastasia Derevenko," he began, and then proceeded to tell Teddy how they had met, and everything there was to know about Anastasia.

When he had finished, Teddy said, "I can't wait to meet her, and she is obviously a very exceptional young woman, from what you say—and comes from a very good family. I—"

"They're not Jewish, Teddy," he said quietly, quickly cutting in, "Just in case you think they're Russian Jews—Ashkenazim—they're not. I hope that's not going to upset you, or trouble you." Maxim put one hand on her arm as she spoke, and his dark eyes, leveled on hers, were searching.

Teddy sat very still, returning his piercing stare. Finally she said slowly, "No, I don't suppose it does disturb me too much. I would have liked you to marry a Jewish girl, of course. It's always so much easier bringing up children when the parents are of the same religious persuasion, but to me your happiness is more important than anything else. If Anastasia is going to make you happy, then so be it." Her smile was full of love as she added, "After all you could marry a Jewish girl and end up being miserable. It's better that you marry a Gentile girl and have happiness."

Maxim felt enormous relief, and the strained look of a moment ago left his face. "I knew I could count on you, Teddy. I knew you would view the situation most intelligently, and not let religion cloud the issue. After all, you never shoved it down my throat when I was growing up, and Mark isn't particularly religious, is he?"

"No, nor has he ever been, as you well know. He never insisted that you be bar mitzvahed, for example. Still, even though his parents are Reform, they are quite religious, traditional. And you *know* Aunt Ketti is, Maxim. But let's not worry about them—you're twenty-five years old, and if anybody knows what he's doing, it's you." Besides, she said to herself, I don't give much thought to religion these days. Not after what God has done to us. God abandoned the Jews a long time ago. *If* there is a God, and I can't but wonder about that when I think of the Holocaust.

Maxim reached out and squeezed her hand. "Thank you, Teddy. And thank you for being you. There's just no one like you, there really isn't."

"I can say the same about you, darling. And so, getting back to Anastasia, I give you my blessing, and so will Mark, I know. Now, most important, when are we going to meet her?"

"In August. She's coming to stay with her grandmother, who lives not far from you, in Chester Street. I thought you could give a little dinner at home, just the four of us. Unless you want to go out somewhere?"

"We can decide that later, can't we?"

Maxim nodded. "Are you busy immediately after lunch?"

"Not really, why do you ask?"

"I'd like to get into the safety deposit box at the Rossiter bank, to look at Mutti's diamond ring. Perhaps Mark could have it cleaned and reset. I'd thought of giving it to Anastasia as her engagement ring."

"What a lovely idea, Maxim, and we can go to the bank straight from here, and while we're there today I wish you'd take over that box. I've been asking you to do so for ages—I don't know why you won't."

"It's such a nuisance, I prefer to leave it in your name, Teddy."

"The box should be in yours," she insisted.

"Oh, all right, then, since you think it's best. We'll do it this afternoon."

"Good. You should also take a look at your mother's other jewelry. You may want to give that to Anastasia as well."

"Good thought. Now, shall we order lunch?"

"I think perhaps we'd better, if we want to get to the bank before three."

Maxim motioned to one of the waiters hovering nearby, who instantly came to the table with the menus. Teddy buried her head behind it, thinking not of food but of Ursula's letter written in Paris twenty years ago. Teddy had never been able to give the letter to Maxim or reveal the contents to him, not even when he was twenty-one. It was still in a second safety deposit box at the bank; long ago she had taken the precaution of separating it from Ursula's jewelry.

If he's old enough to marry, he's old enough to have that letter, Teddy now thought. I *will* give it to him. I *must*. Yes,

I'll give it to him before he gets married. She experienced such a sudden surge of relief as she made this decision after years of vacillating, it was as if a huge weight had been lifted from her shoulders at long last.

Quickly she scanned the dishes that were listed, looked over the top of the menu and smiled at Maxim. "I'd like potted shrimp to start with, and then grilled sole."

"Snap!" Maxim exclaimed, laughing. "I had just decided on the same."

After he had ordered for them, they went on talking animatedly, and Teddy reveled in his happiness. Caught up as she was in Maxim and his plans, she put the letter out of her mind, thinking she would deal with it later.

She had no way of knowing then that later she would lose her nerve yet again, and that the letter would remain locked up in the Rossiter Merchant Bank in Berkeley Square, still unread by Maxim.

43

$\cal{M}$AXIM'S SUCCESS IS REMARKABLE, ISN'T IT?" MARGOT Derevenko said, looking across at Alexander.

Her husband sat in his favorite chair near the window, at the other side of the *petit salon* in the house on the Faubourg Saint-Germain. It was a warm and pleasant evening at the end of July in 1961, and the Derevenkos were enjoying an aperitif before dinner.

Alexander, who was nursing a scotch and soda, took a swallow before saying, "Yes, it's incredible. What an extraordinary achievement it is to have made a million pounds before the age of thirty. One has to take one's hat off to him."

"He's been good for Anastasia," Margot murmured, then shook her head and laughed softly, almost to herself. "And to think I had my doubts about him, when they told us they wanted to get married two years ago."

"You know very well that *I* never did," Alexander said. "And I certainly didn't believe all that nonsense about his being a playboy." Chuckling, he threw his wife a wise and knowing glance. "In fact, to be honest with you, Margot, I rather hoped Maxim *had* sown his wild oats before he met Anastasia, so that he wouldn't be sowing them at some future date, after they were married. I'm a great believer in a man getting all that sort of thing out of the way before he settles down to matrimony."

"Oh, I agree wholeheartedly there!" Margot exclaimed. She sank into the beige silk of the small Louis XV sofa, crossed her elegant legs and sipped her champagne reflectively. After a little while she remarked, "Maxim is very clever, isn't he, Alex?"

" 'Clever' is a gross understatement, my dear. I believe him to be a genius—a financial genius."

Margot stared at Alexander. "Why? How? I mean, what *makes* him a financial genius, in your opinion?"

"That's a hard one to answer." Her husband was thoughtful for a few minutes. Then, placing his scotch on the antique table next to the chair where he was sitting, he pushed himself to his feet and hurried across the room. At the doorway he swung around and beckoned to her. "Come here a minute, Margot," he said, and disappeared into the hall.

Margot who had been watching him in bewilderment, got up and hurried out after him.

He stood in front of the Degas painting of ballet dancers in green dresses, and as she came up to him, he turned to her and waved his hand toward the painting, saying, "What is that?"

"A painting, of course."

"Yes, but it is also the outcome, the *result*, if you like, of artistic genius. Westinvest, the company Maxim created from nothing, is the *outcome* of financial genius. Do you understand what I'm getting at?"

Margot nodded.

He went on, "Now, I can no more explain to you the creative impulse, what it is inside a painter that makes him capable of producing a breathtaking work of art such as this, than I can explain to you what it is inside Maxim that enables him to put together an incredibly successful company or a stunning deal." Alexander shook his head, and smiled a little wryly. "Nor can

I explain to you the genius of Rachmaninoff or Puccini, or William Shakespeare or Emily Brontë."

"It's a gift." Margot said, her eyes lighting up. "Artistic genius is a great gift! A person cannot acquire it, but is born with it, and it has always been there since infancy, becomes apparent in childhood, and flowers in adulthood. And just as a great artist, writer or composer is born with genius, then so was Maxim born with it. Teddy once told me he was a mathematical wizard when he was six or seven years old. A prodigy."

"Yes, so I remember. But there's a lot more to it than being brilliant with figures, I believe." Alexander took her arm and led her back into the small sitting room. He murmured, "In my opinion, Maxim is preternaturally sharp, has great shrewdness and intelligence, and perhaps more important, extraordinary vision."

"For someone who said he couldn't explain financial genius, I think you may have just done so," Margot said, eyeing him lovingly.

"No, I haven't, not really, Margot. I've only scratched the surface, given you a few of his character traits. I won't pretend that I could ever get to the bottom of Maxim, understand what makes *him* tick, because I am fully aware that that is an impossibility."

Margot gave an understanding nod. "I'm sure nobody will ever be able to do that. He's far too deep a man, and very complex. Even Anastasia has mentioned this to me."

Alexander looked at her swiftly, his eyes sharp. "No problems, I hope?"

"No, darling, none whatsoever. They're madly, crazily, blissfully in love. But then you know that. It was simply a remark she made to me in passing."

"With his history, I'm not surprised he's complex," Alexander muttered, and then, glancing at his wife, confided: "I sometimes think Maxim has a genie telling him things. I'll never know where he gets his ideas from, what prompts his decisions, or why he makes his moves when he does, but they are all brilliant. In fact, Margot, everything our son-in-law does in business is dazzling. There are no doubts in my mind that Maxim will amass a gigantic fortune and immense power. Selling West-invest now, and making himself a clear profit of one million pounds, is merely the beginning. Let's not forget that he's only twenty-seven years old."

"He's proving to be a remarkable provider," Margot said. "And certainly a very loving and adoring husband, so I know he's going to be the best father, Alexander. Nothing less than wonderful. The signs are already there. He simply worships little Alix."

"And speaking of our baby granddaughter, let's go upstairs and take a peek at her before we go out to dinner, shall we?"

Margot's response to his suggestion was a vivid smile, and she sprang to her feet at once. She led the way out of the sitting room and they climbed the stairs to the next floor, where Anastasia's old bedroom was located. It had recently been redesigned by Margot, and was now a nursery for the four-month-old baby.

Jennifer, the English nanny, appeared in the doorway of the room next to the nursery when she heard their steps on the stairs; she stood there smiling, waiting for them to cross the landing.

"May we have a look at Alix before we go out to dinner, Jennifer?" Margot asked.

"Of course, Madame Derevenko. She's sleeping soundly, as usual." The young nanny smiled. "She's such a good baby, never a whimper out of her."

Margot and Alexander tiptoed across the carpeted floor of the dimly lit nursery, and stood looking down at their grandchild sleeping so peacefully in the pink wicker crib trimmed with pink satin ribbons and bows.

After a moment they raised their heads; their eyes met across the crib, and they smiled at each other with pleasure and pride. Then they tiptoed out quietly so as not to awaken the baby.

As they went downstairs to the *petit salon* Alexander murmured, "I'm glad they've gone to Venice for a second honeymoon. With a little luck, perhaps they'll make us another grandchild. A boy this time."

Margot merely smiled.

Venice was like a mirage, floating, dreamlike, blues and grays mingling, soft vaporous mists lifting from the lagoon and the canals. Ancient buildings rising up, inchoate images in the muted light. And everywhere a sense of tranquillity and serenity.

La Serenissima, Anastasia whispered to herself, using the name by which the Venetians had called their city for hundreds of years. *La Serenissima* . . . so hauntingly beautiful in its splendid isolation, trapped between sea and sky, her favorite place, which she had loved since she had first gone there as a child. Every aspect of it fascinated and intrigued her, and she was forever held in its thrall, a captive to its mystery and everlasting beauty and wondrous dreamlike quality.

Anastasia stood at the window of their suite in the Danieli, staring out across the lagoon, which was still hazy with early morning fog. She so brimmed over with happiness that she hardly dared contemplate it, for fear of losing it. Tempt not the jealous gods, she thought, moving closer to the window in her bare feet, resting her forehead against the glass, still half asleep as she drifted with her thoughts. Maxim was at the center of them. He was her dream and her reality. He was her world—the sun, the moon, the stars—without him she would have nothing.

She sighed under her breath. Soon they would have to leave Venice. They had already been here a week and time was running out; their short summer holiday would soon be over. But every single day had been miraculous, perfect, a replaying of their honeymoon, except that everything was better than before, if that was at all possible. He was a wonder, her beautiful husband. She loved him so much there were moments when she thought she could not endure it, and she could hardly bear to be away from him, wanted always to be at his side.

A fragment of a verse from the Song of Solomon ran suddenly through her mind: "My beloved is mine and I am his." That was the truth, that was exactly the way it was with them. They belonged to each other. And then she remembered another line from the same book in the Bible: "I am *sick* with love." How apt those words were. She quite often felt ill, feverish, weak in the legs, trembling all over, filled with yearning for him. There was never a moment in a day when she did not long for his hands on her body, ache for his presence. He was a most wondrous lover, a wondrous husband. . . .

She was so caught up in her thoughts of him that she did not hear him get out of bed and cross the floor; she started in surprise when she felt his strong cool hands on her bare shoulders.

"What are you doing up so early, my love?" Maxim murmured against her long blond hair in his warm and mellifluous voice, and turned her to face him.

"I couldn't sleep," she whispered, touching his cheek with one hand, staring up at him, her eyes moist with emotion, spilling over with her love.

He leaned closer to her and she to him, mouth seeking mouth. They kissed, and Maxim pulled her even closer, encircling her with his arms. After a moment of clinging together, he released her, then slid his hands down her silk-clad back, let them rest on her rounded buttocks, then pressed her into him. Their bodies fitted perfectly together. He thought: Two halves to make a whole. He parted her lips, slipped his tongue into her mouth to touch hers. Anastasia was overcome with desire for him, and she felt the heat rising inside her. It was a fierce and tingling heat that enveloped her entire body. Maxim could feel it through their thin nightclothes. He drew away from her, took her hand in his and led her back to the bed, aware now of how much she wanted him. They sat on the edge of the bed and he brought his mouth to hers, sucking at it gently, and they fell back on the eiderdown, their kisses growing in intensity and passion.

Maxim was as hungry for her as she was for him, but within seconds he stopped their kissing and, raising himself up on one elbow, bent over her, smiling into her luminous eyes. Lightly, gently, fleetingly, he kissed her forehead, her eyelids, her nose and her cheeks. She opened her arms and stretched them out to him, and he came into them, lay against her and suddenly his kisses were as passionate as they had been a few minutes before. He crushed his lips to hers, his teeth grazing against hers as he devoured her mouth. Anastasia's response was ardent as ever, and she met his passion with a fervor that more than matched his, her whole body quivering for him.

Inflamed himself, he pulled away momentarily, stared down at her, marveling at her beauty. Her head was thrown back, her long white neck exposed to him. There was something vulnerable and tender about her throat and he brought his lips to it, nuzzled his face against her neck. His hand reached out for one of her breasts, and he began to stroke it tenderly. Within an instant the nipple hardened under his touch, was taut and pointed against the silk of the nightgown.

He felt himself stiffen and his erection was enormous, as it always was with her. A groan escaped his throat and he slid his hand down over her concave stomach, lifted the filmy silk fabric covering her.

Maxim had learned every part of her body well since their marriage, and now he sought the center of her, found it at once, let his fingertips flick delicately against the core of her. Anastasia moaned and arched slightly toward him, all the heat of her body centered in the core of her womanhood.

To Maxim the moist warmth of her was irresistible. He wanted to sink himself into her, take her to him, possess her completely and with every bit of his strength, yet he held back, needing to give her pleasure first. He pulled at her silk nightgown, it slipped off her shoulder and he reached for her breast, cupped his hand around it. Her flesh was pearly-tinted in the pale light of early morning, and cool as marble to his mouth. She sighed deeply as he let his lips linger on her flesh. He sat up abruptly, lifted her bodily and pulled the nightgown over her head, then shed his pajamas, his movements swift and urgent.

Naked, they stretched out together on the bed, lying on their sides so that they faced each other, their bodies barely touching. His brilliant dark eyes impaled hers, and he said in a hoarse voice thickened by desire, "I love you, Anastasia, you'll never know how much, my darling. I can't find the words to tell you. To say 'I love you' just doesn't seem enough somehow."

"I know, I love you in the same way," she whispered, stretching out her hand, stroking his cheek lovingly, wanting him.

He turned her onto her back, raised himself above her, looked down into her huge gray-blue eyes. "You're my life," he said.

She half smiled at him, stretched her body voluptuously, slightly parting her legs, and closed her eyes, and he leaned over her long slender body, enjoying its perfection and youthful beauty. He began to give her pleasure, kissing her breasts, first the one and then the other, until the nipples stood high and the breasts were taut. And then he brought his mouth onto her stomach, trailing his lips down and down and down until they came to rest between her thighs. He caressed her lightly with his tongue and fingers, and she opened herself to him, flowed out to him, and after a moment he felt her stiffen and begin to quiver as she called his name over and over.

He braced himself above her on his hands, and she took him into her lovingly, her face full of adoration as she gazed up into his eyes. She ached to possess him now, just as he did her.

Maxim let out a long sigh as he thrust deeply into her, and she cleaved to him, then wrapped her legs around his back. He put his hands under her body, lifted her closer to him, and they instantly found their own rhythm as they had since the first night of their marriage. They were finely tuned to each other, and they soared upward and upward together as their passion mounted, and as he came to her finally he cried out her name in his need, and they fell away into infinity together.

Later, as they lay in each other's arms, Maxim said, "Last year when we were here you became pregnant with Alix. I hope we've done it again, my darling."

"You and Daddy both," she laughed, resting her head against his chest, throwing one arm over his body possessively. She looked up into his eyes, said with mock solemnity, "Unfortunately, I don't think we *have*. Not yet. Shall we do it again? It's wonderful, trying to make babies, I really can't think of anything I like doing better."

Maxim smiled against her hair, forever enchanted by her. "You're insatiable, Mrs. West."

"If I am, it's your fault. You're the one who has led me into my wicked ways, and taught me everything I know." She let out a tantalizing laugh, slid her hand over his thighs, took hold of him gently.

"And what a willing, enthusiastic and able pupil I've had," he murmured thickly, every part of him wanting her again. He lifted her face to his, kissed her deeply, and began to make love with her once more.

At noon they took a boat to Torcello, one of the many islands in the lagoon that had once been a fishing village. They strolled through the ancient streets until they came to their favorite little trattoria and went inside. They were greeted warmly by Giovanni, the friendly proprietor, who knew them, and who led them outside to the gardens.

"Two Camparis with soda, please, Giovanni," Maxim said, after he had seated them at one of the tables.

"*Sì, Signore*," Giovanni said, smiling and bowing and hurrying away.

Their table stood under a wide canopy made of plaited straw matting, and fingers of sunlight trickled through the woven material, turning Anastasia's hair to molten gold, casting delicate shadows across her face. Maxim stared at her, and recited, " 'She walks in beauty, like the night / Of cloudless climes and starry skies; / And all that's best of dark and bright / Meet in her aspect and her eyes.' "

"Byron," she said, looking across at him. "A poet one should quote in Venice, I suppose, since he loved this city. And thank you . . . how you do flatter me, my darling."

"He might have written those words for you, Anastasia. God, you're beautiful! And oh God, how I love you!"

"Me too, you," she said, smiling at him, settling back, relaxing in the chair. She loved this small trattoria, so casual and unsophisticated, and charming in its rustic simplicity. The shaded area where they were sitting fronted on wide lawns and many flower beds resplendent with honeysuckle, roses and azaleas, the last the color of dark burgundy wine. There were trees in abundance, all offering welcome shade in the intense heat of this August day—stately cypress and willows and, close by their table, a giant magnolia tree with flowers the size of a man's hand, the dark-green leaves so glossy they might have been polished that very morning.

"Oh, Maxim!" she exclaimed suddenly. "Isn't it beautiful here? So peaceful and relaxed. I've never been so *happy*. Never."

"I'm always happy with you, *wherever* we are," Maxim replied, meaning every word. "You help to make the pain go away." He regretted these words the moment he uttered them, having never said anything remotely like this to her before. He tended to keep certain thoughts to himself; he was an intensely private man.

She sat staring at him, a small knot of perplexity settling between her eyebrows; she opened her mouth and was about to say something when a waiter arrived with their drinks.

"*Grazie, grazie*," Maxim said, and he lifted his glass, touched it to hers, then took a swallow. "That tastes good," he said. "Very refreshing."

Anastasia followed suit, then put her glass down and gave him a keen look. "What did you *mean* when you said I help to make the pain go away?"

What a stupid slip of the tongue, he chastised himself, wondering how to answer her. "I honestly don't know what I meant," he lied, and then added quickly, with adroitness, "I was always so disappointed in love, disappointed with the women I took out before I met you. I was a bit lonely I would say, looking back. Yes, that's what I meant. . . ." He reached out, squeezed her long, tapering fingers. "And you have changed all that."

She beamed at him. "I'm so glad, Maxim. I can't bear to think that you were ever unhappy or sad. Were you lonely as a child?"

He shook his head. "Of course not!" he exclaimed a little too heartily. "I had Teddy, and good old Stubby."

At this moment Giovanni appeared to announce the day's specialties, and took their order. When the proprietor had hurried off to the kitchen, Maxim started to speak to Anastasia about his impending trip to Berlin to see Irina Troubetzkoy. "And I thought you might like to go with me," he finished. "I plan to leave about the tenth of the month."

"I *want* to go, and I can't *bear* the idea of being away from you," Anastasia said with another small frown. "But I don't want to leave Alix again. Not so quickly after this trip to Venice. You don't mind, do you?"

"Naturally, I mind, but I understand." He gave her a most loving smile, and his eyes were tender as they rested on her.

Their lunch arrived a few minutes later, and it was delicious. They commenced with warm polenta, accompanied by the tiniest of fried shrimps, herbed and seasoned most delicately. They were slightly oily, and so soft they melted like butter in the mouth. Next, they had *fritto misto*, tiny little fried fish of all kinds, crisp and succulent; the fish went well with the simple green salad and crisp local bread. Maxim had ordered chilled white wine; it was light, clear, greenish, a young wine and one he had drunk before in Venice, and it was the perfect choice.

"Wasn't that good!" Anastasia exclaimed when they had finished. "But I would still like something else. Do you think I'm eating for two?"

"Possibly *three*, the way we've been going at each other since we got here," Maxim responded with a wicked smile. "And I certainly hope so. Twins would please me very much."

She laughed delightedly, and when the waiter reappeared to take their plates away and enumerate the desserts, she settled for the tiny wild strawberries indigenous to France and Italy, slightly perfumed and tasting their very best when eaten without cream or sugar. Maxim ordered a sliver of Bel Paese cheese with grapes for himself, and black coffee for them both.

After lunch they took a boat across to Giudecca Island at the other side of the lagoon.

They went walking along the street facing the Giudecca Canal, and the Grand Canal beyond, the two waterways flowing into the lagoon.

Maxim stood with his arm around Anastasia's shoulders, staring out into the distance. Venice lay across the wide expanse of water, and the whole of the city stretched out before them—resplendent, glorious, magical, gleaming in the afternoon sunlight.

"It's the most wonderful view I've ever seen," Maxim said, suddenly turning to her. "Look at the perfect alignment of spires and towers and cupolas."

Their eyes swept over the Palace of the Doges and the great palaces of long-dead Venetians, the Palladio churches and the salt houses, where salt from the lagoon had been dried centuries before. And they were both struck by the breathtaking beauty of the city, which appeared to float on the water before their eyes.

"No wonder Canaletto and Turner wanted to paint Venice," Anastasia said. "What artist wouldn't want to capture this splendor on canvas!"

"It does have a timeless beauty, and it's unique," he said, a hint of awe in his voice.

They sauntered on, hand in hand, to the end of the Giudecca, and then retraced their steps and eventually took a boat back to the Danieli.

They lay together in the deep bed, reclining on huge soft feather pillows, the kind he remembered from his childhood in Berlin.

They were lazy and languorous after their lunch and the boat trips, but the bedroom was cool and restful, shaded from the hot sun by the slatted wooden shutters.

Maxim ran his lips down her bare arm, enjoying the feel of her silken skin, the smell of her. Anastasia's body was fragrant from the sun, and it held a tinge of salt from the sea wind that had blown up on their boat ride back to the hotel from Giudecca island. Golden skin, the color of an apricot, and just as smooth, he thought, running a finger from her shoulder to her wrist. But it has the bloom of the rose upon it.

Anastasia turned her huge eyes to him and smiled lazily; she was satiated from their lovemaking of the last hour, and sleepy from the wine at lunch.

"Have a nap," he suggested, bending down to kiss her hair.

"Mmmmm, I think I will," she said, nestling into the pillows, pulling the sheet up over her naked body.

He rested on one elbow, continuing to contemplate her for a while, loving her so much. She was the most extraordinary girl, full of enormous warmth and joy, and so very generous and giving of heart. She was sensual and voluptuous, too, a discovery that had delighted him, given him tremendous satisfaction.

Very erotic, my little Botticelli angel, he thought, smiling inwardly, remembering their honeymoon. Virgin though she had been when he had married her, she had taught him more about sexuality than any other woman he had known intimately. There was no coyness or false modesty about her, and after the first few months of marriage he had come to understand her needs and desires, since she made it clear what pleased her the most. Also, in a curious way she had taught him about his own body, had made it come alive as never before. She adored his body and told him so, took all the pleasure she wanted from it and from the fulfillment he gave her. She pleasured him in return as no woman ever had, and they cried out in their mutual need, in the excitement and ecstasy of their lovemaking, and there was no restraint between them.

Maxim slid off the bed and walked over to the window, and stood where Anastasia had stood that morning, gazing across the water, marveling at the incredible beauty spread out before him in the fading light of late afternoon.

He would never forget their times in Venice, would always

remember the softness of the air here . . . the serenity . . . the mists and the blue-gray skies the color of her eyes . . . the balmy nights . . . the lapping sound of the canals as the water slapped against the pilings while they slept. And Venice would always be associated in his mind with his exquisite Anastasia, his beautiful dreamer, the girl of his dreams, his true love, his dearest wife, the only wife he would ever want.

44

ᒍHANK YOU FOR A WONDERFUL LUNCH, YOU OUTDID yourself," Maxim said, smiling at Princess Irina Troubetzkoy. He placed his napkin on the table, pushed the chair back and crossed his long legs.

"I'm glad you enjoyed it," she said, also smiling, her bright-blue eyes lighting up with pleasure at his compliment.

"I always do, but I still think it was far too hot a day for you to be in the kitchen. You should've let me take you out, as I wanted to."

"No, no, I insist on making one meal for you while you're in Berlin, *Liebling*. You're so good to me, it's the least I can do."

"But I am taking you out tonight, Aunt Irina. We'll have dinner at one of your favorite restaurants, and then, if you like, we'll go dancing afterward. I know how much you enjoy that."

"You spoil me, Maxim, and you make me feel young again," she said with a gay laugh.

"You're not old!"

"I was fifty in March, don't forget."

"That's still not old, and you certainly don't look anywhere near fifty," he answered in absolute truthfulness, thinking how beautiful Irina was today, slender and elegant in a delphinium-blue silk dress that exactly matched the color of her vivid eyes.

Her auburn hair was as burnished as ever—no doubt it owed a great deal to the skill of the hairdresser these days, but it did not look dyed and was as becoming as it had always been with her clear pink-and-white complexion. But perhaps the most remarkable thing about her was her face, which was still lovely and relatively unlined, despite the very hard life she had had.

"You're staring at me," Irina said, her expression questioning as she gazed back at him.

"But admiringly so, Aunt Irina. You do look extremely well, you know."

"Thanks to you and your love and care, and the help you have given me over the years, and Teddy, who has also been so affectionate. You've both been wonderful to me, I can never thank you."

"Thanks are not necessary, we're your family," he replied. "Now, how about a glass of lemon tea? After that *Schwarzwälder Kirschtorte* of yours I really need it."

Irina laughed at his expression. "I didn't force you to eat it, and it is your weakness, you know," she said, laughing again. "You've loved it since you were a child."

"Chocolate and cherry tart with lashings of cream might be permissible when you're four years old, but it helps to put the weight on when you're twenty-seven."

Irina shook her head, saying slowly, "I keep forgetting how old you are. It seems like only yesterday that I held you on my knee and rocked you to sleep, when I used to stay with your parents at the villa in the Wannsee."

"Time flies, Aunt Irina, doesn't it?"

"It truly does. Just imagine, your father was your age when I first met him. Goodness me, so long ago . . . before you were even born." Irina suddenly averted her face, stared into the distance, then stood up abruptly. "I had better go and ask Hilde to make the tea, if you'll excuse me for a moment," she said, hurriedly walking away from the table.

Maxim, who had risen with her, said, "Let's have it in the living room, shall we?"

"Why not, it's much cooler in there anyway," she replied as she rushed across the dining room, making for the kitchen.

Conscious of the sudden change in her mood, he stared after her in puzzlement. Then, shrugging, he strode out to the entrance hall, and then to the living room through an arched doorway. It was spacious and airy in feeling, and looked down onto the Lützowufer and the Landwehrkanal. He strolled up to the windows and stood staring out across the canal, his eyes focused on the leafy green treetops of the Tiergarten beyond.

He and the baron, Irina's stepfather, had bought this apartment for her in 1956. When he and Teddy had flown to Berlin to see it, both women had laughed because the new building was so close to the spot where Irina's "little abode" had once been. He had never seen her "hole in the ground," but he had heard about it from Teddy, and it sounded like an appalling place for anyone to live, especially a Romanov princess.

When he had come back to Berlin for the first time since his childhood, in 1950, Irina was already ensconced in the studio off the Ku'damm, a place that Mrs. Reynolds had found for her in 1949. This had been merely adequate, in his opinion, and even the larger studio on the Budapesterstrasse, which she had moved into later, had seemed cramped and dismal. And so when this apartment had come up for sale, he had been delighted to help pay for it, having always wanted her to have someplace that was gracious and comfortable, and that she could make into a proper home.

Through an arrangement with the Deutsche Bank in Frankfurt, established by the Rossiter Merchant Bank, he had been sending money to Irina since he was sixteen. She had not asked for anything, nor was she aware that he had anything to give, as far as he knew, but the conditions under which she was living at the time, and her plight in general, had so disturbed him, he had been determined to assist her. Teddy, as his legal guardian, had agreed, and the banks had worked out a way to transfer the money directly to her. Her stepfather, although not a rich man, helped out as well; also, Irina had been earning money herself for several years, had become a respected freelance translator for various German publishing houses. Maxim did not care whether she worked or not. He was delighted to support her. She had been very close to his parents, and he knew that had he been alive, his father would have done exactly the same thing under the circumstances.

What gratified Maxim the most was the way she had created comfort, beauty and charm in the flat, using furniture the baron had given her from the castle in the Black Forest—plus much flair and ingenuity. Maxim's eyes swept around the living room, and he noticed a few new additions since his last visit: handsome silk cushions on the big cream brocade sofa and several silk-shaded lamps. Also new were the framed photographs of his baby daughter, Alix, arranged on the piano along with the other pictures.

Walking over to the piano, Maxim bent forward and peered at them. To one side were replicas of his own favorites, which he had had since boyhood, and which Teddy had had copied for Irina years ago. Mutti and Papa in evening dress—the famous "portrait" taken in 1935—and the family group that commemorated his fourth birthday. The third picture was the one of Mutti and Teddy and himself standing outside the Plaza-Athénée in Paris in 1939. His marriage to Anastasia was well represented; he picked up a silver-framed photograph of his wife and himself on their wedding day in Paris, stood looking at it, admiring her, thinking how beautiful she was in her lace wedding gown, flowing white veil and coronet of orange blossoms.

After a moment he put it back in its place and swung around as Irina came gliding back into the living room, carrying two glasses of steaming lemon tea on a tray.

She set this on the coffee table in front of the sofa and said as she sat down, "I had a rather nice letter from Margot and Alexander Derevenko the other day. They've invited me to stay with them in Cannes—the last week of September."

"I think you should go, it'll do you good," Maxim told her, sitting down in one of the two armchairs on either side of the sofa.

"I was going to accept—they're a lovely couple, and I enjoy being with them."

Maxim said, "Alexander just bought an extraordinary painting at auction—another Degas. I must say, he is acquiring an impressive collection of art—" Maxim broke off, reached for the glass of tea Irina had placed in front of him and took several sips before sitting back in the chair. He looked pensive and appeared to be momentarily distracted.

Irina studied him intently while the silence lengthened. Finally she said softly, "You're thinking about the Westheim Art Collection again, aren't you?"

He nodded. "I don't suppose we'll ever know what happened

to the Renoirs and all the other great works my family collected."

"I'm afraid not . . . they're gone, lost without a trace. But so many valuable paintings and objects of art belonging to so many people disappeared during the war, Maxim. Some were destroyed in the bombing raids, or were confiscated by the Nazis. *Stolen* is perhaps a better word to use."

Maxim focused his dark, penetrating gaze on her. "I'll never understand why my father didn't leave Germany in the early thirties, when so many Jews *were* getting out."

"You've said that to me every year since you were sixteen, and I've never had a proper answer for you, or an explanation. And I still don't, I never will."

"He was such a brilliant man, an international banker," Maxim muttered. "And he knew so much about everything. As long as I live, I will never be able to fathom *why* he lingered the way he did, why he left it until it was too late."

"So many did, Maxim. Millions of German Jews thought nothing would, or *could*, happen to them, especially those of wealth and standing and position. It was a terrible misjudgment, of course."

"I know, and you've told me that so many times in the past. But I still cannot comprehend how my father could have ignored all the signs—"

"Your father wasn't the only one who miscalculated. Millions made the same mistake. If they hadn't, if they'd left Germany, they would have escaped the Holocaust."

"Yes, so I realize."

"When he did decide to get out, to get the entire family out, we thought there was enough time, Kurt and I, Reinhard and Renata. We were quite sure we could get you all to safety with the help of Admiral Canaris and Colonel Oster . . . but, of course, I've told you all this before."

"I'm sorry to keep mentioning it every time I come to Berlin. I suppose I just can't help myself."

"I understand. There are so many memories for you here, and you're bound to think of your mother and father." Irina's eyes strayed to the photographs on the piano and she stared at the portrait of Ursula and Sigmund for a long moment, then, with a faint smile, she murmured, "You look so much like he did when he was your age. He—" Irina cut off her sentence.

Her mouth trembled and tears suddenly brimmed. She brought her hand up to her mouth and turned her head away.

"Aunt Irina, what is it?" Maxim asked, full of concern.

It took her a while to regain her equilibrium. Finally she turned back to Maxim and said in a very soft voice, "I loved him, you know. Oh, please don't misunderstand, there was never anything between us, he only had eyes for your mother. In fact, he never knew how I felt, I kept my feelings very carefully hidden." She paused, a faint smile flickered. "We were such good friends, he and I, and that's how he thought of me, only as a friend. I was, well, a sort of chum to him. A pal. But I fell in love with him when I first came to Berlin, when I first met Sigi and Ursula. I was so very fond of her too, she was my dear, dear friend." Irina sighed and looked at Maxim with eyes still moist. "Your father is the only man I've ever loved."

Maxim went and sat next to her on the sofa. "Oh, Aunt Irina, Aunt Irina," he said quietly, taking her hand in his, staring into her face. "Whyever didn't you tell me before?"

"I don't know. Perhaps I felt it was inappropriate. And anyway it's so long ago now. . . ."

"Yes, it is," he said, holding her hand tighter than ever. "Now I know why you never married."

"Yes, you do."

He put his arm around her and held her close, filled with compassion for her.

After Maxim left, Irina sat down on the sofa again, leaned back and closed her eyes, hoping to quiet her rapidly beating heart.

Every year that he came to Berlin to see her, Maxim talked to her about the same thing, and every time she answered him in the same way. She always wished she had new and different answers for him, but she did not. Time changed nothing. And God knows she lived with the same questions herself, and there was not a day that went by that she did not think about Ursula and Sigmund and their tragic fate: Sigi executed in the most foul way at Buchenwald, Ursula beaten to death in Ravensbrück. She had always been relieved that Teddy had never told Maxim the truth about the way his mother had died, grateful that she had withheld the facts from him. How could the boy then, the man now, bear to hear anything as horrendous as that, cope with such awful knowledge?

Her friend from their resistance group, Maria Langen, who had been in Ravensbrück with Ursula and Renata, had told her many things when she had been released finally in the summer of 1944. Things she could hardly bear to hear at that time, or remember now. Unspeakable things. But remember she did; she could not get them out of her mind.

Maria had told her about a wall in Ravensbrück—a punishment wall. Women were taken to it and beaten unmercifully by the wardresses in the camp, beaten senseless, and then they were made to stand against the wall, even though they had no strength left. Maria had told her that their screams and cries and moans went on all day and all night, and that they were left against the wall in the rain and the most freezing weather, were never given anything to eat or drink, not even a drop of water.

According to Maria, Ursula had been taken to that wall so many times and beaten so relentlessly, Maria did not know how Ursula had lived as long as she had. Renata and Maria had crept out to the wall at night, trying to comfort Ursula, bringing her water, tending to her bleeding and battered body as best they could with bits of cloth torn from their own clothing. Every time they did this they themselves were sent to the punishment wall the next day, and were beaten and left there with Ursula, but they had not cared about their punishment. They had always returned to look after Ursula, and they had continued to do so very defiantly until the day she died against the wall in Renata's arms.

They had such courage, Irina thought, unbelievable courage. They were both heroines and they paid with their lives, Renata in Ravensbrück, Maria after her release.

The manner in which Ursula and Sigmund had died was Irina's nightmare, and it was one that never went away. At least, not for very long. And it haunted her, year in and year out, and it would continue to haunt her until the day she died.

45

≡

$\mathcal{M}$AXIM'S MIND WAS FOCUSED ON IRINA AS HE RODE
back to the Kempinski Hotel in a taxicab.

Her confession that she had been in love with his father had
startled him, then he had experienced a rush of sympathy for
her. Unrequited love was such a sad circumstance of life. He
had not known what to say to her, how to comfort her. Perhaps
there was no comfort to give after all these years. Certainly she
must have learned to live with her pain by now.

He glanced out of the window as the cab raced down the
Kurfürstendamm.

Berlin, he thought. It was forever nagging at the back of his
mind when he was not there. Sometimes he felt that the city
held a special secret for him, although in relation to what he
did not know. There were times when he believed that he was
pulled back because of nostalgia, his memories of his parents,
his early life. But he was also aware now that he returned to
see Irina Troubetzkoy.

When he had first gone back to the city of his birth in 1950,
he had strongly sensed that she needed him. Now he truly understood why. He was the link to his parents, specifically to
his father, apparently the love of her life.

In actuality, she represented the same thing to him . . . the
link to the past. Irina had been his parents' contemporary, their
close friend, always in their company. Therefore she could tell
him so much about them. More than Teddy could tell him, in
certain ways. Irina and he had always talked about his parents,
often at great length, and she frequently reminisced about the
times they had spent together, and in a way this kept them
alive. At any rate, it made them live again in her mind, and

also in his, and thus it gave comfort to them both, and that was all that mattered.

It suddenly struck him that because he was his father's son she might conceivably see him as her own child, the child she might have had with Sigmund, if the circumstances of their lives had been different.

Oh, the complexities of the human heart, he thought, and he was suddenly pleased that he had been taking care of her financially, and coming to see her every year. He was positive he helped her to feel less lonely and alone.

Maxim and Irina spent a wonderful evening together, as they always did when he came to Berlin. They talked and laughed, thoroughly enjoyed each other's company over dinner, and then he took her dancing at one of the clubs on the Ku'damm, as he had promised earlier.

They were still laughing and talking when they left the club at two o'clock in the morning. Maxim took hold of her arm affectionately, and together they strolled along the Kurfürsten-damm, enjoying the air. As was usual on a Saturday night, the club had been jammed with people and full of cigarette smoke, and in the last hour the atmosphere had become unbearable in the confined quarters of the club. And so even though it was still hot in the streets in the early morning hours of this August Sunday, they were both relieved to be outside.

They walked for about ten minutes, and then Maxim hailed a passing cab. They had hardly settled back on the seat when the driver turned his head, stared hard at them in the dim light of the taxi, and said, "They're building a barricade."

"Who are?" Maxim asked, frowning, not understanding what the man meant.

"The East Germans," the cabdriver answered. "The Communists."

Maxim felt Irina stiffen on the seat next to him, and he glanced at her quickly before saying, "*Where?* Where are they building this barricade?"

"On the Potsdamer Platz."

"We want to go in that direction anyway, so please take us there. I'd like to see what's happening!" Maxim said.

"Right away," the driver replied, starting his engine.

The cab rolled down the Ku'damm, making for the Lützowufer, one of the streets leading into the Potsdamerstrasse, which in turn flowed into the Potsdamer Platz, at the juncture of the two zones.

Suddenly Irina said, "Too many people have been leaving East Germany this past year. Over two hundred thousand actually, and most were young people."

Maxim looked at her alertly. "Are you saying what I think you're saying?"

"Yes. They're not building a barricade to keep West Berliners *out*, it's to keep East Berliners *in*, to prevent them from crossing to the West Zone." She laughed hollowly. "That's the Communist regime for you. They have to encircle their people with barbed wire to keep them from fleeing."

"Irina, I think you're absolutely right."

Within minutes the cab was cruising down the Potsdamerstrasse, and Maxim and Irina saw that a large crowd was already gathering in the area. They exchanged worried glances.

"We'll get out here," Maxim said to the driver, who pulled in close to the curb and braked. After helping Irina to alight, Maxim paid the cab and the two of them hurried off in the direction of the Potsdamer Platz.

They were at once startled and dismayed at the sight that met their eyes. As they pushed through the crowds of people milling around, Maxim and Irina saw that immense rolls of barbed wire had been stretched across the square to block all movement between the East and West zones. Border guards were still in the process of putting the wire in place; they worked to the sound of loud and ferocious jeering and catcalls and derisive whistling from the West Berliners who stood at the other side of the wire in the Western sector, watching them. The guards erecting the barbed-wire barricade worked by the light of gigantic lamps, and they were backed up by tanks and heavily armed troops, who were now coming in by the truckload.

"This whole thing has the look of a military operation," Maxim said, turning to Irina.

She clung to his arm and he felt her shivering, despite the warmth of the August weather. "You can see that they mean business," she muttered. "What we're going to have is a totally schizophrenic city. It was bad enough before, but it will only get worse from now on." She shivered again, clutched his arm more tightly. "Please, take me home, Maxim."

"Of course. Come on, let's go, it's getting very late."

They swung around and walked away from the barricade, making for the Lützowufer. Irina said in an ominous voice, "Barbed wire won't be enough for them. You'll see, they'll build a wall to divide Berlin."

And Princess Irina Troubetzkoy was right, they did.

The Wall stretched for over one hundred miles and was nine feet in height. On one side, in the Eastern sector, it was painted an antiseptic white; on the other, in the Western sector, it was covered with colorful graffiti.

Maxim took Anastasia to look at the Wall when she came to Berlin with him in June of 1963. She had not been to Berlin for several years, and so she had not seen it before; like everyone else, she was not prepared for it, or for the feeling of revulsion it evoked in her.

"But it's so wrong!" she cried, glancing from Maxim to Irina, who was accompanying them. "Totally and utterly wrong."

"Yes, it is," Maxim agreed.

"Many people have been shot, trying to escape over that wall," Irina explained. "But many thousands more *have* made it over safely, *have* escaped to freedom here in the Western Zone." She shook her head and said derisively, "Communists! They make me sick."

"And me, too, Aunt Irina," Maxim remarked, and said to Anastasia, "Come on, let me show you the graffiti, I think you'll find it interesting. In places it's truculent, in others disparaging. It's also humorous, sad, defiant. It runs the gamut, really." He took hold of Anastasia's arm and Irina's, and together the three of them walked along, inspecting the colorful display.

"The graffiti has been called the longest cartoon in the world," Irina told her. "Because, as you can see, it stretches for miles and miles."

"Some of the items are almost works of art," Maxim added, "they have been quite brilliantly executed."

Since she painted herself, and was artistically inclined, Anastasia was fascinated by the graffiti, and she lingered in front of the Wall for quite a while. Later, Maxim took her up onto

one of the viewing platforms that was twenty feet in height and
enabled her to look down into East Berlin on the other side
of the Wall.

"How dismal and unfriendly the streets seem," Anastasia
muttered to Maxim, who stood next to her on the platform.
"So desolate and empty. Where are all the people?"

Maxim shrugged. "I don't know . . . working, most probably.
And I suppose there's no special reason for those who are not
working to be outside. I've noticed the streets every time I've
come up here and looked over the Wall—so empty and depress-
ing."

"It's like a no-man's-land," Anastasia said. "Different from
West Berlin, where there's so much life and activity and excitement."

The three of them remembered Anastasia's words the following day, when she and Maxim and Irina made their way to the
Rudolf Wilde Platz. Maxim's and Anastasia's visit to Berlin
coincided with that of President Kennedy, who was on a European tour, and hundreds of thousands of West Berliners were
flooding into the streets, also making for the Schöneberg Town
Hall in the platz. It was here that the president was going to
speak, after his own visit to the Wall and the signing of the Golden Book in the town hall.

When President Kennedy finally came out, accompanied by
Mayor Willy Brandt and West German Chancellor Konrad
Adenauer, the crowd cheered and shouted, clapped and waved,
and generally showed their approval of him. When he began
to speak they fell silent, and there was not a sound to be heard
in the square, except for his words.

Anastasia craned her neck to see the handsome young American president, and carefully listened to what he was saying.

Kennedy said, "I know of no town, no city, which has been
besieged for eighteen years that still lives with the vitality and
force, the hope and determination of the city of West Berlin.
While the Wall is the most obvious and vivid demonstration
of the failures of the communist system, for all the world to
see, we take no satisfaction from it. . . . "

President Kennedy paused, then concluded dramatically,
"All free men, wherever they may live, are citizens of Berlin,
and, therefore, as a free man, I take pride in the words '*Ich
bin ein Berliner.*' "

The crowd went crazy on hearing these words, screaming and shouting wildly, and many of the West Berliners and foreigners alike had tears streaming down their faces. Anastasia, Maxim and Irina were also cheering the president of the United States, the three of them as touched and moved by Kennedy's speech as everyone else.

But suddenly Maxim sensed a feeling of hysteria growing in the air, and instinctively, protectively, he put his arms around Anastasia and Irina, pulled them closer to him. He could not help wondering if he had been wrong to bring them to this square today, which was jammed now with hundreds of thousands of people. How easily they could be trampled underfoot and hurt, if the crowd went out of control. And it was not until he had brought the two women safely back to the suite in the Kempinski Hotel that he breathed easy again.

But a few months later he was to recall vividly those words he had heard in the Rudolf Wilde Platz in Berlin, and was truly glad that he had gone to hear John Kennedy speak on that warm summer day in June.

46

*I*T WAS A RADIANT DAY. THE SKY WAS A HIGH BLUE AND clear, and the sun was brilliant.

To Anastasia, Manhattan looked as if it had been well and truly polished. The skyscrapers and other buildings appeared to shine on this crisp Friday morning as she walked across Fifth Avenue in the direction of Bergdorf Goodman.

Within seconds she was pushing through the revolving doors into the exclusive store and taking the elevator up to the children's department. Yesterday, when she had been browsing, she had noticed a pretty party dress she hoped would be the right size for two-year-old Alix and several other items that had looked perfect for the new baby. Their son, Michael, was now eighteen months old and growing rapidly.

Anastasia smiled to herself as she thought of them. The Venetian babies, Maxim called them, since both of their children had been conceived in Venice, Alix in July on their honeymoon, Michael in August, when they had gone there for a second honeymoon.

She missed her children terribly, even though she and Maxim had been in New York for only a week; she worried about them, despite the fact that they had their nanny, Jennifer, with them, and also Mrs. Woodson, the housekeeper-cook who looked after the whole family so well. Plus her mother, who had flown over from Paris to stay at the Mayfair house while she was with Maxim on this business trip.

I shouldn't be so jittery, she thought, as she stepped out of the elevator. They're in such good hands. Even so, she hated to be parted from her children, who, along with her husband, were her whole world. She wanted little else except the three of them. She loved them so very much.

To Anastasia's delight the pink organdy dress was still on the display stand, and she stood eyeing it appraisingly for a moment, picturing her blond blue-eyed little daughter wearing it.

A moment later a saleslady was by her side, confirming that the dress was the right size and taking it off the stand. While the dress was being wrapped in tissue paper, placed in a silver box and tied with a purple ribbon, Anastasia looked at romper suits and tiny shirts for Michael, and purchased three of each.

Twenty minutes later she was riding down in the elevator carrying two large shopping bags. She glanced at her watch as she left the store. It was a few minutes to one and she would be exactly on time to meet Maxim. They had arranged to have lunch together in the Oak Room of the Plaza Hotel, just across the little square from the store.

As she went up the steps and into the hotel, Anastasia was not aware of the flurry she created, nor did she notice the admiring glances cast in her direction. At twenty-two she was more beautiful than ever, her skin glowing and full of health and vitality, her long blond hair upswept on top of her head today. She wore a dark ranch mink coat that Maxim had bought her several days ago, high-heeled black patent pumps and long cream suede gloves. Small diamonds sparkled in her ears and a pearl choker encircled her neck.

After leaving the shopping bags and her coat in the ladies' cloakroom, Anastasia crossed the lobby of the hotel and made her way to the Oak Room.

Maxim saw her come in and rose as the captain escorted her to the table, beaming at her.

How handsome her husband looked in his dark-gray pin-striped suit and pale-blue shirt. He was the best-looking man in the room. And she could tell from the brilliance of his dark eyes that he had had a very successful morning, that his meetings on Wall Street had gone well. And why wouldn't they? Her husband was a genius. Everyone said so, that he seemed to have the Midas touch. Whatever business deal he went into, he always made money, lots of it, and came out the big winner. Her father said he was the most brilliant and gifted business-man and entrepreneur he had ever known, and coming from Alexander Derevenko that was praise indeed.

Still smiling, Maxim kissed her on the cheek as she arrived at the table. He said, "You look fabulous. You should wear red more often, darling, it really suits you."

"Why, thank you, kind sir," she answered, giving him a flirtatious look. "And obviously you charmed your business associates and the bankers, got your own way in Wall Street this morning, from the look on your face."

He leaned into her, dropped his voice. "As long as I get my own way with you, that's all that matters, Stassy, my love. In case I haven't told you lately, I absolutely adore you. I have great plans for this afternoon—for *us*. My work is finished for the day, so I'm all yours. After lunch we're going to meander back to the hotel and—" He leaned even closer, whispered in her ear, "Make wonderful love together. And who knows, perhaps we might even make another baby."

She laughed, and a slight flush tinted her face a pretty pink. Her luminous eyes grew more luminous than ever. "What a gorgeous idea. And I adore you, too." Reaching out, she squeezed his hand, then eyed his glass. "Is that a drink?" she asked, sounding surprised.

"It is. I know it's not like me to drink during the day, but I ordered a bottle of Sancerre. I thought it might be nice to celebrate my little deal. It's only worth about twenty-one million dollars, but it's just the beginning."

"Oh, darling, how wonderful! Congratulations! And what do you mean, *just the beginning?*"

"Of West Investments in America. Will you have a glass of white wine with me, to drink to that?"

"I certainly will."

Maxim motioned to the waiter hovering a few feet away, and the man hurried over and filled her glass. As he replaced the bottle in the bucket he asked if they wished to order lunch.

"In a few minutes, thank you," Maxim said, turned to Anastasia and raised his glass. "Here's to the big adventure we're going to have in New York." He touched his glass to hers.

Anastasia looked at him curiously. "*Adventure?*"

"I want to spend more time in the States, eventually open an office here, perhaps even take an apartment on Fifth Avenue or Park or Sutton Place. Wherever you wish. Would you like to live in Manhattan part of the year?"

She hesitated only momentarily, then said, "If you want to, then yes, of course. New York is a most exciting city. But . . . look, what about the children? About their schooling? Things like that?"

"Darling girl, they're still babies! We've lots of time to worry about schools and the like. And you're correct, it *is* an exciting place, and in many different ways. It's especially exciting in business. This is where the future is—in my opinion. That's what I meant when I used the word 'adventure.' "

"Everyone says you have great vision and wisdom, and I know you do." She paused, gave him a small smile. "So I am with you all the way."

He grinned at her, his expression one of genuine delight. "Thank you for that marvelous vote of confidence, my love. You're the best wife I've ever had."

"And the *only* one you will ever have!" she shot back, laughing with him.

"Perhaps we ought to look at the menus," Maxim suggested, handing her one.

"Thank you." She put it down in front of her, said, "Actually, I know what I'm going to have. Clam chowder and then grilled Boston scrod."

"I'll also have the soup, but I think I'd enjoy a bit of that roast beef the waiter is carving on the trolley. It looks delicious."

After Maxim had given the order, Anastasia said, "You've been very secretive about your new deal. Can't you tell me what it is, now that you've closed it?"

"Of course I can. I've bought a company called the Allandale Group, based here in New York."

"What is that?" She stared at him blankly. "It doesn't mean a thing to me."

"The Allandale Group is a company with rather diverse holdings. For example, it owns Marianna Montevecchio, a small cosmetics company, real estate in Manhattan and Long Island, a tool and die company and a large bakery, one that supplies half the stores in the city and suburbs. As I said, it *is* rather diverse, and that's its basic problem. I plan to sell off the nonprofitable bits, keep only the divisions that make money."

"Which ones are they?"

"The real estate division and the cosmetics company. Those are the two I'm going to reorganize. I plan to launch the Montevecchio cosmetics line in England and Europe next year. I know it will do well, the product is superior." He gave her a little smile, one that was full of confidence. "That's the art of the takeover, knowing what to sell and what to keep."

"You like these little takeovers of yours, don't you?"

He stared at her. "*Little.* They're not so little, Peach Melba."

She threw him a sharp look. "I wish you wouldn't call me that," she chastised.

"Why, it's the perfect name for you. After all, you're good enough to eat." His charming, lopsided smile flashed and he leaned over, kissed her cheek, then went on: "The takeover is the most marvelous invention. It's such a fabulous shortcut, saves all those years of slowly building a company, and it yields wonderful profits. It's also very exciting, finding the right company to take over, and then pursuing it."

"I suppose that's the part you love the most."

He shook his head. "I admit it's thrilling, but I like wrestling with the financial problems, and then reshaping the company, being creative, making it into something bigger and better. I'm not a paper chaser, I don't want to build an empire out of paper. Nor am I an asset stripper. I prefer to keep the companies I've bought and run them, once the fat's been trimmed. Anyway, I—"

Maxim broke off as the waiter placed a bowl of clam chowder in front of each of them.

"And you think that this cosmetics company has a future?"

"Very much so, here as well as in Europe, actually. You see, it's been mismanaged, and it also needs new packaging, a fresh marketing approach. The product is excellent and—" Maxim stopped abruptly, his attention caught by a small commotion near the entrance to the Oak Room. Two waiters were speaking to the captain. One was gesticulating excitedly, the other was openly weeping, and Maxim noticed that the captain seemed dazed, had turned white.

"How very odd. I think something's wrong," he said to Anastasia, his brow furrowed. "Look at the captain. He appears to have had a terrible shock. The waiters don't seem to be helping either."

"Perhaps someone's been taken ill in the restaurant." Anastasia glanced around. She caught the attention of a waiter hurrying out of the service entrance from the kitchen and beckoned to him.

The waiter came to a halt at their table.

Anastasia could not miss the expression on the man's face. It was grave, and there was a stunned look in his eyes.

"What's going on?" she asked in a low voice. "Is there something wrong? We couldn't help noticing the—"

"He's been shot," the waiter told her, his voice shaking, and it broke as he added, "The president's been shot."

"The president," Maxim repeated, peering at the waiter, noting his acute distress. "You don't mean President Kennedy, do you?"

The waiter nodded, unable to speak. His eyes filled with tears and his face twisted in a terrible grimace of pain, and he turned on his heels and fled back into the kitchen.

Maxim and Anastasia sat gaping at each other, for a moment not comprehending what they had just been told.

But the news was spreading fast through the room. People were turning to each other, leaning across to other tables, speaking to strangers. In an instant the room was a babble of voices.

Maxim threw his napkin on the table, pushed back his chair

and leaped to his feet. "Come on!" he cried, and moved across the room with such speed Anastasia had to run to keep up with him.

When he reached the captain, Maxim demanded in a quiet but rasping voice, "Is it true? Has President Kennedy really been shot?"

The captain's face was grief-stricken. "In Dallas. At about one-thirty. Bulletins are coming in over the radio in the kitchen."

Maxim and Anastasia were both speechless.

Reaching into his jacket pocket, Maxim pulled out his wallet, extracted two one-hundred-dollar bills and gave them to the captain. "This should take care of my check," he mumbled, and taking hold of Anastasia's hand he left the Oak Room, dragging Anastasia in his wake.

Maxim and Anastasia stood in the middle of the sitting room of their suite at the Pierre, just across the street from the Plaza, staring at the television set.

Incredulity, shock and disbelief were written all over their faces and they were rooted to the spot as they listened to Walter Cronkite delivering all the facts about the shooting of the president.

A muscle in Cronkite's face twitched, and his voice was shaken, solemn, as he repeated what he had just said, apparently recapping the news for viewers who had just turned on their sets.

John Fitzgerald Kennedy, the thirty-fifth president of the United States, was dead. The back of his head had been blown off by an assassin's bullet as he rode in his motorcade through the streets of Dallas. His body lay in Parkland Memorial Hospital in the Texas city.

Maxim still found it hard to accept. The facts would not quite sink in, and he kept changing the stations, going from CBS to NBC and ABC, and back again, wanting to glean bits of additional information from the other newscasters, who were as stunned and grieving as Walter Cronkite.

At one moment Anastasia glanced down and the skirt of her brilliant red dress caught her eye. She thought: Oh God! It's the color of blood! And clapping her hand over her mouth, she fled into the bedroom as the tears began to flow again. She was almost sobbing as she unzipped the red dress, stepped out of it, and quickly put on a dark-blue cashmere sweater and matching skirt, and returned to the sitting room.

So absorbed was Maxim in the news on television, she realized that he had not even noticed her brief absence. Moving across to the sofa, she sat down, and after a moment Maxim joined her, and they sat together watching the broadcast, holding hands.

He suddenly turned his stricken face to hers and said in a hoarse voice, "*I can't believe it*. We just saw him in Berlin this summer, speaking outside the Schöneberg Town Hall. It hardly seems possible that he's dead."

Anastasia's attention was riveted on Maxim, and she saw that his eyes were full of tears, and she pressed her hand against his. Maxim groped for his handkerchief and wiped his eyes, leaned back against the sofa, feeling wrung out.

She said softly, "He looked so young that day in Berlin, and so handsome with his reddish-blond hair glinting in the sunshine. '*Ich bin ein Berliner,*' he said. . . . "

"I remember . . . I remember it very well."

"Why, Maxim? Why? Why was he killed?"

Maxim shook his head. He had no answer, at least not one that would make any sense.

"Why would anybody want to kill Jack Kennedy?" she asked again, more insistently.

"I don't know, Stassy, I just don't know."

"What a horrible world we live in today!" Anastasia cried.

"It always has been," Maxim mumbled.

"Yes. Yes, I know, darling," she whispered, thinking instantly of the way his parents had died, and of the Holocaust.

Maxim and Anastasia sat together in front of the set for many more hours. They did not say very much to each other through their long vigil, caught up as they were in the news, straining to hear every detail of this senseless killing, the most horrific murder in the history of the United States.

Lyndon Johnson appeared on the television screen at six-fifteen that evening of Friday, November 22. As the new president he made his first statement to a grieving nation reeling from the incomprehensible act of violence in Dallas.

"He's dead," Maxim muttered, more to himself than to Anastasia. "John Kennedy *is* dead." And he sighed heavily, finally accepting it.

"*Ich bin ein Berliner. Ich bin ein Berliner. Ich bin ein Berliner.*"

Maxim awakened with a sudden start, Kennedy's words and voice reverberating in his head. He blinked in the darkness of the bedroom, adjusting his eyes to the gloomy light, glancing at Anastasia, who was on her side, sleeping peacefully, her breathing even. He lay for a moment, endeavoring to go back to sleep. When he realized that he was wide awake, he slid out of bed and padded to the living room, closing the bedroom door behind him.

The sitting room of their suite overlooked Fifth Avenue. He walked over to the window and stood staring out at the trees in Central Park. He moved his head slightly to the left and focused for a brief moment on the Plaza opposite. The lights from the hotel shone brightly, illuminating the square in front of the wide steps. The streets were deserted, looked bleak and wintry in the pale lamplight.

Maxim sighed and turned away from the window, walked over to the sofa and lay down, a multitude of thoughts running through his mind.

The assassination of President Kennedy did not make sense, not to him or to anyone else, if the television commentators were anything to go by. Had it been the act of a single man working alone? A crazy man? Or had it been a conspiracy? Fascists? Communists? Who could really say for sure? Who would ever really know. But *evil* had run amok in America earlier today, and the country had been savaged by an insane act of the most terrible and senseless violence.

He had always known that evil lurked around corners, even from the time he was a little boy. Somehow he had understood this after Teddy had told him that bad things were done to Jews in Nazi Germany. Teddy was ambivalent about the Germans. But he had no particular feelings, certainly not hatred. Only an insatiable curiosity about them. Furthermore, even as a Jew, whose parents had been victims of the Third Reich, he did not believe this generation should be blamed for the crimes of the last.

Often when he went back to Germany to see Irina Troubetzkoy he would look at people in the streets, or in cafés and stores, and wonder how it was that such a strong and noble people as the Germans could have been deluded into following a man like Hitler. Of course that megalomaniac had blinded them with the power of his personality, his high-flown rhetoric, his promises of economic security, a better life, a strong and stable Germany free of Communism. The majority of Germans had followed him unquestioningly, seeing not the charlatan that he was but a charismatic leader who would lead them to prosperity and glory.

After mathematics and languages, history had been Maxim's favorite subject at St. Paul's. He had studied it well, had come to understand that Hitler had been the embodiment of pure evil, had created the most evil regime in the entire history of the world, a regime of bigotry, racism, brutality, oppression and murder. For twelve years and four months the Third Reich had trampled over, intimidated and dominated Europe in a reign of terror of a magnitude hitherto unknown to man. It had been a machine of destruction and death, operated by ruthless and cruel men with evil intent in their hearts and the minds of criminals.

When the criminals take over the prison, then chaos and bloody murder reign, he thought. He wondered how it had come to pass. . . . He would never know. That was not strictly true. Diabolical men such as Hitler and his cohorts always played on the ignorance, weakness and fear of people. The Germans were a cultured and civilized race, and yet they had espoused Hitler's policies of anti-Semitism. Maxim sighed and continued to lie on the sofa in the dark, his mind racing. Evil men can engender hatred and prejudice in others, he thought. He knew that from his history books, which he had studied so diligently at school. Atrocities had leaped off those pages—the Spanish Inquisition, the Russian pogroms, the Turks slaughtering Armenians. Atrocity had been around for centuries, perpetrated by supposedly civilized men against other men.

Who will be next? he asked himself.

Maxim rose, went over to the small sideboard where several bottles of liquor were standing on a tray. He poured himself a brandy and carried it back to the sofa. As he sipped it he acknowledged with a terrible sadness that nothing had changed since the beginning of time. And nothing would ever change. There would always be men of evil out to dominate and subdue others. Until one day one of them, caught in the grip of insanity, would push a button and blow the world to smithereens.

As for Jack Kennedy, a young and brilliant man had been cruelly struck down in the prime of his life, and all the world would mourn as America mourned. As he mourned now. Maxim got up and turned on the television set. The network was running a film of Jack Kennedy made in Berlin this past June, when the President had made his now famous remark, *"Ich bin ein Berliner."*

There he was on television, standing before Maxim as he had in reality only six months earlier, his hair ruffled by the light breeze, smiling his little smile, looking slightly amused. A man capable of warmth and irony and humor.

Maxim felt the tears prick the back of his eyes at the sight of the fallen president as he had been in life. God damn the sons of bitches who did it, he cursed, and slammed his fist into the back of the chair in his fury and grief.

47
===

"THE PHENOMENAL SUCCESS OF THE ALLANDALE GROUP has certainly been an extraordinary achievement for Maxim, hasn't it?" Margot Derevenko said, putting *Time* down on the table and looking across at her daughter. "And this article about him is full of accolades."

Anastasia was silent. She sat staring out into the lovely garden that her mother had created so painstakingly over the years, thinking what a haven of beauty and tranquillity it was, and right in the heart of Paris. Peaceful, she thought. So very, very peaceful. Anastasia suppressed a sigh, not wishing her mother to ask if something was wrong. Because it was. She felt so tired, exhausted, and drained of all energy. She had been feeling like this for the longest time now. Years.

Margot said, "Darling, didn't you hear me?"

Anastasia roused herself, gave her mother a small reassuring smile and said, "I'm sorry, I'm afraid I was daydreaming for a moment."

"I said the article on Maxim had wonderful things to say about him, and I simply remarked that the success of the Allandale Group is quite extraordinary."

"Yes, he's turned it into a conglomerate of no mean proportions in the past seven years. But it's also the cross I have to bear," Anastasia replied in a flat, dull voice.

Margot looked at her, frowning. "What a peculiar thing to say."

"It's at the root of our problems—" Anastasia began, and stopped with abruptness, regretting the remark immediately.

"*Problems!*" Margot exclaimed, sitting bolt upright in the garden chair. "What on earth do you mean?"

"Oh, Mother, I don't really want to go into it, not now. Please, forget I said anything."

"I can't forget it, Anastasia. You haven't looked well this past year, and your father and I have been worried about you, if you want to know the truth. I was delighted when you said you were going to come and stay with us for a few weeks." She squeezed her daughter's fingers, and said, "Please, can't you confide in me? We've always been such good friends." When Anastasia made no response, Margot added, "Your father and I feel you haven't been yourself for ages, but we didn't think for one moment that you and Maxim had problems."

"Perhaps we don't, Mother. Perhaps the problems are all in me."

"What do you mean?" Margot asked.

"I feel so tired all the time. Debilitated, actually, as if I've been ill. And I don't seem to have any spark left."

"No spark!" Margot cried, looking at her askance. "But you're only twenty-nine, for heaven's sake!"

"I realize it sounds ridiculous, but it's the truth. I have no energy, and I'm always depressed these days."

Margot Derevenko was horrified by this last statement, and she searched her daughter's pale face, saw at once that she meant what she said.

Sympathy quickly replaced incredulity. "Anastasia . . . darling . . . *you*, of all people, have no reason to be depressed.

You are young and very beautiful. You have a handsome and charming husband who adores you, one who is a millionaire, who showers you with every possible thing you could want. You have two lovely and clever children, as well as doting parents. Aside from all this, you have a house in Mayfair that is a showplace, a lovely villa in Beaulieu and an apartment on Fifth Avenue." Margot shook her head. "If *you* feel depressed there is obviously something radically wrong. It must be physical. I think you ought to see a doctor."

"I don't need a doctor, Mummy. Frankly, I don't know what I need." Yes I do, she thought to herself. I need Maxim to be the way he was when we were first married. I can't reach the man he has become. He's not the same anymore. I don't know why, but we've lost each other.

"Sometimes depression is caused by a diet deficiency. What about going to a nutritionist?" Margot suggested.

Anastasia shook her head.

Her mother's expression became thoughtful, and she reflected for a moment before saying slowly, "Now that both of the children are away at boarding school, perhaps you're feeling a little lonely."

"I don't think it's that."

"A moment ago, when we were talking about the Allandale Group, you said it was at the root of your problems. Please tell me what you meant, it's the only way I'll be able to help you."

Anastasia turned to face her mother, and when she saw the love and concern reflected on Margot's still-pretty face, her eyes welled with tears. "I *am* lonely, Mummy," she admitted. "But not so much for Alix and Michael. It's Maxim I miss. He's away so much. Constantly flying to New York and back, it's been like that since he bought Allandale. And then he's always rushing to Hong Kong or Australia or Los Angeles. Or *somewhere*. It seems to me that in the past six years he's never been off a plane, and all because of Allandale. Oh, it's the basis of his empire, and he's turned it into a huge success. But at what price?" She sighed, and finished in a low voice. "The price of our marriage, in my opinion."

"*Anastasia* . . . I just didn't realize . . ."

"His work comes first. Always. It always has and it always will. It consumes him entirely. I know that now. He's not normal, you know, not when it comes to work. Maxim is beyond a workaholic, Mother. They haven't invented a name for a person who works the way he does. *Around the clock*. He has the stamina of a bull, and the most extraordinary concentration."

"I don't suppose one can fault him for working hard. However, it does strike me that he may be neglecting you."

"I suppose he is. Even when he's with me he is preoccupied, lost in his business deals. Oddly enough, he's grown more withdrawn in certain ways, and less communicative," Anastasia confided.

"But you've always said he was intensely private, and a complicated man."

"That's true." Anastasia laughed hollowly and shook her head. "Believe it or not, after ten years of marriage I still don't know what makes Maximilian West tick."

"Anastasia dear, I hope you don't mind my saying this, but perhaps you should travel with Maxim more than you have been doing. Go to New York more frequently, especially now that both children are away at school."

"My going to New York doesn't change very much, Mummy. Maxim leaves for the office very early, and stays there until all hours at night, and our social life is nonexistent. I'm bored when I'm in New York. I don't have that many friends there. And anyway, Maxim's liable to fly off to Los Angeles for a day or two, and then I'm left to fend for myself."

Margot gave Anastasia a very pointed look, and said quietly, "Are things . . . are things all right between you? I mean in the bedroom . . . sexually?"

"If you're asking me if we still sleep together, the answer is *yes*, we do. Maxim is a very physical man, and passionate, and we do make love. Not as frequently as we once did, though, even when he is at home."

"I see," Margot muttered, sounding and looking suddenly worried. "You don't think there could possibly be another woman, do you?" she finally ventured.

Anastasia shook her head.

"Are you *sure* he doesn't have a mistress in New York?"

"I doubt it. Oh, look, Mummy, maybe he's had one-night stands—after all, he's away from me a great deal, more than half the year these days. But I don't think he's emotionally devious—" She stopped, bit her lip, glanced away.

Margot exclaimed, "What is it? You've thought of something, haven't you? Or, more correctly perhaps, *someone*."

"Not really. It's just that a few weeks ago, when Maxim was in London, I saw him going into Claridge's with a woman. I was passing the hotel in a cab at the time. I suppose he was taking her to lunch."

"Who was it, do you know?"

Anastasia hesitated then blurted out, "Camilla Galland."

"Camilla! But she just remarried recently!"

"Don't be naive, Mother. Marriage vows don't preclude adultery."

"So you *are* suspicious?"

"I don't know. No, that's not true. I *do* know, and I absolutely give Maxim the benefit of the doubt. I don't think there's anything between him and Camilla Galland. It's just that . . . well, to be honest, I've never really liked her, and perhaps because I've never *trusted* her."

"Don't start building a case against Maxim, just because you saw him entering Claridge's with her. Nobody knows men and their *curious*—for want of a better word—ways than I do. But ever since you married Maxim I've felt he was true-blue."

"Before we married you thought he was a womanizer."

"That was then. This is now." Margot leaned forward and squeezed her daughter's arm. "I'm going to help you to organize your life with Maxim better, and when he comes to the South of France next month, you must tell him you plan to travel with him more often."

"Oh, I don't know . . . " Anastasia's voice trailed off.

"Are you suggesting he will object?"

"No, but—"

"No buts, Anastasia. The matter is settled."

It was a hot hazy day, and earlier Maxim had thought the mistral might be blowing up, but now the light wind had dropped and the air was balmy, the sea as calm as a pond.

He stood on the terrace of La Serenissima, their villa in Beaulieu-sur-Mer, between Nice and Monte Carlo, looking out across the long stretch of green lawn, past the swimming pool to the Mediterranean beyond.

The month he had spent here with his family had done him good, he knew that. He felt renewed and relaxed, full of vigor and vitality. It had given him enormous pleasure to spend time with Anastasia and the children. After a whole week of doing nothing but lazing around, he had made several quick trips to London to deal with business, but had returned almost immediately. From that point on, he had stayed put, had worked from his office here at the villa. It had just recently been completed for him, and it contained all the latest equipment, and was a communications center as well, which enabled him to stay in touch with his offices in London, New York, Paris and Hong Kong.

"Daddy! Daddy!"

He turned his head and saw Alix coming up the steps from the beach, swinging a towel and waving to him. Her brother, Michael, carrying a bucket and a fishing net, followed closely on her heels.

How beautiful his children were.

At nine Alix was a small replica of Anastasia, blond and fair of complexion, with the same delicate bone structure as her mother. But her eyes were a smoky gray-green, and she was going to be much taller than Anastasia. She was long and lean and coltish, and something of a tomboy at this age. Eight-year-old Michael was his boy, so like him in appearance with the same dark hair and eyes, his build, and Michael would probably be as tall as he was when he grew up. Both children were bursting with health, energy and high spirits; to Maxim they seemed more beautiful than ever with their young limbs tinted golden-brown by the summer sun.

They ran across the lawn, to join him on the terrace.

Michael said, "Are we going to have the bonfire, Dad?"

"Of course," Maxim responded, suddenly remembering the papers he had to destroy. At breakfast he had told Michael he was going to have a fire, since the shredding machine in the office was broken.

"Can I help too, Daddy?" Alix asked, gazing at him appealingly, her head on one side, wrinkling her nose prettily.

"Why not? And I think we'd better get to it well before lunch. I don't think your mother will appreciate a smoky atmosphere when we're eating, especially since guests are coming. Why not go and find Marcel, tell him to start the fire, and I'll go and get the papers. I'll meet you at the back near the little wood in a few minutes."

"Come on!" Michael said to his sister, and the two of them sped across the lawn at breakneck speed, heading for the back of the villa.

Maxim walked inside, crossing the main salon, thinking how cool and restful it was, with its mixture of pale colors—creams and whites and café au lait, with a hint of peach here and there, and touches of lime green. Anastasia had inherited her mother's flair for decorating, and the entire villa was a tribute to her immense taste and talent.

He ran into her in the marble hall, and he caught his breath, thinking how lovely she was this morning. She wore a pale-green cotton sundress with a ruched strapless bodice, a large cream-colored straw hat with poppies and cornflowers clustered on the band, and carried a basket of flowers. Her golden hair, lighter than ever from the sun and sea, hung down her back almost to her waist. Her arms and shoulders were tanned golden, as were her legs, her feet in sandals.

She smiled at him, he smiled back, and then he reached for her, brought his arm around her waist and pulled her to him, held her very tightly. Nuzzling his face against her neck, he mumbled, "You're very Peach Melba–ish this morning, honeybunch."

She laughed and pushed him away gently. "*I* have flowers to arrange."

"And *I* have papers to burn."

"See you at the pool for a swim before lunch?"

"Absolutely," he said, winking at her.

They went in different directions. Anastasia walked along the corridor to the kitchen; Maxim veered to his left and hurried into his office. He had been placing the papers in two huge shopping bags for days, and he picked these up and took them out to the back of the house.

Alix and Michael were waiting for him, and Marcel, the gardener, had already started the fire. The four of them stood around it, and Michael and Alix fed the papers into the flames.

"Why are you burning them, Daddy?" Alix suddenly asked.

"Because they're *confidential*," Michael answered before Maxim had a chance to respond.

"Yes, I know. But why not simply lock them up in the safe, Daddy?" she asked.

"There are too many, to begin with, *Schatzi*. And secondly,

I don't need them anymore. Rather than having them floating around, it's better to destroy them like this, or in the shredder."

"I see," Alix said, and added, "Because you don't want anybody else to see them or get them, isn't that right?"

"Smart girl," Maxim said, squeezing her bare shoulder.

"She's the smartest girl *I* know," Michael announced, sounding proud. "In fact, she's so smart, Dad, we might even take her into the business with us."

"It's certainly worth considering," Maxim said, his mouth twitching with a hidden smile, realizing his son meant this seriously. "If Alix wants to come into the business with us, of course she can."

"I might," Alix said, beaming at them both, rather flattered by her brother's unexpected compliments. "I'll have to think about it. I haven't really made my mind up about a career yet."

Maxim and Michael exchanged knowing masculine glances, and went on burning the papers.

Later that morning, after he had made his business calls to London, Maxim went swimming with the children in the pool. He enjoyed being with them, and they reciprocated his feelings; there was a bonding between the three of them that was very special.

When Anastasia came down to the pool an hour before lunch, she stood at the edge, watching them cavorting in the water, smiling indulgently.

"Aren't you coming in, Mummy?" Alix cried, bobbing up and down next to Michael, holding a large rubber ball in her hands.

"Yes, Mums, come on in!" Michael yelled, beckoning.

"I don't think I will, not at the moment, angels," Anastasia said, and walked over to one of the poolside lounging beds. Taking off her toweling robe, she threw it over the back of the chaise and sat down. She picked up *Nice-Matin* and began to read it.

"Do you feel all right, Stassy darling?" Maxim asked a few minutes later, standing in front of her, looking down with a worried frown.

"I'm wonderful, but not up to pool antics, suddenly."

He flopped down onto the chaise next to hers, and stretched out his long legs, put his hands under his head and stared up at the clear blue sky. "Isn't this weather glorious? And hasn't our holiday been simply marvelous this year?"

"Yes, it has," she answered, giving him a wide and loving smile. She thought: *Thanks to you. The holiday has been perfect because you have been with us most of the time, and not so preoccupied as in the past few years.* The whole of July had been exceptional in every way, as far as Anastasia was concerned. She had not been as happy as this in a long time, not since before Maxim had purchased the Allandale Group.

Lifting her newspaper, she began to read it again, her heart light, her mind at peace.

Maxim closed his eyes, enjoying the warmth of the sun on his body. The sun was like a tonic to him; he could not get enough of it. The one regrettable thing about England was the poor weather.

His mind turned to the new company he was about to form. He was going to call it West International. It was to be a holding company for future takeovers and acquisitions, and there were quite a few of those on the horizon. One company in particular. One he really wanted, planned to go after.

He was about to make the big leap into the truly big time.

The mere idea of it excited him in a way that nothing else did. In a sense, business was his aphrodisiac. He knew that only too well, and it was something he could not change in himself. If only Anastasia could understand this.

For a split second he contemplated telling her about the new company, and instantly changed his mind. She wouldn't be interested, and in any case, business bored her. It always had. But he didn't mind that. She had so many other remarkable attributes, and he loved her so very much.

"Stassy . . . "

"Yes, darling, what is it?" She glanced at him, and put down the newspaper.

"On my last trip to London two weeks ago, I stopped in at Camper and Nicholsons in Berkeley Street."

"You did! Oh, darling!" She sat up straighter on the chaise, then swung her legs over the side and stared at him. "Are you going to charter a yacht from them next summer? As you've been promising?"

Maxim did not answer. He also swung his legs to the floor, and sat facing her. A wide smile slowly spread across his face.

"Tell me!" she cried excitedly, grasping his arm. "Tell me!"

"I've commissioned them to *build* a yacht. A beautiful yacht for my beautiful wife."

"Oh, Maxim!"

"They have the best naval architects, engineers, yacht stylists and electrical designers in the world, in my opinion. They've been in business since 1782, so they must be doing something right. In any case, the designs will be done first, for our approval, then they will start building her, once they have the go-ahead from me."

"When will she be ready?"

"Not for several years. Two and a half, three maybe. And once she's finished, I want you to do the interior design, with your mother's help, if you wish."

"Oh, she'll be so thrilled, Maxim."

"More important, are you, Peachy?"

"*Very*."

He leaned forward, took her face between his hands, kissed her on the lips. Then he leaped to his feet, pulled her up and walked her over to the outside bar at the far end of the pool area.

"I'm going to crack open a bottle of my best Roederer Cristal to toast the yacht."

"I'll toast her with you!"

She sat down on a stool as he brought the bottle of champagne out of the refrigerator underneath the bar and carefully began to unwind the wire.

"Incidentally, who's coming to lunch today?" he asked.

"Just a bunch of locals," she laughed.

"Teddy and Mark, I'll bet, and your parents."

"Correct. And Yvette and Philippe Arnaud. And Stubby, of course, with his latest lady love. He just phoned to tell me."

"I wish that old reprobate would settle down and get married."

Anastasia laughed again. "So does his mother."

Maxim poured the Cristal into two flutes, pushed one toward Anastasia and lifted his glass. "Here's to your yacht, Peachy."

"To *our* yacht, my darling," she said, giving him the most dazzling smile.

48

$\mathcal{H}$E CALLED HER *BEAUTIFUL DREAMER*. SHE WAS ONE OF
the most magnificent oceangoing yachts ever designed by the
best naval architects there were, custom-built to Maxim's precise specifications by Camper and Nicholsons, the great British
yacht builders.

Sleek of line, elegant and equipped to sail anywhere in the
world, her overall length was 213.9 feet and her cruising speed
fifteen knots per hour. Originally, Maxim had intended to have
a smaller, shorter yacht designed, at first opting for maximum
speed and greater maneuverability over size and spaciousness.
Rather quickly, he had come to realize that much of the pleasure and fun of owning a yacht was to invite guests aboard to
cruise with them part of the time.

With the extended family he and Anastasia had, a large number of staterooms and cabins were an absolute necessity. Aside
from Anastasia and himself, and their children, he required
comfortable accommodation for those he loved and cared
about: Anastasia's parents, Teddy and Mark, and their children, to whom he was close and who were his siblings, in a
sense. Kay, now twenty-four, worked for him at West International in London, and her brother, David, who was twenty-two,
had recently come down from Oxford and was about to enter
the family diamond and jewelry business with Mark. David and
Kay had always looked up to him, and he was like an older
brother to both of Teddy's children. Then there were two other
very important people in his life to consider and include, his
beloved Irina Troubetzkoy and his dearest friend, the faithful,
ever-devoted Stubby.

When she was completed, after an expenditure of several

million pounds, *Beautiful Dreamer* could accommodate twenty people, plus twenty in crew.

She was the ultimate in luxury. Apart from three grand staterooms, there were seven other bedrooms, each one with its own private bathroom en suite, an elegant main salon and a large dining room—both for more formal entertaining—a library, Maxim's study, plus a completely equipped communications center next to an office for his secretarial staff. A swimming pool and the fore and aft decks provided facilities for swimming, outdoor activities and sunbathing, while the boat-deck lounge served as a games room and a place for casual dining. To Maxim a helicopter pad was imperative; this had been included in the ship's overall design so that he could come and go on his helicopter as he wished.

Beautiful Dreamer was almost three years in the building. And it took Anastasia and her mother another year to furnish and decorate her appropriately. When they finally finished their work, the yacht was exquisite—stylish and opulent yet without being pretentious or intimidating. Pale colors, French and English antiques, impressive objects of art and fine paintings abounded. To Maxim's immense satisfaction the interiors of the yacht had comfort, great charm and distinction, and were in perfect taste.

He took delivery of her in July of 1974, and when he saw her moored in one of the best berths in Monte Carlo harbor he was overcome by her beauty. He stood admiring her from the dock, along with Anastasia, Alix and Michael, marveling at her lovely rakish lines, her high streamlined prow, her overall gracefulness. She gleamed brilliantly white against the glittering deep-blue sea in the intense morning sunlight, and as far as he was concerned she was without doubt the best-looking yacht in the port of Monte Carlo—the *Atlantis*, owned by the Greek shipping magnate Stavros Niarchos, notwithstanding.

"She was worth waiting for, eh, Stassy?" he said as they walked up the gangplank.

"Indeed she was. A great deal of time, talent and love has gone into her creation," Anastasia replied quietly. "I'm only sorry she wasn't ready for your fortieth birthday."

"I think we ought to forget *that*," Maxim laughed as he stepped onto the deck, and helped Anastasia on board. Together they walked forward to greet the captain, who was waiting for them with other members of the crew.

That weekend *Beautiful Dreamer* sailed up the Mediterranean coast, heading for Saint-Tropez. Maxim had invited Margot and Alexander Derevenko and Teddy and Mark to join Anastasia, the children and himself on this short maiden cruise. After four glorious days at sea the yacht turned around and sailed back to Monte Carlo, in readiness for the first party they were going to give on board. It was to be a supper dance for seventy guests on Saturday night.

Anastasia filled the yacht with flowers, decorated it with glittering fairy lights, hired the best trio on the Côte d'Azur, ordered cases and cases of Roederer Cristal champagne, and planned a menu of delicious food with her two French chefs. She then proceeded to throw *the* party of the 1974 season.

Halfway through the evening everyone was already congratulating her, telling her she had *two* grand successes on her hands: the beautiful yacht and the spectacular supper dance.

Anastasia thanked them graciously, smiled, and went on smiling for the rest of the evening, even though her heart ached and she was filled with pain inside. Things were not at all right between her and Maxim; they had not been right for several years. And tonight, of all nights, she felt as if she were on the verge of a nervous breakdown, at best some sort of physical collapse.

Now she stood at the far side of the dance floor watching him closely. He was dancing with Chedlya El Bahi, the young Moroccan woman who had been brought by David Maines, a friend of Stubby's who had become part of their crowd. Maxim looked impossibly handsome tonight, his sun-bronzed face, dark hair and brilliant dark eyes emphasized by his cream raw-silk dinner jacket. He was gazing down at Chedlya, chatting and laughing, listening attentively to every word she had to say.

He has time for everyone but me, Anastasia thought bitterly. Charming and dazzling the world at large, with his charisma, his power, his immense wealth. He even paid more attention to my father when we were cruising up to Saint-Tropez. He certainly had little to say to me, except to issue orders in his imperious way. Duke Maximilian indeed.

She bit her lip, blinking rapidly as she saw him lean closer to Chedlya, whisper something in her ear. The young woman laughed, looked up at him, smiling into his face. There has always been something hypnotic about him, Anastasia thought miserably, and a seductiveness. Most people do fall under his spell. To her dismay she noticed that Maxim and Chedlya suddenly appeared to be dancing much closer, and, in a swift rush of the most blinding jealousy, she felt as if a sharp knife were being twisted in her stomach. It was an emotion that had become only too familiar.

Anastasia had no peace of mind these days. The empty ache inside her was always present and she was lonely and depressed. These feelings were caused by Maxim's life-style and behavior, she was fully aware of that. He was absent almost constantly, more than ever before, in fact—always on the run, on the wing, in and out of London and Paris, rushing to New York or Los Angeles or God knows where else. Because of his long separations from her, she found it increasingly difficult to believe that he did not have his flings, become embroiled with some woman somewhere. Casual sexual encounters were probably a part of his life now, the norm, she suspected, while she sat and waited. Waited for him to come home when it suited him.

It struck her that she had been doing a great deal of waiting over the past few years. Waiting for Maxim. Waiting for the yacht to be built. Waiting for the furnishings to be delivered—the antiques, the art, the fabrics, the carpets, all the trappings required to create the floating palace he wanted. Waiting, waiting, waiting. And worrying. Worrying herself to death.

She thought back to the summer of 1970, when she had had the heart-to-heart talk with her mother in Paris, and had then spent a lovely holiday with Maxim and the children at the villa in Beaulieu. It had been idyllic. At the end of the summer, following her mother's advice, she had begun to travel with him. At first it had worked but eventually it had become far too difficult for her to sustain. His schedule, the very nature of his wheeling and dealing in the world of big business, had a certain unpredictability. Sometimes they would arrive in New York only to spend a couple of days there, even though their stay had been planned for much longer. Unexpectedly they would have to fly straight back to London, for business reasons. Or they might have to leave for another city in the States. Or Hong

Kong. Or Australia. Or some far-flung corner of the globe where he had a deal. She did not have Maxim's penchant for flying, nor his immense unflagging stamina. The strenuous routine soon wearied and debilitated her, and took its eventual toll on her health.

Then there were the other demands on her, which necessitated her presence in England and France. A large house in Mayfair and the villa in Beaulieu to run; a variety of staff problems in these homes, constantly needing to be ironed out; the children to tend to during school breaks and holidays.

After a year she had had to stop being his traveling companion; it had become too much for her. Then before she even had a chance to take a breath there had been the yacht to deal with. She had had to cope with countless details herself, since Maxim was forever away, in board meetings somewhere in the world.

Inevitably, their separations became longer, and weeks went by when they didn't see each other. Frequently the weeks turned into months. If she saw him half of the year now, she was lucky.

He's drifting away from me, Anastasia thought, and she was suddenly terribly frightened.

Focusing her gaze on her husband, the man she loved beyond all reason, she saw that he still held the Moroccan girl in his arms. Her stomach began to churn as she continued to observe him intently. She felt herself beginning to tremble with anger and jealousy, and had to exercise enormous control to get a grip on her emotions. *In jealousy there is more self-love than love*, she reminded herself, thinking of the line by La Rochefoucauld.

With a flash of clarity and true objectiveness, she thought: Maxim's got the kind of mesmerizing charm and devastating looks women find utterly irresistible. Without his doing anything to encourage them, *they* fling themselves at *him*. And what man can resist that kind of temptation?

And I bet he doesn't, she added under her breath, still unable to tear her eyes away from him and the Moroccan girl, whom she had now begun to detest.

Maxim caught sight of her and smiled, but Anastasia swiftly averted her face, pretending not to have noticed his acknowledgment of her.

She swung around and began to walk away from the dance

floor, seething inside, her jealousy rampant, her anger spiraling into a towering rage.

David Maines was making a beeline for her, and there was no way she could veer to her right or her left, at least not without giving offense to this very nice man. A screenwriter, and now a best-selling novelist, he had been an acquaintance of her father's for ages, having always been around the film clique in Paris and London. Stubby had taken up with him some time ago, and David had been drifting in and out of their lives for about five years. He always seemed to be in the South of France when they were there, and frequently dined, partied or played tennis with them. Two years ago they had been his guests at his beautiful villa on the top of a hill in Tangier, where they had spent a long weekend with him. Before the advent of Chedlya.

David stopped in front of her, bowed gallantly and said, "My friend Chedlya seems to have commandeered your husband, so I think it's only fair and just that I do the same with you. Please come and dance with me, Anastasia."

"Oh but I don't—" she began, then realizing that as hostess she could not be rude to one of her guests, she said, "I'd love to, David."

He led her out onto the dance floor, complimenting her on the fabulous party as they fell into step. "As for the yacht, it's the epitome of beauty and faultless taste," David remarked.

"Thank you. The party was a bit easier to produce than the yacht, though." She forced a smile and added, "My mother should get a lot of credit, you know, she's enormously talented as an interior designer."

"So are you," David said, smiling down at her, his eyes full of admiration. Aside from her artistic skills, she radiated beauty, and he could not help thinking how lucky Maximilian West was to have this superb woman as his wife.

"And I hadn't realized you were a painter," David remarked as they glided around the floor. "I was very taken with the watercolors in the main salon earlier, and Stubby told me you painted them."

"Years ago. I just sort of putter around," she murmured dismissively, looking over his shoulder, her eyes scanning the area for Maxim. He seemed to have disappeared.

"If that's puttering, then you can putter anytime for me,"

the writer said. "Look, Anastasia, if you ever have a show, or if any of your paintings are ever for sale, do let me know. I'd love to buy a few for the house in Tangier."

"How nice of you, David," she said distractedly, wondering where Maxim had gone with David's girlfriend. "But I don't paint very often, it's not even a hobby." She longed to escape. Her heart had begun to race, and she was frantic, panic-stricken, her face taut. Had Maxim taken the girl somewhere to be alone with her? To make love to her?

She said a little abruptly, "David, would you mind awfully if we stop dancing now? I've just remembered something I must tell the chef at once."

"Of course not, and thank you," he said, immediately leading her off the floor. "Ah, there's Chedlya! Obviously looking for me, I've no doubt. See you later, darling."

Anastasia gave him a small smile, excused herself and hurried away, wishing the pounding in her chest would cease. Out of the corner of her eye she saw Maxim at the bar with her father and Stubby, laughing at some joke, and she felt a surge of relief. Nevertheless, having told David Maines that she had to speak to one of the chefs, there was no way she could linger here.

Avoiding the bar, and her mother and Irina, who were both waving to her, trying to catch her attention, she flew along the main deck to Maxim's and her stateroom, and went straight into the bathroom. She was shaking so much she could barely lock the door. After she had managed to do so, she stumbled over to the mirror and looked at herself.

Sadly, she did not see her great beauty, but saw only the panic in her eyes, her grim mouth and strained expression, the beads of perspiration on her face and neck. But in all truth, at thirty-three Anastasia was at her loveliest. Tonight she wore a draped strapless gown of white chiffon, designed by Madame Grès, and a magnificent diamond necklace that Maxim had just given her. Both the dress and the necklace were set off to great advantage by her golden-brown skin; her blond hair was swept up in a mass of curls on top of her head, and she had an ethe-realness about her this evening that was breathtaking.

But blinded as she was by insane jealousy, anger and hurt, she saw nothing as it truly was. All she could think about were Maxim's neglect of her, his protracted absences, his preoccupation with his business and his detached attitude to her well-being.

She broke out in another cold sweat and reached for a towel to pat herself dry. *I love him too much,* she thought. *He is my whole existence, but I am only part of his, just a fraction of it, and that's the basic problem.* Tears came into her smoky-blue eyes and she strove hard to push them back, peering at herself in the mirror again. *Perhaps there's something wrong with me. Not perhaps, there* is. *I'm sick. I am sick with love.* For him. She recalled those other words from the Bible: "My beloved is mine and I am his." Except that he's not mine, not anymore, she thought. Even though I am his and will always be his.

Oh, why couldn't he have been just an ordinary man? Why did he have to be a business genius, this brilliant tycoon of vision and daring? She sighed and slowly the tears trickled down her cheeks. She wanted their marriage to be the way it had been in the beginning. She wanted all of him. But that was not possible, because Maxim could not give all of himself to her.

She thought: *I can't go on like this. I have to do something. I can't stand the pain of loving him.*

Remembering her guests, she pulled herself together as best she could. She reached for a tissue and patted her eyes before hurrying through into their stateroom.

Seating herself at the dressing table, she applied fresh eye makeup and lipstick, sprayed herself with perfume, pushed a curl into place. Rising, she took a deep breath, managed to regain her composure, and returned to the dance and her guests.

"Congratulations, Peachy," Maxim said a few hours later. He took off his cream dinner jacket and draped it on the back of a chair.

Anastasia stood at the other side of the stateroom. Slowly she turned around, stood staring at him. She loved him so much, wanted him so much. But it was not to be. She was losing him. Just as she had known when they first met fifteen years ago that it was their destiny to be together, so she now knew that it was their destiny to part. *Qué sera sera . . .* what will be *will* be.

She had not been able to stand those women pawing him throughout the evening, clutching at him, flinging themselves at him, draping themselves all over him, kissing him flagrantly when they left at the end of the evening. She hated each and every one of them.

Nausea rose up in her. She thought her legs were going to buckle.

Maxim undid his bow tie, dropped it on the chest and unbuttoned his shirt while continuing to look at her. He smiled his charming lopsided smile. "The party was a spectacular success, the yacht is superb, and the diamond necklace looks gorgeous," he said, and smiled at her again.

She felt something cracking and splintering inside her, and she reached out to hold on to the back of a chair. "That's all I am to you these days, isn't it? The giver of your parties, the decorator of your homes, the wearer of your diamonds," she said coldly.

Maxim was flabbergasted, and could only gaze at her blankly, startled by her extraordinary words, her curious icy voice. Recovering himself quickly, he said, "You are also the recipient of my love, Stassy."

"Recipient of your love! That's a joke. Me and how many others?"

"What on earth do you mean?" he asked, his tone instantly changing. He gave her a sharp look, annoyance replacing bafflement.

"Oh, come on, don't play the injured innocent with me. I know you have affairs with other women."

"I certainly do not!" he exploded, infuriated by her unjustified accusation.

"You don't expect me to believe that a passionate, very physical man like you doesn't become involved in little liaisons when he's away from home, do you? I know you very well, Maxim, and sex has always been extremely important to you. Very necessary, I would say."

"If you can accuse me of philandering, then you don't know me at all!" he shouted back, his voice rising to a higher pitch. "There are no other women in my life, and there never have been. I have always been true to you!"

"And what about Camilla Galland, God's greatest gift to the English stage?" she shot back, her voice acerbic.

"Camilla Galland," he spluttered and laughed disbelievingly. "What an outrageous suggestion. You can't mean that seriously, Anastasia."

"I most certainly do. Quite aside from the fact that I've seen you with her over the years, others have spotted the two of you together."

"You've seen me with her," he gasped. "When?"

"In point of fact, this spring, going into the Ritz. And several years ago, going into Claridge's. You seem to have quite a few luncheons with that lady. Not to mention dinners in New York. You've been seen, you know, so don't deny it."

"I wasn't going to deny it, Anastasia. Why should I? Camilla and I are friends, have been for years. It's no secret. I have had lunch with her in London, and I sometimes speak to her on the phone, as you well know. And I have had dinner with her in New York, yes, when she's been in a play on Broadway. I've been giving her advice about her investments off and on over the years. And incidentally, as far as the dinners in New York are concerned, her husband has always joined us. In case it's slipped your mind, Camilla married Peter Jarvis five years ago. She's still *very* married to him."

"Husbands are generally the last to know about extramarital affairs! As indeed are wives. Don't think you can pull the wool over my eyes by flinging her marriage at me, because you can't."

Maxim, more furious than ever, took a step toward her and cried, "Ask Stubby. Go down the corridor to his cabin *now*, and ask him, goddamn it! He'll tell you I've been advising her on her investments. He was the one who suggested it in the first place."

"*Ask Stubby!*" she exclaimed, her icy voice dripping sarcasm. "Well, well, well, that's the joke of the century. *Ask Stubby indeed*. How preposterous you are, Maxim. Stubby will say anything to protect you. He'd sell his own mother to protect you. Why, Stubby thinks you're God."

"What *is* all this about?" Maxim demanded frantically, truly not understanding why she was ranting and raving at him. His face had turned gray under his tan. "What's brought this on, Anastasia, after our lovely few days together? And the wonderful party tonight?"

"The party may have been wonderful for you, but not for

me. I was left alone to fend for myself, while you paid court to Chedlya and every other woman present."

"You're being utterly stupid. I danced with Chedlya once. And I was the host, remember. I had to dance with our women guests."

Anastasia's face suddenly contorted into an ugly grimace, momentarily obliterating her great beauty.

He sucked in his breath, hardly recognizing her. She might have donned a mask.

She cried, "Things are not right between us anymore, Maxim. You're always *away*. You don't share your life with me. You shut me out years ago." As her pent-up rage flooded her she began to shake uncontrollably and clung to the back of the chair to support herself.

"I have never shut you out!" he protested, his face livid. "You're not interested in my business, that's why I don't discuss it with you. It bores you. It always has. I do my level best to be with you as much as I can. You don't want to travel with me, because you say you can't take the pace, that it exhausts you. What in God's name do you want from me?"

She did not answer.

"You know I love you, Stassy," he said, softening his voice and his manner, moving closer to her. "I've only ever loved *you*. You're the only one I've *ever* wanted. I try to show you how I feel in every way. You yearned for a yacht over the years, so I had one built for you. I called her *Beautiful Dreamer*, because that's what you've always been to me . . . my beautiful dreamer," he murmured placatingly, his smile loving.

"I don't want your yacht!" she screamed. "I don't want your diamonds!" Losing control, she pulled at the clasp, wrenched the necklace off and threw it on the bed. "I don't want it, do you hear!"

Maxim flinched and drew back. He felt as if she had kicked him in the stomach, and a terrible coldness swept through him. He genuinely had no idea what this was all about, what had triggered it. All he knew, at this moment, was that he had to get out into the fresh air. He felt the bile rising in his throat, thought he was going to be sick.

Without uttering another word, he turned and walked out, slamming the door behind him.

"I only want you, Maxim! That's what I meant! I only want

you! Material things don't matter to me!" she shouted after him, staring at the door. But he did not come back. She threw herself on the bed and began to sob, repeating over and over again, "I only want you, my darling, I only want you."

But Maxim did not hear her.

49

MAXIM WALKED DOWN THE MAIN DECK. IT WAS EMPTY; everyone had gone to bed. Leaning against the rail, he stood looking out across the dark sea to the dim horizon, taking great gulps of air and trying to still his shaking limbs. He felt sickened by her words.

Anastasia had hurt him so much he could hardly stand it. The accusations she had flung at him were so ridiculous they were laughable. But he could deal with those. What had cut him deeply, like a lash, and caused him great pain, was the way she had flung the necklace on the bed, screaming that she did not want it.

The diamond necklace was quite extraordinary and it had cost a small fortune. This did not matter to him. What *did* matter enormously was the *love* he had invested in its creation. He had gone to Mark and asked him to make something truly unique for her, and Mark's most gifted designer at Tannen and Graf had created an exquisite design. Then Mark had spent over a year searching the world for flawless blue-white stones. Maxim had wanted the diamonds and the necklace to be perfect for Anastasia, because he loved her so much, and Mark had understood this, and had set out to create a masterpiece.

During the entire time the necklace was being made, Maxim had gone to Mark's prestigious jewelry shop on Regent Street whenever he could, wanting to watch the craftsman working, mounting the stones in the intricate lacy web of white gold. He had hardly been able to contain himself until it was finished, until he could finally present it to Anastasia and see it enhancing her beauty.

He had given it to her after they had boarded the yacht for the first time the other day, and sailed up the coast to Saint-Tropez. It had looked stunning on her and she had been thrilled, or so he thought. But only a few minutes ago she had flung it back at him. He now realized that the action in itself did not mean much. It had been an expression of anger, anger with him. What he did not understand was the reason *why* she was so furious with him, what was at the bottom of her anger.

Sighing under his breath, Maxim walked over to the bar and poured himself a glass of water. He carried it back to the rail, where he stood drinking it, trying to sort out his troubled thoughts. Aside from her anger, there had been her outrageous and unfounded accusations to contend with. He could not imagine what had brought on her strange outburst, or prompted her to make the statements she had made.

Like most married couples, they had had their quarrels in the past, but none of them had ever been quite like this one. He had never seen her so hysterical, so . . . *irrational*. Her behavior had been very much out of character. She was normally composed and serene.

She's overtired, he thought, worn out after all the work she had done on the yacht in the past year. It *has* been a backbreaking task, even with her mother's help. What Anastasia needs now is complete rest, relaxation, me, and my companionship and love. Yes, she needs me to be with her, to take care of her. She's really quite fragile, my beautiful dreamer.

Maxim was suddenly glad he had planned a cruise to the Greek islands as a surprise for her. They would be leaving in a few days and would be sailing around the Aegean for about three weeks. It would do them both good, and maybe with a little luck it would be as idyllic a holiday as the one they had had four years ago. That summer at the villa had been so sublime, it had glowed in his mind ever since.

Once the cruise was over he would attempt to structure his life differently, in order for them to spend more time together. He had been planning to do that anyway; he truly wanted to make her happy.

It was a warm night, and Maxim stayed out on the main deck for several hours, thinking and making plans for their future.

When he finally returned to their stateroom, Anastasia was sound asleep.

He was relieved that she was, for he had not relished the possibility of another quarrel with her. He crept into his dressing room quietly, took off his clothes and prepared for bed, reassuring himself that tomorrow, after a good night's rest, his wife would be her normal self.

And over breakfast he would tell her about the cruise to the Greek islands. He knew how much this would please her, and he was looking forward to it himself.

"Daddy! Daddy! Wake up! Wake up!" Alix cried, pummeling his arm.

Maxim sat up in bed with a start, and stared at his daughter, who stood with her brother at the side of the bed.

"What's the matter?" he asked, their agitation immediately apparent to him. "*What is it?*"

"Mummy just left. She's going to the Nice airport," Michael announced, pointing to the porthole. "She's taking off now in the copter, Dad."

As Michael spoke, Maxim heard the roar of the helicopter as it hovered for a moment above the yacht. Throwing back the sheets, he jumped out of bed and raced across the room to peer out of the porthole. To his dismay he saw his helicopter whirling up and away into the sunny blue morning sky.

"She's going back to London, Daddy," Alix informed him, running to Maxim, catching hold of his arm. "She was crying this morning," Alix went on unsteadily, gulping, her eyes filling. "You're not going to get a divorce, are you, Daddy? Michael and I don't want you and Mummy to get a divorce!"

Maxim was thunderstruck, and exclaimed, "Of course we're not getting divorced! Don't be so silly, *Schatzi*." He bent down, hugged her, then beckoned to Michael. His twelve-year-old son came running into his arms, and the three of them stood holding one another. He adored his children, and it tore at him that they were upset and disturbed by Anastasia's actions, her sudden dramatic departure.

Finally he straightened, released his children from his tight embrace and said, "Everything's going to be all right. I don't want either of you to worry about anything. *Understand?*"

"Yes," Alix said. "But why has Mummy left?"

"I honestly don't know," Maxim answered truthfully. "Now scoot, the two of you, and let me take a shower, shave and get dressed."

Michael said, "What are you going to do, Dad?"

"I'm going to fetch Mummy back. I love her very much. Therefore that is what I *must* do."

"For God's sake, let me drive, Duke," Stubby exclaimed. "You're going to have Margot's Roller and *us* in the drink if you're not careful. *Slow down!*"

Maxim eased his foot off the accelerator of his mother-in-law's new Rolls-Royce, which he had borrowed, and dropped to a lower speed. "You're right, Stubby, and I don't know why I'm racing like this. By the time we get to Nice airport, the plane Anastasia's booked on will have taken off anyway. If Margot hasn't been able to charter one for me, I'll have to wait for the next commercial flight."

"I'm certain Margot will have managed to get hold of a private plane for you by the time we get to the airport, even though it is Sunday," Stubby said reassuringly. "But in any case, when you get to London, Anastasia will have calmed down, take my word for it. You know what women are. Skittish, like thoroughbred horses."

"I hope she's more like herself," Maxim mumbled. "God only knows what brought this on. I still haven't the slightest idea what the row was about. I'm truly puzzled."

"She was pushing hard to get the yacht finished for your birthday in June, and even though she didn't succeed, and was late, she worked damned hard. Maybe the pressure and the stress got to her," Stubby suggested. "She's probably exhausted, you know."

"That's what I've been thinking myself." Maxim tightened his grip on the steering wheel, then confided, "Stassy accused me of having an affair with Camilla Galland, of all things."

There was a small silence, then Stubby said, "You haven't, have you?"

"Oh come on, Stubby, don't be such a bloody fool! Of course I haven't. You ought to know that better than anybody."

"What I *do* know is that Camilla has had quite a thing about you for years. To put it succinctly, she's had the hots for you, two husbands notwithstanding."

Maxim threw him a quick glance out of the corner of his eye and snorted in disbelief. "That's ridiculous!"

"Take my word for it, give her a wink and she's yours."

"You're wrong, and in any event, I'm certainly not interested in Camilla, and I never have been."

Stubby was quiet. After a moment, he ventured, "You don't think Anastasia's heard gossip about you, do you?"

"*Gossip?* What the hell do you mean?"

"You know, gossip about you and other women."

"What other women?"

"The ones you've had affairs with."

"I've only had a couple of one-night stands in my entire married life," Maxim snapped. "That's hardly having *affairs*, as you put it!"

"Sally Batterson lasted more than one night, Duke. I remember *her* very well, since I was in New York with you at the time."

"It lasted a big three weeks! It was a *prolonged* one-night stand, that's all. The whole thing was meaningless. And you, Stubby, my friend, are the only person who ever knew about it."

"Except for the lady involved."

Maxim threw him a scathing glance, said nothing.

"Sally knew," Stubby pointed out.

"*She's* hardly likely to have told anybody."

"How do you know? Some women like to boast, and let's face it, you're worth boasting about."

"Please believe me, Sally never told a soul about our brief dalliance, such as it was. She was engaged to be married at the time, although I didn't know it until a few months later. When I received an invitation to the wedding."

Stubby laughed cynically. "Cold-blooded creatures women are at times, don't you think?"

Maxim concentrated on the traffic ahead, braking as they came to a bend in the lower Corniche, the road running parallel with the sea. Once they had a clear stretch of road ahead of them again, he gunned Margot's Rolls, anxious to get to the airport. "No, Anastasia can't possibly have heard any gossip about me, for the simple reason that there is no basis for it," Maxim remarked, after a moment. "I've led a blameless life for a very long time. In fact, I've always led a blameless life, if you really think about it." He laughed hollowly. "I realize there are those who would like to make me out to be a playboy, a cross between Porfirio Rubirosa and Aly Khan, but nothing could be further from the truth."

"God rest their souls," Stubby murmured. "They both died young, but oh, what lives they lived!" He sighed, then after a pause, went on, "I know you're not a womanizer, you don't have to sell me on your fidelity to Anastasia. I've been a witness to it, and you've been nothing if not a devoted husband and father. Hell, I'm sorry I ever asked you to help Camilla sort out her investments. But that twit of a husband was only creating a bigger muddle than she already had." Stubby frowned. "By the way, what prompted Anastasia to seize on poor old innocent Camilla?"

"She apparently saw me going into the Ritz with Camilla this past spring. We were meeting her accountant there for lunch. Also, I gather some friendly friend told Stassy that she'd seen me dining with Camilla in New York." Maxim shook his head, grimaced. "Whoever *that* troublemaker was forgot to mention Camilla's husband was with us."

Stubby said, "Just goes to show how careful you've got to be when you're a married man. Thank God I'm a bachelor. And that's the way it's going to remain. Actually, I enjoy being the eternal fiancé."

Maxim laughed. "If anybody's the playboy, it's you! I'll never understand why they've always wanted to pin the label on me."

"You *look* the part more than I," Stubby pointed out, grinning. "Dashing, gorgeous, glamorous, et cetera. Most people think of me as your bumbling sidekick."

"Good God, if they only knew! Fast women, fast cars, fast boats, fast roulette wheels. But just watch your step, old son, as far as the fast cars and boats are concerned. I don't want to lose you."

"Listen who's talking! You're the one who always has his foot down on the pedal. But never fear, I plan to be around a long time." Stubby settled back in the seat with a thoughtful expression in his pale-blue eyes.

Maxim drove on in silence for a while.

Suddenly Stubby said, "She's always been possessive of you."

"I suppose so."

"And a bit jealous. I have a deep affection for Anastasia, she is the most wonderful girl, but she gets upset if you even so much as *look* at another woman."

Maxim glanced at Stubby, and then his brows came together in a puzzled frown. "Do you really think so?"

"Yes, I do."

"But surely she knows how much I love her. I've always *adored* her."

"I know, but women can be funny." Stubby hesitated, then said, "There's another thing. She hates you to be away from her. . . . This may sound odd to you, but I think she resents your business, resents the time you devote to it."

Maxim was startled, and exclaimed heatedly, "But I can't just stop! I've built an enormous empire in the last few years. I have a responsibility to thousands of people, employees, major stockholders, and the public, not to mention myself. I happen to enjoy my work."

"I'm sure she's aware of that," Stubby said quickly. "And I'm not saying she wants you to get rid of your business empire. She's far too intelligent a person to expect you to do such a thing. What I'm trying to say is . . . well, you *do* spend a lot of time away from her. What woman wouldn't get fidgety?"

Maxim nodded. "Point well made, Stubby. I must agree. I'm going to have to organize my work schedule a little better."

He sighed so heavily and looked so worried, Stubby exclaimed, "Hey, come on, Duke, everything's going to be fine. You'll see, when you get home to London, Anastasia will be calmer. I'm sure I'll be driving the Roller back to Nice tomorrow, or the day after, to pick you both up."

"I hope so, I can't stand it when things are not right between us."

They patched things up and sailed around the Aegean, and for a while the marriage worked. But within the year it was in trouble again. And for all the same reasons. Inevitably, Anastasia became nervous and run-down, her fragile psyche shattered by innumerable problems, some real, some imagined. Without meaning to do so, she created a rift between them and, unthinkingly, never gave Maxim a chance to bridge it. In 1976, unable to take the stress and pressure of his life, she insisted on a trial separation. At first he fought it, but finally he had to agree. Loving her the way he did, he was afraid of endangering her health.

When Anastasia divorced him in 1977, Maxim was stunned and heartbroken, their children hurt and baffled, their families and friends shocked and saddened.

PART FIVE

Camilla

TANGIER

1981

Wherefore the king said unto me,
Why is thy countenance sad,
seeing thou art not sick?
This is nothing else but sorrow of the heart.

—Book of Nehemiah

50

CAMILLA GALLAND SAT WAITING FOR DAVID MAINES IN the cool marble-lined bar of the El Minzah Hotel in Tangier, where she was staying.

It was that quiet time of day when the bustle in the streets outside had subsided. The sun was dropping low in the sky, mottling the dark-blue sea with speckles of gold and mauve, and she knew that in a moment night would swiftly descend, as it usually did here.

Camilla had always liked this particular hour in North Africa, when it was neither day nor night. The *gloaming* it was called in Scotland, where she originally came from. It was a gentle time.

The silence in the bar was broken only by the muffled whirring of the ceiling fans, the faint plaintive voice of the muezzin calling the faithful to prayer from the minaret of the mosque, echoing to her across the Casbah walls.

In the splintered half-light of the bar she saw David walking toward her—tall, thin, deeply tanned from years of living here. Stopping at her table, he took both of her hands in his and drew her to her feet, hugging her to him. "Camilla! It's wonderful to have you here in my backyard! Welcome!"

"It's lovely to see you, David," she said, meaning it.

They sat down at the table, eyed each other appraisingly, then burst out laughing. They had always enjoyed working together on movies, several of which he had written especially for her; in a sense, they shared battle scars, were like old comrades-in-arms.

"I never thought I'd see you in Tangier alone," David said, settling back in his chair.

"I'm divorced from Peter Jarvis, you know, and I have been for almost two years."

"So I read in the gossip columns. What I meant is that the last news I had of you was from Alan Trenton. He told me you were heavily involved with Maxim West. So where is the great Maxim? Off making some stupendously big deal somewhere, I've no doubt."

Caught off guard, she stammered, "It must be a while since you heard from Stubby. Maxim and I haven't seen each other for the last six months." She reached for her glass of wine to hide her confusion and gulped it down.

His quick writer's eye took in everything. "Oh dear, I've put my foot in it, haven't I? I'm such a clumsy fool. Do forgive me." He smiled at her warmly and rushed on, "Let me go and get us a drink, and then we can catch up with all the gossip. Another white wine?"

"Yes, please."

He strode to the bar, and she heard him murmuring in Arabic to the barman. In the moment he was away she caught hold of herself and tried to compose herself. She wished she had written him a note from Paris before she left. At least she would have been spared the embarrassment about Maxim, and, more important, the painful thoughts of him. She could not help equating him with pain these days. He had hurt her terribly.

"Want to talk about it now? Or shall we leave it until later?" David asked when he came back to the table and lowered himself into the chair.

"I don't mind." She shrugged her shoulders lightly, made a little moue that had a hint of regret to it. "There's nothing much to tell. I ran into Maxim in New York last September, and we became involved. For three months! Then, suddenly, he dropped me." She forced a laugh, shook her head. "Anyway, *you* know what he's like—after all, you've been a friend of Stubby's and his for quite a few years. He's always rushing off to make a big deal somewhere, that's one of the problems."

"There's no question the man's a workaholic," David remarked.

"Very much so," Camilla agreed. "Anastasia was right about him there."

David glanced at her sharply. "Is that the reason they got a divorce?"

"I don't know. Maxim doesn't reveal much. He's the strong silent type. And very secretive. Actually, I found him rather enigmatic, hard to get to know, *truly* know. He mystifies me, he really does. Despite our nice friendship over the years, and then our closeness, our intimacy for those three months, I can honestly tell you I have no idea what that man is all about."

David had seemed puzzled as he had listened to her, but he asked no further questions, merely said, "I'm sorry you and he broke up. Maxim appeared to be so lonely after the divorce . . . the loneliest man in the world, to me."

Camilla made no comment, although she tended to agree.

David said, "Ah, here's Mohammed with our drinks."

The smiling waiter placed the glasses of icy white wine in front of them, bowed and backed away.

David touched his glass to hers. "Down the hatch," he said, laughed, and winked at her.

"Down the hatch!" She took a sip of the wine, then volunteered, "Maxim *is* lonely, David. I worry about him, and I still care what happens to him . . . he has that quality."

"I understand." David leaned back in the chair, focused his keen intelligent gaze on her, and changing the subject, he asked, "Tell me what you're doing in Tangier."

"I'm seriously thinking of buying a house here," Camilla said. "I love the climate, it's within easy reach of Paris and London, if I have a film or a play to do, yet it's sort of—off the beaten track." She laughed at David's startled face, and added, "I'm like you, my darling, I crave a bit of solitude now and again."

"Camilla, this is wonderful news, and it'll be great to have you here. There's a nice little English-American community, and you'll be welcomed with open arms. But they'll leave you alone when you want peace and quiet. That's the beauty of Tangier. I love the place."

"I'd hoped you would be able to steer me in the right direction, David, help me to find a real estate person."

He grinned, and exclaimed, "The *right* real estate person. *That's* very important here. And yes, I know a wonderful Frenchwoman who found my villa for me. I'll phone her tomorrow, invite her to lunch with us. I'm presuming you're free."

"As a bird. But it's your turn now. Tell me all of *your* news. Do you still have that lovely girlfriend? The Moroccan girl . . . "

"Chedlya El Bahi. And no, I don't. She married several years ago. A young Moroccan painter. They live here part of the time, and in Casablanca. I'm fancy-free, as they say." He sipped his drink, and continued, "Actually, I'm enjoying not being involved, for once in my life."

Neither spoke for a moment, then he said, "Incidentally, congratulations again on winning the Oscar for best actress. I did drop you a note in April, I hope you received it."

"Yes, thank you," Camilla replied, smiling, and then she began to tell him about the making of the movie for which she had won the Oscar. David ordered more drinks, and they sat talking shop and reminiscing for another hour or so, until at last David said, "Come on, let's get out of here and go to dinner."

They walked through the dimly lit, mosaic-tiled lobby of the hotel and out into the main street of Tangier. It was dark. The high black sky looked almost luminous, chipped with thousands of tiny stars and hung with a pale moon.

David lifted his head, touched her arm, pointed to the sky. "Great set decorator we have, eh, Camilla?"

She laughed, as always enjoying him, and together they walked down to the sea road, making for his favorite restaurant at the top of one of the highest buildings in the city. "It's not all that high," he explained. "Hardly a Manhattan skyscraper. But the restaurant has a huge plate-glass window, floor to ceiling, and you can see the whole of the town, and beyond, on a clear night. It's as if you've been suspended in the sky above Tangier."

They passed the Socco Chico and the Grand Socco, the two markets. A few Moroccans sat at one of the cafés, their heads close together as they talked, their djellabas pulled closely around them, their glasses of mint tea neglected on the table.

The dark alleys leading into the Casbah looked mysterious and uninviting. Camilla shivered and drew closer to David. "Those streets do look sinister," she said, slipping her arm through his.

He laughed, patted her hand resting on his arm. "You're with me, Camilla, and we're quite safe, I assure you."

As they reached the sea road she relaxed. The cafés facing the ocean were in full swing, packed with Moroccans and Europeans. Their colored lights threw bright rays onto the road, illuminating their way. A huddle of Berber women straggled past, their haiks wrapped around them like tight cocoons of brown fabric, their bare feet slapping the sandy road as they made their way back to the hills. A reluctant donkey followed in their wake, his back laden with a precarious mountain of parcels.

"It was market day today," David explained, as her eyes followed the weird little band of women. "They probably brought down vegetables and flowers. Now they're going back with tea and cloth, and, if they've had a lucky day, sugar and flour."

"How strange that they're not wearing veils," Camilla remarked as she and David caught up with the mule train.

"The country women never do. But they sometimes pull their haiks—their robes—around them to cover their faces. Actually, quite a few of the city-dwelling Moroccan women are emancipated now, don't wear the veil either these days. Ah, here we are." He led her forward toward the building where the restaurant was located.

Camilla looked back at the Berber women. They seemed like creatures from another age, their beady black eyes darting back and forth, staring out from their wrinkled brown faces, which she thought looked like polished walnuts. Or they could be baby sparrows, she added under her breath.

David escorted her through the lobby of the apartment building. It was extremely modern, with gleaming marble floors, mirrored walls and crystal chandeliers. They took the elevator up to the top floor, and went through glass doors into the flower-filled restaurant.

The maître d' greeted David cordially and showed them to a corner table. As David was ordering a bottle of white wine, Camilla took in the magnificent view through the wall of glass. By turning slightly she could see the whole of Tangier: the port and the harbor, the strange cubelike composition of the houses of the Casbah, the dark hills beyond. And straight ahead in front of her, the sea and sky merging endlessly.

She caught her breath and exclaimed, "David, it's fantastic!"

"Isn't it just. And it makes you feel like God looking down." He smiled at her affectionately. "There's Tangier for you, Camilla, at your feet."

"I'm so glad I came, David. I think I'm going to enjoy it here. I do hope I'll be able to find a house. The right house."

"I'm sure you will. In the meantime, I have an idea. Why not move into the villa, stay with me while you're here? My place is huge, and rather beautiful, even though I say so myself."

"Why, how generous of you . . ." Her voice trailed off, and she hesitated.

He said, "Go on, say yes. You'd be wonderful company for me."

"All right, then, you've got a deal!" she agreed suddenly, beaming at him.

"Good girl! Now, let's order dinner. I don't know about you, but I'm starving."

"So am I, to be honest."

David ordered for them both. He selected a French country pâté to start with, a local fish baked *en papillote* with herbs and spices, and a selection of steamed vegetables.

They sipped the chilled Pouilly-Fuissé as they waited for the food, and David filled her in with details about Tangier and the life he led there. And then during dinner he told her about the screenplay he was writing, and unexpectedly suggested she might like to star in it.

"It's a great part for you, Camilla," David said between mouthfuls of fish. "I'll be honest, I didn't have you in mind when I started it. I didn't have any actress in mind. But now that you're here, and I'm looking at beautiful you, I know how marvelous you'd be."

"Beautiful me and all of my forty-seven years!"

"But the story is about an older woman, if you'll forgive the expression," he explained, grinning at her, thinking how beautiful she did look tonight. She wore a pale-green silk dress and emerald earrings; with her reddish-blond hair, green eyes and pink-and-white skin she was an English rose. What a fool Maxim is to have thrown her over. Aside from her lovely looks, she is a very nice woman, and extremely bright. Some men don't know when they're lucky, he thought.

Camilla said, "You're staring at me."

He nodded. "Yes, I am, and I was just thinking that you could easily pass for thirty-six." He leaned across the table and fixed his cool gray eyes on her. "Know what! You might look too young for the part."

She burst out laughing.

"I'm being serious. Honestly I am."

"Shut up and tell me the story," she answered. "A good part might be exactly what I need to cure what ails me."

Later, as she lay between the cool sheets in her bed in the hotel, Camilla thought about the film. David Maines told a story well, and he had intrigued her. Perhaps she ought to let him suggest her to the producer. Yes, it *was* worth considering. And she had meant it when she had said to him that a good part would cure what ailed her.

Camilla Galland loved her work, and her acting career had always been the most important thing to her. Certainly it had given her the most satisfaction above everything else in her life. Her two husbands had never been able to understand this, hence her two divorces. They had felt threatened by her career, her fame, her immense success. Only Charles Mallingham had understood her acting, her deep-seated need to perform on a stage or in front of a camera, and in so doing enlighten and entertain. She had met Charles early in her career, and had been engaged to him when he had suddenly dropped dead of a heart attack at the age of forty-nine. She had been twenty-three. But she had never noticed the age difference between them, had been grief-stricken by his death. A prominent investment banker, who was widowed and childless, Charles had left her the bulk of his fortune and had made her a very rich young woman.

Charles had been the only man she had ever loved, except for Maximilian West. When she first met Maxim in Paris in 1959, she had been very taken with him, and had fallen heavily. But he had never even noticed her, had only had eyes for Anastasia. And so, being pragmatic, she had got on with her life, buried her feelings for Maxim, and eventually married two other men. Her first husband had been Roland Vickers, an English actor; her second, Peter Jarvis, a stage director of small talent. She and Maxim had become friends over the years, and he had helped her from time to time, giving her advice about her investments. But there had never been anything between them, much to her disappointment. Until September of 1980, just ten months ago, when they had run into each other in New York.

Maxim had asked her out to dinner several times, and suddenly, to her enormous surprise and joy, they were involved in an affair. She had been ecstatic. He had been so warm and attentive, seductive and charming, ever the ardent lover, sending her flowers and books, and he had even given her an expensive piece of jewelry. In December he had sent her a diamond brooch from Cartier, just before flying off to London, where he had gone to spend Christmas with Anastasia and their children.

When he returned to New York in January, he had been cool, unresponsive to her, showed no real interest in her anymore. Quite unexpectedly, and with an abruptness that was startling, he had explained that it was all over between them. When she had asked for a reason, he had been evasive, had turned icy cold and uncommunicative. She had seen a toughness in him, a ruthlessness even, that had been dismaying. Nonetheless, recognition of these traits had not changed the way she felt about him. But she had had no alternative but to put up a good front for the world and get on with her life.

The play she was starring in on Broadway had closed in early March, and she had flown to California to attend the Academy Awards. Two months later, proudly carrying her Oscar, she had flown from Los Angeles to Paris, where she had an apartment, which had been her home for a number of years.

Camilla turned over restlessly. Sleep still eluded her. Again her mind focused on the script David was writing, and she thought, Yes, I *am* going to do it, and to hell with Maxim West. At the thought of Maxim her eyes filled with tears, and she began to weep into the pillow, her anguish surfacing. Deep down, within herself, she knew why he had broken off their relationship. He still loved Anastasia. She had known this even when they were romantically involved. He would always love Anastasia and only her.

Impatiently throwing off the bedclothes, she went into the bathroom, where she found a box of tissues. She dried her eyes and blew her nose, splashed cold water on her face.

Loving a man who did not love her was a waste of time. And she had never quite recovered from the indifference he had shown her this past January, upon his return from London. To hell with him, she muttered again under her breath, and she firmly resolved to do the film. She would tell David tomorrow when he came to pick her up to move her into his villa.

Work will help to assuage my sorrow, she told herself as she turned off the bathroom light and went back to bed.

51

*I*T HAD BEEN DIFFICULT TO EXPLAIN TO THE TAXI DRIVER where she wanted to go. It still had no name, this vast white villa on the hill, David's home, filled with his books and paintings and all the other precious trophies he had collected over the years in his worldwide meanderings as a writer.

She paid the driver and pushed open the huge iron gates. The bell tinkled and she nodded to the *gardien*, who came to the door of his gatehouse when he heard the chimes. The old man bowed low, touching his dark-red fez. Camilla smiled back and nodded, and went up the drive, the gravel crunching under her feet as she walked at a brisk pace.

The villa stood on a rise, its pure-white marble columns glinting in the afternoon sunlight, the lawns glistening with water from the many sprays David had installed, the shrubs and trees bright with blooms of vivid color. She had been staying at the villa for three weeks, since moving from the El Minzah, and she was still not accustomed to the beauty of David's house as it was viewed from the main gates and the driveway.

When she reached the steps that led up to the portico and the front door, she turned, and as usual a smile of pleasure crossed her face as she looked down.

Rolling steeply away from the villa were more verdant grassy lawns, bordered by eucalyptus and orange trees, and beyond the stone wall surrounding the property the rooftops of Tangier were just visible. Still farther beyond were the pale sandy beaches of the coastline and the aquamarine Mediterranean.

The villa was silent when she went inside.

She dropped her packages on an ancient pearl-inlaid loveseat in the marble hall, and pushed open the door to the sitting room. The shutters were closed to keep out the bright sun, and she blinked as she focused her eyes in the cool darkness.

Camilla had given this room a name when she had first arrived. She had dubbed it the mint-tea room because of its lovely mixture of greens against the white walls, hung with pale, lime-green silk draperies. Deeper-green rugs lay on the white marble floor; silk pillows in various shades of green were arranged on the white sofas and Louis XV chairs, also upholstered in white heavy cotton. Enormous rubber plants and other tropical species with dark-green leaves grew in brass tubs standing near the many windows. The only splashes of vivid color in this cool room were the modern paintings on the walls, the shelves of books, the masses of flowers in white ceramic urns that had been grown in the little plantation at the back of the house.

She laughed to herself when her eyes fell on the low Moroccan brass table set with an ancient silver teapot and tea glasses in silver filigree holders.

"You called this the mint-tea room and that's what it's going to be from now on," David had said to her several weeks ago, and since then either Fatma or Menoubah set the table every afternoon. It was a new ritual obviously meant to be kept, although she and David did not always observe it.

Closing the door of the sitting room, Camilla walked along the hall in the direction of David's library. She heard the sound of his typewriter as he tapped out new words for his screenplay. He still wrote on an ancient electric machine—no newfangled word processors for this wordsmith.

He was going at full speed, and she wondered whether to disturb him, hesitating before knocking. Suddenly his voice rang out through the heavy brass-inlaid doors just as she raised her hand.

"Camilla, come in, I know it's you. I heard your high heels. Fatma and Menoubah just slap around in their bare feet. Unless of course"—the door was jerked open in her face—"I have some unexpected lady visitor."

"Am I disturbing you?" she asked, staring up at him.

He led her into the library. "No, absolutely not. And I have very sharp ears, Camilla, and I actually miss the sound of your little feet tapping around this great old place. I just sit and wait for you to come back, when I'm not working."

"David, you have been so wonderful to me, and this place is so fabulous . . . I never want to leave."

"You don't have to leave, Camilla. You can stay as long as you wish."

"That's so sweet of you, darling, but I must find my own house."

"I know. . . . Any luck?"

She shook her head. "Janine is still scouring Tangier. As yet I haven't really liked anything I've seen. But then I'm spoiled by this place, it's so heavenly."

"The thing is to take your time, you'll eventually stumble on the perfect villa when you least expect it. Now, how about a drink? It's almost six and I was just about to pour myself some champagne—Pommery and Greno, pink version. I've earned it after my day in the salt mines—"

"More like the gold mines, wouldn't you say?" she cut in.

"*Touché*," he laughed, and walked across to the bar at the far end of the library. "Want a glass?" he asked as he bent down behind the bar and, opening the refrigerator, took out the bottle of pink champagne.

"Why not? It sounds like a grand idea, thank you."

A moment later he came back carrying the two glasses and a pack of the thin black cigarettes he occasionally smoked.

"What sort of secret mission took you into Tangier after lunch?" he asked, and winked wickedly as he sat down. "I know you weren't looking at villas today. Janine told me she was off to Fez with a rich American client."

She laughed. "Don't be such a fool! I went to buy a pair of babouches, so that I can slide around the house silently like Fatma and Menoubah. And some books."

"I hope you bought at least one David Maines. I need the money," he teased.

"No. But I bought a book *for* David Maines, my most generous and loving friend." She rose and left the library before he could respond, and as she hurried through into the hall she hoped he would like her gift. She had spent most of the afternoon searching the shops and the souks for it, wishing to present him with something special to show her appreciation for his many kindnesses to her.

When she returned and gave it to him, he opened the package excitedly like a small boy with his first important gift.

"Camilla, you shouldn't have, but I can't say I'm not thrilled because I am. The only girl who gives me presents is my twenty-year-old daughter, Polly." He pulled off the last piece of wrapping paper and exclaimed in delight, "An old Moroccan Koran! Wherever did you find it? I've looked for one of these for years. Why, darling, it's perfectly beautiful." He looked through the ancient book, turning the pages carefully, fingering the Moroccan-leather binding tooled in gold, appreciating its rarity.

"It *is* old, isn't it?" she asked anxiously. "I did want to find one that was genuine."

"It is indeed, and it's a masterpiece, in my opinion. It's from Fez, the old university city. Thank you, Camilla, thank you so much." He put the Koran down on a table nearby, hugged her, kissed her cheek.

"It comes with much love, David."

He smiled, went and sat down on the sofa again and lighted one of his thin black cigarettes. "Come on, darling, drink your champers before it gets warm."

Taking the chair opposite him, Camilla lifted her glass from the heavy mahogany table inlaid with brass and took a quick sip of the pink champagne. "Mmmm, that's good, it was very hot in the town this afternoon. You were certainly hard at it, pounding away when I came in. How's the screenplay going?"

"Very well, I'm pleased with it, Camilla. I should have the first draft finished in a couple of days, and then I want you to read it. I've spoken to Dick Tomlinson, and he's itching to have you star in it."

"I can't wait to read it, David."

They sat and talked about the script for a short while, and drank another glass of champagne each, and then David said, "I forgot to tell you, I'm expecting guests for dinner."

"Anyone I know?" she asked, looking across at him, lifting a shapely blond brow.

"No, you haven't met them—the Marrons from Casablanca. They're in Tangier for a few days with their son, Michel, and his Moroccan wife, Leyla. They called this morning and I invited them for supper. You'll like them, they're very charming. And, not unnaturally, they're excited about meeting you. They're fans of yours."

Camilla smiled at him, then glanced at her watch. "I suppose they're about to arrive, and here am I looking very grubby and sticky in an old cotton frock."

"They won't be here for about an hour and a half. You have plenty of time to dress. But I'd better go into the kitchen and poke old Fatma in the ribs. She's slower than ever these days." As he spoke he rose, and so did Camilla.

Together they strolled out into the hall. Camilla picked up her bag and the rest of her packages and walked toward the wide, curving staircase.

As she walked past the kitchen she heard Fatma, his cook-housekeeper, chortling merrily at his instructions in Arabic and Spanish.

David had given her the bedroom Camilla considered to be the best in the villa. Large and light, with three French windows opening onto a terrace, it overlooked the gardens and the sea.

At first she had protested, feeling quite certain that she was turning him out of his own room. But he had sworn he had never used it as his, and she had believed him. It was much too feminine for a man. Later he had shown her his own suite, a series of adjoining rooms, rather masculine and furnished somewhat sparsely. They had been designed, like his library downstairs, for writing, and a bachelor's existence.

He had bought the villa and much of the upstairs furniture from a French banker who had quit Tangier. "Got it for a song," David had told her, the first day she was there. "Poor bastard! It held too many tragic memories for him. I almost felt guilty, I got it so cheaply." According to David, the banker had built the villa for his mistress, a young Algerian girl, who had been fatally killed in a motorboat accident in the bay of Tangier. The room Camilla occupied had been hers, and quite often, in the weeks she had been here, Camilla had caught herself wondering about the girl, trying to visualize her face.

The room had a stark, almost virginal quality to it. Vast and high, with white walls and a white marble floor, it was furnished with a large four-poster bed, a huge armoire and a dressing table. All were Spanish in feeling, made of black wood with gilt inlays. The rugs and draperies were also white, but David had given life to this virginal boudoir with some of his colorful paintings, and Menoubah filled huge Moroccan pottery jugs with fresh flowers every day.

Camilla took a bath in the grand mosaic-tiled bathroom adjoining her bedroom, and thought about what she would wear for the dinner this evening. It being July, Tangier was hot, and so she decided on a short pale-gray chiffon dress that was strapless, had a draped bodice, and a full floating skirt. It was gossamer-light, and cool.

After her bath she wrapped a towel around herself, sat at the dressing table and brushed her reddish-blond hair. She swept it up into a chignon on top of her head and anchored it firmly in place with two antique silver combs she had found in one of the souks.

Her weeks in the Tangier sun had given her a light tan, and she needed no makeup other than a touch of brown mascara, silver eye shadow and bright-red lipstick. After spraying herself with Joy, she put on pale-gray lace underwear, pale-gray stockings shot through with silver, and then the dress. She stepped into high-heeled gray silk pumps, wound a long matching scarf around her neck and let the ends fall down her bare back.

Camilla liked the pale-gray image of herself that stared back at her from the mirror. It was soft and gentle, and the gray chiffon was perfect with her tan, far more subtle and becoming than white or pale blue would have been. She realized she did not need much jewelry. "Let's not gild the lily," she muttered out loud. Large mabe pearl earrings and her diamond evening watch were the only pieces she selected from her small traveling jewelry case.

A moment later she hurried out. Glancing at her watch, she noted it was twenty to eight, which meant that, thankfully, she was only a few minutes late. She loathed arriving after everyone else, making an entrance, because as a famous actress she knew everyone—at least, strangers—expected it of her.

She came down the wide staircase and headed for the sitting room, which opened on the long terrace where David usually served cocktails. Walking in, she could see him talking to someone through the French windows, which stood ajar.

As she pushed open the doors and glided out, she exclaimed,

"There you are, David, I do hope I haven't kept—" She broke off and stood gaping at him and his companion.

It was Maximilian West.

Maxim stood there smiling at her. His lean and handsome face was deeply sunburned, and he wore an impeccably cut cream silk suit, a cream Swiss voile shirt and a dark-blue tie. Everything about him seemed to gleam, from the tips of his highly polished brown shoes to his dark and brilliant eyes. He was forty-seven and gorgeous, all six foot one of him. And, as always of late, he had the appearance more of a movie star than of a business tycoon.

Rarely ever at a loss for words, Camilla was now speechless. She stood rooted to the spot, so startled to see him she had not even returned his smile. She began to shake inside and her legs felt unexpectedly weak.

David said. "Have a nice evening, you two. See you later."

Finding her voice at last, Camilla exclaimed, "But, David, where are you going?" and she was furious with herself as she heard the shrillness in her voice.

"I have a date," David replied, winking at her. "Enjoy yourselves." With a nonchalant wave of his hand he was gone, disappearing through the French doors.

"It looks as if we're on our own, Camilla," Maxim said, moving away from the balustrade and walking toward her slowly.

52

_I_'VE BEEN SET UP!" CAMILLA SAID FIERCELY. "YOU AND David set me up. That's not fair. In fact, I resent it."

"No, you don't, you haven't got a resentful bone in your beautiful body," Maxim said, his smile full of warmth as he sat looking at her across the small table on the terrace. "And it's not the way it appears, truly it isn't, Camilla."

"Which way is it, then?" she asked crisply.

He was silent, and then he pushed himself to his feet and offered her his hand. She took it automatically, then flinched inside at his touch, instantly aware that he had the same devastating effect on her as he always had. Clamping down on her feelings for him, she stood up and allowed him to lead her over to the balustrade at the edge of the terrace.

"What do you see out there?" Maxim asked, looking down at her before turning to look toward the grounds.

"Nothing unusual," she replied, puzzled, her eyes scanning the garden. "Lawns, trees, flowers."

"Beyond the garden . . . look toward the sea."

She followed the direction of his gaze, and exclaimed, "Oh! It's your boat, isn't it?"

"Ship," he corrected with a faint smile. "Yacht, to be exact. And yes, it's *Beautiful Dreamer.* I was cruising with a few friends, and Stubby had the bright idea of sailing over to see our old chum David. As a surprise, so to speak. We finally got here late yesterday, and dropped anchor out there."

Maxim waved his hand in the direction of his yacht and continued, "Stubby telephoned David last evening, to announce our arrival. And, in typical Stubby fashion, invited us all over here for lunch today. Only to be told, in no uncertain terms by David, that we couldn't come for lunch. Because you were his house guest and he didn't want you upset."

There was a small pause. Maxim's gaze was very direct as he finished, "Upset by *my* presence, to be precise." A mirthless little laugh escaped him, and he added as an afterthought. "David did call Stubby back to say that I shouldn't take offense."

"Did you?"

"Not really. But it brought me up short, and made me start thinking. I realized I owe you an apology, Camilla."

"Is that why you're here?"

"Sort of."

"What does *that* mean?" Camilla probed, eyeing him, all of her senses alerted for trouble. Swiftly she raised her defenses. This was the most lethally attractive man she had ever known. Furthermore, she had been in love with him for years. He could quite easily be her ruination. She must be on her guard.

Maxim made no response at first to her question, then he

said slowly, his voice soft, contrite, "I am sorry, Camilla, very sorry. I behaved badly toward you, and certainly you didn't deserve to be treated in such a cavalier manner. It was very wrong of me."

When she remained quiet, he asked, "Do you accept my apology?"

"Yes."

Maxim flashed her his lopsided smile. "Then let's kiss and make up."

"Oh no!" she cried. "No kissing." She shrank back, held out her hand. "Let's *shake* and make up."

Amused, he laughed, shook her hand rather formally, then unexpectedly he bent his head and kissed her fingers.

The touch of his mouth on her skin unnerved her. She snatched her hand away, stepped over to the table and reached for the glass of champagne he had poured for her earlier. She tried to conceal her panic and said in a voice pitched unnaturally high for her, "If David was so adamant about your not upsetting me, then how on earth did Stubby talk him into letting you come over here this evening?"

"Stubby had nothing to do with it," he said, moving closer to her. "I phoned David from the yacht early this morning. I told him I wished to see you. I explained that I owed you an apology, that I also wished us to be friends again. And so he suggested I stop by at seven-thirty. For drinks."

"He agreed as easily as that?" she asked incredulously, thinking that David was obviously a pushover.

"Not at all. He was very tough with me. In fact, I had to do quite a lot of talking and persuading. But he finally gave in."

Oh yes, Camilla thought, *you can be very persuasive when you want to be. As I know only too well.* But she said, "I still feel as if I've been well and truly set up by the two of you."

"Please don't feel that way, Camilla. And don't be angry with David. That lovely man is genuinely very fond of you, and he thought he was doing the right thing. He really did mean well, as, indeed, do I."

The glance Camilla now gave him was cool, appraising. "When I asked you a moment ago if you were here to apologize, you said 'sort of.' I'd like to know what you actually mean."

"Look here, Camilla, I didn't come here only to apologize. I wanted to see you again, talk to you, invite you to dinner."

"I'm afraid I can't!" she cried, that sense of panic washing over her once more. "Quite aside from the obvious reasons, I happen to know that dinner has been prepared for me. I'm dining here. *Alone*."

He merely smiled at her.

Maddened, she said in a cold voice, "Anyway, hasn't it occurred to you that I don't want to have dinner with you?"

Ignoring her question, he remarked evenly, "David arranged for the cook to prepare couscous. It's one of my favorite dishes, and it has been for years. I used to eat it at the El Djazier in the Rue de la Huchette in Paris." He smiled at her again. "We're both dining here, actually."

She took a step backward, wanting to put distance between them. Glaring at him, she snapped, "I was right! You did set me up."

It was obvious to Camilla that David had been a willing conspirator. As if the villa and the gardens were not beautiful enough in themselves, David had gone out of his way to make the setting even more fabulous.

He had arranged for them to dine in the garden by candlelight, where they were served by Aly and Menoubah, his butler and housekeeper. As soon as it had grown dark, just before dinner, Aly had turned on the hidden spots, so that the fountains, orange trees and flower beds were illuminated, thrown into prominence in the most spectacular way. The garden became a magical place. Aly had also turned on the sound system, and romantic music, selected by David earlier, played softly in the background while they dined.

The circular table had been set up near a cluster of eucalyptus trees at the edge of the lawn, which swept down to the dark sea, silvered now by moonlight. It was a breathtaking kind of evening, the dark-blue sky clear, cloudless, full of stars, the air warm, heavy with the scent of jasmine.

Aly kept filling her crystal goblet with chilled white wine, and Camilla found herself starting to relax. She discovered that she was not particularly hungry, ate only a few forkfuls of couscous now and again, picked at her green salad.

Against her will and her better judgment, she was falling

under Maxim's spell once more, mesmerized by his charisma and seduced by his charm, his hypnotic voice, his looks and his immense warmth. Having been in love with him for half of her life—since she was twenty-five, in fact—she knew she was extremely vulnerable to him. She found herself laughing at his stories, listening to him eagerly, and enjoying being with him, swept up by the force of his magnetism.

He was so open and honest with her, at one moment during dinner Camilla was on the verge of asking him why he had disappeared from her life so abruptly in January. But she refrained. She was afraid of his answer—in fact, did not want to hear it. For she was not sure she would be able to handle it if he said it was because he was still in love with Anastasia. This thought brought her up short, and she reminded herself that she had vowed earlier not to succumb to his charms. But there was no denying he was at the top of his form this evening. He dazzled her. And so when he kissed her lightly on the cheek after she had made him roar with laughter about something, and then when he lifted her hand from the table and kissed her fingertips, she did not pull away or protest.

But much later, over the tiny cups of strong, sweet coffee, Camilla looked at him carefully in the candlelight, shrewdly assessing him and his motives. He was here for a reason, not just to apologize, talk to her and dine.

After a very long moment, as he returned her gaze unblinkingly, she said, "What do you want?"

"I want you, Camilla."

"For how long?"

"For tonight. For the next two weeks—while I'm in these parts."

"And then?"

"I don't know."

"Well, at least you're honest, Maxim."

"I want to be honest with you, Camilla. Nothing less would do for you. Not now. Well? Give me an answer."

"I want you too, I won't deny it. But . . . I'm afraid."

"Don't be. I promise I won't hurt you again."

"You will hurt me if you make love to me, engage my emotions, then go off and leave me."

He was absolutely silent. Not a muscle moved in his darkly handsome face.

She held herself quite still.

They stared at each other, wanting each other. They recognized this in each other's eyes.

"I won't be your mistress," she said.

"I know that," he answered, his voice as soft as hers. Pushing back his chair, he rose. "Let's go for a walk through the gardens," he said as he helped her up out of the chair.

He took her hand, and she allowed herself to be led by him. She felt as if she had no willpower as far as Maximilian West was concerned. He suddenly stopped walking, and putting a hand on her bare shoulder, he turned her around to face him, stared down into her face and touched it lightly with his fingers.

"You're so lovely, Camilla, and I want you so very, very much. But I won't force myself on you. It's your decision."

"I want you too, Maxim," she whispered.

He leaned into her and kissed her very lightly on the lips, and immediately pulled away. "Shall we go in?"

Camilla could only nod.

Maxim locked the bedroom door, turned around and leaned against it, staring at Camilla, holding himself in check.

She had walked in ahead of him and stood in the center of the room, as motionless as a statue, caught in the corridor of brilliant moonlight streaming in through the open window.

His chest tightened as he continued to look at her. She was a very beautiful woman, a typical English rose because of her fair coloring, serene and ladylike in her demeanor. But underneath that façade of gentility she was earthy, sensual, very sexual. It was these contrasts in her that excited him, started the fire racing through his blood. The first time he had made love to her he had instantly understood that she had a strong sexual drive, therefore the power to excite him over and over again, to bring him to climax repeatedly in one night.

In the three months they had been together last year, she had satisfied him completely every time they had made love, in a way no other woman ever had except for Anastasia, who was lost to him. He pushed aside the thought of his wife. *Ex-wife.* To dwell on her now would be disastrous. If he carried an image of Stassy across the room, he would be rendered impotent. He had not come all this way searching for Camilla, wanting to go to bed with her again, to rekindle their liaison, only to flounder because of thoughts of the past. Frustration was the last thing he needed. He had lived with that for the last six months. And if he was correct in his assessment of her, so had she. Camilla was not a promiscuous woman, and he was certain there had been no other man in her life since him.

"Oh, Maxim . . ." She spoke softly, holding him with her eyes, taking a step forward.

He threw his jacket on a chair, took off his tie, began swiftly to unbutton his shirt as he walked across the room toward her.

When he stood in front of Camilla, he smiled faintly, then slowly unwound the long chiffon scarf wrapped around her neck, let it fall to the floor, took the silver combs out of her hair, so that it cascaded around her face.

Touching the bodice of her strapless dress, he said softly, "Take this off."

Unzipping it, she let it drop to her feet, stepped over it and into his arms, her bare breasts pressed against his bare chest.

Maxim kissed her lightly on the lips as he had a moment ago in the garden, before bending to kiss her breasts. They were small, rounded, taut and high, a young girl's breasts, and he kissed them fleetingly while leading her over to the bed. Easing her down onto it, he leaned over her, removed her shoes, threw them to one side and slipped off her gray lace panties. He unfastened her garters one by one, carefully slid each stocking down her leg, one after the other.

Her eyes did not leave his face.

He said, "I've thought of you constantly, wanted you constantly, for months. I don't want to rush it now."

"Yes," she whispered. Her heart was beating at an excessive rate, and she trembled inside. The heat was rising in her as it never did with any other man. Only with Maxim West. He merely had to glance at her to excite her. The manner in which he was removing her underwear, so delicately, so slowly, drove her crazy, heightened her desire for him. She closed her eyes, curbed the moan of desire rising in her throat, not wishing to break the tension mounting in him, in them both, by making the slightest sound. *I want you now,* she thought. *At once. Immediately. Now. Take me. I love you. I love you. Maxim. Maxim. I've only ever loved you. All my life. I've only ever loved you. Take me. Take me.* The words repeated themselves over and over in her head, like a Bach fugue, endlessly, endlessly repeated themselves.

He had been caressing her body; he stopped, moved away from her. She heard him walking across the tiled floor; she opened her eyes and saw him unzipping his trousers. He stood near the chair, undressing rapidly. She watched him closely, sensually savoring every contour and line of his body: the wide shoulders, slender hips, long legs. Naked, he walked back to the bed, and to her. And her heart missed a beat when she saw how excited he was.

Maxim lay down next to her, took her in his arms, kissed her deeply, his warm mouth enclosing hers. She felt his soft, sweet tongue on hers, and she seemed to draw his breath into her deeply as they clung together.

Camilla lay against the cool sheet, luxuriating in the pleasure of him. She had vowed she would never let him near her again. Now she wondered why she had ever made that vow. This was all that mattered really. Making love with each other like this, his mouth on hers, his hands on her body. His lovely hands. They were sensitive, gentle, fluttering over her, touching her breasts, moving down over her thighs, seeking and loving that most secret part of herself.

She opened her eyes, watching him as he kissed her stomach, her thighs, his lips grazing her gently as they moved on and finally came to rest where they always did. His hands were fluttering once more, joining with his lips to pluck at the kernel of her womanhood, bringing her to climax, and quickly so, as he knew how. But once the trembling started she tried to hold back.

"Don't fight me," he whispered, lifting his head for a moment, looking at her intently. And so she allowed him to do what he wanted with her, let herself go, felt herself flowing out to him. And no longer able to restrain herself, she cried out in her passion, pleasure and excitement, "Maxim! Oh, Maxim!"

He took her swiftly, fiercely, moving into her hard. As he thrust himself forward, her body arched to his and her arms encircled his broad back. He slid his hands under her body, lifting her closer and higher to him . . . higher and higher, and she flung her legs around his waist, welded herself to him. They moved together in perfect unison.

Every one of Maxim's senses was clamoring for her after

months of longing to hold her in his arms like this. Sex with her was pure pleasure. Suddenly he had the need to possess her completely; he must drive her on to that point of physical ecstasy that he was swiftly climbing to himself. He pushed his body against hers, moving faster and faster at an accelerated rate and she took his lead, quickening her speed to rise and fall with him.

Their passion exploded around them suddenly. She cried his name again, but he made no sound at all as he abandoned himself to her and to oblivion.

Later, as they lay side by side on the bed, Maxim raised himself up on one elbow, looked down at her, moved a strand of golden hair away from her face. "Would you have been upset if Stubby and I, and our friends, had landed on you for lunch today?"

"Yes, I would. But I could've handled it. And none of you would have known how I felt. I'm a good actress, you know."

"Not good—*great*." He kissed her nose. "But you haven't been acting for the last hour. This was real."

"It was."

"I wasn't acting either."

"I know."

Maxim hesitated, then said, "You don't have to believe this, but I haven't slept with another woman since you. Not since we broke up in January."

Slightly startled by this admission, she said, "I believe you. What would be the point of lying to me now. But why not?"

"I haven't had time."

"*Bastard!*"

A mischievous glint entered his eyes. "That's only partially the truth. Although I have been swamped with business, I really haven't wanted to sleep with anyone but you." He pushed his face into her hair, murmured against her ear, "You're wonderful, Camilla."

She smiled, and slithered off the bed. Going into the bathroom, she reappeared with a large towel, paused to turn on the ceiling fan and glided back to the bed. She dried his body with the towel, then wiped her own.

"It's so warm in here, we're both covered with perspiration," she said. "You don't mind the fan, do you? I thought it would cool us off."

"It won't cool me off, not when you're around," he replied, giving her a boyish grin.

A secretive, knowing smile slid onto Camilla's face. She crouched next to him, began to flutter her hands over his body as he had done to her earlier. And slowly, joyously, she began to make love to him with her hands and her mouth, until his breathing became shallow, harsh. And when he could no longer stand her ministrations, thought he was going to explode, he quickly moved onto her, braced himself over her body, and took her again.

"Am I too heavy?" Maxim asked.

"No, I like to feel you on top of me."

Nevertheless, after kissing her cheek, he rolled off her body, and fell back against the pillow. "Is there a bottle of water up here, Cam?"

"Yes, I'll get it. I'm thirsty myself." Camilla went to the chest near the window, poured two tall glasses and brought them back to the bed.

He said, after a moment, "I've a confession to make."

"What?"

"It wasn't Stubby's idea to come here to visit David. It was mine. I was in Paris at the end of June. I kept phoning your apartment, before I flew down to Monte Carlo to pick up the yacht. I tried for several days. Finally I got your maid. She told me you'd gone to Tangier, that you were staying at the El Minzah. So I phoned the hotel, only to be told by them that you'd checked out. I pressed them for a forwarding address, and they said you were staying with David Maines."

"Why were you looking for me?"

"Surely you know."

She did not answer him.

He said, "You can't deny there's a strong sexual attraction between us."

"Is that why you came, then?"

"Yes."

"You were awfully sure of me, weren't you?" she remarked, staring at him sharply.

"Not really. But I'm forty-seven years old, and so are you, and we're not children. There's a tremendous sexual bonding between us. In fact, leave us alone together for a few minutes and we inevitably end up in bed."

She continued to stare at him without uttering a word.

"Admit it, Camilla. You know very well how much we excite each other, and satisfy each other in bed."

"Yes," she said at last. *But she was in love with him. That was the difference between them.* Still, she had no intention of telling him how she felt about him. Obviously, he did not love her. He was fond of her, she knew that. But that was all.

"There was another reason I was trying to find you. I wanted to invite you to join us on the cruise." He reached out, slid a finger along her cheekbone, gave her an affectionate smile. "Will you join us for the next couple of weeks?"

"Why?"

"I need you, Cam."

"But for how long will you need me?"

"I just told you, we'll be sailing around for two more weeks."

"I didn't mean that, and you know I didn't, Maxim. I told you earlier, in the garden, I won't become your mistress."

"It's marriage you want, I realize, but I can't promise you that. Let's go slowly, see what happens, how we get on in close proximity for two weeks on the yacht. Will you come?"

"I'll think about it."

He shook his head. "You're maddening," he muttered, bending over her, bringing his mouth to hers. And slowly, expertly, he began to make love to her again.

53

I'M VERY GLAD YOU CAME WITH US ON THE CRUISE, DARling girl," Stubby said to Camilla one morning, as they sat having coffee in the boat-deck lounge. This had become a daily ritual with the two of them, since they both wanted to avoid the glaring morning sun and preferred the cool shade of the lounge.

"So am I," Camilla replied, smiling at him. "The last two weeks have been marvelous for me."

"You've certainly done Maxim good. I've noticed he's much more relaxed when you're around. He's been lonely since the divorce, Camilla. You're very attentive to him, to his needs, you make him feel good, I can tell."

"I love him," she blurted out before she could stop herself, then sat back in the chair, shook her head. "Oh dear, I do have a big mouth, don't I? I didn't mean to tell you that, Stubby."

"Oh, but I knew, I've known for years. You've been in love with the Duke since 1959. Right?"

Camilla was startled by his remarks and asked swiftly, "Has it been so very obvious?"

"Not at all. But you were never interested in *me* in those days, certainly not sexually, when we were . . . er . . . stepping out, shall we say? You were forever asking me questions about him. One day the penny dropped. But your secret's safe with me." Stubby grinned, squeezed her arm. "You're a good kid, Camilla."

"Some kid," she laughed.

"Anyway, I hope you're going to stick around."

"I'm not sure what you mean by that."

"After the cruise. There *is* life after this, you know," he pointed out with a chuckle.

"David wants me to star in the film he's writing—"

"I know," Stubby cut in. "He tells me so every day at lunch. And I'll say this for him, he's very dedicated, even on the cruise. Locked up in his cabin all morning, every morning, hard at it. However, I was actually referring to Maxim . . . what I meant was, I hope you're going to stay with him."

"I have no idea . . . I don't know what's going to happen."

Stubby looked at her carefully. "Stay with him, Camilla. He needs you."

Camilla gave her old friend a hard stare, a thoughtful expression crossing her face. Eventually she said, "I wish I knew what he truly felt about me. Maxim is very closed off, doesn't reveal his feelings."

"He has great affection for you, anyone can see that," Stubby reassured her. "The two of you seem to be very compatible and you obviously enjoy being together. Look here"—Stubby leaned forward, fixed his pale-blue eyes on her—"if two people are still on speaking terms, after close confinement on a yacht for several weeks, then they've got it made, in my opinion."

"I notice you haven't mentioned the word *love*, Stubby."

"Don't quibble, you're not seventeen, and neither is Duke. You're both forty-seven. And, actually, I think you're damned lucky to have what you have together, in this lousy world we live in. The two of you *do* have a lot going for you, which is more than I can say about most couples I know."

"Hasn't Maxim ever said anything about me to you? Mentioned the way he feels?"

"No," Stubby fibbed. After a moment he cleared his throat, and said, in all truthfulness, "Maxim *is* a very private man, he'd never confide anything like that, discuss in detail the intimate side of his life. He's a gentleman, you know."

Camilla nodded, drew closer to Stubby, murmured, "It's just . . . Frankly, Stubby, I don't want to end up being his mistress. As much as I care for him, that role's not for me."

"I understand. Still, I do think you ought to stick around. If not for Maxim's sake, then for another excellent reason."

"What's that?"

"For your own sake, Camilla. He's very good for you too. You're looking wonderful, better than I've seen you look in years, and there isn't an ounce of strain left in you. In fact, you're positively blooming. Ask David. He agrees with me."

"Oh, so you've been talking about me behind my back, have you?" she exclaimed, but there was a hint of jocularity in her voice.

"And very fondly so."

Camilla smiled at him but made no response. She sat quite still, staring through the door toward the deep-blue Mediterranean, admitting that Stubby spoke the truth. Maximilian West *was* good for her. She had never felt so happy in her life. From the moment she had stepped on board *Beautiful Dreamer*, Maxim had treated her affectionately, and with respect, had shown her every consideration. His gallant treatment of her aside, they laughed a lot, talked endlessly about a variety of things, thoroughly enjoyed each other's company. And then there were their nights of passionate lovemaking. His desire for her had not waned—in fact, he did not seem able to get enough of her. She felt the same about him.

She had quickly begun to realize that she had never really known Maximilian West properly. Their friendship over the years had been rather superficial. He had been a married man, not in the least interested in her, and so she had carefully buried her feelings for him. Then again, during the three months they had been involved in New York last year, their time together had been limited. Snatched moments, an evening or two a week, Sundays. The chief reason for the infrequency of their meetings was their conflicting hours. She was starring in a hit Broadway play; he was running a billion-dollar empire. As he was going to bed she was walking off a stage, ready to go out to dine and relax. They had always been out of sync somehow, as far as time was concerned.

But in the two weeks they had been cruising around the Balearic Islands and Sardinia, they had been together constantly, hardly ever out of each other's sight, except when Maxim worked in the morning and in the early evening before dinner. In consequence, she had acquired a better understanding of him. She had always been in love with him; now she genuinely liked him, saw his many qualities as a human being—his kindness, his integrity, his compassion for people. He was a good man. She was aware that he could be tough and hard-nosed about business, perhaps even a bit ruthless. Nonetheless, he was a man of character and honor, and she admired him.

Maybe Stubby is right, Camilla now thought. Maybe I should stay with Maxim. He wants me to, he's said so several times. And what's wrong with being his mistress? *The gossip*, she thought. *I don't want to cope with the gossip, the publicity.* Oh, to hell with all that—who cares what the rest of the world thinks. I can't live my life for the world. I must be true to myself—*I want to be with Maxim* . . .

"Penny for your thoughts," Stubby said.

"You can have them for nothing." Camilla flashed him a lovely smile. "I was thinking that perhaps . . . Well, I might take your advice, and stick around. After all, who cares what the world thinks."

Stubby was momentarily startled by this comment. His brows knitted. "You're too mature to worry about that sort of nonsense, love. Too big. And far, far above it. Besides, Maxim hasn't compromised you in any way on the yacht. You have your stateroom, he has his own cabin—"

"Speaking of that, there's something I've been meaning to ask you," Camilla interrupted. "Maxim moved out of his stateroom when I came on board and gave it to me. Which was lovely of him, very considerate. But I don't understand why he doesn't have a stateroom of his own. I thought there were three on this yacht."

"There are. You have one. Marcia and I have the other. The third is kept permanently locked."

"Why?"

"It belongs to Anastasia. Only she uses it."

Camilla stared at him, perplexed. "I still don't understand."

"When they got divorced, Maxim said she could have anything she wanted. The house in Mayfair, the villa in Beaulieu, the Fifth Avenue apartment, this yacht. Literally anything. *Everything*, if she so desired. But the only thing she asked for was her stateroom on the yacht. To use when she came on board to go cruising with Maxim and the children. She also told him she would prefer it if no one else used it. He respects her wishes. It's locked. Unless she's around, of course."

"Why only the stateroom? Why didn't she ask for the yacht?"

Stubby leaned forward, said in a confiding voice, "Anastasia didn't want *anything* from Maxim, except enough money to live on comfortably. None of the grand homes, nor this yacht. She didn't divorce him because she hated him, you know. She divorced him because she loved him far too much, so she wasn't out to skin him alive. Actually her love was rather obsessive, and possessive. Anastasia built her life around him, made him the be-all and end-all of it, the center of her existence." Stubby pursed his lips, shook his head sadly. "Not healthy. For anyone concerned. She eventually realized this, and she left him, to save herself, in a sense."

"But Maxim must have loved her. Surely she knew that," Camilla ventured.

"She did. However, she couldn't cope with his life, his business, his work schedule. He's not a nine-to-five man, and he never has been. He's driven, ambitious, and brilliant at what he does—"

"Why does he do it? Why does he keep acquiring more and more companies, expanding his business?"

"He's an empire builder by nature, the maker of a dynasty. And he can't help the way he's made, Camilla. He's also brilliant at it, as I just said."

"But surely he has enough money by now. He's a multimillionaire."

Stubby half smiled. "It has nothing to do with money. It has to do with his need to create, the excitement of wheeling and dealing, of meeting immense challenges, plus the satisfaction he derives from what he does. Listen, it's rather like asking why a mountaineer wants to climb Mount Everest."

"Why does he?"

"Because it's there to climb. To conquer. Maxim has to conquer, too."

"But didn't Anastasia understand that?" Camilla asked softly, raising a brow.

"I think she did. But understanding didn't make it any easier to accept. At least not for her. I've always felt she has a very fragile psyche—I think a woman's got to have a streak of toughness in her to cope with Maxim's way of life." He paused, then added, "You could do it. You could cope."

"Are you saying I'm tough?" she exclaimed, throwing him a challenging look.

"I hope to God you are! Yes, you do have a certain toughness in you, Camilla, you're a survivor. Please don't misunderstand me. When I say *toughness* I mean resilience, strength, the will and the capability to bounce back. Don't confuse the word *tough* with the word *hard*. There's a big difference. A woman who has a bit of toughness in her can also be emotional, feminine, sensitive, soft and loving. All the things you are—"

"Thanks for those nice words, Stubby."

He smiled. "On the other hand, a *hard* woman is totally without emotion, or feelings. *Hard-bitten*."

"What you're saying is that Anastasia wasn't resilient enough to cope with the pressures and stresses of Maxim's life, the demands his business makes on his life."

"Exactly. Plus his total dedication to it, his absorption in it. But look, that's all water under the bridge. As you probably know, Anastasia had a nervous breakdown just before the divorce, but she's much better now, making tremendous strides."

"They're friends, he told me. . . . "

"Yes. She still loves him, worships the ground he walks on, actually. But it's an arm's-length friendship. I think that's the only way she can handle it, loving him the way she does. I'm sure she doesn't want to expose herself to his life-style again."

Camilla nodded, remained silent. She was longing to ask Stubby if Maxim was still in love with Anastasia, but she held her tongue. She preferred not to know what his feelings were about his former wife.

David Maines suddenly walked into the boat-deck lounge, exclaiming, "Good morning! Good morning!" and so curtailed any further conversation about Anastasia.

David said, "Phew! It's bloody hot out there this morning. *Blistering*. Mind if I join you for a cup of coffee? Or is this a private confab?"

"Of course it isn't," Camilla replied and immediately rose, went to the sideboard to pour a cup of coffee for David. She placed it on the table next to him, and he said, "Thanks, darling."

"How's the script coming along?" Stubby asked.

David raised his thumbs. "Pretty terrific. I've discovered I like writing on a yacht. There's a splendid isolation about it, no distractions."

At this moment, Maxim appeared in the doorway, holding a sheaf of documents in his hands. He lolled against the doorframe nonchalantly. "Good morning, everybody. I'm just off to do a few hours' work, but before I disappear I wanted you to know I'm considering extending the cruise for another ten days. Who's game?" Although he addressed them all, his brilliant dark eyes were leveled on Camilla as he spoke.

"I am, darling," she said at once with a loving smile.

David said, "Count me in, Skipper."

"What a splendid idea, Duke!" Stubby exclaimed. "Marcia and I would love it."

Maxim beamed at them. "The Lanes and the Turners are disembarking tomorrow, as planned, to fly back to London and the States. So it'll just be the five of us."

54

THE TEN DAYS BECAME TWO WEEKS. *BEAUTIFUL DREAMER* sailed down to Sicily, went on to Malta, and ventured into the Ionian Sea, where she dropped anchor at several Greek islands. Eventually she turned around and cruised back the way she had come, heading in the direction of Tangier.

Now that the other guests had left, it seemed to Camilla that Maxim was even more relaxed and at ease. Furthermore, much to her delight, he was spending a great deal of time with her, did not seem able to get enough of her company. Although he worked every day during the week for a few hours, he was attentive, considerate of her needs, full of warmth. At night, in the privacy of her stateroom, he was as passionate as he had been a month ago when he had first arrived in Tangier looking for her.

One evening after dinner, when the others had straggled off to bed, Maxim lingered longer than usual at the bar on the main deck. Once the crew also retired, and they were finally alone, he said in a low voice, "I want to talk to you about something, Camilla."

"Yes, of course, what is it? You sound serious, and you look troubled, Maxim."

"No, no, I'm not troubled. But I am serious." He held her gaze steadily for the longest time before saying, "Would you consider marrying me?"

Camilla was thunderstruck. This was the last thing she had expected, and she could only sit and gape at him stupidly.

He chuckled. "You do look startled, my pet. *Speechless*, actually. But before you say *yea* or *nay*, let me explain that there would have to be a few ground rules if we married. May I tell you what they are?"

Camilla nodded. She did not care what his ground rules were; she would agree to anything so long as they married. She was so much in love with him she was besotted, had been about to accept him on any terms, to become his mistress, if necessary, rather than lose him.

"If you marry me, I wouldn't want you to give up your career," he said. "It's always been a vital part of your life, Cam, and it's very necessary to me that you continue to act. In films, on the stage. Also, I'd like you to do David's film in January."

"What you're saying is that you'd prefer *me* to be busy, while *you're* running your empire."

"Yes. But it's also better for you. You're a great actress, you're at the height of your talent, your career is flourishing. You're a big name, a very big name. I wouldn't want you to give it up, sacrifice what you've worked for, striven for, all these years—to marry me. I want you to have that success, a sense of fulfillment."

"I *have* to work, Maxim, just as you have to—they'd take me away in a straitjacket if I didn't. Anyway, I wouldn't know what to do with myself if I didn't act."

"I know what you mean. But to continue, Cam, I need plenty of space. In fact, I must have it in order to do my work properly. I don't want you clinging to me, making me the core of your existence. I have to travel a great deal, and I hope you understand this. Of course, you can come with me on the extended trips. I'd love it, love to have you with me. But not on the short, quick trips. They're too hectic, and I'm always locked up in meetings. I don't want distractions. Or to be deflected from what I have to do because I'm worrying about my wife. I've always had great direction, tunnel vision, concentration. I can't change. Business is a huge and vital part of my life."

"I know that."

"Also, there are certain periods when I have to see Anastasia and our children, be with her, Alix and Michael. Birthdays, some holidays. You wouldn't be upset, would you?"

"Of course not. I would think it odd if you didn't see them, under the circumstances. And what *about* Alix and Michael? How are they going to take it, if you marry me? Second wives aren't always popular."

"There'll be no problem. They're both mature. Alix is twenty now, Michael nineteen, remember. They're grown-up."

She nodded. "All right, keep going. What are the rest of your ground rules?"

"There are no more—that's the lot."

Camilla was silent, looked thoughtful.

"What about you? Perhaps you have some ground rules?" A dark brow lifted quizzically.

"No, I don't, Maxim."

"Will you marry me?"

"Of course I'll marry you." She did not say that this was the only thing she had ever really wanted, but she certainly thought it.

His face lit up, and, sitting next to her on the sofa, he put his arms around her. "I'm not cut out to be a bachelor, you know. I'm far too monogamous by nature," he said, touching her cheek lightly. "And I'll always be good to you, Camilla."

"I know you will," she answered, her face radiant.

He bent forward, kissed her deeply and whispered against her hair, "Shall I break open a bottle of champagne to celebrate our coming nuptials? Or shall we do that in bed?"

She did not speak. Extricating herself from his embrace, she rose and held out her hand to him, gave him a small meaningful smile.

Maxim took her hand and together they walked to her stateroom.

He could hardly wait to get her undressed and into bed. His passion for her raged through him, exploded almost as soon as he took possession of her, and for the first time, in all the weeks of their lovemaking, he cried out her name as he climaxed and flowed into her.

Much later that night, after he had made love to her again, slowly and more leisurely, and given her satisfaction, he sat up in bed, propped himself on one elbow and looked down into her face. "Let's not wait, Cam. Let's get married immediately."

"Whenever you want," she said, reaching up, brushing his hair back. Her face was brimming with love for him.

"We'll do it tomorrow," he announced authoritatively with a big smile. "Or the day after. We'll be arriving in Tangier in a few hours. The British consul will marry us. I'll make all the arrangements first thing. Is that all right with you?"

"Everything's always all right with me when I'm with you, Maxim."

It was a golden November day, an Indian summer day.

The sun shone brightly in a perfect sky that was vividly blue, blameless, without a cloud. Camilla paused on the steps of Maxim's Mayfair house, where she now lived with him since their marriage, sniffing the air, breathing deeply, thinking what a glorious day it truly was. An ideal day to go to the country.

As she stepped forward, Maxim's chauffeur, Humphrey, got out of the Jaguar and came around to open the door for her. "Good morning, Mrs. West," he said, with a polite smile as he helped her in.

"Good morning, Humphrey. Isn't it a lovely day? Hardly like winter at all."

"It's beautiful, madam." Humphrey closed the car door, returned to the driver's seat. "Are we going down to East Hendred again, Mrs. West?" he asked, glancing over his shoulder. "Mr. West told me this morning that I'd be driving you to the country today."

"Yes, we are," Camilla said, settling back against the seat. "And we've plenty of time. I have an appointment at the new house with the interior designers, but they're not expecting me before noon."

"Very good, Mrs. West," he said, pulling away from the curb.

Camilla's thoughts drifted aimlessly on the drive to East Hendred, the little hamlet in Oxfordshire, where she had recently bought a lovely old Queen Anne manor house. She and Maxim had found it at the beginning of September, before they had flown off to New York together on one of his business trips. They had both liked it the moment they had seen it, had decided to buy it on the spot. When she had insisted on paying for it, Maxim had protested, and had been highly amused at her insistence about this. But she had won, and after she had bought the house she had given it to him as a wedding present. He had been deeply touched by this gesture, had accepted her gift with grace.

Even though the manor had stood empty for two years, because the previous owner now lived in Barbados, Lacey Court was in relatively good condition. The interior designers she had hired were already hard at work, creating the comfortable, unpretentious country look she and Maxim preferred. It was going to be a wonderful weekend retreat for them both, especially for Maxim. The way he worked, he needed a place to unwind occasionally in peaceful surroundings.

She leaned her head against the seat, momentarily closed her eyes, suddenly thinking of her husband, the man she had loved since she was a girl, whom she had always believed to be beyond her reach. Never in her wildest dreams had she thought she would ever be married to him. Or so incredibly happy with him. He was the most glorious man. Deep down inside, she knew he did not love her in the same way she loved him, but this did not matter to her anymore. Maxim was passionate in bed, caring and affectionate at all times, generous to a fault. Since their marriage in August, he had showered her with beautiful gifts—exquisite jewels, fine paintings, valuable antiques and silver for the new house.

If there were odd moments when she longed to hear him say, "I love you," these had become few and far between. She constantly remembered Stubby's words, when she had mentioned love to him on the yacht. "Don't quibble," he had said. "You're damned lucky to have what you have together. . . ." It was true, they were. Besides, Maxim had started to express his feelings for her lately, murmuring things like "I adore you," or "You're my special lady," and when he did so his voice was loving, his dark eyes full of warmth.

Her thoughts shifted to their wedding day at the British consulate in Tangier. If the others were surprised that Maxim had not asked the captain of his yacht to marry them, she was not. He had built *Beautiful Dreamer* for Anastasia. To marry *her* on it would have been inappropriate in his eyes. He was sensitive in so many different ways. And she knew that Anastasia still owned a large part of Maximilian West, and of his heart. The real reason for the location of the wedding had obviously struck Stubby at one moment, for he had looked at her swiftly and smiled, his eyes conveying his support of her, his understanding. She hadn't minded where they married.

Stubby had also finally tied the knot at long last, his playboy days at an end. The wedding had been in September, after she and Maxim had returned from the States. He had taken the lovely Marcia Bell to be his bride, and the wedding had been at Caxton Hall. Maxim had been best man; she had been matron of honor; afterward Maxim and she had given the wedding breakfast at the Mayfair house.

Teddy and Mark Lewis had been present at Stubby's wedding, and much to her delight they liked her, seemed to be happy that she had married Maxim. Furthermore, so were his children, much to her gratification. Neither Alix nor Michael had apparently been upset to learn of their father's marriage to her—quite to the contrary. And she was starting to develop a lovely relationship with Alix, who was such a beautiful, intelligent young woman.

I'm so lucky, Camilla thought, I'm the luckiest woman in the world. I really do have everything I've ever wanted. Maximilian West. My wonderful career. Even children now, since his appear to have taken to me. As an only child, whose parents were dead, and childless herself, she felt as if she had a proper family at last.

A radiant smile slipped onto her face without her realizing it, and happiness and contentment shone in her expressive green eyes.

Opening her handbag, Camilla took out her small diary, checked her appointments for the rest of the week. She was looking forward to their dinner with David Maines this evening. He had arrived in London yesterday, bringing with him the shooting script of the new film. She had agreed to star in it, and she was anxious now to read the final version.

A little over two hours after Humphrey had driven away from Chesterfield Hill in Mayfair, he was turning into the winding driveway that led up to Lacey Court.

The Queen Anne manor stood in a small dell, surrounded by a copse that grew on a slight rise above it, and it had a lovely timeless quality. This morning its many windows winked in the sunlight, and its ancient gray stones were mellow and gentle against the dark winter landscape, the backdrop of leafless trees.

Humphrey parked opposite the front door, newly painted a shiny pristine white, and instantly the two young interior designers came rushing out onto the broad front steps.

Never one to stand on ceremony, Camilla opened the door,

got out of the Jaguar before Humphrey had a chance to assist her, and hurried forward to meet them.

Alison Dixon and Tony Campbell, the designers she had always used in the past, were full of smiles as they greeted her and escorted her into the house.

"Everything's going marvelously well," Tony told her, stepping back to let her walk around the large entrance hall. "And the fabrics you selected are going to look fabulous. It's easier to tell how they're going to blend in now that the walls are painted in all the rooms. The house is really coming together, Camilla, and has a lovely cohesion to it."

"I can't wait to see everything," Camilla responded, smiling at the talented young team, glancing around the hall, liking the deep-salmon shade they had used for the walls, the botanical prints in dark wood frames, the gilt Georgian mirror, and antique crystal and bronze chandelier.

"You're going to get a lovely surprise when you see the rest of the house," Alison told her. "We've made tremendous strides this past week."

Steering her into the library, Alison continued, "Most of the rooms have been painted, as Tony told you, the wood floors cleaned and refinished—oh, and the beds came from Harrods yesterday. And this room, as you can see, is practically finished. The only things missing are the chesterfield sofa, the books and accessories."

Camilla stood in the center of the library, her eyes sweeping around appraisingly, missing nothing. She kept nodding her head approvingly. The paneled walls of the lovely old room had been cleaned and restored, as had the bookshelves; a Georgian desk and chair, comfortable armchairs, a savonnerie rug, and brass lamps with cream-silk shades were all in place. There was even one of her favorite horse paintings hanging over the fireplace.

"Congratulations!" Camilla exclaimed delightedly, looking from one to the other. "As you know, this room is for Maxim, and I'm so glad you did it first. At least I know he has somewhere to work, even if other parts of the house have to be completed after we've moved in."

They took her on a general tour, and then headed back downstairs to the kitchen. Tony said, "We think we can have the house ready by the middle of December, Camilla, since we're making such good progress." He held open the kitchen door for her, and as she went in he added, "Oh, and by the way, rather than go to one of the pubs in the area for lunch, we brought a picnic with us. We thought it would be much nicer—also we can show you some of the fabrics we selected for the antique wicker furniture, and the tiles for the guest powder room, while we eat."

"What a good idea," Camilla said. "But I'd better pop outside, tell Humphrey to go and find a pub and have a snack. He can come back for me in a couple of hours, since we've more things to go over. Please excuse me."

"Will you have a glass of wine, Camilla?" Alison asked, taking the bottle out of the wicker picnic hamper.

"Why not. Thank you," Camilla said and hurried out.

After sending the chauffeur off for lunch, Camilla paused for a moment outside, glancing around, thinking that she must engage a gardener as soon as possible. Even though it was late November, when nothing could be planted, the garden was somewhat overgrown, a wilderness that needed sprucing up before the spring. I'll put daffodils over there, she thought, have them planted at random under those trees. And crocus and snowdrops. And I'll have lilac bushes put in. Maxim loves lilacs.

It would be wonderful if we could spend the Christmas holidays here, Camilla thought, going back inside. Maxim had told her Alix would be with them, while Michael went to Jamaica with Anastasia. She walked along the corridor to the kitchen, paused when she came to the door of the basement, thinking suddenly of Maxim's main Christmas present. She had decided to have part of the basement turned into a fully equipped wine cellar for him, intending to stock it with the very best wines. Stubby had been helping her to select Maxim's favorites, as well as the champagnes he preferred, which he liked to have as an aperitif rather than hard liquor. Although he was not a big drinker himself, he did insist on serving his guests only the very best vintages. Stubby had already been to one wine auction for her, and they were making excellent progress. The wine racks had been ordered and were due any day.

Deciding to take another look at the basement while Tony and Alison were setting up the picnic lunch in the kitchen, Camilla opened the basement door. She switched on the light and started down the long wooden staircase, which was shallow and very steeply pitched.

She had descended only a few steps when the heel of one of her pumps caught in a crack on the wooden step. Not realizing what had happened, she tried to continue down the steps and was jerked backward as the shoe heel remained stuck in the step. She lost her balance, and as she twisted and then catapulted forward she let out a terrified scream, grabbed wildly for the banister, which ran down the side wall. It was rotten and came away from the bricks in her hand. She screamed again as she went hurtling on down the steep staircase and landed with a heavy thud on the concrete floor at the bottom. She lay absolutely still.

Alison and Tony heard her screams and came racing out of the kitchen. They flew down the corridor, immediately saw the door to the basement open and went to it. Tony stood on the top step looking down, and let out a cry of horror. "Oh my God! Camilla's fallen down the steps!" he exclaimed, going cold all over. He went down the staircase gingerly, his heart in his mouth.

He found her shoe, the tip of the high heel still caught in the crack on the step, and he knew at once how the accident had occurred.

Alison, who was shaking uncontrollably, was chalk-white. She followed her partner down the stairs, so frightened and upset she could barely walk. When she arrived at the bottom of the steep staircase, which she now realized was dangerous, Tony was kneeling next to Camilla.

Her body lay awkwardly, and looked oddly askew on the basement floor. Her beautiful face was white, her eyes closed. Blood seeped out from underneath her golden hair.

"She's badly hurt," Alison whispered, her voice barely audible. She crouched down to Tony, endeavoring to control her shaking limbs.

Tony looked ghastly. "I don't think we ought to move her," he said unsteadily. "We might injure her even more. I'll stay here with Camilla. You go and phone for an ambulance."

Alison nodded, mounted the stairs at a snail's pace, discovering that her legs were as heavy as lead.

Tony watched her disappear through the door at the top of the stairs, then turned back to Camilla. Although he had not said so to Alison, he was quite sure Camilla had broken her neck when she fell, and that she was no longer alive.

Maxim could not accept that Camilla was dead.

It was only after her funeral had taken place that it sank in. The finality of her death struck him a hard blow. He could not believe that the lovely, vibrant, gifted and loving woman he had so recently married was gone from him forever. He was devastated.

It was his daughter, Alix, who helped him the most, although Stubby, Teddy and David Maines also tried to give him solace in his grief.

The day after the memorial service had been held for Camilla, Maxim and Alix were sitting together in his Mayfair house. Alix put her hand on his arm, and said gently, "I liked Camilla a lot, Daddy, and we became good friends. She told me she thought of me as the daughter she'd never had, asked me if I minded. I told her I didn't, I was flattered actually."

Maxim looked at her swiftly but made no comment.

Alix returned his glance, thinking how terrible he looked. Her father was gray under his permanent tan, and his dark eyes, usually so brilliant, were dulled by sorrow. Alix took a deep breath, went on, "After Mummy, Camilla really was the nicest woman I've ever known. I'm so sorry she had that hideous accident, and I want you to know I'm here for you whenever you need me."

Maxim was still unable to speak. But he took hold of his daughter's hand, held it tightly. At last he said, "Camilla was very special. . . ."

"Yes. And she loved you so much, Daddy."

"And I loved her. Not in the same way I love your mother . . . it's just not possible to love two people like that in one lifetime. But I did love Camilla, in a different kind of way, and she was important to me, gave me a lot of happiness these last few months. She helped to make the loneliness go away—" His voice broke. He was unable to continue.

After a few minutes Maxim regained his composure, and said softly, "I never told her I loved her, Alix. Not once. I'll never forgive myself for that." Tears came into his eyes, and he quickly tried to brush them away with his fingertips.

Alix put her arm around his shoulders, rested her head

against his arm. "I'm sure Camilla *knew* you loved her, Daddy."

"It was wrong of me, I should have spoken," he muttered, his voice a harsh rasp.

"A woman always *knows* whether a man loves her or not. Honestly she does," Alix soothed, her heart aching for him, going out to him in his pain. "She feels it in her bones. And anyway Camilla was so happy with you."

He turned to his daughter, searched her face. "Do you really think she was, Alix?"

"Yes. *You made her very, very happy.* She told me that only a few days before the accident."

Maxim leaned back against the sofa and closed his eyes. His daughter's words gave him some comfort—but not enough.

Not long after Camilla's death, Maxim disappeared from any sort of public life. He buried himself in his work more than ever before, curtailed his social life completely, saw only his colleagues, business associates and his immediate family. There had been a great deal of publicity about Camilla's death, their marriage, her life, and his. It all sickened him. He hired a battery of aides to keep the press at bay and his name out of the gossip columns.

Maximilian West retreated and pulled the drawbridge up behind him.

PART SIX

Adriana

NEW YORK

1987

Every wise woman buildeth her house:
but the foolish plucketh it down with her hands.

—The Proverbs

55

$$\equiv\equiv\equiv$$

*A*DRIANA MACKLIN WEST STOOD IN THE CENTER OF THE drawing room of the Wests' Fifth Avenue apartment, surveying it with jaundiced eyes.

She did not like it. She never had, not since the first moment she had set foot in it eighteen months ago. The proportions of the room were superb, and it was airy, spacious and light-filled, with extraordinary panoramic views of Central Park. Unfortunately, it had been decorated by Maxim's first wife, and she found the furnishings abysmal—old-fashioned, outdated, washed out, and totally lacking in style. She had been itching to redecorate since her marriage to Maxim, but whenever she broached the subject he waved his hand dismissively, told her he liked it exactly the way it was. These days he cut her off every time she mentioned the word "decorating," would not even listen to her reasons for wanting to make the changes.

She had even offered to pay for everything herself, but he had told her money was of no consequence, that this was hardly the issue.

Adriana's dark-brown eyes swept around the room again, carefully assessing each item as she had done so often of late. The problem with the room was that it was far too austere, almost cold in its overall feeling, with an overabundance of pale colors, pale fabrics, pale woods, and delicate paintings. What it needed were vibrant colors, rich fabrics, expensive wall-to-wall carpeting, handsome Chinese porcelain lamps, exciting new paintings and eye-catching objects of art. Those things would give it the necessary pizzazz, the feeling of glamour she wanted to create, the chic New York look, which had always been a feature of her other apartments in the past. It was a look she adored, for it proclaimed to the world that the owner had money, power, success.

Dropping her eyes to the yellow pad she was holding, Adriana began to scribble down her ideas for the renowned international interior designer she had hired that afternoon. He had met with her in the executive offices of the cosmetics company she owned, Empress Eugenia Beauty, of which she was president and chief executive officer.

She had liked Valentine Lubbock the moment he had walked in, and the feeling had been mutual. They had understood each other within the first ten minutes of meeting. She knew that Valentine had superb taste, since she was well acquainted with his work, and she had absolutely no doubts that he was going to produce the expensive and glamorous ambience she deemed appropriate for her station in life as Mrs. Maximilian West.

Valentine did not come cheap, and there was no question that the apartment was going to cost a bundle of money, between four and five million dollars, to redesign, revamp and redecorate. But she could afford it, since she was a millionairess in her own right. If money was of no consequence to Maxim, then certainly it was not to her either. Her second husband, Arthur Macklin, had left her a fortune when he died four years ago, as well as the cosmetics company, which was one of the largest in the United States.

She had told Valentine Lubbock that she wanted him to redesign every room, not only this one where she now stood. The library, the dining room, Maxim's study, her den, and all of the bedrooms were to undergo a complete overhaul. Valentine was meeting her here tomorrow with his design team, and they were going to spend the entire day going over every inch of this . . . this . . . mausoleum.

She was well aware that Maxim was going to object when she informed him of her decision tonight. But she would explain her reasons, talk him into it somehow. She had a knack of twisting him around her little finger, getting her way with him, especially when they had been in bed. He seemed more open, receptive and vulnerable to her then, certainly easier to handle. She had come to understand he was a difficult man, not easy to know or live with, and secretive.

Adriana sighed. The problem was they had not been to bed lately. His sexual interest in her had waned of late, and she did not understand why. When they had first met he had been like a young stud, going at her all the time, unable to get enough of her, and for the first six months of their marriage he had continued to be insatiable. But he had not touched her for months and months now. Of course, he *had* been away a great deal, traveling on business; she herself had had to make several trips to California, Texas and Rome, so they had been separated quite frequently. However, he had now been in Manhattan for the whole month of March, and he had still not made love to her since his return from London. When she had tactfully hinted that it was time they went to bed, he had brushed her off politely with a variety of excuses: he was preoccupied with his latest deal, a major acquisition, exhausted, or not in the mood. And he always retreated to his own bedroom these days, or rather, nights, and never came to hers anymore. She had not liked the idea of separate bedrooms, had balked at it from the beginning, but he had insisted when they had arrived in New York after their marriage in France.

"My hours are so erratic," he had said. "I get up at the crack of dawn to deal with my offices in London and Paris. It's better this way. I don't want to disturb your sleep." He had kissed her, flashed her his dazzling smile that always devastated her and murmured, "There'll be plenty of nights when I sleep in your bed, Adriana, don't make any mistake about that. But this is the way I've always lived. I need my own room, please don't worry about it."

Well, she did worry, and she was not sure she believed him when he implied he had his own bedroom with his other wives. And he certainly had been coming to hers less and less. If she didn't know him so well, she might start suspecting he had a mistress. But that was not his style, and he was such a workaholic he surely did not have time for another woman.

A painting that was slightly askew on the wall caught her attention, and she walked across the Aubusson rug intending to straighten it, but paused when she came to the Louis XV console, on top of which was a silver-framed photograph of herself and Maxim on their wedding day in September of 1985. They had been married in the town hall of the Fourth Arrondissement in Paris because he had been detained there on business. She had worn a pale-blue outfit by Givenchy and afterward Maxim had given a dinner for ten at Lasserre. She picked up the photograph, thinking how well he looked at fifty-one, the age he had been when they married. So lean and hand-some and tanned.

When her investment bankers had tried to buy Marianna Montevecchio from him in 1984 and had failed, she had dropped the idea of expanding Empress Eugenia for the moment. Instead she had gone after Maximilian West, finding him a fascinating and exciting man, not to mention an eligible bachelor. In the summer of 1985 she had managed to maneuver an introduction to him in Monte Carlo, through a friend who knew him. To her immense delight and gratification he had fallen for her at once, obviously stimulated by her keen business mind as well as her beautiful face and perfect body. They had had a whirlwind courtship of six weeks, and to the stunned surprise of his family and friends they had married at the end of that summer. She was aware his son and daughter did not particularly approve of her or like her, and she was not overly enthusiastic about them either, considered them to be stuck-up little prigs. As for that ex-wife of his, Anastasia, she was a real pain in the rear end. Always wanting to talk to him about something, or needing to see him about something. And off he trotted, like an obedient pet dog. She had tried to put a stop to those excursions, only to incur his terrible wrath, and he had told her in no uncertain terms never to mention the name Anastasia again. That bitch had some sort of hold on him, although she had no clue what it was. The children most likely. She often wondered what a man like Maximilian West had ever seen in that faded, wimpish, mealy-mouthed blonde. His second wife, the actress who had fallen down the basement steps and broken her neck, had not been much better-looking either.

Adriana placed the photo on the console, stepped over to the small painting by Manet and straightened it, then glanced at her watch. It was almost six o'clock. Maxim had told her that he would be home by seven, and wanted to eat in the apartment. It was Thursday, and both the cook and the butler were off. Usually Maxim took her to Le Cirque, La Grenouille, La Caravelle or the Four Seasons, or some other smart New York restaurant. But before he left for the office this morning he had explained that he had a mountain of work to get through by tomorrow. And so she had had the cook prepare a cold supper of salad, smoked salmon, cold meats and chicken, cheeses and fresh fruit—the things he enjoyed the most.

Hurrying out of the drawing room, Adriana went down the corridor to the kitchen, opened the refrigerator door, checked that there were several bottles of Dom Pérignon on ice, plenty of caviar, then raced back along the corridor to her bedroom.

She took off her dark business suit, hung it in the wardrobe, stripped off her expensive underwear and went into the bathroom. After flinging handfuls of her own brand of bath beads into the tub, she turned on the faucets, stepped over to the mirror and pinned up her hair, wondering what to wear tonight. Something sexy. She must make herself look tempting and irresistible for her husband, get her own way with him tonight . . . in every way.

Her mind stayed focused on Maxim for a few minutes as she lay luxuriating in the hot perfumed tub. She considered her marriage to him to be the coup of the century. And it was. She was the wife of one of the richest men in the world, a billionaire who happened to be in the prime of life, and gorgeous as well as brilliant. Not bad for a rather ordinary middle-class girl from Westchester, who had a typical middle-class upbringing, a boring first marriage to a childhood sweetheart, a second slightly less boring marriage to a rich, older man.

Her thoughts veered to Arthur Macklin. She had been married to him for ten years before he died in 1983 of complications following a stroke. He had been seventy, she thirty-one. She had been extremely fond of Arthur. He had been her stepping-stone into a whole new world.

After her divorce from her first husband, Larry Tucker, she had moved to Manhattan, found a small apartment and become a model.

Her grasp on success had been swift. After being photographed by Scavullo and becoming a cover girl with her face on every magazine from *Vogue* to *Mademoiselle,* Arthur Macklin had noticed her, had instructed the advertising agency he used to hire her to be the Empress Eugenia Girl. Six months later her face had suddenly been on billboards, on television, in magazines and newspapers, and displayed on giant posters in department stores. Her arresting, exotic movie-star looks had been the exact image Arthur Macklin had been seeking to promote his beauty products. Those looks also captivated the owner of the company. The Empress Eugenia Girl became *his* girl. He pursued her, paid court to her most attentively, lavished her with gifts, from jewelry to furs, divorced his wife of thirty years and married her before she had had time to catch her breath, or shake the Westchester dust off her feet.

She had continued to be the Empress Eugenia Girl for a couple of years, and became the spokesperson for the company. Arthur, a shrewd self-made man, rapidly discovered that his great beauty also had brains. Since he had no children, he brought her into the business, personally trained her to be his successor, and bequeathed the company to her in his will. When he was felled by a stroke in the spring of 1983, she had looked after him tenderly and diligently, and had run the company as he would have himself. But after his death she had charted a new course, steered Empress Eugenia into the big time. After buying up several smaller cosmetics companies and merging them with hers, she had repackaged the products, had perfumiers in France invent several new scents for her, and hired chemists to create a whole line of herbal and natural products. She had called this new line Body Beautiful, had opened Body Beautiful boutiques all over the country. In the process her company had outstripped many of its competitors, including Marianna Montevecchio, a division of the Allandale Group, which Maxim owned. Once she had wanted to acquire that company, to merge it with Empress Eugenia, but she had no desire for it any longer. The odd thing was, Maxim had lately started to accuse her of being competitive with him, and at first she had laughed, believing him to be teasing her. But she had begun to realize that he was serious. She was competitive by nature, she couldn't help herself, and of course she competed with the Montevecchio line just as she did with Lauder and Arden and Revlon. It was nothing personal. He apparently thought otherwise. Six months ago they had each gone after the same small house that manufactured a variety of products for the care of hands. It was a sort of friendly rivalry on her part, and she had thought it to be a wonderful joke. He had not. The head of his acquisition team in New York, Peter Heilbron, had been furious.

She sat up with a little start in the tub. Was Maxim holding a grudge? Surely not. She laughed out loud. Surely he wasn't depriving her of sex in the manner of a disgruntled wife who seethed over some imagined insult. No, that couldn't be. He was far too big a man for such silly games. He was not sleeping with her at the moment because of his preoccupation with his current deal. Passionate and highly sexed though he was, he could be remarkably disciplined when he so wished. And he could abstain for months, indeed, *years*. He had told her, in one of those rare moments when he had chosen to confide in her, that he had been celibate for two years after his second wife's death. It not only had startled her but had illustrated to her the extraordinary willpower of the man. *My man*, she added under her breath, and climbed out of the bath.

Walking over to the floor-to-ceiling mirror that she had installed on one of the bathroom walls, she stood regarding herself for a long moment, turning from side to side, checking out her figure. It was still perfect, without an extra ounce of flesh, yet she was not a walking skeleton like some of the New York women she knew. Most of them made her shudder, especially those who put little or no food into their mouths, starved themselves into wraiths. She had a decent covering of flesh on her bones, yet without being fat. Because she was quite tall, just over five feet eight inches in her stocking feet, she did not have to panic if she put on an additional half pound now and then. She turned slowly once more, glad that her exercise trainer came twice a week to put her through her paces. She was in good shape. Her breasts were a little heavy, in her opinion, but well shaped, and voluptuous enough to excite Maxim. She had realized when she lost weight last year that he had been turned off by her boniness.

Reaching for the Empress Eugenia lilac-perfumed body lotion, she smoothed it all over her body, sprayed herself with lilac perfume, one of Maxim's favorite scents, and brushed her thick dark-brown hair. After slipping on a silk robe, she walked into her bedroom.

Seated at the dressing table, she stared at herself in the mirror, wondering what kind of makeup would appeal to him tonight. Should she create a soft girlish look with a pretty pink foundation, blushes, powders and light pastel-colored eye makeup, or turn herself into a more dramatic-looking woman?

Leaning forward, she examined herself closely. She had a wide, full face, with a broad forehead, slightly slanting eyes, shapely dark brows and a rounded chin with a dimple. I'll be myself, she thought, reaching for the pale almond foundation lotion, spreading it on across her high cheekbones. That's who he fell for. *Adriana Macklin.* Anyway, I'm at my most alluring when I'm myself. All thirty-five years of me.

56

*M*AXIM BRACED HIMSELF BEFORE PUTTING THE KEY IN the lock of his Fifth Avenue apartment and opening the door. He was intensely preoccupied with business and not in the mood to cope with Adriana tonight. But cope he must.

Apparently Adriana had heard him come in, and was rushing out of the library to greet him before he even had a chance to remove his trench coat.

"There you are, angel!" she exclaimed, gliding forward, her exquisite purple-and-gold caftan floating around her like a cloud.

"Hello, Adriana," he said mildly, putting his briefcase on the small Louis XV bench in the foyer, giving her a half-smile.

She locked her arms around his neck and planted a kiss on his mouth. "Mmmm. *Yummy.*"

He winced, shrugged out of his coat and hung it in the hall closet, then retrieved his briefcase.

"I have champagne on ice, a cold supper waiting," Adriana murmured in a silky voice, taking his arm, strolling along the spacious hall with him. "I thought I'd open the champagne now, so that we can have a glass before dinner. Would you like that, honey?"

"Not now, Adriana. I'm going to take a shower, change into something more comfortable, and then perhaps I'll have a drink." As he spoke he walked toward his bedroom. "I'll see you shortly," he added quietly.

"I'll be in the library, angel." She watched him disappear

into his room, frowning to herself. He closed the door behind him, shutting her out rather pointedly, and she stood for a moment staring at it, trying to assess his current mood. Thank God, he seemed less bad-tempered and irritable, which was the way he had been for the past few weeks, since his return from Europe. If he was not in a good mood, he certainly wasn't in a *bad* one. *Neutral*, she thought. *He's in a neutral frame of mind.* She smiled to herself, confident that she would be able to handle him very well this evening. A little tender loving care, soothing words, champagne and caviar, soft music, a few gentle kisses. She would soon win him over about the redecoration of the apartment, she had no doubt about that. Later, once she had him in a mellower mood, she had every intention of taking him to bed.

Maxim undressed, went into his bathroom, took a steaming hot shower, stretching and flexing his arms above his head, twisting his shoulders from side to side, moving his neck in circles, attempting to ease some of the tension. It had been building in him throughout the long day at his office. He thought of the last conversation he had had with Graeme Longdon just before leaving tonight. She agreed they should drop the current deal they were working on, although Peter Heilbron had been against making any drastic moves for the time being. "Let's not be rash," Peter had said, walking Maxim to the elevator a short while ago. He had told Peter he would sleep on it. What he needed now, after his shower, was total relaxation. He wasn't sure he would get this with Adriana, who was irritating him more than ever these days. But he must let go of this deal mentally, clear his head for several hours. He felt like a few drinks, a bit of mindless television and six hours of deep sleep. It was imperative that he be fresh tomorrow morning when he made a final decision about his latest business proposition. He was in the middle of a hostile takeover bid for a major American corporation, Palmyra-Kettelson, and suddenly he was not sure that he wished to continue.

Maxim reached for the soap—immediately the perfume of lilacs permeated the shower stall. Adriana really is too much, he thought. He laughed hollowly, acknowledging that she was extremely heavy-handed at times, and in a variety of different, not to mention startling, ways. And yet she was one of the most striking women he had ever seen; he was unable to deny her dark exotic beauty.

The first moment he had set eyes on her in Monte Carlo he had been captivated, instantly swept off his feet. Her incredible face, so full of sensuality, her perfect body and long shapely legs, and the potent sexuality that seemed to literally exude from her had excited him enormously. That summer, a year and a half ago, he had been ripe, an easy target. For the first time since Camilla's death he had been ready to get involved, had truly wanted to bed down with a woman, become completely immersed in her. And this was exactly what he had done with Adriana. On one occasion, during their courtship of six weeks, they had stayed locked up in a suite at the Carlton Hotel in Cannes for three days and nights, unable to tear themselves away from each other sexually.

Adriana had been a departure for him, he had to admit, so very different from the other women he had known and married. He had always fallen for refined, gentle-looking blondes; she was a dark-haired, sloe-eyed siren with truly exotic overtones. And she was different in other ways, too; she had had an earthy, almost raunchy, sense of humor, which at first he had found entertaining, but now abhorred, and he had quickly discovered a number of equally dismaying traits. She was opinionated, stubborn to the point of rigidity, abrasive and brash. Furthermore, that keen sense of business, her understanding of his world of finance, no longer fascinated him as it had initially. And underneath all that exotic beauty and glamour she was curiously masculine.

Masculine, he repeated under his breath. What an odd word for him to use in relation to Adriana, but true, nonetheless, he realized with a jolt. Was that the reason he could no longer get an erection with her? Did she turn him off *because* of that streak of masculinity? His raging lust for her had been swiftly satisfied. Six months after their nuptials in Paris their marriage was over, at least as far as he was concerned. Taking her for his wife had been terribly flawed judgment on his part. He ought to have known that the burning rage to bed her, his immense lust fueled by hers for him, would burn out with amazing swiftness. It certainly had.

His impotence with Adriana had come as something of a shock, and it had worried him at first. He had even wondered if he was losing his touch, had considered going to see a doctor. But he had strayed one night with an old acquaintance, had discovered to his profound relief that his touch was as sure as it ever had been. When he was with a blonde, he had commented to himself. The fault lay not with him but with Adriana apparently.

Now he no longer felt fragile about his ego. All of his mechanisms were in working order. He smiled to himself. A man never got an erection without having his mind and psyche at the back of that erection, as well as his body. Most men were much more delicate psychically than most women, that's why men and women were so different. There had to be at least a little desire in a man in order for him to get an erection, have a sexual encounter. But a woman could make love without desire. All she had to do was lie down and wait for the man to perform. If he couldn't, she blamed him, never herself. Well, rarely herself.

Because he had become impotent with Adriana, he avoided any kind of sexual contact with her these days, wishing to sidestep embarrassment. This was difficult, in that she was hot-blooded and forever on his trail, but fortunately he somehow managed to outmaneuver her. Most of the time.

A year ago he had thought of announcing his intention of getting a divorce, and then changed his mind. He had still not done so. He traveled a great deal, and was away far more than he was in New York, and it suited him to remain married to her for the moment, if only in name. Having a wife was a safeguard, and certainly marvelous protection against other predatory females. Also, he was too involved and immersed in his business for emotional scenes or upheavals.

He would bide his time, and deal with Adriana later.

After dressing in dark-gray flannel slacks, a black turtleneck sweater and black cashmere sports jacket, Maxim left his bedroom, crossed the entrance foyer and walked into the library.

Adriana was nowhere in sight.

Soft music played on the tape deck. A bottle of Dom Pérignon stood open in the silver ice bucket on the small chest. The low coffee table in front of the fire burning in the hearth had been set for supper. No doubt Adriana was in the kitchen, preparing a tray of caviar, lemon wedges and toast, which she now served on the cook's night off with boring regularity.

Stepping up to the chest, he lifted the bottle, poured himself a glass of champagne, and took a long swallow, savoring it. He blinked in the dim light, and realizing the room was far too dark, he walked over to the desk near the window and turned up the lamp. The yellow pad caught his attention at once, and he stood staring down at it, reading Adriana's large scrawl. The name *Valentine Lubbock* leaped out, hitting him between the eyes. Lubbock was the most expensive interior designer in the world. Bending his head, Maxim peered at the pad and continued to read the long list she had made.

At this moment Adriana was returning from the kitchen with the tray of caviar. She stopped dead in her tracks in the doorway, cursed herself silently for being so stupid, for carelessly leaving the pad on the desk. Dismay swamped her; it rapidly turned to alarm when he lifted his head and glared at her. His expression was one of such intense dislike it frightened her.

Maxim's brilliant black eyes blazed in his face, which was livid. He waved the pad at her, demanded angrily, "What's all this? Planning to redecorate, are you?" He threw her a scathing look.

"No, no, of course I'm not. It's just that—"

"Just *what?*" he thundered, and not giving her a chance to respond, he rushed on furiously. "Under no circumstances are you going to make any changes in this apartment! It is perfectly beautiful, and in superb taste, and it suits *me* very well! Not one single item is going to be removed or changed, do you hear me!"

"You don't have to shout. I only wanted to redecorate your *study*. As a birthday present for you," she said, improvising quickly, sidling into the room, placing the tray on the coffee table. She moved closer to the desk, gave him a wide, flashing smile and added, "The study is starting to look a bit shabby, Maxim, you must admit that."

"So what! I don't give a damn. As for redecorating it for my birthday, that's a load of crap! On this"—he waved the pad in her face again—"you have listed every room. I'm not stupid, you know. My mother-in-law is a decorator—"

"*Ex-mother-in-law!*" she exploded, giving him an icy stare.

He ignored her comment, and continued in a frigid tone,

"And through her I know Lubbock, who is also based in Paris. He wouldn't touch *one room* with a barge pole. He only decorates entire apartments!" He flung the pad down on the desk disdainfully. "You don't learn, do you. I told you, I'm not going to have you turning this apartment into an expensive, overdecorated, glitzy imitation of some garish Miami hotel, with the help of the overrated, overpriced and undertalented Mr. Lubbock! Trust you to pick a flashy, tasteless incompetent like him."

"*He is brilliant!* Anyway, who the hell do you think you are? Suddenly you're the great expert on decorating!" she cried shrilly, losing her temper. "Some expert! I've only got to look around this cold, colorless, outdated dump, this mausoleum, to understand you know nothing about decorating."

He did not deign to respond but merely glared at her.

Shaking with rage, frustrated with him on many levels, she hissed, "It's far too French. It has no style."

He blinked, did a double take, threw back his head and guffawed. "The French invented style, you nitwit!"

"I fully intend to make some changes in this apartment whatever you say," Adriana exclaimed, drawing herself up to her full height, hating him suddenly for his superiority and breeding.

He walked over to her and peered into her face, his eyes narrowing, said in the iciest voice, pitched very low, "If you have this *compulsion* to decorate an apartment, with the help of the overrated Mr. Lubbock, I suggest you find an apartment of your own. *Tomorrow.* You are not going to touch *my* apartment. Never. If and when it needs redoing, my mother-in-law will fly over from Paris, and she and Anastasia will take it in hand."

"You bastard! Always flinging that ex-wife of yours in my face," she screeched, all the color draining from her face. "I'm not going to stand for it."

"And what do you intend to do about it?" He gulped down his champagne, put the glass on the end table and walked out of the library.

She ran after him, followed him down the hall, watched him as he opened the closet, took out his trench coat, threw it over his arm.

"Where are you going?" she cried, her eyes widening.

"Out."

"Where?"

"For a walk. I need some air."

"A walk! I don't believe you. I know you, Maxim, I know what a sexy, physical guy you are. You never sleep with me these days, so you must be sleeping with another woman. It's obvious you have somebody stashed away. Some blond hustler."

"This town is full of hustlers, Adriana. Blondes, brunettes and redheads. They come in all colors, sizes and shapes." He walked out, slamming the door behind him.

His temper cooled within minutes of hitting the street. He walked down Fifth Avenue at a moderate pace, more annoyed with himself than with her, for flaring up in the way he had. Anger was such a waste of valuable energy. He needed his strength for more important things at this moment. A wry smile flickered on his mouth as he walked. *Time*, he mused, a commodity I cannot afford to squander at present. I didn't spend enough time with Adriana to get to know her properly. *Marry in haste, repent at leisure*, he added under his breath, recalling Teddy's words after his wedding. Deep within himself he knew that she had not approved of Adriana. But his dearest Teddy loved and respected him far too much to interfere in his life, tell him what to do. I need my brains tested, he thought dismally. I should never have married Adriana Smith Tucker Macklin, and I must extricate myself as soon as I've solved my other problems. That's the bottom line.

His mind, always sharp, finely honed, zeroed in on his hostile takeover bid for Palmyra-Kettelson, a gargantuan beauty-products company and a major American corporation, international in scope. He had been buying its stock for some time, now owned 12 percent of the company and had recently informed the chief executive officer he was prepared to purchase as many more shares as he needed to give him control of the company. The offer had been rejected. The executives had gone into a tailspin. A battle was under way. But he did not want to do battle, despite Peter Heilbron's urging. The head of his acquisition team in New York was encouraging him to continue, predicted he would win, be the *big* winner ultimately.

Turning up the collar of his trench coat and pushing his

hands into his pockets, Maxim walked on, lost in concentration, which was one of his most formidable assets and part of his genius.

As he crossed Seventy-second Street and continued on down Fifth, he finally came to his decision. *He would pass.* Tomorrow morning he would phone the president of Palmyra and call off his hostile bid for the company, offer to sell his stock in the company back to them. He had about $500 million invested. He would probably come out with a huge profit, maybe $90 million, and he would probably be accused of greenmail. *So what.* He had to unload. He did not want the company. Peter would be disappointed, but he could not help that. Graeme would be relieved. She was with him on this, understood his reluctance to invest any further in America at this moment.

He had a peculiar uneasiness about the economy here. Leveraged buyouts and junk bonds were beginning to sicken him; junk bonds were going to turn out to be just that: junk paper, worthless in the long run. West International was secure, the Allandale Group was secure, and the two huge conglomerates were profitable, completely in the black. He did not want to extend himself further.

Maxim's mind switched to his personal investments in the American stock market. He had hundreds of millions of dollars tied up in stock in other companies. He would start unloading that tomorrow. Slowly, carefully. He did not want to start a panic in the Street. He would sell his shares over a period of months, and by August or September he would be liquid. He had a strong suspicion that the economy in the States might possibly start lurching in the fall or winter of this year. He did not know how or why he suspected this, because he never knew where his premonitions about business came from. Gut instinct perhaps. And his gut instinct told him to sell. He did not want to be caught if the stock market *should* fail, God forbid.

Unexpectedly, he felt lighter, the heaviness in his chest dissipating. It came as no surprise. He generally experienced this rush of relief when he had made final decisions about business problems that had troubled him for weeks.

He lifted his head and saw to his surprise that he was at Fifty-seventh Street and Fifth. He went to the nearest telephone, dropped a quarter in the box, dialed quickly.

"Hello?"

"It's me, darling."

"Where are you, Maxim?"

"On the corner of Fifty-seventh and Fifth. I'm coming over."

"I can't wait. I'll give you a couple of minutes."

"About twenty. I want to walk to Sutton Place. See you, babe."

Blair Martin dropped the receiver back in the cradle and spun around. Her eyes took in every detail of the living room, which overlooked the garden, the East River and a portion of the Fifty-ninth Street Bridge.

She nodded to herself, both relieved and pleased that the room looked perfect. Maxim was such a stickler for neatness, but everything was in its given place; she had no cause to worry. A tranquil haven of soft pastel colors and fine French furniture, it looked particularly lovely tonight, filled with the flowers he now sent her several times a week since they had become lovers. All of the silk-shaded lamps had been turned on, a fire burned brightly in the grate, and there was a warmth and a mellowness to the setting.

Blair walked across the room, thinking how lucky she was to live in this house. Maxim had bought it for his daughter, Alix, two years ago, as a peace offering after their quarrel in 1985, in the hope of patching things up with her. Anastasia and Maxim had then decorated the house together; they both had superb taste and that was why the house on Sutton Place was so beautifully appointed throughout.

But Alix had spurned the house, had refused to accept it. Silly girl, Blair thought, shaking her head, as always somewhat mystified by the foolishness and impracticality of others. She was very much a pragmatist herself.

A housekeeper had looked after the house for a while but had eventually left, finding the existence too lonely, Maxim had explained. He had suggested Blair move in about ten months ago, not long after they had started their love affair. He had pointed out that quite aside from needing someone to occupy it for security reasons, he preferred her to live in a private house where he could come and go freely and with impunity. The prying eyes of apartment-building doormen alarmed him. "It's much more discreet, better for me, if you live at my Sutton Place house," he had pointed out. When she had seen the house she had accepted at once. The building where she lived was going co-op and she could not afford to buy her apartment. In fact, she had been in a dilemma about where she would live. And so the arrangement was perfect for them both.

As she ran upstairs Blair thought of Maxim. She was crazy about him and he was mad about her. Odd that she had known him off and on since 1982 and had frequently dated him, but that he had become involved with her only after his marriage to Adriana Macklin. Gorgeous woman, so beautiful, the epitome of glamour. But a bitch on wheels, horrendous, really, and abrasive, with a tendency toward flashiness at times. Blair could not stand women who had diamonds dripping from every pore.

Blair went into the bedroom, stripped off her pants and silk shirt, raced into the bathroom. After spraying herself with perfume, she brushed her short reddish-blond curls into a halo around her heart-shaped face, refreshed her pink lipstick, and smeared a little pale-gray eyeshadow on her lids. This color always made her blue eyes look bluer. Once she had touched up her blond lashes with mascara, she returned to the bedroom.

Opening the armoire, she took out a pale-green silk pajama suit by Trigère, slipped into the wide floating pants, put on the long jacket, tied the broad sash and stepped into a pair of matching silk shoes.

After a quick glance at herself in the mirror, she closed the armoire door and headed out of the bedroom toward the kitchen. There was plenty of champagne on ice, and she had bought fresh salad and vegetables earlier that day. She was a good cook; he loved her spaghetti primavera. That's what she would make, and they could finish the meal with cheese and fruit. Maxim was a simple eater, not faddy about food, which made life easier for her, since she was a working girl; she ran her own small public relations firm.

Halfway down the stairs, Blair remembered her birth control pills. The last thing she wanted was to get pregnant. Swinging around, she sped up the stairs and into the bedroom. Jerking open the drawer of the bedside table, she took out the pills, dropped one into her hand. It was halfway to her mouth when she stopped, stared down at Maxim's photograph on the table, a reflective look crossing her face. Why don't I want to get pregnant? she asked herself, frowning slightly. I'm already almost thirty. I ought to get pregnant, in fact. And there was no good reason why she should not. In fact, she would like to have a baby. She'd also like a husband. Maxim West, to be precise. She was beginning to get tired of being his lover, or, to use a more old-fashioned word, his mistress.

Taking very determined steps, Blair Martin walked into the bathroom, emptied the birth control pills into the toilet, then flushed it, threw the empty box into the wastepaper basket. She went back into the bedroom, walked over the bedside table and closed the drawer.

For a very long moment she stared at Maxim's photograph in its silver frame, one she had taken here in the garden last summer. Then she brought three fingers into the palm of her hand, and pressed her thumb and forefinger together to form the shape of a gun.

Smiling to herself, she aimed her thumb and forefinger at his photograph.

"I gotcha, Maxim. Gotcha, gotcha, gotcha."

PART SEVEN

Maximilian

LONDON-BERLIN
1989

A man of many lives. A man who
had his own center, something
untouchable about him,
something he did not know about
himself . . .

—Melvyn Bragg, *Richard Burton: A Life*

57

I'M SO GLAD YOU WERE FREE, DADDY," ALIX SAID, SMILING at Maxim.

"So am I." He smiled back, patted her hand, then reached for one of the menus Joseph had just placed on the table. The two of them sat together on a banquette in Mark's Club, where he had brought her for lunch after she had shown up at his office in Grosvenor Square a short while before. "Now, Alix, do you know what you want?"

"Nothing first, thank you. Then I'll have the liver and bacon, please."

"I'll join you." Maxim motioned to Joseph, ordered, and then turned to face his daughter. "Well, I must say, it's either feast or a famine with you, *Schatzi*," he remarked, reverting to his pet name for her from childhood.

"What do you mean?" Alix asked, staring at him in puzzlement.

"For four years you kept me at arm's length and behaved as if I were Attila the Hun. Now I don't seem able to get rid of you. Wherever I am, there *you* are, popping up all over the globe. Just think, on Monday you were in New York, as I was, and now, on Wednesday, here you are in London. I'm beginning to think you're following me, Alix."

She drew away from him slightly, gave him a sharp look through narrowed pale-green eyes. "Am I being a nuisance? Is that what you're implying?"

"Of course not," he laughed. "And don't look so worried. I'm only teasing. You ought to know by now that I love all the attention you've been giving me for the past six months or so. You're spoiling me. I shall miss it, you know, when you up and marry and leave me to my own devices."

She also laughed. "I'm not likely to do that. There are no men on *my* horizon at the moment."

"What's happened? Has the entire male population gone blind?"

Alix shook her head. "I just haven't met the right man, Daddy."

"He'll come along, Alix, and when you least expect it. That's the way it usually happens."

"Talking of men. I've never admitted this to you before, but you *were* right about Jeremy Vickers, he *was* after my money. Of course, I didn't see that. Remember, I was only twenty-three at the time."

"He was also after *you*, darling girl. You're a pretty tempting package. Young, beautiful, intelligent and rich. I wouldn't blame any man for going after you. The problem was, Vickers is the worst kind of playboy, and a gambler, to boot. A son of a bitch in general. It was his foul reputation that bothered me—his reputation for being a rough customer, violent. I couldn't bear that you were entangled with such—rubbish."

"He never laid a finger on me, Daddy. You and Michael would have been the first to know about it if he had ever hurt me. Anyway, I'm glad you were so tough about him with me, that you really played the heavy father. Looking back, I realize I wasn't too crazy about your attitude five years ago, but I am now, and I have been for ages. Thanks, Dad."

Maxim squeezed her hand. "I always trusted you, Alix. I knew that ultimately you wouldn't do anything silly or rash, behave in a foolish way. But I did have to let you know what my feelings were, tell you how much I disapproved of that man, even at the risk of antagonizing you."

"I know, and your approval has always been important to me. I wouldn't have married Jeremy over your objections. And, actually, I wouldn't marry anyone today if you didn't approve, even though I am now twenty-eight."

"Stop! You're making me feel old," Maxim said.

"Oh, come on! You old! *Never*."

"Have you forgotten I was fifty-five this past June?"

"You don't look it! In fact, you look terrific. Tall, dark, handsome, tanned, and raring to go. That's my *old* dad," she teased, laughing.

He laughed with her, took hold of her hand, kissed her fingertips. "You do your old dad's heart good, *meine kleine Maus*, you really do."

Alix leaned into him, kissed his cheek lightly, whispered in his ear, "Those two men over there are really intrigued by us. I actually believe they think I'm your mistress."

"I'm flattered they would think an old geezer like me is deserving of a stunning beautiful blonde such as you. However, I'd prefer it if you didn't mention the word 'mistress.' I'm afraid I break out in a rash when I hear it these days."

"Oh, sorry, Daddy." Alix eyed him carefully, ventured in a low, cautious voice, "If I'm prying, you can tell me to shut up, but out of curiosity, what *is* happening with Blair Martin?"

"Nothing much."

"I meant how is she? What's her attitude to you?"

"Hostile, naturally. She wants me to divorce Adriana and marry her. Obviously she wants the baby to have my name, and she's very much playing the injured party, the damaged woman, insists that I do the right thing by her."

"Injured woman! Honestly, Dad, nobody has to get pregnant in this day and age. Not if they don't want to—take my word for it."

Maxim returned his daughter's loving gaze steadily, and nodded his head slowly. "I realize that, Alix. I'm not stupid. And Blair and I had an understanding right from the beginning of our relationship. At least, so I thought. She promised to take precautions. Certainly she knew my feelings about that subject very well. When she told me in the summer of 1987, after I returned to New York from London, that she was pregnant, I was dreadfully upset, and chastised her about it."

"How did she explain her pregnancy, if she was supposed to be looking after the situation?"

"Her answer was that it took two to tango."

An angry glint entered Alix's luminous misty-green eyes. "But it doesn't take two to swallow birth control pills. Or use some other method of protection. I think Blair set you up, Daddy, I really do."

Set me up, Maxim thought. A strange look came onto his face, and his eyes suddenly held a faraway expression as he stared into the distance, for a split second lost to Alix.

"What's the matter? Is something wrong?" she asked, scrutinizing him intently.

"No." Maxim smiled faintly. "I thought of Camilla all of a sudden, just then. *She* once accused *me* of setting her up. In a different way than we were discussing, obviously."

"Did you?"

"Oh yes, very much so. But I had my reasons."

"And Blair Martin set *you* up, and *she* had *her* reasons."

"I believe you're quite correct, Alix. . . . I can't begin to tell you how many times I've asked myself lately why I got involved with her. . . . I think perhaps because she reminded me of Camilla. Blair does have the same coloring, is a similar physical type, isn't she?"

"But she's not half as nice as Camilla was! Camilla was a lovely person."

"How terribly tragic that she died. For all of us," he murmured, thinking out loud, sorrow touching his face.

"Thank God, *you* didn't die, Daddy. As long as I live, I'll never forget the way I felt when you were lying in Mount Sinai, at death's door after you were shot. I was in agony. I realized how stupid I'd been over the Jeremy Vickers situation, understood that you'd only always had my welfare at heart. All I wanted was for you to get better so I could make it up to you."

"And you have, my darling girl."

She smiled at him, leaned closer, "Thank goodness. And you do look fabulous. This summer on the yacht did you a lot of good, didn't it?" Alix said.

"I think it truly turned me around," Maxim replied, nodding several times. "I felt very weak after I got out of the hospital in February, even though I didn't say anything to you and your mother, or Teddy. But I'm from strong stock, and I bounce back very quickly. I'm as good as new now. Never felt better, in fact. Ah, here's our lunch, Alix. I don't know about you, but I'm starving."

After lunch Alix walked with Maxim back to the West International offices in Grosvenor Square. She tucked her arm through his, and shrugged deeper into her thick tweed coat, muttered, "Gosh, it's cold for October, I hope we're not going to have a bad winter."

He glanced down at her. "You sound as if you're planning to stay here in London. I thought Manhattan was now your home. All those rich clients you tell me you have, anxious to give you barrels of cash for art objects and paintings, and old French furniture."

Alix groaned, shook her head. "Not anymore. Well, I do have my regular clients, the top-drawer interior designers, the old money, of course. But a lot of my others, the nouveaux, fell by the wayside, what with the Wall Street crash in October of 1987, and some of the other Wall Street economic problems. Yuppies aren't such ready spenders anymore."

"I shouldn't think they are."

"And what about you, Dad? Are you going to be in London for the next few months?"

"It's more than likely. I might make a couple of quick trips to New York, but I won't be staying long. Actually, I'm planning to spend Christmas in London. Care to join me, *Schatzi*?"

"I'd love to, Daddy!"

"It's a deal," he said, beaming at her, stopping in front of his office building.

Alix smiled at him in return, her face radiant. She reached up, kissed him on the cheek, gave him a bear hug. "I love you, daddy of mine."

"And I love you, too, daughter."

"Good afternoon, Sir Maximilian," the uniformed doorman said, holding the door open for him as Maxim hurried forward after saying good-bye to Alix.

"Afternoon, Jim. Everything all right with you? With the family?"

"Very good, thank you kindly, Sir Maximilian."

Maxim nodded and rushed on, heading for the bank of elevators. He got in, rode up to his executive suite on the eleventh floor.

His secretary, Faye Miller, looked up as he came barreling through the door and exclaimed, "Oh, Sir Maxim! You've just missed Graeme Longdon. Shall I get her back?"

"Not now, Faye, thanks," Maxim said. "New York can wait awhile . . . until later in the day." He strode toward his inner sanctum, swung around and asked, "It wasn't anything urgent, was it? Did she say what it was about?"

Faye shook her head. "No, only that you could return the call anytime, that it was nothing vital."

"Fine." Maxim went inside, closed the door, took off his trench coat, hung it in the coat closet.

Once he was seated behind his desk, he glanced at two folders on his blotter, then picked up the phone and dialed his son's extension.

"Michael West here."

"It's me, Michael."

"Yes, Dad?"

"Can you please come to my office for a moment?"

"I'll be right there."

Within minutes his twenty-seven-year-old son was walking into the room, his face as serious as always, his dark and brilliant eyes as compelling as Maxim's. He gets to look more like me every day, Maxim thought, studying Michael closely as he strode across the room and lowered himself into the chair near the desk.

Michael crossed his long legs, settled back in the chair and gave his father a direct look. "What did you want to see me about?"

"These," Maxim said, lifting the folders, showing them to Michael, then placing them on the desk again.

A dark brow lifted, a gesture unconsciously copied from his father, and Michael stared hard at Maxim. "What are they?"

"Never mind, for the moment. We'll get to them later. First I want to talk to you about something else."

"All right, Dad. Shoot."

"For the last few years you've been angry with me, disgruntled, hostile—"

"Dad, how can you say that!" Michael interrupted, his voice rising slightly, his eyes flashing.

"I can say it because it's true," Maxim shot back, leaning forward, fixing his steady, unblinking gaze on his son. "In fact, things were pretty damned difficult between us, even though we both kept up some sort of pretense of cordiality. Until I was shot earlier this year. And when I almost died, your attitude changed toward me. Some of your anger seemed to fall away, at least to dissipate. True or not?"

Michael was silent for a moment.

The two men stared hard at each other.

Michael finally said, "Yes, it's true."

"But there is still hostility in you, Michael . . . hostility toward me. And that's one of the things I wanted to talk to you about, discuss with you now."

"I'm not hostile, Dad!" Michael protested. "My God, I was heartbroken when you were lying there in New York unconscious, when we didn't know whether you'd live or die. I was so desperately worried about you I couldn't see straight!"

There was a short pause. Michael cleared his throat, said in a low voice, "I love you, Dad."

"I know you do, Michael, and I love you. Look here, I'm not being critical of you, even though it may sound as if I am. I was merely leading up to something, and it's this—I want to say that I truly understand *why* you've been angry and hostile in the past." Maxim propped his elbows on the desk, steepled his fingers, looked over the top of them at Michael.

Michael sat perfectly still in the chair, waiting for his father's next pronouncement, wondering what was coming. He was silent. He knew better than to make the slightest sound when his father had that intense, concentrated expression in his eyes.

At last Maxim spoke again. He said, "You had every right to those emotions, because, in certain ways, I haven't been fair to you over the years. For one thing, I haven't given you enough responsibility, enough power." Maxim let out a heavy sigh, shook his head. "I've clutched the power to me, but without realizing I was doing so. Unconsciously, if you like. Just too preoccupied with all the deals, that's been my main problem over the years. So preoccupied with the deals I've neglected a lot of things I should have paid attention to. In fact, I've been selfish, especially to some people. However, that's another story, we won't go into it. I asked you in here now so that I could tell you things are about to change, Michael. As my only son, and heir to this gargantuan empire, I think it's about time you started sharing more of the work load, the responsibility, the power."

Michael was flabbergasted. Astonishment swept across his face. He continued to stare at his father disbelievingly.

"Aren't you going to say something?" Maxim asked at last, with a brief laugh.

"Are you serious, Dad?" he finally gasped.

"Do I ever say anything I don't mean, when it comes to business?"

"No. But, Dad . . . I mean, gosh, Dad, thanks." As the facts sank in, a huge smile spread across Michael's face. "This is fantastic news for me. I have been anxious to do more in the company, and I won't let you down."

"I know that, Michael. And let me just add that you're a brilliant businessman. The problem is, you've been operating in my shadow. Now's the chance for you to go out there and shine."

"Go out *where*?"

"New York. I'd like you to go to New York and run West International for me. And with me, of course."

Michael was further stunned, but managed to say, "Dad, this is great, wonderful."

Maxim tapped the two folders. "These are the details of the two small deals I've been working on with Grae and Peter, plus a number of memos from me about the New York office, what to expect from certain people."

Michael frowned. "But you'll be there, won't you?" he asked swiftly, staring at his father.

Maxim shook his head.

"You mean you're throwing me in at the deep end? Alone? To sink or swim?"

"You won't sink, you'll swim. You're my son. We're winners. I've no worries about you. And don't look so troubled, it's what you've always wanted, isn't it?"

"But, Dad—"

Maxim held up his hand. "That's it, Michael. I've made the decision. You've always wanted the power. And the New York office. Take them both. Grae and Peter will back you all the way. You can trust them, they won't steer you in the wrong direction. In any case, I'll be at the end of a phone."

"But where?" Michael asked, frowning. "Where will you be?"

"Here in London. Or on the yacht. Perhaps even in New York, sitting two doors away from you in my office. The point is, I want you to run the American end of West International from now on. Will you do it?"

"Yes, of course I will, Dad. I was only *momentarily* startled. You seem to be giving up so much all of a sudden, and so unexpectedly." There was a moment of hesitation on Michael's part, and then he said, "May I ask you why?"

"Of course. First of all, West International will be yours one day. You know the London operation inside out; I think the time has come for you to totally understand the American end of the company. I will guide you, always be there for you, whenever you need me. However, I do want you to start *running* it, Michael. Put very simply, it's your turn now."

Michael nodded. "I understand."

"Secondly, I want to take it a bit easier. I've rushed and pushed and driven myself hard for years and years. Since I was eighteen, actually. I think I should slow down a bit." With a wry smile, he confided quietly, "My brush with death made me realize that there are more things in life than big deals."

"There are, and I'm glad you want to relax, Dad. However, I hope you're not thinking of retiring yet. You're only fifty-five."

"No chance of that, Michael," Maxim said, grinning. "I'd miss the excitement of wheeling and dealing. However, I don't have to work twenty-four hours a day—I've come to realize that."

"When do you want me to go to New York?"

"Whenever you can clear your desk here. Shall we say immediately?"

"I can leave this weekend. There's not much on the back burners here. Will you be going with me?"

"No, but Graeme and Peter are expecting you, eagerly waiting for you. I'm leaving for Berlin next week. I'm going with Teddy to see Aunt Irina."

"It's a strange time to go, isn't it, Dad?"

"What do you mean?"

"All the demonstrations, the unrest in East Berlin, in East Germany, in all of the Eastern bloc countries."

"It's also a fascinating time. We're going to see some extraordinary changes in the next few months, Michael, mark my words. Russia's in trouble economically, and that's part of what's behind Gorbachev's overtures to the West. He's not so concerned with saving the Communist party these days, but with saving his country, his people. And also his attitude to the Eastern bloc governments is going to lead the way to a great deal of reform. You'll see."

"Three years ago, when I was with you in Berlin, you told me the Berlin Wall had to come down, and that it would, one day. Do you think that will happen?"

Maxim shrugged. "I don't know. It should come down, it's an abomination."

"If it did, do you think there would be reunification in Germany?"

"I don't know, and that's not as easy as it sounds. It would be pretty complicated to achieve."

A reflective look crossed Michael's face. "A reunited Germany? How will people react to that?"

"I don't know. But let's not forget that the Germans of today think of themselves as Europeans, and in 1992 there are going to be *no borders* in Europe. We're going to be as one, in a sense. A sort of united commonwealth."

"I understand what you're saying. . . . however, there will be those who will overreact, who will see German reunification as a threat."

Maxim laughed. "I know, but those who think in this way simply don't understand European politics, and, moreover, the European economic situation as it is today. And anyway, the Germans have been bending over backwards to expiate their crimes for the past forty-four years. They're going to be very careful. They want world approval."

"New generation, new values. Is that what you're saying, Dad?"

"I suppose I am." Maxim stood, picked up the folders, walked around his desk.

Michael jumped up, took the folders from his father as they were handed to him. "Thanks for this tremendous vote of confidence, Dad. I won't let you down."

"I know you won't, Michael." As Maxim spoke he put his arm around Michael's shoulders and walked him to the door.

"Mr. Trenton will be coming for a drink before we go out to dinner, Marco," Maxim told the butler who ran his Mayfair house.

"Shall I serve the usual Roederer Cristal, Sir Maxim?"

"Yes, please, Marco. And Mr. Trenton will be arriving around seven-thirty. We'll have drinks in the downstairs library."

Marco inclined his head. "Would you like anything now, Sir Maxim? A cup of tea perhaps?"

"No, thank you," Maxim murmured, walking over to a chair and picking up the *Evening Standard*.

"Very good, sir." Marco slipped out of Maxim's upstairs study, which was part of his bedroom suite, and closed the door quietly behind him.

Maxim glanced at the front page and put the paper down, not being in the mood to read. He leaned back in the chair, closed his eyes and thought of the day's events. His daughter's sudden arrival in London had been a surprise and a delight. One of the things that had given him the most satisfaction in the past nine months since the shooting was the healing of the rift between them. That had been Alix's doing: she had been at his side constantly during his stay in the hospital, and afterward. He had been about to instigate a reconciliation himself, at the beginning of the year, when he had flown to New York to see her, only to discover she was on the Coast. They were truly good friends again, closer than they had ever been. And now perhaps he would be able to enjoy the same kind of relationship with his son. His thoughts turned to Michael, whose stunned shock had been something to behold. He really had been knocked for a loop this afternoon. Maxim smiled inwardly, happy that he had finally handed over some of his power and responsibility. Quite aside from anything else, Michael was deserving. He'll do just fine, Maxim said to himself. He'll truly come into his own, running the New York office.

New York. The thought of the mess there filled him with dismay and apprehension. But it would have to be dealt with sooner or later. Suddenly he remembered something Camilla had once told him years ago. "We write our own scripts, then act them out," she had said, and she had been correct. He had written all of those New York scenes himself. There was really no one else to blame, and ultimately he must take the responsibility.

Next week he was going to Berlin with Teddy. From there he would fly to New York. He experienced a surge of relief as he came to this decision. Once in New York he would put things right. He had no alternative but to do that; so many lives were involved.

He had survived the shooting by the skin of his teeth, and he had made a promise to himself to bring order to his unorthodox private life when he was fully recovered. And he had been doing this slowly. His recuperation had taken longer than he had expected; then in June there had been the investiture at Buckingham Palace, when he had been knighted. And after that, following his doctor's advice, he had taken a long cruise on his yacht, sailing around the Mediterranean with his immediate family during July and August: Alix, Michael and Anastasia, Teddy and Mark, the Derevenkos, Stubby and Marcia—those he was closest to, loved and cared about the most, and who loved him. In September he had flown to Japan on urgent business, had stopped off in Australia and Hong Kong, before returning to London.

He had been here for the whole of October, supervising acquisition of a French perfume and cosmetics company. Then working on his plans for Michael's eventual succession as head of West International a few years from now, when he finally retired. But obviously the time had come to settle matters in New York.

Maxim rose, stood with his back to the fireplace, an abstracted expression on his face. He was still as tortured by inner conflicts and doubts as he had been at the beginning of the year, before the shooting. His brush with death had only made him more acutely aware of them. Most nights he lay awake, prowling the dark labyrinths of his soul, seeking meanings for his life and all that had happened to him. He still had no answers for himself, no new wisdom.

He had been filled with a deep sadness for years, ever since his childhood. Anastasia's departure from his life had only underscored that sadness, the immense sense of loss he had carried inside him.

The sadness would always be there, he had come to understand and accept that. He could only pray that one day he would find the peace that had eluded him for so long, and that when he did he would be at ease with himself and his life at last.

Maxim heard the doorbell ringing, roused himself from his thoughts and went out of the study. He ran lightly down the stairs as Marco was opening the door to Stubby.

He's been my friend for forty-seven years, Maxim thought. *My best friend.* Loyal, staunch, devoted and wise. Whatever would I have done without him?

58

"WHAT TIME IS IRINA EXPECTING US AT HER FLAT?"
Maxim asked, walking out of the bedroom of his suite in the
Kempinski Hotel in Berlin.

"Not for a couple of hours," Teddy answered.

He glanced at his watch. "It's only five o'clock. I must have
misunderstood you. I had it in my head that we're supposed
to be meeting her shortly."

"You didn't misunderstand anything, Maxim," Teddy said.
"I did tell you we should be ready by five o'clock. However,
we're not going to Irina's just yet—I'm expecting a guest."

"Who?"

"A friend of . . . a friend of Mutti's," Teddy began, and
stopped, staring up at him, suddenly seeing him objectively for
once in her life. She could not help thinking what a striking
and handsome man he was, and how well he looked after his
ordeal. When he was shot she had been out of her mind with
worry. And she who had lost her faith had begun to pray again;
she had prayed every night for him, and when he recovered,
her faith in God had been restored.

Maxim said, "You're looking strange, Teddy. What's the
matter?"

"Nothing. To tell you the truth, I was just thinking how
wonderful you're looking at the moment. So very healthy."

He smiled at her. "It's the tan. But seriously, I do feel very
well, Teddy. And who is it that you're expecting?"

"I told you, a former—" Teddy stopped, stood up abruptly
at the sound of knocking and hurried to open the door before
Maxim had a chance to do so. "Good afternoon, thank you for
coming," she said, and opening the door wider, Teddy escorted
her guest into the suite.

Maxim stood in the center of the room, slightly taken aback when he saw the woman with Teddy. She was a nun dressed in a dark-brown habit and a black veil. He was puzzled, and gave Teddy a quick, questioning look.

Teddy said, "Sister Constanza, I would like to introduce you to Maximilian West. Maxim, this is Sister Constanza of the Sisters of the Poor of Saint Francis."

Maxim inclined his head, wondering what the association between Mutti and the Catholic sister could possibly have been.

The nun walked forward, smiling, her hand outstretched.

Maxim took it, smiling in return, thinking that he had never seen such a peaceful face on anyone before in his entire life. "I'm pleased to meet you, Sister Constanza."

The nun was small, dainty, her eyes warm, her voice gentle when she said, "I am delighted to meet you at last. Teddy has written to me for many years, and has told me so much about you."

Maxim's bafflement increased and he stared at Teddy expectantly.

Teddy ignored his quizzical expression, turned to the nun and said, "Please do sit down, Sister Constanza."

"Thank you," the sister responded and lowered herself into a chair.

"May I offer you some sort of refreshment? Coffee or tea?" Maxim asked, looking across at the nun, and then at Teddy.

"No, thank you," the sister said.

"And what about you, Teddy?"

"Nothing, thanks, Maxim. Come and sit here with me." Teddy patted the sofa, where he joined her, frowning slightly, wondering what this was all about.

Clearing her throat, Teddy said, "There's something I've wanted to tell you. For years and years, Maxim." She held him with her eyes, then continued after a moment, "And I *should* have told you . . . a long time ago, actually. But I didn't." She took a deep breath. "In 1939, before we left Paris, Ursula gave me a letter for you—"

"Yes, I still have it," he interrupted, a hint of impatience creeping into his voice.

"And Ursula also gave *me* a letter, which I was instructed not to open except in the event of her death. That is the first thing I did when I came back from Berlin in 1945. There was information in the letter that she wanted me to have, something she wanted me to know. She said I had to use my discretion . . . about telling you or not, when you were old enough to understand. But I never did tell you, or show you the letter."

"What did it say?" Maxim asked, his curiosity fully aroused.

"I'll tell you in a moment," Teddy replied. "When you almost died earlier this year, I regretted that I had never given you the letter. I suddenly realized how wrong I had been to . . . well, to play God, in a sense. You had every right to know what was in the letter."

"What *was* in it?" he demanded.

Teddy reached out, took hold of his hand, held it very tightly in hers. She said softly, "Ursula Westheim was not your birth mother, Maxim. She adopted you. . . . she and Sigmund adopted you when you were a day old."

Maxim sat back gaping at Teddy. He was stunned by her extraordinary words. For a moment he was unable to say anything, endeavoring to digest what she had just said, to fully comprehend her words.

But at last he managed to ask in an unsteady voice, "Then who *was* my mother?"

Teddy returned his penetrating stare but did not answer him.

There was a sudden, painful silence in the room.

Very softly, in that same gentle voice, Sister Constanza said, "I am your mother, Maxim. I gave you life."

Maxim's jaw dropped and his eyes focused on the nun, remained riveted on her. He was reeling from shock, still unable to absorb the things he was hearing.

"But how can you be my mother?" he gasped hoarsely. "You're a nun." He looked from Sister Constanza to Teddy, his eyes dazed.

Sister Constanza said, "I was not always a nun, and I *am* your birth mother, Maxim, truly I am."

"But I don't understand!" he exclaimed. "You are a Catholic, the Westheims were Jews. How did they come to adopt me?"

"I would like to tell you the story," the nun replied. "May I?"

"Of course! *I must know . . . everything!*"

"My name before I became a nun was Dorothea Schubert. I went to work for Ursula Westheim in 1931, when I was sixteen, as her social secretary. She liked me very much, and was always very good to me. When I became pregnant out of wedlock, in 1933, my parents disowned me, threw me out of the house. You see, they were staunch Catholics, very religious, and they felt that I had brought terrible shame upon them."

Sister Constanza shifted slightly in the chair, smoothed a hand over her habit, and continued, "I had no one to turn to in my terrible distress, no real friends to help me, and certainly the rest of my family were against me. It was Ursula who befriended me, allowed me to live at the house in the Tiergartenstrasse for a few months. During that time I began to realize I could not keep my child, that I would have to have the baby adopted. I knew Ursula was unable to have children. One day I went to her, and I asked her if she would adopt my baby."

"And my mother agreed?" Maxim said.

"Not at first," Sister Constanza responded. "She said she must think about it and very deeply . . . mostly because I was Catholic and she was Jewish. I pointed out to her that we were not talking about religion, but about love. I told her that I knew she and Herr Westheim would give my child the greatest love and affection, and so many things that I could not."

"And so they finally agreed?"

"Yes. Frau Westheim took a small apartment for me, just off the Ku'damm, so that I could have my privacy away from the mansion. She and Herr Westheim moved to the villa in Wannsee. It was important that neither of us was in the mansion in the city, because of the servants."

"And then after my birth you gave me to the Westheims immediately . . . Teddy did just say I was adopted when I was a day old," Maxim stated.

Sister Constanza inclined her head, gave him a long and thoughtful look. "It was better for everyone to do this quickly. You were such a beautiful boy, I knew I would not be able to give you up if I held you in my arms for too long. They came for you on June the thirteenth, and took you home with them. They were so happy. I told them that I wanted them to have you above any other couple in the whole world—because I knew what good and wonderful people they were. I knew they would bring you up with love and kindness, and shower you with everything that money could buy."

"They did," Maxim said softly, remembering his mother and father with the greatest of love.

Teddy noticed that Sister Constanza looked pale, drained, and she continued her story: "Sister Constanza went away from Berlin, Maxim. She had decided to go into a religious order, a nursing order of nuns, and she went to Aachen, to the Motherhouse of the Sisters of the Poor of Saint Francis, where she became a novice."

"*Aachen*," Maxim murmured. "What a strange coincidence. That was the border town we stopped at when we were fleeing Germany in 1938."

"Yes," Teddy said, and went on slowly, "In Ursula's letter to me, she told me all of this, and gave me the name and address of Sister Constanza, asked me to stay in touch with her, to write to her with news of you. Discreetly, of course."

"And she did . . . all these years," the sister added, leaning forward in the chair, clasping her hands. "I realize you have suffered greatly, and have had great sadness in your life, because of the way you were separated from Ursula and Sigmund. And because of the way your parents died in the death camps. But I believe that I did the right thing for you, in spite of this."

"Yes, I agree with you," he said, his voice barely audible, meaning every word. "You did the only thing you could at the time. You were not to know what would happen."

"I hope you will see it in your heart to forgive me," the nun said.

"But there's nothing to forgive." Maxim gave her a swift glance. "I loved my parents, and they loved me very much, and that's all that matters in the end."

"Yes," she said. "You speak the truth there."

"Who was my birth father?" he asked.

"His name was Karl Neuwirth."

"Was he also a Catholic?"

"Yes."

"Why didn't he marry you?"

There was a tiny silence before she said, "He was a married man."

"Is he still alive?"

"No, he was killed in the war. He was a soldier on the Russian front. And his wife and two children were killed in a bombing raid."

"I see." Maxim stared at Teddy. "Why didn't you tell me years ago?"

"I kept meaning to . . . and quite a few times, Maxim. But I always lost my nerve. . . . I was afraid, I didn't want to cause you pain." She cleared her throat. "I had to tell you finally, because I thought it was wrong to withhold this information from you, as I explained a moment or two ago. And anyway, I felt that at the age of fifty-five you are mature enough to understand everything."

For the first time a faint smile flickered in his eyes. "Yes, I think I'm old enough to understand, Teddy."

At this moment, quite suddenly, Sister Constanza stood up. "I must leave now," she announced.

Maxim jumped up. "But can't we offer you tea, something before you leave, Sister Constanza?"

She shook her head. "You are kind, but I really must get back."

"Do you have far to go?"

"No. It will only take me about half an hour on the train. The convent is just outside the city."

"Please let me send you in my car—"

"No, no," she cut in, touching his arm lightly. "I must lead my life the way I have always led it. But thank you for your kindness." She stretched out her hand.

Maxim took it, held it in his.

Sister Constanza stared up into his face. Her dark-brown eyes were full of love. She said, "Be at peace with yourself, Maxim. And may God bless you always."

He felt a stirring in his heart for this gentle, religious woman, who had given birth to him, and he impulsively leaned down and kissed her on the cheek.

Her eyes filled with tears, then she smiled at him, and her face was radiant.

59

"ARE YOU ANGRY WITH ME?" TEDDY asked a short while later, after Maxim had read Ursula's letter, written so long ago, which he had handed back to her.

"How could I ever be angry with you, my dearest Teddy?"

"Upset, then?"

"No." His expression was as loving and devoted as it always was.

"Then what *are* you feeling?" Teddy pressed, concerned about the effect the nun's revelations had had on him.

"*Startled, stunned, shocked.* I think anybody would feel those things under the circumstances, don't you?"

"Yes," Teddy agreed quietly, continuing to observe him.

"You could have shown me the letter years ago, you know," Maxim said, returning her gaze evenly, his expression neutral.

"The main reason I didn't, Maxim, is that I thought it would hurt you."

"What I just heard from Sister Constanza does not change anything in my life, Teddy. Mutti will always be my lovely Mutti, my fairy-tale mother from my childhood. I'll never stop loving her, and the memory of her will remain precious to me until the day I die. And no matter whose male genes I have in me, Sigmund Westheim is still my father. He will always be my father to me. He is the one who gave me love, and my standards, my code of honor. I have lived by the rules he set out for me when I was a child, to the best of my ability, all the days of my life."

He paused, gave Teddy a small, almost shy smile, and confided, "I still have the little bits of paper he gave me when I was four years old. I've kept them all these years. In fact, I copied his words down on white postcards, in order to preserve them along with the little carved horse. And, incidentally, I passed on my father's standards, his rules of conduct to Michael, and to Alix. I gave them copies of his words."

"Oh Maxim, what a lovely thing to do, and you never told me!" Teddy exclaimed.

"I have to keep a few secrets from you," he replied, his voice lighter, teasing all of a sudden. Teddy studied him for a moment. "Well, now at last you know who you really are, Maxim, know that you were born a Catholic of Catholic parents."

"No, Teddy, my parents were Jews. *And I am a Jew.* I was brought up a Jew, I feel like a Jew, therefore I am a Jew."

Taken aback momentarily, Teddy stared at him, made no comment. Slowly she began to nod her head. "Yes, Maxim, you are right. You are a Jew."

Maxim went over to the sofa and sat down next to her. He took her hand in his, looked deeply into her face. She was still a beautiful woman, even though she was now seventy years of age. There were fine wrinkles around her green eyes, etched at the corners of her gentle mouth, and her hair had turned snow-white. But there was a serenity and a loveliness about her that age could never dim. He loved her so very much at this moment he thought his heart was going to burst. She had been there for him every day of his life, his sweet and loving devoted Teddy.

He said, very softly, "There's something else I want to say to you."

"Yes, what is it, dear?"

"Sister Constanza may have given birth to me, and Mutti will always be so very special to me. *But you are my mother, Teddy.*"

She stared at him speechlessly. Her eyes filled with sudden tears.

He touched her cheek with the greatest of tenderness, remembering all she had done for him for fifty-four years of his life. He told her, "You have looked after me since I was one year old. You took care of me when I was small, took me to safety in England. Protected my life at the risk of yours, brought me up, raised me to be the man I am today. Whatever good there is in me I owe to you, Teddy. You're the very best part of me. Yes, my dearest, *dearest* Teddy, you *are* my mother.

I love you very much, and I thank you from the bottom of my heart for everything you have done for me."

Profoundly moved, Teddy felt the tears rolling down her cheeks. She clung to Maxim's hand, and her voice was brimming with emotion as she said, "I've loved you as my own child. I never thought of you in any other way. You were always my firstborn—in my heart."

Maxim put his arms around Teddy. "Yes, I know that. I always knew it, I think."

They held each other close, remembering so many little things about the last fifty years, lost for a moment or two in their own private thoughts, bonded as mother and son.

And then Maxim said, against her snowy hair, "It's odd, but so much has become clear to me in the past few days. I have been so mixed up inside myself, so conflicted, and I've been full of doubts . . . about myself, my life. I haven't been able to see straight, actually. And one night, before the shooting, I had wondered who I was, why I was here on this planet, what the hell life was all about."

"I know you've been troubled for a very long time," she said.

"And then last week, a day or two before we left London, I had a flash of extraordinary insight, a revelation . . . you might say it was my epiphany. I suddenly understood so many things about myself, understood that I had been yearning after Mutti for most of my life, searching for her even in other women perhaps. Yes, I truly did understand myself at that moment. . . . I realized I was the lost boy Hans."

Teddy eased herself away from him, looked up into his familiar, handsome face. "What do you mean?"

"When I was a little boy here in Berlin, so long ago now, you read a story to me about a boy called Hans. Do you remember the story?"

"Vaguely."

"His mother lost Hans, and she could never find him again, so he was lost forever, wandering around the world, with nobody to love him. That story really made an impression on me. When we were in Paris in 1939 I asked Mutti not to lose me. And then she did. At least, so I thought, because I never saw her again." He looked into her face, and finished, "I've always been the lost boy."

Sadness fell like a shadow across Teddy's face and her heart ached for him. But she said in the gentlest tone, "You lost. Never." She shook her head. "You've been mixed up, yes, and your private life is now in the most ghastly mess, but I refuse ever to think of you as lost."

"But deep within myself that *is* the way I've felt, although I suppose I only recognized this the other night, when I was having dinner with Stubby in London. He made a remark to me that triggered everything off in my head."

"What did he say?" Teddy asked, her eyes searching his face.

"He said that the women in my life had hurt me badly, let me down in the worst way, whether they had done so intentionally or not. I asked him what he meant, and he pointed out that Mutti was wrenched from me at a tender age, that Anastasia left me against my will, and that Camilla also left me—because she died on me. He then added that Adriana failed me and Blair Martin betrayed me."

"All that's true," Teddy agreed, thinking that Stubby had acquired wisdom in middle age. She had had a soft spot for Stubby since his boyhood, was very fond of him.

Maxim explained, "It occurred to me that in the same way Mutti was wrenched from me, all of the women in my life *abandoned* me, in one way or another, in a sense."

"I can't argue with you there."

"And that same night I understood that you were the only woman who had never hurt me, never let me down. You've always been there for me, and you've been my rock. When I was going in and out of unconsciousness in New York, in the hospital in January, I remember opening my eyes at one moment. And do you know what I saw?"

She shook her head.

"I saw my first wife, my third wife, my mistress, my daughter. *And my mother.* That's what I thought, when I saw you. *Mother.* And then I started drifting off into unconsciousness again, and you, as you are today, as you look today, disappeared. In place of the silver-haired seventy-year-old Teddy, I saw the Teddy of my childhood. I kept thinking that Teddy would come soon, come and save me as she had when I was a child."

"I would always try to save you, Maxim, but there are times in life when we must save ourselves, when no one can do it for us, and that's the way it is now with you."

"What are you getting at?"

"I think you must save yourself by clearing up that frightful, upsetting mess in New York. Those women, Maxim. Adriana, Blair. The baby, Viveca. You mustn't let that situation continue to drift the way it has been drifting since you were shot. It's simply not right."

"Oh, I know that. I plan to bring some order to the chaos in my life as soon as possible. I don't love Adriana. She doesn't love me. Only my status. I plan to divorce her, give her anything she wants, if necessary. We have a prenuptial agreement, but as far as I'm concerned, I'm prepared to renegotiate if it frees me."

"And then what are you going to do? About Blair Martin and her child?"

"I'm certainly not going to marry her, if that's what you're getting at. I'm sorry there's an innocent child involved, but I'm not going to sacrifice myself, get myself into another marital trap with the wrong woman. I don't love Blair either, nor does she love me. Only my money."

"You'll provide for the baby, even though you have no positive proof she is yours?"

"Why not? I'm a rich man. And what if the child *is* mine? I'd hate to think of my offspring in need, wanting for something, wanting for anything."

"You've obviously done a great deal of thinking in the last week. Things didn't seem quite so clear-cut to you, Maxim, when we had lunch a fortnight ago. You sounded muddled, and you troubled me, worried me."

"I told you, the other evening with Stubby gave me such insight—it was my epiphany."

There was a sudden sharp knocking on the door.

Startled, Maxim turned, then looked back at Teddy.

"I wonder who that can be?" he muttered, rising.

Teddy said, "Oh dear, I forgot to tell you, I'm expecting another guest."

"Who?" he asked.

She ignored his question. "I'm afraid I've been playing God again," she said.

Striding to the door, Maxim opened it, and for the second

time that day his jaw dropped. But with remarkable swiftness he recovered himself, and a dazzling smile spread across his face. "Anastasia!" he exclaimed, and he stepped forward, took hold of her arm and escorted his ex-wife into the suite.

60

$\mathcal{P}$RINCESS IRINA TROUBETZKOY GREETED THEM EXCITedly when Maxim, Teddy and Anastasia walked into her apartment that same evening.

"I'm sorry we're so late," Teddy began, only to be silenced by Irina's raised hand.

"You don't know, do you? You haven't heard, have you?" Irina cried, her eyes focused on them.

Teddy looked bewildered, Anastasia intrigued. Maxim said, "Heard what, Irina?"

"The news from East Berlin!"

"No," he answered.

Anastasia took charge. "Let's go into the sitting room, Irina, and you can tell us about it." She slipped out of her coat, placed it on the bench in the hallway.

"Of course! How rude of me to keep you standing here in the foyer. Please take off your coats. Teddy, give me your mink—Maxim, hang your overcoat in the closet," Irina instructed, bustling around them.

A few seconds later, when they were seated in front of the fire in Irina's living room, the three of them sat back, stared at her expectantly.

Irina was far too worked up to sit, and she stood near the fireplace, one hand resting on the mantelpiece. She said, in the same tense, excited voice, "A little earlier today, Gunter Schabowski, head of the East Berlin Communist party, had a press conference. He said that starting at midnight *tonight* East Ger-

mans can leave if they want." Irina's voice shook, tears welled.
"They can leave without special permission . . . for a few hours,
a few days, *forever*, if they so wish. They are free! Free at last,
out of bondage!" She was so overcome she began to weep, and
groped in her jacket pocket for a handkerchief.

Maxim went to her, put his arm around her shoulders.

After a moment she said to him, "You were always right.
The Berlin Wall *is* going to come down, as you predicted it
would."

"I never thought I'd live to see this day!" Teddy exclaimed.

"Neither did I, Teddy," Irina murmured, patting her eyes
again, pulling herself together.

Maxim truly had been surprised. He said to Irina, "Teddy
and I have been tied up for several hours, with an old friend . . .
then Teddy and I had things to discuss; suddenly Anastasia arrived, I missed the evening news on television. Naturally, we
were in the dark when we arrived here. But what wonderful
news this is."

"I have canceled the table at the restaurant," Irina said. "We
are going to have dinner here, and later, around eleven, we
must go out into the streets. We must be there when the crossing points are opened along the Berlin Wall."

"That's right!" Maxim exclaimed. "We can't miss this historic event. Why, history is shifting under our feet at this very
moment. We are seeing history in the making, in fact. Nothing
is ever going to be the same again. . . ."

"What do you mean?" Anastasia asked.

Maxim had instantly understood the implications, seen into
the future, and he said in a voice as excited as Irina's had been,
"I believe we are about to witness the fall of the Communist
regimes in Europe. You're going to see—one by one they'll all
come tumbling down. Freedom and democracy are on the
march."

"Do you really think so?" Teddy asked. He was rarely
wrong. At least, about business or politics.

"Yes, I do," Maxim replied. "It is Mikhail Gorbachev. He
has opened the way to this, with his *perestroika*, and by preach-
ing reform. Believe me, it couldn't have happened without
him."

"The wheel of history," Irina said softly. "How it turns,
sometimes slowly, sometimes so fast. I am seventy-eight, and

all of my life I've lived under the menacing shadow of Communism. The Bolsheviks slaughtered my family—my father, my Romanov uncle, Czar Nicholas, his wife, Czarina Alexandra, my cousins. When I was only a small child I fled Russia with my mother." She sighed. "Over seventy years I've waited, praying that Communism would fail . . . that somehow the people would rise up, and that in their desire for freedom and justice they *would* ultimately prevail."

"They *are* prevailing," Maxim told her. "For months now there have been demonstrations—in Leipzig and all over East Germany. And East Germans have been pouring out, through Hungary and Czechoslovakia, into West Germany, at an amazing rate. It was only a matter of time before the Berlin Wall came down. But look, what about a drink, Irina? We must make a toast on this historic occasion."

"How stupid I am! Hilde put champagne on ice before you came. It's over there, Maxim, on the chest with the glasses. Would you open it, please?"

He strode across the room, opened the bottle and poured the champagne. Anastasia joined him, picked up two glasses when they were filled and carried them over to Teddy and Irina.

A moment later they were all toasting each other.

"To freedom!" Irina exclaimed, lifting her glass high.

"Freedom!" Teddy, Maxim, and Anastasia said in unison, raising their glasses.

"It's November the ninth today!" Teddy said, a look of sudden comprehension crossing her face. "November the ninth, 1989. Fifty-one years ago tonight it was Henrietta Mandelbaum's twenty-first birthday . . . and the night the Nazis torched the Central Synagogue. November the ninth, 1938, was *Kristallnacht*. I'll never forget it . . . racing through the streets on the back of Willy Herzog's motorbike, fleeing from the raging mob of storm troopers. Tonight is the fifty-first anniversary of *Kristallnacht*!"

"How extraordinary that the Wall is coming down tonight," Maxim said. "History truly has come full circle."

Irina nodded in agreement. "If Hitler had not come to power, there would have never been a war. Berlin would never have been divided into East-West zones. Nor would the country have been divided; there would have been no Communist regime running East Germany. Everything harks back to the

Nazis, doesn't it? Only now, as the Berlin Wall crumbles, are we truly seeing the end of the legacy of the Third Reich."

"*Tor auf! Tor auf! Tor auf!*" the crowds bellowed at eleven-forty-five. "Open the gate!" they repeated over and over again. And they continued to taunt the East German border guards for another fifteen minutes, as they waited for midnight at Checkpoint Charlie in West Berlin's American sector.

Maxim stood with his arm around Teddy; Anastasia had hers linked through Irina's. The four of them were among the thousands thronging the streets, impatiently waiting for the stroke of midnight.

At exactly twelve the crowds went wild, cheering, shouting and screaming as East Berliners began to stream through the gate at Checkpoint Charlie, many of them coming over into the West Zone for the first time in their lives. The whistling, the shouting, the cheering continued unabated; West and East Berliners hugged and kissed one another, and wept, overcome by joy. They danced in the streets, shared the champagne and beer the West Berliners had brought with them. It was a grand and glorious night as they celebrated freedom.

All manner of mixed emotions crowded in on Maxim as he stood watching the Berliners go crazy around him. Many of them were now clambering up onto the Wall, where so many had died trying to escape to freedom; others had begun to chip away at it with hammers and picks, intent on breaking it down, this hideous wall of shame.

Berlin. The city of his birth and childhood. It had forever pulled him back, and he had always believed it held a secret for him. And so it had: the secret had been revealed today. He thought of Ursula and Sigmund Westheim, who would always be his Mutti and Papa, and the sadness swelled up in him when he thought of their persecution, the way they had died so horribly in the death camps. Rage engulfed him, but he pushed it aside; it served no purpose now. Instead, he clung to the image of them in his mind's eye, saw Ursula's blond beauty, Sigmund's dark head bent over the piano, heard her laughter, heard his glorious music that had filled the house in the Tiergartenstrasse. They would live on in his heart forever, their memory clear, profoundly pure, intact, unchanged by anything he had heard today. His mind swung to Sister Constanza. He did not believe he would see her again. He was quite certain she had no need or desire to meet with him for a second time. She had come today only because Teddy had asked her. The nun had her God and was at peace with herself. He had understood this about her the instant he had met her. Absolute peace dwelt in that innocent, sweet face.

He had told Teddy many things today. *He had spoken the truth. She was his mother. He was her son. He was a Jew.*

It suddenly struck him how curious it was that Teddy had insisted they come to Berlin this week to see Irina, that today, as the Berlin Wall tumbled, the walls in his mind had tumbled.

"It's like New Year's Eve!" Teddy shouted above the noise, clinging to his arm.

"Or Bastille Day!" Anastasia suggested.

"Celebration . . . revolution . . . no matter what we call it, this is a night to remember!" Irina cried. "The last time we were in a huge crowd like this was in 1963, when we heard President Kennedy speak in front of the Schöneberg Town Hall."

" *'Ich bin ein Berliner,'* " Anastasia said, quoting John Kennedy, looking at Maxim as she did.

"If only he were still alive to see this," Maxim murmured, and then he hugged Teddy to him, brought Irina and Anastasia into the circle of his arms. He thought of the night he had been shot; he thanked God he had survived, that he was alive.

It was almost two o'clock in the morning by the time Maxim, Teddy and Anastasia came back to the Kempinski Hotel, after they had taken Irina home.

At the door of her suite, Maxim kissed Teddy good-night, and so did Anastasia.

"It's been quite a day," Teddy said, turning around on the threshold of her room. "A memorable day. A memorable night."

"Yes, Teddy, it has, indeed," he agreed.

Teddy went in and closed the door without another word.

Maxim and Anastasia stood alone in the corridor, staring at each other. "Where's your suite?" he asked.

"Just along here, not far from yours," she replied.

They walked down the corridor together in silence. When they came to her suite, she inserted the key, opened the door and turned to him. "Would you like a nightcap, Maxim?"

"Why not?" he answered, following her inside.

After they had shed their coats, Anastasia went to the small bar. "What would you like?"

"No more champagne," Maxim said.

"How about a brandy, then?"

"Good idea. Are you having one?"

"Yes."

She poured two glasses, handed him one and sat down in the chair opposite his.

They raised their glasses to each other but said nothing.

After a moment Anastasia remarked, "Michael told me how generous you've been with him, Maxim. Giving him so much power and responsibility, and the New York office to run. He's elated. Thank you."

"I suppose occasionally I do do something right."

"I'm not sure I'm following you."

"Don't pay any attention to me, forget it," he mumbled and walked across the room. He glanced out the window into the street; below, the Ku'damm was still full of milling crowds celebrating. He felt her eyes on him and slowly swung around to look at her.

She sat holding the brandy snifter, a quizzical expression on her face.

He felt bound to explain his last remark, and so he said, "I seem to make a mess of things most of the time these days. I've certainly got a mess going for me in New York . . . in my private life."

Anastasia made no comment.

He said slowly, "How on earth did I get myself trapped between those two women?"

"I think it was my fault," Anastasia answered without hesitation.

"Now *I'm* not following *you*."

"I should never have divorced you, Maxim."

"I agree with you there, Anastasia."

"It was the biggest mistake of my life."

"True." His eyes did not leave her face. "I've never been in love with any other woman but you."

"And I've never been in love with any other man."

"There is only you, Anastasia."

"There's only you . . . for me, Maxim."

"I've just had a wonderful idea, Peachy," Maxim said.

"What is it?"

He began to walk toward her. "Come with me. . . ."

"Where to?" she asked.

"*Venice.*"

"When?"

"Tomorrow. My plane is at Tempelhof Airport. Waiting."

Anastasia stood up. "Yes," she said as she walked into his outstretched arms. "Yes, yes, yes."

She looked up into his face and smiled her incandescent smile.

It filled the empty places of his heart. The sadness inside him slipped away. He knew it would not come back ever again.

Common Yiddish Terms

====

Ashkenazi—The name applied to the Jews of Central and Eastern Europe; a term used since the sixteenth century.

Ashkenazim—Plural of Ashkenazi.

bar mitzvah—A ceremony in a synagogue in which a thirteen-year-old boy reaches the status of a man.

bubeleh—Term of endearment, such as darling, honey or sweetheart, deriving from *buba*, the Russian-Yiddish word for doll.

Chanukah—The feast of lights, a Jewish festival that usually falls just before Christmas.

chollah—A braided soft loaf, glazed with egg white.

chuppah—The wedding canopy under which the bride and groom stand for the wedding ceremony.

chutzpa—Audacity, nerve; incredible gall.

Goy—A Gentile, anyone who is not a Jew.

Goyim—Plural of Goy.

haimisher—Cozy, warm, unpretentious.

kiddush—The prayer and ceremony that sanctifies the Sabbath and Jewish holy days—not to be confused with kaddish.

kinder—Children.

kop—Head.

landsman—A person from the same town in Europe, a countryman.

landsleit—Plural of landsman.

mama-loshen—Mama's language; "Let's talk mama-loshen" means "Let's get to the heart of it" or "Let's talk straight."

megillah—A rigmarole; a story that is far too long.

mensch—Someone of consequence, to admire and even to emulate.

meshuggeneh—Crazy, absurd; can be applied to a person or an idea.

oy vey is mir—Oh, woe is me; poor me.

Shabbes—Sabbath.

Shabbat—Sabbath.

shadchen—A professional matchmaker.

Torah—The scroll containing the five books of Moses: Genesis, Exodus, Leviticus, Numbers and Deuteronomy.

tsuris—Troubles, worries, woes.

Translation of Hebrew prayer: Blessing over Sabbath candles on page 104

Blessed art Thou, O Lord our God, King of the universe, who hast sanctified us by Thy commandments and commanded us to kindle the Sabbath-light.

An excerpt from the new novel

Remember

By **Barbara Taylor Bradford**
Available in bookstores in November

Published in hardcover by Random House.

Read on to the compelling opening chapter by
this brilliant storyteller.

One

SHE LAY IN THE DARKNESS, TRYING TO EMPTY HER HEAD OF every thought, troubling or otherwise, but still, sleep eluded her. Bone tired though she had been earlier, when she had stripped off her clothes and fallen into bed, now she was wide awake. All of her senses were on the alert; she realized she was straining to catch any untoward sounds from outside. At this moment, though, very little noise penetrated the walls of the plush hotel suite. Nevertheless, she found it curious, and ominous, that silence outside.

I should be out there now, she thought. Outside.

Certainly, yes, that was where she belonged; that was where her heart and mind were. Outside, with her crew: Jimmy Trainer, her cameraman; Luke Michaels, her sound engineer; Arch Leverson, her producer. They usually spent all their time together, like any good news team on foreign assignment.

And she was usually with them. But tonight, at dinner, she had been so weary, her eyelids drooping, after several nights with little or no sleep, that Arch had insisted she go to bed for a few hours. He had promised to wake her in plenty of time for her to prepare for her nightly broadcast to the States. Common sense plus fatigue had prevailed; she had agreed; but now she found she was unable to relax and drop off, even though it was a relief to lie between cool sheets.

She felt tense, expectant, and suddenly she knew the reason why. Her intelligence and instinct, combined with her considerable experience as a war correspondent, were all telling her the same thing: Something was going to happen out there tonight. The crackdown that had been in the wind for days—it was going to happen tonight.

Involuntarily she shivered. Blessed with an unusual degree of prescience, she had learned not to doubt herself, and she shivered again at the thought of violence. Blood would be shed if the People's Army moved against the people.

Pushing herself up against the pillows, she switched on the bedside lamp, and glanced at her watch. It was a few minutes before ten. Throwing back the covers, she got out of bed and hurried across to the window. Opening it wide, she stepped out onto the balcony, anxious to see what, if anything, was happening in the streets of Beijing.

Her suite, on the fourteenth floor of the Beijing Hotel, overlooked Changan Avenue, also known as the Avenue of Eternal Peace, which led into Tiananmen Square. Below her on this wide boulevard, illuminated by cluster lights shaded in green, people were moving along steadily in a continuous flow. As they passed through the pools of light cast by the lamps, she saw that they were mostly wearing white shirts or tops; and they moved so quietly, so silently, she found it eerie.

They were heading for Tiananmen Square, that vast rectangle of stone dating back to 1651, early in the Qing Dynasty; the square had been built to hold a million people in its one-hundred-acre expanse. She had come to understand that Tiananmen Square was the symbolic heart of political power in China, and over the centuries it had been the site of some momentous events in the country's turbulent history.

The air was clear; she sniffed but could detect no hint of tear gas, nor of the smell of the yellow dust that perpetually blew in from the Gobi Desert and was normally all-pervasive in the congested capital. Perhaps the light wind was carrying both smells away from the hotel, or perhaps tear gas had not been used tonight. Glancing quickly up and down the long avenue, her eyes shifted back to the crowded pavement below her balcony, and to the people walking toward the square in such an orderly fashion. Everything appeared to be normal, and the military were nowhere to be seen, at the moment.

Why do I believe this is the calm before the storm, she thought dismally as she turned and went back into the suite.

She switched on the rest of the lights in the bedroom, hurried into the bathroom, splashed cold water on her face, and began to brush her hair in swift, even strokes.

The face surrounded by the soft blond hair was wide, with a strong jawline, and its individual features were classic, clean cut, well defined—high cheekbones, straight nose, pretty mouth, chin that was firm and resolute without being pugnacious. The eyes, set wide apart under arched blond brows, were large and clear, their color a light sea-blue that was almost but not quite turquoise. The features came together to create a face that was unusually attractive and lively, vivid with intelligence and humor, and highly photogenic.

In her bare feet, as she was now, she stood five feet six inches tall; slender of frame yet surprisingly strong, with long legs, her body possessed a willowy grace.

The young woman's name was Nicole Wells. Known as Nicky to the world at large, she was called Nick by her family, her closest friends and her television crew.

At thirty-six she had become a superstar in the media, who was at the height of her profession, as war correspondent for the American Television Network, with headquarters in New York. Renowned as a brilliant investigative reporter and as a chronicler of war, and respected for her spectacular coverage of world events, Nicky Wells had a reputation for being courageous, even intrepid. On camera she was mesmerizing, incredibly charismatic.

Now, she put down her brush, tied her hair straight back in a ponytail, and reached into her makeup kit for a lipstick. Once she had outlined her mouth in pink, she leaned closer, grimacing at herself. She thought she looked washed-out, pallid, without makeup, but she was in too much of a hurry to bother with it. Besides, she would not be on camera tonight. When martial law had been declared on May 20, almost two weeks ago, the Chinese government had turned off the satellite; furthermore, television cameras had been banned in the square. Without that satellite feed or Jimmy behind his camera, there would be no more live-spot location shots. At least not in Tiananmen Square. And that was where the story was—at the center of the action. Once again, she would have to make do with a phoned-in report.

The ATN suite served as a makeshift newsroom/office for Nicky Wells, her cameraman and crew. When the cameraman Jimmy Trainer opened the door, he brightened when he saw Nicky, then frowned. "Hey, Nick," he said, "you're supposed to be grabbing some sleep."

"I know. But, Jimmy, I couldn't sleep. I have a premonition . . . something . . . it's going to blow tonight. My instinct tells me there's going to be a crackdown tonight."

Catching the tension in her voice, noting her expression and the seriousness of her words, Jimmy looked at her alertly. After five and a half years of working with her in the trouble spots of the world, he had learned to trust her intuition. Her judgment had rarely been flawed.

"If you say so, Nick, and you know I'm with you all the way. But look, it *seems* pretty quiet out there. At least, it was twenty minutes ago."

Nicky looked at him quizzically. "Nothing's happening in the square?"

"Not really. The kids in the tent encampment were starting to come out of their tents, mingling with each other and talking, sort of sharing experiences, I suppose, as they do every night." For a moment he was thoughtful before he went on, "To tell you the truth, I was reminded of Woodstock tonight, but without the drugs, of course. Or, if you prefer, one of those summer street festivals we have in New York. Everything seemed relaxed, friendly, easygoing."

"Well," Nicky said, sitting down heavily in a chair, "I've been doing a lot of thinking, and analyzing, and I believe that Deng Xiaoping is at the end of his rope. He's been provoked and frustrated by the students for some time now, and I'm sure he's about to make a move. It'll be a bungled move, just as he and the government have bungled the whole Tiananmen Square affair ever since it began. He'll have no compunction, you know, about ordering the troops to move on the students." She sighed, and said in a low, sad voice, "I'm afraid it's going to end in a bloodbath."

He stared at her. "Would Deng go that far? He wouldn't *dare*. He won't risk condemnation from the whole world."

Nicky shook her head. "Oh James, he'll do it all right. And I'll tell you something else. I don't think Deng gives a damn about the rest of the world, its leaders or what anybody thinks of him."

Jimmy said, "But Nicky, those kids are so young, so idealistic!" His voice rose as he rushed on, "And they're *peaceful*. All they want is to be listened to . . . they just want to be *heard.*"

"That's never going to happen," Nicky replied. "You know as well as I do what the students call Deng and his cohorts . . . the Gang of the Old. And they're absolutely right. Deng is eighty-five and far, far too old to understand the way it is today. He's completely out of touch with this generation. All he's interested is in clinging to power. We know the students are not making unreasonable demands, and anyway, wanting freedom and democracy is a pretty normal thing, to us."

Jimmy nodded. He took a deep breath. "Okay, so what do you want to do, Nick?"

"I want to be out there. I want to be right in the middle of it when it happens. That's why we're in here, in Beijing, isn't it? To report the news, to bring the news to the people, to tell the outside world the way it is in China, on Friday night, the second day of June 1989."

———